THE UNDYING PAST

By ORVILLE PRESCOTT

THE UNDYING PAST

MID-CENTURY: AN ANTHOLOGY OF DISTINGUISHED
CONTEMPORARY AMERICAN SHORT STORIES

THE FIVE-DOLLAR GOLD PIECE:
THE DEVELOPMENT OF A POINT OF VIEW

IN MY OPINION: AN INQUIRY INTO
THE CONTEMPORARY NOVEL

THE
UNDYING
PAST

Edited and with an introduction by

ORVILLE PRESCOTT

DOUBLEDAY & COMPANY, INC.

GARDEN CITY, NEW YORK,

1961

PERMISSIONS

Permission to use the following material is gratefully acknowledged by Mr. Prescott and the Publisher:

PLOWING EVE From *The Corn King and the Spring Queen*, by Naomi Mitchison. Reprinted by permission of the publishers, Marzani and Munsell, Inc., successors to Cameron Associates, and Jonathan Cape, Ltd.

THE DEATH OF PERICLES From *Achilles His Armour*, by Peter Green. Reprinted by permission of John Murray and Curtis Brown, Ltd.

NEWS FROM SYRACUSE From *The Last of the Wine*, by Mary Renault. Copyright © 1956 by Pantheon Books, Inc., New York, and Longmans Green & Co., Ltd., London. Reprinted by permission of the publishers.

ACROSS THE ALPS From *Hannibal of Carthage*, by Mary Dolan. Copyright 1955 by Marie M. Dolan. Reprinted by permission of the Macmillan Company.

JULIUS CAESAR TO LUCIUS MAMILIUS TURRINUS From *The Ides of March*, by Thornton Wilder. Reprinted by permission of the copyright owner.

CLAUDIUS' TRIUMPH From *Claudius the God*, by Robert Graves. Copyright 1935 by Harrison Smith and Robert Haas, Inc. Reprinted by permission of Random House, Inc., Robert Graves and Methuen & Co., Ltd.

THE PROCURATOR OF JUDAEA From *Mother of Pearl*, by Anatole France, translated by Frederic Chapman. Reprinted by permission of Dodd, Mead & Company, Inc., and The Bodley Head, Ltd.

PALUS THE INCOMPARABLE From the book *Andivius Hedulio*, by Edward Lucas White. Copyright 1921 by E. P. Dutton & Co., Inc. Renewal, 1949 by Ethel C. White. Reprinted by permission of the publishers.

ON THE GREAT WALL From *Puck of Pook's Hill*, by Rudyard Kipling. Copyright 1906 by Rudyard Kipling. Reprinted by permission of Mrs. George Bambridge, the Macmillan Company, Canada, and Doubleday & Company, Inc.

THE FOUNDING OF THE KINGDOM OF WESSEX From *Conscience of the King*, by Alfred Duggan. Copyright 1951 by Alfred Duggan. Reprinted by permission of Coward-McCann, Inc., publishers, and Curtis Brown, Ltd.

HOW KING HARALD BLUETOOTH CELEBRATED YULE From *The Long Ships*, by Frans G. Bengtsson. Copyright 1954 by Frans G. Bengtsson. Reprinted by permission of Alfred A. Knopf, Inc.

HASTINGS From *The Golden Warrior*, by Hope Muntz. Copyright 1949 by Charles Scribner's Sons, and Chatto and Windus, Ltd.

7

THE SACK OF MAGDEBURG From *Memoirs of a Cavalier,* by Daniel Defoe. Reprinted by permission of E. P. Dutton and Co., Inc., and J. M. Dent & Sons, Ltd.

ENDICOTT AND THE RED CROSS From *Twice Told Tales and Other Short Stories,* by Nathaniel Hawthorne. Reprinted by permission of Washington Square Press, Inc.

THE APPRENTICE From *The Eye Witness,* by Hillaire Belloc. Reprinted by permission of A. D. Peters.

MRS. OLIVER CROMWELL From *Bloodstock and Other Stories,* by Margaret Irwin. Copyright 1953 by Margaret Irwin. Reprinted by permission of Harcourt, Brace & World, Inc., and A. D. Peters, Ltd.

THE FAMOUS MR. JOSEPH ADDISON From *The History of Henry Esmond,* by William Makepeace Thackeray.

RETREAT FROM ST. FRANCIS: THE LAST FOUR DAYS From *Northwest Passage,* by Kenneth Roberts. Copyright 1936, 1937 by Kenneth Roberts. Reprinted by permission of Doubleday & Company, Inc.

THE LAST OF THE JACOBITES From *Red Gauntlet,* by Sir Walter Scott. Reprinted by permission of E. P. Dutton & Co., Inc., and J. M. Dent & Sons, Ltd.

THEY FIGHT THE SERAPIS From *His Fifty Years of Exile* (Israel Potter), by Herman Melville, with an introduction by Lewis Leary. Copyright © 1957 by Hill & Wang, Inc., (American Century Series). Reprinted by permission.

MONSEIGNEUR IN TOWN
THE FALL OF THE BASTILLE From *A Tale of Two Cities,* by Charles Dickens. Reprinted by permission of E. P. Dutton & Co., Inc., and J. M. Dent & Sons, Ltd.

TEN THOUSAND AND FIVE FRANCS From *Good-bye My Son,* by Marjorie Coryn. Copyright 1943 by D. Appleton-Century, Inc. Reprinted by permission of Harold Matson Company.

THE DARK COUNTRY
THE LITTLE TYKE From *The Trees,* by Conrad Richter. Copyright 1940 by Conrad Richter. Reprinted by permission of Alfred A. Knopf, Inc.

H. M. S. SUTHERLAND From *Ship of the Line* (Captain Horatio Hornblower), by C. S. Forester. Copyright 1938 by Cecil Scott Forester. Reprinted by permission of Little, Brown and Company and Harold Matson Company.

BORODINO From *War and Peace,* by Leo Tolstoy, translated by Louise and Aylmer Maude. Copyright 1938 by The Limited Editions Club, Inc. Reprinted by permission of The George Macy Companies, Inc., and the Oxford University Press.

THE WARRIOR'S SOUL From *Tales of Hearsay,* by Joseph Conrad. Reprinted by permission of J. M. Dent & Sons, Ltd.

For
Jennifer, Anne and Peter
Who share my interest in history, my enjoyment of fiction
and my delight in fine historical fiction

CONTENTS

Introduction

This book is a collection of dramatic episodes, glimpses of typical ways of life and portrait sketches taken from the world's finest historical fiction. For the last fifteen years I have been thinking about it and planning it. Since I was ten years old I have been unconsciously preparing it. The actual labor of reading or rereading about four times as many historical novels and short stories as are represented here was one of the most enjoyable and rewarding experiences of my life. It confirmed my long-held conviction that historical fiction is one of the great subdivisions of literature. Many of the world's most distinguished and most critically admired writers have written it. Why then has historical fiction so bad a reputation in some circles?

The answer is easy. Today hundreds of cheap, clumsy, superficial and sensational historical novels are published every year. Without merit of any kind, they amuse only the totally uncritical. But these sub-literary atrocities are so numerous the fine historical novels are often overlooked. People who rightly despise the trash are usually unaware of the existence of the works of art.

What is an historical novel? The only definition I know which seems accurate to me I wrote myself in a book of criticism called "In My Opinion: An Inquiry Into The Contemporary Novel" which was published nine years ago. There I said that an historical novel "is any novel in which the action takes place before the author's birth so that he must inform himself about its period by study. Whether actual historical personages are the protagonists or whether the entire cast is imaginary is irrelevant. What matters is the all-important fact that the author is not writing from personal experience; he is trying to write creative fiction about men and women who lived and loved and died in a world completely different from his own."

This is not easy to do. Certain basic attributes of human nature are timeless. But people vary immensely from era to era. They believe in different

16

gods and in different values. They abide by different customs. Their emotional responses are conditioned by the world in which they live and at various periods differed greatly from what ours would be. Today no man would laugh when another man's hands were cut off. But the Vikings did. Today few would consider political treachery and murder justifiable ways of achieving political power. But many people in Renaissance Italy did. Today we are less cruel as individuals than our remote ancestors; but some of our national states have been crueler than any of their predecessors.

So the serious writer of historical fiction must not only make his characters human and interesting; he must make them creatures of their own times. And only in comparatively recent years have novelists learned the most effective way to do this. Novelists used to insert into their narratives long passages of explanation and description which were clumsy as well as dull.

A better way to re-create the past is to write from the point of view of the people then alive who took their world for granted. What seems strange to us was natural and familiar to them. By artfully casual indications of what his characters believe, what customs and conventions they follow, how they fight or worship, the novelist can make them and their age seem as understandable and vitally alive as our own.

And so the sense of the past is recaptured through the vicariously felt emotions of fictional characters. Historians and biographers can provide facts and interpret events and circumstances. But not even the finest works of history and biography can provide that emotional identification and sense of personal participation which is the special magic of fiction. The true artist in historical fiction can make the past live again and if he is skilful enough his words may continue to live long after his death. I do not claim that all the selections I have made have a chance of immortality. But some have and so there is a double reason for calling this book "The Undying Past."

Most of the selections printed here were written in English, some in French, German, Russian, Swedish and Norwegian. They are arranged chronologically according to the dates of the events described and range from antiquity to the American Civil War. I have chosen only selections which I admire and believe to be the best of their kind; but I could only choose excerpts which could stand alone without much explanation and which are dramatic units in themselves. This meant that I could not include anything from a number of excellent works, such as Marguerite Yourcenor's "Hadrian's Memoirs" and the novels of Willa Cather and Bryher. They can't be cut without damaging a complex emotional unity.

Many novelists of imperishable fame have written historical fiction and are not represented here, among them: Bulwer-Lytton, Charles Reade, George Eliot, Thomas Hardy, Conan Doyle, Victor Hugo, Gustave Flaubert, Stendhal, Alexandre Dumas, James Fenimore Cooper, Mark Twain, Ellen Glasgow, John Steinbeck, John P. Marquand and William Faulkner. Some of these authors wrote wretched stuff when they tried their hands at historical fiction; some did quite well. But none, in my judgment, wrote anything good enough or of the right quotable nature for this volume.

I was surprised when I reread Reade's celebrated "The Cloister and The Hearth" to find it clumsy and sentimental. And I was surprised even more when I reread Dumas, whom I loved as a boy, to find my dearly cherished d'Artagnan tiresome and unconvincing.

But even with these deliberately conspicuous omissions you will find many writers of world fame in these pages and many fine contemporary writers who deserve to be more famous than they are. If I had had several volumes to fill instead of one I could have included much else of nearly equal interest. The field is vast.

But these are my choices, carefully considered, read repeatedly with pleasure. If they can give others only a little of the enjoyment they have given me I shall be satisfied. And if, after making their acquaintance here, any readers feel moved to seek out the books from which these excerpts are taken I shall be delighted.

ORVILLE PRESCOTT

THE UNDYING PAST

Plowing Eve

by Naomi Mitchison

In the beginning were the barbarians. Tarrik was chief of the Scythian kingdom of Marob on the Black Sea. He was also Corn King, the divine incarnation of the principle of fertility which made the grain grow. Erif Der, his wife, was a witch and Spring Queen, divine also in her role as representative of the earth's annual rebirth in the spring.

The snow had melted almost everywhere, uncovering the evergreen leaves and the very young leaves and the brown, soft hummocks of earth, rested and sweet after the winter. If you went outside the town and listened, you heard water all round trickling and soaking away towards the sea. If you listened better still, as Erif listened, you would hear the murmur of the great waters fretting and foaming among mud islands and channels far to the south. She stood beside Tarrik and watched him pressing his hands into the cold sticky clay. He liked it. She felt an absurd, mild annoyance at his absorption with it. 'Tarrik!' she muttered impatiently, 'Tarrik, stop, get up!' He looked at her with smiling, possessive eyes, and spoke softly and thickly as though the stickiness of the soil and the early spring fogs were clinging about his tongue and lips. 'Plowing Eve! We will make a good furrow, Erif!'

It was always the same, year after year, as winter began to loosen and soften, and Plowing Eve got nearer. People came out of their houses more and talked more, looking at one another, men and women, with sudden discovery, and felt a growing and brightening of the senses, keener sight, smell, taste, hearing, touch, not quite a falling in love and yet comparable with it, as though perhaps it were a falling in love with the young, young spring, the incredibly pale and remote and maiden season, still wrapped about with snow. Children felt it as well. Fewer people died at that time of year. They watched the comings and goings of the Corn King and the Spring Queen, looking for signs of the godhead that was ripening in both of them, and getting into touch with it themselves.

Tarrik was used to it and expected it, and yet every year it was equally exciting. They began to give him odd and traditional foods, and hid away all his coats except those of red and yellow. He began to feel extraordi-

21

narily strong and gay and sure of himself. As he walked through the streets
he would suddenly bound towards people, women mostly, and touch their
faces or hands. Even if they had been looking ill or unhappy before, their
answer to him for the moment would be laughter and happiness. Childless wives put themselves in his way; often they had luck afterwards. It
was good to be able to do that. In his security and confidence he said one
day to the Council that he would not care now if Harn Der came back
tomorrow; he would not so much as frown at the old man with no power.
Of course, no one quite took what the Corn King said at these times as
anything binding, but all the same Harn Der's friends looked at one another and felt it was something to start on.

He went to his own Place and did various things there. The new plowshare had to be made by the best of the metalworkers, a friend of Berris, a
man so much interested in his actual craft that he was scarcely interested
at all in the directions which Tarrik gave him. Most of the time while it
was being made, Tarrik hung about the forge, handled tongs or bellows,
helped with the cooling. He knew a good deal about the smith's trade, but
had never taken the trouble to go through with making any big thing —
and small ones bored him. He found himself talking a great deal about
Greece. It was odd, but he did not try to stop himself in anything that
came naturally to his mind or body just before Plowing Eve. Though he
had put out of his thought as much as possible of the people and ideas,
yet some of the things stayed, the things Berris had shown him in Athens,
and the mountains, and the dry, deep summer colours everywhere. So he
talked and talked, and sometimes the man who was working on the plowshare listened to him, and sometimes he was too deep in his work. The
snow outside reflected quantities of light into the spark-jetted cave of the
forge. When the plowshare was finished absolutely rightly, Tarrik wrapped
it in a piece of new linen and took it back by night and in silence to
its place.

In the morning of Plowing Eve, every one went up to the fallow field
in their best clothes. There were thick clay jars standing about, filled with
a brownish drink that was made out of fermented wheat and only used on
feast days. As it was rather nasty it was usually mixed with honey. Early
in the day it had been raining, but by the latter part of the morning it had
stopped, and the clouds rose and parted. The people stood and sat and
lay about the edges of the damp field, with the coloured rods standing
upright in it for the plowing marks. They got drunk, but this stuff, instead
of making them softly drunk, as their usual herb-steeped mead did, made

them drunk and hard and excited. After a time, in one and then another and another part of the ring round the field, the excitement grew and flared to a point, a violence, but, instead of wanting to fight, the man would want to shout, would begin shouting for the Corn King to come, for the plowing, for the year to begin. The shouting ran in waves, round and round. They clapped their hands on their thighs. The shouting took rhythm, became a double song of men and women, deep and shrill. It beat across the fallow field, and on to the plowshare at the side of it.

Now it was noon. At opposite sides the ring parted, huddled back on to itself as the song dropped to satisfied eagerness. From the south came the Spring Queen, with her eyes straight and held, unseeing, unsmiling, past men and women she knew well, brushing by her friend Disdallis, more apart than a bride, and so into the middle of the field. She sat down quietly there and hung her hands over her knees and dropped her head forward on to her wrists. She had a white dress with hundreds and hundreds of little coloured wool flowers fastened on to it all over by long wool stalks. As she walked slowly over the fallow field she was almost shapeless with the hanging mass of them, dropping over her fingers and down from the hem nearly over her feet. Her hair hung behind her in a tight single plait.

From the north end of the field came the Corn King, leading his white plow-oxen with painted horns. He himself wore a curious garment, long strips of coloured stuff over his naked body from neck to knee, belted at the waist, but splitting everywhere as he moved. Tarrik, wearing it, knew that his body was all shivering with no more than this between it and the March wind. All round the ring every one still wore furs and felt. Yet it was scarcely cold that he was. He did not look towards the Spring Queen, but yoked his oxen to the plow and began to drive them along the outer edge of the field. The ring of people were singing and dancing: the plow went in a square, inside their circle; it moved slowly past them like a knife-blade scraping along flesh. In the dance they too began to move slowly round the field, slower than the plow. Birds hovered, crows and seagulls, but did not dare to settle in the furrow for fear of the people. Tarrik pressed on the plow-beam, in, in to the hard, sticky reluctant earth. After he had made and closed the full square about the field, he did not plow it all, only went parallel with his first lines and then suddenly inward on a sharp turn just as his immanent godhead and the sight of one of the plow marks might move him. After a time he began to talk to the Spring Queen in the middle, over his shoulder, in a loud, impersonal voice.

He talked about the plowing. He said: 'This is my field. Mine.' He said: 'Other things are mine. Everything I think of is mine, everything I name. Under the plow. They go under. The plow is a ship. It goes through thick water. It is bringing gold to Marob. I am the plow. It is my body. It is hard and strong. It leaps on the closed sod and plunges through. Soon comes the seed.' And every time he said one of these things the crowd would sigh after him: 'Plow hard! Plow deep!'

At first the Spring Queen said nothing. She seemed asleep. Then she raised her head a little from her knees and began to answer: 'Though you plow the field it is not your field. Why should the field hear? The closed soil has no pleasure of the plow, and cold and hard it will be to the seed. Why should the spring come?' But the people of Marob cried at her softly from the edges of the field: "Spring Queen, be kind, be kind!"

So they went on until the middle of the afternoon. Tarrik was the plow, the seed, the warmth and force of growth. Erif was the hard, fallow field; the cold, reluctant spring. The words they said were in no set form or order, only, on every Plowing Eve since the beginning of Marob, the same kind of loud, unhurrying talk had gone on between the sweating Corn King and the still, shivering Spring Queen, with the same implications behind it. It would go on happening for countless years longer. This way, in Marob at least, the food and wealth of the people was made to grow. It was better not to make the talk into a plain repetition, a formula; the life might go out of it. Now as it went on the people divided up more and more, the women shouting at the Corn King to plow deep and hard, the men calling on the Spring Queen to be kind.

Tarrik had done all this at Plowing Eve since he was a boy. And afterwards, if he thought about it, he could never understand how he got the strength for the whole day, the plowing and dancing and shouting. When it was over he always slept dreamlessly and deliciously, yet not for longer than usual. He remembered that for the first few years he had been afraid, when the day came, that he would not be able to go through it rightly; but he always did. Now he had no fears. Only it was difficult to wait through the morning, after every one had left the Chief's house and gone up to the field, to wait there by himself, doing nothing, getting more and more aware of the smell and texture of the brown earth of the fallow field lying ready for him. He did not think of the day when he would begin to feel his strength go. Why should he? It was no part of him yet. As he plowed and talked and pressed and ached and held hard for the plow marks and felt the furrow opening and the wave of earth turning, the dark, torn clods and crumbs tumbling and settling, he knew that the Spring Queen was in the middle of the field and he was coming towards her. He had forgotten that she was also his wife, Erif Der.

This was her third Plowing Eve. The first time she had been a young girl, proud and confident and sure of her strength and her magic, deeply excited, but yet underneath always herself and her father's daughter, working for the moment with the seasons and with Tarrik, but ultimately not surrendered and prepared to work against Tarrik whenever she chose, later on, although at the moment she was doing the thing she liked, for fun. Last year it had been with her brother, Yellow Bull, and it had all seemed wrong and twisted. There had been something very queer about his plowing; even the oxen had noticed it, and she had seen at once through her half-shut eyes. And she was ill then, full of pains that suddenly took her and swept away everything else. She knew that she had fainted once or twice during her wait in the middle of the field, and once or twice had heard herself speaking as she became fully conscious again, and was only thankful that the godhead was still with her enough to move through her senses. When she had realised that, she had let herself go into a sort of dim condition in which it possessed her and did and said the things for her, and she could look on and bear the pain that she thought then was coming from Tarrik's child, but was really the poison with which Yersha was trying to kill her.

This time she was relaxed again to her own godhead, but without pain. The child in her had not begun to stir yet. It was still tiny, a little queer worm at the base of her body, sending small messages of shock and disturbance. But also it was security. If everything else about her was appearance, if she grew so uncertain of her own existence that it became no difficult or unlikely step between life and death, then this thing which was her and yet not her, anchored her, nailed her down to some kind of reality. It was good to feel secure, good to be part of the seasons, budding and ripening with them.

She raised her head a little to give another answer and saw that the plow-oxen were quite near, that the fallow field was almost plowed. Suddenly Erif Der was unreasonably and beautifully glad. Her voice, as the crowd was hoping it would, grew louder. She was the spring and she would come with flowers and small leaves and lambs and a growing child. The plow came again across her field of vision and then turned inward towards her. She did not know at all how violently she was shivering. The painted horns of the oxen swung together and apart. She saw the Corn

King's eyes over the backs of the beasts. The plow came at her. The singing stopped. At the last moment she leapt to her feet, ran under the horns
of the oxen, between their panting flanks, and leapt the plowshare itself
as it made the last furrow right through the centre of the fallow field,
tearing apart the warmed, flattened grass where she had been sitting.

At once the singing began again, men and women together, and the
ring swept inwards, nearer to the middle of the field and across the first
belt of plowing, so that their feet trampled stickily into the brown, turned
sods, the flesh of earth. 'The spring is awake!' they cried. 'Awake! Oh,
awake and truly awake! The year is beginning again!' Then bagpipes
took it up, then small drums. Then men ran into the centre with poles
and planks which they fitted together into a booth, raised a little way from
the ground and about ten feet square. Long sticks twined with ivy and
stuck with red and yellow wool roses went up from the corners and were
bent and tied together overhead into a kind of canopy. It took an amaz-
ingly short time, just long enough for Tarrik to throw himself on the ground,
into his new furrow, and lie there with his eyes shut and allow one set
of images to die out of him and another to take possession. The Spring
Queen stood at the other side of the booth while they sang at her and threw
sharp, heavy corn ears, left over from last year; some of them like tiny
arrows hit her face and hands, others stuck in her hair; they pricked her
flesh to movement.

When the stage was finished, all hammered together, the voices stopped,
but the pipes and drums went on. The Corn King and the Spring Queen
went up on to it and stood facing one another. Then they began a dance
of courting. In that confined space it was necessarily very formal and cur-
tailed. Sometimes even they were quite still for long moments in an attitude of gazing, the Corn King pressing back the wrists of the Spring Queen
from the ends of her long arms stretched straight over her head, leaning
over and close to her, staring down into her eyes. Sometimes one or both
of them spun round and round. When the Spring Queen did this the wool
flowers on her dress flew out in a curious widening shower, and then, as
she stilled, folded themselves back on to her. Sometimes the Corn King
just jumped, by himself, as some sorts of birds do, showing off to their
mates. The strips of stuff that he wore were always jumping out and apart.
Underneath he was earthy with clay of the furrows over his nakedness.
He felt it everywhere, clay that had been cold now warm against his body.

The drums and bagpipes went on continuously, and the sharp, hollow
handclapping from the crowd. They spun in the blast of noise. The dance

became the climax of the courting between Corn and Spring. He leapt at her. She gave at the knees and all along her body and fell on the floor of the booth, not painfully, for she was all slack to it. Then before the eyes of all Marob he jerked the strips of stuff sideways and away from himself. For one moment all the growers of corn could look on the hard and up-right sign of the godhead on their Chief and Corn King. Then, still to the squealing of pipes he threw his hands up like a diver and all his body curved and shot downward towards her. She did not feel his weight be-cause of the tension in her own skin from head to heels. In the conven-tion of the dance and in a solid noise of drums the Corn opened the Fur-row, broke into the Spring, and started the Year.

It lasted only long enough for this final idea of the dance to get into the minds and bodies of the Marob people. By some curious process, and in spite of the movements he went through in this sacred mimicking of life, all desire of doing it in reality and not only in the dance had left the Corn King. It did not come into his intense but limited consciousness that the Spring Queen was a woman, partner and satisfier of a man's desire. He was not himself a man seizing in ultimate necessity on woman's flesh, but a god making plain his power. Being now this image himself, he was satisfied with an image. Later on that day, as always, the actual thing would happen, but he did not even consider it; he was not yet the person who would be and do that.

Drums and pipes stilled. Suddenly all the people of Marob rushed at the booth of the dancing and at the Spring Queen, lying still and with her eyes shut on the floor. They began to pull the flowers off her dress, snapping the wool stalks, one flower for every household. As they surged round and over her with small rustlings and tuggings, her body quivered and leapt again and again. The Corn King turned her over for them to pluck the flowers from her back. Her shut eyes rested on her hands, damp with sweat that slowly cooled and chilled. He stood back; she was the sacrifice. During the dance her hair had come unplaited; it lay in tangles round her head. People trod on it. The most eager ones would stoop and pull out one of her hairs to go with their flower. Each had a piece of new white cloth for wrapping. Folding it up, hiding it away, satisfied, under a belt, or in the breast of a coat, one after another the householders stepped back and climbed down off the stage. At last all had gone.

The booth was taken to pieces just as quickly as it had been put up. Girls dressed bridally in green and white, with very large hats like in-verted peg tops, led the dishevelled Spring Queen away to a covered cart and laid her on a deep pile of furs. She went to sleep almost at once and did not wake, however bad the long jolting back to Marob was. She scarcely stirred when they carried her out, back into the Chief's house. Here they undressed her and smoothed her hair, cutting out and keeping for luck the entangled corn ears, and put her to bed and took turns to stay by her with a light through the evening and night. But she slept very soundly and softly, with her fingers clasped unstirringly under her chin, and did not turn over in bed even once.

In the field the Corn King took off his belt and ducked out of his odd, ragged dress. The men brought warm water and poured it over him, rubbing off the clay till he was clean again. Then he put on fresh clothes, coat and breeches of red stuff sewn all over with little plaques of gold, tiny rayed suns, and the same on his boots. He wore a crown with spikes; below each spike stared out a rounded and ringed cat's-eye-stone. By now it was sunset; the red light was reflected separately in every one of the flat pieces of gold as he moved or breathed. He was taking the power and glory of the day into himself. They brought him wine, and honeycomb on a golden dish. He took a piece of the honeycomb in his mouth and crushed it between tongue and palate. The golden honey oozed over his lips and down his throat. The dusk of evening closed over the plowed field, but the Corn King himself was the sun now.

Torches were stuck all round and others were carried, whirled and tossed about. Trails of sparks blew across the evening. Half the men of Marob formed themselves into the eight spokes of a wheel, of which the Corn King with the honey in his mouth was centre and giver of motion. They began to sing and wheel. The inner ones turned slowly, the outer, who were all the younger men, bounded hand in hand, stumbling and recovering and leaping in the furrows, knocking down the thin gay plowing marks when they met them. The Corn King was, at the same time, turning slowly and moving step by step onwards along the edges of the field, so that the circle should roll round it, sungates, touching it everywhere. As the spokes of the wheel tired and dropped panting, others from the crowd sprang in and joined hands and made them up again. By now all had drunk deeply of the wheat brew and eaten much honey with it that made them thirsty for more drinking. The torches were seeming to roar and flare behind their eyes now. The wheel throbbed, expanding and contracting. The plowed field rocked and leapt under their feet with pain and pleasure of its plowing.

As the sun ring went on and began to come back to its first place, a good many of the women left the crowd and slipped off homewards, among them most of the young wives and quite young girls. It was thought no dishonour to stay in the plowed field this day of all the year, and no husband or father could well complain, but all the same they might mind, and one does not want to hurt those one loves. Still, quite enough women stayed for the men to be able to work their own and only magic and help the Corn King to help the year. Among these women, too, the bowls of drink were passed round, and dizzily, too, for them to welcome it and stirred up the torches and waved red and yellow ribbons and stamped. The wheel swept through its path to the end and slowed down and broke up sweating and panting. The hub of it, the Corn King, the sun himself, stood in a furrow with his arms stretched out; anyone who looked at him could see that his eyeballs were swinging still from side to side, and clearly he could not see much. But that came right. His arms lifted a little, his shoulders squared back, his gold scales glittered and he grew bigger and fuller of heat and power. He threw up his head and laughed. Then he went forward among the women and made his choice. The night of Plowing Eve had begun.

As it went on and on and the magic of the men was let loose over the plowed field, so Tarrik lost more and more of his godhead. It was fun, it made him laugh in great bursts that every one heard. It started the year well; it was easy. But it had not the sacredness of the sham thing. Between times he began to remember other sorts of ideas. He began also to try and count up how many more times, with the best of luck, this would happen. It only happened once a year: twenty — thirty times more perhaps — three or four times beyond that with any luck. But once you look at a thing and see it is finite, how very little that extra three or four times matters! He used not to mind, used not to think of himself as anything apart from Marob, which went on for ever. It was the Greek part of him standing up in his heart and whispering. The Corn King would always be there, but Tarrik only for a few more years. No, no! Woman, make me forget, rub against me, light fires to burn up all this useless thought!

Gradually the torches burnt down and smouldered out. The full moon of Plowing Night cruised slowly over them and then sank into films and layers of cloud. Men and women got to their feet and breathed cold air and left the well-plowed field. Everything would go right this year. His luck had come fully back to the Corn King.

The Death of Pericles

by Peter Green

> 429 B.C. Pericles, leader of the Athenian democracy
> and creator of the Athenian empire, was dying. For
> several years he had been estranged from his learned
> and brilliant mistress, Aspasia — ever since his discov-
> ery of her infidelity with his young ward, Alcibiades.
> The disastrous Peloponnesian War was already two
> years old.

As the weeks went by Pericles' strength steadily ebbed away. There was nothing violent about his symptoms: rather a slow draining of energy and will-power, a dissipation of the intellect, a weakening and wasting of the body. He coughed ceaselessly, and began to have frequent bouts of vomiting. His mind was clouded with melancholy, and he became a prey to agonizing fits of remorse and despair. He went seldom to the Assembly: but when he did, however great the effort, he walked. Much of the business he would normally have transacted in the Council Chambers he now had sent to his house, where he lay for hour after hour on a day-bed, shivering, wrapped in furs even in the warm September midday. Much remained unread; much he delegated to his subordinates. When he had to take a decision himself it cost him untold effort.

All the time Aspasia cared for him, managed his estate, bullied the slaves, argued with his steward and supervised the running of the household. In political affairs she now never intruded; she made no attempt to alleviate the agony of mind through which this man with whom she had lived for nearly twenty years was passing. They seldom exchanged a word. An insuperable barrier had sprung up between them, built from failure and distrust and despair; aggravated by betrayal, sealed by resignation. The crumbling of Pericles' proud ideals, the ravages and human suffering the plague had brought, and which he had failed to comprehend, the forbidden desire which still raged in her bones had all combined to destroy the noble image round which her life had for so long revolved.

Aspasia, perhaps more clearly than anyone, saw that whether Athens won or lost the world it stood for was gone for ever. It depended on the will and belief of one man: and that man lay slowly dying before her eyes. And, as events ground relentlessly forward, they destroyed not only the

30

present but the past. The jackals were fighting for the scraps which the dying lion had husbanded; and it seemed to her now only natural that there should be nothing left but jackals, that the world Pericles had built out of his beliefs could have had no other ending. She had passed far beyond blame or anger; but as she watched the lonely struggling figure, day by day, she knew herself at one with the common people who, lacking his vision, yet kept a firm grasp on the truth which he had missed. She had a violent nostalgia for the home she had nearly forgotten, the voices of her own countrymen. But when she looked in her mirror she saw an embittered middle-aged woman, set in her ways, committed to the life she had chosen despite herself. It is too late, she said calmly: I shall live and die in Athens now. I have made my choice.

As the September twilight faded she sat and watched Pericles' face. He was sleeping uneasily, muttering and twisting, the light throwing grotesque shadows on his sunken cheeks and the bony, wasted contours of his face. Flecks of foam started from the corners of his mouth. Mechanically she wiped them away. For the first time she began to consider what would become of her: yet objectively, almost as if she were an alien person, not involved in her own dilemma. They will probably kill me, she thought without fear or rancour. Perhaps that would be for the best. There is no reason now for my living.

As if in a dream, she began to think of Alcibiades, torturing herself with her own memories. The woman who renounced her love out of loyalty is not I who sit here today. And he is not the impetuous youth who left me. This war is like a potter's kiln. It hardens all it touches. Alcibiades will take the legacy Pericles bequeathed him and turn it to his own ends. Athens had become an obsession with him, a symbol of power. His power, his to make or destroy. He will let nothing stand in the way of his ambition. Least of all the woman who loved him.

There was a groan from the bed. Pericles was awake, the sweat pouring off his face. He cried out in agony. Aspasia had seen many men die of the plague. The expression on Pericles' face was one with which she was familiar from night after night of vigil. Calmly she summoned a slave, and told him to send messages to the War Council and Pericles' surviving relatives to come at once. She hesitated only for a second, and added Alcibiades' name to the list. The slave, frightened, hurried out. Aspasia sat down again, her eyes fixed on that tortured writhing face. After a while he became delirious.

They all came silently into the darkened room: Hagnon; Nicias; Pericles' wastrel brother Ariphron, awed by the company he found himself in. Aspasia stood by the bedside and greeted them by name. Pericles himself lay quite still. At first glance Hagnon thought he was already dead; but an imperceptible motion of the coverlets showed that he was still breathing. A junior member of the Board of Generals came in late, on tiptoe. No one spoke. Hagnon looked round at the haggard faces. There were not many of them. At the beginning of the year there had been eight generals. Now four were dead; and Phormio was fighting a lonely battle in the Gulf; and the greatest of them all lay on his narrow bed, unconscious and uncaring.

The silence became intolerable. They sat round the bed scarcely daring to breathe, their eyes fixed on that immobile face. Then Pericles sighed in his sleep, and his head turned slightly on its pillow. This single movement seemed to relax the atmosphere. Nicias began to make an almost formal eulogy of the dying man, recalling his great achievements, subtly changing the atmosphere from naked tragedy to the predictable and comforting formulas of official mourning. And how he's enjoying himself, thought Hagnon savagely in his solitary detachment. Each death is a triumph for him. Because he's still alive. I know nothing so horrible as old men at a funeral. It is as if they sucked the very life-blood from the corpse. And the greater the death, the greater the triumph.

Nicias stopped speaking. His words were taken up by all the rest. They spoke of his devotion to the city, his prowess as a general, remembering all his achievements, his early struggle for power, his unfailing good counsel.

Hagnon listened in silence. They seemed to him like puppets, actors in some drama whose words were memorised and rehearsed, mouthpieces for an incomprehensible oracle. How men forget in the face of death: the last gesture of generosity before the unknown, the self-protection against the end that will overtake all of them in turn. Never look for a man's life on his gravestone. What will they find on his? Not the dream of empire, not the plague, not the generals who cannot be here today or any day, not the thousands upon thousands of dumb anonymous men who lie in their shallow graves because of him. No, not these. Nine trophies as general. Sixteen terms of office. And the Parthenon as his memorial.

The leaden eyelids fluttered, raised themselves with tremulous effort. Pericles smiled gently at the circle of faces round him. One hand moved slowly to his neck, where an amulet hung. The hushed voices died away into silence. His eyes focussed slowly on Hagnon. When he spoke he could scarcely be heard.

'Such . . . woman's folly,' he said dreamily. 'Amulets . . . I must be very ill to put up with such nonsense . . .' He struggled for breath. Tiny beads of sweat gleamed on his forehead in the light of the lamp that hung from the ceiling. He went on, his lips hardly moving: 'I . . . have been . . . listening . . . to what you said. Forgive me . . . I had not . . . strength . . . to interrupt you. You have been . . . more than generous. But . . . but, you must not . . . speak what is . . . untrue.' He tried to pull himself up into a sitting position; but the effort was too much, and he sank back, panting. 'You . . . should speak only . . . the truth of me . . .' Hagnon looked at him imploringly. Not now. Not at this final moment. Don't say it, I beseech you, don't say it. But the thin voice went on: 'I am . . . amazed . . . that what I have done . . . stirs you to such praise . . . It was not . . . my doing. Fortune and the Gods . . . govern us all. And there are many . . . many . . . who have done as much as . . . more than . . . I have. Do not . . . deceive future . . . generations.' Hagnon relaxed. This was not a confession. Yet even he was not prepared for Pericles' final words.

'But . . . when you speak of me . . . there is one thing . . . I would have you . . . remember. One thing . . . you have not said.' He gathered his last remaining strength, and for an instant the old fire flashed in his eyes, and his voice became strong. 'No living Athenian,' he cried, 'ever put on mourning . . . because of me.' As he uttered the last words a dreadful rattling cough seized him. For a moment he struggled, choking. Then with an odd, abrupt movement, his head fell back on the pillow. Hagnon slowly rose to his feet; and the others followed him.

There was nothing to be said. One after another they knelt before the dead man; and then passed quietly out into the night. Only Nicias hesitated for a second, looking back at the lonely figure standing motionless at the head of the bed, the folds of her robe heavy, as if carved from stone, her face expressionless. Then he too went, and she was alone.

She stood thus for perhaps ten minutes, insensible to the passing time, numbed and remote. She did not hear Alcibiades' horse stamping on the cobbles outside, nor his knock at the door. When he came in, his face flushed, his step still unsteady, a spatter of wine like blood on the whiteness of his tunic, it was as if he had been created out of air by the dark processes of her labyrinthine dream.

Alcibiades looked from one face to the other in the flickering half-light. They bore a horrible resemblance; to his wandering vision they appeared as a double mask of death. Then he began to laugh.

'I see I have kept my promise to the letter,' he observed at length. Aspasia flinched, but said nothing. Her eyes searched this strange scarred face, hard even in its drunkenness; the bloodshot eyes, the drooping, cruel mouth. Alcibiades moved slowly towards the bed — he might have been wearing armour, so ponderous and precise were his steps — and stared for a long time into Pericles' face. He stepped back and straightened his shoulders, and it seemed he was no longer drunk. Then he began to speak, his eyes steady and bloodshot, his hands hanging straight at his sides.

'I ought to feel sorry for him, or hate him. But I don't. A month ago they cursed him. Now they'll follow his funeral, and beat their breasts, and tear their garments. I've no doubt there have been some most impressive things said here tonight. I can guess them all. We are all . . . unoriginal in the face of death. To me this death isn't . . . personal. It's a problem. A road that may lead several ways. For you it's different. I suppose you think I've changed. That I've become hard. It may be true.' He stared at her challengingly. 'I shall waste no tears over this death. To me it means work to be done.' Conscious that he was repeating himself, he broke off from his train of thought, and said: 'I often thought of how it would be when we met again. Anger, perhaps, or love, or sadness. Now the moment has come, I can feel no passion, no regret even. Only an emptiness.' His mood changed abruptly. 'You've no need to worry. There are at least two men who want you. Nicias' — his lip curled in disgust — 'and a man you don't know yet. His name is Lysicles. He's honest, respectable, well off — and a popular party leader.' Alcibiades did not smile; he might have been reciting for any difference in emphasis with which he treated these last words. Aspasia still said nothing. 'A year ago I would have . . . added myself to them. After what has happened . . . it's as if we had never known each other . . .' For the first time he stumbled in his speech. 'Things are so different now. We've both changed — we're both older, if you like.' He looked, without either pity or vindictiveness, at the lined white face and greying hair. 'I have a task to do. A task which — I freely confess it — you made possible. I shall not face it in the way which . . . either you or he would have wished. It is a different world I have to deal with. Different people. What Pericles fought for can still be won. But not in the same way. There's no room in this world for honour or trust. We're all at each others' throats. It's the price we have to pay for . . . his greatness, if you like. Nicias, Cleon, Axiochus — they're all ordinary men. With ordinary desires and ambitions. Personal ambitions. This war has offered us all a prize. I intend to win it for Athens. And for myself.'

Alcibiades suddenly faltered. 'This may be . . . the last chance we shall have to talk together. Aspasia, why don't you leave Athens? Now, tonight. There is nothing here for you any more. I can put you aboard a ship that's sailing at dawn tomorrow. For Miletus . . .' His words died on his lips as he looked at the stony mask confronting him. He pulled himself together and resumed his old brusque manner. 'Very well. I've done all I can.' The idiotic words fell into the stillness. Impatiently Alcibiades strode to the shutters and threw them open. The moonlight streamed in; the night air brought a whiff of flowers and cooking food, the murmur of the City, to dilute the stillness of death. He went out without another word.

Phormio's courier, who had ridden a hundred miles in less than two days, found Pericles' household conversing in hushed whispers, and the house itself in confusion. He threw the reins to a slave and asked old Evangelus, the steward, to announce him at once to the General. He tapped the wallet he carried slung over his shoulder. 'I must see the General at once,' he said. He brushed through the crowd, not listening to what they had to say; knocked on Pericles' door, and entered at once. He stopped short at what he saw.

'My lady . . . I did not know . . . What can I say?' The courier swore afterwards that Aspasia had smiled. She said: 'You are from Phormio, aren't you? I heard you outside. Give me the dispatches. I will see that they reach the right hands.' The courier fumbled in his wallet and handed over the package.

Alone again, Aspasia broke the seals and began to read.

'I am happy to report,' wrote Phormio, 'that with the Gods' aid and a stroke of luck of which I will write in its place, we have inflicted a signal defeat upon the enemy off Naupactus . . .'

The dispatch still in her hands, Aspasia looked for a moment at the still face from which death had erased all the lines and harshness. Then she began to read again. The shutters swung idly to and fro in the night breeze.

News from Syracuse

by Mary Renault

> 413 – 412 B.C. The Athenian invasion of Sicily to at-
> tack the city of Syracuse was one of the greatest dis-
> asters in military history. Here Alexias, a young aris-
> tocrat and warrior, tells how he heard about it. Lysis
> was his best friend.

One day we were walking in the Agora, both feeling a little weak
and sick; Lysis was feverish from his wound, and I had not long got on
my feet again. We heard a great clamour from the other side, and went
to see, not hurrying much, because it hurt us to be jostled in crowds. As
it happened, however, the man who had caused the commotion was coming our way, and bringing it with him. He was a metic, a Phrygian, with
a barber's apron on. He was spreading his hands, calling on the gods to
witness his truth, and demanding to be taken before the archons.

I remember the look of him well: short, smooth and paunchy, with a
ruby in his ear, and a black beard crimped to display his art. Having come
some way in a hurry, he was sweating like a pig from his hair down into
his beard; he looked the kind of little man who gets a roar in a comedy
by pretending to have dirtied himself with fright. But no one was laughing, unless the gods were, as they sat above the clouds. They, it may be,
were saying, "We sent you Perikles to counsel you, and was not that dignity enough for your City? We sent you omens and prodigies, and writing
in the stars, and the gods in your streets were wounded for a sign; but
you knew better, you Athenians. You would tread upon purple; you would
be greater than Necessity and Fate. Very well; take this in your face."

He came towards us, out of breath, with a brawl about him, as if he
might have cut a customer he was shaving, or overcharged. Seeing us he
outran the men who were shouting at him, and panted, "Oh, sir, I can
see you're a gentleman, sir, and a soldier; speak to them, sir; the City's
given me a living these seven years, and what call would I have to leave
my shop on a busy morning with a ship just in, and make up such a tale?
I swear, sir, the man left me not an hour ago, and I came straight here,
the gods be my witness. Stand by me, sir, you and the noble youth your
friend, and take me to the archons, for people take liberties, sir, with a
foreigner, though seven years I've . . ."

So Lysis turned to the people, and said they ought to leave the man to the law, whatever he had said, and anyone was welcome to come and see justice. Then they grew quieter, till an old man in leather, an armourer, said, "And how many more will he tell on the road? Stop his mouth with pitch, I say. It's well enough for you, son of Demokrates, to keep your temper, but I've three sons with the Army, three sons, and how many more like me won't close their eyes tonight for this liar's tale? All to make himself somebody for a day, the foreign bastard, and cry up his stinking shop." Then the noise broke out again worse than before; the little man ran in between Lysis and me, like a chicken under a hen's wing, and we were forced to walk with him where he was going. He chattered in our ears, and crowd shouted behind us, and called to others who shouted in their turn and joined the press. And the barber wheezed and panted out his tale, between the names of patrons who would put in a word for him, or sometimes broke it off to promise us a hair-trim or a shave for nothing.

Such was the messenger the gods sent to the Athenians, to tell us that our Army in Sicily had perished from the earth.

He had a shop in Piraeus, by the wharf where the traders come in from Italy. The colonists used to go there when they landed, to get polished up after the voyage. A ship was in, and one of the passengers sat down on the bench to wait his turn. And getting into talk with the men beside him, he said, "Last time I came to your City it was a time of festival; garlands in the streets, torches at night, and the wine flowing. Now I dread to see the friends I made then, for what can one say to people in such calamity? I thought the war a mistake myself, for living at Rhegium I know something of Sicily; I doubted if the Athenians would come off with much to show; but, by Herakles, if anyone had told me that all would be lost, two great armies, two fleets of ships, the good Nikias and the brave Demosthenes both dying as wretchedly as thieves; yet what are they after all beside so many brave men, all butchered, or, what is worse, enslaved . . ." At this all the people in the shop stopped him with an outcry asking what he meant; and he looking about him in amazement said, "But has it not reached you here? Has no one heard? All Italy talks of nothing else." So the barber had flung down his razor, and run all the way from Piraeus, and here he was. And Lysis and I believed him no more than the rest.

We saw him safe to the Prytaneion, for it is not good that Hellenes living under law should deal out punishment on hearsay in the street. We left him there and went away. I saw that Lysis' cheeks were flushed along the bone, and his eyes bright with fever. "You have walked too long," I said. — "It's nothing, only that my wound is hot." I made him come home, and bathed it with the infusion the doctor had ordered, and wrung out warm cloths and bound them on; while I worked my shoulder ached again, more than it had for days. All this time we were saying how the barber ought to be made an example of, for upsetting the City with false news. Yet it was as if our bodies knew the truth.

The archons were severe with the barber. Rumour was running like yeast, and he could not name his informant nor say where the man had gone. He was racked in the end, not being a citizen; this getting no sense out of him, they thought him punished enough, and let him go. About nine days later, another ship came from Italy; and the men she brought did not sit down at the barber's first, although they needed it. They were fugitives from the Army in Sicily, who throwing away their shields had saved themselves in the woods. Then we knew that the barber had let us down lightly, compared with the truth.

When Demosthenes came out to the Army, he had been like a man after long absence visiting a friend. The family says, "He has been ailing this last year"; but the fresh eye sees death behind the chair. The Syracusans held both horns of the harbour, and the heights above; he had taken the bold line, and attacked the heights. For a while it had been anyone's battle; but darkness fights for the man who knows the land. Even then, Nikias would have delayed, seeing a lifetime of honour about to close in disgrace; but Demosthenes, being sounder in body and nobler in mind, shamed him into decision. He agreed to go. With prudence and secrecy, everything was made ready; the Syracusans had no word of it; only a dark night was needed for the ships to flit away. It was the great moon of Athene's feast-day. Here in Athens we had a cloudy night, but there she shone clear upon the sea and the rocky headlands; till at her zenith, her face was seen to grow less, and to be cut away, and at last all darkened, as if a great shield had been held before her.

You might have thought Nikias would have raised both hands to heaven, and vowed a hekatomb of oxen to Athene, who had cared for her people so well. For it happened on the night of her feast, when the prayers of all the Athenians were lifted up to her; and it has always seemed to me that to reject her gift, the shelter of her shield, was as great an impiety in its own way as that of Anaxagoras, who pretended that Helios is only a glowing stone. Yet Nikias would see nothing in the omen but calamity, and he carried so many with him that Demosthenes was overruled. They decided to wait another full course of the moon, before they sailed.

So they waited; and the Syracusans attacked the ships again, and sank many more than they could still afford to lose. While they were debating what to do, the enemy strung his own ships across the harbour mouth and linked them with a boom. Then they needed no divination to know they must break out, or die. They prepared for battle.

As if just wakened from a drugged sleep, Nikias worked like two men, seeing the ships made ready, exhorting the trierarchs and the soldiers. He recalled to them the famous words of Perikles, that they belonged to the freest people in the world; as if the Syracusans had been subjects of a tyrant, and not Hellenes themselves, resolved to be free or die. For two years they had seen the fate of Melos hanging over them. They manned their ships along the shore, and waited.

It was Demosthenes who led out our ships to break the boom. They fell on it with such courage that they stormed the boom-ships, and were even casting off the ropes and chains; but then the Syracusan fleet fell on them from behind.

They say two hundred ships fought that day in the Great Harbour. The water was choked with them, ramming and boarding, and drifting while grappled into ships already engaged, so that battles merged and joined in unutterable confusion; hoplites springing from deck to deck and, as they fought, being struck by javelins from their own ships; rudders crushed in the press, the lame ships fouling friend as well as foe; the din so great, and quarters so close, that men hardly knew if the orders they heard came from their own trierarch, or the enemy's.

Meanwhile on shore the Athenians watched the battle as if it were a game of dice, with their lives the stake. They swayed this way and that, crying out in triumph or gasping in despair as their own glimpse of the fight looked well or ill. But the Syracusans held four-fifths of the beaches; they could put in anywhere, if they were pressed; the Athenians had only the tiny strip Gylippos and his men had left them. They were trapped on all sides; the ships that were not sunk were driven back to land. At the sight of them returning, the waiting Army gave one great groan of anguish, and stared from the sea strewn with wreckage and with dead, to the hostile land.

To the land they turned their faces at last, leaving the dead unburied; and as if the reproaches of the homeless shades were not enough, they had to abandon the wounded and the sick. It was that, or stay and die with them. They dragged themselves on the flanks, clung to their friends till they could neither walk nor crawl; and then lay pleading, or cursing, or calling out last messages; their voices hung above the Army along with the ravens and the kites. The walking remnant marched on over the stony land, empty, thirsty, harried by the enemy on either side, until the end. At the last they came to a steep-banked river. They poured down into it, to cross over and to drink; and the Syracusans closed in, before and behind. As the Athenians struggled in the water, stones and darts and arrows rained on them. The river was churned to mud and ran with the blood of the dying. But such was their thirst that those who could reach it lay in it and drank, till others trampled them and they drowned.

Demosthenes fell on his sword, but was taken alive to give the enemy the pleasure of killing him. Nikias too they put to death, no one knows how. Of the rank and file, many thousands perished on the spot; many were dragged off by Syracusan soldiers, to sell for gain. The rest were the common spoil of the State. The fugitives, hiding in the woods, saw them driven away like starved cattle, and knew no more.

They had gone out from the City with women wailing, and flowers strewn in the streets. But one may weep aloud when Adonis dies; for crying eases the heart, and the gods return.

In the silent streets, a man who saw his friends approaching would cross to the other side, lest speech be asked of him. Sometimes as you passed a house you could hear a woman weeping alone, a dull sound, moving as she dragged herself about her work. I had heard it at home, and fled at last into the City. Lysis and I drew together like animals in winter; for hours at a time we hardly spoke.

* * *

Not very long after this, I was brought at last the news of my father's death.

It was Sokrates who prepared me for what I was going to hear, and led me to Euripides' house. For he had one, like anyone else, in the City, not far from ours, though one hears everywhere lately a silly tale that he lived in a cave. This has grown, I suppose from his having had a little stone hut built on the shore, where he went to work and be quiet. As to his being a misanthrope, I think the truth is that he grieved for men as much as Timon heated them, and had to escape from them sometimes in order to write at all.

He greeted me with gentleness but few words, looking at me with apology, as if I might reproach him for having no more to say. Then he led

me to a man whom, if I had not been forewarned, I should have taken
for some beggar he had washed and clothed. The man's bones were staring from his skin, the nails of his hands and feet broken and filled with
grime; his eyes were sunk into pits, and he was covered with festering
scratches and with sores. In the midst of his forehead was a slave-brand
done in the shape of a horse, still red and scabby. But Euripides presented
me to him, not him to me. He was Lysikles, who had commanded my
father's squadron.

He began to tell me his tale quite clearly; then he lost the thread of it,
and became confused among things of no purpose till Euripides reminded
him who I was, and who my father was. A little later again he forgot I
was there, and sat looking before him. So I will not relate the story as he
told it then.

My father, as I learned, had been working in the quarries at the time
of his death. That was where the Syracusans took the public prisoners
after the battle, and where most of them ended their lives. The quarries
at Syracuse are deep. They lived there without shelter from the scorch-
ing sun or the frosts of the autumn nights. Those who could work quarried
the stone. They all grew grey with the stone-dust which only the rain
that sometimes fell on them ever washed away. The dust filled their hair,
and the wounds of the dying, and the mouths of the dead whom the Syracusans left rotting where they lay. There was nowhere in the rock to dig
them graves, if anyone had had the strength to do it; but because a fallen
man takes up more room than one on his feet, they piled them into stacks;
for the living had scarcely space to lie down and sleep, and in this one
place they lived and did everything. After a time not much work was
demanded of them, for no overseer could be got to endure the stench.
For food they were given a pint of meal a day, and for drink half a pint
of water. The guards would not stay to give it out, but put down the bulk
and let them scramble for it. At first the people of Syracuse used to come
out in numbers to look into the quarry and see the sight; but in time they
grew weary of it and of the smells, all but the boys who still came to
throw stones. If any citizen was seen from below, those who were not already resigned to death would call out to him, begging to be bought into
slavery and taken anywhere. They had nothing worse to fear than what
they suffered.

After about two months the Syracusans took away the allied troops from
among them, branded these in the forehead, and sold them off. They kept

the Athenians in the quarry; but at this time they removed the dead, among whom was my father. His body had then been lying there some weeks: but Lysikles had recognised it while it was still fresh.

On this he paused and drew his brows together, as if trying to recall what it was he had omitted. When his forehead wrinkled, the legs of the horse, which was branded on it, seemed to move. Then he remembered and offered me a condolence on the loss of my father, such as a man of breeding makes to a friend's son. You might have thought it was I who had given the news to him. I thanked him, and we sat looking at one another. I had made his memory live for him and he had made it live for me. So we stared, both of us, with an inward eye, seeking blindness again.

His own story he did not tell me, but I heard it later. He had passed himself off as an Argive, having picked up some of their Doric, and having been branded with them was sold. He had been bought for a small price by a rough master; and at last, preferring to starve in the woods, he had run away. When too weak to go further, he had been found by a Syracusan riding out to his farm. This man guessed he was an Athenian, yet gave him food and drink and a place to sleep; then, when he was somewhat recovered, asked him whether any new play by Euripides had lately been shown in Athens. For of all the modern poets, it is he whom the Sicilians value most. And living so much out of the way, they are the last to hear of anything new.

Lysikles replied that the year before they sailed, Euripides had been crowned for a new tragedy upon the sack of Troy, and the fate of the captive women. Whereon the Syracusan asked him if he could repeat any of it.

This is the play Euripides wrote just after the fall of Melos. I did not hear it myself; for my father, having thought his former work unorthodox, did not take me. Phaedo once told me that he heard it. He said that from the moment when he was struck down in battle, through all he saw on the island and while he was a slave at Gurgos', that was the only time he wept. And no one noticed him, for the Athenians were weeping on either side. Lysikles had both heard the play and read it; so as much as he knew, he taught the Syracusan, who in payment gave him a bag of food and a garment and set him on his way. This was not the only case of the kind; Euripides had several visits from Athenians who came to tell him that one of his choruses had been worth a meal or a drink to them. Some, who had been sold as house slaves at the beginning, were promoted to tutors if they knew the plays, and at last saw their City again.

But for my father, who had liked to laugh with Aristophanes, there was no returning. I did not even know if a handful of earth had been sprinkled over him at last, to put his shade at rest. We performed the sacrifice for the dead at the household altar, my uncle Strymon and I; and I cut off my hair for him. In only a little while, when I became a man, I should have been offering it to Apollo. This was the god my father had always honoured most. As I laid the wreath on the altar, with the dark locks of my hair tied into it, I remembered how his had shone in the sunlight like fine gold. Though he had turned forty when he sailed for Sicily, the colour had scarcely begun to fade; and his body was as firm as an athlete's of thirty years.

I told Strymon that my father had died of a wound in the first days of his captivity; for I could not trust his tongue, and this was the story I had given my mother.

*　　*　　*

One fine summer morning in the City, I had just put the last touches on our house, which I had been fresh-whitening. I had been doing it each daybreak till people were about; for though everyone knew nowadays that his neighbour was putting his hand to slaves' work, no one cared to have it noticed. Still, now it was done I was well pleased with it; so was my mother, especially with the courtyard, where I had painted the tops of the columns red and blue. I had had a bath, dressed my hair, and put a clean mantle on; I was carrying the walking staff I used in the City, a good blackwood one that had been my father's. After the dirty work, I felt the pleasure of trimness, as I paused in the porch to take a last look at my handiwork. When I turned my face to the street, I saw a stranger approaching the house.

He was a raw-boned old man, who had been tall when he was straight; he walked halting, and leaning on a stick cut from the thicket, one of his feet being hurt and wrapped in a dirty rag. His white hair was ragged, as if he had trimmed it himself with a knife, and he wore a short tunic of some drab stuff such as poor workmen wear, or slaves. He was dirty enough for either of these, yet bore himself like neither. He was looking at our house, making straight for it; and seeing this, I felt the sinking of some unknown fear; he seemed to me like the messenger of bad news. I stepped forward from the porch, waiting for him to speak; but when he saw me, he only stared. His drawn and bony face with its month-old stubble was weathered nearly black; his eyes being grey, showed in it piercingly. I had been about to hail him, and ask him whom he was looking for. At first I did not know what it was that kept me from asking. I only knew I must not ask.

His eyes moved past me to dwell on the courtyard. Then he looked again at me. I felt before his silent expectation a creeping in my flesh. He said, "Alexias." Then my feet carried me down into the street; and my voice said, "Father."

I don't know how long we stood there; I daresay not many moments. I said, "Come in, sir," scarcely knowing what I did; then collecting myself a little, praised the gods for his preservation. On the threshold he stumbled with his lame foot; I reached out to help him, but he righted himself quickly.

He stood in the courtyard, looking about him. I remembered Lysikles, and it seemed strange to me now that I should have taken his word without any doubts, seeing how broken the man had been and how his tale had wandered. What had put me in mind of him was the sight of my father's hand, calloused and knotted, with dirt sealed into the cracks and scars. My mind was at a stop. I groped for words to say to him. I have felt this painful dumbness in war, at the sight of a brave enemy flung down before me in the dust; but in youth one does not recognise such thoughts, nor indeed ought one to understand them. I made again, in different words, the speech about the gods I had made before. I said we had despaired of this happiness. Then, beginning to come to myself I said, "I will go before you, sir, and tell Mother."

"I will tell her myself," he said, and limped towards the door. He moved quite fast. In the doorway he turned and looked at me again. "I did not think you would grow so tall." I made him some answer. I had grown a good deal; but it was the bowing of his back that had brought us eye to eye.

I reached the doorway behind him, and then paused. My heart was pounding, my knees felt like water and my bowels were loosened within me. I heard him go into the women's rooms, but I could not hear anyone speak. I went away; at last, after what I thought must be a proper time. I went through to the living room. My father was sitting in the master's chair, with his foot in a bowl of water whose steam smelled of herbs and of a putrid wound. Before him knelt my mother, with a cloth in her hands, cleaning the place. She was weeping; the tears were running down, her hands not being free to dry them. It came into my mind for the first time that I ought to have embraced him.

The walking-stick was still in my hand. I remembered the corner where I had found it first, and put it back there.

Drawing near them, I asked him how he had come. He said from Italy, in a Phoenician ship. His foot was puffed up to twice its size, and green matter came from it. When my mother asked if the shipmaster had trusted him for the fare, he said, "They were short of a rower."

"Alexias," said my mother, "see if your father's bath is ready, and that Sostias has not forgotten anything." I was going, when I heard a sound come near, and the breath stopped in my throat; it was I who had forgotten something.

The child Charis came in, singing and chattering. She was holding a painted clay doll I had brought her from Corinth, which she was talking to; so she had come into the middle of the room before she looked up. Then she must have noticed the smell, for she stared with round eyes, like a bird. I thought, "Now he sees how pretty she is, surely he will take pleasure in what he made." He leaned forward in his chair; my mother said, "Here is our little Charis, who has heard so many tales of you." My father drew down his brows; but he did not seem very angry or surprised, and my breath came easier. He held out his hand and said, "Come here, Charis." The child stood still; so I came forward, to lead her up to him. But as soon as I tried to move her, her face grew red, and her mouth turned downward; she hid herself in the skirt of my mantle, wailing with fright. When I tried to carry her to him, she clung to my neck and screamed. I dared not look at him. Then I heard my mother say the child was timid, and cried at any strange face; the first lie I had ever heard her tell.

I took my sister away, and went to look at the bathroom. Poor old Sostias, in his confusion, had made a bad job there; I found razors and comb and pumice, and carried in the clean towels and mantle my mother had laid out. She said, "I will come with you, Myron; Sostias is too clumsy for today"; but he said he would manage for himself. I had seen already that his head was lousy. He went off, using the stick I had laid by. As my mother cleared away the cloths and bowl, she talked quickly to me of how sick he was and what he should eat, and which doctor to get for his foot. I thought of the miseries he had endured, and it seemed to me that my heart must be made of stone, that I had not wept for him as she had done. I said, "At least he will let me trim his hair and beard for him. He won't want a barber to see them as they are."

When I entered he looked ready to order me out again; but after all he thanked me, and told me to close-crop his head, for nothing else would get it clean. Taking the razor I went behind him; then I saw his back.

Eumastas the Spartan would have been humbled before it, and owned himself a beginner. I don't know what they had used on him; it must have had lead or iron tied into it. The scars went right round his sides.

At this sight, I felt all the anger that a son ought. "Father, if you know the name of the man who did this, tell me. One day I might meet him." — "No," he said, "I don't know his name." I worked on him in silence. Presently he told me that he had been taken out of the quarries by a Syracusan overseer, to sell for himself. He had changed masters several times; "but that," he said, "can wait."

His head was so filthy and scabby that it made me feel sick; luckily I was out of his sight. When I had finished, I rubbed him down with some scented oil of my own. It was good stuff from Corinth, which Lysis had given me; I only used it for parties myself. He sniffed at it and said, "What's this? I don't want to smell like a woman." I apologised and put it by. When he was dressed, and one no longer saw his hollow ribs and flanks, he looked nearly presentable, and not much above sixty.

My mother bound his foot with a dry bandage and set food before him. I could tell it was hard for him not to snatch at it like a wolf; but he soon had enough. He began to question me about the farm. I had pulled things together as well as one could expect to; but I found he knew little about the state of Attica; he seemed to suppose I could have given it all my time. I was going to explain that I had other duties; when, as if answering my thought, the blast of the trumpet swelled over the City. I sighed, and got to my feet. "I'm sorry, sir; I had hoped they would leave me longer than this with you. It's some days now since we had a raid."

I ran out shouting to Sostias to make my horse ready; then, coming back in my riding-kilt, reached down my armour from the wall. I could see him following me with his eyes, and hoped, after what he had said about the oil, that I now looked enough like a man to please him; but at the same time my mind was running on the raid, thinking of one way or another the Spartans might be coming, and where we could head them off. My mother, who was used to these alarms, had gone, without my asking her, to get my food ready. Now she came back and, seeing me fight with a twisted shoulder-buckle, went to help me. My father said, "Where is Sostias? He ought to be here for that." — "In the stable, sir," I said. "We lost the groom." It was too long a tale to begin on. Just then Sostias came to the door and said, "Your horse is ready, Master." I nodded and turned to take leave of my father. He said, "How is Phoenix?"

Suddenly I remembered him, standing to arm himself on the spot where I stood now. It seemed like half a lifetime gone. "Overworked, sir, I'm afraid," I said, "but I've kept him for you as well as I could." I should have liked to pause and think, and to say more; but the trumpet had blown and the troop had never yet had to wait for me. I kissed my mother; then, seeing his eyes on me and glad this time not to have forgotten my duty, I embraced him before I left. He felt strange to the touch, bony and stiff. I don't think I had embraced him since my grandmother died, except on the dock when he went to Sicily.

Across the Alps
by Mary Dolan

218 B.C. Hannibal, the Carthaginian hero and patriot
who nearly defeated Rome with vastly inferior resources, was one of the greatest soldiers of all time.
Here his friend and former slave, Sosylos the Greek,
describes one of Hannibal's greatest feats, his crossing
of the Alps with an army which included elephants.

Some say that there are shorter ways across the Alps than by the
route the General selected. But it is easy to be wise after the fact, and
men who could not even contemplate the deed will afterward correct
the doer. I say, in spite of all that happened, that we took the best and
wisest course. For after hurrying up the Rhone to join the troops, we moved
through settled, cultivated land, where there was food for sale and where
the General, by dipping in a quarrel between two factions (for all of
Celtica is rife with factions of some sort) engaged the friendship of one
Brancus, a chief who gave us shoes and winter clothes and guidance to
the towers of the Alps.

We marched into the sunrise, trudging upward through a broad and
gentle valley, with the rugged mountains standing off on either side. And
it was pleasant, winding through the poplar groves and growths of aro-
matic fir. We passed by grain fields almost ready for the harvest. We
camped by rushing little rivers that were icy cold and looked like green-
gray agate frothed with white. Sometimes we waded waist-deep among
grasses starred with daisies. The mountains all this while appeared remote,
and even the white waterfalls cascading down their sides seemed motionless, as though arrested in mid-air.

But gradually, as we marched, the valley narrowed and the mountains
closed around us, until finally we camped below our first high barrier in
the Alps. That afternoon the guides of Brancus said farewell and went
off happy with the gold and gifts which Hannibal distributed. We waved
to them and watched them go, and little thought how soon we were to
wish them back among us.

Next morning we broke camp beneath the shadow of the mountains.
Mists swirled about the rugged, rocky summits. The men spoke quietly
in lowered voices and cast stealthy glances at the heights we were to

48

climb. For now we had to reckon with those unknown Powers that watched and waited on the lofty peaks.

The General, that morning, was like some joyful god, exulting in the work before him. He raced along the line on his black horse, raising his arm to greet the cheering soldiers as he passed. He stopped to judge the footgear of one marcher, the balance of another's pack. He tried the guide ropes of the mules, advised upon the loading of a cart.

"It's steep and rocky," I heard him say with relish, as if a rocky steepness were the very thing to be desired. "Lower that load and draw the lashings tight. I want no overturning carts to block the path." And off he sped, far down the line to where the drivers were readying the elephants, to where the rear guard was assembling. Then he was back again, and everywhere he passed his energy and eagerness put life into the men. Yet he was not too much engrossed to note the Roman prisoner, Alimentus, loaded with my spears, my battle helmet, and my pack.

"Sosylos," he called sharply, drawing up, so that the horse reared as he spoke. I came running.

"Get an armor-bearer from the Spaniards," he said. "Don't trust that fellow with your weapons. Let him take the cooking kettles."

He galloped off, and I obeyed his order gloomily, while marveling that I must have the General himself point out my carelessness. But since I was a slave, I had none under me to do me service save this Roman prisoner, and no man can maintain the quick pace of the cavalry if he must manage extra weapons in the bargain.

This was the way I gained the services of Arrio, a boy bred in the Spanish mountains, who ran away from home to seek adventure. Perhaps the Spaniards sent him to me; perhaps he chose to come himself; at any rate, before I had a chance to seek a bearer, he was there, his round head capped with shags of coarse black hair, his stout round body girt in dingy tatters, his round face beaming with a black-eyed eagerness to take all things in charge. I sometimes wondered afterward if I belonged to Hannibal or Arrio. I had no time to wonder then, because the line began to move before I finished giving him instructions.

The cavalry led out the march and threaded slowly up across the mountain's face. A vagrant wind dispelled the mist. The troops began to sing out as they fell in step.

The air grew colder as we plodded upward on the gritty path. Before the sun had crossed the mountaintop, the army was entrained and climbing in the shadow. Far down the trail the line extended: men and horses, cattle and supplies. Below, a bending of the road concealed it; lower down, it thinned to a mere thread and vanished in a wood. Beyond it, dizzyingly far below, the valley spread out, green with summer, wide and smiling in the sunshine. Around us and above us were the clouds, rolling like smoke, from hidden places in the mountains.

The line crept upward with exasperating sloth. The General held his peace, but I could see that he fretted with impatience. Finally he sent me back along the trail to seek the reasons for our laggard's pace, and it was after this that he abandoned all the carts and carried goods by pack alone.

It was late afternoon when I returned. To my surprise, I found the vanguard settled in a glen, with walls of brush raised high, and cooking kettles slung above the fires, though there was still a mile of marching time left in the day. Something had gone amiss. The General had stopped the train and left the camp with Maltho, a Celtic scout he had picked up, the gods knew where, for Maltho was not one of Brancus's men.

I made some notes upon our progress, with the help of Captain Gisco. I roamed about the camp. I saw the Roman, Alimentus, chained down for the night. I scanned the rocks that rose about us, and once or twice I felt suspicion of a shadow shifting where there was no cause, and of a branch that quivered where there was no wind. Uneasiness beset me, but I charged it to the absence of the General.

It was with some relief, therefore, that I caught sight of Hannibal while he was circling the camp. I noticed that he stationed sentinels upon the rocks and flung an extra guard around the stores. I saw him stop before the fire of a Spanish company and jest with them about the kettle they were stirring. At once, he was presented with a bowl. He dipped it in the mess and ate with gusto, nodded his approval, and wiped his hands upon some leaves when he had finished. As he strode on, the Spaniards set to eating heartily. I thought about those clever cooks who make such mystery of a flavor; they would have been confounded had they seen how easily the General improved the taste of stew.

He was the unifying force in that conglomerate army. He understood the ardent Spaniards, the wild Numidians, and his lone, logic-ridden Greek with equal ease. And if I tell you that he sometimes jested as he went among us, you will understand that thus he taught the men to mock at hardships which he bore so cheerfully. His reputation for grim hardihood was such that nothing was esteemed too dread for Hannibal to dare, nothing too savage to inflict on one who failed him. He utilized this reputation and upheld it, to the enormous admiration of his men. Perhaps it is the reason there was never a rebellion in his army.

He was a man astonishingly great. And he was shrewd. And yet, for all his competency, he was unable to forestall the harm that threatened us. For Brancus's men had left us, and we were without a sponsor in the mountains.

Now, on the upper reaches of the height we were ascending, the road edged out upon the very lip of an abyss which dropped so far into the misty depths that you could scarcely see the patterning of fields upon the distant floor. This drop was on the left, and on the right the rock rose like a wall and then shelved back to form a kind of terrace. Up there the native mountaineers were waiting to attack us. With enemies so well disposed, the road led nowhere but to death. Nor could the General refuse the challenge of these natives, for by doing so he would invite a like reception from each tribe upon his route.

What might have happened under other leadership I cannot say. It was that passion of the General's to know details about the enemy which prompted him to send the Celtic Maltho to the mountain settlement that night. The mountaineers were Celts, and they accepted Maltho without question. They were carousing gleefully and swilling mountain ale in celebration of the loot they meant to seize. The talk was loud and boastful, and while he drank the ale and slapped away the fleas inhabiting the straw on which he sat, Maltho discovered that the mountaineers had watched our march for several days, with special interest in the tools and weapons that we carried.

These facts were not surprising, for the mountaineers employ the crudest of equipment, and indeed few nations of the world can rival the Phoenician skill at manufacturing. What startled Maltho, and sent him streaking back to Hannibal as soon as he could take his leave, was this: at night these thirsty Celts deserted their position on the rocks, and did not take guard again till daylight.

The next night Hannibal built all the fires high, and called for merrymaking in the camp. Under the cover of these noisy celebrations, he withdrew the Spanish archers. They drifted quietly by twos and threes into the shadows, and with the General went up to occupy the height. I managed to accompany this expedition. We set out in the utter darkness, where a chance misstep might send us hurtling in space. I quickly lost my selfassurance, and only prayed that if I fell I might have courage to fall silently, without a cry that would betray the enterprise.

We gained the rock, and scaled it with the aid of ropes, and blindly waited out the night in aching immobility. Dawn showed us nothing of our situation. Our blindness merely changed from black to white. Engulfed in mist, we waited silently, and strained both eyes and ears for the approaching Celts, who soon would be upon us. No sight. No sound. The drip of moisture from the cold wet rocks. The idiot comment of a cuckoo. Nothing more.

Suddenly the General was at my shoulder, peering toward the settlement. It was the purest fortune that a fitful wind swept through the mist and showed us the advancing Celts. But still we made no sound, if you except the whistle of the arrows as they left our bows. The deadly silence of the volley did as much to stop the Celts as deadly aim, and when they rallied, we leaped out yelling on the rocks and drove them down. They swarmed from every side, and still we forced them off, till finally they withdrew, leaving their dead askew upon the stones. It was now rosy daybreak.

"Listen," hissed Ildebil, the Spanish captain.

We heard the clump of hoofs, the clink of armor, the snorts of horses scrambling up the trail below our rock. The cavalry moved briskly into view, with big rough Captain Marr well in the lead. The Carthaginians, the dark Numidians, the Spanish riders trotted by. It was full daylight now, and we could see the empty depths of the abyss beyond the road. The Celts had long been quiet, but some of them crept out upon the shelving rocks between us and the trail, just as the elephants came loping past. At sight of them, the natives seemed to freeze in their positions. They looked uneasily at one another and rasped out cautious whispers of alarm. Maltho was near me. He began to chuckle silently.

"Tails before and tails behind them," he quoted mockingly. At once, the General was there beside him.

"What are they saying?" he demanded.

"The elephants. They think there must be mighty spirits in the elephants." Maltho paused to listen. "The Druids say the souls of fallen warriors inhabit animals. They think these must be souls of fallen gods, and they're afraid."

Just then an irreligious Celt let fly an arrow. It struck upon the shoulder of an elephant and fell to earth. The great beast merely tossed his head and flicked his trunk to brush the stricken spot, as if a gnat annoyed him. There was an awed moan from the mountaineers. They backed away and left the slope, to let the strange procession pass.

They could do little else. The General was in command of the position. It was a matter of mere time until we passed the danger of that place. Then there occurred one of those accidents which no one can foresee. The infantry marched by, and after them some strings of extra horses took the path. Long trains of pack mules followed after them. The barebacked mounts were led in clusters, crowding up the trail. They jostled one another as they struggled for a footing, and suddenly one horse slipped off the path. The three attached to him went over, one by one, into the emptiness. They spun out, screaming, pawing vainly as they plunged. Panic erupted through the line. The Celts, seeing their opportunity, dashed out upon the tilted rock, shouting and stoning the excited animals.

Some of the horses wheeled, milled crazily upon the path, and charged against the mules behind them. A section of the pack train went into the void. We watched it from above, unfurling like a live and shrieking ribbon on the air. The drivers spun down, flailing arms and legs like tiny spiders. On the road, the men and beasts were fighting one another wildly for a footing. Dust swirled up from the trail and hid the struggling mass of bodies, but the horrible inhuman cries shrilled on the air. A second mule train, with its precious load of food, plunged downward. The Celts now charged upon the trail itself and tried to snatch some portion of the goods they coveted.

The General could stand aloof no longer. Despite the risk of adding to confusion, he had to rescue what was left of his supplies. To rout the Celts was easy, for they fled. But it was not so easy to subdue the animals and bring some order to the madness raging on the trail. At last, calm was restored. The quiet ranks resumed their march with slow and fearful caution.

When all the train was safely past the precipice, the General led us from the height and down a rocky footpath to the village. The Celts were not to go unpunished for the havoc they had caused.

We reached the settlement but it was empty. The angry Spaniards poured into the glen and found no sign of life except the yapping of a few excited dogs. They overran the town and quickly searched the huts on either side of the small stream. A crippled crone in charge of two flea-bitten infants was the only occupant. She did not seem afraid and she was willing to explain that all the villagers had set off down the mountain to retrieve our lost supplies.

The General turned to his men and grinned. "You see how shrewd they are," he said. "They leave their storerooms full of food and hides; they leave their cattle grazing in the meadow. All that they need to keep them through the winter stands unguarded, while they go hunting in the rocks for knives and battered kettles. Let them go. We'll camp here for two days and resupply the army."

We rested during those two days, and many men and animals that had been counted lost came straggling into camp. But the Roman, Alimentus, remained among the missing. I thought he had been killed or taken by the Celts, and wasted no concern upon him. I have made many wrong appraisals in my time, but none more careless than my estimate of Alimentus.

We stripped the village bare, and left the Celts with nothing to sustain them through the cruel Alpine winter. Wherever they would steal or beg or migrate in their destitution, they would carry warning of the vengeance of the General. You might think this was punishment enough, and for the General himself I think it would have served. But to his men he must appear both unrelenting and implacable, and that was why he left the town in flames. I saw it later from a distant height — a black and smoking ruin.

From that day when we left the burning settlement, it grew more difficult for me to keep a record of our progress. Our route began to twist and turn, to rise and fall beyond all reckoning. I tried to fix on landmarks to identify our way; the queer shape of a mountain peak, the lonely outflung branches of a tree that grew out of some crevice in a cliff. But with a single turn in the trail, the peak would alter, the outline of the tree would disappear in the flat wall. On every side the mountains seemed to surge, as baffling and as trackless as the sea.

But though the disappearance of my landmarks was confusing, their reappearance, after two days' march, was terrifying. This happened some time after we had left the burning village. At first I doubted my own eyes. I hurriedly unstrapped my notes and scanned the record, then hastened from the camp to get a clearer view on higher ground. There it was: the same craggy profile in the distant rock, the same dark marking for the eye hole, the murky blotch I fancied for a mole upon the chin. And still I hoped my eyes and wits had played some trick upon me.

For in these latter days new urgency had sped the march. The General was moving with one eye upon the stores in fear of hunger, and one upon the skies in fear of snow. Our rests were shorter and less frequent. Our food was carefully dispensed, and heavy guards protected the supplies. Against these small and scrupulous economies was I to fling the news of two days' loss? Two days of toiling in a wasteful circle? It almost seemed that by discovering the error I took upon myself the guilt of causing it. Torn with uncertainty, I peered again at the familiar rock, when suddenly the General stood beside me.

"What do you see?" he said, with more demand than question in his voice. He stood there with his legs apart, his fists upon his hips, as men will sometimes halt to catch their breath. He did not look at me, but toward the mountains.

"I hope I may be wrong," I said unhappily, and pointed to my landmark. "Out there, I see a portrait in that crag: the blunt nose, the eye socket, the mole upon the chin." He nodded with no change in his expression. "That is my landmark for two days ago. The same position; almost the same distance."

"I thought as much," he said, and this time there was grimness in his tone. "The guides will pay for this," he said, and then he slowly added, "but who has paid the guides?" After a moment's silence he continued. "Tell no one of this landmark. If anyone should recognize it, you must contradict him. I cannot have the men discouraged now."

He disappeared as quickly as he had come, and I was there alone, to face the certainty that we were lost. Below me I could hear the noises of the camp: the rumble of men's voices, the crackle of the brushwood gathered for the fires, the clangor of stacked armor, the stamp and whinny of the horses.

They were dead men, down there, I thought. Dead men, but for a while they could not die. They must climb on, hauling their useless burdens after them, turning away from one blind walled-in trail to find another quite as mocking. Then the starving. Then the freezing. Then the snows. It was like that gruesome fable of the folk in hell, where men push wearily at rocks that never reach the hilltop, or strain their bonds for water that never wets their lips. A wise man's course was plain to see, and I could take it there and then. I need not wait the last extremes of misery. One step beyond the rock on which I stood would send me spinning to oblivion.

That step I could not bring myself to take. I have not left the theater, in all my life, before the play has ended. I must see all of it; that is the Greek in me. Moreover, there was still the cunning brain of Hannibal, who willed that we should live and come to Italy. And to be sure, there was no lack of peaks from which to fling myself whenever life became unbearable. At last I turned and made my way down to the camp.

I wondered if the guides had somehow taken Roman gold to lead us to our deaths. And so, I think, did Hannibal. I know he tried to learn the truth of it, for he had meant to take the Romans by surprise. He was not present at the mess that night. And later, in the dark, I heard a tortured groaning, oft repeated. Three times I heard the long and slowly dying wail a man expels when plunging from a height. But from the General, not then nor afterward, did I learn anything. Next morning Maltho was the only guide in camp. He had been waiting for us far ahead, much puzzled by our failure to appear, and spent the night in coming back to find us. The other guides were thought to have deserted.

That was the day I came on Gorlas the Numidian striving obscenely with the garments which the Celtic prince had given us. They were in truth an odd contrivance. A man must step inside and draw them upward, for they were forked and made a casing for the legs which was good proof against the cold but hellishly discomforting. Gorlas grinned while struggling with the garment, for he had only two expressions for his face: a stolid look for commonplace occasions and a twisted grin for every kind of stress. I watched, and it was comical to hear him curse so sorely while he grinned so happily. He knotted the leg pieces on his chest. And as he gathered up the weapons he had set aside, I saw he had acquired a Celtic knife. It was a curious design, one I had fancied when I saw it in its owner's hands. It was a knife belonging to a Celtic guide who had deserted, so they said, the night before.

We made good progress after that, and came soon to a high plateau, well settled and well planted. Here we were welcomed, given princely gifts of food and cattle, and guided amicably through the land. Whatever offerings the people brought were well bestowed, because they purchased safety for their flocks and fields. Meanwhile we hurried on, having no time for pillage nor for feasting. At length the plateau was behind us. The General bade farewell to these complacent guides and promptly changed the order of the march. He placed the elephants first in the line (no tribe, so far, had dared to attack the elephants), and brought the baggage from the rear to come between the cavalry and a strong afterguard on foot.

The General did nothing without purpose, and there was speculation in the ranks as to the meaning of this new formation. Time and again my stocky Spanish armor-bearer Arrio found reasons to approach me, offering me water or a change of weapons, and hovering close by as long as possible. It struck me then that Arrio must glory in his new assignment. Of all the Spaniards, this young runaway was closest to the General's staff; it would be odd indeed if he did not pretend to having secret information. I thought I saw a new importance in his bearing, as would befit a lad who had been nothing but a roustabout and now was made a witness to official matters. No doubt his countrymen depended on his news, and looked to Arrio for explanations of our change of march.

I must have smiled at these reflections as we jogged along, for Mago, riding past me down the line, wheeled round and asked me what I found amusing. He had been friendly to me ever since that day in Spanish Carthage when he was made captain. And, in truth, Mago was much improved. He had grown more discreet, though not less talkative. Adventure and experience brought out a lively humor in him which brightened many an evening in the camps. As Mago spoke, the march came to a halt, and while I told him about Arrio the boy himself came running up the line.

"Is this Arrio?" said Mago in a stern official voice.

Arrio stopped short; his mouth fell open with surprise at being known to the exalted officer.

"I hear that Arrio's eye is keen," said Mago in a deep portentous tone, as if he were pronouncing oracles. "He has an eye to see, a mind to ponder on his observations." Poor Arrio could understand but little of all this, but none the less he nodded, open-mouthed. "Use them, use them, young Arrio!" cried Mago with the fervor of an orator. "Be on the watch for hidden danger! Imagine every peril that might befall us, and know beforehand how you mean to meet it. A good soldier is a ready soldier. Hold your place in line, but keep a watchful eye for *danger!*"

Arrio's head bobbed eagerly and he was off like an arrow down the line, while Mago laughed and vowed that now at least the Spaniards would be kept on the alert. But even when we jest, we use the subjects topmost in our minds, and I believe this fancying of danger and defense was one of Mago's own employments. Surely his words to Arrio were opportune, and I had reason to be grateful for them before the day was spent.

It was early afternoon when we came to the gorge. As we approached, we skirted a white rock which rose about three hundred feet in air. Beyond this rock the road ran like a thread into a narrow cleft from which the mountain walls sprang up on either side. Between these walls the way climbed steadily until it reached the pass. The place was deathly quiet. In the lead the elephants were plodding stolidly into the gloom of the defile. After their padded tread the clumping of the horses' hoofs, the scuff-scuff of the marching men were all that broke the stillness. The mounted troops followed the elephants, and you could see their ranks close in before they disappeared into the hushed and shadowed gorge. The pack mules bobbed behind the cavalry.

This was the order we were keeping when the sleepy stillness was shattered by a piercing screech. Celts seemed to spring out of the very roadside. The air was split with savage yelling. It rang with the clangor of spear on steel and hissed with the whip of arrow and dart. The Celts fell on the troops, all up and down the line. It was fend and thrust, swing and strike, heave and throw your weapons without any plan at all except the frenzied will to stay alive. Many a shout that swelled the lungs escaped the throat in a feeble death gasp. Bodies writhed where men had stood erect a moment since. I plunged my spear into a Celt and lost it as he wrenched away. My wicker shield collapsed under a Celtic club. I would have fallen then and there had Arrio not been at hand with battle weapons. I seized them as I swerved my horse to trample on a Celt. I speared another, while Arrio flipped an arrow from his quiver and ran to a position on the rocks. Then I made for the General, who shouted in the thick of it.

"Bostar!" he called the captain of the guard. "Move up! Hold the mouth of that passage!" The guards were already cutting and thrusting the enemy back off the roadside.

"Hanno, ride ahead to Maharbal! Tell him to make full speed up the gorge. Keep the line going all night if need be! He's to get it through to safety."

The young captain raced forward with the message.

After the first onslaught the Celts had momentarily withdrawn. Hannibal rallied his guard. "Gisco, send the slingers and the archers up on that white rock. They can dominate the road from there."

The cavalry had seemed to leave the world behind when they had entered in the gorge. The deeper they advanced into that rocky cleft, the more the quiet oppressed big Captain Marr. For days he had been haunted by the sense of hidden eyes watching from the still rocks and the motionless thickets. Now it was worse. In this narrow crevice of a trail, he felt not only watched but straitened. The gorge was hardly wider than the road, if you except the stream that trickled underneath an arching ledge. They were walled in. Marr looked ahead and saw the trail congested with the elephants. Their tails swung and their hind quarters heaved in clumsy haste. His last thought dwelt upon a well fleshed company of ambulating females, when the clash of the attack broke out behind him. In a moment Hanno came pounding up the trail.

"Make haste to the top of the pass!" he began to shout as he approached them.

Marr was lifting his arm to give the order when some trick of light above him changed the signal to a quick leap sideward, underneath the ledge. It was pure instinct. The earth shook with a thunderous impact. A boulder rocked and settled dustily upon the very spot the captain had abandoned. Marr peered back along the line. Most of the riders huddled under cover, as stones and logs continued to smash down on the roadway. Marr set to cursing with a violent passion. The tribes of the plateau had been well treated. They had nothing to resent and nothing much to gain by this delayed attack. It was pure malice, and it had to go unpunished. Marr raged profanely as he waited for a lull, then waved his troops from cover. He sent them forward at a gallop, counting as they passed.

He glanced behind them where a mule train hustled up the trail. Even as he looked, another boulder caromed downward, mangling the animals. Some of the mules broke loose, dashed wildly against the rock walls. Packs broke open; their contents littered the floor of the passage. In the narrow confines of the gorge, the shrieking of the beasts and pinioned men was torture to the ears. Marr raced down the road and seized the guide ropes of the second mule train. Shouting and cursing, he urged the small beasts onward, and sent them up the trail, lashing at their flanks as they scrambled over the debris on the path.

Meanwhile, Hanno came tearing back to the General with news of the disaster in the gorge.

"Ildebil," ordered Hannibal, "take your men up the mountains. Go after those devils; stop that slaughter on the trail!"

The Spaniards cast off cloaks and packs and ran toward the ascent.

Some of the Balearic slingers had already scrambled up the high white rock. They let loose a volley of stones and leaden pellets upon the rallying Celts. Their aim was murderously accurate. In childhood, on their cave-pitted islands, the Baleares learned to split a hair at twenty paces. If any boy should fail in marksmanship, he forfeited his meals. The slingers were well able to protect the entrance to the gorge.

The Celts were back again like a cloud of hornets, but the strong rear guard had now come up to drive them off. By this time the entrance to the passage was strewn with the dead. The sun had long since disappeared below the mountains; the pack train had vanished into the gorge. The

General sent part of the rear guard after it, but did not follow with the rest. As long as he controlled the entry, he could protect the rear of those en route. Darkness was coming on. The Celts withdrew. Returning to the rock, the General called up the captains of the guard.

"We'll camp here," he announced. "We'll have no food until we can rejoin the baggage train. Those who have anything to eat will share it with their comrades."

As he finished speaking, a thin cold rain began to fall. It hissed into the fires that sprang up near the rock; it dampened the firewood; it ran down in chill trickles from cold metal helmets. It fell on soddening cloaks and tunics. It kept on falling, lightly, quietly, remorselessly, all through the night.

As for the General, I do not think he slept at all that night. Each time I stirred out of the lethargy that settled on me, I saw him moving through the bivouac. Many a soldier, squirming in his soggy wrappings, looked up to see the General beside the hooded fire. The moisture dripped from his battered headpiece and his beaked nose; it beaded on his woolen cloak. He grinned down mockingly upon the shivering forms before him. Dulled as they were with hunger and exhaustion, they seemed to come alive at sight of Hannibal. Sometimes he merely nodded and moved on. Sometimes he bent over a wounded man or gave some order for his benefit. But he performed no kindly ministry among the injured. He gave no sympathy. He merely showed that he was with his men, a soldier subject to the same discomforts as themselves. And neither then nor afterward did I hear any murmur of complaint, or even of regret, for all the misery of that night beside the rock. The soldiers spoke of it with pride as of a time when each had matched the fortitude of Hannibal.

Nor have I said one word against their pride till now. For it was good and helpful and it was precisely what the General intended. But I say now that no man living in those hours could have matched the courage of the General. I think they were among the blackest in his whole career. Here Hannibal, the master of surprise attack, allowed himself to be surprised. Already lacking in supplies, he lost provisions. Already dangerously late, he met delay. The situation now was desperate. Hunger was unavoidable. Snowfalls upon the peaks were now a certainty. He had set out to punish Rome. What would he bring to pit against her might? A feeble, staggering army? A demoralized army? Quite possibly he was leading a dead army.

Hannibal knew on that night that he had failed his aim, which was to cross the mountains by a march so well provided and so ably planned that it would merely be a difficult maneuver. That hope was lost. The whole affair was now the wildest hazard. It might be wisdom to turn back and save his army for the war in Spain. It might be best to seize the Celtic towns and winter in the mountains. I watched him, wondering what he would do. And I betray my ignorance of Hannibal when I admit I wondered. For I know now he would have gone to Italy alone if necessary, abandoning his men, his comrades, and his brother as they failed or fell. It was the purpose of his life to strike at Rome; and he would strike at her most vulnerable side, with Punic armies if he could, with Celtic allies if he must, with every kind of wile and weapon in his reach, and he would go on striking till the day he died. Few men in all the generations of humanity have known so well what they were born to do.

They were desperate times, indeed, that followed the disaster at the gorge. We climbed forever upward. We led our mounts and picked our way on narrow, rubbly paths where a loose rock or crumbled footing might dispatch a man to death. The wind shrilled down upon us from the heights above. It slammed against our shields, tugged at our wraps, and whistled in our aching ears. Supplies dwindled and hunger griped our bellies. Many a man, light-headed from privation and dizzied in the high thin air, mistook his footing and crashed down upon the jagged rocks below. Many another one lagged far and farther in the rear, and it was piteous to see these weak ones creeping into camp long after all the rest were lost in sleep. And still we struggled on, drawn close by that vast loneliness through which we traveled, spurred by the dread of being left forsaken on those heights.

The General let the cold and desolation work for him. Desertion was unthinkable. The only danger was despair, and he could see it gathering like a cloud. Each night the list of missing men grew longer as he stood to hear it in the torchlight, taking the officers' reports. In these days he wore a bulky cloak of spotted fur, a gift from Brancus, and he would fling it backward from his shoulders as the officers approached, and nod impassively to hear the toll of lagging men, and men considered lost.

"Save their rations for them," he would say as he dismissed his captains. "The stragglers may come in by morning." This done, he settled himself on the ground, still in the torchlight, and he would eat his dole of meal with relish, munching long and thoroughly, and drinking from the common store of sour wine. At first I thought this was a leader's trick, a heartening example to his men. Then I recalled that Hannibal had never dined except from hunger. It struck me suddenly that he was quite as gaunt and shrunken as the rest of us, for all his carefree manner.

The meal done, he would quench his torch, roll in his cloak, and stretch out on the rocks, and soon the camp would follow his example. Sleeping men do not dismay one another with their fears, and rested bodies carry stouter hearts. When all the camp was quiet, the General might rouse again, and go off to consult with Maltho. Or he might prowl among the sleepers, trying to decide how many days of marching could be got from those exhausted bodies. I sometimes wondered if he ever felt a storm of pity rise and shake him inwardly, when looking at the wasted figures of the men who trusted him. But I think now that he had long controlled all feelings till they came to him on call, and never dared intrude without a summons. Instead of pity, he would be obsessed with planning how to drive his men to their survival, and what to do when they would fail to rise at dawn, but rather choose to lie and let death take them.

Lively spirits and cheerful tempers were swiftly recognized in these hard days. Thus Arrio, my onetime armor-bearer, was promoted to the fighting ranks, and he assumed the swagger he thought fitting for the post. Mago was given more authority, and I am glad to say that I, Sosylos, was now freed and made a captain. I must admit that in my case the General mistook my curiosity for courage. For there are some who, even in the face of Death, must scrutinize that lady to see if she be equal to her reputation.

I watched our hardships sharpen and our strength expire. There came a night when I was sure, as we made camp, that we would never march from where we lay. It was not mutiny; it was the loss of hope. We were like men enduring tortures on a road to nowhere. I ate my dole of food in silence and stretched out upon the stones, half wishing that I need not ever rise again.

Arrio stood sentinel above the sleeping camp and looked into the wide and glittering sky. To city men, who rarely cast a glance aloft, the heavens are a sparkling enigma. To such as Arrio (and to the greater portion of mankind) they are a mere utility. Time must be measured, and what else can count the hours, or trisect the month, except the heavens? What else gives notice of the changing year? When Taurus rises early, with the Pleiades aspangle in his mane, what shall a man expect, if not the winter? Arrio looked at the Pleiades and gave no thanks for their unnecessary warnings. His nostrils had already felt the crisp invasion of the frost. He wrapped himself more snugly in the wolfskin cape that gave his head the furred shape of a prick-eared animal. It had been Vilbo's cape: Vilbo, his fellow runaway and laughing comrade. The boy had slipped and fallen on the heights, and Arrio had snatched at him in vain, grasping the empty cape while Vilbo spun down through the void. Poor Vilbo! Yet Arrio was glad the cape, at least, was saved. So many good things went with men who had no need for them. A month ago, no mangy cloak could have consoled him for the loss of Vilbo. Now, like the rest of us, young Arrio would find no fault with anything that aided his survival.

He stamped his rag-wrapped feet upon the icy stone. Even firewood was hard to find. The boy looked down at the ruddy splotch below, where hoarded embers glowed against the dark. He thought of leaping fires built in former camps, when we were down below the timberline. Arrio shivered and breathed steamily upon his fingers. He listened to the wide, lonely silence. There was a scrape and rustle on the rock below him.

"Who's there?" the boy cried fiercely to the dark.

"A friend; a fellow soldier," came the answer.

"Give the watchword."

"Feasting in Italy." The phrase was uttered in a Spanish dialect like Arrio's own.

"One day sooner," was the boy's reply. "That watchword, now," reflected Arrio aloud. "Who makes up all that nonsense?"

"Some officer," the voice suggested carelessly. "Why?"

"Who's feasting and where's Italy? Does anybody know?" scoffed Arrio. "And as for you, you'd better get back to your company," he said. "It's dangerous to wander in the dark. You step too close to the supplies, and you've a knife between your ribs. Those Africans on guard will roast you for their breakfast."

"It's not so bad as that," said the voice in the dark. "We get a handful of meal and some wine every day, don't we? A man can't take much food in this thin air."

"Stop talking like an officer," said Arrio in disgust. "How much worse can it be? How long can we live on these rations? We don't even know where we are. We're freezing and we have no fires to warm us. By morning we're as stiff as gravestones. Even our beards are brittle with the frost. It stands to reason," Arrio went on, as though he were accustomed to consult the laws of reason, "if we knew where to go, we would have gone there before now. Go on, get back to sleep," he added loftily.

"Keep a sharp watch," the soldier said.

Arrio could hear him moving off, down the rock. The young sentry felt better. He was comfortably unaware that he had just been bullying the General. The boy's dark, pessimistic talk, far from discouraging himself, gave Arrio new confidence. He saw himself now as a veteran campaigner, and, warm with self-approval, turned his thoughts to happier themes. His hand stole tentatively toward his downy chin.

I, Sosylos, slept ill upon these heights and I awoke when Hannibal returned. He sat there, hunched upon the stone, his knees drawn up within the circle of his arms. I went to him, and for an answer to my whispered question he merely shook his head.

"They're spent." He said this in an undertone. "Excepting Marr and Mago and a few like you and your young Spaniard. They've only one more effort left, and it's the last," he said, "the one men seldom realize they have. It comes out of their spirits."

"Spirits?" I said in some perplexity. My head was ringing so that I had hardly caught his words. "A company of ghosts will do you little good at Rome."

"Yes, *Rome*," he snarled, and I was startled at the sudden venom in his voice. "Noble, self-righteous Rome," he mocked. "We must remember Rome. Coiled like a fat snake in the Tiber's mud; a torpid snake too stupid to survive, except by swallowing its neighbors. Shall all good things be offered up to Rome? Can nothing prosper without sharpening Rome's appetite? Was it for Rome Phoenicians braved the unknown seas and set their trading posts on lonely islands? Was it for Rome that Carthage built and manned her fleets? Was it for Rome my father toiled and died in Spain? Shall all the world give up its gains to Rome, and sweat to keep Rome sleek and fat because the Romans feel this is no more than right? I say Rome must be beaten down and crushed! I say these ragged skeletons of mine shall do it. For they *must*. Who else is there to stop the Romans, except us?"

He turned on me as if I spoke against him, but I had never been at such a loss for words. The General was always moderate in speech; he was in every way a man of discipline. He scoffed at ranting orators, yet here he crouched, talking so like a tragic poet that I scarcely knew him. All powerful emotion seems naive, and I was suddenly abashed to see my stern commander thus exposed.

He was not waiting for any word from me. He had a tougher wisdom than my own. Within himself, the General was rousing up the spirit that sets men doing what cannot be done.

Early next morning, if anyone had been awake, he might have seen young Arrio making for the water casks with the air of a man on a mission. The army was asleep, and that was just as well, in Arrio's opinion. There were not many mirrors in the camp, but issues as momentous as a sprouting beard require watching. He often used these early secret moments to turn his head this way and that, over his image in the water. He had discovered that his face made an absorbing study. In Spain he was a jolly pudding of a lad with all the menace of a dimpled cupid. The new Arrio was different, and the vision of the new Arrio enchanted him. The round face was drawn to a taut triangle. The dark eyes were sunken into deeply shadowed sockets. The chubby frame was lean and spare. The new Arrio was a desperado, a cutthroat, a man to beware of. He often leered back from the water casks with horrible expressions on his face.

But now, alas, an icy crust obscured the water. When Arrio had broken it, he still could catch no clear reflection of his face. He had no time to lose; the men would soon begin to wake. The lad moved forward on the trail, seeking the brook which he was sure to find near any camp. He had no way of knowing that the stream he found was not the one that filled our water casks.

This water was not frozen because it was a small, fast-running brook, but it was rippling too busily to yield an image. Arrio squatted there among the wet pebbles, hopefully feeling his chin and looking down at the swift-moving water. There was something different about it. Only a mountain lad would read its signal. Suddenly Arrio whirled and pelted toward the camp as quickly as his trembling legs could carry him.

Morning had roused no brisk activity among the soldiers. Exhausted and near-starved, they huddled apathetically, unwilling to begin the task of breaking camp. Arrio shouted wildly as he swerved among them.

"The stream!" He pointed back excitedly. "The stream runs east instead of west! We've crossed the peaks!"

The skinny, tattered troops staggered erect. They shivered in the wind and gave a feeble cheer. As if by order, they stumbled toward the stream. Soon nearly all the army was assembled, grinning fatuously at the little brook.

The General herded us eastward, beyond the camp, circling the rocks to where the ground began to fall away.

"Over there is your Italy," Hannibal exulted. "Within a five-day march. In five short days you'll reach the teeming fields, the fat cattle, the rich and well-stocked towns of Italy. All yours for the taking! Compare that with the cheap spoils you could get from cattle raids in Spain! Yes, you've had a long march," he admitted, "and short rations. But it was worth it. Now the worst is over. For now you can forget the hardships and think of the rewards to come. No one can stop an army that has overcome the Alps."

It comes to me that I have said no word about the women on this journey, yet was there ever any march of men that did not have its following of women? The Spanish women left us at the Pyrenees. The Celts began to join us at the Rhone and some came on with us from Brancus' settlement. And many disappeared or died along the way, and others came to us from hostile tribes and helped us with devices for survival in the mountains.

I have said nothing of them because this is the story of the General, and for the General these women hardly had existence. As for myself, from the beginning of my manhood I formed the habit of avoiding traffic of this sort, with women and with boys. For in my early years I followed closely in the Stoic regimen, in which Anthon directed me. And after I was sent to Spain, I was in close companionship with Hannibal and shared in the austerity he practiced. Some may consider that my circumstances made an oddity of me in this respect, but I regard the matter as irrelevant, excepting as it may explain my negligence in speaking of the women. Only a very few of them survived, and I suspect that as they failed and lagged behind they fell a prey to other appetites than those of venery.

It was just growing light when Hannibal again looked from his tent. The snow had stopped, but the hushed stillness was a threat above the camp. The blind, blank white lay everywhere. Mounds of white, where the soldiers slept. Peaks of white, where the tents pushed up beneath their fluffy caps. And down the slopes he must traverse out of this featureless locale, nothing but smooth, trackless white.

After we crossed the peaks, and all but saw our way down into Italy, the worst misfortune had befallen us. Of all the dire predictions made against this crossing, the grimmest and the gravest was the threat of snow. Fifteen, twenty, thirty feet of snow might pile in drifts, they said, to smother us, immobilize our march, obliterate our roads. Then we would feel the grip of real disaster. Comrades would look upon each other, not as men but as meat. The happiest would die by murder; some would freeze; the rest would starve. Next spring, after the thaws, the vultures could rejoice at Barca's folly.

In all the years that I had known the General, this was the first time I could read his face. The sparkling mockery was gone. Without that bright vitality the face was old. It was closed and bleak; but even as I watched him the jaws stiffened and anxiety gave place to resolution.

Only speed could save us. This first snowfall was more ominous than heavy. With a swift march downward, between storms, we might escape. As he stood watching there, the trumpets sounded.

Happily, the day dawned clear. The sun struck on the snow with a blinding glare that pierced the eyeballs and set colored spots to dancing in the eyes. In starting from the camp, we had to cross a long and gentle slope that suddenly fell off into a steep descent. The Spaniards, born to mountaineering, were to lead the way. They had to test each step. There was no way to tell, under that treacherous white blanket, where the footholds lay. The Spaniards started delicately, stepping sidewise against the incline. I saw young Arrio among the first.

Test the footing . . . step. Test . . . step. Test . . . step. They looked like shaggy devotees of some weird dancing cult as they inched downward. Suddenly Arrio's feet flew out from under him, and he shot downward, faster, and faster toward the drop. He twisted, he clawed desperately at the snow, but each move only sped him down the swifter. In a last hope he freed his short sword from its sheath and drove it powerfully in the ground. It held. Arrio swung to a stop, and a cheer went up from the watching men. Still clinging to the sword hilt, the lad tried cautiously to gain his footing, but beneath the soft new snow lay the glazed layer of last year's fall. He slipped and floundered helplessly, till someone flung a rope, and drew him back to level ground.

They tried again. This time they hacked and stamped the icy crust so that a man could crush a foothold into the surface. They strung a guiding rope along the way. Finally, a detachment of foot soldiers made its way down. Next, the General chose to try a string of pack mules on the trail. They started carefully. I wondered if the burdens, however firmly bound, would not destroy the balance of the little animals.

"Gently, now; take it slowly," the General called as they moved down. It would work, we thought; it was going to do —

"Hold fast!"

One mule lost its footing, and the whole string skimmed down the slope, tipping the soldiers over like toys. Ropes broke, animals screamed, mules threshed on the slippery grade. Some of them, pawing frantically, broke through the crusted surface with their sharp hoofs and stood rooted in the ice. Just as the uproar subsided, word came back that the trail below was impassable.

The General, with Mago and Captain Marr, slipped and sidled down the snowy slope and made the steep descent where the soldiers hacked some steps into the incline. I clambered after them. This passage leveled out upon a broad and winding ledge which made a fair roadway. The General pushed on, to round the turn, and stopped.

The whole ledge ended abruptly in mid-air. An avalanche had swept a great slice of the mountain down to lie in stones and rubble some thousand feet below. The road was gone. Instead, the rocky wall rose straight into the sky.

We were trapped. The General saw it clearly. We were perched on the bald knob of an icy mountain and there was no descent. We had almost no food, no firewood, no pasturage. By now, snow clogged and hid the passes through which we had come. Any wind might blow a new snowstorm upon us. Retreat was impossible.

Mago stood in hopeless silence. Maharbal was cursing with elaborate detail, under his breath. Hannibal moved to the edge. Could we notch a roadway into the face of this mountain? He kicked at the snow clinging to the vertical wall. It fell away and showed the solid rock.

Anger and rebellion seemed to seethe inside the General. We were within three days of Italy. We had borne all the terrible sufferings of the journey. Now we were at the end of our strength, we were on the threshold of safety. Now slow, inglorious Death mocked us across that gaping void. Hannibal stared bitterly at the rock. To him it was a new kind of enemy: impersonal, inanimate, immovable. Flesh and blood were powerless against it. Man could make the buoyant sea support him. He could make the soft earth yield for him. But who had ever overcome the rock?

Who, indeed? The General began to chuckle, then to laugh aloud. Why else had the Phoenicians come to Spain, if not to rob the very rocks? What were those mines that honeycombed the Spanish hills, if not a conquest of the rocks? The irony of his predicament brought on another gust of laughter. The rocks gave echo to the sound, and it was horrible to hear them laughing back at us, long after he was silent. From near and far, from high and low, we heard the strange, wild chorus of derision.

I must confess it set my flesh acrawl. For there are tales of men who dare too much and rouse the anger of the unseen Powers, and they are generally driven mad before they are destroyed.

Mago and Marr were looking anxiously at Hannibal, and so was I. If he had lost his wits, there was no hope for any of us. Marr hurried to the General and took his arm.

"Come back," he urged. "There must be some way out of this. Come back to camp and see what can be done."

The General looked up in sharp surprise. He saw dismay upon our solemn faces, and instantly, he played the self-assured commander.

"No need to go up there," he said. "Here is the place to do what must be done. We're going to cut a road in that rock."

Cut the rock, indeed! I felt despair and it was physical; it twisted me inside and sent the bitterness upgushing in my throat.

"Mago" — he turned to his bewildered brother — "send me any miners serving in the army; send me the masons and the smiths and the siege engineer. We'll cut that rock. If there were gold in it, we'd split it soon enough."

Mago set off, not knowing whether he had heard a madman's raving or a sane man's final, desperate resort.

"Zoos, General," Marr said, regaining his assurance, now that he had a plan of action, "those smiths and masons are too clever. They know how far they'll fall if they should lose their footing. Call my Numidians down here. They're ignorant. They haven't sense enough to think of anything except the road."

The General nodded. He was gazing far across the gap to where the interrupted road resumed its course.

"I know," he said. "We may be forced to use them, but let's try the others first. We'll go and see what Mago has collected."

The General had to set his men to work before the story of the laughing echoes spread despair among them. He gave them little chance to speculate upon their plight.

"You're up here on a slippery mountain and you must get down," he barked at them. "There isn't any road, and so the only thing to do is make one. And by the great god Baal, you'll make it! What's more, you'll have to clear this slope of snow and ice, so that the elephants can move down quickly when the road is cut.

"I want every man to go through his kit and bring me anything that

can be used as a chisel and anything that can be melted down to make a
chisel. Pile them up here before my standard.

"I want every scrap of wood that can be used for kindling. Stack them
here: roots, brush (if you can find it), tent poles, war towers, camp chairs,
litters, everything we have that will take fire. We're going to heat that
frozen rock and crack it. We're going to chip at it until we've cut a road.
We're going to march down and away like soldiers when the task is done.
Get to work, now, all of you!"

They worked all day. They cleared the slope of ice and graded the descent.
They forged the chisels and the picks to hew the rock. But, true to Marr's
prediction, it was the Numidians who actually cut the road. While the
professionals demurred and peered at the abyss, Gorlas spat showily upon
his hands and swung his pick. He was a capering comedian whom everybody watched with interest, as I had watched him on the day he tried the
Celtic breeches. Now, as then, his face was twisted in a grin, and soon he
chipped a fragment from a crevice in the rock. His fellow soldiers stood
in line to follow him and all the men took heart from his example. Before
the night closed in, a narrow track was nibbled partially across the cliff.

But those Numidians! They were in fact as single-minded as their captain promised. They did not stop for darkness. They built a fire on the
ledge, and as they cut the rock they raked the fire forward. In its light
you caught the gleam of melted frost oozing from the stone. The wind
scooped and scoured at the face of the precipice, but the Numidians clung
there like bats. Each time the wind died down, you heard the flat clink
of the iron on the rock.

Above us, in the camp, the soldiers huddled close for warmth and tried
to sleep. But I could no more sleep than Captain Marr. We watched there
at the road's end, stamping in the cold and nursing a small fire, scarcely
brighter than a cat's eye in the darkness.

SSSSSssssss! A cloud of steam purled upward from the ledge and hid
the path, the workers, and the fire in a rosy glow. It came from the boiling wine poured on the frozen stone to crackle it. Behind the steam an
agonizing shriek rose, high and piercing. It quavered off into a sobbing
wail. Then everything was quiet.

"What's wrong?" cried Captain Marr. "What happened?"

The Numidians were strung along the ledge, each working to enlarge
his section of the path. It was impossible for one to pass another on that
narrow track. Word came back from mouth to mouth along the rock.

"It's Gorlas, Captain."

"Scalded his feet."

"The flesh is hanging from his bones."

"Bring him back here," raged the captain. "Come off that rock, all of you. Bring Gorlas. Pull him by his shoulders." The big captain waited impatiently while the order was relayed forward, and the reply came slowly back.

"He won't come, Captain. He's fighting with the man who wants to bring him. And there's no room to fight, out there."

"Clear that damned snake path!" shouted Captain Marr. "Come off, now. All of you!"

Slowly the Numidians began to pass their picks and hammers backward, then to inch their way along the ledge to broad, safe ground.

The captain started forward. He was the only one whom Gorlas would obey, and I could see Marr was determined not to lose the man. Perhaps I should have tried to stop the captain, but I too had watched these fearless little fellows all day long, and felt some shame that I must owe my safety to their unrequited courage. I knew what sent the captain forward on the narrow ledge.

Marr was too big a man to fit the track of the Numidians. He was almost a fourth again as tall as they, and large in every way. His mere height seemed to overbalance him, inclining him above the black abyss upon the right. I watched, expecting him to crouch down on his hands and knees, in common caution, but he moved erect. And how could he do otherwise? Numidians had sidled back and forth along that cliff all day. Before such men a captain may not crawl. He stepped deliberately forward.

Look straight ahead, I urged him in my mind, as he moved off. Don't look at the abyss; look straight ahead. Try not to think, I pleaded silently; I knew that there are times when a man's body serves him better than his brains.

The captain's right foot slipped and missed the ledge. He staggered forward and froze rigidly. I felt the sweat start out beneath my clothing, while the shock of my alarm churned through me. I stopped my breath and held as still as did the captain. Then, up from far below, we heard the faint click of the stone that rolled and fell away beneath Marr's tread. He straightened slowly, and we all released our breath. He took the final steps and reached his goal.

The ledge was wider at the place where Gorlas lay, as if the picks had struck a crumbling texture in the rock. The little man was propped against the wall, his head thrown back, the scalded feet thrust forward in a puddle fed from the upended kettle. The fire was dying down, and it would shortly vanish into blackness.

"Light more torches, there!" the captain bellowed. But the winds tossed his words together, and we heard nothing but a vague halloo. Then he picked up an ember from the fire and waved it as he slowly called, "Lights! Torches! Hurry!"

We kindled all the firewood and held it high. But as it wavered in the wind, the rough ledge seemed to writhe and throb among the shadows thus created. Then I heard a familiar voice behind me.

"Wait a moment, Captain."

It was Arrio, of course, who frequently traced down my whereabouts. He took an arrow, thrust it through a daub of pitch, and set the whole alight. He shot it arching through the dark, and lodged it nicely in a crevice of the rock above the path.

Marr grasped the dazed Numidian beneath the arms. He sat down on the trail and made a kind of sled, to carry Gorlas on his own long legs. Then he began to snake his way backward drawing the scalded soldier up to him with every move.

I hoped that Gorlas was unconscious, for any sudden movement on that narrow ledge would tip them into space. They were beneath the flaming arrow when the wind, which had been quiet, tore at them with aggravated fury. It plucked the arrow from the crevice just above them and, shrilling like a hundred demons, dashed the lighted brand down on the chest of the Numidian. Gorlas screamed, jerked from Marr's grasp, and lurched toward the abyss. The captain's fist struck upward under Gorlas's chin; the captain's body rolled him toward the wall. Marr brushed away the burning arrow. It fell down, down, still flaming, till we could see it only as a pinpoint gleam below.

The two were now in darkness. Marr seemed to wait, to let the glare die from his eyes. Then we could hear the slide and scrape again, and soon the captain moved into our torchlight and soon we helped him and Gorlas safely off the ledge.

The captain sat there for a moment, drawing up his knees and leaning forward, with his head upon them. Then he rose, and shot a rueful, grinning glance at me before he turned to the Numidians.

"Get back to work," he told them with easy unconcern. "Go back out there and make that road. I'll see to Gorlas." He took the little fellow in his arms and carried him to Synhalus, the surgeon.

They chipped and hammered at that mountain all night long. Late the next day, they had a perilous, narrow foothold cut across the precipice. The scouts went over it barefooted. Mountain troops could follow. But for the regulars, the precious horses, elephants, and the equipment, a much wider track was needed.

The General spurred the men and scanned the skies. Snow clouds swirled and blackened over the peaks, and he observed them with a stolid face. We stood there where the new-hewn road began, and watched the swinging picks of the Numidians. And in an instant, without warning, the air was white with snow. It did not merely fall; it seemed to be hurled down upon us with the vengeful swiftness of attack. We could no longer see the workmen on the rock. Within a moment hoods and cloaks were caked and whitened, and each hollow in the road was fluffed with white. The winds shrieked and whistled and drove the snow in shaking veils across the chasm. One of these flying clouds swept past us, and above its whine we heard the high shrill scream of a Numidian, torn from the ledge and dashed to death beneath that white malevolence. One by one the dull clink of the picks was stilled. One by one the Numidians came off the rock, groping their way on hands and knees, looking like strange, white furry quadrupeds.

No one said anything. I hardly dared to look at Hannibal, nor did he look at us, but stared out on the swirling void where yesterday the very stones had mocked him. We seemed to stand there an eternity, as if we were already frozen in our final postures, while the road ledge filled with snow and all the demons of the air howled out their triumph over us.

And then, as suddenly as it began, it ended. The sun came out. The ledge was briskly cleared, and the Numidians resumed their work. I think each one of us was glad he had kept silence in that dreadful interval.

Late that same day the ledge was wide enough for horses, and the skinny animals were led to pasture in the glens below. On the third day the road was broadened so that it could bear the starving elephants. The great, dispirited beasts seemed to have withered in the cold. They moved slowly, in an enormous melancholy. Trunk to tail, they linked themselves in mournful comradery and crossed along the precipice.

When the last of the train moved off the mountaintop, the General and Captain Marr were haggard but triumphant. Thanks to the brave Numidians, the worst and final peril of our passage was behind us.

Julius Caesar to Lucius Mamilius Turrinus
by Thornton Wilder

45 B.C. The greatest of Romans, Julius Caesar, was
not only a general and statesman. He was also an orator, a writer on various topics and a poet. What some
of the private opinions of this many-sided genius
might have been are suggested in these imaginary letters by one of the most versatile and distinguished of
modern writers.

(*On religious rites*)

I enclose in this week's packet a half-dozen of the innumerable
reports which, as Supreme Pontiff, I receive from the Augurs, Soothsayers,
Sky Watchers, and Chicken Nurses.

I enclose also the directions I have issued for the monthly Commemoration of the Founding of the City.

What's to be done?

I have inherited this burden of superstition and nonsense. I govern innumerable men but must acknowledge that I am governed by birds and
thunderclaps.

All this frequently obstructs the operation of the State; it closes the
doors of the Senate and the Courts for days and weeks at a time. It em-
ploys several thousands of persons. Everyone who has anything to do with
it, including the Supreme Pontiff, manipulates it to his own interest.

One afternoon, in the Rhine Valley, the augurs of our headquarters forbade me to join battle with the enemy. It seems that our sacred chickens
were eating fastidiously. Mesdames Partlet were crossing their feet as they
walked; they were frequently inspecting the sky and looking back over
their shoulders and with good reason. I too on entering the valley had been
discouraged to observe that it was the haunt of eagles. We generals are
reduced to viewing the sky with a chicken's eyes. I acceded for one day,
though in my capability of surprising the enemy lay one of my few advantages, and I feared that I would be similarly impeded in the morning.
That evening, however, Asinius Pollio and I took a walk in the woods;
we gathered a dozen grubs; we minced them into fine pieces with our
knives and strewed them about the sacred feeding pen. The next morning

74

the entire army waited in suspense to hear the will of the Gods. The fateful birds were put out to feed. They first surveyed the sky emitting that chirp of alarm which is sufficient to arrest ten thousand men; then they turned their gaze upon their meal. By Hercules, their eyes protruded; they uttered cries of ravished gluttony; they flew to their repast, and I was permitted to win the Battle of Cologne.

Most of all, however, these observances attack and undermine the very spirit of life within the minds of men. They afford to our Romans, from the street sweepers to the consuls, a vague sense of confidence where no confidence is and at the same time a pervasive fear, a fear which neither arouses to action nor calls forth ingenuity, but which paralyzes. They remove from men's shoulders the unremitting obligation to create, moment by moment, their own Rome. They come to us sanctioned by the usage of our ancestors and breathing the security of our childhood; they flatter passivity and console inadequacy.

I can cope with the other enemies of order: the planless trouble making and violence of a Clodius; the grumbling discontents of a Cicero and a Brutus, born of envy and fed on the fine-spun theorizing of old Greek texts; the crimes and greed of my proconsuls and appointees; but what can I do against the apathy that is glad to wrap itself under the cloak of piety, that tells me that Rome will be saved by overwatching Gods or is resigned to the fact that Rome will come to ruin because the Gods are maleficent?

I am not given to brooding, but often I find myself brooding over this matter.

What to do?

At times, at midnight, I try to imagine what would happen if I abolished all this; if, Dictator and Supreme Pontiff, I abolished all observation of lucky and unlucky days, of the entrails and flights of birds, of thunder and lightning; if I closed all temples except those of Capitoline Jove.

And what of Jove?

You will hear more of this.

Prepare your thoughts for my guidance.

The next night.

(The letter continues in Greek.)

Again it is midnight, my dear friend. I sit before my window, wishing that it overhung the sleeping city and not the Trasteverine gardens of the rich. The mites dance about my lamp. The river barely reflects a diffused starlight. On the farther bank some drunken citizens are arguing in a wine shop and from time to time my name is borne to me on the air. I have left my wife sleeping and have tried to quiet my thoughts by reading in Lucretius.

Every day I feel more pressure upon me, arising from the position I occupy. I become more and more aware of what it enables me to accomplish, of what it summons me to accomplish.

But what is it saying to me? What does it require of me?

I have pacified the world; I have extended the benefits of Roman law to innumerable men and women; against great opposition, I am extending to them also the rights of citizenship. I have reformed the calendar and our days are regulated by a serviceable accommodation of the movements of the sun and the moon. I am arranging that the world be fed equably; my laws and my fleets will adjust the intermittence of harvests and surplus to the public need. Next month torture will be removed from the penal code.

But these are not enough. These measures have been merely the work of a general and of an administrator. In them I am to the world what a mayor is to a village. Now some other work is to be done, but what? I feel as though now, and only now, I am ready to *begin*. The song which is on everyone's lips calls me: father.

For the first time in my public life I am unsure. My actions have hitherto conformed to a principle which I may call a superstition: I do not experiment. I do not initiate an action in order to be instructed by its results. In the art of war and in the operations of politics I do nothing without an extremely precise intention. If an obstacle arises I promptly create a new plan, every potential consequence of which is clear to me. From the moment I saw that Pompey left a small portion of every venture to *chance*, I knew that I was to be the master of the world.

The projects which now visit me, however, involve elements about which I am not certain that I am certain. To put them into effect I must be clear in my mind as to what are the aims in life of the average man and what are the capabilities of the human being.

Man — what is that? What do we know of him? His Gods, liberty, mind, love, destiny, death — what do these mean? You remember how you and I as boys in Athens, and later before our tents in Gaul, used to turn these things over endlessly. I am an adolescent again, philosophizing. As Plato, the dangerous beguiler, said: the best philosophers in the world are boys with their beards new on their chins; I am a boy again.

But look what I have done in the meantime in regard to this matter of

the State religion. I have bolstered it by re-establishing the monthly Commemoration of the Founding of the City.

I did it, perhaps, to explore in myself what last vestiges of such piety
as I can discover there. It flatters me also to know that I am of all Romans
the most learned in old religious lore, as my mother was before me. I confess that as I declaim the uncouth collects and move about in the complicated ritual, I am filled with a real emotion; but the emotion has no
relation to the supernatural world: I am remembering myself when at
nineteen, as Priest of Jupiter, I ascended the Capitol with my Cornelia at
my side, the unborn Julia beneath her girdle. What moment has life since
offered to equal that?

Hush! There has just been a change of guard at my door. The sentries
have clashed their swords and exchanged the password. The password tonight is CAESAR WATCHES.

(On Cleopatra and her visit to Rome.)

Last year the Queen of Egypt began requesting permission to pay a
visit to Rome. I finally granted it and have offered her for residence my
villa across the river. She will stay at least a year in Italy. The whole matter is still a secret and will not be announced to the City until the very
eve of her arrival. She is now approaching Carthage and should be here in
about a month.

I confess that I look forward to this visit with much pleasure and not
only for the reason which first leaps to the mind. She was a remarkable
girl. Even at twenty she knew the loading capacity of each of the major
wharves of the Nile; she could receive a deputation from Ethiopia and
refuse all of its requests and make the refusals appear to be benefits. I
have heard her scream at her ministers' stupidity during a discussion of
the royal tax on ivory and she was not only right, but right with a wealth
of detailed and ordered information. Indeed, she is one of the few persons I have known who have a genius for administration. She will have
become a still more remarkable woman. Conversation, conversation will
be a pleasure again. I shall be flattered, understood and flattered, in a
realm where few are capable of understanding my achievements. What
questions she asks! There are few pleasures equal to that of imparting to
a voracious learner the knowledge that one has grown old and weary in
acquiring. Conversation will be a pleasure again. Oh, oh, oh, I have sat

holding that catlike bundle on my lap, drumming my fingers on ten brown toes and heard a soft voice from my shoulder asking me how to prevent banking houses from discouraging the industry of the people and what are the just wages of a chief of police relative to those of the governor of a city. Everyone in our world, my Lucius, everyone is lazy in mind except you, Cleopatra, this Catullus, and myself.

And yet she is lying, intriguing, intemperate, indifferent to the essential well-being of her people, and a light-hearted murderess. I have been receiving a series of anonymous letters warning me of her propensity to murder. I have no doubt that the lady is not long separated from a beautifully wrought cabinet of poisons; but I know also that at her table I need no taster. The prime object of her every thought is Egypt and I am its first security. If I should die, her country would fall a prey to my successors — patriots without practical judgment or administrators without imagination — and this she knows well. Egypt will never recover its greatness; but Egypt, for what it is, lives by me. I am a better ruler over Egypt than Cleopatra; but she shall learn much. During her stay in Rome I shall open her eyes to things that no Egyptian ruler has ever conceived of.

(Again, on Cleopatra and her visit to Rome.)

Cleopatra can never do a thing without pomp. She asked to be permitted to bring a court of two hundred and a household of a thousand, including a large royal guard. I have cut down these numbers to thirty and a retinue of two hundred, and have told her that the Republic will undertake the responsibility of guarding her person and her party. I have directed, also, that outside of her palace grounds — my villa has already been renamed the Palace of Amenhotep — she may not employ the insignia of royalty except on the two occasions of her official welcome on the Capitoline Hill and of her official leave-taking.

She informed me that I was to appoint twenty ladies of the highest birth, headed by my wife and my aunt, to constitute for her a company of honor for the illustration of her court. I replied that the women of Rome are free to enter into whatever engagements of this kind they may wish to and I sent her a form of invitation which she might forward to them.

This did not please her. She replied that the extent of her domains, which are more than six times as large as Italy, her divine descent — which she now traces back, in the greatest detail through two thousand years to the Sun — entitle her to such a court and that it is unbecoming that she *re-*

quest the ladies of Rome to attend her receptions and routs. The matter rests there.

I have had a part in the formation of these swelling claims. When I first met her, she was proud to state that there was not one drop of Egyptian blood in her veins. This was obviously untrue; descent in the royal house to which she belongs had always been confused by substitutions and adoptions; the effects of consanguineous marriage having been fortunately mitigated by impotence on the part of the Kings and gallantry on the part of the Queens, and by the fact that the beauty of Egyptian women far surpassed that of the descendants of the Macedonian mountain brigands. Moreover, Cleopatra at that time, apart from participation in a limited number of traditional functions, had not deigned to interest herself in the customs of the ancient country over which she ruled. She had never seen the pyramids, nor such temples on the Nile as were farther removed than an afternoon's journey from her palace at Alexandria. I advised her to make public the fact that her mother's mother was not only an Egyptian but the true heir of the Pharaohs. I persuaded her to wear Egyptian costume at least half of the time and I took her on a journey to view the monuments of a civilization that dwarfed, by Hercules, the woven huts of her Macedonian ancestors. My instructions succeeded beyond my reckoning. She is now the true Pharaoh and the living incorporation of the Goddess Isis. All the documents of her court are in hieroglyphs to which she appends, in condescension, a Greek or Latin translation.

All this is as it should be. The adherence of a people is not acquired merely by governing them to their best interests. We rulers must spend a large part of our time capturing their imaginations. In the minds of the people, Fate is an ever-watching force, operating by magic and always malevolent. To counter its action we rulers must be not only wise but supernatural, for in their eyes human wisdom is helpless before magic. We must be at once the father they knew in their infancy who guarded them against evil men and the priest who guarded them against evil spirits.

Perhaps I have forgotten to tell you also that I directed that she bring in her train no child under five years, neither hers nor one belonging to any member of her company.

(The Divine Attributes of Mortal Rulers)

The Queen of Egypt and I have been quarreling. It is not the quarrel habitual in boudoirs, though it frequently arrives at a termination which cannot be said to be new.

Cleopatra declares that I am a God. She is shocked to discover that I have not long since come to acknowledge that I am a God. Cleopatra is very certain that she is a Goddess and the worship of her people confirms her daily in this belief. She assures me that the divinity which lives in her has endowed her with unusual perspicuity in recognizing divinity. Through that endowment she is in a position to assure me that I am one also.

All this makes for conversation of a very flattering sort, interrupted by droll byplay. I pinch the Goddess and the Goddess squeals. I put my hand over the Goddess's eyes and, by the Immortal Gods, she is unable to see a thing. She has answers for all these sophistries. It is the one subject, however, on which the great Queen is not accessible to reason and on which I have learned not to permit our conversations to take a serious turn. On that subject alone she is, perhaps, oriental.

Nothing seems to me to be more dangerous — not only for us rulers, but for those who gaze upon us with varying degrees of adoration — than this ascription of divine attributes. It is not difficult to understand that many persons will feel at times as though they were inflated by unusual powers or caught up into currents of some inexplicable rightness. I had this feeling frequently when I was younger; I now shudder at it and with horror. How often I have had it thrown back at me, generally by flatterers, that I said to the timid boatman in the storm: "Have no fear; you bear Caesar." What nonsense! I have had no more exemption from the ills of life than any other man.

But that is not all. The history of nations shows how deeply rooted is our propensity to impute a more than human condition to those remarkable for gifts or to those merely situated in conspicuous position. I have little doubt that the demigods and even the Gods of antiquity are nothing more than ancestors about whom these venerations have been fostered. All this has been fruitful; it expands the imagination of the growing boy and it furnishes sanctions for good manners and public institutions. It must be outgrown, however — outgrown and discarded. Every man that has ever lived has been but a man and his achievements should be viewed as extensions of the human state, not interruptions in it.

There is no one but you with whom I can talk of this. Every year this discomfiting deification increases about me. I remember with shame that there was a time when I endeavored, for administrative reasons, to fan it: sufficient evidence that I am a man and a most fallible one, for there is no human weakness equal to that of trying to inculcate the notion that one is a God. I had a dream one night that Alexander appeared at the door of my tent with sword lifted, about to slay me. I said to him: "But you are no God," and he vanished.

The older I grow, dear Lucius, the more I rejoice in being a man — mortal, mistaken, and unabashed. Today my secretaries timidly brought me a succession of documents on which I had made various kinds of errors (to myself I call them Cleopatra-errors, so obsessive is that enchantress). I corrected them one after one another, laughing. My secretaries frowned. They could not understand that Caesar would be delighted at his mistakes. Secretaries are not exhilarating companions.

The words "divinity" and "God" have been in use among us for some time. They have a thousand meanings and for any one person a score.

The other night I found my wife under strong emotion imploring the Gods to send a sunny day for her trip to Lake Nemi. My aunt Julia is a farmer and she does not believe that they will alter the weather for her convenience, but she is certain that they are watching over Rome and have placed me here as governor. Cicero does not believe that they would hesitate to let Rome glide into ruin (he would not wish to share with them the honor of having saved the state from Catiline), but he has no doubt that they placed the conception of justice in men's hearts. Catullus probably believes that men have developed an idea of justice from quarreling with one another over property and over boundary lines, but he is certain that love is the only manifestation of the divine and that it is from love, even when it is traduced and insulted, that we can learn the nature of our existence. Cleopatra holds that love is the most agreeable of activities and that her attachment to her children is the most compelling emotion she has ever experienced, but that these are certainly not divine — divinity for her resides in the force of one's will and the energy of one's personality. And none of these meanings are meanings for me, though at various times in my life I have held all of them. With the loss of each of them I have been filled with an increased strength. I feel that if I can rid myself of the wrong ones, I shall be coming closer to the right one.

But I am an aging man. Time presses.

Claudius' Triumph

by Robert Graves

44 A.D. The Emperor Claudius, an intellectual who stuttered and wrote history, never expected to be Emperor. Deaths and murders in the imperial family raised him to the purple. During his reign part of the island of Britain was conquered and Claudius, of course, celebrated a triumph in Rome. This is his account of it taken from the autiobiography he might have written.

I duly celebrated my triumph at the New Year. The Senate had been good enough to vote me five further honours. First they had voted me a Civic Crown. This was a golden oak-leaf chaplet, originally only awarded to a soldier who, in battle, went to the rescue of a comrade who had been disarmed and was at the mercy of an opponent, killed the opponent and maintained the ground. The honour was more rarely won than you would suppose; because a necessary witness was the man who had been rescued and whose duty it would be to present the crown to his saviour. It was very difficult to make a Roman soldier confess that he had been at the mercy of an enemy champion and only owed his life to the superior strength and courage of a comrade; he was more likely to complain that his foot had slipped and that he was just about to leap up again and finish off his opponent when this ambitious fellow had officiously broken in and robbed him of his victory. Later the honour was also granted to regimental or army commanders who by their heroism or good generalship saved the lives of troops under their command. I was given the Crown in this sense, and really I think that I deserved it for not listening to the advice given me by my staff. It was inscribed *For saving the Lives of Fellow-Citizens.* You will remember that when I was first proclaimed Emperor the Palace Guard had forced me to wear a similar chaplet, the one with which Caligula had been pleased to honour himself for his German victories. I had no right to it then and was much ashamed of wearing it (though really Caligula had had no right to it either), so it was a great pleasure to me now to wear one that was rightfully mine. The second honour was a Naval Crown. This crown, decorated with the beaks of ships, was awarded for gallantry at sea — for example, to a sailor for being the first to board an enemy ship or to an admiral for destroying an enemy fleet. It was voted me because I had risked my life by putting to sea in dangerous weather with the object of reaching Britain as soon as possible. I afterwards hung both these Crowns on the pinnacle over the main entrance to the Palace.

The third honour the Senate gave me was the hereditary title of Britannicus. My little son was now known as Drusus Britannicus, or merely as Britannicus, and I shall henceforward always refer to him by that name. The fourth honour was the erection of two triumphal arches in commemoration of my victory: one at Boulogne, because that had been my base for the expedition, the other at Rome itself on the Flaminian way. They were faced with marble, decorated on both sides with trophies and bas-reliefs illustrative of my victory and surmounted with triumphal chariots in bronze. The fifth honour was a decree making the day of my triumph an annual festival for all time. Besides these five honors there were two complimentary ones awarded Messalina, namely, the right to sit in a front seat in the Theatre with the Vestal Virgins, next to the Consuls, magistrates and foreign ambassadors, and the right to use a covered carriage of state. Messalina had now been voted every one of the honours awarded my grandmother Livia in her lifetime, but I still opposed the granting to her of the title Augusta.

The sun consented to shine brightly for the day of triumph, after several days of unsettled weather, and the ward-masters and other officials had seen to it that Rome was looking as fresh and gay as so venerable and dignified a city could possibly look. The fronts of all the temples and houses had been scoured, the streets were swept as clean as the floor of the Senate House, flowers and bright objects decorated every window, and tables heaped with food were set outside every door. The temples were all thrown open, the shrines and statues were garlanded, incense burnt on every altar. The whole population, too, was dressed in its best clothes.

I had not yet entered the City, having spent the night at the Guards Camp. At dawn I ordered a general parade there of the troops who were to take part in the triumph and distributed the bounty-money that I calculated was due to them from the sale of the spoil we had taken at London and Colchester and elsewhere, and from the sale of prisoners. This money amounted to thirty gold pieces for every private soldier and proportionately more for the higher ranks. I had already sent bounty-money on the same scale to the soldiers in Britain who could not be spared to return for the triumph. At the same time I awarded decorations: neck-chains for distinguished conduct on the field, to the number of one thousand; four hundred frontlets (gold medallions in the shape of the forehead-amulets of horses) reserved for gallant cavalry-men or for infantry soldiers who had succeeded in killing an enemy cavalry-man or charioteer; forty massive gold bracelets given in recompense for outstanding valour — when awarding these I read out an account of each of the feats which had earned them; six olive garlands conferred on men who had contributed to the victory, though not actually present at it (the commander of the base camp and the admiral commanding the fleet were among those who won this honour); three Rampart Crowns, for being the first man over the stockade into an enemy's camp; and one Untipped Spear — Posides's — which was granted, like the Civic Crown, for saving life, and which he had earned ten times over.

The Senate, on my recommendation, had voted triumphal ornaments to all men of senatorial rank who had taken part in the campaign — that is to say, to all regimental commanders and senior staff-officers. It was a pity that Aulus could not be spared, or Vespasian, but all the others had come. Hosidius Geta and his brother Lusius Geta, who had commanded the eight Guards Battalions in Britain, were both honoured: I think that this was the first time in Roman history that two brothers have worn triumphal dress on the same day. Lusius Geta became my new Guards Commander, or rather he held the appointment jointly with a man named Crispinus whom Vitellius had appointed temporarily in my absence. For Justus, the former commander, was dead. Messalina had sent an urgent message which reached me on the eve of the battle of Brentwood to tell me that Justus had been sounding various Guards officers as to their willingness to stand by him in an armed revolt. Trusting Messalina completely and not daring to take any risks, I sent an immediate order for his execution. It was years before I learned the true facts: that Justus had got wind of what was going on in Messalina's wing at the Palace in my absence and asked one of his colonels what he had better do about it — whether he ought to write to me at once, or wait for my return. The colonel was one of Messalina's confidants, so he advised Justus to wait, for fear that the bad news might distract me from my military duties and then went straight to Messalina. Justus's death, the cause of which was soon known throughout the City, was a general warning not to let me into a secret which finally everyone but myself knew — even my enemies in Britain and Parthia, if you can believe it! Messalina had been going from bad to worse. But I shall not record her behaviour in detail here because I was, so far, wholly ignorant of it. She had come to Genoa to meet me on my return from France and the warmth of her greeting was one of the things that was now making me feel so happy. In six months, too, little Britannicus and his baby sister had grown out of all recognition and were such beautiful children.

You must realize how much this day meant to me. There is nothing in this world, I suppose, so glorious as a Roman triumph. It is not like a triumph celebrated by some barbarous monarch over a rival king whom he has subdued: it is an honour conferred by a free people on one of their own number for a great service he has rendered them. I knew that I had earned it fairly and that I had finally disproved the ill opinion that my family had always had of me as a useless person, born under the wrath of Heaven, an imbecile, a weakling, a disgrace to my glorious ancestors. Asleep in the Guards Camp that night I had dreamed that my brother Germanicus came up to me and embraced me and said in that grave voice of his: "Dear brother, you have done excellently well, better, I confess, than I ever thought you would do. You have restored the honour of Roman arms." When I woke in the early morning I decided to abrogate the law that Augustus had made limiting triumphs to the Emperor himself and his sons or grandchildren. If Aulus continued the campaign in Britain and succeeded in the task I had given him of permanently subduing the whole southern part of the island I should persuade the Senate to give him a triumph of his own. In my opinion, it seemed that to be the only man who could legally be awarded a triumph rather detracted from the glory than added to it. Augustus's enactment had been designed to keep his generals from inciting border tribes to warfare in the hope of winning a triumph over them; but surely, I argued, there were other ways of restraining generals than making the triumph, which had once been open to everyone, a mere family rite of the Caesars?

The decoration-ceremony over, I gave three audiences: the first to all governors of provinces, for whose temporary attendance at Rome I had asked the Senate's permission, the next to the ambassadors sent me from allied kings, and the last to the exiles. For I had won the Senate's permission for the return from their places of banishment of all exiles, but only for the duration of the triumphal festivities. This last audience was rather a sad one for me, because many of them looked very feeble and ill and they all begged piteously to have their sentences revised. I told them not to despair, for I would personally review every case and if I decided that it was to the public interest for the sentence to be cancelled or mitigated I would intercede with the Senate on their behalf. This I afterwards did, and many of those whose recall I could not recommend were at least allowed a change of their place of banishment — in every case a change for the better. I offered Seneca a change, but he refused it, replying that while he lay under Caesar's displeasure he could not desire any amelioration of his lot; the perennial frost that (according to the fables of travelers) bound the land of the brutish Finns, the perpetual heat that scorched the sands of the deserts beyond Atlas (where Caesar's victorious armies had penetrated in defiance of Nature and in expansion of the map of the known world), the fever-ridden marshy estuaries of Britain now subjugated, no less than the fertile plains and valleys of that distant and famous island, by Caesar's outstanding military genius, nay, even the pestiferous climate of Corsica where the unfortunate Seneca, author of this memorial, had now languished for two years — or was it two centuries? — this frost, this fire, this damp, this Corsican three-in-one medley of damp, fire and frost, would pass as evils scarcely noticed by the exile, Stoic-minded, whose one thought was to bear in patience the crushing weight of the disgrace under which he laboured, and make himself worthy of Caesar's pardon, should this supreme gift ever, beyond expectation, be bestowed upon him. I was quite ready to send him to his native Spain, as his friend my secretary Polybius pleaded for him, but if he himself insisted on Corsica, why, Corsica it must be. Narcissus learned from the harbour officials at Ostia that among the mementoes of his visit to Rome this brave Stoic took back in his luggage gem-studded golden drinking-cups, down pillows, Indian spices, costly unguents, tables and couches of the fragrant sandarachwood from Africa, inlaid with ivory, pictures of a sort that would have delighted Tiberius, quantities of vintage Falernian and (though this falls into a somewhat different category from the rest) a complete set of my published works.

At ten o'clock it was time to be on our way. The procession entered the City from the north-east by the Triumphal Gate and passed along the Sacred Way. Its order was as follows. First came the Senate, on foot, in its best robes, headed by the magistrates. Next, a picked body of trumpeters trained to blow triumphant marching tunes like one man. The trumpets were to call attention to the spoils, which then followed on a train of decorated wagons drawn by mules and escorted by the Germans of the Household Battalion dressed in the Imperial livery. These spoils were heaps of gold and silver coin, weapons, armour, horse-furniture, jewels and gold ornaments, ingots of tin and lead, rich drinking-vessels, decorated bronze buckets and other furniture from Cymbeline's palace at Colchester, numerous examples of exquisite North-British enamel work, carved and painted wooden totem-poles, necklaces of jet and amber and pearl, feather head-dresses, embroidered Druidical robes, carved coracle paddles and countless other beautiful, valuable or strange objects. Behind these wagons came twelve captured British chariots, the finest we could choose, drawn by well-matched ponies. To each of these was fixed a placard, on poles above the head of the driver, giving the name of one of the twelve conquered British tribes. Next came more wagons, drawn by horses, containing models in painted wood or clay of the towns and forts we had captured, and groups of living statuary representing the yielding of various river gods to our troops, each group being backed by a huge canvas-picture of the engagement. Last of this series was a model of the famous stone-temple of the Sun God of which I have already spoken.

After these came a body of flute-players playing soft music. They introduced the white bulls that came along behind, under charge of the priests of Jove, roaring angrily and causing a lot of trouble. Their horns were gilded and they wore red fillets and garlands to show that they were destined for sacrifice. The priests carried pole-axes and knives. The acolytes of Jove followed, with golden dishes and other holy instruments. Next came an interesting exhibit — a live walrus. This bull-like seal with great ivory tusks was captured asleep on a beach by the guard of our base camp. The walrus was followed by British wild cattle and deer, the skeleton of a stranded whale, and a transparent-sided tank full of beavers. After this, the arms and insignia of the captured chiefs, and then the chiefs themselves, with all members of their families that had fallen into our hands, followed by all the inferior captives marching in fetters. I was sorry not to have Caractacus in the procession, but Cattigern was there and his wife, and the wife and children of Togodumnus, and an infant son of Caractacus, and thirty chiefs of importance.

After these came a company of public slaves, marching two and two, carrying on cushions the complimentary golden crowns which had been sent me by allied kings and states in token of grateful respect. Next came twenty-four yeomen, dressed in purple, each with an axe tied in a bundle of rods, the axes crowned with laurel. Then came a four-horse chariot which had been built at the order of the Senate, of silver and ebony: except for its traditionally peculiar shape and for the embossed scenes on its sides, which represented two battles and a storm at sea, it was not unlike the chariot which I had broken up in the Goldsmiths' Street as being too luxurious. It was drawn by four white horses and in it rode the author of this history—not "Clau-Clau-Claudius," or "Claudius the Idiot" or "That Claudius" or "Claudius the Stammerer" or even "Poor Uncle Claudius" but the victorious and triumphant Tiberius Claudius Drusus Nero Caesar Augustus Germanicus Britannicus, Emperor, Father of the Country, High Pontiff, Protector of the People for the fourth year in succession, three times Consul, who had been awarded the Civic and Naval Crowns, triumphal ornaments on three previous occasions and other lesser honours, civil and military, too numerous to mention. This exalted and happy personage was attired in a gold-embroidered robe and flowered tunic and bore in his right hand, which was trembling a little, a laurel bough, and in his left an ivory sceptre surmounted with a golden bird. A garland of Delphic laurel shaded his brows and, in revival of an ancient custom, his face, arms, neck and legs (as much of his body as showed) were painted bright red. In the Victor's chariot rode his little son Britannicus, shouting and clapping his hands, his friend Vitellius, wearing the Olive Crown, who had ruled the State in the Victor's absence, his infant daughter Octavia, held in the arms of young Silanus, who had been chosen as her future husband and who in company with young Pompey, married to the Victor's daughter Antonia, had brought the Senate the laurel-wreathed dispatch. Silanus had been voted triumphal dress and so had young Pompey, who also rode in this chariot and held Britannicus on his knee. Beside the chariot rode young Pompey's father, Crassus Frugi, who had now worn triumphal dress twice, the first time having been after Galba's defeat of the Chattians. And we must not forget the public slave who stood in the chariot holding over the Victor's head a golden Etruscan crown ornamented with jewels, the gift of the Roman people. It was his duty to whisper in the Victor's ear every now and then the ancient formula, "Look behind thee: remember thyself mortal!"—a warning that the Gods would be jealous of the Victor if he bore himself too divinely, and would not fail to humble him. And to avert the evil eye of spectators a phallic charm, a little bell, and a scourge were fastened to the dash-board of the chariot.

Next came Messalina, the Victor's wife, in her carriage of state. Next, walking on foot, the commanders who had been awarded triumphal dress. Then the winners of the Olive Crown. Then the colonels, captains, sergeants and other ranks who had been decorated for valour. Then the elephants. Then the camels, yoked two and two and drawing carriages on which were mounted the six thunder-and-lightning machines of Caligula's

invention, which had been put to such apt use by Posides. Then came the
Heron King on his stilts, a golden bracelet twisted about his neck. I am
told that, after myself, the Heron King earned more cheers than anyone.
After him walked Posides with his Untipped Spear, and the Spanish ocu-
list, wearing a gown, for he had been rewarded with the Roman citizenship.
Then came the Roman cavalry, and then the infantry in marching order,
their weapons adorned with laurel. The younger soldiers were shouting
"Io Triumphe!" and singing hymns of victory, but the veterans exercised
the right of free speech which was theirs for the day, indulging in sar-
castic ribaldry at the Victor's expense. The veterans of the Twentieth had
composed a fine song for the occasion:

> *Claudius was a famous scholar,*
> *Claudius shed less blood than ink.*
> *When he came to fight the Britons*
> *From the fray he did not shrink,*
> *But the weapons of his choice were*
> *Rope and stilts and camel stink.*
>   O, O, Oh!

> *Rope and stilts and stink of camel*
> *Made the British army shake.*
> *Off they ran with yells of horror*
> *And their cries the dead would wake —*
> *Cries as loud as Claudius utters*
> *When he's got the stomach-ache.*
>   O, O, Oh!

I am told that at the tail of this column there were bawdy songs sung
about Messalina, but I did not hear them where I was; indeed, if they had
been sung by the yeomen walking just ahead of me I should not have
heard them, the crowd was raising such a tremendous din. After the infantry came detachments of auxiliaries, headed by the Balearics and Nubians.

That ended the procession proper, but it was followed by a laughing
and cheering rabble giving a mock triumph to Baba, the clown of Alexandria, who had come to Rome to improve his fortunes. He rode in a public dung-cart, to which had been yoked in a row a goat, a sheep, a pig
and a fox. He was painted blue, with British woad, and dressed in a fantastic parody of triumphal dress. His cloak was a patchwork quilt and his

tunic an old sack trimmed with dirty coloured ribbons. His sceptre was a cabbage-stick with a dead bat tied to the end of it with a string, and his laurel branch was a thistle. Our most famous native-born clown, Augurinus, had recently consented to share the government of the Society of Vagabonds with Baba. Baba was held to resemble me closely and therefore always played the part of Caesar in the theatricals that the two of them were constantly giving in the back streets of the City. Augurinus played the part of Vitellius, or a Consul of the year, or a Colonel of the Guards, or one of my ministers, according to circumstances. He had a very lively gift for parody. On this particular occasion he represented the slave who held the crown over Baba (an inverted chamber-pot into which, every now and then, Baba's head disappeared) and kept tickling him with a cock's feather. Baba's sack-tunic was torn behind and disclosed Baba's rump, painted blue with bold red markings to make it look like a grinning human face. Baba's hands trembled madly the whole time and he jerked his head about in caricature of my nervous tic, rolling his eyes, and whenever Augurinus molested him struck back with the thistle or the dead bat. In another dung-cart behind, under a tattered hood, reclined an enormous naked negress with a brass ring in her nose, nursing a little pink pig. The spoils of this rival triumph were displayed on handcarts wheeled by ragged hawkers — kitchen refuse, broken bedsteads, filthy mattresses, rusty iron, cracked cooking-pots, and all sorts of mouldy lumber — and the prisoners were dwarfs, fat men, thin men, albinos, cripples, blind men, hydrocephalitics and men suffering from dreadful diseases or chosen for their surprising ugliness. The rest of the procession was in keeping: I am told that the models and pictures illustrating Baba's victories were the funniest things, in a dirty way, ever seen at Rome.

When we came to the Capitoline Hill, I dismounted and went through a performance which custom demanded but which I found a great physical strain: I ascended the steps of the Temple of Jove humbly kneeling on my knees. Young Pompey and Silanus supported me on either side. At this point it was the custom to lead aside the captured enemy chiefs and execute them in the prison adjoining the temple. This custom was the survival of an ancient rite of human sacrifice in thanksgiving for victory. I dispensed with it on grounds of public policy: I decided to keep these chiefs alive at Rome in order to give others in Britain who were still holding out against us a demonstration of clemency. The Britons themselves sacrificed war prisoners, but it would be absurd to commemorate our intention of civilizing their island with an act of primitive barbarism. I would grant these chiefs and their families small pensions from the public funds and encourage them to become Romanized, so that later when regiments of British auxiliaries were formed there would be officers to command them capable of acting in friendly co-operation with our own forces.

Though I failed to sacrifice the chiefs to Jove I did not at any rate fail to sacrifice the white bulls, or to give the God an offering from the spoils (the pick of the golden ornaments from Cymbeline's palace), or to place in the lap of his sacred image the laurel-crown from my brow. Then I and my companions in triumph, and Messalina, were entertained by the college of the Priests of Jove to a public banquet while the troops dispersed and were entertained by the City. A house whose table was not honoured by the presence of at least one triumphant hero was an unlucky house indeed. I had heard unofficially, the night before, that the Twentieth were planning another drunken orgy like the one in which they had taken part during Caligula's triumph: they intended to launch an assault on the Goldsmiths' Street and if they found the doors of the shops barred they would use fire or battering-rams. I thought at first of defending the street with a corps of Watchmen, but that would only have meant bloodshed, so I had the better idea of filling the flasks of all the troops with a free wine-ration with which to drink my health. The flasks were filled just before the procession started and my orders were not to drink until the trumpets gave them the signal that the sacrifice had been duly made. It was all good wine, but what I gave the Twentieth was heavily doctored with poppyseed. So they drank my health and that put them so soundly to sleep that by the time they woke up the triumph was over: one man, I regret to say, never woke up. But at least there was no serious disturbance of the peace that day.

In the evening I was guided home to the Palace by a long torchlight procession and the corps of flute-players, and followed by enormous crowds of cheering and singing citizens. I was tired out and after washing off my red paint went straight to bed, but the festivities continued all night and would not let me sleep. At midnight I rose and with only Narcissus and Pallas as my companions went out into the streets. I was disguised as an ordinary citizen in a plain white gown. I wanted to hear what people really thought of me. We mixed with the crowd. The steps of the Temple of Castor and Pollux were dotted with groups of people resting and talking, and here we found seats. Everyone addressed everyone else without ceremony. I was glad that free speech had returned to Rome at last, after its long suppression by Tiberius and Caligula, even though some of the things I heard did not altogether please me. The general opinion seemed to be that it had been a very fine triumph but that it would have been still finer if I had distributed money to the citizens as well as to the soldiers, and increased the corn-ration. (Corn had been scarce that winter again, through no fault of mine.) I was anxious to hear what a battle-scarred captain of the Fourteenth sitting near us had to say: he was with a brother whom he had apparently not seen for sixteen years. At first he would not talk about the battle, though his brother pressed him to do so, and would only discuss Britain as a military station: he thought that with luck he could count on very pretty pickings. Soon he would be able to retire, he hoped, with the rank of knight: he had made quite a packet of money in the last ten years by selling exemptions from duty to the men of his company, and "on the Rhine one doesn't get a chance of spending much money — it's not like at Rome." But in the end he said: "Frankly speaking, we officers of the Fourteenth didn't think much of the Brentwood fighting. The Emperor made it too easy for us. Wonderfully clever man, the Emperor. One of these strategists. Gets it all out of books. That trip-rope, now, that was a typical stratagem. And that great bird, flapping its wings and making weird sounds. And getting the camels forward on the flank to scare the enemy's ponies with their stink. A first-class strategist. But strategy isn't what I call soldiering. Old Aulus Plautius was going straight at that central stockade, and be damned to the consequences. Old Aulus is a soldier. He'd have given us a better bloody battle if it had been left to him. We officers of the Fourteenth like a good bloody battle better than a clever bit of strategy. It's what we live for, a bloody battle is, and if we lose heavily, why, that's a soldier's luck and it means promotion for the survivors. No promotion at all in the Fourteenth this time. A couple of corporals killed, that's all. No, he made it too easy. I had a better time than most, of course: I got in among the chariots with my leading platoon and killed a good few British, and I won this chain here, so I can't complain. But speaking for the Regiment as a whole, that battle wasn't up to the standard of the two others we fought before the Emperor came: the Medway fight was a good one, now, nobody will deny that."

An old woman piped up: "Well, Captain, you're very gallant and we're all very grateful and proud of you, I'm sure, but for my part I've two boys serving in the Second, and though I'm disappointed that they didn't get home leave for to-day, I'm thankful they're alive. Perhaps if your General Aulus had had his way, they'd be lying there on Brentwood Hill for the crows to pick at." An old Frenchman agreed: "For my part, Captain,

I wouldn't care how a battle was won, so long as it was well won. I heard two other officers like yourself discussing the battle to-night. And one of them said: 'Yes, a clever bit of strategy, but too clever: smells of the lamp.' What I say is, did the Emperor win a splendid victory or did he not? He did. Then long live the Emperor."

But the Captain said: "*Smells of the lamp,* they said, did they? That was very well put. A strategical victory, but it smelled of the lamp. The Emperor's altogether too clever to rank as a good soldier. For my part, I thank the Gods that I never read a book in my life."

I said shyly to Narcissus as we went home: "You didn't agree with that captain, did you, Narcissus?"

"No, Caesar," said Narcissus, "did you? But I thought he spoke like a brave and honest man and as he's only a captain, perhaps you ought to be rather pleased than otherwise. You don't want captains in the army who know too much or think too much. And he certainly gave you full credit for the victory, didn't he?"

But I grumbled: "Either I'm an utter imbecile or else I'm altogether too clever."

The triumph lasted for three days. On the second day we had spectacles in the Circus and in the amphitheatre simultaneously. At the first we had chariot-races, ten in all, and athletic contests, and fights between British captives and bears; and boys from Asia Minor performed the national sword-dance. At the other a pageant of the storming and sacking of Colchester and the yielding of the enemy chiefs was re-enacted, and we had a battle between three hundred Catuvellaunians and three hundred Trinovants, chariots as well as infantry. The Catuvellaunians won. On the morning of the third day we had more horse-racing and a battle between Catuvellaunian broad-swordsmen and a company of Numidian spearmen, captured by Geta the year before. The Catuvellaunians won easily. The last performance took place in the Theatre — plays, interludes and acrobatic dancing. Mnester was splendid that day; and the audience made him perform his dance of triumph in *Orestes and Pylades* — he was Pylades — three times over. He refused to take a fourth call. He put his head around the curtain and called archly: "I can't come, my Lords. Orestes and I are in bed together."

Messalina said to me afterwards: "I want you to talk to Mnester very sternly, my dearest husband. He's much too independent for a man of his profession and origin, though he *is* a marvellous actor. During your absence he was most rude to me on two or three occasions. When I asked him to make his company rehearse a favourite ballet of mine for a festival — you know that I have been supervising all the Games and Shows because Vitellius found it too much for him, and then I found that Harpocras, the secretary, had been behaving dishonestly, and we had to have him executed, and Pheronactus whom I chose in his place has been rather slow in learning his business — well, anyhow, it was all very difficult for me, and Mnester instead of making things easier was most dreadfully obstinate. Oh no, he said, he couldn't put on *Ulysses and Circe* because he hadn't anyone capable of playing Circe to his Ulysses, and when I suggested *The Minotaur* he said that Theseus was a part he greatly disliked playing but that on the other hand it would be below his dignity to dance in the less important part of King Minos. That's the sort of obstruction he made all the time. He simply refused to grasp that I was your representative and that he simply *must* do what I told him: but I didn't punish him because I thought you might not wish it. I waited until now."

I called Mnester. "Listen, little Greek," I said. "This is my wife, the Lady Valeria Messalina. The Senate of Rome thinks as highly of her as I do: they have paid her exalted honours. In my absence she has been taking over some of my duties for me and performing them to my entire satisfaction. She now complains that you have been both unco-operative and insolent. Understand this: if the Lady Messalina tells you to do anything, however much obedience in the matter may happen to hurt your professional vanity, you must obey her. *Anything*, mark you, litttle Greek, and no arguments either. Anything and everything."

"I obey, Caesar," Mnester answered, sinking to the floor with exaggerated docility, "and I beg forgiveness for my stupidity. I did not understand that I was to obey the Lady Messalina in *everything*, only in certain things."

"Well, you understand now."

So that was the end of my triumph. The troops returned to duty in Britain, and I returned to civil dress and duty at Rome. It is probable that it will never happen to anyone again in this world, as it is certain that it had never happened to anyone before, to fight his first battle at the age of fifty-three, never having performed military service of any sort in his youth, win a crushing victory, and never take the field again for the rest of his life.

The Procurator of Judaea

by Anatole France

57 A.D. One of the most celebrated short stories in French literature, this is a study of the mind of a typical Roman official. It demonstrates with brilliant irony how difficult it is to understand the significance of events alien to one's own traditional outlook.

L. Aelius Lamia, born in Italy of illustrious parents, had not yet discarded the *toga praetexta* when he set out for the schools of Athens to study philosophy. Subsequently he took up his residence at Rome, and in his house on the Esquiline, amid a circle of youthful wastrels, abandoned himself to licentious courses. But being accused of engaging in criminal relations with Lepida, the wife of Sulpicius Quirinus, a man of consular rank, and being found guilty, he was exiled by Tiberius Caesar. At that time he was just entering his twenty-fourth year. During the eighteen years that his exile lasted he traversed Syria, Palestine, Cappadocia, and Armenia, and made prolonged visits to Antioch, Caesarea, and Jerusalem. When, after the death of Tiberius, Caius was raised to the purple, Lamia obtained permission to return to Rome. He even regained a portion of his possessions. Adversity had taught him wisdom.

He avoided all intercourse with the wives and daughters of Roman citizens, made no efforts toward obtaining office, held aloof from public honors, and lived a secluded life in his house on the Esquiline. Occupying himself with the task of recording all the remarkable things he had seen during his distant travels, he turned, as he said, the vicissitudes of his years of expiation into a diversion for his hours of rest. In the midst of these calm employments, alternating with assiduous study of the works of Epicurus, he recognized with a mixture of surprise and vexation that age was stealing upon him. In his sixty-second year, being afflicted with an illness which proved in no slight degree troublesome, he decided to have recourse to the waters at Baiae. The coast at that point, once frequented by the halcyon, was at this date the resort of the wealthy Roman, greedy of pleasure. For a week Lamia lived alone, without a friend in the brilliant crowd. Then one day, after dinner, an inclination to which he yielded urged him to ascend the incline, which, covered with vines that resembled bacchantes, looked out upon the waves.

Having reached the summit he seated himself by the side of a path beneath a terebinth, and let his glances wander over the lovely landscape.
To his left, livid and bare, the Phlegraean plain stretched out towards
the ruins of Cumae. On his right, Cape Misenum plunged its abrupt spur
beneath the Tyrrhenian Sea. Beneath his feet luxurious Baiae, following
the graceful outline of the coast, displayed its gardens, its villas thronged
with statues, its porticoes, its marble terraces along the shores of the blue
ocean where the dolphins sported. Before him, on the other side of the
bay, on the Campanian coast, gilded by the already sinking sun, gleamed
the temples which far away rose above the laurels of Posilipo, whilst on
the extreme horizon Vesuvius looked forth smiling.

Lamia drew from a fold of his toga a scroll containing the *Treatise upon
Nature,* extended himself upon the ground, and began to read. But the
warning cries of a slave necessitated his rising to allow of the passage of a
litter which was being carried along the narrow pathway through the
vineyards. The litter being uncurtained permitted Lamia to see stretched
upon the cushions as it was borne nearer to him the figure of an elderly
man of immense bulk, who, supporting his head on his hand, gazed out
with a gloomy and disdainful expression. His nose, which was aquiline,
and his chin, which was prominent, seemed desirous of meeting across
his lips, and his jaws were powerful.

From the first moment Lamia was convinced that the face was familiar
to him. He hesitated a moment before the name came to him. Then suddenly hastening towards the litter with a display of surprise and delight —

"Pontius Pilate!" he cried. "The gods be praised who have permitted
me to see you once again!"

The old man gave a signal to the slaves to stop, and cast a keen glance
upon the stranger who had addressed him.

"Pontius, my dear host," resumed the latter, "have twenty years so far
whitened my hair and hollowed my cheeks that you no longer recognize
your friend Aelius Lamia?"

At this name Pontius Pilate dismounted from the litter as actively as the
weight of his years and the heaviness of his gait permitted him, and embraced Aelius Lamia again and again.

"Gods! what a treat it is to me to see you once more! But, alas! you call
up memories of those long-vanished days when I was Procurator of Judaea
in the province of Syria. Why, it must be thirty years ago that I first met
you. It was at Caesarea, whither you came to drag out your weary term
of exile. I was fortunate enough to alleviate it a little, and out of friend-

ship, Lamia, you followed me to that depressing place Jerusalem, where
the Jews filled me with bitterness and disgust. You remained for more than
ten years my guest and my companion, and in converse about Rome and
things Roman we both of us managed to find consolation — for your mis-
fortunes, and I for my burdens of State."

Lamia embraced him afresh.

"You forget two things, Pontius; you are overlooking the facts that you
used your influence on my behalf with Herod Antipas, and that your
purse was freely open to me."

"Let us not talk of that," replied Pontius, "since after your return to
Rome you sent me by one your freedmen a sum of money which repaid
me with usury."

"Pontius, I could never consider myself out of your debt by the mere
payment of money. But tell me, have the gods fulfilled your desires? Are
you in the enjoyment of all the happiness you deserve? Tell me about
your family, your fortunes, your health."

"I have withdrawn to Sicily, where I possess estates, and where I cultivate wheat for the market. My eldest daughter, my best-beloved Pontia,
who has been left a widow, lives with me, and directs my household. The
gods be praised, I have preserved my mental vigor; my memory is not
in the least degree enfeebled. But old age always brings in its train a long
procession of griefs and infirmities. I am cruelly tormented with gout.
And at this very moment you find me on my way to the Phlegraean plain in
search of a remedy for my sufferings. From that burning soil, whence
at night flames burst forth, proceed acrid exhalations of sulphur, which,
so they say, ease the pains and restore suppleness to the stiffened joints.
At least, the physicians assure me that it is so."

"May you find it so in your case, Pontius. But, despite the gout and its
burning torments, you scarcely look as old as myself, although in reality
you must be my senior by ten years. Unmistakably you have retained a
greater degree of vigor than I ever possessed, and I am overjoyed to find
you looking so hale. Why, dear friend, did you retire from the public service before the customary age? Why, on resigning your governorship in
Judaea, did you withdraw to a voluntary exile on your Sicilian estates?
Give me an account of your doings from the moment that I ceased to be
a witness of them. You were preparing to suppress a Samaritan rising
when I set out for Cappadocia, where I hoped to draw some profit from
the breeding of horses and mules. I have not seen you since then. How

did that expedition succeed? Pray tell me. Everything interests me that
concerns you in any way."

Pontius Pilate sadly shook his head.

"My natural disposition," he said, "as well as a sense of duty, impelled
me to fulfill my public responsibilities, not merely with diligence, but even
with ardor. But I was pursued by unrelenting hatred. Intrigues and cal-
umnies cut short my career in its prime, and the fruit it should have looked
to bear has withered away. You ask me about the Samaritan insurrection.
Let us sit down on this hillock. I shall be able to give you an answer in
few words. Those occurrences are as vividly present to me as if they had
happened yesterday.

"A man of the people, of persuasive speech — there are many such to
be met with in Syria — induced the Samaritans to gather together in arms
on Mount Gerizim (which in that country is looked upon as a holy place)
under the promise that he would disclose to their sight the sacred vessels
which in the ancient days of Evander and our father, Aeneas, had been
hidden away by an eponymous hero, or rather a tribal deity, named Moses.
Upon this assurance the Samaritans rose in rebellion; but having been
warned in time to forestall them, I dispatched detachments of infantry
to occupy the mountain, and stationed cavalry to keep the approaches to
it under observation.

"These measures of prudence were urgent. The rebels were already lay-
ing siege to the town of Tyrathaba, situated at the foot of Mount Gerizim.
I easily dispersed them, and stifled the as yet scarcely organized revolt.
Then, in order to give a forcible example with as few victims as possible,
I handed over to execution the leaders of the rebellion. But you are aware,
Lamia, in what strait dependence I was kept by the proconsul Vitellius,
who governed Syria not in, but against the interests of Rome, and looked
upon the provinces of the Empire as territories which could be farmed
out to tetrarchs. The head-men among the Samaritans, in their resentment
against me, came and fell at his feet lamenting. To listen to them, nothing had been further from their thoughts than to disobey Caesar. It was
I who had provoked the rising, and it was purely in order to withstand
my violence that they had gathered together round Tyrathaba. Vitellius
listened to their complaints, and handing over the affairs of Judaea to his
friend Marcellus, commanded me to go and justify my proceedings before the Emperor himself. With a heart overflowing with grief and resentment I took ship. Just as I approached the shores of Italy, Tiberius,
worn out with age and the cares of empire, died suddenly on the self-

same Cape Misenum, whose peak we see from this very spot magnified in the mists of evening. I demanded justice of Caius, his successor, whose perception was naturally acute, and who was acquainted with Syrian affairs. But marvel with me, Lamia, at the maliciousness of fortune, resolved on my discomfiture. Caius then had in his suite at Rome the Jew Agrippa, his companion, the friend of his childhood, whom he cherished as his own eyes. Now Agrippa favored Vitellius, inasmuch as Vitellius was the enemy of Antipas, whom Agrippa pursued with his hatred. The Emperor adopted the prejudices of his beloved Asiatic and refused even to listen to me. There was nothing for me to do but bow beneath the stroke of unmerited misfortune. With tears for my meat and gall for my portion, I withdrew to my estates in Sicily, where I should have died of grief if my sweet Pontia had not come to console her father. I have cultivated wheat, and succeeded in producing the fullest ears in the whole province. But now my life is ended; the future will judge between Vitellius and me."

"Pontius," replied Lamia, "I am persuaded that you acted towards the Samaritans according to the rectitude of your character, and solely in the interests of Rome. But were you not perchance on that occasion a trifle too much influenced by that impetuous courage which has always swayed you? You will remember that in Judaea it often happened that I who, younger than you, should naturally have been more impetuous than you, was obliged to urge you to clemency and suavity."

"Suavity towards the Jews!" cried Pontius Pilate. "Although you have lived amongst them, it seems clear that you ill understand those enemies of the human race. Haughty and at the same time base, combining an invincible obstinacy with a despicably mean spirit, they weary alike your love and your hatred. My character, Lamia, was formed upon the maxims of the divine Augustus. When I was appointed Procurator of Judaea, the world was already penetrated with the majestic ideal of the *Pax Romana*. No longer, as in the days of our internecine strife, were we witnesses to the sack of a province for the aggrandisement of a proconsul. I knew where my duty lay. I was careful that my actions should be governed by prudence and moderation. The gods are my witnesses that I was resolved upon mildness, and upon mildness only. Yet what did my benevolent intentions avail me? You were at my side, Lamia, when, at the outset of my career as ruler, the first rebellion came to a head. Is there any need for me to recall the details to you? The garrison had been transferred from Caesarea to take up its winter quarters at Jerusalem. Upon the ensigns of the legionaries appeared the presentment of Caesar. The inhabitants of Jerusalem, who did not recognize the indwelling divinity of the Emperor, were scandalized at this, as though, when obedience is compulsory, it were not less abject to obey a god than a man. The priests of their nation appeared before my tribunal imploring me with supercilious humility to have the ensigns removed from within the holy city. Out of reverence for the divine nature of Caesar and the majesty of the empire, I refused to comply. Then the rabble made common cause with the priests, and all around the pretorium portentous cries of supplication arose. I ordered the soldiers to stack their spears in front of the tower of Antonia, and to proceed, armed only with sticks like lictors, to disperse the insolent crowd. But, heedless of blows, the Jews continued their entreaties, and the more obstinate amongst them threw themselves on the ground and, exposing their breasts to the rods, deliberately courted death. You were a witness of my humiliation on that occasion, Lamia. By the order of Vitellius I was forced to send the insignia back to Caesarea. That disgrace I had certainly not merited. Before the immortal gods I swear that never once during my term of office did I flout justice and the laws. But I am grown old. My enemies and detractors are dead. I shall die unavenged. Who will now retrieve my character?"

He moaned and lapsed into silence. Lamia replied — —

"That man is prudent who neither hopes nor fears anything from the uncertain events of the future. Does it matter in the least what estimate men may form of us hereafter? We ourselves are after all our own witnesses, and our own judges. You must rely, Pontius Pilate, on the testimony you yourself bear to your own rectitude. Be content with your own personal respect and that of your friends. For the rest, we know that mildness by itself will not suffice for the work of government. There is but little room in the actions of public men for that indulgence of human frailty which the philosophers recommend."

"We'll say no more at present," said Pontius. "The sulphureous fumes which rise from the Phlegraean plain are more powerful when the ground which exhales them is still warm beneath the sun's rays. I must hasten on. Adieu! But now that I have rediscovered a friend, I should wish to take advantage of my good fortune. Do me the favor, Aelius Lamia, to give me your company at supper at my house tomorrow. My house stands on the seashore, at the extreme end of the town in the direction of Misenum. You will easily recognize it by the porch, which bears a painting representing Orpheus surrounded by tigers and lions, whom he is charming with the strains from his lyre.

"Till tomorrow, Lamia," he repeated, as he climbed once more into his litter. "Tomorrow we will talk about Judaea."

The following day at the supper hour Lamia presented himself at the house of Pontius Pilate. Two couches only were in readiness for occupants. Creditably but simply equipped, the table held a silver service in which were set out beccaficos in honey, thrushes, oysters from the Lucrine lake, and lampreys from Sicily. As they proceeded with their repast, Pontius and Lamia interchanged inquiries with one another about their ailments, the symptoms of which they described at considerable length, mutually emulous of communicating the various remedies which had been recommended to them. Then, congratulating themselves on being thrown together once more at Baiae, they vied with one another in praise of the beauty of that enchanting coast and the mildness of the climate they enjoyed. Lamia was enthusiastic about the charms of the courtesans who frequented the seashore laden with golden ornaments and trailing draperies of barbaric broidery. But the aged Procurator deplored the ostentation with which by means of trumpery jewels and filmy garments foreigners and even enemies of the empire beguiled the Romans of their gold. After a time they turned to the subject of the great engineering feats that had been accomplished in the country; the prodigious bridge constructed by Caius between Puteoli and Baiae, and the canals which Augustus excavated to convey the waters of the ocean to Lake Avernus and the Lucrine lake.

"I also," said Pontius, with a sigh, "I also wished to set afoot public works of great utility. When, for my sins, I was appointed Governor of Judaea, I conceived the idea of furnishing Jerusalem with an abundant supply of pure water by means of an aqueduct. The elevation of the levels, the proportionate capacity of the various parts, the gradient for the brazen reservoirs to which the distribution pipes were to be fixed — I had gone into every detail, and decided everything for myself with the assistance of mechanical experts. I had drawn up regulations for the superintendents so as to prevent individuals from making unauthorized depredations. The architects and the workmen had their instructions. I gave orders for the commencement of operations. But far from viewing with satisfaction the construction of that conduit, which was intended to carry to their town upon its massive arches not only water but health, the inhabitants of Jerusalem gave vent to lamentable outcries. They gathered tumultuously together, exclaiming against the sacrilege and impiousness, and, hurling themselves upon the workmen, scattered the very foundation stones. Can you picture to yourself, Lamia, a filthier set of barbarians? Nevertheless, Vitellius decided in their favor, and I received orders to put a stop to the work."

"It is a knotty point," said Lamia, "how far one is justified in devising things for the commonweal against the will of the populace."

Pontius Pilate continued as though he had not heard this interruption.

"Refuse an aqueduct! What madness! But whatever is of Roman origin is distasteful to the Jews. In their eyes we are an unclean race, and our very presence appears a profanation to them. You will remember that they would never venture to enter the pretorium for fear of defiling themselves, and that I was consequently obliged to discharge my magisterial functions in an open-air tribunal on that marble pavement your feet so often trod.

"They fear us and they despise us. Yet is not Rome the mother and warden of all those peoples who nestle smiling upon her venerable bosom? With her eagles in the van, peace and liberty have been carried to the very confines of the universe. Those whom we have subdued we look on as our friends, and we leave those conquered races, nay, we secure to them the permanence of their customs and their laws. Did Syria, aforetime rent asunder by its rabble of petty kings, ever even begin to taste of peace and prosperity until it submitted to the armies of Pompey? And when Rome might have reaped a golden harvest as the price of her goodwill, did she lay hands on the hoards that swell the treasuries of barbaric temples? Did she despoil the shrine of Cybele at Pessinus, or the Morimene and Cilician sanctuaries of Jupiter, or the temple of the Jewish god at Jerusalem? Antioch, Palmyra, and Apamea, secure despite their wealth, and no longer in dread of the wandering Arab of the desert, have erected temples to the genius of Rome and the divine Caesar. The Jews alone hate and withstand us. They withhold their tribute till it is wrested from them, and obstinately rebel against military service."

"The Jews," replied Lamia, "are profoundly attached to their ancient customs. They suspect you, unreasonably, I admit, of a desire to abolish their laws and change their usages. Do not resent it, Pontius, if I say that you did not always act in such a way as to disperse their unfortunate illusion. It gratified you, despite your habitual self-restraint, to play upon the contempt with which their beliefs and religious ceremonies inspired you. You irritated them particularly by giving instructions for the sacerdotal garments and ornaments of their high priest to be kept in ward by your legionaries in the Antonine tower. One must admit that though they have never risen like us to an appreciation of things divine the Jews celebrate rites which their very antiquity renders venerable."

Pontius Pilate shrugged his shoulders.

"They have very little exact knowledge of the nature of the gods," he said. "They worship Jupiter, yet they abstain from naming him or erecting a statue of him. They do not even adore him under the semblance of a rude stone, as certain of the Asiatic peoples are wont to do. They know nothing of Apollo, of Neptune, of Mars, nor of Pluto, nor of any goddess. At the same time, I am convinced that in days gone by they worshipped Venus. For even to this day their women bring doves to the altar as victims; and you know as well as I that the dealers who trade beneath the arcades of their temple supply those birds in couples for sacrifice. I have even been told that on one occasion some madman proceeded to overturn the stalls bearing these offerings, and their owners with them. The priests raised an outcry about it, and looked on it as a case of sacrilege. I am of opinion that their custom of sacrificing turtle-doves was instituted in honor of Venus. Why are you laughing, Lamia?"

"I was laughing," said Lamia, "at an amusing idea which, I hardly know how, just occurred to me. I was thinking that perchance some day the Jupiter of the Jews might come to Rome and vent his fury upon you. Why should he not? Asia and Africa have already enriched us with a considerable number of gods. We have seen temples in honor of Isis and the dog-faced Anubis erected in Rome. In the public squares, and even on the race-courses, you may run across the Bona Dea of the Syrians mounted on an ass. And did you never hear how, in the reign of Tiberius, a young patrician passed himself off as the horned Jupiter of the Egyptians, Jupiter Ammon, and in this disguise procured the favors of an illustrious lady who was too virtuous to deny anything to a god? Beware, Pontius, lest the invisible Jupiter of the Jews disembark some day on the quay at Ostia!"

At the idea of a god coming out of Judaea, a fleeting smile played over the severe countenance of the Procurator. Then he replied gravely — —

"How would the Jews manage to impose their sacred law on outside peoples when they are in a perpetual state of tumult amongst themselves as to the interpretation of that law? You have seen them yourself, Lamia, in the public squares, split up into twenty rival parties, with staves in their hands, abusing each other and clutching one another by the beard. You have seen them on the steps of the temple, tearing their filthy garments as a symbol of lamentation, with some wretched creature in a frenzy of prophetic exaltation in their midst. They have never realized that it is possible to discuss peacefully and with an even mind those matters concerning the divine which yet are hidden from the profane and wrapped in uncertainty. For the nature of the immortal gods remains hidden from us, and we cannot arrive at a knowledge of it. Though I am of opinion, none the less, that it is a prudent thing to believe in the providence of the gods. But the Jews are devoid of philosophy, and cannot tolerate any diversity of opinions. On the contrary, they judge worthy of the extreme penalty all those who on divine subjects profess opinions opposed to their law. And as, since the genius of Rome has towered over them, capital sentences pronounced by their own tribunals can only be carried out with the sanction of the proconsul or the procurator, they harry the Roman magistrate at any hour to procure his signature to their baleful decrees, they besiege the pretorium with their cries of 'Death!' A hundred times, at least, have I known them, mustered, rich and poor together, all united under their priests, make a furious onslaught on my ivory chair, seizing me by the skirts of my robe, by the thongs of my sandals, and all to demand of me — nay, to exact from me — the death sentence on some unfortunate whose guilt I failed to perceive, and as to whom I could only pronounce that he was as mad as his accusers. A hundred times, do I say! Not a hundred, but every day and all day. Yet it was my duty to execute their law as if it were ours, since I was appointed by Rome not for the destruction, but for the upholding of their customs, and over them, I had the power of the rod and the axe. At the outset of my term of office I endeavored to persuade them to hear reason; I attempted to snatch their miserable victims from death. But this show of mildness only irritated them the more; they demanded their prey, fighting around me like a horde of vultures with wing and beak. Their priests reported to Caesar that I was violating their law, and their appeals, supported by Vitellius, drew down upon me a severe reprimand. How many times did I long, as the Greeks used to say, to dispatch accusers and accused in one convoy to the crows!

"Do not imagine, Lamia, that I nourish the rancor of the discomfited, the wrath of the superannuated, against a people which in my person has prevailed against both Rome and tranquillity. But I foresee the extremity to which sooner or later they will reduce us. Since we cannot govern them, we shall be driven to destroy them. Never doubt it. Always in a state of insubordination, brewing rebellion in their inflammatory minds, they will one day burst forth upon us with a fury beside which the wrath of the Numidians and the mutterings of the Parthians are mere child's play. They are secretly nourishing preposterous hopes, and madly premeditating our ruin. How can it be otherwise, when, on the strength of an oracle, they are living in expectation of the coming of a prince of their own blood whose kingdom shall extend over the whole earth? There are no half measures with such a people. They must be exterminated. Jerusalem must be laid waste to the very foundation. Perchance, old as I am, it may be granted me to behold the day when her walls shall fall and the flames shall envelop her houses, when her inhabitants shall pass under the edge of the sword, when salt shall be strewn on the place where once the temple stood. And in that day I shall at length be justified."

Lamia exerted himself to lead the conversation back to a less acrimonious note.

"Pontius," he said, "it is not difficult for me to understand both your longstanding resentment and your sinister forebodings. Truly, what you have experienced of the character of the Jews is nothing to their advantage. But I lived in Jerusalem as an interested onlooker, and mingled freely with the people, and I succeeded in detecting certain obscure virtues in these rude folk which were altogether hidden from you. I have met Jews who were all mildness, whose simple manners and faithfulness of heart recalled to me what our poets have related concerning the Spartan lawgiver. And you yourself, Pontius, have seen perish beneath the cudgels of your legionaries simple-minded men who have died for a cause they believed to be just without revealing their names. Such men do not deserve our contempt. I am saying this because it is desirable in all things to preserve moderation and an even mind. But I own that I never experienced any lively sympathy for the Jews. The Jewesses, on the contrary, I found extremely pleasing. I was young then, and the Syrian women stirred all my senses to response. Their ruddy lips, their liquid eyes that shone in the shade, their sleepy gaze pierced me to the very marrow. Painted and stained, smelling of nard and myrrh, steeped in odors, their physical attractions are both rare and delightful."

Pontius listened impatiently to these praises.

"I was not the kind of man to fall into the snares of the Jewish women," he said; "and since you have opened the subject yourself, Lamia, I was never able to approve of your laxity. If I did not express with sufficient emphasis formerly how culpable I held you for having intrigued at Rome with the wife of a man of consular rank, it was because you were then enduring heavy penance for your misdoings. Marriage from the patrician point of view is a sacred tie; it is one of the institutions which are the support of Rome. As to foreign women and slaves, such relations as one may enter into with them would be of little account were it not that they habituate the body to a humiliating effeminacy. Let me tell you that you have been too liberal in your offerings to the Venus of the Market-place; and what, above all, I blame in you is that you have not married in compliance with the law and given children to the Republic, as every good citizen is bound to do."

But the man who had suffered exile under Tiberius was no longer listening to the venerable magistrate. Having tossed off his cup of Falernian, he was smiling at some image visible to his eye alone.

After a moment's silence he resumed in a very deep voice, which rose in pitch little by little:

"With what languorous grace they dance, those Syrian women! I knew a Jewess at Jerusaelm who used to dance in a poky little room, on a threadbare carpet, by the light of one smoky little lamp, waving her arms, as she clanged her cymbals. Her loins arched, her head thrown back, and, as it were, dragged down by the weight of her heavy red hair, her eyes swimming with voluptuousness, eager, languishing, compliant, she would have made Cleopatra herself grow pale with envy. I was in love with her barbaric dances, her voice — a little raucous and yet so sweet — her atmosphere of incense, the semi-somnolescent state in which she seemed to live. I followed her everywhere. I mixed with the vile rabble of soldiers, conjurers, and extortioners with which she was surrounded. One day, however, she disappeared, and I saw her no more. Long did I seek her in disreputable alleys and taverns. It was more difficult to learn to do without her than to lose the taste for Greek wine. Some months after I lost sight of her, I learned by chance that she had attached herself to a small company of men and women who were followers of a young Galilean thaumaturgist. His name was Jesus; he came from Nazareth, and he was crucified for some crime, I don't quite know what. Pontius, do you remember anything about the man?"

Pontius Pilate contracted his brows, and his hand rose to his forehead in the attitude of one who probes the deeps of memory. Then after a silence of some seconds:

"Jesus?" he murmured, "Jesus — of Nazareth? I cannot call him to mind."

Palus the Incomparable
by Edward Lucas White

191 Marcus Aurelius, the philosopher-emperor, was succeeded by his brutal son, Commodus, the greatest chariot driver and gladiator who ever lived. This account of Commodus killing for fun and to display his superlative skill is the best description I know of the spectacles which delighted and debased the Roman populace.

After my return to the City the chief topic of conversation among persons of all grades of society and the pivot, so to speak, on which the spectacles of the amphitheater revolved was Palus the Gladiator.

I may set down here that I, personally, am now, as I was when I saw him appear as a charioteer for the last time, certain that Palus was Commodus in person. And I set this down as a fact. It will be seen later that I had more opportunity than any man in Rome, outside of the Palace, to know the facts.

Many people then believed and not a few still maintain that Palus was merely a crony of Commodus. Some whispered that he was a half-brother of Commodus, a son of Faustina and a favorite gladiator, brought up by the connivance of her too-indulgent husband; which wild tale suits neither with Faustina's actual deportment, as contrasted with the lies told of her by her detractors, nor with the character of Aurelius. Others even hinted that Palus was a half-brother of Commodus on the other side, offspring of Aurelius and a concubine. This invention consorts still worse with the nature of Aurelius, who was one of the most uxorious of men and by nature monogamic and austere, almost ascetic. Some contented themselves with conjecturing that Palus accidentally resembled Commodus, which was not so far from the truth.

For I knew Ducconius Furfur from our boyhood and I solemnly assert that Palus was Commodus and that, whenever Palus appeared in the circus and, later, in the amphitheater, while the Imperial Pavilion was filled by the Imperial retinue, with the throne occupied apparently by the Emperor, the throne was occupied by a dummy emperor, Ducconius Furfur, in the Imperial attire, and Commodus was in the arena as Palus.

Anyone who chooses may, from this pronouncement, set me down as a credulous ninny, if it suits his notions.

When Palus drove a chariot in the circus he never appeared with his face fully exposed, but invariably wore over its upper portion the half-mask of gauze, which is designed to protect a charioteer's eyes from dust and flying grains of sand. Similarly, when Palus entered the arena as a gladiator he never fought in any of those equipments in which gladiators appear bareheaded or with faces exposed: as a *retiarius*, for instance. He always fought as a *secutor* or *murmillo*, or in the armor proper to a Samnite, Thracian, or heavy-armed Greek or Gaul; all of which equipments include a heavy helmet with a vizor. Palus always fought with his vizor down.

It seems to me that the plain inference from these facts corroborates my opinions concerning Palus: certainly it strengthens my belief in my views. And these facts were and are known to be facts by all who, as spectators in the circus or in the amphitheater, beheld Palus as charioteer or as gladiator.

As a gladiator he was more than marvellous, he was miraculous. I was present at all his public appearances from the time of my return from Baiae. Also I had seen him closer, from the Senatorial boxes in the amphitheater, three several times during my impersonation of Salsonius Salinator. Moreover I had seen him as a gladiator not a few times before that, since Falco, soon after we came to Rome from Africa, because of his affection for me and his tendency to indulge me in every imaginable way and to arrange for me every conceivable pleasure, had contrived to use the influence of some new-found friends to make possible my presence at shows in the Colosseum, and that in as good a seat as was accessible to any freeborn Roman not a noble or senator.

The very first time I saw Palus in the arena I felt sure he was Commodus in person, for he had to a marvel every one of his characteristics of height, build, outline, agility, grace, quickness and deftness and all his tricks of attitude and movement. The two were too identical to be anything except the very same man.

It will occur to any reader of these memoirs that Palus was a left-handed fighter, and that Commodus not only fought left-handed, but wrote, by preference, with his left hand and with it more easily, rapidly and legibly than with his right. But I do not lay much stress on this for about one gladiator in fifty fights left-handed, so that the fact that Palus was left-handed, while it accords with my views, does not, in my opinion, help to prove them.

What, to my mind, much more tends to confirm my views, is the well-known fact that Palus was always equipped with armor and weapons more magnificent and more expensive than any ever seen on other gladiators. Everything he used or wore was of gold of heavily gilt; even his spear heads and sword blades were brilliantly gilded; so were his helmets, shields, bucklers, corselets, breastplates, the scales of his kilt-straps when he fought as a Greek, and his greaves, whether of Greek pattern or of some other fashion. If he appeared in an armament calling for arm-rings, leg-rings, or leg-wrappings, these were always also heavily gilt. So was his footgear, whether he wore thigh-boots, full-boots, half-boots, soldiers' brogues, half-sandals or sandals. His shoulder-guards (called "wigs" in the slang of the prize-ring) were, apparently, of pure cloth of gold, which also appeared to be the material of his aprons when his accoutrements did not include a kilt.

Now it may be said that this merely indicates that his equipment was the most extravagant instance of the manner in which opulent enthusiasts lavished their cash on the outfitting of their favorites in the arena. To me it seems too prodigal for the profusion of any or all of such spendthrifts: it appears to me more like the self-indulgence of the vainglorious master of the world. Palus often wore a helmet so bejeweled that its cost would have overtaxed the wealth of Didius Julianus.

I consider that my opinions are corroborated by the well-known fact that whenever Palus appeared as a gladiator in the amphitheater, Galen was present in the arena as chief of the surgeons always at hand to dress the wounds of victors or of vanquished men who had won the approbation or favor of the spectators or of the Imperial party. True, Galen was often there when Palus was not in the arena, for he was always on the watch for anatomical knowledge to be had from observation of dying men badly wounded. But, on the other hand, while he was often in the arena when Palus was not there, he was never absent when Palus was fighting.

Similarly, after Aemilius Laetus was appointed Prefect of the Palace, he was always present in person in the arena whenever Palus appeared in it. This, too, makes for my contentions.

The first fight in which I saw Palus revealed to me, and brought home to me with great force, the reason for his nickname, its origin and its astonishing appropriateness. The word "*palus*" has a number of very different meanings: manifestly its fitness as a pet name for the most perfect swordsman ever seen in any arena came from its use to denote the paling of a palisade, or any stake or post. Palus, in a fight, always appeared to

stand still: metaphorically he might be said to seem as immobile as the
post upon which beginners in the gladiatorial art practice their first at-
tempts at strokes, cuts, thrusts and lunges. So little did he impress beholders as mobile, so emphatically did he impress them as stationary, that
he might almost as well have been an upright stake, planted permanently
deep in the sand.

I first saw him fight as a *secutor*, matched against a *retiarius*. This kind
of combat is, surely, the most popular of all the many varieties of gladiatorial fights; and justly, for such fights are by far the most exciting to watch
and their incidents perpetually varied, novel and unpredictable. It is exciting because the *retiarius*, nude except for one small shoulder-guard and
a scanty apron, appears to have no chance whatever against the *secutor*
with his big vizored helmet, his complete body-armor, his kilt of lapped
leather straps plated with polished metal scales, his greaves or leg-rings
or boots and his full-length, curved shield and Spanish sword. The *secutor*,
always the bigger man and fully armed and armored, appears invincible
against the little manikin of a *retiarius* skipping about bareheaded and
almost naked and armed only with his trident, a fisherman's three-tined
spear, with a light handle and short prongs, his little dagger and his cord
net, which, when spread, is indeed large enough to entangle any man,
but which he carries crumpled up to an inconspicuous bunch of rope no
bigger than his head.

Yet the fact is the reverse of the appearance. No one not reckless or
drunk ever bet even money on an ordinary *secutor*. The odds on the *retiarius* are customarily between five to three and two to one. And most
secutors manifestly feel their disadvantage. As the two men face each
other and the *lanista* gives the signal anyone can see, usually, that the
retiarius is confident of victory and the *secutor* wary and cautious or even
afraid. Dreading the certain cast of the almost unescapable net, the *secutor* keeps always on the move, and continually alters the direction and
speed and manner of his movement, taking one short step and two long,
then three short and one long, breaking into a dog-trot, slowing to a snail's-
pace, leaping, twisting, curving, zigzagging, ducking and in every way
attempting to make it impossible for the *retiarius* to foretell from the movement he watches what the next movement will be.

Palus behaved unlike any other *secutor* ever seen in the arena. He
availed himself of none of the usual devices, which *lanistae* taught with
such care, in the invention of which they gloried and in which they drilled

their pupils unceasingly. He merely stood still and watched his adversary. The cunning cast of the deadly net he avoided by a very slight movement of his head or body or both. No *retiarius* ever netted him, yet the net seldom missed him more than half a hand's breadth. When the disappointed *retiarius* skipped back to the length of his net-cord and retrieved his net by means of it, Palus let him gather it up, never dashed at him, but merely stepped sedately towards him. If the *retiarius* ran away, Palus followed, but never in haste, always at a slow, even walk. No matter how often his adversary cast his net at him, Palus never altered his demeanor. The upshot was always the same. The spectators began to jeer at the baffled *retiarius*, he became flustered, he ventured a bit too near his immobile opponent, Palus made an almost imperceptible movement and the *retiarius* fell, mortally wounded.

I was never close enough to Palus to see clearly the details of his lunges, thrusts and strokes. I saw him best when I was a spectator in the Colosseum while impersonating Salsonius Salinator, for in my guise as colonial magnate I sat well forward. Even then I was not close enough to him to descry the finer points of his incomparable swordsmanship. Yet what I saw makes me regard as fairly adequate the current praises of him emanating from those wealthy enthusiasts who were reckoned the best judges of such matters. By the reports I heard they said that Palus never cut a throat, he merely nicked it, but the tiny nick invariably and accurately severed the carotid artery, jugular vein or windpipe.

I can testify, from my own observation, to his having displayed comparable skill in an equally effective stab in a different part of his adversary's body. As is well known, a deep slash of the midthigh, inside, causes death nearly as quickly as a cut throat; if the femoral artery is divided the blood pours out of the victim almost as from an inverted pail, a horrible cascade. Most of the acclaimed gladiators use often this deadly stroke against the inside midthigh, slashing it to the bone, leaving a long, deep, gaping wound. Palus never slashed an adversary's thigh; in killing by a thigh wound he always delivered a lunge which left a small puncture, but invariably also left the femoral artery completely severed, so that the life-blood gushed out in a jet astonishingly violent, the victim collapsing and dying very quickly. Such a parade requires altogether transcendent powers of accuracy from eye and hand.

Besides fighting as a *secutor* against a *retiarius* Palus in the same accoutrements fought with men similarly equipped, or accoutred as Greeks,

Gauls, Thracians, Samnites, or *murmillos;* also he appeared in the equipment of each of these sorts of gladiators against antagonists equipped like himself or in any of the other fashions.

In all these countless fights he was never once wounded by any adversary nor did he ever deliver a second stroke, thrust or lunge against any: his defence was always impregnable, his attack always unerring; when he lunged his lunge never missed and was always fatal, unless he purposely spared a gallant foe.

Besides the exhibitions of bravado and self-confidence traditional with gladiators, all of which he displayed again and again, Palus devised more than one wholly original with himself.

For instance, he would take his stand in the arena equipped as a *secutor,* the *lanista* would have in charge not one *retiarius,* but ten, or even a dozen. One would attack Palus and when, after a longer or shorter contest, he was killed, the *lanista* would, without any respite, allow a second to rush at Palus; then a third; and so on till everyone had perished by the *secutor's* unerring sword. No other *secutor* ever killed more than one *retiarius* without a good rest between the first fight and the second. Palus, as was and is well known, killed more than a thousand adversaries, of whom more than three hundred wore the accoutrements of a *retiarius.*

Palus was even more spectacular as a *dimachaerus,* so called from having two sabers, for a *dimachaerus* is a gladiator accoutred as a Thracian, but without any shield and carrying a naked saber in each hand. Such a fighter is customarily matched against an adversary in ordinary Thracian equipment. He has to essay the unnatural feat of guarding himself with one sword while attacking with the other. Such a feat is akin to those of jugglers and acrobats, for a sword is essentially an instrument of assault and cannot, by its very nature, take the place of a shield as a protection. Everybody, of course, knows that showy and startling ruse said to have been invented by the Divine Julius, which consists in surprising one's antagonist by parrying a stroke with the sword instead of with the shield and simultaneously using the shield as a weapon, striking its upper rim against the adversary's chin. But this can succeed only against an opponent dull-witted, unwary, clumsy and slow, and then as a surprise. A *dimachaerus* has to depend on parrying and his antagonist knows what to expect.

Palus was the most perfect *dimachaerus* ever seen in the Colosseum. Without a shield he fought and killed many Thracians, Greeks, Gauls, *murmillos,* Samnites and *secutors.* He even, many times, fought two Thracians at once, killing both and coming off unscathed. I saw two of these exhibitions of insane self-confidence and I must say that Palus made good his reliance on his incredible skill. He pivoted about between his adversaries, giving them, apparently, every chance to attack simultaneously, distract him and kill him. Yet he so managed that, even if their thrusts appeared simultaneous, there was between them an interval, brief as a heart-beat, but long enough for him to dispose of one and turn on the other, or escape one and pierce the other. I could not credit my own eyes. With my belief as to the identity of Palus I marvelled that a man whose life was dominated by the dread of assassination, who feared poison in his wine and food, who hedged himself about with guards and then feared the guards themselves, who distrusted everybody, who dreaded every outing, who was uneasy even inside his Palace, felt perfectly at ease and serenely safe in the arena with no defence but two sabers, and he between two hulking ruffians, as fond of life as any men, and knowing that they must kill him or be killed by him. In this deadly game he felt no qualms, only certitude of easy victory.

The controversies over the identity of Palus have produced a whole literature of pamphlets, some maintaining that he was Commodus, others professing to prove that he was not, of which some rehearse every possible theory of his relationship to Aurelius or Faustina. Among these the most amazing are those which set forth the view that Palus was Commodus, but no skillful swordsman, rather a brazen sham, killing ingloriously helpless adversaries who could oppose to his edged steel only swords of lath or lead.

This absurdity is in conflict with all the facts. Manifestly the antagonists of Palus were as well armed as he, both for defence and attack.

And, what is much more, the populace clamored for Palus, booed and cat-called if Palus did not appear in the arena; cheered him to the echo when he did appear; yelled with delight and appreciation at each exhibition of his prophetic intuition as to what his adversary was about to do, of his preternaturally perfect judgment as to what to do himself, of the instantaneous execution of whatever movement he purposed, of its complete success; and applauded him while he went off as no other gladiator ever was applauded. It was the popular demand for him which made possible and justified the unexampled fee paid Palus for each of his appearances in the arena. The managers of the games were obliged to include Palus in each exhibition or risk a riot of the indignant populace.

Now no sham fighter could fool the Roman populace. A make-believe swordsman, such as the pamphlets which I have cited allege Commodus to have been, might, if Emperor, have overawed the senators and nobles of equestrian rank and compelled their unwilling applause of sham feats. But no man, not even an Emperor, could coerce the Roman proletariat into applauding a fighter unworthy of applause. Our populace, once seated to view a show of any kind, cannot be controlled, cannot even be swayed. No fame of any charioteer, beast-fighter or gladiator can win from them tolerance of the smallest error of judgment, defect of action, attempt at foul play or hint of fear: they boo anything of which they disapprove and not Jupiter himself could elicit from them applause of anything except exhibitions of courage, skill, artistry and quickness fine enough to rouse their admiration. They admired Palus, they adored him.

This is well known to all men and proves Palus a consummate artist as a gladiator. Not only would the populace howl a bungler or coward off the sand, they know every shade of excellence; only a superlatively perfect swordsman could kindle their enthusiasm and keep it at white heat year after year as did Palus.

Palus, I may remark, was always a gallant fighter, and a combination of skill and gallantry in an adversary so won his goodwill that he never killed or seriously wounded such an opponent. If his antagonist had an unusually perfect guard and a notably dangerous attack, was handsome, moved gracefully, displayed courage and fought with impeccable fairness Palus felt a liking for him, showed it by the way in which he stood on the defensive and mitigated the deadliness of his attacks, played him longer than usual to demonstrate to all the spectators the qualities he discerned in him, and when he was convinced that the onlookers felt as he felt, disabled his admired match with some effective but trifling wound.

Then, when his victim collapsed, Palus would leap back from him, sheath his sword, and saw the air with his empty left hand, fingers extended and pressed together, thumb flat against the crack between the roots of the index finger and big finger, twisting his hand about and varying the angle at which he sawed the air, so that all might see that he wished his fallen adversary spared and was suggesting that the spectators nearest him imitate his gesture and give the signal for mercy by extending their arms thumbs flat to fingers.

Except Murmex Lucro I never saw any other gladiator presume to suggest to the spectators which signal he would like them to display; and Murmex had the air of a man taking a liberty with his betters and not very sure whether they would condone his presumption or resent his insolence;

whereas Palus waved his arm much as Commodus raised his from the Imperial throne when, as Editor of the games, he decided the fate of a fallen gladiator concerning whom the populace were so evenly divided between disfavorers and favorers that neither the victor nor his *lanista* dared to interpret so doubtful a mandate.

The most amazing fact concerning Palus was that his audiences never wearied of watching him fence. It is notorious that the spectators in the Colosseum always have been and are, in general, impatient of any noticeable prolongation of a fight. Only a very small minority of the populace and a larger, but still small, minority of the gentry and nobility, take delight in the fine points of swordsmanship for themselves. Most spectators, while acclaiming skilled fence and expecting it, look upon it merely as a means for adding interest to the preliminaries of what they desire to behold. Even senators and nobles admit that the pleasure of viewing gladiatorial shows comes from seeing men killed. Contests are thrilling chiefly because of their suggestion of the approach of the moment which brings the supreme thrill.

The populace, quite frankly, rate the fighting as a bore; they do not come to watch skilled swordsmen fence; they want to see two men face each other and one kill the other at once. It is the killing which they enjoy. The upper tiers of spectators in the amphitheater seldom give the signal for mercy when a defeated man is down and helpless, even though he be handsome and graceful and has fought bravely, skillfully and gallantly. One seldom sees an outstretched arm, with the hand extended, fingers close together and thumb flat against them, raised anywhere from the back seats; their occupants habitually, in such cases, wave their upraised arms with the hands clenched and thumbs extended, waggling their thumbs by half rotating their wrists, to make the thumb more conspicuous, yelling the while, so that the amphitheater is full of their insistent roar and the upper tiers aflash with flickering thumbs. They weigh no fine points as to the worth of the vanquished man, they do not value a good fighter enough to want him saved to fight again, they come to see men die and they want the defeated man slaughtered at once.

They are habituated to acquiescing if the Emperor — or the Editor, if the Prince is not present — or the nobility contravene their wishes and give the signal for mercy when a gallant fighter is down by accident, misadventure or because he was outmatched. But there is often a burst of howls if the signal for mercy comes not from the Imperial Pavilion or the whole *podium,* but merely from some part of the nobility or senators.

Generally, if the Emperor has not given or participated in the signal for mercy, scattered individuals among the proletariat proclaim their disappointment by booings, cat-calls, or strident whistlings.

Now Palus was so popular, so beloved by the slum-dwellers, that whenever he showed a disposition to spare an opponent, the whole mass of the populace were quick with the mercy-signal: the moment they saw Palus sheathe his blade their arms went up with his, almost before his, thumbs as flat as his, never a thumb out nor any fingers clenched.

More than this, no spectator, while Palus played an adversary, ever yelled for a prompt finish to the bout, as almost always happened at the first sign of delay in the case of any other fighter. So comprehensible, so unmistakable, so manifest, so fascinating were the fine points of the swordsmanship displayed by Palus that even the rearmost spectator, even the most brutish lout could and did relish them and enjoy them and crave the continuance of that pleasure.

Most of all the Colosseum audiences not only insisted on Palus appearing in each exhibition, not only longed for his entrance, not merely came to regard all the previous fights of the day as unwelcome postponements of the pleasure of watching Palus fence, but were manifestly impatient for the crowning delight of each day, the ecstasy of beholding a bout between Palus and Murmex Lucro, which contests were always bloodless.

Customarily, while Palus flourished, each day began with beast-fights, the noon pause was filled in by exhibitions of athletes, acrobats, jugglers, trained animals and such like, and the surprise; then the gladiatorial shows lasted from early afternoon till an hour before sunset. Palus and Murmex appeared about mid-afternoon and were matched against the victors in the earlier fights. Each located himself at one focus of the ellipse of the arena, at which points two simultaneous fights were best seen by the entire audience. There they began each fight, not simultaneously, but alternately, till all their antagonists were disposed of, most killed and some spared. The spectators seldom hurried Murmex to end a fight; they never hurried Palus. His longest delay in finishing with an adversary, even his manifest intention to exhaust an opponent rather than to wound him, never elicited any protest from any onlooker. All, breathless, fascinated, craned to watch the perfection of his method, every movement of his body, all eyes intent on the point of his matchless blade.

Last of the day's exhibitions came the fencing match between Palus and Murmex, at the center of the arena, empty save for those two and their two *lanistae*. All others in the arena, including the surgeons, their helpers and the guards, drew off to positions close under the *podium* wall.

Murmex and Palus fenced in all sorts of outfits, except that neither ever fought as a *retiarius*. Mostly both were equipped as *secutors,* but they fought also as *murmillos,* Greeks, Gauls, Thracians, Samnites, and *dimachaeri,* or one in any of these equipments against the other in any other.

Sometimes they delighted the populace by donning padded suits liberally whitened with flour or white clay, their *murmillos'* helmets similarly whitened, and then attacking each other with quarter-staffs of ash, cornelwood or holly. A hit, of course, showed plainly on the whitened suits. As neither could injure the other in this sort of fight, and as they were willing to humor the populace, each was careless about his guard and reckless in his attack. Even so hits were infrequent, since each, even when most lax, had an instinctive guard superior to that of the most expert and cautious fencer among all other contemporary fighters. Even when, very occasionally, if Palus happened to be in a rollicking mood, each substituted a second quarter-staff for his shield and, as it were, travestied a *dimachaerus,* as what might be called a two-staff-man or a double-staff-man, hits were still not frequent. Each had a marvelously impregnable defence and they were very evenly matched in the use of the quarter-staff in place of a shield as they were in everything else. Palus fought better with his left hand attacking and his right defending, Murmex better the other way, but each was genuinely ambidextrous and used either hand at will, shifting at pleasure. When, amid the flash of their staffs, either scored, the hit brought a roar of delight from the upper tiers, even from the front rows, for the most dignified senators caught the infection of the general enthusiasm and so far forgot themselves as to yell like street urchins in their ecstasy.

Except in this farcical sort of burlesque fight neither ever scored a hit on the other, in all the years throughout which their combats finished each day of every gladiatorial exhibition. Yet the audience never tired of their bloodless bouts and, while the nobility and gentry never joined in, the populace invariably roared a protest if they saw the *lanistae* make a move to separate them, and yelled for them to go on and fence longer.

The interest of the populace was caused by the fact, manifest and plain to all, that, while Murmex and Palus loved each other and had no intention of hurting each other, their matches had no appearance whatever of being sham fights. From the first parade until they separated every stroke, feint, lunge and thrust appeared to be in deadly, venomous earnest and each unhurt merely because, mortal as was his adversary's attack, his guard was perfect.

It seemed, in fact, as if each man felt so completely safe, felt so certain that his guard would never fail him, and at the same felt so sure that his crony's guard was equally faultless, that there was no danger of his injuring his chum, that each attacked the other precisely as he attacked any other adversary. It was commonly declared among expert swordsmen and connoisseurs of sword-play, as among recent spectators, when talking over the features of an exhibition after it was over, that practically every thrust, lunge or stroke of either in these bouts would have killed or disabled any other adversary; certainly it appeared so to me every time I saw them fence and especially while watching their bouts after I returned from my year at Baiae, for after that I never missed a gladiatorial exhibition in the Colosseum. To my mind Palus and Murmex were manifestly playing with each other, like fox-cubs or Molossian puppies or wolf-cubs; yet the sport so much resembled actual attack and defence, as with nearly grown wolf-cubs, that it gave less the impression of play between friends than that of deadly combat between envenomed foes. Many a time I have heard or overheard some expert or connoisseur or enthusiast or provincial visitor, prophesy somewhat in this fashion:

"Some day one of those two is going to kill the other unexpectedly and unintentionally and by mistake. Each thinks the other will never land on him; each thinks the other has a guard so impregnable that it will never be pierced; each uses on the other attacks so unexpected, so sudden, so subtle, so swift, so powerful, so sustained, so varied that no third man alive could escape any one of them. It is almost a certainty that that sort of thing cannot go on forever. One or the other of them may age sufficiently to retire from the arena, as did Murmex Frugi, safe and unscarred, as he was not. But it is far more likely, since both are full of vitality and vigor, that neither will notice the very gradual approach of age, so that they will go on fighting with eyes undimmed, muscles supple and minds quick, yet not so quick, supple and keen as now: but the preternatural powers of one will wane a bit sooner than those of the other. And sooner or later one will err in his guard and be wounded or killed."

Most spectators agreed with such forecasts. What is more, most of the spectators admitted that, as they watched, each attack seemed certain to succeed; every time either man guarded it seemed as if he must fail to protect himself.

This, I think, explains the unflagging zest with which the entire audience, senators, nobles and commonality, watched their bouts, revelled in them, gloated over the memory of them and longed for more and more. Consciously or unconsciously, every onlooker felt that sometime, some bout would end in the wounding, disabling or death of one of the two. And so perfect was their sword-play, so unfeigned their unmitigated fury of attack, so genuine the impeccable dexterity of their defence that every spectator felt that the supreme thrill, even while so long postponed, was certain to arrive. More, each felt, against his judgment, that it was likely to arrive the next moment. It was this illogical but unescapable sensation which kept the interest of the whole audience, of the whole of every audience, at a white heat over the bouts of Murmex and Palus. I myself experienced this condition of mind and became infected with the common ardor. I found myself rehearsing to myself the incidents of their last-seen bout, anticipating the next, longing for it: though I never had rated myself as ardent over gladiatorial games, but rather as lukewarm towards them, and considered myself much more interested in paintings, statuary, reliefs, ornaments, bric-a-brac, furniture, fine fabrics and all artistries and artisanries. Yet I confessed to myself that, from the time I saw first a bout between them, anticipation of seeing them fence, or enjoyment of it, came very high among my interests and my pleasures.

To some extent, I think, the long and unequaled vogue of their popularity was due to the great variety of their methods and almost complete absence of monotony in their bouts.

Palus was left-handed, but for something like every third bout or a third of each bout he fought right-handed, merely for bravado, as if to advertise that he could do almost as well with the hand less convenient. Murmex was right-handed, but he too fought often left-handed, perhaps one-fifth of the time. So, in whatever equipment, one saw each of them fight both ways. Therefore as *murmillos* they fought both right-handed, both left-handed, and each right-handed against the other fighting left-handed. This gave a perpetually shifting effect of novelty, surprise and interest to every bout between them. They similarly had four ways of appearing as Greeks, Gauls, Samnites, Thracians, *secutors* or *dimachaeri*.

Their bouts as *dimachaeri* were breathlessly exciting, for it was impossible, from moment to moment, to forecast with which saber either would attack, with which he would guard; and, not infrequently, one attacked and the other guarded with both. When they fought in this fashion Galen, it always appeared to me, looked uneasy, keyed up and apprehensive. Yet neither ever so much as nicked, flicked or scratched the other in their more than sixty bouts with two sabers apiece.

More than a dozen times they appeared as Achilles and Hector, with the old-fashioned, full-length, man-protecting shield, the short Argive sword and the heavy lance, half-pike, half-javelin, of Trojan tradition. Murmex threw a lance almost as far and true as Palus and the emotion of the audience was unmistakably akin to horror when both, simultaneously, hurled their deadly spears so swiftly and so true that it seemed as if neither could avoid the flying death. Palus, true to his nickname, never visibly dodged, though Murmex's aim was as accurate as his own; he escaped the glittering, needle-pointed, razor-edged spear-head by half a hand's-breadth or less by an almost imperceptible inclination of his body, made at the last possible instant, when it seemed as if the lance had already pierced him. It was indescribably thrilling to behold this.

Besides fencing equipped as Gauls, Samnites, Thracians and *secutors* they appeared in every combination of any of these and of Greeks and *murmillos* with every other. Palus as a *dimachaerus* against Murmex as a *murmillo* made a particularly delectable kind of bout. Almost as much so Murmex as a Gaul against Palus as a Thracian. And so without end.

After my return from Baiae Falco pampered me more than ever and, in particular, arranged to take me with him to all amphitheater shows and have me sit beside him in the front row of the nobles immediately behind the boxes of the senators on the *podium*. This does not sound possible in our later days, when amphitheater regulations are strictly enforced, as they had been under the Divine Aurelius and his predecessors. But, while Commodus was Prince much laxity was rife in all branches of the government. After the orgies of bribe-taking, favoritism and such like in the heyday of Perennis and of Cleander, all classes of our society became habituated to ignoring contraventions of rules. Under Perennis and later under Cleander not a few senators took with them into their boxes favorites who were not only not of senatorial rank, nor even nobles, but not Romans at all: foreign visitors, alien residents of Rome, freedmen or even slaves, and the other senators, as a class exquisitely sensitive to any invasion of their privileges by outsiders, winked at the practice partly because some of them participated in it, much more because they feared to suffer out-and-out ruin, if, by word or look, they incurred the disfavor of Perennis while he was all-powerful or, later, of the more omnipotent Cleander. When a senator saw another so violate propriety, privilege and law, he assumed that the acting Prefect of the Palace had been bribed and so dared not protest or whisper disapprobation.

Much more than the senators the nobles obtained secret license to ignore the rules, or ignored them without license, since, when so many violated the regulations, no one was conspicuous or likely to be brought to book. Falco, being vastly wealthy, probably bribed somebody, but I never knew: when I hinted a query he merely smiled and vowed that we were perfectly safe.

So I sat beside him through that unforgettable December day, at the end of which came the culmination of what I have been describing.

The day was perfect, clear, crisp, mild and windless. It was not cold enough to be chilling, but was cold enough to make completely comfortable a pipe-clayed ceremonial toga over the full daily garments of a noble or senator, so that the entire audience enjoyed the temperature and basked in the brilliant sunrays; for, so late in the year, as the warmth of the sun was sure to be welcome, the awning had not been spread. I, in my bizarre oriental attire, wore my thickest garments and my fullest curled wig and felt neither too cold nor too warm.

I never saw the Colosseum so brilliant a spectacle. It was full to the upper colonnade under the awning-rope poles, not a seat vacant. Spectators were sitting on the steps all up and down every visible stair; two or even three rows on each side of each stair, leaving free only a narrow alley up the middle of each for the passage in or out of attendants or others. Spectators filled the openings of the entrance-stairs, all but jamming each. In each of the cross-aisles spectators stood or crouched against its back-wall, ducking their heads to avoid protests from the luckier spectators in the seats behind them. The upper colonnade was packed to its full capacity with standees.

The program was unusual, gladiatorial exhibitions from the beginning of the show; and nothing else. The morning was full of brisk fights between young men; provincials, foreigners and some Italians, volunteer enthusiasts. The noon pause was filled in by routine fights of old or aging gladiators nearly approaching the completion of their covenanted term of service. It ended with a novelty, the encounter of two tight-rope walkers on a taut rope stretched fully thirty feet in the air. It was proclaimed that they were rivals for the favor of a pretty freedwoman and that they had agreed on this contest as a settlement of their rivalry. Certainly the two, naked save for breech-clouts and each armed with a light lance in one hand and a thin-bladed Gallic sword in the other, neared each other with

every sign of caution, enmity and courage. Their sparring for an opening lasted some time, but was breathlessly interesting. The victor kept his
feet on the rope and pierced his rival, who fell and died from the spear-
wound or the fall or both.

During the noon pause the Emperor had left his pavilion. When he
returned I, from my nearby location, was certain that Commodus himself
had presided all the morning, but that now Furfur was taking his place.
Certainly Palus and Murmex entered the arena soon after the noon pause
and gave an exhibition almost twice as long as usual, killing many adversaries. Before the sun was half way down the sky, as Palus finished an
opponent with one of his all but invisible punctures of the thigh-artery,
the upper tiers first and then all ranks acclaimed this as the death of the
twelve-hundredth antagonist who had perished by his unerring steel.

The daylight had not begun to dim when Murmex and Palus faced each
other for the fencing bout which was to end the day. Each was equipped
as a *secutor*, Murmex in silvered armor, Palus all in gold or gilded arms.
Their swords were not regulation army swords, such as *secutors* normally
carried, but long-bladed Gallic swords, the longest-bladed swords ever
used by any gladiators.

They made a wonderful picture as the *lanistae* placed them and stepped
back: Murmex, burly, stocky, heavy of build, thick-set, massive, with
vast girth of chest and bull-neck, his neatly-fitting plated gauntlet, huge
on his big right hand, his big plated boots planted solidly on the sand,
his polished helmet, the great expanse of his silvered shield, his silvered
kilt-strap-scales and silvered greave-boots brilliant in the cool late light;
opposite him Palus, tall, lithe, graceful, slim, agile, all in gleaming gold,
helmet, corselet, shield, kilt, greave-boots and all. They shone like a composite jewel set in the arena as a cameo in the bezel of a ring. And the
picture they made was framed in the hoop of spectators crowding the slopes
of the amphitheater, all silent after the gusts of cheers which had acclaimed
the two as they took their places.

If possible, their feints and assaults were more thrilling than ever, unexpected, sudden, swift, all but successful. As always neither capered or
pranced, Murmex not built for such antics, Palus by nature steady on his
feet. But, except that their feet moved cannily, every bit of the rest of
either's body was in constant motion and moved swiftly. The gleam and
flicker of thrust and parry were inexpressibly rapid. Even the upper tiers
craned, breathless and fascinated; and we, further forward, were numb
with quivering and excitement.

I have heard a hundred eye-witnesses describe what occurred. There was close agreement with what I seemed to see as I watched.

Palus lunged just as Murmex made a brilliantly unpredictable shift of his position. The shift and lunge came so simultaneously that neither had, in his calculated, predetermined movement, time to alter his intention; Murmex, you might say, threw his throat at the spot at which Palus had aimed his lunge. The sword-point ripped his throat from beside the gullet to against the spine, all one side of it. He collapsed, the blood spouting.

Palus cast the dripping sword violently from him, the gleaming blade flying up into the air and falling far off on the sand. The big shield fell from his right arm. Both his hands caught his big helmet, lifted it and threw it behind him. On one knee he sank by Murmex and, with his left hand, strove to staunch the gushing blood.

Before Galen, before even the *lanistae* could reach the two, Murmex died.

Palus staggered to his feet and put up his gory hand to his yellow curls, with a convincingly agonized gesture of grief and horror.

He uttered some words, I heard his voice, but not the words. Folk say he said:

"I have killed the only match I had on earth, the second-best fighter earth ever saw."

The audience, I among them, stared, awe-struck and fascinated, at Commodus laying a bloody hand on his own head; we shuddered: I saw many look back and forth from Palus in the arena to the figure on the Imperial throne.

The guards ran, the surgeons' helpers ran, even Galen ran, but Aemilius Laetus reached Palus first, and, between the dazed and stunned *lanistae*, picked up the big golden helmet and replaced it on his head, hiding his features. The distance from the *podium* wall to the center of the arena is so great, the distance from any other part of the audience so much greater, that, while many of the spectators were astounded, suspicious or curious, not one could be certain that Palus was, beyond peradventure, the Prince of the Republic in person. Palus stood there, alternately staring at his dead crony and talking to Laetus and Galen.

The heralds had run up with the guards. Laetus, without any pretense of consultation with the dummy Emperor on the throne, spoke to the heralds and each stalked off to one focus of the ellipse of the arena. Thence each bellowed for silence, their deep-toned, resonant, loud, practiced voices carrying to the upper colonnade everywhere. Silence, deep already since Murmex received his death-wound and broken only by whispers, deepened. The amphitheater became almost still. Into the stillness the heralds proclaimed that next day the funeral games of Murmex Lucro would be celebrated in the Colosseum where he had died; that all persons entitled to seats in the Colosseum were thereby enjoin to attend, unless too ill to leave their homes: that all should come without togas, but, in sign of mourning for Murmex, wearing over their garments full-length, all-enveloping rain-cloaks of undyed black wool and similarly colored umbrella hats; that any person failing to attend so habited would be severely punished; that the show would be worth seeing, for, in honor of the Manes of Murmex, to placate his ghost, no defeated fighter would be spared and all the victors of the morning would fight each other in the afternoon.

Surely the tenth day before the Kalends of January, in December of the nine hundred and forty-fourth year of the City,* the year in which Commodus was nominally consul for the seventh time, and Pertinax consul for the second time, saw the strangest audience ever assembled in the amphitheater of the Colosseum. I was there, seated, as on the day before, next my master, my gaudy Asiatic garments, like his garb of a noble of equestrian rank, hidden under a great raincoat and my face shaded by the broad brim of an umbrella hat.

The universal material conventional for mourners' attire is certainly appropriate and proper for mourning garb. For the undyed wool of black sheep, when spun and woven, results in a cloth dingy in the extreme. The wearing of garments made of it suits admirably with grief and gloom of spirit, deepens sadness, accentuates woe, almost produces melancholy. And the sight of it, when one is surrounded by persons so habited, conduces to dejection and depression. This equally was felt by the whole audience. Instead of being a space glaring in the sunlight shining on an expanse of white togas, the hollow of the amphitheater was a dingy area of brownish black under a lowering canopy of sullen cloud, for the sky was heavily overcast and threatened rain all day, though not a drop fell. The windless air was damp and penetratingly chilly, so that we almost shivered under our swathings. The discomfort of not being warm enough and the dispiriting effect of the grim sky and gloomy interior of the amphitheater was manifest in a sort of general impression of melancholy and apprehension.

Apprehension, or, certainly, uneasiness, pervaded the audience and, as

*191 A.D.

it were, seemed to diffuse itself from the Imperial Pavilion, crowded, not, as usual, with jaunty figures in gaudy apparel, all crimson, blue, and green picked out and set off by edgings of silver and gold, but with a solemn retinue, all hidden under dingy umbrella hats and swathed in rain-cloaks. To see the throne occupied by a human shape so obscured by its habiliments gave all beholders an uncanny feeling in which foreboding deepened into alarm. The appearance of the whole audience, still more of the Imperial retinue, was one to cause all beholders to interpret the garb of the spectators as ill-omened, almost as inviting disaster.

In the center of the arena was built up the pyre which was to consume all that was left of Murmex. It was constructed of thirty-foot logs, each tier laid across the one below it, the lower tiers of linden, willow, elm and other quick-burning woods, their interstices filled with fat pine-knots; the upper tiers of oak and maple, at which last I heard not a few whispered protests, for the old-fashioned folk felt it almost a sacrilege that holy wood should be used to burn a gladiator, a man of blood. The pyre was thus a square structure thirty feet on a side and fully twenty feet high; each side showing silvered log-butts or log-ends, with gilded pine-knots all between; its top covered with laurel boughs, over which was laid a crimson rug with golden fringe, setting off the corpse of Murmex, which lay in the silver armor he had worn in his last fight, high on the mound of laurel boughs.

At each focus of the arena was placed a round marble altar, one to Venus Libitina, one to Pluto. By these the heralds took their stands and proclaimed that no offerings would be made at the altars except one black lamb at each, that every man slain in the day's fighting would be an offering to the Manes of Murmex, since the day would be occupied solely with the celebration of funeral games for the solace of his ghost.

The games began with a set-to of sixteen pairs of gladiators fighting simultaneously. After this was over the sixteen victors drew off towards one end of the arena and sixteen other pairs fought simultaneously. After them the victors of the first set paired off as the *lanistae* arranged and the eight pairs fought. The eight victors again rested while the survivors of the second set simultaneously fought as eight pairs. So they alternated till only two men survived. A third batch of thirty-two gladiators then fought in sixteen pairs; then the two survivors of the first and second batches fought. The heralds proclaimed that the sole survivor of the first sixty-four would fight again in the afternoon.

To my eyesight the figure on the throne, even under that broad hat-brim and enveloped in that thick rain-cloak, was manifestly Commodus in person. Unmistakably his was every Imperial gesture as he presided as Editor of the games.

During the noon interval, as usual, the Emperor retired to his robing-room under the upper tiers of the amphitheater. When again, after the noon interval, the throne was reoccupied, I felt certain that its occupant was Ducconius Furfur.

At any rate Palus appeared at once after the noon interval and the first fight was between him and the survivor of the sixty-four wretches, who had begun the day's butchery. Palus, of course, killed his man, but with more appearance of effort and less easily than any adversary he had ever faced under my observation. The people cheered his victory, but not so enthusiastically as usual. He did not appear again till the last event of the day, which was a series of duels between champions in two-horse chariots, driven by expert charioteers, they and the fighters equipped with arms and armor such as was used by both sides at the siege of Troy. Horses are seldom seen in the Colosseum and these pairs, frantic at the smell of blood, taxed to the utmost the skill and strength of their drivers, particularly as they were controlled by the old-fashioned reins of the Heroic period, the manipulation of which calls for methods different from those effective with our improved modern reins.

The charioteers were capable and their dexterous maneuvering for every advantage of approach and relative position won many cheers. Eight pairs fought, then the eight victors paired off, then the four victors, then the two. The sole survivor then retired and while he was out of the arena there entered a superb pair of bay horses, drawing a chariot of Greek pattern, in which, to the amazement of all beholders, was Narcissus, the wrestler, himself, habited as Automedon and acting as charioteer; while beside him, magnificent in a triple crested crimson-plumed helmet of the Thessalian type, in a gilded corselet of the style of the Heroic age, with gilded scales on its kilt-straps, with gilded greaves, with a big gilded Argive shield embossed with reliefs, and holding two spears, manifestly habited as Achilles, stood Palus.

When his refreshed antagonist re-entered in a Trojan chariot and ar-mored and armed as Hector of Troy, Palus handed his two spears to his Automedon, leapt from his chariot, walked over to Hector's, and spoke to him. I heard it reported afterwards that he said:

"It would spoil the program for Hector to slay Achilles, but you have as much chance of killing me as I of killing you. I am so shaken by Murmex's death that I am not the man I was yesterday morning and up till then. I never felt so nearly matched as by you, not even by Murmex. Attack and spare not. I have given orders that, if you kill me, you shall not suffer for it in any way. I don't want to live, anyhow, now Murmex is dead."

Whether he said this or something else, he spoke earnestly and walked back to his chariot nearby, without any elasticity in his tread.

Narcissus, the wrestler, to the astonishment of the spectators, proved himself a paragon horse jockey. Everyone knew him as a wrestler, as reported the strongest man alive, as claimed by his admirers to have a more powerful hand-grasp than any rival, as the favorite wrestling-mate of the Emperor; all the notabilities had seen him and Commodus wrestle in the Stadium of the Palace; all Rome knew him for a crony of the Prince; yet no one had ever heard him praised or even mentioned as a charioteer. Yet he showed himself a matchless horseman. Hector's charioteer was a master, yet Narcissus outmaneuvered him, gained the advantage of angle of approach and, after many turns, gave Palus his chance. The two great lances flew almost simultaneously; but, as Achilles dodged, Hector fell dying of a mortal wound in the throat.

What followed was, apparently, according to the prearranged program and was indubitably in keeping with the equipment of the two champions and their charioteers; yet it horrified me, and I think all the senators and nobles as well as most of the audience. As Hector sprawled horridly on the sand Narcissus veered his pair and, as they passed the fallen man, Achilles leapt from his chariot. Drawing his Argive sword he slashed the dying man across his abdomen; then, sheathing his blade, he stood, one foot on his adversary's neck and, raising his lance and shield, shouted: "Enalie! Enalie! Enalie!" the old Greek invocation to the war-god. Then he threw aside his lance and shield and stripped off the armor from the dead. Arena-slaves carried it to the pyre and placed it upon it, by Murmex.

Narcissus had wheeled the chariot in a short circle and halted it as near Palus as he could keep it and control the frantic horse. Palus took from one of the hand-holds at the back of the chariot-rail a long leathern thong. With his dirk he slit each foot of the corpse between the leg-bone and the heel-tendon; through the slit he passed the thong, knotting it to his liking. The doubled thong he tied securely to the rear rim of the chariot-bed. Retrieving his lance and shield he posed an instant, every inch Achilles, stepped over Hector's naked corpse and mounted the chariot. From Automedon he took the reins and the whip, passing him his lance, yet retaining his great circular shield, nowise hampered by which he drove the chariot round and round the pyre, the picture, as all could see, he felt, of Achilles placating the ghost of Patroclus.

This exhibition shocked the whole audience, upper tiers and all. The ghost of a hiss breathed under the tense hush of the silent beholders. A shudder ran over the hollow of the amphitheater, as the dragged corpse, mauled by the sand and turning over, became a mere lump of pounded meat. The chill of the onlookers appeared to reach Palus. He halted his team near the pyre, arena-slaves dragged away Hector's corpse, one brought a lighted torch and Palus himself kindled the pyre at each of its four corners, walking twice round it. When it was enveloped in crackling flames, he mounted the chariot and Narcissus drove him out; drove him out, to the horror of all beholders, by the Gate of Ill-omen.

After he vanished through that gate no amphitheater ever again beheld Palus the Gladiator.

When he was gone all eyes were fixed on the kindling pyre. The flames blazed up all round it and above it, the smoke mounted skyward in a thick column, the crackle and roar of the flames was audible all over the amphitheater; so deep was the solemn stillness. I shall carry to my last living hour the vivid recollection of that picture: under the grim gray sky, framed in by the sable hangings which draped the upper colonnade, and by the dingy audience, against the yellow sand, that column of sooty smoke and below it the red glare of the blazing pyre.

On the Great Wall

by Rudyard Kipling

385 Dan and Una were the luckiest children in England because Puck, "the last of the People of the Hills" and the wisest of fairies, was their friend. Through his magic they met several of his oldest friends who told them about the England they had known. In this story Parnesius, a Centurion of the Thirtieth Legion, tells of the last sad days of Roman power.

'When I left Rome for Lalage's sake
　　By the Legions' Road to Rimini,
She vowed her heart was mine to take
　　With me and my shield to Rimini —
　　(Till the Eagles flew from Rimini!)
　　　　And I've tramped Britain and I've tramped Gaul
　　　　And the Pontic shore where the snow-flakes fall
　　As white as the neck of Lalage —
　　As cold as the heart of Lalage!
　　　　And I've lost Britain and I've lost Gaul,'
　　　　(the voice seemed very cheerful about it),

'And I've lost Rome, and worst of all,
　　I've lost Lalage!'

They were standing by the gate to Far Wood when they heard this song. Without a word they hurried to their private gap and wriggled through the hedge almost atop of a jay that was feeding from Puck's hand.

'Gently!' said Puck. 'What are you looking for?'

'Parnesius, of course,' Dan answered. 'We've only just remembered yesterday. It isn't fair.'

Puck chuckled as he rose. 'I'm sorry, but children who spend the afternoon with me and a Roman Centurion need a little settling dose of Magic before they go to tea with their governess. Ohe, Parnesius!' he called.

'Here, Faun!' came the answer from Volaterrae. They could see the shimmer of bronze armour in the beech crotch, and the friendly flash of the great shield uplifted.

'I have driven out the Britons.' Parnesius laughed like a boy. 'I occupy their high forts. But Rome is merciful! You may come up.' And up they three all scrambled.

'What was the song you were singing just now?' said Una, as soon as she had settled herself.

'That? Oh, "Rimini." It's one of the tunes that are always being born somewhere in the Empire. They run like a pestilence for six months or a year, till another one pleases the Legions, and then they march to that.'

'Tell them about the marching, Parnesius. Few people nowadays walk from end to end of this country,' said Puck.

'The greater their loss. I know nothing better than the Long March when your feet are hardened. You begin after the mists have risen, and you end, perhaps, an hour after sun-down.'

'And what do you have to eat?' Dan asked, promptly.

'Fat bacon, beans, and bread, and whatever wine happens to be in the rest-houses. But soldiers are born grumblers. Their very first day out, my men complained of our water-ground British corn. They said it wasn't so filling as the rough stuff that is ground in the Roman ox-mills. How-ever, they had to fetch and eat it.'

'Fetch it? Where from?' said Una.

'From that newly-invented water-mill below the Forge.'

'That's Forge Mill — our Mill!' Una looked at Puck.

'Yes; yours,' Puck put in. 'How old did you think it was?'

'I don't know. Didn't Sir Richard Dalyngridge talk about it?'

'He did, and it was old in his day,' Puck answered. 'Hundreds of years old.'

'It was new in mine,' said Parnesius. 'My men looked at the flour in their helmets as though it had been a nest of adders. They did it to try my patience. But I — addressed them and we became friends. To tell the truth, they taught me the Roman Step. You see, I'd only served with quick-marching Auxiliaries. A Legion's pace is altogether different. It is a long, slow stride, that never varies from sunrise to sunset. "Rome's Race — Rome's Pace," as the proverb says. Twenty-four miles in eight hours, neither more nor less. Head and spear up, shield on your back, cuirass collar open one hand's breadth — and that's how you take the Eagles through Britain.'

'And did you meet any adventures?' said Dan.

'There are no adventures South of the Wall,' said Parnesius. 'The worst thing that happened me was having to appear before a magistrate up North, where a wandering philosopher had jeered at the Eagles. I was able to show that the old man had deliberately blocked our road; and the magistrate told him, out of his own Book, I believe, that, whatever his Gods might be, he should pay proper respect to Caesar.'

'What did you do?' said Dan.

'Went on. Why should I care for such things, my business being to reach my station? It took me twenty days.

'Of course, the farther North you go the emptier are the roads. At last you fetch clear of the forests and climb bare hills, where wolves howl in the ruins of our cities that have been. No more pretty girls; no more jolly magistrates who knew your Father when he was young, and invite you to stay with them; no news at the temples and way-stations except bad news of wild beasts. There's where you meet hunters, and trappers for the Circuses, prodding along chained bears and muzzled wolves. Your pony shies at them, and your men laugh.

'The houses change from gardened villas to shut forts with watch-towers of gray stone, and great stone-walled sheepfolds, guarded by armed Britons of the North Shore. In the naked hills beyond the naked houses, where the shadows of the clouds play like cavalry charging, you see puffs of black smoke from the mines. The hard road goes on and on — and the wind sings through your helmet-plume — past altars to Legions and Generals forgotten, and broken statues of Gods and Heroes, and thousands of graves where the mountain foxes and hares peep at you. Red-hot in summer, freezing in winter, is that big, purple heather country of broken stone.

'Just when you think you are at the world's end, you see a smoke from East to West as far as the eye can turn, and then, under it, also as far as the eye can stretch, houses and temples, shops and theatres, barracks and granaries, trickling along like dice behind — always behind — one long, low, rising and falling, and hiding and showing line of towers. And that is the Wall!'

'Ah!' said the children, taking breath.

'You may well,' said Parnesius. 'Old men who have followed the Eagles since boyhood say nothing in the Empire is more wonderful than first sight of the Wall!'

'Is it just a Wall? Like the one round the kitchen-garden?' said Dan.

'No, no! It is the Wall. Along the top are towers with guard-houses, small towers, between. Even on the narrowest part of it three men with shields can walk abreast, from guard-house to guard-house. A little curtain wall, no higher than a man's neck, runs along the top of the thick wall, so that from a distance you see the helmets of the sentries sliding back and forth like beads. Thirty feet high is the Wall, and on the Picts' side, the North, is a ditch, strewn with blades of old swords and spearheads set in wood, and tyres of wheels joined by chains. The Little People come there to steal iron for their arrow-heads.

'But the Wall itself is not more wonderful than the town behind it. Long ago there were great ramparts and ditches on the South side, and no one was allowed to build there. Now the ramparts are partly pulled down and built over, from end to end of the Wall; making a thin town eighty miles long. Think of it! One roaring, rioting, cock-fighting, wolf-baiting, horse-racing town, from Ituna on the West to Segedunum on the cold eastern beach! On one side heather, woods and ruins where Picts hide, and on the other, a vast town — long like a snake, and wicked like a snake. Yes, a snake basking beside a warm wall!

'My Cohort, I was told, lay at Hunno, where the Great North Road runs through the Wall into the Province of Valentia.' Parnesius laughed scornfully. 'The Province of Valentia! We followed the road, therefore, into Hunno town, and stood astonished. The place was a fair — a fair of peoples from every corner of the Empire. Some were racing horses: some sat in wine-shops: some watched dogs baiting bears, and many gathered in a ditch to see cocks fight. A boy not much older than myself, but I could see he was an officer, reined up before me and asked what I wanted.

' "My station," I said, and showed him my shield. Parnesius held up his broad shield with its three X's like letters on a beer-cask.

' "Lucky omen!" said he. "Your Cohort's the next tower to us, but they're all at the cock-fight. This is a happy place. Come and wet the Eagles." He meant to offer me a drink.

' "When I've handed over my men," I said. I felt angry and ashamed.

' "Oh, you'll soon outgrow that sort of nonsense," he answered. "But don't let me interfere with your hopes. Go on to the Statue of Roma Dea. You can't miss it. The main road into Valentia!" and he laughed and rode off. I could see the statue not a quarter of a mile away, and there I went. At some time or other the Great North Road ran under it into Valentia; but the far end had been blocked up because of the Picts, and on the plaster a man had scratched, "Finish!" It was like marching into a cave. We grounded spears together, my little thirty, and it echoed in the barrel of the arch, but none came. There was a door at one side painted with our number. We prowled in, and I found a cook asleep, and ordered him to give us food. Then I climbed to the top of the Wall, and looked out over the Pict country, and I — thought,' said Parnesius. 'The bricked-up arch with "Finish!" on the plaster was what shook me, for I was not much more than a boy.'

'What a shame!' said Una. 'But did you feel happy after you'd had a good —' Dan stopped her with a nudge.

'Happy?' said Parnesius. 'When the men of the Cohort I was to command came back unhelmeted from the cock-fight, their birds under their arms, and asked me who I was? No, I was not happy; but I made my new Cohort unhappy too. . . . I wrote my Mother I was happy, but, oh, my friends' — he stretched arms over bare knees — 'I would not wish my worst enemy to suffer as I suffered through my first months on the Wall. Remember this: among the officers was scarcely one, except myself (and I thought I had lost the favour of Maximus my General), scarcely one who had not done something of wrong or folly. Either he had killed a man, or taken money, or insulted the magistrates, or blasphemed the Gods, and so had been sent to the Wall as a hiding-place from shame or fear. And the men were as the officers. Remember, also, that the Wall was manned by every breed and race in the Empire. No two towers spoke the same tongue, or worshipped the same Gods. In one thing only we were all equal. No matter what arms we had used before we came to the Wall, on the Wall we were all archers, like the Scythians. The Pict cannot run away from the arrow, or crawl under it. He is a bowman himself. He knows!'

'I suppose you were fighting Picts all the time,' said Dan.

'Picts seldom fight. I never saw a fighting Pict for half a year. The tame Picts told us they had all gone North.'

'What is a tame Pict?' said Dan.

'A Pict — there were many such — who speaks a few words of our tongue, and slips across the Wall to sell ponies and wolf-hounds. Without a horse and a dog, and a friend, man would perish. The Gods gave me all three, and there is no gift like friendship. Remember this' — Parnesius turned to Dan — 'when you become a young man. For your fate will turn on the first true friend you make.'

'He means,' said Puck grinning, 'that if you try to make yourself a decent chap when you're young, you'll make rather decent friends when you grow up. If you're a beast, you'll have beastly friends. Listen to the Pious Parnesius on Friendship!'

'I am not pious,' Parnesius answered, 'but I know what goodness means;

and my friend, though he was without hope, was ten thousand times better than I. Stop laughing, Faun!'

'Oh Youth Eternal and All-believing,' cried Puck, as he rocked on the branch above. 'Tell them about your Pertinax.'

'He was that friend the Gods sent me — the boy who spoke to me when I first came. Little older than myself, commanding the Augusta Victoria Cohort on the tower next to us and the Numidians. In virtue he was far my superior.'

'Then why was he on the Wall?' Una asked, quickly. 'They'd all done something bad. You said so yourself.'

'He was the nephew, his Father had died, of a great rich man in Gaul who was not always kind to his Mother. When Pertinax grew up he discovered this, and so his uncle shipped him off, by trickery and force, to the Wall. We came to know each other at a ceremony in our Temple — in the dark. It was the Bull Killing,' Parnesius explained to Puck.

'I see,' said Puck, and turned to the children. 'That's something you wouldn't quite understand. Parnesius means he met Pertinax in church.'

'Yes — in the Cave we first met, and we were both raised to the Degree of Gryphons together.' Parnesius lifted his hand towards his neck for an instant. 'He had been on the Wall two years, and knew the Picts well. He taught me first how to take Heather.'

'What's that?' said Dan.

'Going out hunting in the Pict country with a tame Pict. You are quite safe so long as you are his guest, and wear a sprig of heather where it can be seen. If you went alone you would surely be killed, if you were not smothered first in the bogs. Only the Picts know their way about those black and hidden bogs. Old Allo, the one-eyed, withered little Pict from whom we bought our ponies, was our special friend. At first we went only to escape from the terrible town, and to talk together about our homes. Then he showed us how to hunt wolves and those great red deer with horns like Jewish candlesticks. The Roman-born officers rather looked down on us for doing this, but we preferred the heather to their amusements. Believe me,' Parnesius turned again to Dan, 'a boy is safe from all things that really harm when he is astride a pony or after a deer. Do you remember, O Faun,' he turned to Puck, 'the little altar I built to the Sylvan Pan by the pine-forest beyond the brook?'

'Which? The stone one with the line from Xenophon?' said Puck in quite a new voice.

'No. What do I know of Xenophon? That was Pertinax — after he had

shot his first mountain-hare with an arrow — by chance! Mine I made of
round pebbles in memory of my first bear. It took me one happy day to
build.' Parnesius faced the children quickly.

'And that was how we lived on the Wall for two years — a little scuffling
with the Picts, and a great deal of hunting with old Allo in the Pict country. He called us his children sometimes, and we were fond of him and
his barbarians, though we never let them paint us Pict fashion. The marks
endure till you die.'

'How's it done?' said Dan. 'Anything like tattooing?'

'They prick the skin till the blood runs, and rub in coloured juices. Allo
was painted blue, green, and red from his forehead to his ankles. He said
it was part of his religion. He told us about his religion (Pertinax was always interested in such things), and as we came to know him well, he
told us what was happening in Britain behind the Wall. Many things took
place behind us in those days. And by the Light of the Sun,' said Parnesius,
earnestly, 'there was not much that those little people did not know! He
told me when Maximus crossed over to Gaul, after he made himself Emperor of Britain, and what troops and emigrants he had taken with him.
We did not get the news on the Wall till fifteen days later. He told me
what troops Maximus was taking out of Britain every month to help him
conquer Gaul; and I always found the numbers were as he said. Wonderful! And I tell another strange thing!'

He jointed his hands across his knees, and leaned his head on the curve
of the shield behind him.

'Late in the summer, when the first frosts begin and the Picts kill their
bees, we three rode out after wolf with some new hounds. Rutilianus, our
General, had given us ten days' leave, and we had pushed beyond the
Second Wall — beyond the Province of Valentia — into the higher hills,
where there are not even any of Rome's old ruins. We killed a she-wolf
before noon, and while Allo was skinning her he looked up and said to me,
"When you are Captain of the Wall, my child, you won't be able to do
this any more!"

'I might as well have been made Prefect of Lower Gaul, so I laughed
and said, "Wait till I am Captain." "No, don't wait," said Allo. "Take my
advice and go home — both of you." "We have no homes," said Pertinax.
"You know that as well as we do. We're finished men — thumbs down
against both of us. Only men without hope would risk their necks on your
ponies." The old man laughed one of those short Pict laughs — like a fox
barking on a frosty night. "I'm fond of you two," he said. "Besides, I've

taught you what little you know about hunting. Take my advice and go home."

'"We can't," I said. "I'm out of favour with my General, for one thing; and for another, Pertinax has an uncle."

'"I don't know about his uncle," said Allo, "but the trouble with you, Parnesius, is that your General thinks well of you."

'"Roma Dea!" said Pertinax, sitting up. "What can you guess what Maximus thinks, you old horse-coper?"

'Just then (you know how near the brutes creep when one is eating?) a great dog-wolf jumped out behind us, and away our rested hounds tore after him, with us at their tails. He ran us far out of any country we'd ever heard of, straight as an arrow till sunset, towards the sunset. We came at last to long capes stretching into winding waters, and on a gray beach below us we saw ships drawn up. Forty-seven we counted — not Roman galleys but the raven-winged ships from the North where Rome does not rule. Men moved in the ships, and the sun flashed on their helmets — winged helmets of the red-haired men from the North where Rome does not rule. We watched, and we counted, and we wondered, for though we had heard rumours concerning these Winged Hats, as the Picts called them, never before had we looked upon them.

'"Come away! come away!" said Allo. "My Heather won't protect you here. We shall all be killed!" His legs trembled like his voice. Back we went — back across the heather under the moon, till it was nearly morning, and our poor beasts stumbled on some ruins.

'When we woke, very stiff and cold, Allo was mixing the meal and water. One does not light fires in the Pict country except near a village. The little men are always signalling to each other with smokes, and a strange smoke brings them out buzzing like bees. They can sting, too!

'"What we saw last night was a trading-station," said Allo. "Nothing but a trading-station."

'"I do not like lies on an empty stomach," said Pertinax. "I suppose" (he had eyes like an eagle's) — "I suppose that is a trading-station also?" He pointed to a smoke far off on a hill-top, ascending in what we call the Picts' Call: — Puff — double-puff: double-puff — puff! They make it by raising and dropping a wet hide on a fire.

'"No," said Allo, pushing the platter back into the bag. "That is for you and me. Your fate is fixed. Come."

'We came. When one takes Heather, one must obey one's Pict — but that wretched smoke was twenty miles distant, well over on the east coast, and the day was as hot as a bath.

'"Whatever happens,"' said Allo, while our ponies grunted along, "I want you to remember me."

'"I shall not forget," said Pertinax. "You have cheated me out of my breakfast."

'"What is a handful of crushed oats to a Roman?" he said. Then he laughed his laugh that was not a laugh. "What would you do if you were a handful of oats being crushed between the upper and lower stones of a mill?"

'"I'm Pertinax, not a riddle-guesser," said Pertinax.

'"You're a fool,'" said Allo. "Your Gods and my Gods are threatened by strange Gods, and all you can do is to laugh."

'"Threatened men live long," I said.

'"I pray the Gods that may be true,'" he said. "But I ask you again not to forget me."

'We climbed the last hot hill and looked out on the eastern sea, three or four miles off. There was a small sailing-galley of the North Gaul pattern at anchor, her landing-plank down and her sail half up; and below us, alone in a hollow, holding his pony, sat Maximus, Emperor of Britain! He was dressed like a hunter, and he leaned on his little stick; but I knew that back as far as I could see it, and I told Pertinax.

'"You're madder than Allo!" he said. "It must be the sun!"

'Maximus never stirred till we stood before him. Then he looked me up and down, and said: "Hungry again? It seems to be my destiny to feed you whenever we meet. I have food here. Allo shall cook it."

'"No," said Allo. "A Prince in his own land does not wait on wandering Emperors. I feed my two children without asking your leave." He began to blow up the ashes.

'"I was wrong," said Pertinax. "We are all mad. Speak up, O Madman called Emperor!"

'Maximus smiled his terrible tight-lipped smile, but two years on the Wall do not make a man afraid of mere looks. So I was not afraid.

'"I meant you, Parnesius, to live and die a Centurion of the Wall," said Maximus. "But it seems from these," he fumbled in his breast, "you can think as well as draw." He pulled out a roll of letters I had written to my people, full of drawings of Picts, and bears, and men I had met on the Wall. Mother and my sister always liked my pictures.

'He handed me one that I had called "Maximus's Soldiers." It showed a row of fat wine-skins, and our old Doctor of the Hunno hospital snuffing at them. Each time that Maximus had taken troops out of Britain to help him conquer Gaul, he used to send the garrisons more wine — to keep them quiet, I suppose. On the Wall, we always called a wine-skin a "Maximus." Oh, yes; and I had drawn them in Imperial helmets.

'"Not long since," he went on, "men's names were sent up to Caesar for smaller jokes than this."

'"True, Caesar," said Pertinax; "but you forget that was before I, your friend's friend, became such a good spear-thrower."

'He did not actually point his hunting spear at Maximus, but balanced it on his palm — so!

'"I was speaking of time past," said Maximus, never fluttering an eyelid. "Nowadays one is only too pleased to find boys who can think for themselves, and their friends." He nodded at Pertinax. "Your Father lent me the letters, Parnesius, so you run no risk from me."

'"None whatever," said Pertinax, and rubbed the spear-point on his sleeve.

'"I have been forced to reduce the garrisons in Britain, because I need troops in Gaul. Now I come to take troops from the Wall itself," said he.

'"I wish you joy of us," said Pertinax. "We're the last sweepings of the Empire — the men without hope. Myself, I'd sooner trust condemned criminals."

'"You think so?" he said, quite seriously. "But it will only be till I win Gaul. One must always risk one's life, or one's soul, or one's peace — or some little thing."

'Allo passed round the fire with the sizzling deer's meat. He served us two first.

'"Ah!" said Maximus, waiting his turn. "I perceive you are in your own country. Well, you deserve it. They tell me you have quite a following among the Picts, Parnesius."

'"I have hunted with them," I said. "Maybe I have a few friends among the Heather."

'"He is the only armoured man of you all who understands us," said Allo, and he began a long speech about our virtues, and how we had saved one of his grandchildren from a wolf the year before.'

'Had you?' said Una.

'Yes; but that was neither here nor there. The little green man orated like a — like Cicero. He made us out to be magnificent fellows. Maximus never took his eyes off our faces.

'"Enough," he said. "I have heard Allo on you. I wish to hear you on the Picts."

'I told him as much as I knew, and Pertinax helped me out. There is never harm in a Pict if you but take the trouble to find out what he wants. Their real grievance against us came from our burning their heather. The whole garrison of the Wall moved out twice a year, and solemnly burned the heather for ten miles North. Rutilianus, our General, called it clearing the country. The Picts, of course, scampered away, and all we did was to destroy their bee-bloom in the summer, and ruin their sheep-food in the spring.

'"True, quite true," said Allo. "How can we make our holy heatherwine, if you burn our bee-pasture?"

'We talked long, Maximus asking keen questions that showed he knew much and had thought more about the Picts. He said presently to me: "If I gave you the old Province of Valentia to govern, could you keep the Picts contented till I won Gaul? Stand away, so that you do not see Allo's face; and speak your own thoughts."

'"No," I said. "You cannot remake that Province. The Picts have been free too long."

'"Leave them their village councils, and let them furnish their own soldiers," he said. "You, I am sure, would hold the reins very lightly."

'"Even then, no," I said. "At least not now. They have been too oppressed by us to trust anything with a Roman name for years and years."

'I heard old Allo behind me mutter: "Good child!"

'"Then what do you recommend," said Maximus, "to keep the North quiet till I win Gaul?"

'"Leave the Picts alone," I said. "Stop the heather-burning at once, and — they are improvident little animals — send them a shipload or two of corn now and then."

'"Their own men must distribute it — not some cheating Greek accountant," said Pertinax.

'"Yes, and allow them to come to our hospitals when they are sick," I said.

'"Surely they would die first," said Maximus.

'"Not if Parnesius brought them in," said Allo. "I could show you twenty wolf-bitten, bear-clawed Picts within twenty miles of here. But Parnesius must stay with them in Hospital, else they would go mad with fear."

'"I see," said Maximus. "Like everything else in the world, it is one man's work. You, I think, are that one man."

'"Pertinax and I are one," I said.

'"As you please, so long as you work. Now, Allo, you know that I mean your people no harm. Leave us to talk together," said Maximus.

' "No need!" said Allo. "I am the corn between the upper and lower millstones. I must know what the lower millstone means to do. These boys have spoken the truth as far as they know it. I, a Prince, will tell you the rest. I am troubled about the Men of the North." He squatted like a hare in the heather, and looked over his shoulder.

' "I also," said Maximus, "or I should not be here."

' "Listen," said Allo. "Long and long ago the Winged Hats" — he meant the Northmen — "came to our beaches and said, 'Rome falls! Push her down!' We fought you. You sent men. We were beaten. After that we said to the Winged Hats, 'You are liars! Make our men alive that Rome killed, and we will believe you.' They went away ashamed. Now they come back bold, and they tell the old tale, which we begin to believe—that Rome falls!"

' "Give me three years' peace on the Wall," cried Maximus, "and I will show you and all the ravens how they lie!"

' "Ah, I wish it too! I wish to save what is left of the corn from the millstones. But you shoot us Picts when we come to borrow a little iron from the Iron Ditch; you burn our heather, which is all our crop; you trouble us with your great catapults. Then you hide behind the Wall, and scorch us with Greek fire. How can I keep my young men from listening to the Winged Hats — in winter especially, when we are hungry? My young men will say, 'Rome can neither fight nor rule. She is taking her men out of Britain. The Winged Hats will help us to push down the Wall. Let us show them the secret roads across the bogs.' Do I want that? No!" He spat like an adder. "I would keep the secrets of my people though I were burned alive. My two children here have spoken truth. Leave us Picts alone. Comfort us, and cherish us, and feed us from far off — with the hand behind your back. Parnesius understands us. Let him have rule on the Wall, and I will hold my young men quiet for" — he ticked it off on his fingers — "one year easily: the next year not so easily: the third year, perhaps! See, I give you three years. If then you do not show us that Rome is strong in men and terrible in arms, the Winged Hats, I tell you, will sweep down the Wall from either sea till they meet in the middle, and you will go. I shall not grieve over that, but well I know tribe never helps tribe except for one price. We Picts will go too. The Winged Hats will grind us to this!" He tossed a handful of dust in the air.

' "Oh, Roma Dea!" said Maximus, half aloud. "It is always one man's work — always and everywhere!"

' "And one man's life," said Allo. "You are Emperor, but not a God. You may die."

' "I have thought of that too," said he. "Very good. If this wind holds, I shall be at the East end of the Wall by morning. To-morrow, then, I shall see you two when I inspect, and I will make you Captains of the Wall for this work."

' "One instant, Caesar," said Pertinax. "All men have their price. I am not bought yet."

' "Do you also begin to bargain so early?" said Maximus. "Well?"

' "Give me justice against my uncle Icenus, the Duumvir of Divio in Gaul," he said.

' "Only a life? I thought it would be money or an office. Certainly you shall have him. Write his name on these tablets — on the red side; the other is for the living!" And Maximus held out his tablets.

' "He is of no use to me dead," said Pertinax. "My mother is a widow. I am far off. I am not sure he pays her all her dowry."

' "No matter. My arm is reasonably long. We will look through your uncle's accounts in due time. Now, farewell till to-morrow, O Captains of the Wall!"

'We saw him grow small across the heather as he walked to the galley. There were Picts, scores, each side of him, hidden behind stones. He never looked left or right. He sailed away Southerly, full spread before the evening breeze, and when we had watched him out to sea, we were silent. We understood that Earth bred few men like to this man.

'Presently Allo brought the ponies and held them for us to mount — a thing he had never done before.

' "Wait awhile," said Pertinax, and he made a little altar of cut turf, and strewed heather-bloom atop, and laid upon it a letter from a girl in Gaul.

' "What do you do, O my friend?" I said.

' "I sacrifice to my dead youth," he answered, and, when the flames had consumed the letter, he ground them out with his heel. Then we rode back to that Wall of which we were to be Captains.'

Parnesius stopped. The children sat still, not even asking if that were all the tale. Puck beckoned, and pointed the way out of the wood. 'Sorry,' he whispered, 'but you must go now.'

'We haven't made him angry, have we?' said Una. 'He looks so far off, and — and — thinky.'

'Bless your heart, no. Wait till to-morrow. It won't be long. Remember, you've been playing "Lays of Ancient Rome." '

And as soon as they had scrambled through their gap where Oak, Ash, and Thorn grew, that was all they remembered.

The Founding of the Kingdom of Wessex
by Alfred Duggan

495 When Roman power collapsed Anglo-Saxon
barbarians poured into England to conquer, to destroy, and to settle. The leader of the most successful
war band was a cynical turncoat named Cerdic, a
Romanized Briton who had joined the winning side.
This is his own story of how he founded the kingdom
which today is ruled by Queen Elizabeth II.

In the morning we penetrated the inland sea, our sails set to a
favourable wind, but with oars ready to keep us clear of the numerous
shoals. We had to steer a winding course, which meant that we were observed from the mainland for some hours before we landed, and the local
inhabitants had plenty of time to gather their forces to oppose us. This
was a disadvantage, for no one fights his best after a tiring and cramp-
ing voyage, and the enemy would bury their valuables before we could
start plundering. But I did not greatly fear any levy that could be raised
on the shores of the Sea of Vectis.

Ever since I can remember that land has been without a ruler. To the
west lies the powerful Kingdom of the Dumnonians, and on the east was
once the Kingdom of the Regni; it is always a sensible plan to have a
desert on your boundary, and neither my father nor the Dumnonian King
had given much help when pirates landed to ransack again the ruins of
the once flourishing city of Portus. That city had suffered a nasty civil
war soon after the Emperor's authority was withdrawn from Britain, and
its trade had vanished when the sea became unsafe for merchants. Presently it had been deserted, like so many other cities of Britain. By the
time I was a young man, twenty-five years before I landed with my army
of Saxons, the whole district had lost its Roman civilization; there was
no central authority, gathering taxes and paying a comitatus, between
Regnum and Dumnonia. That is not to say that the country was entirely
empty. Anyone who took the trouble to clear away the trees would find
rich soil beneath, and there were plenty of Romans who preferred to live
in a land without law; they would be exceptionally tough warriors, but
there ought not to be very many of them, and they would probably not
unite under one leader. We expected that we could face them in open battle.

Soon after midday we rowed up a little creek in the shore of the mainland that I am proud to say is still called Cerdics-ora, meaning Cerdic's
landing-place. The five ships were close together and we were able to
drive the bows into soft mud and run ashore dryshod. A few Romans had
collected to oppose our landing, but we were three hundred strong, much
more numerous than the average party of raiders, and we must have out-
numbered them considerably; we soon drove them from the battlefield,
without ourselves suffering much loss. It was Cynric's first battle, and
the dear boy exposed himself freely; but I had seen to it that he had a
good bodyguard of experienced veterans, and no harm came to him. In
one way it is a good thing to win a reputation for courage in early youth,
for it is very hard to lose afterwards, and gathers good men to the war-
band; but I had a serious talk with him that evening, and explained that
there was no point in my founding a Kingdom if I had no heir to succeed me. He promised to take more care of himself in future.

Now we were established on the coast, and the perennial question of
what to do with our ships had to be settled. Of course, we had made up
our minds to live permanently in Britain, and we did not need them to
take us back to Germany; on the other hand, ships are valuable possessions, and I could not bear to watch them burn. Finally I sent away all
five, with very small crews; four were to be exchanged for good presents, after the German manner of selling, and the largest was to come back
carrying the crews of the other four, and a few recruits as well. We would
have to wait in a fortified camp until it returned; but that would be in
about six weeks, and the neighbourhood would supply us for that time.

We lived peacefully in our camp for two months. There was no local ruler who could bring a regular comitatus into the field against us,
and the Dumnonians were on the defensive now that they had no organized Roman state to the east of them. My present territory was at one
end of the wide belt of devastated country that stretched through the
middle of Britain, I believe right up to the Kingdom of Elmetia somewhere near Eboracum; there was no ruler who felt it his duty to turn me
out at all costs.

All the same, I was not satisfied with our present hunting ground; for
the land immediately north of the Sea of Vectis is so thickly wooded and
so little cultivated that it is a hunting ground and nothing more. A gang
of hunters with wooden clubs, who had forgotten their laws and lived bes-
tially in small family groups, was no sort of inheritance to leave to Cynric.

Also we were too near the coast. I am told that the Empire still lingers on at the eastern end of the Middle Sea, but it will be many generations before a powerful fleet brings law and order to the pirates of the Channel. I have seen from my boyhood what a terrible drain it is on the resources of a Kingdom always to keep a look-out for raiders from the sea; I did not want Cynric to spend his life sitting on the beach waiting for news of pirates, and incessantly driving his cattle to shelter. I must go inland, to a hilly country where beacon-fires would give good warning of the approach of enemies, and where there was open grass for farmers to plough.

But I had to persuade my followers of this, for if I gave them orders that they did not like they could march off and join the South Saxons on our eastern borders. In any case we would have to winter at Cerdics-ora, since it was too late to plant corn. We did not have a very good time, but we managed somehow with deer from the woods and fish from the streams. I kept my men together as much as possible, so that they would feel they were one community, and in the evenings we held long discussions about our future plans, in which I tried to guide them to fall in with my ideas. Cynric was a great help to me; he was always cheerful and active, even when food was scarce, and the younger men would follow him anywhere. He will make a splendid ruler for the organized Kingdom I have founded after so many years of gruelling warfare.

There was another point on which I tried to influence my men to comply with my wishes. The real wild Germans of Germany, who have had no contact with Rome, are in the habit of burying with their dead most of the valuable possessions of the corpse; it is a pious idea, and a strange contrast to their usual appalling avarice. But in our present situation we really could not afford to bury good swords and golden arm-rings in the earth. We needed all the treasure we could muster, and I set myself to alter the religious prejudice of my men.

This was not as difficult as you might expect, for the Germans are not a religious people; they are sensible enough to be nervous about the future, and they take what precautions they can; but they themselves do not believe that their sacrifices have much effect, for the gods are fundamentally hostile to mankind. Furthermore, they have an uncomfortable feeling that other people know more about the supernatural than they do, and any outlandish wizard impresses them enormously. I had been careful not to bring with me any holy men, and of course we could not set up sanctuaries in this new land until someone had dreamt the appropriate dream; we got on very comfortably that winter without any religion at all, and were none the worse for it. I had hopes that when we moved north in the spring they would bury the dead with nothing more than their best clothes; especially as we had no women with us, who are always the conservatives. There was not a single woman in the camp, which was rather unusual; Frideswitha's servant had been drowned as an offering to the ghost of her mistress, and I ordered that no Roman women should be caught alive. I did not want Cynric to get into any entanglement before he was safely married to a Woden-born girl with a good dowry.

Our numbers were slightly greater than when we had landed, for we had lost few men in battle, and there had been no serious sickness; while the ship had arrived with reinforcements. That ship was a great bother; I could not bear to part with it, but I did not want to split the army by leaving it guarded. When we were ready to march in the spring I put on board a small crew, and sent it back to Germany to bring more men. For miles to the north the land was empty and uncultivated, and I could promise good farms to all who joined me. These farmers are not the best type of recruits for serious fighting, being mostly poor and badly armed; but if I picked my way carefully I ought to be able to reach open country without rousing any Roman King against us.

During winter hunting parties had scouted the neighbourhood thoroughly, and I knew the lie of the land. The abandoned ruins of Venta and Calleva lay attractively just to the east of our line of march, but I regretfully decided that it would be unwise to take them over just yet. Nobody lived in them, but the South Saxons might regard them as within their sphere of influence, and I did not want to start a war with the settlers on our eastern border. I could not diverge to the west without bringing the fierce Dumnonians on my track, but there were several alternative routes, since most of the rivers in that land flow southward. Some hunters had found a good track leading overland to the westernmost of these rivers, which was called the Avon (like half the streams in Britain). From the look of the winter floods I guessed it must rise in chalky country, and as the chalk will not bear forest there must be a stretch of open land between us and the Thames valley. This was the gateway to Britain that I chose.

In the beginning of May in the year 496 we set off to found our Kingdom. We were about three hundred and twenty strong, all fighting-men without a single woman or child. Aella had founded South Saxony with less; but that had been on the coast, in sight of the pirate ships that could reinforce him or take him back to Germany. I could not conceal from myself that an attack on the inland country was a more risky undertaking.

We advanced for two days, and had covered about thirty miles when we emerged on to the uplands. These were rugged hills, much steeper than the smooth crests of the land by the Channel, and as always with chalk it was hard to find drinking water; the grass was rougher than I had expected, and there did not seem to be many sheep about.

The inhabitants were the greatest surprise of all. I thought I knew southern Britain and the kind of people who lived in it; if I had been asked to describe them I would have said that they were the ordinary type of citizen, growing more and more barbarous as order decayed, and beginning to copy the Saxon method of fighting; at the very bottom of the scale were a class of coloni who spoke Celtic in their homes, though of course their masters ordered them about in Latin and their tools and methods of cultivation were Roman. But this rugged plain was covered with little hill-top villages where Celts ploughed with the implements that their ancestors used before Caesar came to Britain; they spoke no language but Celtic, and seemed to pay rent to no landowner. The only possible explanation was that no one had ever interfered with such a poor district.

Quite recently someone must have taken an interest in the land, for on its northern border was a great entrenchment that did not look to be a hundred years old. My men were worried for fear the builders of such a mighty work might come and chase them into the sea; but I guessed that it had been built by the Dumnonians when Saxon mercenaries first came to the upper Thames, and abandoned soon after, when they realized that those savages were not dangerous. My followers called it the Ditch of Woden, which to them was a satisfactory explanation of any remarkable object that they could not have made for themselves; it was a complete waste of labour, in any case, and had no influence at all on the course of future campaigns.

I did my best to get into touch with the miserable Celts who lurked on the hill-tops, but without success; they always fled when I sent an envoy to negotiate with them. The trouble is that nowadays no one trusts a Saxon even when he wants to make peace, and of course I was quite unable to persuade my men to spare the life of anyone they caught while he was running away. In that respect Saxons are like greyhounds, and just as impossible to stop once the pursuit has begun. So I learned nothing of the history of that part of the country; probably the brutish Celtic peasants could have told me very little.

That first year we lived well, for the crops had been sown before our invasion began, and we had nothing to do but harvest them as they ripened. But the future was doubtful. We were right in the middle of Britain, and there were organized Roman states on our western border; any day they might send a confederate army to drive us out. That meant that it was unsafe to scatter to different ploughlands. Once again the dream of every barbarian invasion had failed to materialize; it would have been very nice to have ruled as a warrior aristocracy over a population of hard-working peasants, like the Goths in the south, but my men were too savage to refrain from killing the goose that might have laid golden eggs. Luckily we had captured more sheep and cattle than we could eat at once, so we had a little stock of breeding animals to begin the next year. But it was not the kind of life that satisfied my instinct for civilization; nomad shepherds can keep a sort of culture, particularly in military affairs, but isolation in family groups leads to the decay of traditional learning.

I talked over the problem with Cynric. We decided that at all costs we must keep in touch with the coast, and encourage a stream of lower-class immigrants from Germany. We still had the one ship, and sent it on several voyages that summer to bring back working settlers; these began to clear the valleys by the Sea of Vectis.

But the life that I planned was not what the warriors wanted. The whole Empire was a prize for adventurous swords, and in other places more valuable plunder was to be gained than mutton and woollen cloaks. Many nobles left me in the autumn of 497, when they found that I intended to remain in the empty land that I had conquered. I was able to fill their places with other recruits, to whom good food was a greater booty than gold; but these were not so well born or so well armed, or above all so capable of absorbing civilization. I was worried about what would happen if we were attacked by a really good Roman comitatus.

The only thing to do was to keep very quiet where I was, and trust that the increase in the numbers of my following would outweigh the decline in its quality. A professional Saxon raider was a match for three Romans; even peasant spearmen ought to be able to hold their own against equal numbers. These people brought their women with them, for they needed labour on the land; that was a stabilizing influence, since the women made them wash occasionally, and eat meals at stated times, and sleep under a roof. Men alone are always trying to prove how tough they are, and how like brute beasts they can live; without women they would soon run naked and forget how to speak.

I did not marry again. I had brought bad luck to both Gertrude and Frideswitha, and it seemed I did not possess the art of ruling women. I was now forty-six years of age, and quite content to sleep alone most nights. It is unusual for a chieftain to be unmarried, and most of them want as many descendants as possible, but I had put all my eggs into one basket. I thought only of Cynric, who should have an undisputed succession, without kinsmen to intrigue against him. He was still attached to the memory of his unfortunate mother, and that was another reason for my celibacy; a stepmother often clouds the relationship between father and son.

So I settled down as the ruler of a peasant folk; it was a small and backward country, and I did not make myself a laughing-stock by taking the title of King. But every year more settlers came, brought in my own ship and owing obedience to me, and more woods by the Sea of Vectis were cleared for the plough. I myself, with my dear son, lived in the open country to the north, and we herded our sheep from one hill-fort to another; the peasants of the coastland kept us supplied with bread and beer. We fought many little skirmishes with the miserable Celtic squatters, but we had no set battles with rival armies, and we ate abundantly, even in the spring. It was not the sort of life I had planned when I left Germany; then I had dreamed of ruling a subject population of civilized men, the ambition of every German raider; now I was nothing more than the war chief of a very barbarous band of nomads. But at least I had won the complete independence that had been my object since I was a child; the orders I could give my men were circumscribed by a thousand customary rights and obligations, but nobody could give me any orders at all.

Every spring I led out small parties of scouts; we were careful not to attack any place that was guarded by well-armed men, but of course we destroyed any village that could not defend itself. In this way we won definite borders for our infant state, and our neighbours grew accustomed to having us there. To the south our country stretched to the sea, to the west there were the Roman states that were best left alone, and to the east, after many miles of empty forest and ruined farms, one would come to the outposts of the men of Kent. On the north we had no defined border; Londinium was now a deserted ruin, and there were no Roman cities south of the Thames, though war-like bands of Romans dwelt on the high hills north of it. In the valley itself the sons of the Saxon mercenaries I had led under Count Ambrosius still lived in peace in their riverside clearings. They now paid tribute to no ruler, and had settled down to a very savage and poverty-stricken life of fishing and hunting; when their weapons broke they had no metal to make new ones, and they had interbred with the lowest class of coloni, so that they had degenerated from even the low level of culture that they had managed to retain when I first knew them. They were a useful object-lesson of what happens to men who try to live an independent life without women of their own kind, or a competent ruler. But it fascinated me to think that they had come to their present home by the rivers that flow out on the east coast, and that we had met them coming from the south. The German invasions, after fifty years of steady infiltration, had mastered all the southeast of Britain, and there was not a walled city or a properly-run villa anywhere east of the territory of Corinium.

I was not afraid of the Romans of the west; they had got used by degrees to owning only half of the island, and they were too busy murdering one another for the thrones of the remaining cities to undertake a war of conquest.

For three years we lived in peace, the quietest period of my middle life. The land I ruled fell into two definite portions; in the north was the open chalk, a broken country of steep slopes and sudden valleys, where armies could move freely in any direction; in the south were the rivers, running through thick forest to the sheltered sea; they were swampy and liable to sudden flood, but small boats could bring new settlers with good German spears. In the north my little war-band of very inferior comrades moved peacefully from one hill-fort to the next; as our sheep ate the grazing; and in the valleys of the south the corn-lands increased year by year where new farmers cleared the woods.

The year 500 passed in that peaceful manner. To me it was a landmark, as such a nice round number, but no Saxons counted the years, and I believe the Romans, hopelessly out of touch with the civilized world, now dated by the regnal years of their ephemeral Kings. I was in my fiftieth year, and Cynric was past his twenty-second birthday; though he was quite content with his position as my heir, and waited patiently for me to die a natural death. I might have ended my days as a petty war chief of the open chalk; but various dangers came upon me one after the other, and the action I was forced to take raised me to my present exalted position.

My first trouble came not from the Romans, but from the side of Germany, and it was one I had long foreseen. In the full summer of the year 501 I was sitting quietly in a little hut of turf in the hill-fort where my band was halted. There was a light drizzle, and I was eating my supper under shelter, for I had already begun to suffer from the rheumatic pains that are the natural penalty of campaigning in the climate of Britain. My men were making the usual disgusting mess of their supper in the rain outside, and I was glad of the excuse to eat neatly and silently, with no companion except my son. German table manners have always been the greatest trial I have had to endure while living among these barbarians, and they still offend me after fifty years. But I could not often indulge in the luxury of private meals; the Saxons know in their hearts that they are rather disgusting people, and they are always on the look-out for fancied insults. My rheumatism had given me the chance of a little treat, and I was enjoying myself talking sense to Cynric instead of bellowing war-songs with my dear comrades-in-arms.

Then a messenger pushed his way, crouching, through the low door of the hut, and sat down beside me. Of course, there was no room to stand up, but a civilized man would at least have asked for permission before plumping himself down. He was only a farmer from the south coast, of the lowest class of Saxon who was counted as really free, but I had to shake him by the hand, and offer him food from my bowl, before I could ask him why he had left his squalid clearing to interrupt my rest. I have always managed to be a good comrade to the shaggiest barbarian, but even after all these years it is a strain, especially with very smelly peasants at meal-times.

As a matter of fact he had important news, and he had done right to come and tell me. Two strange warships had come to land at Cerdics-ora by the Sea of Vectis, and the crews were helping themselves to the pro-duce of the farms near the coast without paying for what they took; so far they had not killed anyone.

My dear Cynric was for blowing the war-horn at once, and summoning the whole countryside to drive them to their ships; since they had come in only two we must outnumber them, and we ought to be able to make their stay uncomfortable, though pirates fight much better than farmers. But I persuaded him to sit quiet and talk it over, for that evening at least; I never start a war until I am pushed into it, and those two ships might be the forerunners of a fleet. My heart sank as I thought that from now on we would face that perpetual watch against sea-borne raiders that had been the most unpleasant feature of my youth in Anderida; I suppose that men who settle down to grow corn in any part of the world are at once the target of every ruffian who would rather fight than dig, but it was a wearisome prospect. I held a council, to see if we could deal with the matter without fighting.

My war-band at this time consisted of no more than fifty warriors who had never stiffened their muscles by doing useful work of any kind, though

of course I could raise a large army of clumsy peasants; most of the ambitious and blood-thirsty men who had come with me from Germany had
moved on in search of better plunder. Those who remained were happy
to be at peace for as long as possible, and nobody enjoys waging war on
pirates, who fight very fiercely and possess no riches, otherwise they would
not have gone to sea. The chief thing in our favour was that we were
hardly worth plundering either; the raiders could not have intended to
come ashore in a German land, where all the craftsmen had long ago been
killed, and the scanty gold and silver traded for weapons and ploughs.
They would either sail farther west, or if they were seeking new corn-
lands they could take axes and go into the forest, where there was room
for all.

So my captains decided, and from their point of view they were sensible; but it might make my position very shaky if an independent leader
shared my territory. We arranged that I should try to get into peaceful
discussions with the new arrivals; I sat up late with Cynric, planning how
I could keep the leadership of my own men, and if possible become the
war chief of the pirates also. It depended on the personality of their present leader. He might be a man who kept his oath, and in that case I could
make him my subordinate and ally, as though he was a barbarian chief
seeking employment from a Roman ruler; but that was how all the trouble
had started between Vortigern and Hengist, long ago, and I knew that
sworn promises seldom checked a leader of pirates if he saw a chance
of bettering his position. I could not make any firm plans until I had met
him and sized him up.

In the morning the whole war-band started south; I went ahead with
the ten best-dressed men as an escort, and we marched openly along the
track, without attempting to scout for an ambush. But half a mile behind
came the rest of the warriors, with a crowd of armed peasants; they marched
with their swords loose in the scabbard, ready to come to our rescue as
soon as they heard the alarm. Cynric led them, and I knew he would do
his best to save us if we were received with treachery. Most rulers would
never have dared to put their safety into the hands of the heir to all that
they possessed; but Cynric was the prop of my old age.

We spent a night in camp on the road, for the journey was longer than
a comfortable day's march, and I had decided against riding the wretched
little ponies that we sometimes used. We would look more impressive if
we walked steadily in close order than if we straggled along the trail on
those cow-hocked, razor-backed nags, that always stopped to nibble the

grass of the wayside when you wanted them to keep together. Even the kindliest critic could not say that Saxons are good horsemen, and a dozen of them riding together are a horrid sight.

On the second day we marched along the track, singing to keep our paces in unison, with a green and leafy branch borne in front of the little procession. So many wars have started by accident, because two bodies of armed men had to approach closely to discuss terms, and some nervous ass drew his sword, out of sheer fright. On the other hand, it would be putting an appalling strain on the honour of a pirate commander if I walked up to his camp by myself, without escort. His sentries would see the army marching half a mile behind; but they would only conclude that they had to deal with a sensible and experienced war-band, that wanted peace but could defend itself at a pinch. For the same reason we pretended not to notice the fresh footprints of their scouts when we passed them on the track, and kept our eyes turned away from the bushes; I gave strict orders that no one was to see a stranger until we had reached the main camp, and begun to parley.

Our peasants, who had fled from the pirates, were also hiding in the woods. They did not show themselves to my small escort, but came out of their refuge to join the supporting force, and Cynric had the sense to send forward a messenger with their news. It appeared that the pirates were not seeking war; they had given everyone time to run away before they pillaged a farm, they had not killed the sick who had to be left behind, and after helping themselves to what they wanted they had left the huts unburned. This information cheered me up; the newcomers would not be so careful to avoid starting a blood-feud unless they intended to have peaceful dealings with us in future.

It was quite late in the afternoon that at last we arrived at the pirates' camp. The track led to a little creek where the woods had been cleared. Just outside we found a small body of pirates; they had evidently been told by their scouts how many men I had with me, for their guard was of exactly the same strength, and their leader stood in front, waving a green branch. I gave a sigh of relief; we had managed to get into touch without fighting; now surely my Roman education would give me the advantage, when it came to negotiating with an ignorant barbarian.

Our respective escorts remained about fifty yards apart, and I met their leader alone. We began, of course, by giving our names, and the names of our ancestors, right back to Woden. He was called Port, and he had with him his two sons, Baeda and Maegla, and two shiploads of lesser warriors, all Saxons. Germans never lie about their descent, and I accepted this quite easily, but the reason he gave for coming to my small and ravaged land was really very extraordinary. He said that he had had the misfortune to kill a peculiarly sacred bear, and that the witch who was the servant and guardian of the animal had told him that to avert the unpleasant consequence of his sacrilege he must sail to a land already called by his own name, where the local priest would have power to cleanse him of his guilt. He had inquired diligently from travellers in his part of Germany, and at last had heard there was an old Roman city on the shore of the Sea of Vectis called Portus. Then he gathered a war-band, including both his sons, and here he was.

I say that this story struck me as extraordinary, although it is a fair example of barbarian witchcraft. That is because he was the first German I had met who put himself to inconvenience for religious motives; the Germans have a great quantity of religious beliefs, and a whole crowd of competing gods and goddesses; but no great poet has ever brought order into their Pantheon, as Homer did for civilized men, and they worship whichever Divine Power they find most handy. The normal German thing to do, if you have the misfortune to kill the sacred bear of Freya, is to switch over at once and worship Thor instead. Germans have an enviable capacity for proving to themselves that whatever they did was really right, or at least that it was the fault of someone else; Port was the first who had ever to my knowledge suffered from remorse.

Of course, I pretended to credit everything that he said; if I had not, the fighting would have begun at once. I pointed out politely that I had a prior claim to anything of value that might remain in the deserted city of Portus; but the whole land was underpopulated, and he was welcome to dwell there, if he would come to my war-band and be my faithful companion. I ought soon to be able to learn whether he was really a priest-ridden ass, or whether some deep scheme lay at the back of this astonishing tale.

He was delighted to be given his spiritual home without having to fight for it, and we embraced before the two escorts. Then we all went into his camp, and feasted on cattle stolen from my farms; but in future we arranged that he should pay, or at least owe, for the food his men needed until they had harvested their first crop. After supper, Port spoke again of the need to get himself cleansed from the blood-guilt of the sacred bear. His earnest request for the services of the local priest put me in a difficult position. For the last six years I and all my followers had got on very well without any holy men at all; now here was my new ally inquiring earnestly for a priest, who would have to perform a fairly complicated ritual.

I filled the gap myself; I did not want to detail a comrade to act as a temporary priest, for it might have put ideas into his head; a ruler must always beware of those who pretend to know the will of the gods, and take it upon themselves to proclaim what the laity should do. We have no bears in the south of Britain, otherwise the obvious thing would have been to order Port to sacrifice pretty heavily to the first bear he met; but I made up a most colourful and impressive ritual. I made him fast for a whole day, and sacrifice his jewelled sword-belt by hanging it in a tree where I could retrieve it later; he also provided a Roman, though they were scarce in the neighbourhood, who was burnt in a large fire at midnight; I then recited as much as I could remember of the Penitential Psalms; as a climax to the whole proceeding I baptized him. The joke is that the baptism was probably valid, for I am a baptized Christian myself; if there is any truth in what I was taught as a child, Port must have been very surprised when he died shortly afterwards.

When the religious nonsense was finished we made a satisfactory treaty. Port and his measly little war-band were allowed to dwell in Portus and the country round about, and he remained in authority over them, an authority he might transmit to his heirs; of course, subject to my supreme command in time of war. This brought in the danger of separatist tendencies in my new state, a thing that I had always tried to avoid up to now; I think my comrades were surprised that I conceded it so easily. There was a reason. I had taken Port's measure. I knew he was a fool, and I was confident that I could eliminate him before he became a nuisance.

We had one more day of feasting and drinking, and then I marched back to the open sheep-runs of the north. I had decided to wait for at least a year, to lull any suspicions that the Portingas might harbour, and then I should not be at all surprised if a sad accident befell that intrusive religious nincompoop. There was no hurry at all, for my men would never desert me to follow him; the danger would come in the next generation, if he left a capable son.

We remained at peace, living comfortably on our flocks and the corn from the southern valleys. We even began to plough the sheltered ravines of the open country, wherever there was water; the Roman peasants had clung to the infertile hill-tops, which were bare by nature, but our heavy ox-drawn ploughs did better on deep soil, and we had good axes to cut down the trees. Huts were built near the new fields, and they were warmer and more comfortable than the hill-forts, which were presently left to the shepherds. I have noticed the same thing in other lands permanently occupied by Saxons; after a few years the whole pattern of settlement is changed, until you would have to dig to find traces of the Roman inhabitants.

Port and his little self-governing settlement in my territory still rankled. I did not want to pick a quarrel and wipe out the whole war-band; if Port and his two sons died suddenly his followers would be useful reinforcements for my own army. What made the whole enterprise difficult was that I dared not take an accomplice into my confidence. Cynric must continue to believe that I was an honourable chief, otherwise he might start plotting to succeed me. Also the plan must arrange for the deaths of Baeda and Maegla at the same time as their father; the two young men had no religious scruples and were governed by nothing but self-interest; to allow one of them to inherit his father's power would merely be exchanging King Log for King Stork. I racked my brains in vain; the stock arrangement on these occasions is a hunting accident, but the objection to that was that I wanted to kill three people, and it would be altogether too much of a coincidence if I shot all three of them in mistake for a deer.

I suppose my mind had grown flabby during the years of peace we had enjoyed, for it took me a long time to remember that I possessed one great advantage; I was the only German in Britain who could read and write, and no one among my following suspected that I had acquired so much effeminate and useless learning. I could safely arrange by letter the deaths that were necessary for the peaceful succession of my son.

Once I had thought of this solution it was easy to work out the details. Only Romans could read the letters I must write, so I would have to get into touch with a band of Roman outlaws, capable of killing three well-armed Saxon nobles; and I would have to arrange matters so that they got some advantage from the murder, or thought they were going to, which would do just as well. I listened carefully to the reports of our scouts on the Roman outlaws who hung around the outskirts of our settlements. They were mostly dispossessed peasants, who knew that the Dumnonians had no farms to offer them, and who enjoyed the idle life of the woods. The trouble was that probably none of them could read either; but years of outlawry had made them into hardened campaigners, and I thought it likely that exiled Roman noblemen would presently start to form them into a comitatus.

I pretended that the occasional raids of these outlaws were more of a nuisance than they were in actual fact, and appealed to our farmers for information about their depredations. I heard rumours of a Roman leader who sounded like the very man I wanted. In the western woods quite a large band had been formed; it was led by a relative of the King of Demetia, who had left home in a hurry. He was known to my men as Natan-leod, a quite impossible name; but Germans often make the most horrible mess of foreign words, since the strange noises of their ugly language have no parallel in Latin.

I gave out that I was seriously alarmed at the danger represented by this band of half-armed peasants, and offered a reward to anyone who could bring in one of their men alive. Some of our best warriors went out to hunt them, and caught a prisoner. He was an intelligent man, and I talked to him in private; I told him frankly that I wished to get in touch with his chief, and that I would arrange his escape so that he could deliver a letter. He said that the real name of Natan-leod was Venatianus Leoninus, and that he had been a noted warrior of the Demetians until he had been mixed up in an unsuccessful rebellion; a man of that standing would certainly be able to read, so that was one difficulty solved. But there still remained another; what reward could I offer to Leoninus to make him my ally? I could do nothing openly, of course, for my men would not have obeyed me if I told them that a Roman chief must be left in peace, as my friend. I did not dare to lose a battle so that he might win, for men would leave me if I got the reputation of an unsuccessful leader. Besides, though one often hears gossip that the result of a battle was arranged in advance, and that one commander lost on purpose, actually such an affair is very difficult to work out.

Eventually I wrote a long letter. I explained frankly my reasons for wanting to get rid of the Portingas as a separate community, and offered to leave a small flock of sheep in a certain spot as evidence of my good faith. When Leoninus had taken the sheep he was to leave a letter where I could find it, and then we would make a plan to ensure the deaths I wished for. I knew that the sheep would be an acceptable gift to the outlaws, for they were always short of clothing, especially wool.

The prisoner escaped the night before we were to sacrifice him, and after the flock had been taken I found the letter. The rest of the plot was quite easy to fix up, although in the end I had to hand over the reward that I had promised. I possessed very little treasure, but the outlaws were easily satisfied; they were short of weapons and everything made of iron, for they could not trade with the Roman Kingdoms, who made war on them just as we did. Accordingly, I offered a consignment of sword-blades and scrap-iron if Leoninus would carry out the little commission in which I needed his help.

My plans were worked out by harvest-time. Leoninus made a small but very impudent raid on the flocks that grazed outside the hill-fort where I was staying. I summoned Port and his two sons to a conference to decide on measures against these raids, but I told him that we would not take the field until the end of autumn, and that he could leave his followers to get in their crops. I asked him to let me know by what route he was coming, so that I could send an escort; I then passed on this information to Leoninus, and arranged for the escort to go the wrong way. Port, Baeda, and Maegla were killed after a brave defence. Venatianus took away his promised payment in excellent steel, and the Portingas, leaderless, agreed to merge their identity in the common mass of my followers.

Meanwhile we all lived in peace and prosperity, the grazing of the north admirably supplemented by the corn of the south. Each summer several boatloads of new immigrants arrived direct from Germany, until the southern valleys were lined from end to end with fertile farms. Dear Cynric several times suggested that it would be fitting for me to take the title of King, now that I ruled so many men and such rich land; but I was against it. I pointed out that though the number of able-bodied men who came to my annual law-moots was large, they were nearly all stiff and clumsy spearmen. My war-band, who did not work and were supported by the rents of the farmers, was actually smaller than it had been when I first landed. I also said that I thought it silly to announce myself as a King, for no particular reason except that we were growing rich; let us wait until the next war broke out, and I could be properly hoisted on a shield amid the slain.

I was perfectly content to go on with things as they were. I was now too old, in my middle fifties, to enjoy warfare for its own sake; I was at last completely independent, and my nearest equal was far away in the land of the South Saxons. For the rest of my life I had no ambition except to safeguard what I had won.

Cynric was in his twenties, the age when all Woden-born young men delight in war; it was really very good of him to put up so quietly with the peaceful ways of his father, but I have already said that he was a remarkable son. Of course he now led my little war-band when they had to go out after raiders, and he did most of the work that is involved in the defence of a land surrounded by enemies; but he remained faithful to me. I don't know what I have done to deserve such an obedient son, but I long ago made up my mind that there is no justice in the way the world is run, and I sincerely hope there will be none in the next world.

How King Harald Bluetooth Celebrated Yule

by Frans G. Bengtsson

989 The Norse Vikings, pirates, conquerors, and seafarers extraordinary, yearned for fame as well as for loot and took care that poets should chronicle some of their most remarkable exploits. So the cruelty and courage of the Viking code of heroic conduct are a matter of record. What kind of men abided by it is shown in this excerpt from the finest novel yet written about the Norsemen.

Great men from all over the north came to Jellinge to celebrate Yule with King Harald, so that there was less than room enough for them at the tables and in the bedchambers. But Orm and his men did not complain of this overcrowding, for they had received a good price for their slaves and had sold them all before the festival commenced. When Orm had divided up the proceeds of the sale, his men felt rich and free indeed, and they began to yearn for Lister and to know whether Berse's two ships had come home, or whether they themselves were the only survivors of Krok's expedition. They offered no objection to staying in Jellinge, however, until the festival was over, for it was regarded as a great honor, and one that added luster to a man's name for the rest of his days, to have celebrated Yule with the King of the Danes.

The principal guest was King Harald's son, King Sven Forkbeard,* who had arrived from Hedeby with a large following. Like all King Harald's sons, he was the child of one of his father's concubines; and there was little love lost between him and his father, so that in general they avoided each other as much as possible. Every Yule, though, King Sven made the journey to Jellinge, and everybody knew why. For it often happened at Yule, when the food was richer and the drink stronger than at any other time in the year, that old men suddenly died, either in bed or on the drinking-bench. This had been the case with old King Gorm, who had lain unconscious for two days after a surfeit of Yuletide pork and had then died; and King Sven wanted to be near the royal coffers when his father

* The father of King Canute the Great.

158

passed over. For many Yules now he had made the journey in vain, and each year his impatience increased. His followers were a rough crew, over-bearing and quarrelsome, and it was difficult to keep the peace between them and the men of King Harald's household, all the more so now that King Harald had turned Christian and many of his men had followed suit. For King Sven still clung to the old religion and made spiteful mock of his father's conversion, saying that the Danes would have been spared all this folly if the old man had had the sense to know when he had lived long enough.

He did not trumpet his opinions too openly when he was at Jellinge, however, for King Harald was easily roused to anger, and when this hap-pened he was liable to do anything to anybody. They wasted no words on each other once they had made formal salutation, nor, from their seats of honor in the great hall, did they toast each other more than the con-ventions of politeness absolutely required.

There was a snowstorm on Christmas Eve, but it passed, and the weather grew calm and cold; and on Christmas morning, while the priests were singing Mass and the courtyard of the palace lay shrouded in good steam from the preparations afoot in the kitchens, a great long-ship rowed up from the south and made fast to the pier, its sail tattered and its oars glazed with ice. King Harald was at Mass, but they sent a messenger to inform him. Wondering who these new guests could be, he went up the stairs to look at the ship. It was steeply built, with a red dragon's head poised arrogantly upon a curved neck at the prow, its jaws caked with ice from the cruel seas it had passed through. They saw men climb ashore wearing garments barked with ice, among them a tall chieftain in a blue cloak and another, of equal stature, clothed in red. King Harald scanned them as closely as he could from where he stood, and said: "It looks like a Jomsviking or perhaps a Swedish ship, and it is boldly manned, for its crew approach the King of the Danes with no shield of peace upon their masthead. I know of but three men who would dare to come thus: Skoglar-Toste, Vagn Akesson, and Styrbjörn. Moreover, they have brought their ship alongside without removing their dragon-head, though they know well that the trolls of the mainland do not love dragon-heads; and I know of but two men who do not care what the trolls think, and they are Vagn and Styrbjörn. But I see from the ship's condition that its captain dis-dained to seek shelter from last night's storm, and there is but one man who would have refused to bow to such a tempest. It is my guess, there-fore, that this must be my son-in-law Styrbjörn, whom I have not seen these four years; one of them wears a blue cloak, moreover, and Styrbjörn has sworn to wear blue until he has won back his inheritance from King Erik. Who this other with him may be, the man who is as tall as he, I cannot surely say; but Strut-Harald's sons are taller than most men, all three of them, and they are all friends to Styrbjörn. It cannot be Jarl Sigvalde, the eldest of them, for he takes little pleasure in Yule celebrations now, because of the ignominy with which he stained his name when he rowed his ships away from the battle at Jörund-Fjord; and his brother Hemming is in England. But the third of Strut-Harald's sons is Thorkel the Tall, and it may be that this is he."

Thus King Harald surmised in his wisdom; and when the strangers reached the palace and it became evident that he was right, his spirits rose higher than they had been at any time since King Sven arrived. He bade Styrbjörn and Thorkel welcome, ordered the bathhouse to be heated for them at once, and offered mulled ale to them and all their men.

"Even the greatest of warriors," he said, "need something to warm themselves after such a voyage as you have endured: and there is truth in the old saying:

> Mulled ale for the frozen man,
> And mulled ale for the weary:
> For mulled ale is the body's friend
> And makes the sick heart merry."

Several of Styrbjörn's men were so exhausted by their voyage that they were hardly able to stand: but when tankards of mulled ale were offered them, their hands proved to be steady enough, for not a drop was spilled.

"As soon as you have bathed and rested," said King Harald, "the Yule feast shall begin: and I shall go to it with a better appetite than if I had only my son's face to look at across the table."

"Is Forkbeard here?" said Styrbjörn, glancing around him. "I should be glad to have a word with him."

"He still cherishes the hope that some day he will see me die the ale-death," said King Harald. "That is why he has come. But if I ever should die at a Yule feast, I think it will be because I am sick of looking at his misshapen face. You will have your chance to speak with him in good time. But tell me one thing: is there blood between him and you?"

"No blood as yet," replied Styrbjörn, "but as to the future I cannot say.

He has promised me men and ships to help me against my kinsman in Uppsala, but none have yet arrived."

"There must be no fighting in my house during the holy festival," said King Harald. "You must understand that at once, though I know that you will find it tedious to keep the peace. For I am now a follower of Christ, who has been a good ally to me; and Christ will tolerate no strife on Christmas Day, which is His birthday, nor on the holy days that follow."

Styrbjörn replied: "I am a man without a country, and as such cannot afford the luxury of being peaceful; for I would rather be the crow than his carrion. But while I am your guest, I think I shall be able to keep the peace as well as any man, whichsoever gods are presiding over the feast; for you have been a good father-in-law to me, and I have never had cause to quarrel with you. But I have news to bring you: namely, that your daughter Tyra is dead. I wish I could have come with more joyful tidings."

"That is sad news indeed," said King Harald. "How did she die?"

"She took it amiss," said Styrbjörn, "because I found myself a Wendish concubine. She became so wrathful that she began to spit blood; then she languished and, after a time, died. In all other respects she was an excellent wife."

"I have noticed of late," said King Harald, "that young people cling less keenly to life than old people. But we must not allow this grief to weigh down our spirits during the Yule feast; and in any case I have more daughters left than I know what to do with. They are a fine-spirited bunch and will not marry any man who is not of noble birth and high renown; so that you need not remain a widower for long if you should find any girl among them who takes your fancy. You shall see them all — though I fear that, when they hear that you are single again, they may have some difficulty in keeping the Yule peace."

"Something other than marriage is uppermost in my mind just now," said Styrbjörn, "but we can speak of that later."

Many glances were cast at Styrbjörn from doorways and loopholes, as he went with his men to the bathhouse; for he rarely accepted hospitality, and was held to be the greatest warrior that had been seen in the north since the days of the sons of Ragnar Hairy-Breeks. He had a short, fair beard and pale blue eyes, and men who had not seen him before murmured with surprise at finding him so slim-built and narrow-waisted. For they all knew that his strength was such that he cleft shields like loaves of bread and split armed men from the neck to the crotch with his sword, which was called Cradle-Song. Wise men said that the ancient luck of the Uppsala kings was his, and that it was this that gave him his strength and success in every enterprise he undertook. But it was also known that the curse of his family and their ancient ill luck had in part descended on him, and that it was because of this that he was a chieftain without a country; and that it was for this reason, too, that he was often afflicted with a great heaviness and melancholy. When the fit attacked him, he would shut himself away from all company and sit sighing and mumbling darkly to himself for days on end, unable to endure the presence of any of his fellow beings, save for a woman to comb his hair and an old harpist to give him ale and play him sad music. But so soon as the fit passed from him, he would be eager to go to sea again, and to battle, and then he would bring the strongest of his men to weariness and despair by his recklessness and his bad weather-luck.

So he was feared as no other chieftain in the north was feared, almost as though something of the power and majesty of the gods dwelt in him; and there were those who believed that some time in the future, when he reached the zenith of his might, he would sail to Miklagard and crown himself emperor there, and voyage in triumph along the round edge of the earth with his terrible navies.

But there were other who claimed that they could see it written in his eyes that he would die young and unlucky.

At length everything was ready in King Harald's great dining-hall for the Yule feast, and all the men were assembled there in their numbers, seated on benches. No women were allowed to be present at so tremendous a drinking-bout, for it was difficult enough, King Harald thought, to keep the peace when men were by themselves, and it would be many times harder if they had women to brag to in their cups. When everyone was in his place, the groom of the bedchamber announced in a gigantic voice that the peace of Christ and King Harald reigned in the hall, and that no edged implements might be used except for the purpose of cutting up food; any cut, thrust, or open wound caused by weapon, ale-tankard, meat-bone, wooden platter, ladle, or clenched fist would be reckoned as plain murder, and would be regarded as sacrilege against Christ and as an unpardonable crime, and the miscreant would have a stone tied round his neck and be drowned in deep water. All weapons apart from eating-knives had been left by order in the vestibules, and only the exalted personages who sat at King Harald's own table were allowed to retain their swords; for it was felt that they would be able to control themselves even when drunk.

The hall was built to hold a good six hundred men without crowding, and in the middle stood King Harald's own table, with the thirty most eminent of the company seated at it. The tables for the other guests stretched down the length of the hall from one end to the other. Styrbjörn sat on King Harald's right hand, and Bishop Poppo on his left; opposite them King Sven had Thorkel the Tall on his right, and a red-faced, bald old jarl from the Small Islands called Sibbe on his left. The others sat according to their rank, King Harald himself having settled each man's place personally. Orm, though he could not be reckoned as one of the great chieftains, had yet been allotted a better place than he could have expected, and Toke likewise, for King Harald was grateful to them for their gift of the great bell, and was an admirer of Toke's poetry. So Orm sat three places from the Bishop, and Toke four; for Orm had told King Harald that he would like, if possible, to sit next to Toke, in case the latter became troublesome through drink. Facing them across the table were men of King Sven's company.

The Bishop read grace, King Harald having commanded him to be brief about it, and then they drank three toasts: to the honor of Christ, to the luck of King Harald, and to the return of the sun. Even those of the company who were not Christians joined in the toast to Christ, for it was the first of the toasts and they were thirsty for their ale; some of them, however, made the sign of the hammer over their tankards and murmured the name of Thor before they drank. When the toast to King Harald's luck was drunk, King Sven got ale in his windpipe and had a coughing fit, causing Styrbjörn to ask whether the brew was too strong for his taste.

Then the Yule pork was brought in, and warriors and chieftains alike fell silent when they saw it appear, and took a deep breath and sighed with joyous anticipation; many loosened their belts, to save doing so later. For though there were those who whispered that King Harald was in his old age less openhanded with gold and silver than he had been of yore, this accusation had never been leveled at him in the matter of meat and drink, and certainly never by anyone who had celebrated Yule in his palace.

Forty-eight acorn hogs, well fattened, were slaughtered for his pleasure every Yule; and it was his custom to say that if this did not see them through the whole feast-tide, it would at any rate be sufficient to provide a tasty entrée for every guest, and that they could then fill up with beef and mutton. The kitchen servants entered in a long line, two by two, each pair bearing a great smoking pot, except for some who carried troughs of blood-sausage. They were accompanied by boys armed with long forked spits, which, once the pots had been set beside the tables, they plunged into the stew, fishing out large hunks of meat which they gave to the guests in order of precedence, so that each had his fair share; in addition to which, every man received a good ell's length of blood-sausage, or more if he wanted it. There were bread cakes and fried turnips set out on clay plates, and at the foot of each table there stood a butt of ale, so that no man's horn or tankard need ever be empty.

As the pork approached Orm and Toke, they sat quite still, with their faces turned toward the pot, watching the boy closely as he fished for the meat. They sighed blissfully as he lifted out fine pieces of shoulder pork to put on their plates, reminding each other how long it was since they had last eaten such a dinner, and marveling that they had managed to survive so many years in a country where no pork was allowed to be eaten. But when the blood-sausage arrived, tears came into their eyes, and they declared that they had never eaten a meal worthy of the name since the day they had sailed away with Krok.

"This is the best smell of all," said Orm in a small voice.

"There is thyme in it," said Toke huskily.

He plunged his sausage into his mouth, as far as it would go, bit off a length, and slowly closed his jaws; then he swung hastily round, grabbing at the boy's coat as he attempted to move on with the trough, and said: "If it be not contrary to King Harald's orders, give me at once another length of that sausage. I have for some years past now fared indifferently among the Andalusians, where they have no food worthy of the name, and these seven Yules I have longed for blood-sausage and had none."

"My case," said Orm, "is the same."

The boy laughed at their anxiety and assured them that King Harald had enough sausage for everybody. He ladled out on each of their plates a good length of the thickest that he had; then they were contented and began to eat in earnest.

For some time now, nobody spoke, either at the King's table or anywhere else in the hall, except when somebody asked for more ale or mumbled a word between bites in praise of King Harald's Yuletide feast.

On Orm's right sat a young man who cut his meat with a knife that bore an engraved silver hilt. He was fair-skinned and had very long and exquisite hair, carefully combed. He belonged to Thorkel the Tall's company, and evidently came of good family, for he was honorably placed at the King's table although he had as yet no beard; besides which his nobility was apparent from his fine clothing and silver sword-belt. After the first flush of eating was over, he turned to Orm and said: "It is good at a feast to sit next to men who have traveled widely; and I think I heard that you and your neighbor have voyaged farther afield than most of us here."

Orm replied that this was correct, and that Toke and he had spent six years in Spain.

"For various reasons," he added, "our journey took longer than we had anticipated; and many of those who set out with us never returned."

"You must have had many adventures worth the telling," said the other. "I myself, though I have not traveled as far as either of you, have also recently been on a voyage from which few came back."

Orm asked him who he was and what voyage he referred to.

The other replied: "I come from Bornholm, and my name is Sigurd; and my father was Bue Digre, of whom you may have heard, despite your long sojourn abroad. I was with him at Jörund-Fjord when he was killed, and I was captured there, together with Vagn Akesson and many others besides. Nor should I be sitting here tonight to tell the tale if it had not been for my long hair; for it was my hair that saved my life when orders had been given for all the prisoners to be killed."

By this time a number of their table companions had eaten their fill and were begining to regain the freedom of their tongues for the purpose of speech. Toke now joined in the conversation, remarking that what the Bornholmer had just said had an unusual ring about it and promised a good story; for his part, he had always regarded long hair as being more of a handicap to a soldier than an advantage. Thorkel the Tall sat picking his teeth in the aristocratic manner that was now beginning to be fashionable among great men who had traveled widely, with his face turned to one side and the palm of his hand raised before his mouth. He overheard their conversation and observed that long hair had proved unlucky to many a soldier in the past, and that sensible men always took care to bind their hair up carefully beneath their helmets; however, he added, Sigurd Buesson would show by his story how a shrewd man might take advantage of the length of his hair, and he hoped that everyone in the hall would listen to what he had to say.

King Sven, by this time, was in a better humor, the appearance of Styrbjörn having shadowed his spirits for a while. He sat lolling backwards in his chair, gnawing a pig's trotter, the bones from which he spat out on the straw that covered the floor. He noted with satisfaction that King Harald, who was engaged in a discussion with Styrbjörn about women, was eating and drinking more than anyone else. He, too, overheard what was being said farther down the table and joined in the discussion, pointing out that a wise soldier also always remembers his beard, for when a battle was being fought in windy weather a man's beard could easily get into his eyes just when he was preparing to parry a sword-thrust or to avoid a winging spear; wherefore, he told them, he always made a point of having his hair plaited before marching into battle. But now he would be interested to hear how Sigurd Buesson had taken advantage of his long hair, for men who had fought at Jörund-Fjord usually had adventures worth relating.

Bishop Poppo had not succeeded in finishing all that had been placed before him, and the ale that he had drunk had given him hiccups; nevertheless, he was capable of utterance and he, too, joined in the discussion, saying that he would be happy to tell them the story of Prince Absalom, whose long hair had proved to be his downfall. This, he said, was a good and instructive story, which stood written in God's own holy book. But King Sven cut him off promptly with the comment that he could keep such stories for women and children, if he could persuade them to listen to him. Words were then exchanged between him and the Bishop on this score; but King Harald said:

"A feast such as this, which lasts for six days, will allow us all time in which to tell our stories; and few things are better than to listen to good stories when a man has eaten his fill and has ale left in his cup. For it helps the time to pass easily between one meal and the next, and makes for less quarreling across the tables. But let me say this in the Bishop's favor, that he has good tales to tell, for I myself have listened to many of them with pleasure, concerning saints and apostles and the old kings that used to reign in the Eastern lands. He has told me many stories about one of them whose name was Solomon, who was greatly beloved by God and who seems to have been very much like myself, though it is true that he had more women. I think that the Bishop should tell his story first, before the food and drink make him sleepy, for our Yule drinking does not have the same good effect on him that it has on us, since he has not had sufficient time to accustom himself to it. After him, let other men tell of their adventures at Jörund-Fjord, or with Styrbjörn among the Wends, or elsewhere. We have, besides, here among us, men who have been as far abroad as Spain, whence they have sailed to my court bearing with them a holy bell which has been of great service to me; and I wish to hear them tell their story before this feast is done."

They all agreed that King Harald had spoken wisely, and it was done as he suggested; so that evening, after the torches had been brought in, the Bishop told the story of King David and his son Absalom. He spoke loudly, so that everyone could hear him, and he told his tale cunningly, so that all the company except King Sven enjoyed it. When the Bishop had finished talking, King Harald observed that his story was well worth storing away in one's memory, for one reason and another; and Styrbjörn laughed, and raised his glass to King Sven and said: "Be wise, O Prince, and pay heed to this tale, and cut thy hair short as bishops do."

This remark appealed to King Harald, who smote his thigh and fell into such a fit of laughing that the whole bench on his side of the table shook; and when his men and Styrbjörn's followers saw their masters laughing, they all joined in, even those of them who were unaware of the cause, so that the whole hall rang with merriment. King Sven's men, however, were displeased; and he himself glowered sourly and mumbled something into his cup and gnawed his lip-beard and had a dangerous look about him, as though he might at any moment leap to his feet and break into violence. Styrbjörn leaned forward in his seat and stared at him out of his pale eyes, which never blinked, and smiled. There was considerable unrest in the hall, and it looked as though the Christmas peace might shortly be ended. The Bishop stretched out his hands and cried something that nobody heard, and men fixed their eyes upon one another across the table and groped for the nearest thing that might serve as a weapon. But then King Harald's jesters, two small Irishmen who were famed for their skill in trade, jumped upon the King's table in motley-colored tunics, wearing feathers in their hair, and began to flap their broad sleeves and puff their chests and stamp their feet and stretch their necks; then they crew at each other exactly like cocks, so that no man present could remember ever having heard a cock crow as finely as they did; and within a few seconds they had all forgotten their anger and were lolling in their seats helpless with laughter at their antics. So the first day of the feasting ended.

On the next day, when the eating was over and the torches had been carried in, Sigurd Buesson told them of his adventures at Jörund-Fjord, and how he had been saved by his long hair. They all knew about this expedition, how the Jomsvikings, with men from Bornholm, had sailed out in a mighty fleet under the command of Strut-Harald's sons, with Bue Digre and Vagn Akesson, to win Norway from Jarl Haakon, and how few had returned from that enterprise; so Sigurd did not waste many words on this part of his story, and made no mention of how Sigvalde had fled with his ships from the battle. For it would have been churlish to have spoken of Sigvalde when Thorkel the Tall was among his audience, though they all knew Thorkel to be a bold fighter and were aware that he had been struck on the head by a large stone during the battle soon after the opposing navies had come to grips, so that he had not been conscious when his brother had rowed away.

Sigurd had been aboard his father's ship, and confined himself to such parts of the battle as he himself had been directly concerned in. He told them of his father's death; how Bue had fought fiercely, but at last, when the Norwegians had boarded his ship in overwhelming numbers, had received a slash on his face from a sword which had taken away his nose and the greater part of his jaw; and how he had then seized up his great treasure-chest and leaped overboard with it in his arms. He told, too, how Bue's kinsman, Aslak Holmskalle, had gone berserk, casting aside his shield and helmet, which was something one seldom saw nowadays, and hewing about him with both hands, impervious to the touch of iron, until an Icelandic bard, a follower of Jarl Haakon's son Erik, had picked up an anvil from the deck and with it had split his skull.

"After that," continued Sigurd, "for such of us as remained alive on my father's ship, there was little left to do; for we were few in numbers and very fatigued, and all our ships had now been overpowered, save only Vagn's own ship, which still fought on. We were hemmed in the forecastle, so weary that before long we could lift neither hand nor foot; and at last there were but nine of us left, all wounded, and there they pinned us with their shields and so took us. We were disarmed and brought ashore; and soon the survivors of Vagn's ship were dragged to join us, Vagn himself being among them. Two men carried him, and he bore both sword- and spear-wounds, and was pale and weary and said nothing. They made us sit on a log on the beach, with our legs tied together with a long rope, though they left our hands free; and there we sat and waited, while men were sent to Jarl Haakon to discover what should be our fate. He commanded that we were instantly to be put to death, and Jarl Erik, his son, and many of his followers came to watch our end; for the Norwegians were curious to see how Jomsvikings would conduct themselves in the face of death. There were thirty of us on the log, nine from Bue's ship, eight from Vagn's, and the rest from the other ships. Vagn himself sat on our extreme right; and I shall tell you the names of such of the others as were known to me."

Then he gave them a list of all those whose names he knew, in the order in which they sat on the log; and all the company in the great hall listened in silence, for many of those he named were men whom they had known, and some of his listeners had kinsmen among the dead.

He continued: "Then a man came with a broadax and stood in front of Vagn and said: 'Do you know who I am?' Vagn glanced at him, but did not seem to notice him and said nothing, for he was very weary. Then the other man said: 'I am Thorkel Leira. Perhaps you remember the vow you made to kill me and bring my daughter Ingeborg to bed?' Now this was true, for Vagn had vowed thus before setting out, since he had heard that Thorkel's daughter was the most beautiful girl in Norway, besides being one of the richest. 'But now,' continued Thorkel Leira, with a broad grin, 'it looks rather as though I am going to kill you.' Vagn curled his lip and said: 'There are yet Jomsvikings living.' 'They shall not live long,' replied Thorkel, 'and I shall see to it myself, so that there shall be no mistake. You will see all your men die beneath my hand, after which you will shortly follow them.' Then he went to the other end of the log and proceeded to behead the prisoners, one after another as they sat there. He had a good ax and went to work with a will; and he never needed to strike twice. But I think that those who were watching the scene had to admit that Vagn's and Bue's men knew how to conduct themselves in the face of death. Two who were seated not far from me began a discussion as to what it would feel like once one's head was off, and they agreed that it was one of those things that are difficult to foretell. One of them said: 'I have a brooch here in my hand. If my brain is still working after I have lost my head, I shall stick it into the ground.' Thorkel arrived at him; but as soon as the blow fell on his neck, the brooch dropped from his hand. That left only two men between Thorkel and myself."

Sigurd Buesson smiled quietly at his listeners, who sat in silent excitement. He raised his cup and drank a deep draught.

King Harald said: "I see that you still have your head on your shoulders; and anyone can hear by the sound of your swallowing that there is nothing wrong with your neck. But that was a sorry situation you were in on that Norwegian log, and it is no easy thing to guess how you managed to escape to tell the tale, however long your hair. This is a fine story, and do not keep us waiting to know how it ended."

They all raised a shout of agreement, and Sigurd Buesson continued:

"As I sat there on the log, I do not think I was more frightened than the others were; but I felt it would be a pity to die without having done something worthy for men to speak of after I had gone. So when Thorkel came to my place, I said to him: 'I am afraid for my hair; I do not want it to be stained with blood.' So saying, I drew it forward over my head; and a man who was walking behind Thorkel — I heard later that he was his brother-in-law — ran forward and wound my hair round his fingers and said to Thorkel: 'Now, strike!' He did so; but in the same instant, I pulled my head back as quickly as I could, so that the ax fell between me and his brother-in-law and cut off both his brother-in-law's hands. One of them remained hanging in my hair."

Everyone in the hall burst into a great roar of laughter. Sigurd himself laughed with them; then he proceeded: "You may well laugh, but your laughter, loud as it is, is as silence compared with the merriment of the Norwegians when they saw Thorkel's brother-in-law writhing on the ground, with Thorkel standing scowling above him. Some of them laughed so much that they fell over. Jarl Erik came forward and looked at me and said: 'Who are you?' I replied: 'My name is Sigurd, and Bue was my father; there are yet Jomsvikings living.' The Jarl said: 'You are truly of Bue's blood. Will you accept your life from me?' 'From such a man as you, Jarl,' I replied, 'I will accept it.' Then they untied me. But Thorkel, ill-pleased at this, roared: 'Shall it be thus? Then it were best I lose no time in dispatching Vagn.' Raising his ax, he rushed toward him as he sat quietly on the end of the log. But one of Vagn's men, named Skarde, a good man from Kivik, was seated four places from Vagn; and it seemed to him wrong that Vagn should lose his head before his proper turn arrived. So he threw himself forward over the foot-rope as Thorkel rushed by him, so that Thorkel fell full length over his body and lay at Vagn's feet. Vagn leaned forward and took up the ax, and there was little weariness to be seen in his face as he buried it in Thorkel's head. 'I have fulfilled half my vow,' he said; 'and still there are Jomsvikings living.' The Norwegians laughed louder than ever; and Jarl Erik said: 'Will you have your life, Vagn?' 'If you grant it to us all,' replied Vagn. 'It shall be so,' said the Jarl. So they freed us all. Twelve of us escaped from the log with our lives."

Sigurd Buesson was loudly acclaimed for his story, and everyone praised the good use he had made of his hair. They all discussed his story across the tables, admiring his good luck and that of Vagn; and Orm said to Sigurd: "There is much that is common knowledge in these parts which

Toke and I are ignorant of, because we have been out of the country for
so long a time. Where is Vagn now, and what happened to him after he
escaped from the log with his life? From all that you say, his luck sounds
to me greater than that of any other man I ever heard tell of."

"That is so," replied Sigurd, "nor does it stop halfway. We rose high
in Jarl Erik's favor, and after a while he sought out Thorkel Leira's daughter, whom he found to be even more beautiful than he had imagined her;
nor did she offer any objection to helping him to fulfill the remainder
of his promise; so that now they are married, and are well contented.
He is thinking of coming back to Bornholm with her, as soon as he can
find the time to do so; but the last heard of him was that he was still in
Norway and was complaining that it would be many months before he
could return home. For he became master of so many fine houses when
he married the girl, and of so many great estates attached to them, that
it will be no swift matter to sell them for the prices they deserve to command; and it is not Vagn's custom to sell things cheaply when he does
not have to do so."

Toke said: "There is one thing in your story that I cannot help wondering about. I mean, your father's, Bue's, treasure-chest, which he took
with him when he jumped overboard. Did you fish it up before you left
Norway? Or did someone else get there before you? If it is still lying on
the sea-bed, I know what I should do were I to go to Norway. I should
drag the sea for that treasure-chest, for Bue's silver must have been worth
a great fortune."

"They fished long for it," said Sigurd, "not only the Norwegians, but
also such of Bue's men as survived. Many men dragged for it with grap-
pling hooks, but they caught nothing; and one man from the Vik who
dived down with a rope was never seen again. Then all of us concluded
that Bue was such a Viking as would wish to keep his treasure with him
on the sea-bed, and that he would have no mercy on any man who tried
to take it from him; for he was a strong man, and he loved his wealth.
Wise men know that those who dwell in the Great Halls are stronger
than when they were alive; and this may also be true of Bue, though he
does not dwell in the Great Halls but on the deep sea-bed beside his
treasure-chest."

"It is a pity that so much silver should be lost," said Toke. "But, as
you say, even the boldest of men would not willingly choose to be at the
bottom of the sea with Broad Bue's arms locked about his waist."

So that evening drew to its close.

Hastings

by Hope Muntz

1066 No battle in Western history was more decisive than Hastings; few have enthralled men's imaginations more. In this majestic account of the defeat of Harold the Saxon by William, Duke of Normandy, the excitement and exaltation of the men who fought and died and a sense of the tramp of doom itself are conveyed with matchless skill.

Of the Battle-order

There was a little chapel in the Weald hard by the English camp. It was named for Our Lady, St. Mary-in-the-Wood. Abbot Elfwy sang Mass there before the King and his captains, setting at naught the Roman ban. The Mass was but begun when an alarm was sounded. Harold sprang up in dread, calling his men.

The King drew up his array in haste. His battle-order made the fyrd murmur. He bade the men stand close, many ranks deep, the Danes and English heavy-armed before them. The fyrd had expected to charge down from the whole length of the ridge in line of battle, but now they heard that they must hold their ground till nightfall and fight on the defence. Harold bent back the wings as far as the steep northward slopes, making a great shield-burgh, a fortress of armed men. Within it he left open ground, that men might carry word from the commanders and have space for the wounded. The road led back thence towards Caldbec. In the midst of the shield-burgh he set up the Golden Dragon and the Fighting Man, banners and pennons grouped around them.

The Wessex levies and their Thegnhood were upon the right; upon the left those of East Anglia and Huntingdon, and in the centre the men drawn from London and the shires adjoining. The picked Men of Kent had their place where the slope was easiest, for theirs was the right of the first blow in battle. Well forward also were the Men of York, who had come South with Harold, not tarrying for their Earl. These men alone came from beyond the Humber. The Housecarles of London had the right to guard their King in battle. They stood under Ansgar's banner by the Standard where the ground was highest, the good fyrd of Middlesex and Essex backing them. Elsewhere thralls fought beside the levies, but here were none but trained men.

Duke William's spies saw how the English poured out of the forest. They watched the King's array, and spoke together fearfully, gazing on the glittering ranks, the many banners.

"There is a captain yonder," they said. "See how he marshals them."

They drew near as they dared. They saw the towering stature of the Housecarles, their gilded mail, their inlaid bills and axes, their gold-hilted swords, their shields, locked like a wall.

"God help our men," they said, "these giants must be his Knights who fight on foot. These are the victors of Stamford Bridge. What shall avail us?"

They saw archers and slingers set within the shield-burgh and in the woods on either flank. They saw no crossbow men or horse and yet their hearts misgave them. A host on foot seemed to them no longer a thing of scorn. They turned and bore word to the Duke, and told their comrades what they had seen. Duke William heard their words unmoved, but many of his soldiers quaked. No great pitched battle had been fought in Normandy for twenty years. William had won his fights by stratagems and by surprise. This new manner of warfare filled their minds with dread.

When Harold had made all ready, he perceived that the alarm had been a false one. He bade his men take food. The empty alecasks were set within the shield-burgh filled with water, basins and cups and pails beside them.

They ate and were sufficed, and there was still no sight of William. The King spoke. His words were for thralls and the fyrd. The Thegns and Housecarles knew his thought, as he knew theirs. He told the levies of Duke William's archers and his crossbow men, who opened a way for the horse. He told them that for the first time they must meet the charge of mounted men, but that naught could prevail against them, if they stood fast.

The thralls shouted: "When do we charge, lord King?"

At his answer, their faces fell. They took to muttering.

"Men," said Harold, "the Duke comes hither to seize our land. It is his part then to attack, mine to defend. Count the place where you stand as your hearth-stone. Mark your captains' banners. Do not stir from them. To you I give the highest trust. It is the hardest trial for brave warriors to stand and endure while others fight. That trial is yours this day. You must not fail. The battle rests with you."

Then the fyrd murmured, saying: "He packs us here with thralls, like herring in a barrel. He sets Danes before us. Are we to get no fighting and no spoil? What of our threshing?"

With that some of them abode to hear no more; but the most part remained, sorely perplexed and downcast. When the King saw how it was with them, he sweated.

"Hear me, men," he said. "If I should build a sea-wall, would I get a single line of stones to guard the land?"

A man of Romney shouted: "No, but a rampart, King."

"Aye," said Harold, "behind the dressed stones an earthen rampart. Both must hold, or else the sea bursts in and the land drowns. I set you here, Housecarles and Thegns and fyrd, to stem this flood. Mailed warriors and levies, ye are one; the wall and rampart of this Kingdom. Stand then, have patience. Those that fled shall hear your glory and find courage. It is not William's horsemen or his archers that shall save him then. He fears us now. His ships are beached, lest his men fly. This day is a beginning."

When the noise abated, he said again: "By all that you hold dear, I bid you stand. He will feign flight and try to draw you down. By that alone can he succeed; for if you go, what can you do against mailed horsemen? Can stones and earth unjoined hold back the sea? Whether the days of Ethelred must come again, or whether we shall leave our children peace and a proud memory, it lies upon the issue of this field."

They heard him grimly, but they saw him smile.

"We gave the Northmen four-and-twenty ships," he said. "How many for the Normans?"

They answered with a roar of laughter: "Let the bastards swim."

"Aye, let them swim," said Harold. "God be with you. Stand fast, cleave where you can. Do not be tender with them, Danes. My Men of Kent, first blood to you. York, let this be a greater Stamford Bridge. Housecarles, we have the Duke himself against us. Teach him what his Knights are worth. Stand, my fyrd-men, stand fast, my rampart. What says the proverb? 'He that seeks trouble, it were a pity he should miss it.'"

He rode back amidst laughter and cheering to his Standard. There he alighted. His chiefs came to him with eager praise. Harold wiped his brow and said: "Pass the word round. Tell it again."

His messengers went through the host, bidding all men stand firm. The captains were in good heart.

Ansgar said to the King: "You could not have done better. Now they know the issue."

"Aye, they know it now," said Harold. "Poor devils, will they know it when his darts sting them and they have no answer?"

Ansgar and Elfwy and the King's captains and his brothers began to pray him that he would be content to hold command and would have no part in the fighting.

"We shall see," he said.

Their hearts sank.

"It is past reason, brother," said Gyrth.

Harold said: "It is past reason that we stand here."

When he began to mock, they saw that they but wasted breath, yet Abbot Elfwy still pleaded with him. The old man stood there, mail-clad. His face was pinched and blue with cold and weariness. When Harold said that he was all unfit to fight, he answered: "I was never brisker. I would you were as hale."

"We are a sorry crew, uncle," said the King, "but they will rue the day they met us."

The host stood waiting. It was yet early, very cold. They stamped, and blew upon their fingers, and saw their breath rise up like steam. It seemed to them that half the day went by.

The King said to Elfwy: "Uncle, I would that I had stayed."

"You have a good precedent, my child," said Elfwy. "Alfred left his Mass before the victory of Ashdown."

Harold smiled and gave him thanks.

"God Almighty," said Leofwin, "where is the fellow? He must be on shipboard."

Earl Waltheof had brought ivory dice. He and Leofwin sat them down and fell to play. The King and those around watched the game, yawning; sometimes their lids fell and they were near slumber.

At last they heard Duke William's trumpets and saw a stir across the valley. When the hosts saw each other, a mighty shout went up. Then the Duke's first battle came down from the heights in good array, marching to music, at a foot pace. Archers and crossbow men came first. They wore no mail, but jerkins of boiled leather and quilted coats. Then came the mail-clad foot, spear-men with shields and swords; and after them the Knights, pennons and banners flying. This force wheeled to face the English left. King Harold and his men watched them and spoke among themselves.

A second host followed. These men halted over against the English right.

Last came a third battle, greater than the others. The King saw before him William's gold and scarlet banner, and many more that he had known in Normandy. There too, borne next the Duke himself, he saw a mighty Standard, azure and gold and silver, the sign of the Cross. He looked and his eyes widened. A murmur rose among the English.

"God save us," they said, "it is the Holy Cross."

Even among the Housecarles such words passed. The King looked at Gyrth, as though he would have spoken.

"Can you name the captains, brother?" said Earl Gyrth.

After a moment, Harold said: "Yonder in their right battle, Eustace of Boulogne commands, as the Duke's foremost ally. With him I see Ivo of Ponthieu, and lords from Flanders and from France. I see Burgundian banners and a Spanish standard. Some of the Duke's countrymen from Italy are yonder, and Normans from the the Isle of Sicily. There are men too from Normandy with Eustace, the great FitzOsbern captains them. William has set them with the Count for that Eustace is an unsure warrior, bold enough in hope of victory and gain, but one that loves life above honour."

"Who is on the left?" said Gyrth.

The King said: "Alan the Red commands the Breton men. They fight as the Welsh, brother; brave as lions, but they will not stand. He has set to stiffen them the good men of Maine and those of Poitou. Haimer of Thouars is their captain, and no bad one. It was well done to set him by the Bretons."

"What of the centre battle?" said Earl Gyrth.

Harold did not answer.

"One good man I can spy yonder, brothers," said Leofwin. "I can see Malet's banner. It is a shame to see him in that pack."

"Who else is there?" said Waltheof.

Harold said: "William's half-brothers ride with him, Mortain and the Bayeux Bishop. Robert is a good fellow, but no captain. Odo could teach the Duke himself. He is as valiant too, but a foul fighter. Would I might meet him."

With that he named Neal of St. Sauveur who led the men of the Cotentin, Hugh the Constable, and many more.

"It is a famous chivalry," he said, "but take away the captain and one might liefer deem them wolves. By that I measure him."

He mused and said: "It is as though we looked upon the coast of France. Do you see, my lords, what he has done? On the right eastward, Flanders and Boulogne and Ponthieu; then the Normans of the centre, Lisieux and

Caen and Bayeux, then the Cotentin; and on the West the Bretons. So shall his men fight by their neighbours and egg each other on."

Ansgar said: "The Bastard is a captain plainly, but I think he has a task before him."

The King answered: "If it please God to help us, we shall hold him."

Earl Gyrth looked on the ordered ranks, the banners and the lances. His eyes rested on St. Peter's Cross and dwelt upon it; a light came into them like fire.

Leofwin chafed and fretted, and could not be still.

"I would the Duke would fall to work," he said. "My stomach comes and goes."

Earl Waltheof bade him keep his tally when the sport began.

"Look to it, cousin," he said. "I mean to beat you."

"What odds?" said Leofwin.

They laid a wager.

Harold passed his tongue over his lips. He looked up at the sun. The day shone clear and fair. The woods were bright with many hues. They heard far off the old bell of Our Lady's chapel, ringing the Hour of Tierce. The sound came stilly through the trees and died away. The King and his chiefs signed themselves and spoke a prayer. Harold kissed the silver ring and said to them: "Sirs, may God keep you. Let the trumpets sound."

Of the First Onslaughts

Some of the Duke's men had been so faint-hearted that he had bidden them depart. Now he spoke to the soldiers once again.

"Slay everyone you can," he said, "for if we conquer we shall all be rich."

They cheered at that. The English answered, yelling in mockery: "Out, out!"

"Hark," said Odo, "the dogs are barking."

William reined his horse and looked up at the hill. The sun dazzled upon the Standard and the Dragon. The spear-points burnt like flames. Beyond the painted shields the banners shone with silver, gold and scarlet, sky-blue and green; the bright helms winked and glittered. The hill was steep and grown with gorse and brambles and yellow bracken. The rough grass was beset with molehills. Marshy ground and water-course, the Asten and the river Brede, lay upon either flank; before him lay the miry valley. The Duke looked and rubbed his chin.

"He has made it like a castle," said Count Robert. "I never saw such an array of battle."

"The nut has a hard rind," said Odo. "We shall need good teeth."

"Brothers," said William, "I will build my church where Harold stands."

A monk of St. Martin of Marmoutiers cried out: "Sire, name it for the soldiers' Saint."

"I grant it," said the Duke.

He cantered down the ranks of bowmen, giving counsel. He called on God and raised his mace. The host took up the cry: "God help!"

The first ranks of the bowmen began to go forward.

Those who stood at the back of the English array could not see what passed in the valley. When they heard the trumpets, they stood a-tiptoe and craned their necks.

"Are they coming?" they said. "Are they coming?"

Suddenly the shouting was hushed. They heard a whistling like the sound of wings. Then it seemed as though a hail-storm beat against the shield-wall. The shouting broke out again, mingled with shrieks and cries. So it went twice and three times and again, and still continued. The Housecarles stood unmoving.

When the archers fell back, the Duke's heavy-armed foot came to the assault, launching their throwing-weapons, pressing on with spears and swords.

A man in the last rank of Harold's host, seeing an old crab-tree hard by, climbed up to know what might be doing.

"Can you see them?" said his comrades.

"By God," he said, "They are half-way up the hill. Our men are snoring. What ails the fellows?"

They began to shout rudely to the Housecarles, bidding them make show of manhood. The Housecarles answered. "Hold your peace, you midden-cocks. What do you know of warfare?"

When the enemy drew near, the thralls waited for no command, but every man let fly with what he had.

"Shoot, shoot," they cried to the Housecarles.

The Duke's men came on, hurling their darts. On a sudden the King's trumpets spoke. The captains shouted. There was a stir and flash down the whole line of battle. The French battle-cry wavered and died away. A fearful shrieking rose. The English yelled in triumph.

Those who stood by the crab-tree pulled the man down and fought each other for his place. Clarions rang across the valley. A cry was made: "The Knights, the Knights are coming! Stand fast. Keep your ranks."

The men who had swarmed up into the tree stared breathless, seeing a sight of splendour and of terror beyond their dreams. Those who could see nothing heard a man's voice begin a battle-chant. The chorus swelled, awesome and terrible and ever louder. The ground trembled beneath the English, as though they stood above sea-caverns on a day of storm. A single horseman charged the shield-wall singing, tossing his lance on high. Then came a shock that made the whole host reel. The noise of battle roared and thundered and died away at last as a great surf that breaks upon a rock-bound shore. There remained only the sound of crying, more woeful than the voice of sea-birds.

The men of the shield-wall shouted their battle-cry: "God Almighty! Holy Cross!"

They heard no answer.

The levies whooped and hooted their delight, and cried to those in front: "Well fought, well fought, axe-men. You made the bastards skip."

"What did you look for?" said the Housecarles.

They wiped their weapons without haste and took their talk up where they had left it. Anschill of Ware said to his comrade Burchard: "Finn should have wed the wench."

This first onslaught was scarcely beaten back, when the Duke marshalled his ranks again and sent archers and foot to the attack. Then for the second time came the great charge of the horsemen. The heaps of dead before the shield-wall grew, and with them lay the lopped and mangled living. The King's few bowmen, scattered through the host and hidden in the woods on either flank, aimed their shafts at the horses, and as each assault was ended picked off the stragglers toiling down the hill. It went thus till high noon was past, and then a pause came in the battle. None had seen harder fighting than this day. A cold fear struck the Frenchmen at the heart.

King Harold ordered now that all sorely wounded men should go out of the fight. The ranks had stood so close that neither slain nor wounded men could fall.

Some of the wounded jested with the shire-men as they passed, and cursed their luck, that they must leave the work half-done.

"God's truth," said the country fellows, "your luck is more than ours. We have stood here all day like wethers in a pen."

Ansgar the Marshal went out of the battle now. He had been stricken, wounded in the loins. The King bade him command the camp and send the captain to take his place. Ansgar besought him to have no more part himself in the close fighting, saying; "Sire, my heart stood still to see you."

Harold said he had not come there to be idle.

"My dear lord," said Ansgar, "have you not said it is the harder part? We need your head more than your hands."

Before the next assault, the King rode round his array. Many of the shire-men had been stricken by the hail of weapons that passed the shield-wall. They chafed that they had no revenge. He saw a young lad laid on the grass, dying. The lad wept. When Harold spoke to him, he answered: "Lord King, I never struck a blow for you. What will they say at home?"

"Aye," said an old man, "it is not the dying, King. It is the manner of it." So they spoke on every side, yet at his words they quietened.

When the attack began, Harold took his place among them, idle with the rest. No toil seemed to him harder. The valour of the Housecarles seemed to him a lesser thing than this endurance. He spoke his thoughts. His neighbour, Stanwin, grinned, and said: "King, we be slow to rise, but when we rise up, we be something."

Stanwin offered the King half his bread and cheese.

Harold gave him thanks and said: "Your wife bakes bravely."

"Oh, ah," said Stanwin, "bravely as a Queen, but 'tis her tongue that's heavy."

The King laughed. A little man called Breme, upon the other side, offered him drink from a great leathern bottle and pledged him, saying: "I drink your health, King Harold."

With that he wiped his hand across his mouth and passed the bottle.

"Drink hail," said Harold. He drank a thin sour beer, and did as Breme had done. The clarions rang. The King looked over the heads of those before him and forgot his neighbours. He muttered words unknowingly and gripped his weapon. The Knights of Brittany and Poitou charged the shield-wall with lowered lances, shouting in their own speech and calling on their Saints. He saw beyond his battle-line the wild heads of the horses scattering foam, the flash of sword and lance, and the white glaring faces. The line stood firm. The first rank knelt, their bills pointed against the horses' breasts, the second stood close and set their points against the riders. He glanced up at the sun. The day was three-parts spent. He smiled.

Breme shouted up to him: "How do we fare?"

"Better than well," said Harold.

When the first shock of the charge was broken and the lances shivered, the English used both bills and axes. The Knights were hard warriors, but they had never found themselves so straitened. The axemen fought left-handed, so that no shield availed. Mail was shorn through like silk, swords shattered at a blow. Men saw their comrades hewn asunder. They saw their horses headless while they yet bestrode them. The ground grew slippery as in a marsh. Among the fallen the chargers plunged and screamed in a red mire. The axes rose and fell and rose again, scarlet and terrible. The Knights saw themselves weaponless before their slaughterers. They turned and fled, horror upon them.

A cry was raised: "The Duke is slain. Each for himself!"

The flight grew frenzied. The whole host heard the word and wavered. A roar rose from the English. On either wing the levies burst the shield-wall, yelling. The King himself was borne away, as by a flood, down the hill-side.

When the close pressure of the throng released him, Harold stood still and looked about him, panting. Where the ditch spanned the field below, the Breton horse had over-ridden their foot; chargers and men struggled and choked together in the foul water. Thralls were hard at work with bill-hooks, clubs and hatchets. He looked towards the centre and saw the matchless chivalry of Normandy in headlong flight. Beyond them the French banners were borne backward faster yet.

"Oh, God, if it could be!" he said. "Where are the Earls?"

He heard his trumpets sounding the recall unheeded. A standard-bearer of the fyrd leapt down the hill towards him, yelling. Harold seized the staff and felled him. More levies rushed past. He heard the winding of a hunting-horn. A lad hulloed.

"Stand, men," he shouted. "Stand!"

His voice was lost. He saw a trumpeter and roared to him: "Recall, recall. Sound the recall."

The man stopped, staring. The King snatched the trumpet from his hands, and sounded. The shire-men were deaf. He saw that in the centre the fight was checked. The clarions rang. Duke William's banner turned to meet the fleeing Bretons, the Duke himself, bareheaded, galloping before, shouting in fury. The Norman Knighthood massed in wedge array behind him, bearing down upon the hurly-burly at the ditch.

Housecarles and Thegns had gathered to the King. Godric of Fifhide ran up with Ethelnoth of Canterbury.

Godric shouted something and pointed to the valley.

Harold cried: "Back."

They saw the horsemen drive across the field, the levies all unheeding. "Sire, my men!" said Godric.

The King turned. Godric followed with the rest, sobbing forth curses. They heard the sounds of battle change behind them.

The English trumpets up and down the field blared the recall. Upon the left the lines were formed again. The centre stood unshaken. On the right many men were cut off. The King drew on the centre and the left, so that the front ranks yet appeared as strong. The axemen watched, bleak-faced, the bloody struggle in the valley.

A knoll stood out from the hill no great way from the summit on the right. Thurkill of Kingston Bagpuize had fought his way thither with a band of fyrd-men, Stanwin and Breme among them. Before they could win to their comrades the Knights came against them. There was an oak tree on the knoll and round it they made their stand. Even thralls held their own like giants, fighting without helm or mail. They stood within spear-cast of the King's lines and shouted to their side for help. But now no throwing-spears were left, nor stones nor arrows, save those that could be gleaned. Harold forbade any man to leave his place.

"Sire, for the love of Christ," said Godric.

The King said: "Be still."

Before the shire-men were beaten down, Duke William led a new attack against the shield-burgh. This onslaught was more terrible than all, and this too failed.

King Harold had fought on the right. He mounted now and rode round his array. Then he came to his own place. He alighted slowly and leant against his horse. There was a hush like death upon the field. Harold's brothers and his captains had thought him lost. They swore he should not go from them again.

"Are you not wounded, Sire?" they said. "Are you not hurt?"

He shook his head. Earl Leofwin began to curse the headstrong levies. Harold turned on him in fury. Seeing his brother's stricken look, he checked himself. Gyrth brought him water. He drank and said: "Where is the messenger I sent to Ansgar?"

The man came to him. He asked if there were news yet of the Earls, but there was none. Then he asked if the baggage-wagons had been found.

"Sire," said the man, "the Marshal hears they have turned back to London."

All those around stood silent, casting anxious glances on King Harold. He began to laugh.

"Well, sirs," he said, "we have worked for our glory, and we will not share it. If we have no help, neither has the Duke. I dare swear he remembers Rouen kindly."

Seeing that he could jest, their hearts were lightened. The sun was westering, and they reckoned it was no more than three hours till nightfall.

As they were speaking, someone called out that the Knights charged again. They took their posts in haste. They saw, as in the first attack, a single horseman riding on alone, but they beheld no chivalry behind him. Brihtric of Gloucester said: "It is a herald. He will sue for peace."

But as they watched, they could see no white shield or flag of truce. The Knight rode furiously, leaping over furze and brambles, trampling the dead. As he drew near they heard him crying out and calling on his horse.

"Hola, hola," he cried. They saw his bridle broken. A roar of laughter went down the line.

"This way, Frenchman," called the Housecarles. "We will quiet him for you."

The horse came on full gallop. When he saw the lifted axes, he pricked his ears and snorted. Then he spread his fore-feet wide and slithered to a halt, his quarters under him. His rider rose up and clasped him round the neck. So doing, he lost his stirrups.

"Hola," cried the Knight, "God help! St. Michael mercy!"

Two Housecarles sprang out of the line towards him, axes aloft. The stallion squealed and backed and whirled about. He hurtled down the hill faster than he had come. The Knight held for his life, with stirrups flying.

The French observed this exploit in a wrathful silence. The English loudly cheered. The King laughed till he sobbed.

"God Almighty," he said, "one man has won his fame!"

He turned back from the shield-wall and went to see his wounded men. They asked him what had chanced, and when he told them, the story passed from mouth to mouth and made them merry. The tale of the Knight's charge heartened the whole host like good wine. They were still laughing when the archers came on to attack again.

Of the House of Godwin

Abbot Leofric of Peterborough had been wounded by a lance-thrust in the thigh. He lay with other sorely wounded men on the high ground behind the line of battle, where the Dragon and the Standard crowned the hill.

Leofric bore himself bravely. When he heard the trumpets sound for a new onslaught, he said to Erwin, the King's leech, who tended him: "Make haste, for I have three men's work to do."

"Lord Abbot, you can do no more this day," said Erwin.

Leofric said: "By the Apostle, Harold shall not say that all our kindred failed him."

He ground his teeth and said again: "Make haste."

Erwin did for him what he could. The Abbot stretched out his hands and clutched the grass. He lay still, staring up into a cloudless sky. He thought that the air had darkened. On a sudden he cried out and strove to raise himself.

"Lie still, my lord," said Erwin, "I have done."

The day grew loud, as with the flight of starlings. Men looked up. Then the arrow-storm came down upon them, falling from on high. Erwin sank forward across the Abbot and was still. A shrieking rose, as from the souls in hell. The Duke's bowmen had aimed upwards, against the Standard. Upon the Housecarles, upon the men of Middlesex and Essex fell that keen rain. The wounded and those who tended them lay like St. Edmund, pierced in every limb. Between them the barbed shafts thrilled in the ground. Then suddenly as it began, the storm was ended. The host stood dazed.

Abbot Leofric had no hurt, for Erwin's body saved him. He lay a moment as though stunned, not knowing what befell him. He saw the Fighting Man glitter above him, pierced with shafts. As he sought to rise, Abbot Elfwy staggered to him, stricken through the jaws. Leofric would have helped him, but Elfwy tore his hands away, and pointed whence he had come, striving to speak.

Leif the Northman ran up, stumbling across the fallen. He snatched the salves and linen. The water-bowl lay shattered.

"Water," he said, "bring water. Find a leech."

Leofric looked after him and saw where the King stood, bowed together, staying himself upon his shield. Elfwy sank down, groaning. Leofric knew not if he lived or died. His own soul failed within him.

A man ran past with water in a leaking bucket. The Abbot halted after him. The King's brothers and his chiefs pressed round him, and men cried out for a leech.

Leofric said to Gyrth: "I am a leech."

"In God's name then," said Gyrth.

He spoke to Harold. The King held his head between his hands. Blood ran through his fingers and down the shield. He neither moved nor answered.

Earl Waltheof stood with Godwin's sons. The Abbot asked him: "What is the wound?"

And when he heard, he said: "Lord Jesus, he must go out of the battle."

Leif said to Harold: "Foster-son, you must go back."

He did not answer. They took counsel together. Then they sought to lead him back. Harold raised his head and fought them, crying out for Erwin.

"God damn you, where is the leech?" he said.

They loosed him in despair. He staggered, reeling. Leif caught him in his arms and laid him down. They heard the trumpets sound for the onset of the heavy-armed foot following the archers. The King sought to rise. He fell back and spoke Gyrth's name.

"Take the command, lord Earl," said Leif.

Gyrth kissed his brother. He took Harold's shield, that men might think he was the King, and called his chiefs. His calm was changed. They saw him like a lion. Leofwin stood staring upon Harold, his face ashen, Waltheof beside him.

"You too," said Leif. "Back to your work."

When Leofwin would have kissed the King, Harold struck at him. Earl Leofwin followed Gyrth, sobbing. The noise of battle rose again at the shield-wall. The clash of steel on steel was like the clangour of a hundred smithies. The King called on the name of Christ.

Abbot Leofric began his task with shaking hands. He laid aside the helm and put back the coif of ring-mail. A shaft had stricken Harold above the right eye and destroyed it. He had drawn the arrow-head so strongly that the torn flesh hung down. When Leofric touched his hurt, he swooned.

"He gave the Duke good help who sent this gad-fly," said Leif.

The Abbot laboured in silence, sweating as he toiled, for faintness came on him from his own wound. Before the work was done, they heard the coming of the Knights. Harold lay as the dead. Leofric put his hand upon his breast.

"Please God he will live," he said. "He must be borne back to the camp when I have done, and the news hidden if may be. Nothing will hold the men if they get word."

"It will be night ere long," said Leif.

As they spoke, they heard the yelling of the levies, like hounds in cry. Upon the left the host surged forward.

"God help us," said Leif, "this is the end."

He seized his weapons and sprang up, thrusting through the press towards Gyrth's banner. Trumpets sounded vainly.

The King came from his swoon and murmured something.

"Lie still, my son," said Leofric. "The day goes well."

The trumpets rang again, loud as the crack of doom. Harold raised himself up, casting the Abbot from him with a madman's strength. He cried out to those around him: "Get me to my feet."

From the valley on the left the shouts of triumph died before the Norman battle-cry. William had drawn the shire-men down by a feigned flight. The King turned and strove to see how the fight went on his right wing. The sun was low and the light smote him. He groaned and said: "How is it on the right? Do the men stand?"

One of the Housecarles answered: "They stand firm, lord King."

Harold said: "Bid Godric shorten his line. Let him send half his levies. Take up the Standard."

When the Duke led his Knights against the weakened left, he saw the Fighting Man over against him, where he had thought to breach the shield-wall. Sometimes a Knight broke through to find his death, but the line held. It was the hour of sunset when the Knighthood fell back. They rode down the hillside, a ragged band, horses and men forspent.

King Harold had kept his station by the Fighting Man, gripping the banner-staff. When he was told that the assault had failed, he asked men for his brothers.

Leif came to him, and Waltheof, with new wounds.

"Is it you, foster-father?" said the King. "Where are my brothers?"

Seeing him there upon his feet, Leif swore.

"Before God," he said, "are there no men of yours with wits about them? You must be out of the fight, Harold. What do you here?"

"Where is Gyrth?" said the King. "Where is Leofwin?"

When Leif saw that nothing would serve, he fell to praising Harold's brothers. The King had never heard such words from him.

"What would you tell me, Leif?" he said.

Leif told his tidings.

"Fallen?" said Harold. "Leofwin too?"

Earl Waltheof said, weeping: "Oh, cousin, Gyrth threw himself against the Duke and slew his horse. Then the Knights came between us. The Duke struck him down. I saw Leofwin fall."

"What would you, foster-son?" said Leif. "They died like warriors. 'Old age gives no quarter, though the spears may.'"

"And the Duke lives?" said Harold.

Leif said: "The devil guards his own. The man was twice unhorsed. Haveloc's son dealt him a blow that might have felled an ox, yet the Duke slew him. Three times we thought the Bastard ours. He stood alone and fought us like a demon."

The King said: "Is he so great a warrior?"

He bade them to bring his brothers' bodies to the Standards, and they brought them, bloody and trampled. The Duke's mace had fallen on Earl Gyrth, crushing both helm and head. A spear had stricken Leofwin through. He lay as though in wonder.

"Give me to drink," said Harold.

He would not go out of the fight, or yield up the command to any man.

In the next attack, Duke William sent foot-soldiers before the archers. While they cast their spears, the bowmen loosed their arrows upwards. A roof of shields covered the English host. The closed ranks did not part. The dead fell, but the living never stirred. The Housecarles stood like men of iron. The Duke beheld no opening for his horse. Seeing that silent and unmoving host, he signed himself.

When the archers and foot fell back, no clarions sounded. There came a great lull in the battle. Now men on both sides felt themselves spent past endurance. Many were dead of weariness alone. Those that lived could scarcely wield their weapons. The very reason of their warfare was forgotten in the thought of rest. The sun had set behind the western hills, and but an hour of daylight yet remained.

Of the Fighting Man

Duke William summoned his captains to him in the valley. They came in silence, wounded, bone-weary, haggard-eyed. Their stallions trembled with drooped crests and bloody sides lathered with foam and sweat.

The Barons saw no praise in their lord's looks. When they had gathered, he looked round upon them in such a silence that they quailed.

At last he said: "My lords and Barons, you were called warriors once. What shall I call you now? Our bowmen have done better service. Is this the valour of your chivalry? Look yonder. See your victors. A few wounded axemen and a rabble of peasantry without a captain."

They heard him, shamed.

The Duke raged.

"By God's Splendour, sirs," he said, "must I win this day for you single-handed? Have I not fought with Harold, foot to foot, and given him the crown he earned? On foot I fought. I struck the tyrant down. Must I destroy them all? By the Apostle, if you forego the spoils of victory now, you are the laughing-stock of Christendom."

They were silent, with bowed heads.

"Very good," he said. "Fly if you will. It will not save you. I have destroyed the ships."

At that they looked on him wild-eyed.

"Ye fools," he said, "when have you seen me worsted? I tell you the day is won. Harold is dead."

As he was speaking, they heard from the hill a ragged shout, the sound of one man's name.

They hearkened, unbelieving. They heard that name again, and a third time.

"It cannot be," said William. "With mine own hand I slew him."

Count Eustace cried out: "Lord have mercy on us."

Despair took them anew.

"My lords," said Odo, "it seems to me our arrow-storm was on the mark. It must have been his brother who bore Harold's shield. If the King be not dead, then he is wounded."

William threw back his head and laughed.

"Good hearing, sirs," he said. "I feared before. I never yet knew men stand fast when such a captain fell. Now but one life stands between us and triumph."

Eustace said: "Cold comfort. He will not come into the battle, being wounded. And for those Knights of his that fight on foot, we shall not come at him while they are living."

The Duke knitted his brows and said to Odo: "Give us of your cunning counsel, brother. You are the man to help us now."

"Why do you call on me?" said Odo. "Call on Harold."

When the council was ended, the Duke's lords rode back, each man to his own post. Hugh of Montfort, the Constable, upon the right of William's centre battle, had the King's Standard now before him. He called his chiefs and gave them his lord's command.

"We are to seek none but the King himself," he said.

Duke William led his Knights again to the attack. As soon as the horse-men drew near the shield-wall, they began to shout King Harold's name. Some cried in their own tongue, some few in English, taunting the King with cowardice, mocking him that he hid behind his men.

Robert of Vieux Pont rode with the Constable, and with them William Malet. Hugh and Robert shouted loudly. Malet rode in silence.

The Constable cried to him: "Take up the word, Sir Knight. The Duke commands."

"I promised him my sword," said Malet, "not a woman's weapon."

Robert of Vieux Pont answered: "My faith, Malet, you will need all weapons, if you would see Greville again."

Malet said: "I was a Knight before I held Greville."

As they charged, the Knighthood shouted to the Housecarles: "Axemen, where is your King, he that was perjured to the Duke? Does Harold hide himself? He is a dead man if we find him."

The taunts sounded like an unending chant of shame. The King heard them where he stood. He gasped as though he fell into an ice-cold flood.

Leif said, raging: "Give them no heed, my fosterling. This is their guile."

The Knights hurled themselves against the shield-wall. As they fought and as they fell, they cried shame on the King: "Coward, Usurper, Per-juror; show yourself, Harold, if you dare."

He said to those around him: "I will not bear it. Better die."

They laid hands on him and held him back by force.

Patric of La Lande, fighting beside Duke William, shouted: "Where do you hide, Harold FitzGodwin? You were bold enough in Brittany. Come out, Earl Harold. Hear me name you 'perjuror.'"

William roared, as he fought: "Harold, your liege-lord calls you. Traitor, show yourself."

The wounded Housecarles by the Standard dragged themselves up and seized their weapons, stumbling back into the battle. The King struggled, sobbing, cursing those who held him.

"Loose me," he said, "shall these go back and I stand here?"

Leif answered: "Did your brothers die, that he should win this day with words?"

Thereafter Harold was still. He bade them give him his great axe. The keen edge was unturned. He signed the blood-stained steel as though he prayed.

The hue and cry continued. At the sound of it, King Harold's men grew battle-mad. This one thing wrought what the Duke's power could not. Axemen rushed out slaughtering. Housecarles threw away their shields. The Men of Kent and London hurled themselves forward, the shire-men behind them. William saw his Knights go down, his bravest warriors fall.

Patric shouted to him: "Eustace feigns flight again to draw them down."

The Duke saw Count Eustace going back and all his right wing wavering, FitzOsbern shouting to the men in vain.

"By God," he said, "if they fly now, they will not turn to-day."

When Count Eustace saw him coming, with the thousand knights who followed him, he cried: "God help!" And he and his turned back to face the axes.

Duke William fought now beside Count Eustace and his men. Young Robert of Beaumont fought there also, leading a band of horsemen. The Duke marked him. The lad fought like a hero, crying: "Englishmen, where is your King?"

William called to him: "Beaumont, my Knight, your spurs are won this day."

Robert laid on like three men, gasping forth his cry.

The weight of horsemen breached the English line in many places when the ranks were thinned. The fighting was back and forth on the hill-top. The Duke's men thought the day was won. Many turned back to plunder. Then the English drew together round the Dragon and the Standard, and fought more strongly. The battle grew yet harder. Men trod not on the ground, but on the fallen. Those that fell were trampled under foot and stifled. The light began to fail. A spear struck William's horse. The Duke fell headlong and rose dazed. Eustace horsed him, seizing a Knight's charger. Fury came on William. He fought despairing. His sole strength upheld them.

Hugh of Montfort pressed the attack against the Standard with all his might. Twenty Knights took a vow to win the Fighting Man. Robert FitzErneis was their leader. The Men of London broke before them and fell back, fighting like berserks. Robert alone lived till he reached the Standard. A great axe struck him down, but the breach widened. More Knights pressed on. The Housecarles heard a voice they knew, and saw their lord beside them. From either host a shout went up.

William looked westward. Against the after-glow he saw an axeman mightier than his fellows. The Knighthood broke and fled before him, as though the tide of battle turned, now and for ever. The Duke wheeled his horse.

"Eustace," he shouted, "Ponthieu, Giffard, Normans to me!"

They heard that call above the tumult, loud as at morning.

They drew off and threw themselves into a wedge array, and all together charged the Standard.

The King heard the thunder of their coming as he fought. He turned his head and saw the Cross. A sword struck him across the brow unseen. His axe fell from his hand. He sank down on his knee. His foemen yelled. They heard his battle-cry and saw him rising. A Knight bent from the saddle and hewed to the thigh-bone before the shields could close, crying: "God help!"

The Duke drove home his spurs and rode the ranks of Housecarles under foot. He saw his quarry. His lance struck down through shield and mail and breast into the ground. The ashwood splintered. The weight of the charge carried William on. Men fell before the broken lance. With his own hands he cast the Standard down.

Duke William's brothers drew rein at his side. Toustain the White bore after him the banner with the Cross. His bodyguard swept round. His Barons gathered. About them the strife yet raged, disordered, masterless. Where the King fell, Count Eustace and his men wheeled, howling, stabbing down with swords and lances. A man bore to the Duke a broken helm, an arm-ring wet with blood.

William turned and snatched the banner-staff from Toustain's hands. He stood up in his stirrups. Beyond the fury he saw the still woods, the dark heights of Telham. He shouted, weeping, to his men: "Victory, victory with the help of God!"

But when the stars shone they were fighting still.

Of the End

In the camp on Caldbec Hill the wounded heard the uproar of the fighting. Ansgar the Marshal had sent down all who could strike a blow, the boys and the camp-servants. None was left save maimed and dying men, the priests who tended them, and the flock of wives and children and old folk drawn from the country round. The sunset glory faded and yet none knew how the battle went.

As the twilight deepened there came a hush at last. Out of it rose a hoarse shout. It seemed to them the army cried King Harold's name.

"What shout is that?" said Ansgar. "Is the day ours?"

He sent monks to the field. While they were gone the noise arose more hideously, the endless din of battle. Suddenly they heard a very yell of triumph, a Norman cry.

Ansgar said: "Oh, Christ, what is it?"

He raised himself upon his elbow. When he looked down, he saw men running northward; at first a few, then more, then a great rush of the shire-levies. He looked about him as a man distraught.

"A trumpeter," he said, "find me a trumpeter."

As they fled the shire-men heard the trumpet-calls ring out. They thought the Earls were come. They turned from flight and toiled up the steep hill with a new hope. When they beheld no more than Ansgar and his band of wounded and the lone trumpeter sounding his call, many fell down and wept.

Ansgar shouted to them. He had some of the men dragged before him. "You dogs," he said, "why do you fly? Your orders were to stand."

"The King," they said, "the King is gone. Harold is fallen."

"Harold gone?" said Ansgar. "What man commands?"

"Fly, fly," they said, "there is no host, no captain."

"There is a captain here," said Ansgar. "I command. Hold fast. The Earls are coming."

Seeing him so unshaken they began to know themselves again. Ansgar had men bear him to and fro. He ordered the defence as he was able. The stones for the engines lay there. He bade them carry them to the hill's edge, that they might roll them down upon the foe. He bade the trumpets sound as though a host were come. More levies gathered to him. He sent word to the field that he would hold the camp and ordered that all should . fall back.

Sebricht had gone down with the other servants when the fight grew desperate. He was no warrior, yet he pressed on, clutching a dead man's sword. For the first time men fell before him. He heard the cry of the King's death, and Ansgar's bidding reached him. In the same instant he heard a shout of "Holy Cross." A sudden hope made his heart beat. He saw a rush of axemen. He took up the battle-cry and fought beside them. Horsemen came against them and were beaten back. They came again. A third time they rode against the axes and drew off.

Sebricht cried: "The King, is the King with you, Housecarles?"

Leif's voice answered him: "What man is that?"

"It is I, Sebricht," he said. "Where is the King?"

"Gone," said Leif. "There is no joy in living after this day."

Sebricht sobbed out: "Ansgar the Marshal will defend the camp. He sends word to fall back."

Abbot Leofric caught his arm and cried: "Sebricht, are my kinsmen come? Was it their trumpets?"

"What should they do now?" said Leif. "Better to die with Harold than to live without him."

Earl Waltheof was with them. He thrust forward now.

"You are a Northman, Leif," he said. "We have our land yet. We can live to fight."

"Aye, to fight," said Leofric.

They heard the trumpets loud from the hill.

"Hark, they are come," said Waltheof. "Back, my lords."

Brihtric of Gloucester joined them with other men. They fought their way towards the camp. There were many such small bands upon the field. Some few had Ansgar's word. Some turned. The rest fought on. It grew so dark that only by their voices could foes know each other. Godric of Fifhide and Edric the Deacon had joined Alfric of Gelling. He was Waltheof's warrior. Two Hampshire men were with them, Ednoth and Edwy, and others all unknown. A freeman of St. Edmundsbury bore them Ansgar's bidding.

Alfric answerd: "Harold did not fly."

No man would turn away.

Godric the Sheriff said: "Give us a song, Edric. Let the bastards know where to find Englishmen."

Edric began to croak forth the words of the old warrior Brihtwold, in the Song of Maldon:

> "Soul shall be stronger,   spirit be keener,
> Mind shall be mightier   as our might lessens."

Godric and his men took up the battle-chant, hewing as they sang:

> "Here lies our captain   cut all to pieces,
> Good and gone under;   aye may he groan for it,
> He that now from this warfaring   would turn homeward."

At the sound of that grim singing in the darkness, the Duke's men muttered spells against witchcraft and gave ground. The English staggered forward, seeking them. Edric led the chanting still. The freeman fought beside him with a club, Godric with his great axe. Their words came in gasps:

> "I am grown grey-hair'd;   go hence I will not,
> But I here abiding   with my bread-giver,
> By so loved a man   look to perish."

It was near Midnight and the moon had risen when the fighting on the hill was at an end.

Count Eustace and his men had thought it better to chase the fleeing in hope of gain than to fight axemen in the dark, and they had left that labour to the Duke. Now William too pressed on towards Caldbec, for there he heard the sound of a new battle, and the voice of English trumpets.

FitzOsbern cried to him: "Hark to the trumpets. Help has reached them."

William rode on.

A sudden dreadful cry of men and horses smote their ears. It came not from the camp, but from the broken country to the West, where the pursuit spread far and wide. The Duke drew rein. He strained his eyes to see. The English trumpets rang again in triumph from the hill. He turned his head and glared, grinding his teeth. He saw a band of horsemen spurring back, Count Eustace hastening before.

William thrust across their path and shouted hoarsely: "Eustace, stand!"

The Count drew rein beside him, breathless. He leant across and gasped in the Duke's ear: "Sire, save yourself. It is death yonder. A new host is come, with slings and mangonels. My men are cut to pieces."

A missile hurtled from the dark and took the Count between his shoulders. It was so great a blow that the sound rang, for Eustace bore his shield upon his back. He fell against the Duke, blood bursting from his mouth and nose. William roared to his men to take him. None knew whence the blow had come. The Knights drew round Duke William with raised shields.

"On to the camp," he said.

A man rode to him from the West, crying of horsemen overthrown; of a great gulf deep as the mouth of Hell. They could not understand his words. His speech was thick as though he had been drunken.

"Back, back, Sire," said the Barons.

William cursed them. He sent men West, he sent back to the field to call his foot. He waited raging. Word came of a ravine that had betrayed his Knights, and tidings that the camp was held in strength. All counselled that he must turn back. When he had ordered his array the Duke pressed on.

Horsemen and foot toiled up the steep hill-side with bursting hearts, gasping: "God help!"

No stones, no weapons met them. William himself first gained the heights. He found no living foeman. Ansgar had draw off his men into the fastnesses of the great Weald.

Duke William reined his horse by Harold's tent and looked about him, his breath labouring.

Three Guests of Canon de Vannes

by Helen Waddell

1117   Although misery, ignorance and violence flourished in the twelfth century, so also did saints and scholars. The most popular teacher and the greatest religious philosopher was Peter Abelard, whose affair with his brilliant pupil, Heloise, is one of the world's immortal love stories. Gilles de Vannes, an aged and wise canon of Notre Dame in Paris, was Abelard's best friend.

"Put another log on the fire, Pierre," said Gilles. "It is bitter cold. I have no great love for an early Easter. The fast makes one feel the cold."

Pierre de Montboissier stooped to the pile on the hearth, flung a log to the back and turned the block of elm on the fire, so that the radiant bark glowed like burning scales. He stood, leaning against the chimney, and looked anxiously at Gilles. He was stooped forward and the old fine hands stretched out to the heat had gone dead and white at the finger-tips.

"Let me pour you a drink, sir. The fast is not so strict for you. It is not as if it were Good Friday."

"You're a good lad," said Gilles gratefully. Pierre poured the wine carefully, tilting the bottle by slow degrees. He knew how to handle a wine, that youngster. But why, why was he for the cloister? Were those long legs never to grip the sides of a horse with armored knee, but sit muffled in petticoats some day on an abbot's white mule?

"I shall miss you, Pierre," he said crossly. He held out his hand for the goblet, scowling up under puckered brows.

Pierre flushed scarlet with pleasure and embarrassment. He opened his mouth, but only to stammer.

"It is nonsense," went on Gilles, ignoring him. "I do not believe that you could not get another couple of months' leave." He scowled at the young averted face and the splendid throat, rising out of the ugly cowl. "I have always felt for Charles the Fat, when he cursed the man that ever made Tutilo a monk. By the way, did you ever see the ivory he carved, the diptych at St. Gall?"

"I did not," said Pierre. O blessed Gilles, who always spoke of things, and not of sentiment. "But our Abbot told me of it. I think he would sell

196

his soul for it. He wants it copied — you know, the vine leaves and the deer — for a capital in the cloister at Cluny."

Gilles nodded. "There has been a good deal of coveting roused by that same diptych in its time. Did you ever hear how the Abbot Salomo tricked the Bishop of Mainz out of it, and got it for St. Gall? It is a good story, but they don't like to hear it at Mainz."

Pierre sat down with a contentęd sigh. To sit with Gilles was to sit with Time himself, to whom a thousand years were as yesterday. "Hearing you talk," he said suddenly and without embarrassment, "is the best thing I have got out of Paris."

Gilles looked at him with narrowed eyes. "Do not forget," he said, a little sternly, "that you heard Peter Abelard lecture on 'I said: ye are gods.' "

The young face did not redden: it went suddenly expressionless.

"I have not forgotten," he said quietly, but Gilles felt a curious hardness in the voice. Quick anger swept over him. He leaned forward, his hands gripping the arms of his chair, his huge frame half out of it, his jowl thrust into Pierre's face.

"And who," said he, "are you to condemn him?"

The movement was not calculated, but it served. The youngster shrank back, startled out of his frozen mask.

"I'm not condemning him." His voice was sharp with wretchedness. "But — but I worshiped him." He dropped his head on his hands.

Gilles sat back, his brief anger spent.

"I know," he said, "I know. It is hard to forgive one's god for becoming flesh."

Pierre de Montboissier raised his head. He was flushed with the tears he had kept back, but there was no fear of them now.

"It is not that," he said steadily. "St. Augustine himself — But it is what has happened to his mind. It is heavier, like his face now. And he does not care for any of us. He used now and then to stay and talk when the lecture was over. Hours he would talk, and we would never know we were hungry. You do not know what he was like. His lectures, they were like a great wind that leapt suddenly, and you went with it, the trees tearing and shaking. It was like galloping horses — " He stopped breathless. "And now — — "

"And now?"

"It is not fair of me to talk of him like this, but you — you know him utterly. He reads his lectures now, old lectures, and yawns reading them, and every now and then he looks at the hour-glass. None of us ever saw the sand run down. Most of us watch for it now. And they bet if he will stay the last grains of sand. He never gives the extra lecture — you know what they call the *Extra ordinem*. Sometimes it comes back; someone asks a question, and it is like a hawk, you know when the eyelid half closes and suddenly it slides back, and he blazes down at us. But it is oftener to strike than to soar. Even then, just to see him before he stoops —" Pierre's eyes were shining in his head. They suddenly clouded.

"But they are not afraid of him now. If you heard them snickering when he comes to the lecture at six, half awake, about . . . about . . ."

Gilles nodded.

"They've made a song about it," Pierre went on savagely, like one biting on a tooth.

> "Good argument
> Hath Peter in his head,
> But better argument
> Hath Peter —"

"I can supply the rhyme," said Gilles. There was silence between them.

"God knows," the boy went on, arguing with himself, "we are spirit and flesh. But to see the spirit becoming flesh before one's eyes. And *his* spirit."

Again Gilles nodded. "How old are you, Pierre?"

"Almost twenty-two."

"Abelard is thirty-seven. For the seven years of manhood that you have behind you, and the fifteen that are before you till you reach his age, this man never looked on a woman to lust after her." He was glowering at the young man's face, content to see it slowly redden. "He was proud enough and arrogant, but lavish — had he ever a penny? When other men gave the rind of the bacon, he gave all he had. And he would come in here to me famished, because he had forgotten to eat. He came to the age when a man's passion is fiercest, and he has begun to know how solitary his soul is, but still he was like a man walking in a dream, though I thought I saw signs of his waking. Then one day, in this room, he saw Heloise."

Pierre's head was bent, but the back of his neck, his very ears were crimson.

"God help the boy," thought Gilles, in sudden understanding. He waited a moment.

"He is not the only man," he went on quietly, "who would think her worth flinging the world away for, and heaven after it."

Pierre shivered. He did not look at Gilles, but at his twisting hands.

"They make songs," he managed to say at last, croaking, "about her too."

"And do you suppose," said Gilles with a sudden ring of triumph in his voice, "that she cares?"

Pierre looked at him, startled.

"How could she not?"

"You think," said Gilles slowly, "it is the dove and the hawk? I tell you, you have seen the mating of eagles. And yet," the ring of triumph left his voice, "I know, I know. Boy, do you think I am not myself afraid? Never have I seen such madness as this. And I wonder sometimes what the end will be."

The door opened abruptly.

"Will you see Master Alberic of Rheims," said Jehan, "for he came up the stairs after me?"

"Surely," said Gilles. He turned his face to the door. Pierre de Montboissier rose from his stool, and stood in the shadow beyond the chimney, watching a large and portly figure come through the door, and pace with dignity down the room.

"You are welcome, Alberic," said Gilles. "Man, even if I had not heard it, I would know from the very walk of you that they have made you Master of the Schools at Rheims."

"My walk?" said Alberic uncertainly, halting the procession.

"And why not? Should not the spirit be mirrored in the body? It is the sign of an ingenuous soul. How long have you been in Paris?"

"Since Palm Sunday," said Alberic. "And I must go tomorrow. But I could not take my leave without seeing our Nestor." Gilles bowed. "And I had warm greetings for you from the Archbishop."

"Rauol le Vert," said Gilles reminiscently. "But I suppose he is white enough now. Well, tell him from me, if you have not already done so, what a distinguished scholastic he has got. Bless my soul," he went on reflectively, "to think of you sitting in Gerbert's chair."

"I trust," said Alberic, "that the doctrine taught from it will be a little sounder."

"I am sure of it," said Gilles. "Safer, at any rate. No mathematics in it. The common people used to say that the devil made Gerbert a brazen head that answered all inconvenient questions for him. Much better to have it on one's own shoulders. Upon my word, Alberic, at this rate there will soon be an exodus from Paris to Rheims."

"You flatter me, Gilles," said Alberic. "Though indeed," he went on,

pouting his full lips, "if the lecture I heard a day or two ago is a speci-
men of the fare here, it is a stony pasture enough."

A figure stepped out of the shadow. "You were unfortunate, Master
Alberic," said Pierre courteously. "Whom did you hear?"

"The great Abelard himself," said Alberic. He chuckled. "A barren shallow wit. I always knew it. And would you believe it, the lecture I heard
on Monday, word for word, was a lecture I heard him give three years ago
at Laon, before Anselm silenced him."

Pierre de Montboissier made a step forward, but an almost imperceptible
movement of Gilles' hand halted him.

"A marvelous memory yours, Alberic," said Gilles blandly. "It may be —
nay, it must be — the secret of your high success. Yet it must have been
a rare lecture, for you to remember it after three years."

"My memory is indeed tolerably good," said Alberic. "But I have special reason to recall this one. It was the first he had the impudence to
give, and a few of us went to hear him and take note of his impertinences.
It was an unheard-of thing, for a young man, unlicensed, to lecture without permission, setting himself up in opposition to that good old man."

"I am glad to hear the rights of it," said Gilles smoothly. "I had always
understood that he was challenged to it."

"Challenged? Well, in a manner, yes," said Alberic. "He had had the
impudence to declare that a man needs no master in theology but Holy
Writ and the Fathers and his own intelligence."

"A very dangerous doctrine," said Gilles. "The half of us would find
our occupation gone. To whom did he say it? Not, I hope, to old Anselm,
may God rest his soul. He would have had apoplexy."

"It was not to Anselm direct," admitted Alberic. "But he had absented
himself from Anselm's lectures, and some of us observed it and rebuked
him for it."

"I am glad," said Gilles, "that he had so much grace. It is more than
he showed to William here. Poor William; it was a good day for him when
Abelard's seat was empty. But after all, William was forty-five and a fresh
man: it was fine exercise for him. Abelard has a kind of respect for age.
He is very civil to myself. And so you challenged the barren rascal?"

"We did."

"And he lectured, I suppose, to empty benches?"

"There are always lovers of novelty," said Alberic. "And he drew the
lighter sort, till Anselm silenced him."

"That was not like that good old man," said Gilles. "I never thought he looked beyond the first benches, and there, Alberic, he would see your earnest face. But I suppose you reported it to him?"

"We thought," said Alberic uncomfortably, "myself and Lotulf of Novara — —"

"I never liked Lombards," said Gilles absent-mindedly. "But I forget myself. So you chased him? And Paris got the leavings of Laon. What became of Lotulf?"

"He is with me," said Alberic. "I had the good fortune to be able to retain him as my coadjutor."

"They transplant well," said Gilles. "Like Jews. So you are still hunting in couples? Well, my friend Raoul is better off even than I thought. A pair of active hounds. And long may he be able to keep them in leash. Pierre, a cup of wine for Master Alberic. No, Alberic, I insist. It must be after Vespers, and anyhow you have travelers' grace."

Pierre moved to the dresser and came again, offering Master Alberic his cup with a faintly exaggerated courtesy.

"You are a student of Master Abelard," said Alberic, eying him with distaste.

Pierre bowed. "I have that good fortune."

Alberic looked him up and down.

"You are a monk of Cluny?"

"At Vézelay. I had leave from Cluny to hear Master Abelard for the winter."

"If Cluny had been what it was," said Alberic, "I doubt if you would have had it. But it has lifted up its soul to vanity and lies. When it knew the holy Hugh — —"

"It knows the greatest master in Christendom, anyhow," said Pierre. He was trembling.

"Well crowed, bantam," said Gilles. "Now, Alberic, do not have your countenance suffused. May not this one be loyal to his master, as you to the good Anselm?"

"Loyalty where loyalty is due," said Alberic. "But to a masterless man that climbed over the wall into the sheepfold, a wencher and a — —"

"Pierre!" thundered Gilles. The boy's arm had swung back for a resounding smack across the large, white face. It fell to his side, and he stood breathing hard and shivering like an over-ridden colt.

Alberic looked at him, his lips tight. "Perhaps you know," he said, "if they teach you any canon law at Cluny, that that would have meant excommunication?"

Gilles raised his hand. "That will do, Alberic. Pierre, go now, but come and see me tomorrow, before you start on your journey. I have a little present for your Abbot, an Art of Writing that came to me from Monte Cassino. It might interest you too, Alberic."

He lifted his hand in easy farewell to Pierre, as he talked. The young man made him a reverence, and without a look at Alberic, turned and walked across the room. The door latched behind him.

A whistle came from Alberic's pursed lips.

"I trust," said Gilles gravely, "you are grateful to me, Alberic. I feared for a few of those fine front teeth. Man, you would have gone down like a sack of oats."

"He would have paid with a good many stripes for it," said Alberic grimly. "And what midden was that cockerel reared on?"

"His father is the Sieur de Montboissier," said Gilles. Alberic's jaw dropped. "Doubtless it would have salved your hurt," Gilles went on blandly, "to know that you had suffered at so exalted a hand. And if I am not mistaken, you will some day be telling the story in your cups that you once threatened excommunication to the Abbot of Cluny."

"That one the Abbot of Cluny?"

"As soon, I think, as the abbacy is vacant and his years allow. But see here, Alberic, you called Peter Abelard what you meant for an ill name, though when the boy is older he will know how many of us deserve it. What did you mean?"

"If you do not know that, Gilles," said Alberic, "you are the only man in Paris that does not. Except, they tell me, the poor old sheep, her uncle. It met me in the change house at Meaux. And they were singing a bawdy song under my window last night. They tell me it was one of his own. I wonder, Gilles, that you can see the old man's innocence so grossly abused. I tried to hint something of it to him myself today."

"You are sure," said Gilles smoothly, "that you would not prefer to hint something of it to the culprit? For I am expecting him, after Vespers. If a brother be overtaken in a fault, restore such an one in the spirit of meekness. Or would you rather wait for the support of your friend Lupus of Novara?"

"Lotulf," said Alberic mechanically. He had risen, but already a swift foot was coming up the stair. The arras flew back, and Abelard was in the room, filling it with a curious vibration. With the wind that swept from the door, a flame leapt on the crumbling log, and danced on the three faces.

Gilles glanced from one to the other. "God, what a bladder of lard," he thought. "And what a firebrand."

Abelard had gazed for a moment blankly at the stranger. Then his face lit up with impish friendliness.

"Old Alberic!" said he, and reached out a hand to the doctor's hood that hung from Alberic's shoulders. "Well done, man. Rheims has got a good mastiff. And how is the terrier?"

"You speak in riddles, Master Abelard," said Alberic.

"You know him, the little sharp-nosed friend, with pink eyes, like a ferret. He used to find the scent and you gave tongue. And mind you, Gilles, our Alberic has a good bell-mouthed bay. It is the great deep chest he has. But you're putting on flesh, Alberic. And so, they tell me, am I."

Alberic moistened his lips. "If you will excuse me, Gilles," he said formally, "I shall take my leave. I am to sup with the Bishop tonight. I may take your greetings to the Archbishop? Master Abelard, your servant."

Abelard swept his doctor's cap to the knee. The procession formed, and moved out.

"Some men are born to be bishops," said Abelard. "That one walks under his miter already. But what a hill of suet!"

Gilles was wiping his hands on the skin that lay over his knees.

"You were spared that at least," he said. "If godliness makes a man's face to shine, I wish it did not also make his hands to sweat."

Abelard did not answer. He stood leaning against the chimney, just as Pierre had stood, his foot tapping on the floor. The mischief had gone from his eyes, and left them dark and smoldering. "Lucifer," thought Gilles, "but not the Light-bringer tonight. The Prince of Darkness."

"What about a drink, Peter?" he said at last. "Or had you better eat first, if you have been fasting?"

Abelard looked up. "I have been fasting, sure enough," he said, an odd undercurrent of bitterness in his voice. He crossed to the dresser, splashed out a cupful, and drank it at a gulp.

"That's better," he said, and came back to the fire. He was humming under his breath the tune that was over all Paris.

> "Set now your arms on mine,
> Take we our pleasure,
> O flower of all the world — "

"Stop that," said Gilles.

Abelard smiled at him affectionately. "What do you suppose, Gilles," said he, "was the idea of fasting? To keep down the body and bring it into subjection? Or to put an edge on every sense one has? For it seems to me that whatever the body lacks in vigor, the mind makes up for. And I begin to understand the rich temptations of the Desert Fathers. Lord, what an orgy of the mind they had!"

"See here, Peter," said Gilles, "you had better go home, eat the heaviest meal you can put into you, read for a couple of hours, and go to your bed. For you are in the devil's own mood this night."

"Perhaps I am," said Abelard. He sat down by the fire again, shuddering a little. "Perhaps I am." He sat silent, brooding upon the fire. After a long time, he began to speak.

"I saw one man tonight," he said, "that had been fasting long enough. I was coming out from Vespers. He was kneeling below the Crucifix, at the foot of the stairs to the rood-loft; and just as I was passing him, he crumpled up. I hauled him out to Grosse Margot's and got a glass of wine into him before he knew, and when he came to, he could have spat it at me. Poor soul, I had broken a ten days' fast on him. An Irishman, one of Malachy's men from Armagh."

Gilles sat silent. Better let him talk himself out.

"He was half delirious at first, muttering the same words over and over to himself. I could not make out the sense, but it was a good meter. And when I had comforted him a while, and told him that where the mind had not consented the body still kept its integrity, as with the holy virgins that by force lost their virginity — you are squeamish tonight, Gilles? — he got friendly enough. And I asked him what the meter was, and the words. So he translated me the Irish. It was a prayer, but he said if he had been rightly himself, he should not have been praying it till Good Friday."

Abelard had risen and had gone across the room to the far window, faintly luminous now with the rising moon. He stood, looking out, his head resting against the central mullion, his arms stretched along the crossbeams. The long, black sleeves falling from either arm drooped like great wings. "God have mercy," said Gilles to himself, "it's a crucified Apollyon."

He turned back to the room, still leaning against the central bar, but his arms by his side.

"Do you not want to hear it, Gilles?"

"Well?" It was all Gilles could do not to shout at him.

The arms went out again, the face bent forward, the eyes gleaming out of the white devil's mask of the face.

> "May some fruit from the Tree of Thy Passion
> Fall on us this night."

Gilles crossed himself. After a while he spoke.

"Go home, Abelard," he said, as if he spoke to a child. "You are not yourself. And for God's sake, eat your supper and go to bed."

"I'll go to bed," said Abelard lightly. "I promise you that. I'll go to bed. There, Gilles," the mockery had slipped from his voice, "don't fret. Man, you'd think I had been saying a Black Mass instead of a poor Irishman's litany. I'll eat my supper, and read a while, and go to bed. Shall I send Jehan up to you?"

"He will be here with my supper shortly," said Gilles. "Will you stay and have it with me, Peter?"

Abelard shook his head. The faint smoldering came back to his eyes.

"I have fasted long enough," he said. "I'll be getting home. Good-night, Gilles. Sleep." He was gone.

Gilles sat sunk in his chair. *"They say that Paradise and Calvary, Christ's cross and Adam's tree, stood in one place,"* he muttered to himself. Slowly he got out of his chair, and crossed to where his stool was set below the crucifix, lowering himself painfully upon his gouty knees.

O Lamb of God that takest away the sin of the world: have mercy upon us.

O Lamb of God that takest away the sin of the world: have mercy upon us.

O Lamb of God that takest away the sin of the world: receive our prayer.

Jehan, coming in with his dish of trout, stood gazing at a sight he had not seen for fifteen years.

The Tournament at Belleperche

by Jay Williams

> 1209   The three young men met at the tournament
> held by the Baron Gaston of Belleperche in honor of
> his wedding. All three were poor and ambitious; but
> Amauric was set apart by the fervor of his devotion
> to the ideals of chivalry, ideals which most knights
> believed they could not afford to take too seriously.

A space of ground, roughly oval and some fifty yards long, had
been enclosed with a palisade of wood. On one side of it a platform had
been erected, shaded with an awning; here on chairs and benches sat
Gaston with his guests, ladies, squires, pages, and those men who, for one
reason or another, were taking no part in the tournament. All about the
lists a trench had been dug and beyond this, on the hill slope, sat the
country people eating bread and garlic and drinking common wine from
leather skins. At each end of the lists, outside the barrier, were the pa-
vilions of the two leaders, on the northern end the challengers under
Guillaume, and to the south the defenders under Peire. Before each leader's tent hung his shield, Peire's bearing a silver leopard ramping, and
Guillaume's three red martlets. Under each shield stood a king at arms
with the rolls, on which he pricked the names of those knights who chose
to enlist with one or the other commander. A little to one side was a booth
of armorers, and in it a pile of rebated swords, their points and edges
rounded off, for this was no passage of arms to the death but a tourney
of peace for the sake of sport.

Joscelin had gone with his friends to Baron Guillaume's tent, where
they all three entered their names. The baron in glittering mail — it had
been rolled in a barrel of sand to clean the rust from it — and under it an
old-fashioned short tunic which reached to his knees, stood before the
tent with his mail hood thrown back on his shoulders, and greeted the three
as they bowed to him.

"You will ride in the van," he said, "upon the right. I give you this place
of honor for your youth's sake." For a second, his eyes met Joscelin's;
then he looked away. "And also for your merit. Well, a pleasant morning, sirs. Which of you is to win the Lady Alix?"

All three colored and knew not where to look. "The truth is, my lord,"

Guy said, at last, "we fear that with her Gaston will give some trick like that of the goblet, or that eagle that turns its head."

Guillaume looked grave. "Your tongue is overbold, young man," said he. "I can forgive it, for youth forgets sometimes its due to courtesy; I will not chide with you. So, God be with you. We will begin very soon."

They passed on and stood in the shade of the armorers' tent. Guy said, "Ouf! I felt the rake of his spur, then. But I was not so far out, by heaven, Gaston would as willingly laugh at you as save his soul."

"It may be so," said Amauric, "but think, Guy, is it wise to speak so of our host to his bride's uncle? Guillaume said only what he must."

"Yes, yes, you are too pure for me," Guy said impatiently. "I cannot be watching of my speech every instant of the day. Why don't we begin? They wait overlong for the laggards."

His voice was unsteady, and Joscelin looked more closely at him. He was astonished to see that Guy was nervous, that his face was pale and his forehead glistening damp. He himself was as tight-drawn as a bowstring, the palms of his hands wet, his body streaming with cold perspiration, his jaws aching from clenching his teeth. But it was always so with him before any action, and he was used to it; only, he had always thought himself alone in this, for he had never before had close friends. He could not stop the trembling in his knees, and wanted constantly to urinate. It was not fear, but the nervousness of anticipation. He looked at Amauric. The fair young man appeared utterly tranquil. He had not yet tied on his arming-cap, and his long hair stirred in the little breeze and tangled in the rings of his camail; he had his thumbs hooked in his belt and stood with his weight settled on one foot, watching the coming and going of men.

"What are you thinking of, Amauric?" Joscelin asked.

"Last night," said Amauric, "a dream of the night came and stood beside me in the likeness of — of a maiden. She was dressed all in cloth of gold, and she held out a sword to me hilt foremost, and at the same time I thought some manner of great bird, all fiery, flew right across the sky and screamed out, 'So fares it with Amauric as this sword shapes.'"

"Oh, a lucky dream," Guy said. "By heaven, a good omen. I will keep well behind you in the mellay." He clapped his hands and rubbed them together as if it had been winter. "Why do they wait?" he said.

Joscelin asked Amauric, "Have you no fear of wounds or death?"

Amauric, without moving, replied, "I am afraid of showing fear."

"Why, so is every man afraid," Guy said, too loudly. "And before a tourney, of seeming a fool, or awkward, or of doing some stupid thing:

of being, like that unlucky knight of Castres last year, carried away by
his horse that at the onset bolted and tried to leap the barrier and so cast
the poor fool into the ditch, where he broke his neck."

"No," said Amauric. "I mean otherwise, for as the dear Virgin sees
me I do not care if I do well or ill, so long as I do not disgrace my
knightly oath."

"By my hand," said Joscelin, "I think I never saw anyone more watchful of his honor than you." He waved away the midges that swam in the
air before them. "It is a part of your lineage to show this pride, I think."

At this, Amauric moved; he was visibly shaken. He came suddenly to
Joscelin and put both hands on his shoulders. His eyes were dark with
trouble, and he bit at his lower lip. He said, "Alas, Joscelin, do not say
that. For if it is only pride you see in me, I am not fit to wear a sword.
Don't speak of my lineage, it is nothing. Nor my honor. I swear to you,
I do not think of that. Only, for me, knighthood is a sacred thing, given
solemnly, consecrated with God's holy blood and with his holy Vessel,
a thing hard won by ordeal. Surely, you must feel that? God forbid, I
should hold it so cheap as to feel pride in myself or my own honor — — "

Joscelin knit his brows, gripping Amauric by the wrists. "I have never
met a man like you," he said, shaking his head. "You are right. And yet — — "

Guy, rocking from toes to heels with his hands clasped behind his back,
said, "You should understand him, for you are a pair, the two of you, as
any couple of hounds. When I first met you yesterday, remember, I heard
much the same sort of words from you."

Joscelin flushed. He alone knew that his talk was a pose, part of a disguise that he put on as he might a surcoat, to pass among knights as one
of them; he could not begin to feel the awful sense of dedication that
so evidently moved in Amauric, and by that very lack felt himself les-
sened and almost a liar.

He put Amauric's hands off his shoulders, and said roughly, to Guy,
"That is pure clack, and you are a fool."

Guy shrugged. "It is as well we are friends," he replied. "I have leaped
out my bodkin for less."

Upon that, as if it were to put a period to the words, the trumpets
brayed out on either side of the lists and Guillaume of Sabarat, standing before his tent, shouted in a voice of brass, "Mount, sirs!"

Joscelin pulled his coif up over his cap and laced it tight around his
face. He had no helmet, nor did Guy, but Amauric had a flat-topped helm,
closed all around and with slits for his eyes. They all three took swords

from the booth and went to their horses. As Joscelin swung himself into the high saddle all his tenseness dropped away; he settled the heavy, snug mesh of his mail over his knees and shrugged his shoulders against its weight, feeling in each small, accustomed act the gathering within his arms and chest and belly of power and readiness. He slung his shield strap about his neck and dressed his shield on his left arm. Quickly he checked over his gear: all his leather was old and rather worn, his shield grips were frayed, and the cinch strap of his saddle worried him. Experimentally he swung the rebated sword. Its blade was a trifle shorter than his own, owing to the point having been ground off, but it was no toy; in experienced hands it could deal almost as serious a wound as a mace. He took up the reins, patted his horse's neck, and joined Guy and Amauric at Guillaume's tent.

Raimon of Miraval, mounted on a vast black horse, greeted them with a shout. Hot as he normally was, within his gambeson and mail coat he was still hotter, and great pearls of sweat hung on his face and streamed down his cheeks. For this reason, he went bareheaded, "For," as he explained, "if I could not wipe my eyes, my own sweat were like to be my death." He glanced at the clear, bright blue sky, sniffed the air like a dog, and said, "A fine day, sirs, but better fitted to a battle than this play. It has ever been my experience that wars are fought in the worst weather, in rain or sleet, or on days of such heat that the very birds lie panting in the bushes."

Baron Guillaume, erect in the saddle, viewed his followers. There were eighteen knights about him, the greater part of them, in spite of all his and Gaston's care, men of his own region, vassals of Foix. There were the castellans of Rancie and of Ercé, the sieur of Castelet, two or three vavasours of Sabarat, and the old lord of Oust, Bertrand, called the Lion, gray and stern and sour of appearance. Guillaume smiled as he looked at them, and, "Gentlemen," he said, "good morrow and good fortune. I pray you, if you will, since my niece has done me the honor to give me her ensign, use with your own war cries that of 'Capedan,' which I shall myself take for this day."

Raimon, twirling his sword like a juggler, said, "My friend, there is no one here so churlish as to refuse you. If there should be one — — "

"Put by this chatter," growled Bertrand of Oust. "We will be hungry for our dinners before ever we begin the sport."

"Ah, Bertrand, you were ever a boor," Raimon laughed.

"Very well," said Guillaume. "Let us enter the lists, sirs, if it pleases you."

In a single line they rode through the gate, while from the opposite side rode Peire and his following, the sun gleaming redly on their armor, their swords sloping over their shoulders. The two commanders came to the center and saluted Gaston, who waved to them with a smile. Beside him, Elizabeth of Capedan clapped her hands, her lips parted and her cheeks glowing. Alix, on his other side, rested her chin on her hand and watched under lowered lids.

"Ha! there is no better sight, by the Trinity," cried Gaston, "than to see brave men come joyously to the tourney. On my soul, I wish that I were with you. Well, to your places, and God help you both to do your best endeavor."

The country people stood up all along the hill, the better to see. The marshals of the lists took their stations within the enclosure to mark how each knight bore himself, and to keep the rules. The two troops ranged opposite each other and Gaston signaled, whereat a trumpet sounded the onset, and one of the marshals, holding up his baton, cried in a loud voice, "Let them go!" The two double lines of knights moved slowly and ponderously towards the center at a trot; when they met there was a nearly simultaneous clash of sword upon shield.

At that first encounter, the press was so great that for a space the rear ranks had nothing to do but sit their mounts, as the men in the first line exchanged sword strokes. Joscelin was on the extreme wing, knee to knee with Amauric, on whose other side was Guy. A young squire of Peire's company swung his sword at Joscelin, who warded the blow with ease and in his turn struck at the youth's head. Before they could go further into the matter the pressure of the crowd behind pushed them apart, and separated Joscelin from his friends. He exchanged three or four cuts with a man whose armor had been painted black; one of his blows knocked loose a nail from Joscelin's shield, and once Joscelin got in over his guard and hit him on the shoulder, and then they were carried in opposite directions by the mellay.

There were by now two or three men unhorsed and half a dozen badly hurt. Some were dragged free by their squires, and others managed to make their way to the barrier to be helped out of the lists by the heralds. All semblance of lines had vanished and the knights fought man against man, the whole mass pivoting around a rough center, turning like a millpond and throwing up gleams of armor within a cloud of reddish dust, as it had been sparkles from sluggish water. Arms rose and fell, helmets bobbed on the current, and here and there a veil fluttered, some favor from a lady. Gaston had had a largesse distributed to the villeins and they all shouted, "Noël! Noël!" applauding and cheering. Yet over all noises rose the crashing and clangor of steel, the shrill neighing of steeds, and the hoarse war cries.

The castellan of Ercé had engaged Peire of Gardefis, but the younger knight, expert at tourneys, so managed his horse as to bring himself in close upon the other's right hand and with a blow under the arm drove the wind out of Ercé so that he lolled helpless in the saddle. Nearby, the old lord of Oust fended off the attack of a knight of Villefranche; with the flat of his blade he sent his assailant headlong and then himself dismounted to drag the unconscious man clear of trampling hoofs. In the very center of the mellay, Raimon of Miraval, singing lustily one of his own *sirventescs*, "My heart is cast down at the wickedness of the world," lay about him like a madman, swinging his sword with both hands, his shield on his back and drops of water flying from his bare head.

Guillaume of Sabarat overthrew the lord of Bazière, and then, encountering the powerful and renowned young Bastard of le Vernet, beat his helmet from his head, breaking its thongs, and with a terrible back-slash disarmed the man and broke his wrist. In another quarter, the castellan of Rancie was overthrown by Peire's squire, Raoul of Carbonne, who in turn was wounded by his own cousin Roger of Castelflor, who had enlisted under Guillaume.

Joscelin having passed through the opposing ranks, spurred away from the barrier towards which he had been forced. All at once, he saw at a little distance the familiar face for which he had been searching, that of the dark-browed knight of Calzac who had insulted him at dinner. Only an instant he hesitated, to be certain of his quarry, then he urged his mount forward. The knight of Calzac was occupied with another man and, tugging at the reins, was attempting to turn his horse's head when Joscelin reached him. Calzac's opponent was one of Guillaume's squires, and Joscelin shouted to him, "Go! leave this man to me; find you another."

Calzac, without waiting, slashed at Joscelin's face. Only just in time, Joscelin parried the blow with his shield, and with a deadly smile forced his horse on so that his stirrup clashed against that of the other. Dropping the edge of his shield, he struck over it, not once but three or four times, handling the heavy blade as if it were a switch, and so beat down Calzac's shield and gave him no time for recovery. Then he stood up in the stirrups and aimed a blow straight at Calzac's head. Even as he struck, there darted through his mind the thought of lawsuits and blood-gild, and a hundred complications that might ensue if he killed the man; he turned his wrist and the flat of his blade smashed against the side of the man's camail. Calzac's arms went out and he swayed backwards; his body turned, and blood spattered from his nostrils; he toppled forward and sideways against Joscelin's knee and hung head down from the saddle.

Almost in the same moment, Joscelin was attacked by two men, one of them the knight from the Garonne Valley, the other a man with a yellow silk scarf wound round his helmet. They both came at him from the right and he was hard put to it to defend himself, for his horse pressed back against that of Calzac, which stood still with its master limply bent over. So close on him were his assailants that Joscelin could not get his mount's head round. A blow caught him on the upper arm making him drop his sword, he was hit on the thigh, and then, as he leaned his weight away from them, the old leather of his saddle girth parted and he was pitched over. He caught at the other horse as he fell, and was able to pull his right foot from the stirrup. His back was against the body of Calzac. He had an instant of panic, hanging between his horse and the senseless man, clutching Calzac's saddle, thinking that if he could not free his left foot he would be dragged. Then he shook the stirrup loose and slipped, panting, to the ground with his steed between the two men and himself.

They loomed over him, and weaponless he raised his shield to cover his head. Dust choked him, and the rank smell of the horses was overpowering. Behind him, Calzac's horse moved away. He waited stolidly, trying to wipe his eyes.

Someone shouted incoherently. There was a loud clang and the hollow thump of a shield being struck. Peering under his guard, he saw his two foes engaged, one on either side, with Guy and Amauric.

He had forgotten his friends in the flurry of the combat, and he felt hot shame that they had not forgotten him. With that realization, he stooped beneath the neck of his horse and ran towards them. He had been self-possessed before; he was not so now. As if it had been grim war instead of a mock battle, he gave himself up to rage, no longer marking anything clearly, no longer fully conscious of what he did.

Guy and the man with the yellow scarf were circling each other, shield to shield. Joscelin sprang behind the helmeted man and snatched his belt from the left side; with all his strength he plucked the man bodily from the saddle. The helmet rang against the ground, the yellow scarf blew away. Pausing only long enough to seize the fallen man's sword, Joscelin swung himself into the saddle.

He saw Guy's mouth open but no sound reached him. He saw a white shield bearing a red griffon, and the blur of a blade. Even as he caught it on his own sword, he realized that he had lost his shield. Everything was going very fast. He was aware of Guy close beside him, his mail hood loose and open, his face blazing like his hair. There were men all round him and he struck again and again, never troubling to guard himself.

Their group had become the focus of the battle, as first one man, then another came to the rescue of friends on either side. Joscelin hacked down a man on foot who strove to reach him. He heard a confused yelling. He had a glimpse of Raimon of Miraval with blood spotting his yellow surcoat, working like a man chopping wood, his mouth wide in a laugh.

He paused and drew breath. Guy reined in alongside him and put his mailed hand on Joscelin's knee. Amauric drew up on his other side. Without being able to hear each other over the rattle of arms, with no more than a nod and a gesture, they communicated, and understood each other at once; all three abreast clapped spurs to their horses and galloped at a knot of men headed by Peire of Gardefis, which was readying for a charge.

Joscelin saw a tangle of figures, of light surcoats and dark mail emerging from the dust. Then he was among them. A horse crashed down, kicking and whinnying with terror. Amauric was shouting something indistinct, and Guy was standing in the stirrups snarling like a wild beast. Before the three, the half-formed group of Peire's men burst apart and scattered, leaving several fallen. One crawled away on hands and knees; another scrambled up and limped to the barrier leaning on his sword.

Joscelin perceived dimly through the veil of his wild frenzy that he was facing Peire, whom he recognized by the silver leopard painted on his black shield, for the other man's features were concealed by a closed helm. Straight at that leopard he drove his sword, and gashed away the paint so that the brown oxhide showed beneath. Peire's own sword licked out at his unprotected left arm, but Joscelin was unaware of pain. He kicked his mount still closer in, and with a great, wide-armed swing struck with all his force against Peire's shield. The stout wood cracked in two, the steel bands that reinforced the shield flew apart from the rivets, and the top half split off and dangled by the leather face. Joscelin could hear the man grunt with pain. At the same time, Amauric rode in close from the left. Peire's horse reared up, its forefeet lashing, and the knight, dropping his sword, seized the reins to keep from being unhorsed. His left arm hung useless. Joscelin caught the bit and held the steed, while Amauric touched the rounded tip of his sword to Peire's breast.

Joscelin was breathless. But Amauric gasped, "Yield yourself, sir."

They could not see his face, only the glint of eye-whites behind the slits of his helmet. The smooth, impassive steel regarded them and it was impossible to know where the man was looking.

"I yield," he said at last, in a muffled voice. "To you." He pointed to Amauric.

Amauric turned to Joscelin. His face, too, was concealed by his helm, and Joscelin could not tell friend from foe: they were like two figures in a dream, anonymous and inhuman.

Amauric said, "I cannot accept this surrender. It was for Joscelin I asked."

Joscelin shrugged. "For God's sake, have done with knight-errantry," he said hoarsely. "Take him. I'll none of it."

His limbs were shaking, as much from fatigue as anger. At that moment, tourney or no, surrender or no, he would willingly have slain Peire. He gripped the high saddlebow to steady himself.

The marshal had cast down his baton, indicating the finish of the tournament, and the gates at either end of the lists had been reopened. Towards that one over which hung the three martlets of Guillaume of Sabarat, Joscelin slowly walked his horse.

The sun was still high when they gathered once more in the great hall to dine, and the various smokes and steams and savors curled pale in the shafts of light, high up under the beams and vaultings of the ceiling and among the shields and banners that hung on the patterned walls. They were a gay company in spite of bruises and bandages, and as Guy had predicted there were fewer of them, which made the rest more joyous. There was many a knight who wore no cap but a cloth about his head over a lump, and many another who relied on his neighbor to cut his meat for him. Before they began to eat, when the first course of eels and puff pastes, omelets and snails, was set on the board, Gaston stood up and a herald cried, "Listen, barons, knights, squires, and noble dames, I pray you listen!"

With his hands tucked in his belt, the wide sleeves of his green broadcloth blouse thrown back, and a little cap of orfroi covering his thin, sandy hair, Gaston looked a most princely host. His eyes twinkled as he surveyed, with satisfaction, the array of his guests and his household before him, and he laughed his rich and comfortable laugh.

"Hard is it," he said, "to choose but two among so many who acquitted themselves so gallantly. Therefore, I say, I will give to Guillaume of Sabarat and to my kinsman Peire a purse of fifty livres which they may distribute as they will among their followers."

There was much applause at this and Guy said in Joscelin's ear, "Heaven be thanked. It may be I will at last have two coins to knock together and so din down my creditors."

Gaston went on, "Well indeed did all bear themselves. Yet, from what the marshals and heralds have told me, and what my own eyes beheld, I have determined that the golden cup shall be given to Raimon of Miraval, nor will any man quarrel with me, for a more courteous warrior I never yet beheld."

He took from a squire a goblet of Florentine work, a great shell of blue and green glass held by golden bands on which were carved all manner of birds and foliage amazing to see, standing on three golden feet like stag's hoofs. This he passed to Raimon, who held it at once to be filled by his joglar Bayona. This Bayona was a spare, lean man with a seamed face; two deep furrows ran from his nostrils to the corners of his mouth, other furrows ran outwards from the corners of his eyes and struck upwards from between his eyebrows, and in all ways he appeared grim and silent. Yet he had a voice that would move stones, a deep voice like that of some ancient, mellow organ, or like the hum of honeybees, a voice at once capable of stirring up sadness in men's souls or of ringing out like a battle horn, and no small part of Raimon's fame was owed to Bayona's singing of his songs. He served, too, as Raimon's squire, although he wore no weapon of any sort nor ever was seen on any field of war. As he poured out wine into the goblet, he said, "Better were it for my master to win guerdons for his songs than for hacking of helmets."

Raimon smiled and pledged his host, drinking the cupful off as if it were no more than a drop.

Gaston said, "Of young bachelors we saw many a one do good feats of arms. Most excellently, however, did Amauric of Montjoie bear himself, and much honor did he win. And since it was he who received the surrender of Peire, we give him the prize."

Heads turned, and some stood up to stare. Amauric himself sat like a stricken man, his face pale and his eyes blank.

"Come hither," Gaston called. "Come up to the salt. Alix, my dear," he added, beckoning to his daughter, "go, fetch your young knight here and make him welcome by your side."

Alix rose up. Without a word, with her eyes downcast, she walked slowly the length of the table and came to Amauric's seat. As he still remained motionless, Joscelin took him by the arm and said roughly, "Rouse yourself. Do not leave the lady to stand waiting for you."

Amauric held the edge of the table and pushed himself upright. It was not surprise alone that made him clumsy. The truth was simpler: Alix was the maiden who had appeared to him in his dream. Wherever he went, Amauric saw portents and omens; he lived, indeed, in a mysterious world and in every happening he saw not chance but the working of a huge and strange design. When, coming first to Belleperche, he had been greeted by Alix as Joscelin was, he had seen at once in her the living image of that Goddess he worshiped more fervently than anyone suspected. She was, for him, Chivalry Herself, the pure Virgin to whom Amauric had dedicated his arms and to whom, like all knights who were members of the Society of the Grail, he had made his vows. Her image stood in the chapel at Montjoie, with just such round cheeks and long straight nose, and braided hair the gilt of which had faded to just the color of Alix's, and he saw her come alive before him, her bosom rising and falling, the faint marbling of blue veins under the skin of her arms carrying the surge of life. In Her name, the knights of his society swore never to harm the weak and defenseless, and to keep themselves virgin; in Her name they took oath to redress wrongs and show courtesy to womankind, for who better than the Virgin could understand such a need and command it in a world full of wickedness? In their secret ceremonies, it was She who bore before the head of the order the mystic Cup containing the wine of their communion. She had predicted victory to him in a dream, and now, knowing that She had chosen him to be pre-eminent among all the knights who rode in the tourney, Amauric's knees turned to water, his brain swam, and his heart hammered within him.

He took Alix's fingers in his own, and if his were burning, hers were cold and lifeless.

Joscelin watched them, half turned in his seat, and in him two emotions struggled, a deep affection in and pride for his friend, and as well, a kind of bitterness that verged upon hatred. There was no envy in it, nor could he tell why, watching Amauric's slender and graceful figure as he led the girl back to the dais, he should have had all at once and for no longer than the fraction of an instant the image of himself striking that blow at the knight of Calzac that all but killed him— only the face of the knight, in his mind, was the face of Amauric.

His imagination recoiled, and he put the thought out of his mind with horror. He discovered that Guy was speaking to him.

"What?" he said.

"Fortune smiles on those who deserve it most," Guy repeated, with a twisted smile. "I am glad, at least, that it was Amauric."

And Joscelin realized with a shock that exactly the same feelings were in Guy's heart as in his own.

The Pilgrim

by Zoe Oldenbourg

> 1211   Ansiau was old, with one son dead in Palestine and the other openly countermanding his wishes in his own barony of Linnières. And now he was going blind. Scorning a life that was only humiliation, the once mighty warrior became a pilgrim and set forth alone and on foot. He was dependent on the aid of a beggar boy, Auberi.

The Body's Darkness

That day the old man was awakened by the singing of birds and he thought himself in Linnières forest, fording the river very early in the morning on the track of a big boar, and he was astonished to see the spoor so clear in the riverside mud. "I still see clearly, after all," he thought. And the birds outdid each other in singing — *pia-pia-pia-pia, quic-quivic-quic, fiu-fiu-fiu* — *quic-quivic* — it was unending, and then he stretched and opened his good eye.

And it was still dark.

At first he thought that all the birds had gone mad and that this might be a bad sign, something dreadful was going to happen in the country. But the darkness was so black, not a streak of light anywhere on the horizon, not even a star; and the grass was drenched with dew. Suddenly he was terribly afraid, like a little child, and cried out: "Lady, lady, sister," and his own voice, weak and foolish, seemed strange to him and he was ashamed of it.

Then he remembered; the previous evening he had lain down in the grass on the slope of a hill with Auberi; they had been on the move, he was weary, he had a headache — now, at least, his headache was gone. But he could see nothing — not even red blurs or golden arrows. He rubbed his eye. He might as well have rubbed his nose. Nothing. He called: "Auberi."

He could hear the child yawning gently and stretching, his voice was drowned in sleep.

"My lord?"

"Do you think it is late, Auberi?"

"We've certainly slept well," the child said. "The sun is already fully up behind the hill opposite: the trees on the ridge are all golden, the light comes through all combed."

"Auberi, turn me towards the sun."

"But you're facing it," the child said, surprised. And the old man raised his hand before him as if he were trying to touch the sun.

"Auberi, my son, I can see nothing, I don't know what it is, it has never happened to me before. Perhaps it will go off; it's being so tired."

The child took him by the shoulders and looked hard into the wide-open eyes.

"Look — look hard," he said; the old man's fear was infecting him. "But you must be able to see! Your eye is the same as before! No!" he cried, "no! no! You are frightening me. You can see, say you can see!" His voice became whimpering, and still the old man said nothing. He took Auberi's head in his hands and passed his fingers over his face. The child burst into sobs and pushed him away.

"I don't want you to! Don't touch me like that! Don't be like that!"

The old man lay face downwards on the ground, his head on his arms. He, too, was sobbing, great, dry, barking sobs, and his shoulders shook, and it was so painful to hear him that Auberi began to tug at him and put his arms about the old man's neck.

"Don't cry like that. Come, look, it will go away. Come now, we'll go and pray to Our Lady and it's sure to go away."

"Auberi," the old man said, "leave me alone, go away, go back to your home. I want to die."

Auberi clung to him, wailing like a baby. "No, don't die! You must not! I don't want to be left alone!"

An hour later the man raised himself on his elbow, sat up, felt for his bag and his cudgel. Auberi watched him with his mouth open, unable to get used to the uncertain movements of a blind man.

"Auberi, where are you? We will leave here."

"Yes, my lord."

The old man rose with difficulty, took a step forward, leaning on his stick, and stretched out his arm — he thought he could feel holes beneath his feet and he dared not go forward — the earth seemed to crumble and shift in all directions.

"Auberi, give me your arm. Auberi, tell me, what are your eyes like?"

"Grey, I think, my lord. Or yellow."

As they were passing beneath a tree a branch wet with dew touched the old man's face and he started violently, then slowly wiped the dew from his forehead.

They went down towards the valley and every step was a plunge into the abyss.

"Auberi," the old man said, "is the sun up?"

"Yes, my lord, it is just above the mountain. It already hurts the eyes."

"Hurts the eyes," said the old man. "Look well, Auberi, look well. It is so beautiful! . . ."

He had to learn to walk straight and to cut his bread and to drink from a bowl without spilling it over the side — it was not as he had sometimes done it before, at night time — now the certainty of not seeing made all his motions so clumsy that he did everything wrong; seated at some peasant's table, he felt endlessly about to find a bit of bread which was right under his nose and his hand went all round it but could not seize it; if Auberi gave it to him he became angry, because he wanted to learn to find everything for himself.

Yet he had thought that since his sight was so bad he would not lose much if he went blind! Ah! what would he not have given for one bit of grey sky, seen through a half-open door, at evening; to see the moon shiver in a drinking-trough, even to see the sun as a red blur through closed eyelids; but no, nothing, he was like a beast which has never had eyes, just a head of wood with a hole in it to swallow bread.

No matter which way I turn there will be no more sun for me. No matter the hour of my awakening, there will be no more day. All roads will be the same, I shall seen none new; all men will be faceless, I shall see none new.

Friend, friend, you will not see me again. Neither living nor dead.

There was once an old man so blind that he mistook the skin of a kid for the hand of the son he loved and blessed in his stead the son he did not love, and the son became strong, and fathered the twelve patriarchs, for it was not given to the beloved son to be blessed. But my beloved son has long been dust and earth and no longer has eyes, ears nor voice; and it is the one I do not love who will possess all — children and name and land. And it is for that reason I must go out blind on to the roads, to find the child again who has lost eyes of flesh and heart of flesh. Such is God's will.

Ah! may he who has stolen blessing and heritage live in peace and increase and multiply, since it is God who has willed it. I know well that the will of God is not the will of men.

And on the Wednesday following Quasimodo they came to a large township where there was a church dedicated to Saint Peter; since Saint Peter was the patron of Troyes and Ansiau had often prayed to him, he went and knelt before the church porch and asked Auberi to guide his hands to touch the image of Saint Peter carved in the door. He raised his hands and clasped them on Saint Peter's foot and leaned his forehead against the column on which the saint stood. There he stayed, talking to Saint Peter as he would have talked to an uncle or a godfather.

"I have always loved and honored you. In my prayers I have never forgotten your name. In the time of my youth, after each tournament, I made offering to you of a candle. Now I can no longer give you anything. I cannot even see your face, for I am blind. I have nothing to ask of you unless it be the health of my lady and my children. I shall love you faithfully even though I have nothing to ask for myself, better even than before, now that I have need of nothing. With my sad heart I am very happy to find you again, father and friend. There, in your Paradise, before the Mighty King, think of me, a poor pilgrim. In your great church in Troyes remember me sometimes, during the mass. O best of all men, no one loved God as much as you did at the time when He was on earth, and how dearly must we love you, for none has ever been able or will be able to love as you loved. If only I had a small part of your great love for Him, I should surely have the strength to bear all without complaint, father and lord."

The sun beat directly down upon the old man's uncovered head. He was so still that the pigeons which fluttered about the porch began to settle upon his legs and shoulders. And the longer he stayed there, pressed against the column, his hands grasping Saint Peter's foot, the more he desired to remain there forever; he did not feel the blood withdraw from his numbed arms and since he could see nothing he felt his body grow vast and rise and grow in all ways. The column was like an enormous cathedral pillar and Saint Peter's statue a great tower reaching towards the clouds and the door of the church raised itself higher than mountains and dominated the whole country; if he took but a single pace he would bestride the Rhône; he had but to reach out his hand to touch the sea. And, what was strange, this did not frighten him. He experienced neither vertigo nor drunkenness but only a great tranquillity. It was as if he had just understood that this was natural, that he had always been bigger than the mountains without knowing it. He saw immense vistas of mountains bathed in sunshine, their blue darker with distance, their outline strangely jagged, green-banked river bearing fleets of sailing boats, fields of ripe wheat to the horizon and beyond, vast forests of ancient oaks and great hoary pines and beeches with deep hollows beneath their roots, and beneath the coppice wood there were earths where foxes hid with their cubs, stags bounded across the clearings and vultures glided above the summits. He had only to extend his hand to cover all that with its shadow.

As of a dream he wondered what could be the meaning of his vision. Why did God show him, at this particular moment, what he could never see with his eyes? "Are you telling me, Friend, that I still have my heart's eyes and the memory of what I have seen? I know it well but it does not console me; when a man is hungry, is he satisfied with the memory of yesterday's meal? O Friend, why have you taken that from me which you left even to the holy man Job, whom you tried so hard? Why torture me by showing me all the beauty of the world which you created for the delight of our eyes? There it is — I see each leaf on the trees and the small birds in the branches and the dew drops in the grass, and yet, Lord, I see them not. I see them not, I see nothing! If I could only see my hand, my staff. O good Saint Peter, ask God to give me back my eyes. I know well that for Him it is less than a little speck of dust, but for me it is still very much."

Someone touched his shoulder and asked:

"What are you doing here, poor man?" He raised his head. The statue of Saint Peter, and the column, shrank so quickly beneath his hands and arms that he seemed hardly to have time to realize the change. He was aware of his body as a bit of flesh, formless, colorless and so small that he would have to walk and walk forever even to reach Marseilles. The porch of the church, too, felt small; and small the man who spoke to him.

But he could not forget his dizzy ascent; and he stayed there, his face stupidly turned towards the man who had spoken, yet not knowing whether he was still there. Yet for eight days now he had believed himself able to detect people's presence by their breathing.

"What am I doing here? You can see for yourself: I am praying to Saint Peter."

"Are you mad, old man, to speak in that manner to a priest of God? Are
you a heathen?"

"I am blind. I could not see that you were a priest."

"Forgive me, poor old man," the other said, gently. "Come with me,
we will eat together. I have, as it happens, fresh eggs and lettuces."

"There's my boy, somewhere," the old man said. "He should be playing
here, near the drinking-trough. He will certainly be hungry, hungrier than I."

"Come, I will beckon him. Take my hand. There are three steps."

In the priest's little house there was a window cut into the stone, rounded
at the top; the floor, paved with irregular flags, was strewn with herbs.

The two men, seated at a small, square table, were finishing their meal.
The priest offered his guest a cup of water reddened with wine; he was
poor and could not afford wine every day. The table was of well-polished
wood and smelled of wax. The priest's gown was carefully darned, his
face red-brown, lean, and marked with deep lines, like a peasant's, and
his eyes were grave. He talked at length with the man, urging him to confess so that he could receive Communion on the morrow. It would be of
much help to him, he said.

"Confession is too bitter a thing, Father," the old man said, "and if I
were to confess now I should speak rather of others' sins than my own,
for my heart is heavy with them. As for my own sins, God has already
chastised me more than I deserved. I well know that I should not say such
a thing and that He knows better than I what is good for me. But there
it is — I gave up everything of my own free will, my house and my children and my country; and yet I was attached to them. And He has de-
prived me of the only thing I should not have had the strength to sacrifice
myself."

"He will take even more from you, if He judges you worthy, my son,"
the priest said. "Is it for us to haggle with God?"

"Father, I do not haggle, but if you knew how hard it is no longer to
see anything! You are perhaps thinking that since I am old the thing has
hardly any importance. Father, even toads, even flies can see the sun. I
should never have told any man what I am telling you now; I don't like
to complain. But you are more learned than I — tell me why God has done
this to me."

The priest made no answer and Ansiau's head fell lower than ever; since
he had been sightless it seemed to him that all his hidden thoughts were

written on his face and he was ashamed to be so exposed to a man he could not see.

"Son," the priest said, at last, "we are here in the hands of Saint Peter and I see that you honor him and pray to him, which is well. You show good sense, for Saint Peter is so great a saint that the heavy and terrible keys of Paradise are confided to his care, and entry into Paradise to his judgment. Know that, after our most sweet and most pure Lady, Mary, the Crowned Queen, it is he who is our great intercessor with God, for he holds a place in Heaven that no other saint could ever fill, how great soever the marvels which he wrought. For before God there are twelve thrones all made of gold and light, for the twelve holy apostles, and of these apostles Saint Peter is the highest in dignity. And never could you conceive the beauty of these twelve thrones, for you must not think that they are twelve chairs decorated with gems like the thrones of kings and bishops, but surely high, spiritual glories beside whose beauty that worldly beauty which you regret is naught but a dung-heap.

"Do you suppose, my son, that Saint Peter was a sinner like us? Know that he was a man clean of all stain and he came very near to being a perfect man, for he was guilty of only one sin in his whole life. Even so, when he was tempted by the Devil, who came to him in the shape of the high priest's handmaiden, it was not from cowardice that he denied God, nor any other evil feeling, but only because he had trusted overmuch in his own strength and God wished to teach him a lesson. And even so, my son, learn that no sinner, though a parricide, no truly repentant sinner, not even Saint Mary Magdalene, ever wept for his sins as Saint Peter wept for that one backsliding; they were surely tears of fire and blood that he wept for his sin and even until his death he did not forgive himself. As you can see, my son, there is a vast difference between him and you, and yet 'when he was become old one took him by the hand and led him where he did not wish to go.' And do you think that *he* said: 'I have not deserved it?'"

His elbows on the table, Ansiau listened, and his dead eye blinked; he was fighting back his tears.

"And that is the great lesson, my son, which Saint Peter and all the Saints give us. It means that we do not attain to joy by a pleasant life and making good cheer, but by such agonies and martyrdoms that the mere thought of them makes your hair stand on end. If you have ever seen a criminal flayed or quartered, think of it, and do not forget that not otherwise were the holy martyrs treated. And know this, when Saint Peter yielded up his body to the great agony of death, he asked his executioners to crucify him not as Our Lord was crucified — though that is suffering unspeakable — but with his head below his feet, which is harder still and more shameful. That was how he considered that he deserved to be treated, after the most holy life he had led. And after that, friend, what suffering and what shame have you to fear on this earth? Come, do not call yourself unfortunate. And if worse happens to you, do not hold it an evil, but a good thing."

The worthy priest had succeeded in his aim: the old man was now thinking of Saint Peter and his heart contracted with pity. "Simon called Peter, dost thou love me more than these others love me? — When thou art old they shall bind thee and lead thee where thou wouldst not go — Lord, you know well that I love you." Beside such a love what did his own wretchedness for a little ball of flesh and water and a dead nerve amount to? He was not the first nor the last to whom that had happened. And after all he was free and was going where he wished. *Domine, tu scis quia amo te.*

On the morrow the man and the child took the road early in the morning. It was cool, the birds were singing and the sky above the valley was white. A thick white mist hung above the river, slowly rising. In the east the face of the hills began to glow.

The blind man, with his hand on Auberi's shoulder, kept to his rhythmic pace, rather slow, forced to match his long strides to the child's shorter, irregular steps. His head was empty and he was thinking of nothing.

The Songbird

At a couple of hundred paces from the town a man in a red bonnet was lying in the grass of the verge, and another, a muscular ruffian in rags, with a bandaged eye, was engaged in slitting his pockets.

Auberi, very amused and excited by this spectacle, at once began clapping his hands and shouting, "Hi, there! Hi there! Thief! Thief! Murder!" The man with the bandaged eye, seeing the two pilgrims and no doubt impressed by the old man's imposing stature, dropped his knife and made off. The man in the red bonnet, woken by the shouting, jumped to his feet asking:

"Who cries thief?"

As his whole posture was that of a man offering help, Auberi stopped and, bent double, his head thrown back, burst into such a wild peal of laughter that the old man began laughing too, without knowing why. Then Red-bonnet, thinking himself the object of a practical joke, advanced on the child with raised fist.

"I'll teach you to wake folks up for nothing, you urchin!"

Auberi could not stop laughing.

"Look at your pocket, you big goose," he said, between two hiccups, "y-y-your pocket!"

The other, seeing his pocket slit open, grasped what had happened and began to laugh himself.

"So," he said, "I'd have certainly been done for but for you, good people. Thank you. I'll repay that one of these days." He began pulling up his worn hose which hung down his legs like sacs and the two pilgrims resumed their way.

They had hardly taken twenty steps when the man in the red cap overtook them. He put his quick, strong hand on the old man's shoulder.

"Who are you, good people?" he asked. "I can see you are not from these parts. If there is anything I can do for you? — as for money, I've certainly no more than I need but, if you've need of it, we'll share."

"Why, blockhead," Auberi said. "Have you ever seen folks who've no need of money? Come, share it out, and then we'll see."

"I'm speaking to your father, you little Auvergnat piglet," the man said, and pulled the boy's curly hair but without appearing in the least angry.

"My friend," Ansiau said, "we are pilgrims and do not live on alms. If you have money more than your need, I accept willingly. You must have a good heart. But do not be concerned for us."

"At least you're no Auvergnat, old 'un," the other said. "You look to me like a Burgundian. And, by Saint Trophime, you've been a soldier. Now that," he added, "is something I should never want to be. You get old, the captain recruits younger men and out you go to beg your bread on the roads; and then people complain that there are brigands about! By Saint Macaire, a soldier has a stomach to fill, same as any other man, hasn't he, old 'un?"

"It's a trade, like another," the blind man said. "And understand, my lad, that I never served for pay* but to fulfill my oath as a liegeman. I am the son of a noblewoman and my servant is also free born, and you must take a different tone with us."

The man in the red bonnet whistled a little, disconcerted and surprised, and for some time walked at the old man's side in silence. Auberi watched him, rather slily, triumphing in his embarrassment. The man in the red cap and grey jerkin was quite young — he could hardly be twenty-five — handsome of face, with a small, aquiline nose, a strong, rounded chin, a good color in his cheeks and lively blue eyes. A few locks of straw-colored hair strayed from under his bonnet. His lips seemed to smile even when he was serious. He walked with his hands tucked into his belt, whistling the tune of a sad song, and Auberi noticed that he whistled very well. The old man also listened, trying to pick up the tune.

"But," the young man suddenly exclaimed, "by the tripes of Saint Fiacre! you've a queer way of looking straight ahead of you. By Saint Eloi, you're blind!"

"Have you never seen a blind man?" Ansiau asked. "God's grace, they're not scarce like freaks at a fair!"

"And are you going far like that?"

"To Jerusalem."

At that the young man raised his eyebrows and his face expressed pity for the old man's simplicity.

"But Jerusalem is a long way, comrade," he said, smiling. "You don't know the road. You have to cross the whole country as far as the sea, embark in a ship, cross the wide sea; and it's dangerous. And such journeys are costly."

---

* *la solde,* hence *soldier,* one who fights for pay.

"I know a little about it," the old man said. "I've made the journey twice. This will make the third time."

"God!" — the young man crossed himself — "have you travelled so far? As a pilgrim or a crusader?"

"Crusader, my lad. Both times. As you see, I've seen the world."

For some time they walked in silence.

"And you," Ansiau asked, "what's your trade? You've a burgher's manner of speech."

The man seemed somewhat embarrassed.

"Oh, me, I'm not from these parts. I was on my way to Avignon, not that I have any kin there, but they say it's a fine town. I also like seeing the world a bit. I'd willingly go so far as Marseilles. Look," he added brusquely, "I'm going to suggest something: suppose we travel together? It's always safer; and it's pleasanter. What with the war and all these men-at-arms crossing the country, it's always better to be in company — and with a good knife in your belt. There's more than one kind of crusader, as you know. And, after all, you have a child with you."

"Bah!" Ansiau said. "In this season, between Avignon and Marseilles, there's always plenty of people on the road. But as for coming with us, faith, I'll not refuse. The way is not so hard when there's someone to talk to."

Their new companion, who said that his name was Riquet, was a merry-spirited fellow. He sang and jested the whole time. Auberi was glad to have someone young to talk to and moreover happy to make their new fellow traveller realize that he was nobly born, treating him with a certain condescension, and this slightly disdainful and protective manner greatly amused Riquet.

"Now where, exactly, do I find the nobility?" he would say, laughing. "Here he walks on the holes in his sandals and is still at wetting his knickers and yet he puts on all the airs of a bishop! It's like what they say — that a pedigree dog will never drink from the same bowl as a cur." And he would tap Auberi on the cheeks and the child would shrug his shoulders, half-offended, half-won by this affectionate gesture.

They stopped to eat, that evening, near a stone cross, and all three first fell on their knees to say a short prayer.

"Hi!" Auberi said, suddenly, to Riquet. "Heathen! What, is your bonnet stuck to your head or have you a leprosy under it?" And he snatched off the bonnet and threw it on the ground.

Riquet picked it up quickly but Auberi had raised his eyes to the other's head in surprise: in the middle of a crown of tangled golden curls was a circular area covered with short, thick hair like the bristles of a brush.

"What a queer haircut!" Auberi cried, laughing. "Is that the fashion in your parts?"

"Little puppy!" Riquet said, confused, and replacing his bonnet.

"What is it, Auberi?" the old man asked. The child was still laughing.

"Why, that he's a monk," he said, at last. "A fine monk, in his red bonnet! Have you taken a penitential vow to dress like that?"

Hangdog, Riquet sat down beside the old man and began to eat his bread.

"Well, what of it?" he said. "What is it to you that I'm a monk?"

The old man received the news with indifference.

"At least," he said, "there's no risk of your getting yourself hanged."*

The three ate in silence. Finally, Riquet asked the old man:

"Say, Master Peter, good lord, do you still want me for a companion on the road?"

"I don't concern myself with other people's business," the old man said. The young man continued:

"I don't want you to think I've done anything bad. I will tell you the whole story. It's very simple. I was journeying to Valence with another brother, with some crown pieces which the provost owed the father abbot. I had the coins in a belt round my waist. When we came to Saint Matthew's Church the other brother went in to pray while I held our mule. While I'm there a pretty girl speaks to me . . . well, what with one thing and another, come evening, I climbed out of the window of the monastery where we were sleeping and visited the girl. And when I woke up — no girl, no belt and no money. Then I didn't dare return to my companion, and, faith, I threw my frock into a bed of nettles. As you see. That was three months ago."

"That sort of thing happens, when you're young," the old man said. "But you would do better to return to your monastery and confess everything. They won't punish you more than is necessary."

"Oh, I know," the other said, with a deep sigh. "I know it well. The father abbot was so fond of me that I should get off with a few strokes of the lash and three months' duty in the farmyard. The father abbot would never have believed I stole the money, not he! But it's the disgrace! There it is — shame. Ah! misery of me! If ever I were to meet the father abbot, my heart would break. And now, whenever I see a Black Friar on the road,

* i.e., he could always plead "benefit of clergy." *Translator*

I run till there's ten leagues between us, that's what I've come to! Misery!"

He shook his head with an air of such sadness that Auberi was sorry for him and clapped him lightly on the back.

"Never mind," he said, "poor little brother! We shan't like you the worse for it."

In Riquet's company their way was merrier and the days seemed shorter. Riquet chattered like a magpie, and he had a fine voice and a taste for music. During their halts he and the old man sang in harmony, for Riquet had a quick ear for a tune and a good memory for the words and the old man had an inexhaustible repertoire of songs merry and sad, war songs and love songs, songs of Champagne, Burgundy and France. For in camp and garrison, on the eve of tournaments or during rests in the course of hunting, there could be nothing pleasanter than to listen to a good song and to sing the refrain in chorus.

Riquet was the son of a rich peasant from the neighborhood of Montélimar and had become a monk to satisfy a taste for study. He had learned to read and write and to copy music and could compose tunes himself. He sang the songs which the girls of his village sang in their dances, and minstrels' songs heard during feasts at the castle. Since he had been on the road he had often tried to join up with troupes of minstrels, but they were, he said, a rough lot, treated people not of their brotherhood like dirt, were thieves and cheated at games of chance or skill.

He was forever making plans. He could play a little on the rebec — if he could get hold of one he would go from castle to castle on his own account; all that was needed was to learn many love songs to please the ladies. Perhaps he might manage to compose some himself and then he really would do well, and be able to wear cloth and silk — perhaps he might even win some lady's love. There had been troubadours who had been so fortunate, and no more born in a palace than himself.

"For they say," he reasoned, "that a handsome face counts for much — and my own is by no means ugly — but that that's nothing compared with a beautiful voice for arousing a woman's love. They say there's neither charm nor witchcraft equal to sweet words of love well sung."

And then — why, then a famous singer may well be received by a duke or a count, be given rewards and honors equal to a knight's — in short, Riquet had made up his mind to try his luck as a minstrel.

As he had little singleness of purpose, however, there were other days when he dreamed of turning sailor, voyaging to Palestine or Venice — or even joining a ship in the spice trade. He had read books about the Indies and Japan and had such marvels to tell concerning them that Auberi, incredulous, shook his head; Indians there were, half-man, half-dog, others with the heads of birds; flowers grew in those parts so big that they could eat a man; there were winged gryphons with feathers of gold and elephants with a tail growing from their noses so strong that they could root out a tree with it.

"A lot of silly tales," Auberi said.

"No, no, my boy," the old man said, "it is all perfectly true. And there are even greater marvels, only no one has ever seen or told them. For there are things so strange and frightful that a man cannot see them without instantly falling dead. All that Riquet tells us I have already heard, told by older and wiser men than he."

Riquet nodded, half-thoughtful, half-smiling. He said:

"The father abbot was so kind that he let me read all his books. Lord, what fine books he had! And bound in such leather! They were as smooth as oil. And parchment like silk, full of pictures painted in all colors and smothered with gold. We had a brother who did them himself; he did one of the whole history of Alexander."

"I had a son," the old man said, "a monk, who worked at illuminating. He was buried on All Saints' Day. The prior showed me some of his work." He stopped, feeling his voice unsteady.

"Last year," Riquet went on, still among his memories, "the archbishop of Grenoble himself sent our father abbot, out of courtesy, a brand new bestiary, the binding gilt. To read it makes your heart beat with delight, it is so full of instruction. The father abbot liked my voice and made me read it aloud — ah, God! what a good abbot he was! When he was in a good humor he would stop me — " at that Riquet sighed profoundly " — to ask me, 'And what do you think of that, Brother Frotaire?' — they called me Brother Frotaire at the monastery. Yes, it's quite true, it was just like that; he'd say to me 'And what do you think of that, Brother Frotaire?' And I'd tell him what I thought as best I could, and then the father abbot would be quite content. Sometimes he'd say: 'If ever I am ill, don't call a doctor, call Brother Frotaire, he'd revive a dead man.' Oh yes, and there were even some who were jealous of me because the father abbot was so fond of me." And Riquet changed suddenly from smiles to tears, since for him the monastery was now become a place of joy and a haven of peace, the promised land where milk and honey flowed. And, in fact, he had lived well there. Three months of wandering had not been able to efface his air of joyful health, sign of a youth free from hunger.

"Well, there it is, you see what comes of running after pretty girls," the old man said, calmly.

"Ah, well," Riquet said, quickly consoled, "what could I do? I'm young and the Devil is strong. Now, at least, there's no more risk of my losing the monastery's cash. You've been young yourself, you must have loved beautiful girls."

"Oh, I had other things to do. It only happened to me once, and that when I was no longer so young, and God knows it did not bring me happiness. It's not so much a sin, my lad, as foolishness; you always lose a thousand times more than you gain. And I'm saying this chiefly for Auberi's benefit, for I'm not the one to teach *you* anything about it."

"Her name was Talasia," Riquet said suddenly, after a silence. "She had eyes as black as jet."

A troop of crusaders from the north came down the road and the pilgrims had to climb on to the roadside bank and flatten themselves against the rock to let them pass. It took a long time — the horses passed in pairs along the stony road at a light trot, swinging their cruppers and tossing their heads, hooded in canvas: their hoofs clattered, the harness creaked and the iron medallions on the reins clinked together. The horsemen came in single file in their white or grey tunics with a red cross in the center of the breast. They were already wearing their armor and their helmets were protected from the sun by canvas hoods or a scarf of light-colored stuff knotted about the head. They bore themselves upright and stiff, their eyes fixed on the horizon; each squire carried, slung against the side of his horse, his master's long, pointed or oval shield, in bright, crude colors intended to be recognized from a distance — squares, bars or bends, birds, trees and crosses. They were French and many of them also had the royal *fleur de lis* among their arms. Some few were from Champagne or Lorraine and marched behind their own colors. Here and there groups of men were singing. From time to time a lance struck against a shield.

Their whole movement was absorbed into the monotonous clatter of hundreds of hoofs striking the stony road in cadence.

The pilgrims, flat against the rock, were several times brushed by horses' tails and long crupper-cloths or the horsemen's tunics. Ansiau, head high, mouth open, stood there shivering and panting like an old war horse who hears the trumpet sound — and the sounds were so close — the clatter of arms, creaking of saddles and the breathing of horses. They made him wild and since he could see nothing he was lost in it, letting himself go, his heart torn by the sound of them, the old cavalier, blind and naked of arms, without horse or armor and unable to go with them. So strong was the call of familiar sounds and scents, that he wanted to throw himself under the horses' hoofs rather than survive the moment when he would cease to hear them.

"Auberi, Auberi, mark their banners well. Can you see Champagne?"

"There's one that looks like it, blue and silver. But the sun strikes right in my eyes, I can't see very well."

Ansiau was astonished that anyone who still had his eyes could not see very well.

"Blue and silver, how many bars? With crowns or not? Can you see Blois? Bar? Imperial eagles in simple quarterings, cope in sable and azure?"

"They pass so quickly," Auberi whimpered. "I haven't time to see."

"Ah, ah!" The old man was gasping aloud in his suffering. "That I should have such a fool with me — at his age, and nothing learned! Ah, if only I had my sight, misery — brothers, oh brothers — my little ones — my sweet lads — oh, comrades, oh, my blood! — to die, to die! — to go forward with you!"

Now they could see nothing on the road but a distant cloud of white dust and the last banners swinging to the monotonous amble of the horses. The blue sky rested gently upon the green and grey mountains. The road was marked here and there by still-warm yellow dung in which rooks and crows were pecking calmly. Two belated horsemen went by at the gallop, raising a dust, then silence fell upon the road. The three pilgrims walked slowly, without talking, deafened. And the earth seemed still to shake beneath their feet.

And because, after that troop had passed through, there remained nothing to eat in the townships near the road, they had to go up into the hinterland and take to the mountain roads.

The Black Death
by Sigrid Undset

> 1350   After a stormy life full of passion, conflict and
> suffering Kristin Lavransdatter retired as a lay sister
> to the convent of Rein on the shores of Trondheim
> Fjord in Norway. There her son Skule brought her
> tidings of the coming of the plague.

During the mass Kristin called to mind that she had forgotten to
bring in blind Lady Aasa's cloak, from where they had sat together on the
bench outside the priest's door that morning. After the service she went
round to fetch it.

Under the archway stood Sira Eiliv, lanthorn in hand, and Skule. "He
died as we came alongside the wharf," she heard Skule say, in a strangely
wild, despairing voice.

"Who?"

Both men started violently when they saw her.

"One of my ship-folk," said Skule, low.

Kristin looked from one to the other. At the sight of their blank, strained
faces in the lanthorn's glimmer she broke unwittingly into a little cry of
fear. The priest set his teeth in his under-lip — she saw that his chin quivered a little.

" 'Twere best, my son, you should tell your mother. Better that we all
make us ready to bear it, if 'tis God's will this folk too shall be awaked
by so hard a — " But Skule uttered a kind of groan and said no word: and
on that the priest spoke: "Pestilence has come to Björgvin, Kristin — The
great and deathly sickness that we have heard say is laying waste the
lands in the world around — — "

"The black death — ?" whispered Kristin.

"It boots not to try to tell you how things were in Björgvin when I sailed
from there," said Skule. "None can think it that has not seen it. At first
Sir Bjarne took the hardest measures to quench the fire where it broke
out, away in the houses around Jons cloister; he would have cut off the
whole Nordnes from the town with a chain of his men-at-arms, though
the monks of the Michael cloister threatened him with the Church's ban —
There came an English ship that had the pest aboard, and he would not
suffer them to unload the lading or to leave the ship; every man on the

sloop died, and then he had her scuttled. But some of the wares had already been brought to land, and some of the burghers smuggled more ashore one night — and the friars of the Jons church stood to it that the dying must have ghostly comfort — Then folk began to die throughout all the town, so 'twas bootless, we saw — Now is there not a living soul in the city save the bearers of the dead — all flee the town that can, but the pest goes with them — — "

"O Jesus Christus!"

"Mother — mind you the last time 'twas lemming-year at home in Sil? The throngs that rolled along all the roads and paths — mind you how they lay and died in every bush, and rotted, and poisoned every runnel with stench and festering foulness — ?" He clenched his fists; his mother shuddered:

"Lord, have mercy on us all — Praise be to God and Mary Virgin that you were sent hither even now, my Skule — — "

The man ground his teeth together in the dark:

"So said we too, my men and I, the morning we hoisted sail and stood down Vaagen out to sea. When we were come north to Moldö Sound, the first fell sick. We bound stones to his feet and a cross upon his breast when he was dead, vowed a mass for his soul when we came to Nidaros, and cast his body into the sea — God forgive us. We put in to shore with the next two and got them help for their souls, and Christian burial — for 'tis bootless to flee from fate. The fourth died as we pulled into the river, and the fifth last night — — "

"Is it needful that you go back to the town?" asked his mother a little later. "Can you not bide here?"

Skule shook his head, with a joyless laugh:

"— Oh, soon, methinks, 'twill matter naught where one is. Useless to be afeared — a man in dread is half dead. But would that I were as old as you are, mother!"

"None knows what they are spared who die young," said his mother, low.

"Be still, mother! Think on the time when you yourself were three and twenty winters old — would you have missed the years you have lived since then — — ?"

Fourteen days later Kristin saw for the first time one sick of the plague. Rumour that the pest was raging in Nidaros and spreading through the country-side had come to Rissa — how, 'twas not easy to understand, for folk kept their houses, and every man fled to the woods or thickets if he saw an unknown wayfarer on the road; none would open his door to stranger-folk.

But one morning two fishers came up to the cloister bearing a man between them in a sail; when at day-break they came down to their boat, they had found a strange bark at the wharf, and in its bottom lay this man, senseless — he had found strength to make his boat fast, but not to get out of it to land. The man had been born in a house owned by the cloister, but his kindred had all left the country-side.

The dying man lay on the wet sail in the midst of the grass-grown courtyard; the fishermen stood afar off talking with Sira Eiliv. The lay sisters and serving-women had fled into the houses, but the nuns stood in a cluster at the door of the convent hall — a throng of startled, trembling, despairing old women.

Then Lady Ragnhild stepped forth. She was a little, thin old woman, with a broad, flat face and a little round, red nose like a button; her great, light-brown eyes were red-rimmed, and always watered a little.

"*In nomine patris et filii et spiritus sancti,*" she said in a clear voice, then gulped once. "Bear him into the guest-house — — "

And Sister Agata, the eldest of the nuns, elbowed her way through the throng and, unbidden, went with the abbess and the men who bore the sick man.

Kristin went in thither late at night with a remedy she had made ready in the pantry, and Sister Agata asked if she durst bide there and tend the fire.

She deemed herself she should have been hardened — well used as she was to births and deaths, she had seen worse sights than this — she strove to think of all the worst that she had seen — The plague-stricken man sat upright, for he was like to choke with the bloody spittle that he brought up at each coughing-fit — Sister Agata had slung him up in a band passed across his lean, yellow, red-haired chest, and his head hung forward; his face was leaden grey-blue, and fit on fit of shivering shook him. But Sister Agata sat calmly saying over her prayers, and when the cough took him she rose, put one arm about his head, and help a cup below his mouth. The sick man roared loud in his agony, rolled his eyes fearfully, and at length thrust a black tongue far out of his gullet, while his lamentable cries died away in pitiful groaning. The nun emptied out the cup into the fire — and while Kristin threw on more juniper, and the wet branches first filled the room with a stinging yellow smoke, and then burst hissing into flame, she saw Sister Agata settle the cushions and pillows under the sick

man's back and arm-pits, wipe his face and cracked brown lips with vine-
gar-water, and draw the fouled coverlid up about his body. 'Twould soon
be over and done, she said to Kristin — he was cold already; at first he
had been hot as fire — but Sira Eiliv had prepared him already for his
going. Then she sat her down beside him, thrust the calamus root into its
place in her cheek with her tongue, and fell again to prayer.

Kristin strove to overcome the fearful horror that she felt. She had seen
folk die a harder death — But 'twas in vain — this was the plague, a chastisement from the Lord for all mankind's secret hardness of heart, of which
He alone had knowledge. She felt as if she were rocked giddily on a sea,
where all the bitter and angry thoughts she had ever thought towered
up like one huge wave amid a thousand, and broke in helpless woe and
lamentation. Lord, help us, for we perish — —

Sira Eiliv came in late in the night. He chid Sister Agata sharply that
she she had not followed his counsel to bind a linen cloth dipped in vinegar over her mouth and nose. She mumbled testily that 'twas of no avail —
but both she and Kristin had now to do as he bade them.

The priest's quietude and steadfastness put some measure of courage
into Kristin — or awoke a feeling of shame — she ventured out of the juniper smoke and began to help Sister Agata. A choking stench came from
the sick man, that the smoke availed not to deaden — filth, blood, sour
sweat, and a noisome smell from his throat. She thought of Skule's words
about the lemming swarm; once more there came upon her the awful longing to fly, though she knew there was no place whither one could flee
from this. But when once she had taken heart of grace and touched the
dying man, the worst was over; and she helped as well as she might until
he had breathed his last. He was black in the face already when he died.

The nuns walked in procession, with the holy relics, crosses, and burning tapers, round the church and the cloister hill, and all in the parish
who could walk or crawl went with them. But, not many days after, a
woman died near by at Strömmen — and then the deadly sickness broke
out at a stroke on every hand throughout the country-side.

Death and horror and direst need seemed to bear away the land and its
folk into a timeless world — 'twas not more than a few weeks that were
gone by, if one were to reckon the days, and already it seemed as if the
world that had been, ere pestilence and death stalked naked through the
land, was fading from folk's memories, as a sea-coast sinks when one stands
out to sea before a rushing wind. 'Twas as though no human soul could

keep in memory that once life and the daily round of work had seemed
sure and near, death far away — or had the power to conceive that so it
would be again — if so be all men did not die. But "Belike, we shall all
die," said the men who came to the cloister with their motherless little
ones; some said it with dull, hard faces, some with weeping and lamenta-
tions; they said it when they fetched a priest to the dying, they said it
when they bore the corpses to the parish church down the hill and to the
graveyard by the cloister chapel. Often the bearers themselves must dig
the grave — Sira Eiliv had set the lay serving-men — such as were left —
to work at saving and garnering the corn from the cloister's fields; and
wheresoever he went in the parish he admonished the folk to get their
crops housed, and to help one another to care for the cattle, that so they
might not perish in the dearth the plague was like to leave behind when
it had spent its rage.

The nuns in the cloister met the visitation at first with a kind of bewildered calm. They settled them down for good in the convent hall, kept
a fire blazing night and day in the great masoned fire-place, slept there,
and there took their food. Sira Eiliv counselled that great fires should be
kept up in the courts and in all the houses where there were fire-places;
but the sisters were afraid of fire — they had heard so many tales from
the oldest sisters of the burning of the convent thirty years before. Meal-
times and working-hours were kept no longer, and the divers offices of
the sisters could not be kept apart, by reason of the many children who
came from without, praying for food and help. Sick folk were brought in —
these for the most were well-to-do folk who could pay for a grave-stead
in the cloister and for masses for their souls, or the poorest and loneliest
of the poor who could get no help at home. Those of a middle station lay
and died in their own houses. On some manors every human being died.
But amid all this the nuns had as yet made shift to keep up the hours
of prayer.

The first of the nuns who fell sick was Sister Inga, a woman of Kristin's
age, near fifty years; but none the less was she so afeared of death that
'twas horrible to see and hear her. The shivering fit came upon her in the
church during mass, and she crept on hands and knees, shaking and with
chattering teeth, praying and beseeching God and Mary Virgin for her
life — Before long she lay in a burning fever, groaning, and sweating blood
from all her body. Kristin's heart shuddered within her — doubtless she,
too, would be as wretchedly afraid as this when her time came. 'Twas

not alone that death was sure — 'twas the awful horror that clung about
death from pestilence.

Then Lady Ragnhild herself fell sick. Kristin had wondered a little
that this woman had been chosen to an abbess's high office — she was a
quiet, somewhat peevish old woman, unlearned, and, it seemed, lacking
any great gifts of the spirit — but, when death laid his hand upon her, she
showed she was in truth a bride of Christ. Her the sickness smote with boils
— she would not suffer even her spiritual daughters to bare her old body, but
under one of her arms the swelling grew at last as big as an apple, and
under her chin too boils broke out and waxed huge and blood-red, and at
last turned black; she suffered unbearable pains from them, and burned
with fever; but as oft as her mind was clear, she lay there a pattern of
holy patience, sighing to God for forgiveness of her sins, and praying in
fair and heart-felt words for her cloister and her daughters, for all sick
and sorrowful, and for the salvation of all souls who now must part from
hence. Even Sira Eiliv wept, when he had given her the viaticum — and
his steadfastness as well as his unwearied zeal in the midst of all this misery had been a thing to wonder at. Lady Ragnhild had many times already
given her soul into God's keeping and prayed Him to take the nuns into
His ward — and then at last the boils on her body began to burst. But
this proved a turning towards life, not death — and after, too, folk deemed
they saw that those whom the sickness smote with boils were sometimes
healed, but those to whom it came with a bloody vomit, died every one.

It seemed as though the nuns took new courage from the abbess's steadfastness, and from the having seen one stricken with the pest who yet did
not die. They had now to milk and tend the byres themselves, to make
ready their own food, and themselves fetch home juniper and fresh pine
branches to burn for cleansing smoke — each one had to do what came
to her hand. They cared for the sick as best they could, and doled out
remedies — theriac and calamus root had given out; they dealt round gin-
ger, pepper, saffron, and vinegar to ward off the poison; and milk and meat
— the bread gave out and they baked at night — the spices gave out, and
folk must needs chew juniper-berries and pine-needles against the infection. One by one the sisters drooped and died; passing-bells rang from the
cloister church and the parish church early and late in the heavy air; for
the strange, uncanny mist still lay upon the land; there seemed to be a
secret privity 'twixt the fog and the deadly sickness. Sometimes it turned
to a frosty fog and sifted down in small ice-needles and a half-frozen

drizzle, and the land grew white with rime — then came mild weather and the mist again. Folk deemed it a sign of evil omen that the sea-fowl, that else were wont to flock in thousands along the creek that runs inland from the fjord and lies like a river between the low stretches of meadow, but widens to a salt-water lake north of Rein cloister — that they suddenly vanished, and in their stead came ravens in countless numbers — on every stone by the water-side the black birds sat amidst the fog, making their hideous croaking; while flocks of crows, so huge that none before had seen the like, settled on all the woods and groves, and flew with ugly screech-ings over the stricken land.

Now and again Kristin thought of her own — the sons who were scat-tered so far and wide, the grandchildren she should never see — little Erlend's golden head wavered before her sight. But they were grown to seem far off and pale to her. Almost it seemed as though all mankind in this time of need were alike near to each other and alike far apart. And then she had her hands full all day long — it stood her in good stead now that she was used to all kinds of work. While she sat milking, she would find beside her suddenly little starving children she had never before set eyes on, and she would scarce remember to ask whence they were or how things were with them at home; she would give them food and lead them to the shelter of the chapter-hall, or some other place where a fire was burning, then stow them away in a bed in the dormitory.

She marked, with a kind of wonder, that in this time of calamity, when more than ever there was need that all should be vigilant in prayer, she scarce ever found time to meditate or to pray. She would fling her down in the church before the tabernacle when she found a vacant moment, but naught came of it but wordless sighs, and Paternosters and Aves ut-tered by rote. She herself knew not that the nun-like ways and bearing she had fallen into in these two years were dropping from her more and more, and that she was growing ever liker to the housewife of the old days — as the flock of nuns dwindled, the round of cloister duties fell into disarray, and the abbess still lay abed, weak and with half-palsied tongue — and the work grew more and more for the few that were left to do it.

One day she learned by chance that Skule was still in Nidaros — his ship-folk were dead or fled away, and he had not been able to get new folk. He was whole yet, but he had plunged into wild living, as had many young men in this desperate pass. For him who was afraid, death was sure, they said, and so they deadened thought with drink and riot, gambled and danced and wantoned with women. Even honourable burghers' wives and young maids of the best kindreds ran from their homes in this evil time; in company with the women of the bordels they caroused in the inns and taverns amongst the wildered men. God forgive them, thought the mother — but 'twas as though her heart were too weary to sorrow much for these things.

But in the country-side too, for sure, there was enough of sin and distraction. They heard little of it at the cloister, for there they had no time for much talk. But Sira Eiliv, who went about everywhere, without rest or respite, to the sick and dying, said one day to Kristin that the folk's souls stood in yet direr need than their bodies.

There came an evening when they were sitting round the chimney-place in the convent hall — the little flock of folk that were left alive in Rein cloister. Four nuns and two lay sisters, an old stable-man and a half-grown boy, two bedeswomen and some children, huddled together round the fire. On the high-seat bench, where a great crucifix gleamed in the dusk on the light-hued wall, lay the abbess, and Sister Kristin and Sister Turid sat at her hands and feet.

It was nine days since the last death among the sisters, and five days since any had died in the cloister or the nearer houses. The pestilence seemed to be lessening throughout the parish, too, said Sira Eiliv. And for the first time for near three months something like a gleam of peace and hope and comfort fell upon the silent and weary folk that sat together there. Old Sister Torunn Marta let her rosary sink upon her lap, and took the hand of the little girl who stood at her knee:

"What can it be she means? Ay, child, now seems it as we should see that never for long does God's mother, Mary, turn her loving-kindness from her children."

"Nay, 'tis not Mary Virgin, Sister Torunn, 'tis Hel.* She will go from out this parish, with both rake and broom, when they offer up a man without blemish at the graveyard gate — to-morrow she'll be far away — —"

"What means she?" asked the nun again, uneasily. "Fie upon you,

---

* In Norse folk-lore the plague was personified as a hideous old woman carrying a rake and a broom. Where she used the rake, some part of the population survived; where she used the broom, she swept the country-side of every living soul. It would be natural, in the fourteenth century, for the popular imagination to identify her with Hel, the death goddess of the old mythology.

Magnhild; what ugly heathenish talk is this? 'Twere fit you should taste the birch — — "

"Tell us what it is, Magnhild — have no fear" — Sister Kristin was standing behind them; she asked the question breathlessly. She had remembered — she had heard in her youth from Lady Aashild — of dreadful, unnamably sinful devices that the Devil tempts desperate men to practise — —

The children had been down in the grove by the parish church in the falling dusk, and some of the boys had strayed through the wood to a turf hut that stood there, and had eavesdropped and heard some men in it laying plans. It seemed from what they heard that these men had laid hold on a little boy, Tore, the son of Steinunn, that lived by the strand, and to-night they were to offer him up to the pest-ogress Hel. The children talked eagerly, proud that the grown-up folk were paying heed to what they said. They seemed not to think of pitying the hapless Tore — maybe because he was somewhat of an outcast. He wandered about the parish begging, but never came to the cloister, and if Sira Eiliv or any sent by the abbess sought out his mother, she ran away, or she kept a stubborn silence, whether they spoke lovingly or harshly to her. She had lived in the stews of Nidaros for ten years, but then a sickness took hold on her, and left her of so ill a favour that at last she could not win her livelihood so as she had used her to do; so she had forsaken the town for the Rein parish, and now dwelt in a hut down by the strand. It still befell at times that a chance beggar or some such stroller would take lodging with her for a while. Who was father to her boy she herself knew not.

"We must go thither," said Kristin. "Here we cannot sit, I trow, while christened souls sell themselves to the Devil at our very doors."

The nuns whimpered in fear. These were the worst men in the parish; rough, ungodly fellows; and uttermost need and despair must have turned them now into very devils. Had Sira Eiliv only been at home, they moaned. In this time of trial the priest had so won their trust, that they deemed he could do all things — —

Kristin wrung her hands:

"Even if I must go alone — my mother, have I your leave to go thither?"

The abbess gripped her by the arm so hard that she cried out. The old, tongue-tied woman got upon her feet; by signs she made them understand that they should dress her to go out, and called for her golden cross, the badge of her office, and her staff. Then she took Kristin by the arm — for she was the youngest and strongest of the women. All the nuns stood up and followed.

Through the door of the little room 'twixt the chapter-hall and the choir of the church, they went forth into the raw, cold winter night. Lady Ragnhild's teeth began to chatter and her whole frame to shiver — she still sweated without cease by reason of her sickness, and the pest-boil sores were not fully healed, so that it must have wrought her great agony to walk. But she muttered angrily and shook her head when the sisters prayed her to turn, clung the harder to Kristin's arm, and plodded, shaking with cold, on before them through the garden. As their eyes grew used to the darkness the women made out the dim sheen of the withered leaves strewn on the path beneath their feet, and the faint light from the clouded sky above the naked tree-tops. Cold water-drops dripped from the branches, and puffs of wind went by with a faint soughing sound. The roll of the waves on the strand behind the high ground came to them in dull, heavy sighs.

At the bottom of the garden was a little wicket — the sisters shuddered when the bolt, fast rusted in its socket, shrieked as Kristin withdrew it by main force. Then they crept onward through the grove down towards the parish church. Now they could see dimly the black-tarred mass, darker against the darkness; and against the opening in the clouds above the low hills beyond the lake they saw the roof-top, and the ridge turret with its beasts' heads and cross over all.

Ay — there were folk in the graveyard — they felt rather than saw or heard it. And now a faint gleam of light was to be seen low down, as of a lanthorn set upon the ground. Close by it the darkness seemed moving.

The nuns pressed together, moaning almost soundlessly amid whispered prayers, went a few steps, halted and listened, and went on again, They were well-nigh come to the graveyard gate. Then they heard from out of the dark a thin child-voice crying:

"Oh, oh, my bannock; you've thrown dirt on it!"

Kristin let go the abbess's arm, and ran forward through the church-yard gate. She pushed aside some dark shapes of men's backs, stumbled over heaps of up-turned earth, and then was at the edge of the open grave. She went down on her knees, bent over, and lifted up the little boy who stood at the bottom, still whimpering because the dirt had spoiled the good bannock he had been given for staying quietly down there.

The men stood there frighted from their wits — ready to fly — some stamped about on the same spot — Kristin saw their feet in the light from the lanthorn on the ground. Then one, she made sure, would have sprung at her — at the same moment the grey-white nuns' dresses came into sight — and the knot of men hung wavering — —

Kristin had the boy in her arms still; he was crying for his bannock; so she set him down, took the bread, and brushed it clean:

"There, eat it — — your bannock is as good as ever now — And now go home, you men" — the shaking of her voice forced her to stop a little. "Go home and thank God you were saved from the doing of a deed 'twere hard to atone." She was speaking now as a mistress speaks to her serving-folk, mildly, but as if it could not cross her mind that they would not obey. Unwittingly some of the men turned toward the gate.

Then one of them shrieked:

"Stay a little — see you not our lives at the least are forfeit — mayhap all we own — now that these full-fed monks' whores have stuck their noses into this! Never must they come away from here to spread the tidings of it — — "

Not a man moved — but Sister Agnes broke into a shrill shriek, and cried in a wailing voice:

"O sweet Jesus, my bridegroom — I thank Thee that Thou sufferest Thy handmaidens to die for the glory of Thy name — !"

Lady Ragnhild pushed her roughly behind her, tottered forward, and took up the lanthorn from the ground — no one moved a hand to hinder her. When she lifted it up, the gold cross on her breast shone out. She stood propped on her staff, and slowly turned the light upon the ring about her, nodding a little at each man she looked on. Then she made a sign to Kristin to speak. Kristin said:

"Go home peaceably and quietly, dear brothers — be sure that the reverend mother and these good sisters will be as merciful as their duty to God and the honour of his Church will suffer. But stand aside now, that we may come forth with this child — and thereafter let each man go his way."

The men stood wavering. Then one shrieked out as though in direst need:

"Is't not better that *one* be offered up than that we should all perish — ? This child here who is owned by none — — "

"Christ owns him. 'Twere better we should perish one and all than to hurt one of His little ones — — "

But the man who had spoken first shouted again:

"Hold your tongue — no more suchlike words, or I cram them back down your throat with this" — he shook his knife in the air. "Go you home, go to your beds and pray your priest to comfort you, and say naught of this — or I tell you, in Satan's name, you shall learn 'twas the worst thing you ever did to put your fingers into our affairs — — "

"You need not to cry so loud for him you named to hear you, Arntor — be sure he is not far from here," said Kristin calmly, and some of the men seemed affrighted, and pressed unwittingly nearer to the abbess, who stood holding the lanthorn. "The worst had been, both for us and for you, had we sat quiet at home while you went about to make you a dwelling-place in hottest hell."

But the man Arntor swore and raved. Kristin knew that he hated the nuns; for his father had been forced to pledge his farm to them when he had to pay amends for man-slaying and incest with his wife's cousin. Now he went on casting up at the sisters all the Enemy's most hateful lies, charging them with sins so black and unnatural that only the Devil himself could prompt a man to think such thoughts.

The poor nuns bowed them terrified and weeping under the hail of his taunts, but they stood fast around their old mother, and she held the lanthorn high, throwing the light upon the man, and looking him calmly in the face while he raved.

But anger flamed up in Kristin like new-kindled fire:

"Silence! Have you lost your wits, or has God smitten you with blindness? Should we dare to murmur under His chastisement — we who have seen His consecrated brides go forth to meet the sword that has been drawn by reason of the world's sins? They watched and prayed while we sinned and each day forgot our Maker — shut them from the world within the citadel of prayer, while we scoured the world around, driven by greed of great and small possessions, of our own lusts and our own wrath. But they came forth to us when the angel of death was sent out amongst us — gathered in the sick and the defenceless and the hungry — twelve of our sisters have died in this plague — that you all know — not one turned aside, and not one gave over praying for us all in sisterly love, till the tongue dried in their mouths and their life's blood ebbed away — —"

"Bravely speak you of yourself and your like — — "

"I am *your* like," she cried, beside herself with anger; "I am not one of these holy sisters — I am one of you — — "

"You have grown full humble, woman," said Arntor, scornfully; "you are frighted, I mark well. A little more and you will be fain to call her — the mother to this boy — your like."

"That must God judge — He died both for her and for me, and He knows us both — Where is she — Steinunn?"

"Go down to her hut; you will find her there sure enough," answered Arntor.

"Ay, truly someone must send word to the poor woman that we have her boy," said Kristin to the nuns. "We must go out to her to-morrow."

Arntor gave a jeering laugh, but another man cried, uneasily:

"No, no — She is dead," he said to Kristin. " 'Tis fourteen days since Bjarne left her and barred the door. She lay in the death-throes then — — "

"She lay in — " Kristin gazed at the men, horror-struck. "Was there none to fetch a priest to her — ? Is the — body — lying there — and no one has had so much compassion on her as to bring her to hallowed ground — and her child you would have — ?"

At the sight of the woman's horror, 'twas as though the men went clean beside themselves with fear and shame; all were shouting at once; a voice louder than all the rest rang out:

"Fetch her yourself, sister!"

"Ay! Which of you will go with me?"

None answered. Arntor cried:

"You will have to go alone, I trow."

"To-morrow — as soon as 'tis light — we will fetch her, Arntor — I myself will buy her a resting-place and masses for her soul — — "

"Go thither now, go to-night — then will I believe you nuns are chokeful of holiness and pureness — — "

Arntor had stuck his head forward close to hers. Kristin drove her clenched fist into his face, with a single loud sob of rage and horror — —

Lady Ragnhild went forward and placed herself at Kristin's side; she strove to bring forth some words. The nuns cried out that to-morrow the dead woman should be brought to her grave. But the Devil seemed to have turned Arntor's brain; he went on shrieking:

"Go now — then will we believe on God's mercy — — "

Kristin drew herself up, white and stiff:

"I will go."

She lifted the child and gave it into Sister Torunn's arms, pushed the men aside, and ran quickly, stumbling over grass tussocks and heaps of earth, toward the gate, while the nuns followed wailing, and Sister Agnes cried out that she would go with her. The abbess shook her clenched hands toward Kristin, beckoning her to stop; but she seemed quite beside herself and gave no heed — —

Suddenly there was a great commotion in the dark over by the graveyard gate — next moment Sira Eiliv's voice asked: who was holding Thing here. He came forward into the glimmer of the lanthorn — they saw that he bore an ax in his hand. The nuns flocked around him; the men made shift to steal away in the dark, but in the gateway they were met by a man bearing a drawn sword in his hand. There was some turmoil and the clash of arms, and Sira Eiliv shouted toward the gate: woe to any who broke the churchyard peace. Kristin heard one say 'twas the strong smith from Credo Lane — the moment after, a tall, broad-shouldered, white-haired man appeared at her side — 'twas Ulf Haldorssön.

The priest handed him the ax — he had borrowed it from Ulf — and took the boy Tore from the nun, while he said:

" 'Tis past midnight already — none the less 'twere best you all came with me to the church; I must get to the bottom of these doings this very night."

None had any thought but to obey. But, when they were come out on to the road, one of the light-grey women's forms stepped aside from the throng and turned off by the path through the wood. The priest called out, bidding her come on with the others. Kristin's voice answered from the darkness — she was some way along the track already:

"I cannot come, Sira Eiliv, till I have kept my promise — — "

The priest and some others sprang after her. She was standing leaning against the fence when Sira Eiliv came up with her. He held up the lanthorn — she was fearfully white of face, but, when he looked into her eyes, he saw that she was not gone mad, as at first he had feared.

"Come home, Kristin," he said. "To-morrow we will go thither with you, some men — I myself will go with you — — "

"I have given my word. I cannot go home, Sira Eiliv, till I have done that which I vowed to do."

The priest stood silent a little. Then he said in a low voice:

"Mayhap you are right. Go then, sister, in God's name."

Like a shadow, Kristin melted away into the darkness, which swallowed up her grey form.

When Ulf Haldorssön came up by her side, she said — she spoke by snatches, vehemently: "Go back — I asked not you to come with me — — "

Ulf laughed low:

"Kristin, my lady — you have not learnt yet, I see, that some things can be done without your asking or bidding — nor, though you have seen it many a time, I ween — that you cannot alway carry through alone all that you take upon you. But this burden of yours I will help you to carry."

The fir woods sighed above them, and the boom of the rollers away on the strand came stronger or more faint as the gusts of wind rose or died away. They walked in pitch darkness. After a while Ulf said:

" — I have borne you company before, Kristin, when you went out at night — methought 'twere but fitting I should go with you this time too — — "

She breathed hard and heavily in the dark. Once she stumbled over somewhat, and Ulf caught her. After that he took her hand and led her. In a while the man heard that she was weeping as she went, and he asked her why she wept.

"I weep to think how good and faithful you have been to us, Ulf, all our days. What can I say — ? I know well enough 'twas most for Erlend's sake, but almost I believe, kinsman — all our days you have judged of me more kindly than you had a right to, after what you first saw of my doings."

"I loved you, Kristin — no less than him." He was silent. Kristin felt that he was strongly stirred. Then he said:

"Therefore meseemed 'twas a hard errand, when I sailed out hither to-day — I came to bring you such tidings as I myself deemed it hard to utter. God strengthen you, Kristin!"

"Is it Skule?" asked Kristin softly in a little. "Skule is dead?"

"No; Skule was well when I spoke with him yesterday — and now not many are dying in the town. But I had news from Tautra this morning — " He heard her sigh heavily once, but she said naught. A little after he said:

" 'Tis ten days now since they died. There are but four brothers left alive in the cloister, and the island is all but swept clean of folk."

They were come now where the wood ended. Over the flat stretch of land in front the roaring of the sea and the wind came to meet them. One spot out in the dark shone white — the surf in a little bay, by a steep, light-hued sand-hill.

"She dwells there," said Kristin. Ulf felt that long, convulsive shudders went through her frame. He gripped her hand hard:

"You took this on yourself. Remember that, and lose not your wits now."

Kristin said, in a strangely thin, clear voice, that the blast caught and bore away:

"Now will Björgulf's dream come true — I trust in God's and Mary's grace."

Ulf tried to see her face — but 'twas too dark. They were walking on the strand — in some places 'twas so narrow under the bluffs that now and then a wave washed right up to their feet. They tramped forward over tangled heaps of seaweed and great stones. After a while they were ware of a dark hump in against the sandy bank.

"Stay here," said Ulf, shortly. He went forward and thrust against the door — then she heard him hew at the withy bands and thrust at the door again. Then she was ware that the door had fallen inwards, and he had gone in through the black hole.

'Twas not a night of heavy storm. But it was so dark that Kristin could see naught, save the little flashes of foam that came and vanished the same instant on the lifting sea, and the shining of the waves breaking along the shores of the bay — and against the sand-dune she could make out that black hump. And it seemed to her that she was standing in a cavern of night, and that 'twas the forecourt of death. The roll of breaking waves and the hiss of their waters ebbing among the stones of the beach kept time with the blood-waves surging through her, though all the time 'twas as though her body must shiver in pieces, as a vessel of wood falls apart in staves — her breast ached as if something would burst it in sunder from within; her head felt hollow and empty and as 'twere rifted, and the un- ceasing wind wrapped her round and swept clean through her. She felt, with a strange listlessness, that she herself had surely caught the sickness now — but 'twas as though she looked that the darkness should be riven by a great light that would drown the roar of the sea with its thunder, and that in the horror of this she should perish. She drew up her hood, blown back from her head by the wind, wrapped the black nun's cloak close about her, and stood with her hands crossed beneath it — but it came not into her thought to pray; 'twas as though her soul had more than enough to do to work a way forth from its mansion trembling to its fall, and as though it tore at her breast with every breath.

She saw a light flare up within the hut. A little after, Ulf Haldorssön called out to her: "You must come hither and hold the light for me, Kristin" — he was standing in the doorway — as she came, he reached her a torch of some tarred wood.

A choking stench from the corpse met her, though the hut was so draughty and the door was gone. With staring eyes and mouth half open — and she felt her jaws and lips grow stiff the while and wooden — she looked round for the dead. But there was naught to see but a long bundle lying in the corner on the earthen floor, wrapped in Ulf's cloak.

He had torn loose some long planks from somewhere and laid the door upon them. Cursing his unhandy tools, he made notches and holes with his light ax and dagger, and strove to lash the door fast to the boards. Once or twice he looked up at her swiftly, and each time his dark, grey-bearded face grew more hard set.

"I marvel much how you had thought to get through this piece of work alone," he said as he wrought — then glanced up at her — but the stiff, death-like face in the red gleam of the tar brand was set and unmoved as ever — 'twas the face of a dead woman or of one distraught. "Can you tell me that, Kristin?" he laughed harshly — but still 'twas of no avail. "Methinks now were the time for you to say a prayer."

Stiff and lifeless as ever, she began to speak:

"*Pater noster qui es in coelis. Adveniat regnum tuum. Fiat voluntas tua sicut in coelo et in terra —*" Then she came to a stop.

Ulf looked at her. Then he took up the prayer:

"*Panem nostrum quotidianum la nobis hodie —*" Swiftly and firmly he said the Lord's prayer to the end, went over and made the sign of the cross over the bundle — swiftly and firmly he took it up and bore it to the bier that he had fashioned."

"Go you in front," he said. "Maybe 'tis somewhat heavier, but you will smell the stench less there. Throw away the torch — we can see more surely without it — and see you miss not your footing, Kristin — for I had liefer not have to take a hold of this poor body any more."

The struggling pain in her breast seemed to rise in revolt when she got the bier poles set upon her shoulders; her chest *would* not bear up the weight. But she set her teeth hard. So long as they went along the strand, where the wind blew strong, but little of the corpse smell came to her.

"Here I must draw it up first, I trow, and the bier after," said Ulf, when they were come to the steep slope they had climbed down.

"We can go a little farther on," said Kristin; "'tis there they come down with the seaweed sleighs — there 'tis not steep."

She spoke calmly, the man heard, and as in her right mind. And a fit of sweating and trembling took him, now it was over — he had deemed she must lose her wits that night.

They struggled forward along the sandy track that led across the flat toward the pine wood. The wind swept in freely here, but yet 'twas not as it had been down on the strand, and, as they drew farther and farther away from the roar of the beach, she felt it as a homefaring from the horror of utter darkness. Beside their path the ground showed lighter — 'twas a cornfield that there had been none to reap. The scent of it, and the sight of the beaten-down straw, welcomed her home again — and her eyes filled with tears of sisterly pity — out of her own desolate terror and woe she was coming home to fellowship with the living and the dead.

At times, when the wind was right behind, the fearful carrion stench enwrapped her wholly, but yet 'twas not so awful as when she stood in the hut — for the night was full of fresh, wet, cold, cleansing streams of air.

And much stronger than the feeling that she bore a thing of dread upon the bier behind her, was the thought that Ulf Haldorssön was there, guarding her back against the black and living horror they were leaving behind — and whose roar sounded fainter and more faint.

When they were come to the edge of the fir woods they were ware of lights: "They are coming to meet us," said Ulf.

Soon after, they were met by a whole throng of men bearing pine-root torches, a couple of lanthorns and a bier covered with a pall — Sira Eiliv was with them, and Kristin saw with wonder that in the troop were many of the men who had been that same night in the churchyard, and that many of them were weeping. When they lifted the burthen from her shoulders she was like to fall. Sira Eiliv would have caught a hold of her, but she said quickly:

"Touch me not — come not near me — I have the pest myself; I feel it — — "

But none the less Sira Eiliv stayed her up with a hand below her arm:

"Then be of good cheer, woman, remembering that our Lord has said: 'Inasmuch as ye have done it unto one of the least of these my brethren or sisters, ye have done it unto Me.'"

Kristin gazed at the priest. Then she looked across to where the men were shifting the body from the stretcher that Ulf had fashioned to the bier they had brought. Ulf's cloak slipped aside a little — the point of a worn-out shoe stuck out, dark wet in the light of the torches.

Kristin went across, kneeled between the poles of the bier, and kissed the shoe:

"God be gracious to you, sister — God give your soul joy in His light — God look in His mercy on us here in our darkness — — "

Then it seemed to her as 'twere life itself that tore its way from out of her — a grinding, inconceivable pain, as though something within her, rooted fast in every outermost fibre of her limbs, were riven loose. All that was within her breast was torn out — she felt her throat full of it, her mouth filled with blood that tasted of salt and foul copper — next moment her whole dress in front was a glistening wet blackness — Jesus! is there so much blood in an old woman? she thought.

Ulf Haldorssön lifted her in his arms and bore her away.

The Witch and the Lord

by Edith Simon

> 1354   In the Middle Ages the boundary line between witchcraft and medicine was often indistinguishable. So when Hugh, Lord of Bedesford, lay dying his brother was only doing the proper thing when he enlisted the aid of the white witch, Swan Ygern-Jane.

Then Baldwin came to Trefeller Court and said that Hugh was dying, and implored her to lend them her bondwoman that had saved Elizabeth and already proved her skill in Bedesford, too.

"Sister! As you call yourself Christian — as you yourself hope to find mercy on the Last Day! He is your own brother and, good or bad, he is rightful lord over all of us. He is coughing day and night. The men say they cannot bear it much longer, for it sounds as if his insides are raked out of him with iron combs."

"He may be beyond her arts."

"Then at least your conscience will know you did not begrudge him in his extremity. Prior Haakon has not dared give him the sacrament, for that his strength may rally, before the end, enough to make full confession. Even the Benedictines sent a brother with a cask of coltsfoot syrup, Juliana!"

Neither of the Cinqmort brothers had as yet seen Swan Ygern-Jane face to face. To hear a woman dubbed "leech" commonly suffices to render folk incurious as to her looks, and certain of her age. So Baldwin was taken aback when Juliana led her out to him, and found nary a word to say to the woman the whole way.

Since Hugh's illness he had known what had become of their mother's tapestries. They were hung round my lord's bedchamber, rather inexpertly put up, and rather out of keeping in their faded femininity.

All the bed gear was most fine, but had sadly suffered of late. There was a hearth, by which an old woman sat watching a caldron and some cooking bags. The sick man lay moveless under quilts and brocades; his breath soughed through the room.

The first thing Jane asked for was willow boughs, as green as might still be found, to be set all round his bed. Then she stripped Lord Hugh and looked close at his French scar and felt his ribs, and laid her ear to his chest and back. She asked them to bring her a spear which did not belong to Lord Hugh; also a bellows, a frog, some birdlime, more water, more vessels, and a young cat with its eyes open, but yet living with its dam.

While search went on for all these things, Jane took a mortar and pounded linseed, which she mixed with the birdlime and some vinegar, and forced down Lord Hugh's throat, first of all to purge him. Waiting for this to take effect, she clipped his unbarbered beard, pared his nails, gathered up part of the floor straw into which his bloody spittle had soaked, and made sure of catching some of his water. All this she cooked together in a little stewpan. Next she gave Lord Hugh to eat of a paste compounded of red roses powdered and candied, and gillyflowers and pennyroyal treated in the same way, to clear his head that she might talk to him.

He opened his eyes on her whom he did not know, unsurprised.

"Listen to me, lord of Bedesford. I have come here to make you well. This is what I shall do. We must trick the sickness into leaving your lungs. You see this bullfrog? I shall make him swallow a decoction made of parts of you, boiling hot. This will make him croak for a time — a time during which you must preserve absolute silence, and choke sooner than cough, for the sickness is to mistake the frog's voice for yours and him for you. Meanwhile, I shall employ someone to work these bellows without cease close by your chest. This is to strengthen your lungs, even as the bellows are inexhaustible. But you must be quiet, no matter what it cost you. Do you understand? Do not speak. Raise your head and nod if you have understood me and are willing to do your best to help me. Shake it if you deem the sickness stronger than your will."

Lord Hugh was so weak that sweat streamed down his corpse-nosed face with the effort of nodding.

"Now I am going to give a draught to help you be quiet. Close your eyes, lord of Bedesford, and I will seal them down with beeswax, after, when I kill the frog, to make it seem you have died. You must trust utterly in me whatever I may do. You will sleep and yet not sleep. You will hear and yet not hear. You will know and forget."

The frog croaked in Jane's hands, the bellows were worked by two men taking turns; and there was the sound of running water. Jane had set Baldwin to pouring water from one vessel into another continuously, to cool the sick man's burning blood. The kitten purred by the hearth.

Jane made as if she were tending the frog in her lap, speaking to him in a gentle voice steadily growing louder, "O my lord your coughing sounds most sorely. My lord, your skin is clammy. Your eyes are starting out of

your head. Would that I could exchange you, O my lord that I am nursing
in my lap, for yon man lying on the bed, whom nobody cares for, and
whose lungs can be heard working away strong as bellows. But it is not
possible. It is you whom the sickness fills entirely."

Stealthily she rose, still holding, bewailing, caressing the frog. Suddenly,
with one leap, she gained the fire and dropped the frog where the flames
were most dense — taking the sickness by surprise.

She staggered back and had to hold on to the bedpost. Her dress clung
to her in dark, wet patches; strands of damp hair hung about her brow
and temples.

"Keep the bellows working! Keep the water running!"

She took a short knife from its sheath in her belt and went back to the
hearth. She lifted the kitten by the scruff of the neck and carried it, kicking and clawing, to the bed.

"Sit up, lord of Bedesford."

The man who for days had been unable to move without assistance,
sat up. He seemed asleep.

"Open your mouth, lord of Bedesford. You are about to receive health
and life to drink."

Holding the kitten above Lord Hugh's head, Jane cut its throat with
a single stroke of her knife. The kitten's blood, steaming as it met the air,
fell over Lord Hugh's quiet face like a dark, hot, wet cloth unwound off
the bale. As much of it as poured into his mouth he swallowed. His face,
his nostrils, his sealed eyelids did not even twitch.

> "One life of the cat
> I take for leech fee,
> For fee of execution.
>
> The second cat life
> Ends in its own death.
> Trouble us not, second life.
>
> Third life of the cat
> Goes to Lord Hugh.
> Likewise the fourth life.
>
> And the fifth and sixth,
> Seventh and eighth lives.
> Ninth life is Hel's, mother of darkness.

> Second and ninth lives, flee:
> Trouble us not.

Keep the bellows working. Keep the water running. Sleep, sleep, lord of Bedesford."

The sick man fell back and slept on. Jane took a cloth and washed the cat's blood off him. Once more she stoked up the fire and thrust the drained corpse down into it. At length she dropped her arms to her sides with a sigh, and said, "Now we may speak. He will not waken until the cock-crow. Then if, striving to open his eyes, his lids break the wax, he will live. I have done my utmost. Now you must pray all you can."

"The spear you asked for, wise woman?"

"That I shall not use until we are certain the sickness was well and truly trapped in the frog and the fire. You must understand that what I have just done was to drive away his present sickness only. The spear is to heal the lingering hurt from his old wound. It is a pity we cannot have the spear that made the wound; but we can try. I shall bleed him a little and smear the blade with his blood. Therefore, see you, the spear must not be able to recognize him for its owner. Then shall I tend the blade, cooling it, anointing it, as if it were the wound itself. Many wounds have I healed in this fashion, but I never yet tried it with a weapon that was not truly the right one. Yet try it I will. Now it will be best if I rest me. Much power has gone out of me in these hours. And do you watch and pray. Pray for him and pray, if you will, also for me that have wrestled with Darkness and Death."

Jane stayed on in my lord's bedchamber without anyone else to help her, by her own request, save in the way of bringing and taking what was needed.

Nobody thought that there was danger to her chastity, and not only because my lord was still so weak. Mind you how Master Lamb had tried to convince Juliana of the bondwoman's effect on Black Andrew and in-deed all full-blooded men? Well, either it required the sea air, just as the voluptuous flowers of the sea will fade without they are steeped in salt water, or men of the sea alone were prone to the sea-reared intoxication of the pirates, or else fresh baptism had changed the essence of her woman-hood even as it had her name. We could see she was very fair, and stately, but the finest thing about her we deemed was her hair, which she wore covered up, showing solely in her eyebrows and eyelashes. It was inhuman, like strange jewelry, which one may admire but not long to kiss.

"I am awake," Lord Hugh called, in a voice still feeble but clear and dry. "Come and sit by me, woman. Talk to me."

Jane lifted the pot she had been stirring from its hook and placed it on the hearthstone. She fetched her spinning and sat down on the bed step. Her drab garments became one with the curtain dusk, the pale shapes of her feet, hands, and face alone showed up. Slowly the spindle sank and was tucked up again under her invisible arm; slowly the twirling thread emerged and grew.

"Talk to me. Tell me, how long have I to live now? How far will the cat last me? A cat's life is not very long."

Jane smiled. "So you are not satisfied, lord of Bedesford — you that a little while ago had only a few hours left of your own life?"

"There is a carp in my pond that lived there before my father's father's time and outlived the fish murrain before the Black Death. He has a silver ring through one gill. That is how we know him."

"And you would have had me bleed that carp into you? Fish blood is alien to man blood. And, as you cannot make bread without flour, so you cannot make a spell without what happens to be the ingredient proper to it."

"But why a cat?"

"Of all beasts the cat alone has nine lives. With any creature that has only one, life cannot be transferred, merely ended. Nine, which is three times three, is a sacred number, and therefore dangerous. Eight, which is four times two, each two being itself twice one, is like quicksilver and slips through your fingers. Seven is the most powerful number, and will not bend to any will. But six, a pair of threes, is fixed and limited and subject to control; lacking a third three, it is malleable. After all death debts are paid, six lives remain of the cat's nine. We reckon that its original nine lives total up to the span allotted to man. Barring accident, and discounting what amount of life you have already spent, the six hale, whole cat lives you have eaten should bring up your life again to three score and ten. But it is a life like any other, and is not proof against future disease or injury."

Lord Hugh lay still, thinking, for a while. "I was told that you call yourself a king's daughter. Never have I heard of kings' daughters being taught the crafts we leave to lesser folk."

"Ay, and so it took me to save you. Lesser folks' lesser craft availed you nothing."

"Yet should I have thought no king's daughter would willingly live enslaved. If it were I — they would have to keep me in chains. They would have to kill me before they could make me work." He stretched comfortably in his warm bed.

"It is easy to see you have never lain in chains."

"Do you think," Lord Hugh demanded suspiciously, "that now you have gained power over me?"

"Perhaps. If I troubled to use it."

"If anyone but you had answered me thus!"

"There you see it, already."

"What?"

"Anyone but me. I am excepted. It is my power." Jane laughed aloud rarely; she did so now. "Lie down, lie still. This is part of my cure, lord of Bedesford! I make you angry to make you well and strong, for to your soul anger is the elixir of life." After a moment Lord Hugh laughed with her. Such was her power.

The Feast of Peace and Reconciliation

by Pär Lagerkvist

> 1490? Among the arts which flourished during the
> Italian Renaissance was the art of political crime.
> Petty despots and great princes practiced it with
> ostentatious zeal. Treason, treachery, and murder in
> high places were as typical of the age as patronage
> of poets and painters. In this excerpt a court dwarf,
> consumed by hate and misanthropy, describes with
> admiration his prince's finest hour.

Now I shall relate the story of yesterday and, above all, I shall
describe the great feast which concluded the peace ceremonies connected
with the treaty between our princely house and that of Montanza; and
what happened there.

First we assembled in the throne room and the treaty of lasting peace
between our states was read aloud. Its wording was eloquent and high-
sounding, and it also contained clauses relative to the abolishment of the
border fortresses and free trade between our peoples and various agree-
ments to facilitate this trade. Then came the signatures. The princes stepped
forward to the table, followed by their chief nobles, and put their names
on the two large documents which lay there. It was quite impressive. There
followed a blaring fanfare from sixty trumpeters who stood along the four
walls of the hall, at a distance of three paces from each other, clad alternately in our own and Montanza's colors. Then those present trooped into
the great banqueting hall with the master of ceremonies at their head, to
the festal strains of specially composed music. The mighty room was lighted
by fifty silver candelabra and two hundred torches held by lackeys in
gilded liveries and also by lads who had been taken straight from the
streets, dressed in foul rags with their bare dirty feet on the stone floor.
At close quarters they smelled very disagreeable. There were five tables
in the hall, weighed down with silver and majolica and vast dishes of cold
meats and fruit of every hue, and twenty large groups of statuary modeled
in sponge cake, which they told me represented various scenes from Greek
mythology, a heathen faith of which I know little. All the appointments
in the middle of the central table were of gold — candelabra, fruit bowls,
plates, wine ewers and goblets — and here sat both the princes and all the

other persons of royal blood and our and Montanza's chiefest followers. The Prince sat opposite il Toro and beside him was the Princess in a gown of crimson with slashed jeweled sleeves of white damask and heavy gold embroideries over her fat bosom. On her head she wore a silver net studded with diamonds which flattered her ugly chestnut hair and, since she had indubitably spent several hours painting herself, it was for once easy to see that her plump flabby face must one time have been very beautiful. She smiled her own special smile. The Prince wore a simple close-fitting suit of black velvet, the sleeves inset with pleated yellow silk. He was slim and youthful and supple as a rapier. He was rather reserved, but seemed to be in good humor, for time and again he stroked his short black hair as is his habit when pleased. I felt passionately devoted to him. Il Toro was clad in a short, very broad-shouldered coat of dark green cloth and rare sables, and beneath that a scarlet suit with heavy golden chains depending from the collar. In this garb he looked shorter and burlier than ever, and his thick bull neck protruded from the brown sable fur in all its crimson obstinacy. In appearance he was well-bred amiability personified, but one cannot judge by people's faces. It is their bodies which show them as the kind of animals they are.

Of course Don Riccardo was at that part of the table, in one of the best places, though by rights he should have been sitting at one of the other tables. He always pushes himself forward and naturally the Prince cannot do without him — nor the Princess either for that matter. He chattered and showed off from the very beginning, twiddling contentedly at his curly black beard. I gave him an icy glance, which none but myself could interpret. But enough of that.

A little apart — though how could that be, since they too were sitting at the table like all the others — were Giovanni and Angelica, side by side. It was natural that they should have been placed together since they were of much the same age and both of princely blood. At least he is, but she may very well be a bastard. They were the only young things among the many hundred guests and they seemed more like children than adults, and therefore rather apart from the others. It looked almost as though they had come there by mistake. Poor Angelica was making her entry into the great world and was dressed up in a white satin gown with long tight-fitting sleeves of gold brocade and a coif of pearls and thin gold thread on her colorless fair hair. Of course she looked frightful, and for those who were accustomed to seeing her in plain, almost common, clothes, the effect was grotesque and pretentious. Her mouth was agape as usual

and the baby cheeks red with shyness. Her big blue eyes shone as though
they had never seen so much as a wax candle before. Giovanni, too, seemed
rather embarrassed among all these people and kept throwing them bash-
ful glances, but he was a trifle more sophisticated, and the bashfulness
appeared more to be a part of his nature. He was dressed in blue velvet
with a gold embroidered collar and a narrow chain with an oval gold
locket which is reported to contain a portrait of his mother, she whom
they say is in paradise — but who can tell? She may just as well be writhing in purgatory. He is deemed handsome. I heard some of the guests
whisper something about it, but when I then heard them talking about
a "handsome couple" I realized that they must have a very peculiar notion
of beauty. At any rate he is not to my taste. I think that a man should
look like a man. One cannot believe that he is a prince and a Montanza.
How will he ever be able to reign over a people and sit on a throne? Personally, I doubt if he will ever get a chance to do so.

The children took no part in the conversation and seemed grievously
embarrassed when anyone looked at them. Nor did they talk very much
together, but I noticed how they kept looking strangely at each other, and
smiling secretly whenever their eyes met. I was surprised to see the girl
smile, for as far as I remember I have never seen her do so before, at least
not since she was quite small. She smiled very carefully as though feeling
her way. Perhaps she knew that her smile was not beautiful. But then, I
never think that human beings are beautiful when they smile.

After closely watching their behavior, I began to wonder more and more
what might be the matter with them. They scarcely touched their food
and at times they just sat there staring down at their plates. I could see
that their hands were meeting in secret under the table. When anybody
near by leaned against his neighbor and observed them, they became bewildered and red in the face and began to talk very earnestly to each
other. By degrees I realized that there was something special between
them — that they were in love with each other. This discovery had a strange
effect on me. I scarcely know why it upset me so much, and made such
a disagreeable impression on me.

Love is always disgusting, but love between these two who were no
more than a pair of innocent children, seemed to me more repulsive than
anything I had previously known. The mere sight of it made me burn
with wrath and indignation.

But more of this later. I have dallied far too long with these infants who, after all, were not the principal figures at the banquet. I shall continue with my description of the latter.

After the guests had eaten the cold meats of which there was a profusion on the tables, the major-domo appeared in the doorway, mounted on a white mare saddled in purple, and loudly announced the first twelve dishes which were then borne in by numerous camerieri and scalchi, to the strains of a fanfare blown by two trumpeters who led the mare by the bridle. The smoking dishes spread a smell of meat, sauces, and fat which impregnated the whole room, and I, who can hardly endure the stink of food, was within an ace of vomiting. The seneschal arched his back like a cockerel and strutted importantly to the Prince's table, where he began to carve the roasts, ducks and capons, the grease dripping from the fingers of his left hand which held the viands. All the while, he gesticulated with the long carving knife which he held in his right hand, as though he were a famous fencer exhibiting his perilous art. The guests stuffed themselves with food and I began to feel the discomfort, the vague nausea from which I always suffer when I see people eating, especially when they are gluttonous. They gaped in the most disgusting manner in order to make room for the too large bits and their jaw muscles champed in constant unison, while one could see the tongue moving about the food inside the mouth. Il Toro was the unpleasantest of all those who sat at the Prince's table. He ate like a churl, devouring everything with a shocking appetite, and he had a nasty bright scarlet tongue, broad like that of an ox. On the other hand, the Prince did not eat voraciously. He partook of less than usual that evening and scarcely drank at all. Once I saw him raise his glass to himself and, sunk deep in thought, gaze into its greenish depths as though surveying the world through them. The others drank tremendously. The servants kept running around and filling up the goblets and beakers.

Gilded sturgeon, carp and pike were borne in on immense majolica dishes, receiving great applause for their skillful dressing, mighty galantines adorned with wax ornaments so that one could not see what they really were, pasties shaped like the heads of deer and calves, sucking pigs roasted whole and gilded, and sugared and perfumed dishes composed of fowls, quails, pheasants and herons. At last came two pages clad as hunters carrying an entire wild boar, as gilded as the rest, with flames issuing from its jaws which had been filled with a burning substance that smelled most foully. Girls dressed, or rather undressed, as nymphs, ran in to strew the floor with scented powders, in order to get rid of the disgusting stench, but the result was worse than ever, and the air became suffocatingly stuffy. For a space, I could scarcely breathe.

Il Toro accepted a portion of the boar as though he had eaten nothing before, and all the others took huge slices of the dark red flesh which still dripped blood, but was, nevertheless, regarded as a delicacy. It was horrible to see them start their chewing again, while the gravy trickled from their lips and beards; there was something shameless about the spectacle, and I, who always avoid eating in public and never consume more than is absolutely necessary to maintain life, was more and more nauseated by these red swollen oversized creatures who seemed to be all stomach. Then, too, it was horrible to see the boar being opened up by the seneschal and the gory slices cut out of its inside until at last only the skeleton and a few rags of flesh remained.

Don Riccardo, eating left-handedly and with a special servant to cut his meat for him, put away a large quantity and drank deeply. His face was one wide foolish smile, and with his good arm he kept raising his goblet to his lips. His outfit of dark red velvet was meant to personify some kind of passion — he always dresses himself for his mistress. His eyes were brighter and wilder than usual and every now and again he gesticulated and recited some nonsensical poem or other, addressing anybody who would listen to him, except the Princess. High-sounding words about love and the joy of living flowed out of him as soon as the wine had poured down his throat. The Princess' eyes glistened whenever he looked at her, and she smiled her mysterious smile at him. Otherwise, she sat there as usual during a feast, half present and half absent. Sometimes they glanced sideways at each other when they thought nobody else was looking, and then her eyes shone with a moist, almost morbid, luster. I noticed them. I never let them out of my sight, though they had no notions of it. Nor did they guess what was brewing in my soul. Who knows anything of that? Who knows what I, the dwarf, have abrewing in my innermost being, to which none has access? Who knows anything about the dwarf soul, the most enclosed of all, where their fate is determined? Who can guess my true identity? It is well for them that they cannot, for if they did they would be terrified. If they did, the smile would die on their faces and their lips would wither and fade forever. Not all the wine in the world would make them red and moist again.

Is there no wine in the world can make them moist again? Will they never smile again?

I also looked at the damigella Fiammetta who, though not at the Prince's table, was quite honorably placed, better than her position warranted. She is fairly new to the court, and I had not paid much attention to her before, though I cannot think why. In point of fact, she is startlingly handsome, tall and straight, young and yet mature, ripe for the world. Her face is dark and hard and very proud, with pure regular features and coal-black eyes with a deep-lying glint in them. I noticed that the Prince sometimes cast an uneasy glance in her direction, as though trying to discover what was going on behind her immobile face, or guess at her thoughts or mood. She never looked at him.

Now nearly all the lights in the hall were extinguished and a titillating music was heard, though no one knew its source. Twelve Moorish dancers came rushing into the darkness with burning torches between their teeth, and began to perform a mad breath-taking dance. Now they whirled with a ring of fire around their black heads, now they brandished their torches in the air or flung them high and caught them again between their glittering fangs. They played with the fire as though with something dangerous, and everybody stared at them, half fascinated and half scared by their strange demoniac appearance. They swarmed about the place where the princes were sitting and when they flourished their torches the sparks showered over the table. Their dusky faces were twisted into fierce grimaces as they lit the torches, and they resembled spirits of the underworld whence they had brought their fire. And why should they not have lighted them there? Why should they not have dipped their torches in the flames of hell? I stood with my old dwarf's face hidden in the darkness and watched these spirits and their strange demoniac dance which seemed to have had the devil for teacher.

And as though to indicate their origin and recall the kingdom of death to which all must one day return, they ended by turning down their torches and extinguishing them on the floor; then they vanished as though the earth had opened and engulfed them.

There was a grisly feeling in the air before the lights went up again, and my dwarf's eyes, which see better in the dark than the eyes of men, observed that some of the guests sat with their hands on their dagger hilts, as though ready for anything.

Why? It was only a troupe of dancers which the Prince had hired in Venice to entertain his guests.

The hall was illuminated again and immediately the major-domo reappeared in the doorway on his white mare and, to the shrill strains of a fanfare, announced the most exquisite course of the evening: *"Pavoni!"* Whereupon fifty servitors hastened in from every side, bearing aloft huge jeweled silver dishes on which were enthroned as many peacocks, gilded and with their iridescent tails outspread. Everybody manifested the most idiotic delight at the sight, and the depression aroused by the down-turned torches, presaging death, was swept away. These creatures are like children, forgetting one game for another. But they never forget the game I play with them.

Having gaped their fill at the monstrous dishes, they proceeded to devour them, just as they had done with all the other victuals. The banquet began all over again with the appearance of these vainglorious birds which I have always detested and which remind me of human beings, but that may be the reason why men admire them so and regard them as a delicacy. As soon as they had been gobbled up, new courses were brought in, pheasants, capons, quails and ducks again, sturgeon, carp and dripping venison steaks, fresh quantities of food with which they stuffed themselves until my mounting disgust was turned to nausea. Then came mounds of cakes, confectionery, and sweetmeats stinking of musk, which they swallowed as though they had had nothing else to eat throughout the evening. And at last they flung themselves upon the groups of Greek mythological statuary which they had pronounced so rarely beautiful and cut them up and devoured them until only a few morsels remained, and the stained tables looked as though they had been devastated by a horde of barbarians. I looked at the havoc and the hot sweaty creatures with the greatest aversion.

Now the master of ceremonies stepped forward and requested silence. He announced the performance of a superlatively beautiful allegory, composed at the Prince's gracious command by his court poets for the diversion and edification of the honored guests. The skinny sallow scribblers who sat far down at the humblest table pricked up their ears and looked stupider than ever as they eagerly and superciliously awaited the performance of their work of genius, whose profound and symbolic purport was to constitute the climax of the feast.

Mars made his entrance on a stage at one side of the hall, clad in shining armor, and declared that he had decided to compel the two mighty champions Celefon and Kalixtes to a combat which should be renowned throughout the world and crown their names with eternal glory, but above all would tell mankind the power and the glory of himself, the god of war, how at his command gallant blood would flow and heroes fight each other at his will. He concluded by saying that as long as courage and chivalry remained on earth they would be at the service of Mars and none other, and then left the scene.

Now appeared the two champions and as soon as they caught sight of each other they began their sparring, so that their blades flashed through the air, and there followed a lengthy bout of fencing which was much appreciated by those in the hall who understood its subtleties. Even I must admit that they were notable swordsmen and I took great pleasure in that part of the piece. During the duel they pretended to inflict grievous wounds on each other and staggered exhaustedly under them until they sank lifeless to the floor.

The god of war reappeared and perorated about the honorable combat which had caused their heroic deaths, about his irresistible power over the senses of men and about himself, the mightiest on earth of all the Olympic gods.

After his departure a gentle music was heard. Shortly afterward the goddess Venus glided in, followed by her attendants, and found the two knights sadly mangled and, as she herself said, bathing in their blood. The attendant nymphs bent over them, lamenting that two such fine handsome men should have been needlessly bereft of their manhood and should have ceased to breathe. As they wept over this tragic fate, their mistress declared that only the cruel Mars could have incited them to this senseless duel. To this the nymphs agreed, but reminded her that Mars had once been her lover and that despite her celestial gentleness she had held him in her arms. But she asserted that this was a base slander, for how could the goddess of love favor the wild and barbaric deity who was hated and shunned by all, including his own father, the great Jupiter? Then she stepped forward and touched the fallen champions with her magic wand, whereupon they rose up all hale and hearty and pressed each other's hands in token of lasting peace and friendship, swearing that never again would they yield to the fearsome Mars and wage bloody war against each other.

Then the goddess made a long and moving speech about love, praising it as the strongest and gentlest of all powers, as the source and vivifying origin of all things; of its delicate might which imbues strength with gentleness, which dictates heavenly laws for earthly beings, and compels all living creatures to obey them; which can change and purify the hard coarse senses of men, the acts of princes and customs of the people; of brotherly love and charity reigning in a devastated and bloodstained

world with chivalry and magnanimity in their service, bestowing other
virtues on mankind than those of martial glory and feats of arms. Raising
her magic wand she proclaimed that her almighty divinity would conquer
the earth and transform it into the happy abode of love and eternal peace.

If my face had been able to smile I should have done so during this
ingenuous epilogue, but these sentimental outpourings were most flatter-
ingly received and caused many of those present to feel really moved and
enchanted, so that the last mellifluous words were followed by an almost
reverential silence. The scribblers who had achieved this result looked
highly pleased and obviously appropriated to themselves all the credit of
this successful entertainment, although nobody gave them a thought. Undoubtedly they regarded this eloquent and skillful allegory as the only
important item in all the festivities which celebrated the peace treaty between our princely house and that of Montanza. But I wonder if what was
to follow was not the most important of all.

As usual I had my place behind my princely lord, and from the depths
of my experience could guess at his wishes before they were uttered, sometimes before he even formulated them to himself, thus fulfilling his commands as though I were a part of himself. Now he gave me a sign,
imperceptible to all others, which meant that I was to serve il Toro, his
son, and his foremost men with the rare wine which is in my sole keeping
and which I alone know how to prepare. I fetched my golden ewer and
filled il Toro's goblet. He had thrown off his fur-trimmed coat which had
become too warm during all his potations, and there he sat in his scarlet
garb, short and stout and sanguine, his face as red as fire. The golden
chains round his bull neck were tangled together so that he looked as he
were fettered in them. I filled his goblet to the brim. His replete body
exuded an odor of sweat, eructations and wine fumes, and it nearly made
me vomit to be so near such a repulsive bestial creature. I thought: "Is
there anything so vile as a human being?" and continued down the table
to some of his foremost men, commanders and noble lords, who had been
put at the Prince's table. Then I filled Giovanni's gold beaker, while
Angelica looked at me with her stupid bright blue eyes, as foolish and
wondering as in her childhood days when she read in my compressed old
man's face that I did not want to play with her. I saw that she dropped
his hand when I approached and I also saw how she paled, presumably
because she feared that I had discovered their shameful secret. And she
was quite right. With disgust I had observed their growing intimacy, the
more shameful since they belonged to two opposing parties, and were

themselves but innocent children who had allowed themselves to be dragged down into the slough of love. I had observed their blushes, caused by the fire of love within their veins, by concupiscent appetites whose revelation is enough to make one sick. It was with the strongest distaste that I had marked the combination of innocence and carnal desires which is particularly nauseating and whereby love between persons of that age is rendered even viler and more abhorrent than any other kind. I took pleasure in filling his beaker which was only half empty, but that is of no consequence when I add my own wine.

Last of all I approached Don Riccardo and filled his goblet to the brim. It was not part of my mission, but I have missions of my own. I give myself orders to fulfill. When I saw the Prince looking at me I met his eyes with serenity. They were strange. Human eyes are sometimes like that — a dwarf's never. It was as though everything in his soul had floated to the surface and was watching me and my actions with mingled fear, anxiety and desire; as though strange monsters had emerged from the depths, twisting and turning with their slimy bodies. An ancient being like myself never looks like that. I stared straight in his eyes and I hope that he noticed the steadiness of my hand.

I know what he wants, but I also know that he is a knight. I am no knight, but only the dwarf of a knight. I can guess his desires before they have been uttered, perhaps before he has formulated them to himself, and thus I perform his most inaudible commands, as though I were a part of himself. It is good to have a little bravo like that who can render all manner of service.

While I filled Don Riccardo's goblet, which was empty as usual, he leaned back guffawing with laughter so that his beard stood straight out and his mouth with all its broad white teeth gaped open like a crater. I could see right down his throat. I have already mentioned my distaste for laughing people, but the sight of this fool who "loves life" and finds it so irresistibly amusing, roaring with vulgar laughter, was particularly revolting. His gums and lips were wet and the tears swam in the nasty little glands in the corners of his eyes from which radiated small red streaks over the dark brown unnaturally brilliant eyes. His larynx bounced up and down under the short black bristles on his throat. On his left hand he wore a ruby ring which I recognized as one which the Princess had given him when he was ill and which I had carried next my heart wrapped up in one of her nauseous love letters. Everything about him disgusted me.

I do not know what he was laughing at, nor does it matter, for I cer-

tainly should not have found it in the least amusing. Anyhow he never
did so again.

My task was done. I awaited further developments beside this ebullient
fool of a whoremonger, and smelt the stink of him and the velvet of his
dark red suit which was meant to express passion.

My lord the Prince raised his greenish goblet, turning his amiable smile
toward the honored guests, toward Lodovico Montanza and his brilliant
train around the table, but most of all toward il Toro who was sitting
opposite him. His pale aristocratic face was delicate and noble and very
different from the hot and swollen countenances of the others. In gentle
but virile tones he bade them drink a toast to the lasting peace which
henceforth should reign between their two states, between the princely
houses and between the peoples. The long meaningless fighting was at an
end and a new era had started which was going to bring peace and prosperity to us all. The old saying of peace on earth was at last to be realized.
Thereupon he drained his glass and in solemn silence the noble guests
emptied their golden goblets.

Afterward my lord remained sitting with his glass in his hand and his
absent gaze seemed to be contemplating the world through it.

The ripple of voices began again and I do not know exactly how long
it lasted; that kind of thing is difficult to reckon, one loses a sense of time.
I was far too strung up, violently and indescribably so, and furious because Giovanni had not touched his wine. Aflame with wrath I saw Angelica smile faintly and pull it toward her, pretending that she wanted
to drink it herself. I had hoped that they would both do so, that in their
infatuation they would want to drink from the same source; but neither
touched it. Perhaps the accursed girl suspected something, perhaps in
their prurient exaltation they felt no need of wine. I seethed with bitterness. Why should they live? Devil take them!

Don Riccardo on the other hand gulped it down in a single draught.
He emptied this his last goblet to the Princess, saluting the "lady of his
heart" as usual. In a last attempt at wit he gesticulated humorously with
his useless right arm and raised the excellent libation which I had served
him with his left hand, smiling the while that much admired but essentially vulgar smile of his. And she smiled back at him, first rather mis-
chievously, and then with that moist desirous glint in her eyes which I
find so sickening. I cannot understand how anybody can have that kind
of expression in his eyes.

Suddenly il Toro gave vent to a weird howl and stared straight ahead

of him with stiff glaring eyes. Two of his men who had been sitting on
the same side of the Prince's table hastened to him, but simultaneously
began to stagger, seized the edge of the table and collapsed on their seats,
where they writhed in agony, groaning something about having been poisoned. Not many heard them, but one of the others, who was not yet so
seriously affected, shouted to the whole room: "We are poisoned!" Everybody sprang up and confusion reigned. Other members of il Toro's suite
leaped up with drawn daggers and other weapons and rushed to the central table where they attacked our men and tried to push their way through
to the Prince. But his followers had risen in their turn to defend themselves and their lord, and a terrible tumult began. There were many killed
and wounded on both sides and blood flowed in torrents. It was like a
battlefield indoors among the decked tables, between drunken red-faced
warriors who after sitting peacefully beside each other suddenly found
themselves fighting desperately for their lives. Screams echoed from every
side and drowned the groans and sighs of the dying. Appalling curses
summoned all the devils in hell to this spot where the foulest of all crimes
had been committed. I climbed onto a chair so as to get a good view of
what was happening about me and stood there, frenzied with excitement,
surveying the tremendous results of my work: the extirpation by me of
this loathsome race which deserves nothing else. I saw how my mighty
sword went forth over them, pitilessly destructive, demanding vengeance
and punishment for everything. How I dispatched them to burn eternally
in the fires of hell! May they burn forever! All these creatures who call
themselves men, and who inspire such disgust and nausea! Why should
they exist? Why should they revel and laugh and love and overrun the
earth? Why should these lying dissemblers and braggarts exist, these lust-
ful shameless creatures whose virtues are even viler than their sins? May
they burn in the fires of hell! I felt like Satan himself, surrounded by all
the infernal spirits involved at their nocturnal meetings, swarming around
them with grinning faces, dragging their souls still hot and stinking from
their bodies, down into the kingdom of death. I felt my temporal power
with a joy greater than I had ever known, and so acute that I nearly
lost consciousness. I felt how the world had, through me, been filled with
terror and doom, and transformed from a brilliant feast to a place of fear
and destruction. I brew my draught and princes and powerful nobles groan
in their death pangs or wallow in their blood. I offer my potion and the
guests at the lavish tables grow pale and their smiles fade and none raises
his glass again or prates of love and the joy of living. For after my drink

they forget all the beauty and wonder of life and a mist enfolds everything and their eyes fail and darkness falls. I turn down their torches and
extinguish them so that it is dark. I assemble them with their unseeing
eyes at my somber communion feast where they have drunk my poisoned
blood, that which my heart drinks daily, but which for them spells death.

Il Toro sat motionless. His face was blue and his underjaw with its
sparse beard viciously lowered as though he wanted to bite somebody with
his brownish tusks. He was a frightful sight with his eyes bulging yellow
and bloodshot from their sockets. Suddenly he twisted his hunched neck
around as though trying to dislocate it, and the clumsy head lurched over
on one side. At the same time his short bull body arched itself backward
in a bow, jerked convulsively as though stabbed — and he was dead. By
now all his men at the Prince's table were writhing in infernal agony, but
it was not long before they too ceased to give any sign of life. As for Don
Riccardo, he died leaning back with half-closed eyes as though reveling
in my drink, much as he used to do when he had tasted a really rare wine;
suddenly he threw out his arms as though wanting to embrace the whole
world, fell backward, and died.

During the fighting and confusion nobody had any time for those who
were dying, so they had to expire in their own way as best they could.
Only Giovanni, who had been sitting on the same side as il Toro and who,
thanks to the damned girl, had not tasted my potion, hurried forward to
his father and stood bending over his horrible body as though under the
delusion that he could help him. But a burly man with fists like those
of a blacksmith elbowed his way to him just as the old scoundrel breathed
his last, seized the lad as though he had been a feather and dragged him
through the hall. The young coward allowed himself to be taken away and
thus escaped us. Devil take him!

The tables were upset and their furnishings trampled underfoot by the
combatants who were now quite insane with bloodlust. The women had
fled shrieking, but in the midst of all the desolation I saw the Princess
standing as though petrified, with rigid features and glassy eyes. Her ca-
daverous pallor contrasted comically with the paint which still remained
on her middle-aged face. Some of the servants managed to lead her from
that terrible room, and she followed them listlessly, as though unaware
of where she was or whither they were conducting her.

Though inferior in number, il Toro's men still brandished their inade-
quate weapons as they retreated toward the exit doors. The battle continued on the stairs, and they were pursued down them and out into the

square. Here the sorely pressed enemy was relieved by Montanza's body-guard which had been summoned from the Palazzo Geraldi and, under cover of the latter, they contrived to make their escape from the town. Otherwise they would undoubtedly have been mowed down to the last man.

I stood there alone in the abandoned hall, now in semidarkness since all the candelabra had been thrown onto the floor. Only the ragged, apparently half-starved urchins remained, creeping around with their torches and hunting among the corpses for scraps of food and grimy delicacies, which they devoured at incredible speed, simultaneously grabbing as much of the silver as they could hide beneath their tatters. When they judged it unsafe to stay any longer, they threw away their torches and stole out with their booty on padding naked feet, and I was left alone in the room. Undisturbed I gazed around me, sunk deep in thought.

The flickering rays of the dying torches illuminated the mutilated corpses of friend and foe, lying in their blood on the stone floor among the trampled bloodstained napery and the remnants of the great banquet. Their festal garments were torn and dirty and their pallid faces still twisted and evil, for they had died fighting in the midst of their mad fury. I stood there, surveying everything with my ancient eyes.

Brotherly love. Eternal peace.

How these creatures love to discuss themselves and their world in great and beautiful words!

Columbus

by Hermann Kesten

1492 That Columbus sailed the ocean blue in fourteen hundred and ninety-two because Queen Isabella
of Spain pawned her jewels to finance his voyage is
one of the most popular of history's false legends.
How the money really was raised is revealed in the
following account of one of the most misunderstood
episodes in history.

Again Columbus stood before the throne, again he spoke of the
Cross and of gold, of converting the heathen and of the fabulous lands,
Zipango, Mangi, and Cathay on the East Coast of Asia, painting them in
the glowing Byzantine colors of Marco Polo. While he spoke in the Hall
of Ambassadors at Granada, trying to stir the King and Queen to enthusiasm, he was feeling already in advance the terrible disappointment that
he had felt a hundred times already face to face with King Joao of Portugal, the Council of Genoa, the King of France, with all the dukes, counts
doctors and scholars, monks and sailors, into whom he had tried to instill
his enthusiasm and who had mocked him or indolently listened to his words
as to fairy tales. While he delivered his familiar and often-practiced glowing speeches he looked back again over his dreadful failure of a life, his
frustrated greatness, his disappointed dreams.

Born in a weaver's hut in a village near Genoa, ship's boy at the age of
fourteen, Columbus had voyaged to every known part of the earth: at
thirty he had come to rest in Lisbon, married a penniless girl whom he
had seen praying in a convent chapel, had a son whom he called Diego,
lived on the sale of charts and maps which he made himself, studied many
travelers' tales and the papers left behind by his dead father-in-law, a distinguished Portuguese mariner who had colonized and governed the island
of Porto Santo, slowly conceived the idea of discovering the western sea
route to Eastern Asia, corresponded with distinguished scholars about this
project, above all with Paulo Toscanelli of Florence, one of the most learned
men of the day, whose information enlightened him extremely. He worked
out his plans with exactitude, and believed that fame and reward were
already his.

Then began the dreadful round of suffering and humiliation. At last he succeeded in penetrating to King Joao of Portugal. Joao listened to him and heard him out and tried to steal his plans and ideas, and sent other men off secretly as directed by those plans. When King Joao failed in this he dismissed Columbus in disgrace. Columbus fled; his wife died; with his little son Diego on his arm he landed at Palos in Andalusia and knocked on the monastery door at La Rabida for a crust of bread; the abbot, Juan Perez, kindly took him in, saw to his wants, gave him letters of recommendation to the Duke of Medina Coeli, who threw him out, and to the Duke of Medina Sidonia, who looked after him for two years and then sent him away with a barren recommendation to the King and Queen of both the Spains. They heard him and consoled him. He journeyed to Genoa and made his proposals there and was mocked. The King of France wrote him gracious letters.

Before he departed from Spain Columbus went once more to the monastery at Palos to take farewell of his friend, Juan Perez. He had spent seven years in Spain; with his head on the bosom of a poor and beautiful girl, he had felt his disappointments burning only more fiercely and his tears of rage more bitter; his mistress had died leaving him a little son, Fernando; and now he knocked again at the door of the monastery of La Rabida near Palos, in rags, without money, without any real prospects, equipped with nothing but his foolhardy dreams and his derided certainty that his dreams were called to serve humanity better than seventy kings of the kind that treated him as a swindler, as a charlatan, as a dog.

The faithful Prior Perez, who understood little of ships and much of men, had been once confessor to Queen Isabella. He journeyed to Santa Fé, was granted an audience, eulogized his friend, and obtained a small sum of money for Columbus so that he could buy a new pair of breeches, a new cloak and a mule to appear in decently at Court.

Columbus bought himself a pair of breeches, hired a mule, rode to Santa Fé, seized a sword, fought against the Moors, saw Boabdil kissing the hands of the King and Queen, saw the fall of Granada, all the while apathetic and downcast; what did a city more or less matter to him when he proposed to discover half the world, the whole of India, and conquer it? He despised this whole burdensome war with the Moors which was holding him there, devouring the finest years of his life. Meanwhile he bustled about, a little-known man in the barren train of importunate solicitants, brooding in corners of anterooms, indulging his plans of world conquest, a fellow in patched breeches, gray-haired, of vulgar descent, a foreigner, treated almost like a fool. With perfect indifference, more, with profound contempt, he surveyed the noisy jubilations of assembled Christendom over the destruction of a charming city.

At last they called him to an audience. There sat Ferdinand and Isabella, puffed out with the empty pride of victors; there sat their father-confessor, Talavera, the new Archbishop of Granada, a kind and learned man, holding in no account the so-called progress of human knowledge, who thrice before, head of learned commissions of casuists and lawyers, monks and theologians, had insolently snubbed him; in the Council of Salamanca this mild Talavera had designated the plans of Columbus as "vain, impracticable and resting on foundations too weak to deserve the support of the government." Now this same Talavera, raised still higher, regarded the still deeper fallen Columbus, staring maliciously at his coat, newly bought with the alms of the Throne.

Columbus spoke and spoke; before his eyes there swam the encouraging countenances of his friends, Deza, the new Archbishop of Seville, and the new Grand Chancellor and Grand Cardinal of Spain, Mendoza, and Beatrix de Moya, and the Aragonese Santangel and Sanchez, both wealthy baptized Jews; they all seemed transformed into evil caricatures; Columbus was seized by a dangerous fury; these middle-sized figures grew and grew, and he, a thousand times superior, became poorer and smaller. He was already despising himself; he did not know any more whether he himself really believed in his words, in the gold, in the converting of the heathen, in the Byzantine soap bubbles of Marco Polo, in the lofty goal he proposed, which was to use the gold from the lands he would discover to equip a great crusade and free the Holy Sepulcher in Jerusalem — was that really the dream of his life: a grave in Jerusalem? Or did he want to discover the Western Passage, nothing more? There was one, he knew that, he believed in it, he would find it, this very year and now; he held the truth in his hands; the Western Passage, that alone was what he wanted! And was everything else, gold and Cross, mankind and fame, only a light pretext of his dreaming soul? He no longer knew. As through thick walls he heard the friendly tones of the Queen: "And what is your demand, Señor?"

"The Western Passage," he wanted to answer, and "Your death," he wanted to answer; he hated them all, this rabble of dwarfs on the thrones and in the palaces of Europe, this rabble that possessed power and gold and ships and the force of law and which shut him out and suppressed him for so long that other, inferior, men would steal his fame, and the Western Passage to India. He pulled himself together and spoke with dignity:

"I demand for myself and my heirs the titles and the powers of viceroy and admiral over all the lands and islands discovered by me, and a tenth of all the future revenues they may yield."

Talavera, the new Archbishop of Granada, bellowed loudly: "This is presumption! This is impossible for your Majesties! The impudence of a casual adventurer in pump-hose!"

Isabella regarded this curious man who possessed nothing and spoke like a king to kings. She said: "Señor! You are not used to the ways of the Court. You are not dealing here with small shipowners, with tradesman. We can promise you a small title, which is no doubt what you would like — perhaps the title Don and an official position, if it would please you, as captain of one of our ships?"

Columbus stared at her as though she were mad. The Queen suddenly felt the whole man as a monstrous insult. She recognized the rebel in him. He depressed her, he irked her. She glanced at Ferdinand. It was, as always, in vain to try to read his face. His face expressed majesty, nothing more. Unconsciously Isabella compared the face of the adventurer, Columbus, with the face of the King. Suddenly she felt again, as before in previous audiences, pity for this Genoese. She said: "Well, have you considered?"

Columbus answered: "I demand for myself and my heirs the titles and the powers of viceroy and admiral over all the lands discovered by me, and a tenth of future revenues they may yield."

He spoke his sentence to the end although Ferdinand and Isabella rose in the middle of his words and left the Hall of Ambassadors, followed by Mendoza, Deza, Beatrix de Moya, and the whole Court. Meditatively Talavera, Archbishop of Granada, who alone remained with Columbus, gazed at the impudent petitioner. He thought: He is a fool. I'll pray for him. He is no swindler, he is simply mad!

Columbus stared back at him. Talavera explained gently: "The audience is ended, Señor."

With quiet dignity Columbus bowed and left the Hall of Ambassadors and strode through the gardens of the Alhambra until he came to the cathedral where he had tied up his mule, and he untied it and mounted the good beast and rode through Granada and Santa Fé; he rode away, away from Spain! A big man, disappointed, he rode on his mule, swaying from side to side, paying no attention to the way. A wind carried away his hat and he rode on. His hair, threads of it still red, as all his hair had been originally, but for the most part already gray, blew out in the wind.

Columbus rode down the highways, the dust enshrouded him; he rode

and thought: Only to be away from Spain! Ah, half a lifetime lost — am
I a fool, I have spooned wisdom into myself, and what has it done for me?
Born into a marvelous world, a world which has just awakened and rubs
the sleep from its eyes, the thousand-year-old sleep of Faith, with reason
radiant at last as though it were the gay light of the first morning, with
life smiling at last, these Spaniards, old-fashioned knights, new-fashioned
priests, drag this new life back from the dawn of reason into the ancient
darknesses of their false fanaticism. Is that why I have been born into the
finest century of history? Have I had this great, blessed, silent glance into
the promised land simply for a false heaven to rise up against me and
throw down the lofty and only true dream of a finer life? I have lost seven
years! In the bosom of a woman I found likewise a false heaven. Fool that
I am! She is dead and I have a son left, Fernando. India or the bosom
of a woman?

The mule had stopped at the edge of the road, beneath a mulberry tree.
Pensively it stood before a briar. Columbus was oblivious. Pensively he
stared at the wide heavens. The love of a woman, he murmured, or king
of half a world. I have chosen, and I am betrayed! Instead of splendor and
fame, another son, a Fernando to add to a Diego. Dost Thou scorn me,
O God? As Columbus stared at the setting sun with his tired, small, blue-
gray eyes that saw so far, it seemed to him that suddenly a wall fell and
he looked. He saw nothing but the sea, the unending sea, with the waves
crashing down in front of him and running out gentle and smooth; the sea
sparkled green and gold, and he walked dry-footed over it, through the
Western Passage to India!

Then he heard his name called. Who called him? He would not go back.
"Messer Colombo, Señor Colon, Don Cristobal!"

Slowly Columbus turned. Before him on a horse caked with sweat was
Don Luis Santangel, Treasurer of Aragon, a baptized Jew and a favorite
of King Ferdinand.

A patron, thought Columbus, bitterly smiling; what does the fellow
want? With solemn dignity he bowed.

"Messer Colombo! You must come back. Their Majesties have graciously
listened to me. They await you; they agree to everything!"

"No more," said Columbus.

"But, Señor, what are you saying? It is Queen Isabella who calls you
back!"

"Well, you can tell Isabella . . ."

"No, Señor! I am paying for the expedition, I, Luis de Santangel of Saragossa. You have my word and in addition the grace of the King and Queen of Spain."

"You, Don Santangel! Noble patron, how can I thank you . . ."

"No more, Señor. I, Don Luis de Santangel, believe that you will find the Western Passage; understand me, I am doing the biggest piece of business in my life!"

"Ah!" said Columbus. "Do you sniff the gold?"

"Gold I have enough of. I see fame."

Columbus rode back. The King and the Queen were gracious, as kings and queens are. They solemnly signed and sealed with an oath an agreement which they intended, as ever and anon, to break when it proved more advantageous not to keep it; with solemn faces Ferdinand and Isabella sat and sealed and signed at Santa Fé on April 17th, 1492. They, as masters of the seas of the world, appointed the Genoese, Christopher Columbus, Admiral, Viceroy, and Commander in Chief of all the islands and realms which he might discover in the Western Sea. Ferdinand and Isabella signed. Columbus was granted the right to propose three candidates for the governorship of every realm, the Throne to make the final choice of one of these. He was granted exclusive jurisdiction over all matters of trade, a tenth of all products and gains within the boundaries of his discoveries, and another eighth in addition if he, Columbus, bore an eighth part of the expenditure. These benefits were assured to him and his heirs for eternity, together with the privilege of setting the title "Don" before their names. Ferdinand and Isabella signed.

The harbor of Palos received the royal order to deliver two ships as punishment for some transgression. The city of Palos resisted. No single sailor would sail. They said they had no desire to sail to certain death and Hell. The family Pinzon, seamen, of Palos, delivered a third ship, their own property, part of the cost of which Columbus was to bear out of his future gains. A hundred and twenty men shipped in three ships. The total expenses disbursed by the Crown amounted to 17,000 gulden and were lent by Santangel. The three ships together displaced 160 tons. Only one of them, the flagship, called the *Santa Maria* was decked in. The War Fleet, as it was called (and the name was the only pomp about it), was instructed to keep itself well away from the African coast and other overseas possessions of Portugal. On the morning of August 3rd, 1492, Columbus and his seamen, with the exception of the Jews, took Communion, made confession, and said farewell to the Old World, standing out to sail to India.

It was, however, the most trivial undertaking that Isabella ever undertook at sea; she possessed a navy of 120 ships and she had already equipped great ocean-going expeditions, great and stately undertakings. This Columbus was worth only a handful of ducats to her. Ferdinand simply could not stand the fellow.

When the little ships vanished over the horizon there remained a gloomy sadness in the Andalusian town of Palos. It was Friday morning.

The Philosopher's Stone

by Dmitri Merejkowski

1494   The great dream of medieval and Renaissance
alchemists was to find the philosopher's stone which
would transmute base metals into gold. Lodovico
Sforza, Duke of Milan, called Il Moro because of his
dark complexion, was one of the most splendid and
unscrupulous of Renaissance princes. Leonardo da
Vinci was his court artist for seventeen years.

Messer Galeotto had passed all his life in seeking after the Philosopher's Stone.

Having concluded the medical course at the University of Bologna, he
had entered as a pupil, or *famulus*, the service of Count Bernardo Trevisano,
at that time celebrated as an adept of the occult sciences. Subsequently,
during the course of fifteen years, he sought the transmutative Mercury in
all possible substances, — in kitchen salt and ammonia, in divers metals,
in virgin bismuth and arsenic, in human blood, spleen, and hair, in animals
and vegetables. Six thousand ducats of his patrimony had flown up the
flue of the melting furnace. Having spent his own money, he had taken to
that of others. His creditors had put him in jail. He had escaped, and during the following eight years made experiments with eggs, wasting twenty
thousand of them. Next he worked with Maestro Enrico, the Papal Protho-
notary, upon different sorts of copperas, had become ill from their poisonous
vapours, had lain ill for fourteen months, abandoned of all, and had almost
died. Enduring beggary, humiliations, persecutions, he had visited, as an
itinerant laboratorian, Spain, France, Austria, Holland, Northern Africa,
Greece, Palestine, and Persia. At the court of the King of Hungary they
had tortured him, hoping to find out the secret of transmutation. Finally,
already aged, wearied, but not disillusioned, he had returned to Italy, at
the invitation of Duke Moro, and had received the title of Court Alchemist.

The middle of the laboratory was taken up by an unwieldy oven of
fire-clay with a multiplicity of compartments, fire-doors, sumps, and bellows. In one corner, under a layer of dust, flung down in disorder, were
sooty scoria, resembling cooled lava.

Intricate appliances — alembics, stills, chemical receivers, retorts, funnels,
mortars, cucurbits with glass vials, long-necked, serpent-shaped pipes,

279

enormous bottles, and the tiniest of jars — encumbered the work-table. Poisonous salts, lyes, and acids exuded a pungent odour. An entire mystical universe of gods lay imprisoned in the metals, — seven gods of Olympus, seven heavenly bodies: in gold, the Sun; Luna in silver; in copper, Venus; in iron, Mars; in lead, Saturn; in pewter, Jupiter; while in the living, glistening quicksilver, — the ever-mobile Mercury. Here were substances with names barbaric, inspiring terror in the uninitiate: Cinnabar Crescent; Wolf's Milk; Brazen Achilles; asterite; androdama; anagallis; panopticum; aristolochia. A precious drop of Lion's Blood, which cureth all ills and bestoweth youth eternal, — gotten through many-yeared toil, — glowed redly, like a ruby.

The alchemist was seated at his work-table. Spare, small, as wrinkled as an old mushroom, but still irrepressibly spry, Messer Galeotto, propping his head with both hands, was attentively watching a cucurbit, which with a low ringing sound was bubbling and coming to a boil over a rarefied bluish flame. This was the Oil of Venus — *Oleum Veneris,* — of a translucent green colour, like a smaragd. A candle, burning beside it, cast an emerald reflection through the cucurbit upon the parchment of an open ancient folio, the work of the Arabic alchemist Jabir Abdalla.

Hearing steps and voices upon the stairs, Galeotto arose, cast a glance about the laboratory, to see if all were in order, made a sign to the servant, a taciturn *famulus,* that he put additional coals in the melting furnace, and went to meet his guests.

The company was in a merry mood, just after supper and Malvasia. Among the retinue of the Duke were the chief Court Leech, Marliani, a man of great acquirements in alchemy, and Leonardo da Vinci. The ladies entered — and the quiet cell of the man of learning became filled with the fragrance of perfumes, the silken rustling of dresses, frivolous feminine chatter and laughter, — as if with the jargoning of birds. One of them caught with her sleeve a glass retort, sending it to the floor.

" 'Tis naught, signora, — be not perturbed!" spake Galeotto pleasantly. "Allow me to pick up the fragments, lest you cut your dainty foot."

Another took in her hand a sooty piece of iron slag, soiling her light glove, scented with violets, and an adroit cavalier, squeezing her hand on the sly, tried to clean off the stain with a lace handkerchief. The fair-haired, mischievous Donzella Diana, well-nigh swooning from pleasant apprehension, touched a cup filled with quicksilver, spilling two or three drops on the table, and, when they started rolling in shining globules cried out:

"Look, look, signori, here be miracles: liquid silver, running of itself, and alive!" And she almost jumped for joy, clapping her palms.

"Is it true that we shall behold the devil in the alchemic fire, when the lead is turning into gold?" asked the pretty little roguish Filiberta, wife of the old Consul of the Salt Industry. "What think you, messer, — is it not a sin to be present at such experiments?"

Filiberta was exceedingly devout, and it was told of her that she permitted everything to her lover save a kiss on the lips, holding that continence was not entirely violated whilst the lips with which she had sworn at the altar to marital fidelity remained innocent.

The alchemist approached Leonardo and whispered in his ear:

"Messer, I assure you I can appreciate the visit of such a man as you . . ." He pressed his hand hard.

Leonardo was about to protest, but the old man interrupted him and took to nodding his head:

"Oh, of course! . . . 'Tis all a mystery to them, — but surely you and I understand one another? . . ."

Then, with an affable smile, he turned to his guests:

"With the permission of my patron, the Most Illustrious Duke, and also of the ladies, my fair sovereigns, I begin the experiment of divine metamorphosis. Attention, signori!"

In order that no doubts might arise about the genuineness of the experiment, he showed the crucible, — a melting pot with thick sides of fireclay, — requesting that everyone present look it over, touch it, tap its bottom, and become convinced that there was no deception of any sort about it, during which he explained that alchemists at times secrete gold in melting pots with double bottoms, of which the upper one, cracking from intense heat, reveals the gold. The chunks of pewter and of coal, the bellows, the sticks for stirring the cooling slag of the metal, and the rest of the objects, in which any gold could be concealed, — and even those in which, evidently, there was altogether no chance of concealment, — were also subjected to close scrutiny.

He next cut up the pewter into small pieces, laid it in the crucible, and put it in the maw of the oven upon the flaming coals. The taciturn, cross-eyed *famulus* — with a face so pale and gloomy that one lady well-nigh fell into a swoon, taking him in the darkness for a devil — began to work the enormous bellows. The coals burned more intensely under the noisy stream of air.

Galeotto entertained his guests with patter. Incidentally, he aroused general merriment, by styling alchemy *casta meretrix,* — a chaste strumpet, that hath many admirers, yet deceiveth all, and, while she seemeth accessible to all, has up to that time been in the embraces of none, — *nullos unquam pervenit amplexus.*

The Court Leech Marliani, a man corpulent and ungainly, with a bloated, clever and pompous face, frowned angrily as he listened to the alchemist's chatter, and wiped his forehead; finally, unable to endure it, he spoke:

"Messer, is it not time for business? The pewter is boiling."

Galeotto reached a blue bit of paper and unwrapped it carefully. It proved to contain a powder, of the light yellow of a lemon, unctuous, glistening, like roughly ground glass, giving off an odour of burnt sea salt, — this was the much sought tincture, the priceless treasure of the alchemists, the wonder-working Stone of Wise Men, *lapis philosophorum.*

With the sharp edge of a knife he separated a barely perceptible grain, no larger than a rape-seed; he rolled it into a pellet with white beeswax, and cast it into the seething pewter.

"What do you suppose the potency of the tincture to be?" asked Marliani.

"One part to two thousand eight hundred and twenty parts of the metal to be transmuted," replied Galeotto. "Of course, the tincture is as yet not perfected, but I think that in a short while I shall attain the magnitude of a unit to the million. 'Twill suffice to take a grain of powder the weight of a millet seed, to dissolve it in a barrel of water, dip up a nutshell full, and sprinkle it on a vine, in order to have ripe clusters appear as early as May! *Mara tingerem, si Mercurius esset!* I would turn the sea into gold, if there be quicksilver enough!"

Marliani shrugged his shoulders: the boasting of Messer Galeotto maddened him. He began proving the impossibility of the transmutation by deductions in scholastics and the syllogisms of Aristotle. The alchemist smiled.

"Bide a while, *domine magister,* — I shall right soon present a syllogism which you will not find easy to controvert."

He threw on the coals a handful of white powder. Clouds of smoke filled the laboratory. With hissing and crackling the flame leapt up, multicoloured, like a rainbow, — now blue, now green, now red. Confusion arose in the crowd of spectators. Subsequently Madonna Filiberta told that in the purple flame she had seen a devil's phiz. With a long cast-iron hook the alchemist lifted up the lid of the crucible, now at white-heat, — the pewter was boiling, foaming and gurgling. The crucible was covered again.

The bellows whistled, snorted, — and when ten minutes later a thin iron rod was plunged into the pewter, all saw a yellow drop appear on its tip.

" 'Tis ready!" uttered the alchemist.

The clay smelter was taken out of the oven, allowed to cool, and broken, — and, ringing and sparkling, an ingot of gold fell out before the gathering struck dumb with astonishment.

The alchemist pointed to it, and, turning to Marliani, uttered triumphantly: "*Solve mihi hunc syllogismum!* Solve me this syllogism!"

" 'Tis unheard of. . . . Unbelievable. . . . 'Tis against all laws of nature and logic!" mumbled Marliani, spreading his arms out in confusion.

The face of Messer Galeotto was pale; his eyes flaming. He raised them to heaven and exclaimed:

"*Laudetur Deus in aeternum, qui partem suae infinitae potentiae nobis, suis abjectissimis creaturis communicavit. Amen.* Glory to God on high, Who doth bestow upon us, the least worthy of His creatures, a moiety of His infinite power. Amen."

Upon testing of the gold on a touchstone moistened with nitric acid, a yellow glistening streak was left, — it proved purer than the very finest Hungarian or Arabian. All surrounded the old man, felicitating him, wringing his hands. Duke Moro led him aside:

"Wilt thou serve me, truly and faithfully?"

"I fain would have more than one life, in order to dedicate them all to the service of Your Excellency!" replied the alchemist.

"Look thou, then, Galeotto, that none of the other rulers . . ."

"Your Highness, should any find it out, give orders to hang me like a dog!" And, after a short silence, with a fawning obeisance he added:

"If only I might receive — — "

"What? Again?"

"Oh, for the last time, as God is my witness, — for the last time . . ."

"How much?"

"Five thousand ducats."

The Duke after cogitating a while, beat him down by a thousand, and agreed.

The hour was late; Madonna Beatrice might be alarmed. They got ready to depart. The host, escorting his guests, offered a piece of the virgin gold to each one as a memento. Leonardo stayed behind.

When the guests had departed, Galeotto approached him and said:

"Master, how did the experiment please you?"

"The gold was in the rods," Leonardo answered calmly.

"What rods? What would you say, messer?"

"In the rods wherewith you stirred the pewter, — I saw all."

"You yourself inspected them . . ."

"Nay, not those."

"Not those? What mean you, an it please you . . ."

"Why, I tell you I saw all," Leonardo repeated with a smile. "Persist not in your denial, Galeotto. The gold was hidden inside the hollowed-out rods, and when their wooden ends had burned off it fell into the crucible."

The old man's legs gave way beneath him; on his face was an expression both submissive and piteous, like that of a caught thief.

Leonardo approached and laid his hand upon the alchemist's shoulder.

"Fear not; none shall find out. I shall not tell."

Galeotto seized his hand and uttered with an effort:

"Truly, — you will not? . . ."

"Nay, — I wish you no ill. Only why do you do this? . . ."

"O Messer Leonardo!" exclaimed Galeotto, and immediately after his immeasurable despair a hope just as immeasurable began to gleam in his eyes. "I swear by God that even if appearances were against me, remember that my deception is but temporary, for the weal of the Duke and for the triumph of science, for I have really found it, — I have really found the stone of the mystagogues! As yet, of course, I do not actually possess it, but to all intents and purposes it can be said that it exists, inasmuch as I have found the path, — and as you know the chief thing in this matter is the path. Some three or four experiments more, and 'tis accomplished! What else was I to do, master? Can it be that the discovery of the greatest truth does not warrant such a petty lie? . . ."

"What are you and I about, Messer Galeotto, — just as if we were playing hoodman blind?" exclaimed Leonardo, shrugging his shoulders. "You know as well as I do that the transmutation of metals is nonsense; there is no Philosopher's Stone, nor can there be. Alchemy, necromancy, black magic, as well as all other sciences not founded on exact experience and mathematics are either deception or madness, — a banner of charlatans, blown full by the wind, after which the foolish rabble flocks . . ."

The alchemist continued to gaze at Leonardo with clear and wondering eyes. Suddenly he bent his head to one side, slyly closed one eye, and began to laugh:

"Well, now, that is not at all nice, master, — not at all nice, really! For am I not of the initiate, eh? As though we do not know that you are the greatest of the alchemists, the possessor of the most hidden secrets of nature, a new Hermes Trismegistus and a new Prometheus!"

"I?"

"Why, yes, — you, of course."

"You are a jocose fellow, Messer Galeotto!"

"Nay, it is you who are jocose, Messer Leonardo! Ai, ai, ai, what a dissembler you are! I have in my time seen alchemists jealous of the mystery of their science, but never yet to such a degree as yourself!"

Leonardo looked at him attentively, was about to become angry, but could not.

"So, — you really do," he said with an involuntary smile, "you really do believe in such things? . . ."

"Do I believe!" exclaimed Galeotto. "Why, do you know, messer, that if God himself were to come down to me right now and say: 'Galeotto, there is no Philosopher's Stone,' I would reply to Him: 'Lord, even as it is true that Thou hast created me, so is it true that the stone is, and that I shall find it!"

Leonardo no longer contradicted, nor grew indignant, he listened with curiosity.

When the conversation touched on the aid of the Devil in the cryptic sciences, the alchemist with a smile of conquest remarked that the Devil was the poorest creature in all nature, and that there was not a single being in the universe more weak than he. The old man believed only in the might of the human reason, and asserted that all was possible to science.

Then suddenly, as though recalling something amusing and charming, he asked if Leonardo saw frequently the spirits of the elements: but when his companion confessed that he had not seen them once as yet, Galeotto was again incredulous, and, with relish, explained in detail that a Salamander has an elongated body, a finger and a half in length, spotted, thin, and rough; while the Sylphide's is translucently blue, like the sky, and ethereal. He told about nymphs, — Undines, living in the water; of underground Gnomes and Pygmies; plant *Durdallas,* who inhabit plants, and the rare *Diameias,* dwellers in precious stones.

"I could not even convey to you," he finished his narration, "how benevolent they are!"

"But wherefore do the elemental spirits appear not to all, but only to the elect?"

"How could it be posssible for them to appear to all? They fear coarse people, — libertines, drunkards, gluttons. They are to be found only where malice and cunning are not. Otherwise they become timid like the beasts of the forest, and hide from human gaze in their native element."

The old man's face became illumined with a tender smile.

"What a strange, pitiful and endearing fellow!" reflected Leonardo, no longer feeling indignation against the alchemical ravings, endeavouring to speak with him cautiously, as with a child, ready to pretend the possession of any secret desire, that he might not hurt the feelings of Messer Galeotto.

They parted friends.

Messer Niccolo Machiavelli

by Maurice Samuel

1500–1503   Cesare Borgia, the brilliant son of Pope
Alexander VI, is widely believed to have inspired
The Prince by Niccolo Machiavelli. In that world-
famous work it is argued that usurping princes must
make expedient use of fraud and force to maintain
themselves in power. The first of these two short
episodes takes place in Rome early in Cesare's short
career; the second in Assisi after Cesare had suppressed a revolt of his own officers by murdering four
of them at Sinigaglia.

An hour after Cesare had left with Cardinal d'Este, a guard at the
outer door announced: "The honourable envoys of Florence."

"That," thought Giacomo, "must be Messer Francesco Capello, reinforced by some newly-arrived official to give more weight to his tedious-
ness." He looked hastily for the right phrases with which to put the
Florentines off. Beyond any doubt Cesare had made an appointment with
Messer Capello and had deliberately broken it. He was tired of Messer
Capello's monotonous argumentation. Florence was at war with Pisa, and
the French were "helping" Florence; that is, they were delaying action
and collecting salaries. The miserable Bailli of Dijon, the French captain
who had proved such a pest to Cesare at Forlí, was now practicing his
extortionary arts on the Florentines. What the Florentines wanted from
Cesare was a strong plea to his ally, the French King, to put some life
into the troops before Pisa. That, said Messer Capello, would be to Cesare's
advantage, too. Cesare would be needing the French troops himself before
long, for the resumption of the Romagna campaign. If the war with Pisa
was not brought to a close, there would be two of them competing for
King Louis' men. And besides, Florence would prove a grateful friend
and would raise no objections to Cesare's conquest of the Romagna. And
so, and so forth — all of which wearied Cesare who, it now seemed, was
determined to avoid the Florentine envoy for a time.

Giacomo rose from his desk and went into the outer room. He bowed
and said: "Gentlemen, I cannot tell you with what regret — " but as he
looked up he was stricken dumb for an instant. Side by side with Messer

Francesco Capello stood Messer Niccolo Machiavelli. In a single instant
Giacomo traversed the twelve months — were they only months, not years?
— which separated the meetings, saw himself a youngster in the home of
Messer Buonavia, felt about him Forli, Messer Cobelli, Madonna Leonora
and Picina: and in the same instant he recovered: "Gentlemen, I cannot
tell you with what regret the Duke went forth but a little while ago, having received a most urgent call."

Messer Capello, the older and more important man, said without hesitation: "We scarcely hoped that your master would keep his customary
hours on such a day. Will he return this evening?"

Giacomo, who knew that when Duke Cesare went out with Cardinal
d'Este, neither of them would be seen again till morning, answered:

"Sir, I know not." He was still shaken. "He left no word. Nor have I
word from Messer Agapito."

Machiavelli was looking at Giacomo thoughtfully. "Was it not in Forli
that we met?" he asked.

"It was in Forli, Signor Machiavelli, a long time ago."

The expression on Machiavelli's face changed slightly; a strange echo
of the last look that Giacomo had seen on it, by moonlight, the look of
embarrassment, supplication, bravado and complicity, came and went.

"Truly a long time," he said, "if we measure time by events. Yes! Messer
Giacomo Orso! Messer Capello, this young gentleman, who speaks for
Messer Agapito and the Duke, was, but one year ago, in Forli, at the time
of my embassy to the Countes Caterina Sforza, clerking for a merchant.
I do not wonder at finding him here. There was in him even then that
which belongs to courts and princes."

Giacomo smiled his acknowledgment, bowed to Messer Capello, and answered Machiavelli according to the book:

"That is most gracious of you, sir. Gentlemen, I would gladly invite
you to wait at your ease, if such an invitation did not imply that I expect
the Duke to return soon."

"We shall acquit you of all responsibility," answered Messer Capello,
pleasantly and quite obviously aware that Cesare would not come back
that evening. He turned to Machiavelli. "Even though the Duke return,"
he said, "we cannot importune him with our affairs. He must at this moment be moving heaven and earth to find those who attacked his brother-in-
law; and I doubt not that was the urgent business which called him forth."

"Indeed, I doubt not," answered Giacomo, looking straight at Messer
Capello.

"We shall not wait," announced Messer Capello, after a pause.

Machiavelli turned to his fellow-envoy. "Messer Capello, it is a happy chance that I have met Messer Orso again. By your leave and his, I shall wait with him."

When the older envoy had withdrawn Messer Niccolo seated himself at Giacomo's table, and asked: "Do your duties take you far into the night?"

"I have ended for this evening," answered Giacomo, "and the night is my own. If it were not too forward, I would offer you an hour of poor entertainment over a bottle of wine in my lodgings."

Machiavelli smiled, and the smile hinted at many things, such as: "I like the forwardness of a young rooster," and "You need not tell me that the Duke will not return tonight," and "It is a pleasure to be rid of Messer Capello."

Giacomo went into the adjoining room, to announce his departure to Pietro and Bernardo. At the third hour after sunset he left the Chancellery for his lodgings.

Two very remarkable days followed for Giacomo. It appeared that Machiavelli's visit to Rome was, if not secret, more or less unofficial. He had recently left the camp before Pisa, disgusted by the trickery of the French; he would shortly set out for France on a mission to King Louis. He had not expected to be received by Cesare, still less to succeed with him where Messer Capello had failed. What he had really come for — so much Giacomo gathered indirectly from their first conversation — was to find out what line his colleague had taken with Cesare. That was all the business he had in Rome; except, perhaps, a little diversion, a trifling adventure, to console him for the loathsome time he had passed at Pisa. But of course, that did not come under the heading of business, did it? And Messer Niccolo half winked at Giacomo, who, at this point, became as it were stony with embarrassment, blushed, and lost all his courtly composure. Somehow, without being averse to salacious talk, it made him sick to have a man, and especially an older man, intrude on his sexual privacy. Messer Niccolo skipped away from the subject and did not refer to it again. For the rest, he gave freely of his company to Giacomo. That first night they talked into the sixth hour. They ate together the next day at a tavern in the Borgo. The day after, Machiavelli accompanied Giacomo to his fencing lesson. Giacomo felt that the older man had taken a liking to him; chiefly, no doubt, because he listened so eagerly. Machiavelli had also perhaps had a notion that he might pump some information out of the young secretary; if so, he soon abandoned it. He gave rein, instead, to his passion for large and general discourse. It was only at the beginning — after he had retreated hastily from the reference to some lusty little wench who might brighten the nights for him — that he touched on immediate business, criticising, with a frankness which was meant to flatter Giacomo, Messer Capello's propositions.

"I am not by any means of the view of my colleague," he said. "Were your Duke merely ambitious of conquering the Romagna, he might well plead with the French King to help us finish the Pisan war speedily. And Florence might well be content to have il Valentino ruler of the Romagna. Such an arrangement would be more desirable than a Venice established so far south of the Po. But your Duke is a great prince. His ambitions go further. They go very far indeed. And if he lives — — "

He stopped. Giacomo thought once more of the phrase: "Meanwhile Sertorius was assassinated by his own officers."

"If he lives," said Machiavelli, "he will not be content with less than all of Italy. Of what advantage is it to him, then, that there should be peace between Florence and Pisa, or tranquility in any part of Italy which is not yet under his rule?"

Giacomo refilled Machiavelli's cup and remained gravely attentive.

"For if there could be permanent tranquility, there would be no need for anyone to unite Italy. But since there is no permanent tranquility, it would be a disaster that an accidental tranquility should occur precisely when one comes to unite the country. It might even be argued that an inopportune tranquility should be skillfully disturbed when necessary."

Machiavelli looked closely at Giacomo, who felt himself pressed to the wall, and answered: "It is a matter to be considered."

"Have you not seen," asked Machiavelli, earnestly, "how people with a toothache forget their pain sometimes as they approach the barber-surgeon's door, and turn back, thinking themselves cured? It may well be that at the approach of a saviour and unifier of Italy, a factitious and as it were treacherous tranquility would set in, and the saviour, like the surgeon's door, and turn back, thinking themselves cured? It may well so that the patient may submit to the drawing of the tooth. Disorders must be created for the liberator to repress."

Giacomo could not answer with an outright yes to the startlingly simple logic of the argument. Nor could he find a single flaw in it. He moved the discussion a little to one side. He said musingly: "The prince who intends to unite Italy must certainly show that where he rules there is order and justice, while where he does not, there is disorder and injustice."

"Yes," said Machiavelli. "And the greater the contrast between the tranquility in his dominions and the disorder outside of them, the louder will become the clamour for his intervention, and the sooner will unification be achieved."

At this point Machiavelli stood up, and began to pace the room, frowning as he talked:

"Therefore it is not to Cesare's interest to promote tranquility elsewhere, but rather to foment disorder. And he is aware of this. It may be —" Machiavelli paused, frowned more deeply, nodded, then continued — "it may be that this is he — we cannot tell yet — who will unify our country. For he has all that I find necessary in such a one: not to belong to any reigning house, therefore inheriting no ancient quarrels; possessing the necessary greatness of spirit, the *magnanimitas*, the courage; unafraid to do that which has to be done, lest he be called bad names. Has he not taken as his motto: '*Fays ce que doys, avien che pourra*'? 'Do what thou shouldst, let follow what will!'"

Machiavelli was speaking rapidly but tensely, like one who prepares to write something, and rehearses orally. He turned suddenly toward Giacomo:

"Now I remember, it was of this we talked in Forli. And I remember further that afterwards I was discontented with myself that I had not made my thoughts clearer."

"Signor," put in Giacomo, quickly. "I must offer you my apologies, I was unfit to understand you then. I am altogether different now."

"A little sojourn at a court suffices for one who is ready to learn," agreed Machiavelli. "I, too, have learned much since that time. Dost thou hear me, Messer Giacomo," he adopted the familiar form of address almost impetuously, he was so eager to come to grips with Giacomo's mind, "I have learned since then another great truth. It irked me, in Forli, that I had been sent to Madonna Caterina on a mission of such small account. And it irks me that I shall go to the French court as second to Messer della Casa. But I know that my heart-burning is utter foolishness. There is nothing more pitiful than a man's plaint that his gifts are not understood. If thou art not understood, thou fool —" he talked heatedly, as if chiding himself — "if thou art not understood, it is thy fault only. Messer Giacomo, give no heed to one who laments: 'Ah, if they had only followed my plan, all would have been well.' For the plan which does not include, as part of itself, the means to get itself adopted, is no plan at all. I must laugh at the man who says, 'The world does not appreciate me!' 'The world mis-prizes me!' He that, having abilities, cannot persuade others to hire them, is as if he had no abilities."

It was fascinating not only to listen to the man but to watch him. For as he went into a kind of ecstasy, he was visibly finding the words and expressions which conveyed his full meaning, and it was as if a prisoner were liberating himself from chains of speechlessness.

"And that is why the goodness of those that preach goodness is folly. Do you not hear them say: 'Ah, if the world were only good, as I want it to be!' Aye, messer monk or moralist or philosopher, what means hast thou to make the world good? That is what I ask. And thou hast no an-swer." He confronted Giacomo suddenly: "What means hast thou to make the world good?"

"Word and example," answered Giacomo, to play his part.

"And must not the example match the word?"

"Assuredly it must!" replied Giacomo.

"Well then!" cried Messer Niccolo, triumphantly, "what kind of example do the preachers of goodness set? The example of failure! And that is why the preachers of good must defer their success to the end of the world — which they always do. Thus the best of them know only how to dream of miracles and live on dung. I say to the good man, 'Get thee into some private place and practise thy goodness for thy delectation and that of thy friends. But bring it not into disrepute by proclaiming it as the prin-ciple of the management of kingdoms.' For there nothing counts but the doing of that which one sets out to do. Mark well, that the great prince is he that commands — that is, he directs those that can do, that have the *virtù* of doing. So it is with your Cesare. What men has he not already drawn to his side — and that but a beginning? Orsini and Moncadas and de Lorquas and Baglioni — and Cesare himself still young. But he has that about him which promises — success! Philosophers and artists and crafts-men are but instruments, as other men are; it is the ruler, the true prince, the master of the state, who makes them useful. He uses them, then throws them aside. What had Messer Leonardo been without an il Moro to use him? But now, I doubt not, he, and others like him, Messer Michel Angelo, and Pinturricchio, and Messer Vanucci, and Messer Calmeta, and the Unique Aretino — they are but waiting for the word to be used by Duke Cesare — *if* he succeed; as indeed he may."

Giacomo had a pointed question on the tip of his tongue, hesitated with it, and, again filling Machiavelli's cup, so as to cover his embarrassment, said:

"How does it sort with your Florentine loyalty, Messer Niccolo, to speak thus of my master?"

"I know not if I speak of your master," answered Machiavelli, so promptly that it could be seen that he had well considered that question before. "If he is indeed the unifier and saviour of Italy, then he will be the benefactor of Florence not less than of all the other cities and states. And if he is not the unifier and saviour, then none owes him loyalty, and I am not pledged to him."

"And how shall it be known?" asked Giacomo.

"By his success, by his success, by his success!" cried Machiavelli, triumphantly. "It is permitted to a Caesar to do everything — but fail."

Here he stopped abruptly, either because he was exhausted, or his thoughts had begun to crowd on him too fast.

"Messer Giacomo," he said, in a changed voice, "I have taken advantage of your kindness. I must return to my lodgings now, with Messer Capello, and I know not my way. But you and I will surely talk again before I return to Florence."

Giacomo walked the Florentine envoy to the Navone section, then returned to his own lodgings, his mind in a whirl. This man Machiavelli was altogether extraordinary. He was in his way the counterpart of Cesare. Cesare had chosen as his motto: Do what thou shouldst, let follow what will. Machiavelli's motto might be: Think as thou shouldst, wherever it lead.

At their next meeting Giacomo could hardly wait until they had exchanged courtesies before he began to ply Machiavelli with questions.

He wanted to know, first, wherein a man was an instrument, and what it meant that he could be thrown aside.

They were eating together at a small corner table in a tavern, and leaning over toward each other could converse at ease.

"The being thrown aside," said Messer Niccolo, "is the last and greatest service which an instrument must perform for the user. It is thus when the master uses thee for the execution of a policy which he must later disown, placing the blame on thee, and forcing thee to take the punishment."

"Ah — yes."

"Thy master," continued Machiavelli, "uses in the Romagna an excellent and most pliable instrument — one Don Ramiro de Lorqua, to rule

with a harsh hand, to crush the fierce spirits of Romagnuoli who know not
what order and discipline mean. And it can be done in one way only —
ruthlessness. Ruthlessness. Nor is it for the restoration of discipline alone,
but for the teaching of the people to forsake their looseness, their sloven-
liness, their unreadiness to obey, or to obey in time, doing a thing tomorrow, or next week, instead of now, doing it half-heartedly. Now all that
can only be beaten out of a people, burned out of it, by making examples.
But he that does it will be hated. As Don Ramiro is already hated in the
Romagna."

"Yes," said Giacomo.

"Now when his work is done," said Machiavelli, "he, the instrument,
must be cast aside, so that the hatred remain associated with him, and the
sweet effects of the order, the smooth working of things, be associated
with the ruler himelf, with Duke Cesare."

"He must be cast aside," murmured Giacomo. "He must be given other
employment."

Machiavelli shrugged his shoulders. "The manner of his being cast aside
matters not. Given other employment, or perhaps, for the contentment of
the people, beheaded and thrown to the dogs."

"No!" cried Giacomo, starting.

"But that may be the highest service he can, in the end, render for his
prince," said Machiavelli, smiling at the other's horror.

There was no escape from Messer Niccolo's argument. Both that evening, and in the all too brief hour they spent the next day, when Machiavelli went with Giacomo to his fencing lesson, — which Giacomo cut short,
out of eagerness to resume the conversation — Giacomo felt as though a
light on which he did not dare to open his eyes was slowly breaking
through his closed lids, was penetrating even his flesh.

"For we must remember," said Machiavelli, pressing against Giacomo's
reluctance, "that what matters — and naught else besides — is the triumph
of the Prince, and the order and justice within his kingdom; and therefore the death of this one or that one, if it serve that end, in peace not
less than in war, is the highest justice. It is, indeed, as when one makes
a special example of a criminal, or of one who disobeys in a certain matter, though he is not therein worse than others who have committed the
same crime, or have disobeyed in the same manner. But he is chosen, for
no reason within the misdemeanor itself, to be made an example of. Now
I have heard some say that this is injustice. That a man must be punished
for his crime, not for more or less. But it must be seen otherwise. He is

not punished out of blame, but to prevent others from behaving likewise. And I would go further; and I would say that if it be not possible to find him who has committed a given crime, it would be well to take another, and punish him severely in such wise that at least some are deterred, by the belief that the criminal was caught and punished."

"An innocent man?" asked Giacomo, aghast. "An innocent man, one known to be innocent?"

Machiavelli looked at him simply.

"But thou seemest not to know whereof we speak. Is it not of the good of the kingdom? Is it not of order and justice for the kingdom? If thou must kill one man, in order that a thousand others be saved, what right hast thou to consider whether he is guilty or innocent?"

It made Giacomo perspire a little; he could not answer Messer Niccolo. But he thought of something by the next day, when their third and last conversation took place, as they walked in the sunlight from the slopes of Vatican City toward the Tiber.

"Messer Niccolo," he said, "there is in my life but one purpose, but it has two sides, like a shield, and cannot be with one side only. I have given myself, in faithfulness and truth, to Duke Cesare, believing in him, and knowing that he will unite all Italy, and I will do whatsoever he commands, for I know that he commands nothing which serves not that purpose. That is one side. And there is on the other side — " he hesitated — "a search, for one that must be found and punished. One that slew my brother, and murdered sundry people in my village. Now, what justice or order will there be in this our Italy, if that man be not found and punished?"

Messer Niccolo stopped, looked at Giacomo, and answered shortly: "It is always thus with the instruments — they desire to be also the manipulators. Thou hast thy private purpose, to which I have naught to say. For I talk of one thing: the establishment of order and general justice: and whether this or that particular crime, this or that particular criminal, go unpunished or not, concerns me not and concerns not Cesare."

Giacomo said, boldly: "Now I can answer you, signor. For I have spoken with Duke Cesare of this self-same crime; and I have his assurance that it shall be paid for — that being part of the setting up of order. What say you to that?"

"I say naught," said Messer Niccolo, quietly, like a man who says a great deal. And Giacomo thought: "He would answer, 'Thy prince lies to thee,' but dares not."

Giacomo regretted that at Sinigaglia he had missed, among many other things, the sight of Machiavelli overtaken and swamped by Cesare's dazbling coup d'état. But neither then, nor in the confusion of the ensuing days, when Cesare and his headquarter troops were descending on city after city, did a meeting take place between them. Only at Assisi, where there was a brief pause, Machiavelli came to say farewell.

The long-demanded recall had come for him at last — and he did not seem to be happy about it. He had pleaded for it, he told Giacomo frankly once. "Let them," he said, "send someone of high position to establish friendly relations with the Duke. I have not been charged with that mission." Then he added bitterly: "Nor am I well qualified for it. It should be a man of more eloquence and greater reputation, and one who understands the world better than I do." Now he was free to rejoin his Madonna Marietta, and that, perhaps, explained his outburst of eloquence at his farewell meeting. And perhaps it was a recoil from many weeks of confusion and incoherence. Whatever it was, he talked that evening like one inspired, so that Giacomo was once again cast, and this time more deeply than ever, under the spell of his visions.

Three of them, Machiavelli, Giacomo and Pieter Andradi, sat in Andradi's quarters, not far from that garden of thornless roses where Saint Francis once met and routed the devil. Andradi, whose acquaintance Giacomo had made some weeks before, in Imola, was a newcomer on Cesare's staff. He was of Flemish origin, some twenty-five years old, industrious and reliable, an excellent Latinist, with only a fair command of Italian, a silent but not unfriendly fellow. He had confessed to Giacomo that he was homesick, but Giacomo suspected something else: the turbulent life into which he had fallen was not to his taste.

Machiavelli came to them after the evening meal, which he had taken with the new Florentine ambassador, Messer Salviati. He was flushed, in part with drink, and in part with repression; the first they could smell, the second he revealed voluntarily, because he had no sooner greeted them and taken his seat than he burst out:

"Signori, one can not play the prophet at home — so much Holy Writ tells us; but one should not play the prophet abroad, either, when encountering someone from home."

Ah, thought Giacomo, he has been trying to tell the new ambassador something, and has been snubbed for his pains.

Machiavelli continued: "When say you, gentlemen, is the time to make an alliance with a prince; when his star is rising, or when it is at the

zenith?" He did not wait for an answer. "When it is rising, I say, as merchants buy in a rising market. That is no time to be neutral, to hesitate —
if, indeed, any time is fit for neutrality, which I doubt. For a neutral is
despised by the victor and hated by the vanquished. What think you,
gentlemen?"

Giacomo began to say something cautiously, and did not get beyond
the opening. "For my part — "

"What is one to wait for?" interrupted Machiavelli. "Let us mark the
progress of your Cesare since Sinigaglia. A scant two weeks have passed,
and Città da Castello and Perugia have fallen to him. Baglioni and Monte-
feltros and Varanos have fled from before him. It is no secret that he left
Assisi today with the pick of his soldiers and by now he is already at Castel
della Pieve. Siena trembles, and I do not doubt that Petrucci is already
in flight. Cesare moves like lightning. Tomorrow he will be at the zenith,
the greatest man in Italy. I know not — " he turned particularly toward
Giacomo, "in what proportions *fortuna* and genius have collaborated with
him. But his genius is like that of ancient Rome. How did that mighty
city rise to power? By always and ever having the choice in attack, both
as to time and place. But not that alone. To keep one potential enemy
quiescent by skilful assurances, while she pounced upon another, was her
ever-successful method. In this wise the next victims would always deem
that this particular quarrel was not their business; it was a matter too remote for their intervention. Then, when the flames of conquest had spread
to those who had remained neutral, it was too late for them. They had
only their own forces, which did not suffice. Thus it was that the Romans
never had two important wars on their hands at the same time."

He stood up and began to pace back and forth, like a professor before
his class, making point after point.

"They did not attack the Latins till they had crushed the Samnites. They
did not attack the Tuscans till they had swallowed the Latins. Certainly,
gentlemen, *fortuna* played her part. If the Samnites had attacked Rome
while she fought the Volscians and the Aequeans, who can tell what the
issue might have been? But the Samnites said: 'We will not intervene,
it is not our business.' But therein the cunning assurances of Rome also
played their part. Thus it was again when Pyrrhus came into Italy; Carthage
slept the sleep of false security, and did not waken till Pyrrhus was defeated. Ah, but then it was too late. And the Gauls did not awaken until
the Carthaginians were defeated, and again it was too late. All these things
I have considered, and there is no escape from my conclusions."

Machiavelli was trembling with excitement. He stopped walking and gazed into the distance, like a seer. Giacomo began a question, but the Florentine lifted an admonitory finger and burst out:

"And as further proof of the wisdom of the Romans, whereon your Cesare leans: mark that always, before invading a territory, they secured themselves some secret friends there, who should open a way for them, and serve them as administrators and advisers after their arrival, being more skilled in local affairs. Thus the indecision of the deluded neutral is increased, and spreads to domestic affairs. Which means, gentlemen, not that things remain undone, but that they are half done, or first done and then undone. The Romans had no such weakness, nor has Cesare."

What Giacomo wanted to ask, if he could have found diplomatic words, was whether Machiavelli was ready to come over to Cesare's side. He did not get the chance. Machiavelli continued rapidly:

"Signori, I have written a treatise, and its subject is the late rebellion of the people of the Val di Chiana against our Florentine Republic. And I have begun it with the words which Lucius Furius Camillus used in the Roman Senate after he had repressed the rebellion of the Latins. He said: 'I have done, O Conscript Fathers, all that war can do. Now it is for you to assure our future in regard to the rebels.' And the Romans dealt wisely and decisively with the rebels. They utterly destroyed the city of Veliterno, and transferred its inhabitants to Rome. They demolished the ships of the city of Anzio, and colonized the city with loyal Romans. They knew that half measures are worse than no measures at all; for either a people can be won by kindness, or it can not, and in the latter case it must be reduced to harmlessness. Yet what have we done with our rebels of the Val di Chiana? We have not won the Aretines over, after their rebellion; we have only punished them and harassed them. But neither have we rendered them harmless, for we have left their walls standing, and allowed five-sixths of the inhabitants to remain in the city. And so Arezzo will ever be ready to rebel again, as your Duke Cesare well knows, without my telling him. But *he* did otherwise with his conquests. Where he has had to crush, he has crushed without remorse. And where he has deemed it politic to win a people over, he has done it with a generous will."

He paused again. Giacomo repressed his first question; it was difficult to phrase it in the presence of a third person. He said:

"Messer Niccolo, why is it that in our last conversations, here in the Romagna, you cite again and again what the Romans did? Whereas I remember that in Rome, a year and a half ago, and before that, in Forli, you never looked for examples among the ancients."

Machiavelli's face lit up, as a teacher's might when a pupil puts his finger on the core of a problem.

"Why, you have hit it, Messer Giacomo." He began to walk again. "I have, in this last year, read much and thought much, and I have at last perfected my understanding of the management of men. It is a simple secret. Men do not change in character. The world has always been inhabited by men who feel as we do; it will always be inhabited by men who feel as we do. There have always been rulers and ruled; there will always be rulers and ruled. There have always been good subjects and bad subjects; there will always be good subjects and bad subjects; there will always be rebellions and suppression of rebellions. These are eternal laws. And if we study the past, we shall find the laws expressed in the records. The passions which moved the Romans, their desires and ambitions, are the passions which move us. Now though men do not change in character, they change in regard to their abilities — — "

But at this moment, to Giacomo's amazement, Andradi sprang to his feet, and advancing upon Machiavelli as though he were about to assault him, cried out, in his heavy Flemish accent:

"No, no, no, I will not have it! Is it nothing that Christ came into the world? The Romans were pagans, we are Christians. Is that no change?"

Machiavelli responded hotly, poking a finger into Andradi's chest, and forcing him back into his chair:

"Yes! There has been a change, but a change which arises from a misunderstanding of true Christianity, from a false interpretation of our religion. Does our religion anywhere teach that we shall not love, honour, exalt and defend our country? But to defend our country we need strength, and we have so misused the principles of our religion that we are weak. Consider the strength of the Romans, their love of liberty, and the vigour with which they defended their liberties. Whence did these qualities arise? From their religious education and institutions! Now our religion causes us to despise the honours and possessions of this world. Or let me say, the false interpretation of our religion causes us to do so. And nowhere can this be said more boldly than here, in Assisi, where Saint Francis lived. Consider how he turned his back on the world, and taught others to do so, in such fashion that anyone with the slightest will to rule could rise to mastery. Our religious institutions are part of our education. Among the Romans there was the institution of the sacrifices, great and terrible spectacles, which the young, witnessing, understood as the symbol of man's strength. But our sacrifices are of the heart; they are quiet solemnities, without inspiration. We exalt Saint Francis rather than Francesco Sforza; the Romans glorified into their Pantheon, which in a manner of speaking was their congregation of saints, the commanders of armies and heads of republics. We exalt the humble, the contemplative, the weak and the lowly. The Romans saw the highest good in magnificence of soul and of circumstance, in strength of body, in all the qualities which make men to be feared. Thus we are taught to endure injuries, since our reward will be in paradise. I say we are taught thus — " he added rapidly — "and I say that this is a false interpretation of our religion. It is the interpretation of baseness, effeminacy, indolence, and not the interpretation of virtue." He used the word *virtù*, which means manhood, manliness, virility, strength of purpose.

Andradi was suffering. He tried once or twice to interject a question, but could not find the words quickly enough to throw them into the few brief pauses in Machiavelli's impassioned discourse. He burst out at last, with a single word which he repeated desperately over and over again:

"Impossible! Impossible! Impossible! Impossible!"

Machiavelli stopped short, and passed his tongue between his lips, wiping away a thin accumulation of foam at the edges. He overcame an impulse to say something which Giacomo guessed would have been outrageous and blasphemous. Instead, he forced a smile into his face, a crooked, mocking, and at the same time, bitterly hopeless smile.

"Signori," he said, "this was not my intent at all. I came to bid you a peaceable farewell, and not to belabour you with my midnight visions." He held out his hand.

"Let me accompany you to your lodgings, Messer Niccolo," begged Giacomo.

Machiavelli made a friendly gesture of refusal; the smile had acquired a touch of resignation and even of good nature. As he shook hands with the men he sighed: "Is it not a mad thing to fill the hours between enforced labour with voluntary labour? My apologies, signori, and my best wishes."

He did not succeed in relaxing the tension. Almost the instant he was gone Andradi turned on Giacomo as if he held him responsible for the views Machiavelli had enunciated.

"No, Messer Giacomo! Not madness, but devil's talk! Also it is nonsense, because the devil talks nonsense. Full of sillinesses and contradictions!

Such a man I would try for heresy. He is not alone, Messer Giacomo, I have heard others — — "

Giacomo listened with only half an ear. He nodded slowly and appreciatively, so that the other took him to be in agreement, whereas Giacomo only meant: "I know your state of mind, for I remember my own when I first heard him speak. I do not intend to argue with you."

But he was also nodding in secret agreement with words not uttered by Machiavelli. The contradictions in the discourse — Andradi was right, there were contradictions — sprang only from the need for concealment. Machiavelli could not say outright that Christianity itself corrupted and enfeebled the character of citizens; he therefore put the blame on the false interpretation of Christianity. He could not say outright that the paganism of the Romans was the true religion; he therefore had to say that only its methods and institutions had merit.

Far more wildly than after the talks in Rome, Giacomo felt himself uplifted and was renewed. He took leave of Andradi almost rudely, so impatient was he to be alone and to pursue his thoughts. In the cold winter streets of Assisi he paced back and forth, reluctant to enter his lodgings, reluctant to confine himself. There was a secret abroad in the world, the secret of a release from error. It was known to the circle of the elect, but as yet they did not dare to tell each other of it. Some were even afraid to tell it to themselves, but Giacomo told it to himself, and his heart thudded with the daring of it. He would whisper it, if not to others, at least into the night. Cesare *was* the anti-Christ. He was the restorer, the liberator, in a more glorious sense than anyone outside the circle of the elect perceived; he was the liberator not of Italy alone, but of man. Herein, even to the uninitiate, lay his attractiveness, the terror and admiration which he inspired.

Mona Lisa Gioconda

by Dmitri Merejkowski

1505 To be present while the world's most enig-
matic and versatile artistic genius paints the world's
most famous portrait — that is the invitation extended
by the author of the following imaginative sketch.

Leonardo wrote in his *Book of Painting:*
"For portraits thou shouldst have a special studio, — a court, like an
oblong quadrangle, ten ells wide, twenty long; the walls should be painted
black, with a sheltering projection along the walls, and a canvas awning,
the latter arranged so that folding or unfolding, as required, it may serve
for protection from the sun. If you have not attached the awning, paint
only before twilight, or when it be cloudy and hazy. Such light is perfect."

Such a courtyard for portraiture he had arranged in the house of his
landlord, a noble citizen of Florence, the Commissary of the Signoria, —
Ser Pietro di Batto Martelli; a lover of mathematics, a man of intelligence,
and friendly disposed to Leonardo.

The time was a calm, warm and hazy day toward the end of the spring
of fifteen hundred and five. The sun shone through the humid haze of
the clouds, with a dull, seemingly subaqueous light, with soft shadows,
that melted away like smoke, — the light Leonardo liked best, and which,
as he asserted, bestowed an especial charm to feminine faces.

"Is it possible that she will not come?" he mused upon her whose portrait he had been painting for almost three years, with a steadfastness
and diligence unusual to him.

He was preparing the studio for her reception. Giovanni Beltraffio
watched him on the sly and wondered at the perturbation of his expect-
ancy, almost impatience, which were inappropriate in the usually calm
master. Leonardo arranged in order upon their shelf sundry brushes, pal-
ettes, little pots with paints, which had congealed, becoming covered, as
though with ice, by a light film of glue; he took off the canvas cover from
the portrait, which stood on a movable three-legged easel, or *leggio;* he
turned on the fountain erected for her amusement, whose jets in falling
struck against glass hemispheres, turning them and producing low, strange
music; around the fountain grew her favourite flowers, — irises, — planted

and carefully cultivated by his own hand; he brought some sliced bread in a basket for the tame doe, who was wandering through this yard, and which she used to feed out of her hand; he adjusted the deep-piled rug in front of her chair of smooth dark oak, with back and arms done in lattice-work. Upon this rug, his accustomed place, a white tom-cat of a rare breed, brought from Asia and bought also for her amusement, with eyes of different colours, — the right yellow, like topaz, the left blue, like sapphire, — was already curled up and purring.

Andrea Salaino brought notes and began tuning his viol. There arrived also another musician, — one Atalante. Leonardo had known him while still in Milan, at the Court of Duke Moro. He played especially well upon a silvern lute, which the artist had invented, and which bore a resemblance to a horse's skull. The best of musicians, singers, story-tellers and poets, the wittiest of conversationalists, did the artist invite to his studio, that they might divert her, and obviate the ennui which is usual on the faces of sitters for portraits. He studied her face for the play of thoughts and emotions aroused by the conversations, stories and music.

Subsequently the gatherings had become less frequent, he knew that they were no longer necessary; that she would not grow bored even without them. Only the music was not discontinued, since it helped both of them to work, — for *she*, too, took part in the labour of her portrait.

All was in readiness, but still she came not.

"Is it possible that she will not come?" he reflected. "To-day the light and shade seem to be created especially for her. Should I send after her, perchance? But then, she knows how expectant I am. She must come."

And Giovanni saw how his impatient disquiet increased. Suddenly a slight breath of air swayed the jet of the fountain to one side; the glass tinkled, the white petals of the irises quivered under the watery dust. The sensitive doe, stretching out its neck, was poised in expectation. Leonardo listened attentively. And Giovanni, although he himself heard nothing as yet, understood by his face that it was she.

First, with a meek bow, there entered Sister Camilla, a convertite nun, who lived in her house and accompanied her on every occasion to the studio of the artist; she had the ability of obliterating herself and becoming invisible, modestly taking her seat in a corner with prayer book in hand, without lifting up her eyes or saying a word, so that for the three years she and her mistress had been visiting him Leonardo had almost never heard her voice.

After Camilla came in she whom all had been expecting, — a woman of thirty, in a simple dark dress, with a transparently dark, smoky coif coming half down her forehead, — Mona Lisa Gioconda.

Beltraffio knew that she was a Napoletana, of an ancient family, the daughter of Antonio Gerardini, a grandee who had at one time been wealthy, but who had become ruined during the French invasion of 1495; and the wife of the Florentine citizen, Francesco dell' Giocondo, who had married Mona Lisa after being twice a widower. When Leonardo was painting her portrait, the artist was past fifty, while Mona Lisa's spouse, Messer Giocondo, was forty-five. He had been chosen one of the twelve Banuomini, and was slated to become prior soon. This was an ordinary man, such as always and everywhere abound, — not too bad, not too good; businesslike, prudent, plunged in his duties and the affairs of his agricultural estate. The exquisite youthful woman seemed to him the seemliest ornament of his house. But the charm of Mona Lisa was to him less comprehensible than the merits of a new breed of Sicilian bullock, or the benefit of custom duties on undressed sheep-skins. It was said that she had married him not out of love, but only at the will of her father, and that the bridegroom she had chosen first had found a voluntary death on the battlefield. There were also rumours current (perhaps they were but gossip) about other adorers of hers, — passionate, persistent, but whose suit was always vain. However, evil tongues — and of such there were not a few in Florence — could say nothing bad of la Gioconda. Quiet, demure, pious, strictly observant of all the rites of the Church, compassionate toward the poor, she was a good housewife, a faithful spouse, and not so much the stepmother as the tender mother to her twelve-year-old stepdaughter, Dianora.

And that was all that Giovanni knew of her. But the Mona Lisa who came to the studio of Leonardo seemed to him altogether another woman. For three years — time did not exhaust, but, on the contrary, deepened this strange feeling — he experienced a wonder, resembling fear, at her every appearance, as before something phantasmal. At times he explained this feeling by his having become accustomed to seeing her face on the portrait, and the master's art being so great, that the living Mona Lisa seemed to him less actual than the one portrayed on the canvas. But there was something besides, still more mysterious.

He knew that Leonardo had the opportunity of seeing her only during his work, in the presence of others, at times of many invited persons, at times only of Sister Camilla, inseparable from her, — and never alone; and yet Giovanni sensed that they possessed a secret which drew them together and set them apart from all. He also knew that this was not a secret of love, — or, at least, not of that which men are wont to style love.

He had heard Leonardo discourse how all artists were inclined to copy their own body and face in the bodies and faces they portrayed. The reason for this, as the master saw it, lay in the fact that the human soul, being the creator of its body, strove, every time that it was confronted with the necessity of inventing a new body, to repeat in the latter that which it had already at one time created, — and so potent is this inclination that at times even in portraits, through the outward semblance of that which is portrayed, there glimmers at least the soul, if not the actual face, of the artist.

That which was taking place before the eyes of Giovanni was still more striking: it seemed to him that not only she who was depicted on the portrait, but even the living Mona Lisa herself, was coming to resemble Leonardo more and more, as is sometimes the case with people who live together uninterruptedly for many years. However, the chief force of the growing resemblance did not consist so much of the features themselves — although even here also it occasionally amazed him of late — as much as in the expression of the eyes, and in the smile. He recalled, with inexplicable wonder, that this same smile he had seen in the case of Thomas the Doubter, inserting his fingers into the Lord's wounds, in the sculpture of Verrocchio, for which the youthful Leonardo had served as model; and in the case of Our Mother Eve before the Tree of Knowledge in the master's first picture; and in the Angel shown in The Virgin of the Rocks, and in Leda and the Swan, and in many other feminine faces which the master had painted, drawn and modelled, still before he had known Mona Lisa, as though all his life, in all his creations, he had been seeking a reflection of his own charm, and had, finally, found it in the face of Gioconda.

At times, when Giovanni would contemplate for long this common smile of theirs, he would feel eerie, almost afraid, as before a miracle: the reality seemed a dream, the dream — reality, as though Mona Lisa were not a living being, the wife of a Florentine citizen, one Messer Giocondo, the most ordinary of mortals, but that she was a being resembling phantoms, and evoked by the will of the master, — a changeling, a feminine double of Leonardo himself.

Gioconda stroked her favourite, the white cat, which had jumped up on her lap; and invisible sparks ran through the white fur with a barely audible crackling, under her soft, slender fingers. Leonardo began working. But suddenly he abandoned his brush, scrutinizing her face attentively; not the least shadow or change upon this face could elude him.

"Madonna," asked he, "are you perturbed by aught today?"

Giovanni also felt that she did not look like her portrait as much as usually.

Lisa raised her calm gaze to Leonardo.

"Yes, a little," she replied. "Dianora is not altogether well. I have not slept all night."

"Mayhap you are tired, and are not much inclined for my portrait? Would it not be better to postpone the sitting? . . ."

"Nay, 'tis naught. Would you not regret losing such a day? Look, what tender shadows, what a humid sun: 'tis my day!"

"I knew," she added, after a silence, "that you were expecting me. I would have come sooner, but was detained, — Madonna Sophonisba . . ."

"Who? Ah, yes, I know. . . . A voice like that of a street huckstress, and smelling like a perfumer's shop. . . ."

Gioconda smiled.

"Madonna Sophonisba must needs tell me, without fail, of yesterday's celebration at the Palazzo Vecchio held by the most illustrious Signora Argentina, wife of the Gonfaloniere, and what, precisely, was served at supper, and what dresses were worn, and who was attentive to whom . . ."

" 'Tis just as I thought, then! 'Tis not Dianora's illness that had upset you, but the small talk of this chatter-box. — How queer it is! Have you ever noticed, madonna, that at times some nonsense or other, which we may hear from a mere acquaintance, and which nonsense we have no concern with, — common worldly folly or vulgarity, — will suddenly cast a gloom upon the soul, and upset us more than powerful grief?"

She inclined her head in silence, — it was evident that they had long since grown to understand one another, almost without words, at a mere hint.

He again made an attempt to resume work.

"Tell me some story," said Mona Lisa.

"Which shall it be?"

After a little thought, she said:

"Tell me of the Realm of Venus."

He had a few stories which were her favourites, for the greater part from the recollections of himself or others, or of his travels, observations of nature, projects for pictures. He narrated them almost always in the same words, — simple, half childlike, to the sounds of soft music. Leonardo made a sign, and when Andrea Salaino on his viol, and Atalante on his silvern lute that resembled a horse's skull, struck up that music which had been chosen beforehand and invariably accompanied *The Realm of Venus*, he began in his high, feminine voice, as one would an olden fairy-tale or a lullaby:

"Mariners, dwelling on the shores of Cilicia, aver that those who are fated to perish in the waves, at times during the most fearful storms, chance to behold the Island of Cyprus, the realm of the goddess of love. Around it beat tempestuous waves, whirlwinds, and waterspouts; and many mariners, drawn by the beauty of the island, have shivered their ships against the cliffs surrounded by whirlpools. Oh, how many of them have been dashed to bits, how many have sunk! There, upon the shore, are still to be seen their pitiful skeletons, half-covered with the sand, entwined with sea-grasses, — some thrust forth their prow, others, their stern; some, the gaping beams of their sides, like to the ribs of half-rotted corpses; others, the splinters of a rudder. And so great is their number, that this scene resembles the Day of Resurrection, when the sea shall give up all the ships that have perished within it. But, above the isle itself there is a sky eternally blue, and the shining of the sun upon its knolls, flower-decked; and in the air there is a calm, such that the high flame of the censers upon the steps in front of the temple stretches toward the sky, just as straight, as immovable, as the white columns, the black cypresses, reflected in a mirror-smooth lake. No sound is there, save for the sweet murmur of the jets of the fountains, as they flow over the edge and fall from one porphyry bowl into another. And those drowning in the sea behold a-near this placid lake; the wind brings to them the fragrance of the myrtle groves, — and the more fearful the tempest, the profounder the peace in the realm of Cyprida."

He lapsed into silence; the string of the lute and the viol died away, and there fell a silence, which is more beautiful than all sounds, — the silence after music. Only the jets of the fountain murmured, striking against the hemispheres of glass.

And, as though lulled by the music, walled off from actual life by the silence, — radiant, a stranger to everything save the will of the master, — Mona Lisa gazed straight into his eyes with a smile that was filled with mystery, like still water, perfectly clear, but so deep that no matter how much the gaze plunged within it, no matter how it probed, it could not see the bottom, — she was smiling upon him with his own smile.

And it seemed to Giovanni that now Leonardo and Mona Lisa were like two mirrors, which, reflecting themselves in one another, were deepening to infinity.

Mistress Anne Boleyn

by H. F. M. Prescott

1524–1536 Anne Boleyn, the bold young beauty who became Henry VIII's second queen, was beheaded in 1536. She was convicted of adultery, incest and treason — and may have been innocent. Henry, in love with Jane Seymour, was tired of the woman for whom he had defied the Pope in order to obtain a divorce. Thomas, Lord Darcy, who worries about Anne and Henry in the brilliant vignettes which follow, was a conservative nobleman who disliked Cardinal Wolsey, Henry's great minister, almost as much as he disliked Anne.

November 19, 1524

The Court was at Greenwich, and Lord Darcy went there for two days after he had come to London. He landed at the steps and stood with Sir Robert Constable waiting for their people to get ashore. A little farther along half a dozen men were heaving and straining to lift into a barge a great erection of beams and painted cloths, battlemented, and with towers, made to represent a castle. Already the effigy of a unicorn stood in the barge, its brown paper side torn in places and fluttering in the wind, a forlorn sight, except that its painted horn was still gay and fresh. The staging and properties for the last jousts were being taken back to the Wardrobe in London.

They found the King coming away from dinner, and when they had kissed his hand they followed him to the Queen's apartments. There, not being noticed any more by His Grace, they withdrew to a window, and watched the group by the fire, where the King stood, his feet wide apart, swinging a big jewel which hung by a gold lace round his neck, and talking and laughing with a cluster of gentlemen and ladies.

'His Grace,' Darcy murmured in Constable's ear, 'is thickening,' and Constable, looking at the round bulge of the King's jowl above the fine shirt collar worked in gold with a pattern of roses and pomegranates, nodded his head.

'Yet he rides, hunts and plays at tennis.'

Darcy's eyes had left the group at the fire, and looked beyond Constable's head. He said, 'Yea. Yea,' but not as though he heard what was being said to him.

Constable gave a little laugh under his breath, 'And His Grace's father was as lean and little as a smoked herring.'

Darcy said, in a voice as low but with no laughter in it, 'I can remember His Grace's grandfather, King Edward. His Grace is a man much like to him.'

'What are you looking at?' said Constable, and turned, craning his neck to see what it was.

Darcy told him, 'Nothing. Nothing,' and brought his eyes back to the group round the King. But he had been looking to the place where the Queen stood, pleasant and smiling, and with people about her. And yet he thought that she seemed ill at ease, as if she would have come where the King was, and yet, again, would not.

'And the why she would not,' thought Darcy to himself, 'is that young maid in sanguine red,' and he took a good look at the girl who stood up, slim and glowing in her velvet gown, with black hair falling loose over her shoulders. He could see that she had a marvellous pretty throat and neck, and thought that she knew it too, and, young though she was, knew how to show it, for she would let her head droop, now this way, now that, and then she would lift her chin till all the whiteness of her throat was displayed, and then would dip her head again, as graceful as a swan.

Yet she was no languishing beauty who trusted only in her looks to bring down the game. When she turned herself about Darcy saw that her dark eyes were alive and alight with mockery, and her voice as well as her laughter sounded often and merrily. By and by indeed it was her voice and the King's which answered each other, while the rest of those about spoke less and less, as though they found it more absorbingly interesting to listen.

So now Darcy and Constable could catch most of what was being said by the fire. Just what it was about they could not tell, but the girl was certainly asking His Grace for something, now imperious, now wheedling, now saucily feigning a timorous humility.

'Well, then,' said the King at last, 'you shall have it. And if wives are more importunate than maids, God help me!'

'Oh! Sir, Your Grace is the noblest Prince in Christendom. I humbly thank Your Grace,' and she gave him a very low curtsey, and caught his hand and kissed it; Darcy was not the only one who could see how the King seemed to wish to prevent her lips touching his hand. 'And when?'

said she, standing before him again, palm laid to palm under her chin —
'And when?'

The King swore then, by God's Blood, that she was the most insolent
beggar of them all, and when she only laughed at him, he swore again, and
walked a few paces from her, but came back, and stood close to her. 'Some
day,' he said, 'some day.'

'Lord!' she cried, 'what a promise! As they say in France — *"Faictes moi
une chandelle quand je suis morte."* For I fear the fashion may have changed
by then.'

His Grace still stood very close to her, looking down at her laughing
face. But he was not laughing.

'Some day. And it may not be as long time hence as you think.'

He turned from her then and went away down the room. The group
at the fire broke up, and several passed close to the window where Darcy
and Constable stood. Darcy called to one of them, 'Sir Thomas! Sir
Thomas Wyatt!'

The tall bearded man would have gone by if Darcy had not caught him
by the arm. He paused then unwillingly, while his eyes followed the girl
in the blood-red gown. Only when he saw her join those about the Queen
he shrugged his shoulders, and seemed content to linger.

They talked for a while about the Duke of Suffolk, and last year's campaign in France, and Sir Thomas was very caustically witty at the Duke's
expense. Then Darcy asked him — 'Who was that merry, free-spoken
maiden?'

Wyatt looked at him sharply. 'She that was asking the King to give her
a husband?'

'A husband?' said Darcy with his eyebrows up, and Sir Robert Constable
muttered something about a whipping.

'Yes. Mistress Anne's a mad lass. She says she wants to have one of those
billements of pearls, those new things that women are wearing. And since
maids must wear their hair loose, so that without a husband she cannot
have a billement, she says forsooth that she will have both.'

Sir Thomas Wyatt shook his head smiling indulgently, and Darcy had
to remind him that he had not told them who the young gentlewoman was.

'Why!' said he, 'she is Mistress Anne Boleyn.'

Darcy whistled. 'Sister to her that is now Lady Carew and that was
the King's minion a year or two — —'

Wyatt interrupted him. 'You North-country men talk too free.'

'Well,' said Darcy, very much the nobleman, yet with a spice of mockery in his voice, 'perhaps you'll give me leave to say, Sir Thomas, that the King seems to like well that family. But how is your good lady and your bairns?'

Sir Thomas seemed to care for that subject as little as the other. He muttered a hasty answer and moved away. The two watched him pushing through the crowd till he stood beside Mistress Anne Boleyn.

'That manner lass,' said Constable, 'is born to make trouble among men.'

Darcy agreed, and suggested that such should be drowned, like kittens, when young.

October 3, 1526

Although there was a moon outside the window, inside the curtains of the bed it was quite dark. Lord Darcy, wide awake, and restless because of the unseasonable warmth of the night, shifted uneasily, and, because he had a troubled mind, he sighed.

'Sir?' his wife whispered, and, 'Tom?'

'Go to sleep, Sweet.'

'What's amiss, Tom?'

'It's too hot for October,' he told her, but the obvious truth did not put her off. He felt her hand grope for his, and when she had found him she said again, 'What's amiss?'

He broke out, and it was with a great sigh — 'By God's Death! I think all the world's amiss.'

'Is it,' she asked, 'this great battle in the East that the infidels have won?' It was only a little more than a month since the King of Hungary and most of his chivalry had fallen at Mohacz, and the Turk was pouring into the eastern parts of Europe.

He told her it was that, but she asked, 'And what else?'

He said nothing for a moment, and she felt him move in the darkness, and knew that he had shaken his head.

'If you were not a woman who is as secret as any man,' said Darcy, 'I could not tell you. Come near that I can speak low.'

When her head was close to his mouth he told her, in a whisper.

At first she could not believe him.

'The King put away his wife? Divorce the Queen? After all these years? How many? Fifteen or more. He cannot. Why should he wish?'

She was silent, and then murmured, 'How do you know this thing?'

'Never mind how, but I know. There's the Bishop of Bath in Rome treating with the Holy Father of it.'

'Shame on him then — the Bishop I mean.'

'Oh! He likes it as little as any. *"Istud benedictum divorcium,"* they say is what he calls it.'

She took him up. ' "As little as any?" You like it little?'

He moved restlessly. 'God knows — ' he began again. 'If it's the King's will — — '

'Fie on you, Tom,' she cried, 'it can't be God's.'

He stiffened at her rebuke. 'The King needs an heir.'

'The Princess Mary.'

'She's a girl.'

'She's lawful. But there's the bastard boy as well.'

'Hush!' he told her, but she said she was not afraid to speak the truth, and Henry Fitzroy might be Duke of Richmond but certainly he was a bastard.

'And why else,' she persisted scornfully, 'does the King wish it? There was great talk about that niece of Norfolk's, the Boleyn girl. Ah!' She read his silence. 'It's that, is it?'

After a long time she turned suddenly towards him.

'Tom, why will you suffer this as if it would be well?'

He told her, hesitating, at first, but then in a hard tone — 'For an heir for one thing. And for another because, in so great a business as this will be, we may find means to pull down the Cardinal.'

She drew away from him, but he could hear what she muttered to herself. 'God forgive you men!' she said.

May 30, 1527

Darcy was just leaving the Chamber of Presence at Greenwich Palace when he found the Duke of Norfolk at his elbow — not the old Duke, who had died three years ago, but his son Thomas Howard, who had been Earl of Surrey and got himself much honour at the Battle of Flodden. Darcy had never liked him, and liked him no more now that he was Duke, and High Treasurer of England, but Norfolk greeted him with particular courtesy, walked on with him and after a minute or two edged him away into a little closet of painted wainscot. Darcy though he looked very pleased over something.

'Sit, my Lord,' said Norfolk. 'I saw you lean heavily on your stick while we waited for the King.' There was only a stool and a pair of virginals in the closet, but the Duke would have Darcy sit on the stool, while he tucked his own backside on to the virginals, jangling all the keys once in painful discord. Then he inquired with great kindness about my Lord's old disease.

But after a little of this he was silent, and pulled a comical face and laughed.

'Indeed we can see that it is May-time; yea, even in London and at Court,' he said.

Darcy did not pretend to misunderstand him.

'How long will it last? May's but thirty-one days, and then?'

Norfolk shook his head, still smiling, then he narrowed his eyes and looked crafty.

'My niece is a most virtuous and chaste lady. You know the King — how set he is to have his will. Yet here he can have it not. I promise you I could weep for him, to read the letters he writes to her when she has crossed him, or runs away home from Court to be done with the importunities of his suit. "H. R." he will sign himself at the foot, and "*Aultre ne cherche*" between the letters, and right in the midst of all a heart drawn, and inscribed with A. B.'

'Very pretty,' said Darcy sourly. 'But if she will have none of him, and he will not tire, what will be the end of it?'

'Ah!' Norfolk leaned closer. 'She will none of him except lawfully. Yet — if the Queen should become a nun — ' He broke off there as if he had said too much. 'A little while ago,' he went on, 'she sent him a jewel, representing in diamonds a maid solitary in a ship, and the posy "*Aut illic aut nullibi.*" To which he replied somewhat to this end, for she showed me the letter — "My heart is dedicated to you alone, wishing that my body were so too, as God can make it if it pleases Him." '

'Ah!' Darcy remarked, not without malice. 'God?'

The Duke got up and the strings of the virginals whined. 'My Lord, I can see God's hand here, if you cannot. The realm lacks an heir. The Princess? Pooh! We lack a Prince. And one other we have with us that we could well lack.' He came close to Darcy and whispered, 'You and I think alike of the King's prepotent subject, my Lord Cardinal. We should be friends.'

Darcy considered that for a minute, and with it the rest of what the Duke had told him. Then he said:

'You tell me that the King means marriage with your niece?'

Norfolk was looking at the floor. He did not raise his eyes but rustled the strawing with one foot and answered softly that he believed no less.

Darcy also looked down at the Duke's foot, and at a faded head of clover that Norfolk was shifting this way and that; it was as if neither wished to meet the other's eyes. The Duke moved away again, but paused at the virginals, and leaning one hand that held his blue velvet cap upon the painted case of the instrument, with the fingers of the other picked out a shivering sweet chord or two. Then he looked round at Darcy.

'And your niece, Mistress Anne, is of the same mind as yourself, my Lord, towards the Cardinal?' Darcy inquired.

'I promise you,' Norfolk chuckled. 'Sometimes I think a woman can outdo any man when it comes to pure, piercing hatred.'

When the Duke had gone Darcy sat a while alone, turning over what he had heard. Then he shrugged his shoulders and got up. He did not think it likely, on the one hand, that Mistress Anne's virtue would prove as impregnable as Norfolk rated it; nor, on the other, if it did, that even that lively bold slip of a girl was an adversary whom the great Cardinal should fear. She might dance like a dark flame through the maskings at Court in her cloth of gold and with rubies about her neck which Darcy was sure her father had never given her, but the King must go from masking to the Council Table, and there the Cardinal would rule.

October 1, 1527

Lord Darcy was returning out of London to the house at Stepney, when the Duke of Norfolk caught him up, going to try a new hawk in the fields beyond the village. The Duke sent his gentlemen on, and rode softly beside Darcy's horse-litter, talking of the North Country, and of the young Duke of Richmond, the King's son, who had been sent there with a Council and a great Household to learn the trade of a ruler, though he was barely ten years old. 'But,' said Norfolk, 'a singular gracious and wise child as all agree,' and he waited a minute for Darcy to answer, and, when he did not, added that it was a pity his mother had not been the King's lawful wife.

Darcy said rather he thought it was a pity that the boy was not Queen Katherine's child.

'That is what I would say,' Norfolk assured him, but Darcy had an idea that he had put it the other way to try what answer he would get. He wondered what the Duke would be at, and wondered still more when they came to the end of the lane along which Darcy must turn. For the Duke pulled up there, and began to ask about the house. Was it big enough, in good repair, were there stables and grazing in plenty? And every now and then as he talked he would nod and tip his head towards the roof and chimneys that showed above the orchard trees, and he frowned, and then winked one eye, so that Darcy knew that he wanted to be asked to turn in for a while, and see the house, though he could not think why the Duke should want it, nor why he should make such a secret of it. But he said, 'If you will turn in, my Lord, to drink a cup of wine?' and he told his footboy to go on and fetch Norfolk's gentlemen back.

The Duke would gladly turn in, he said, adding that it was as warm as summer, which was true, for, after a wet and windy September, October had come in with a light mist and still blue skies. So, at the Duke's own suggestion, they drank their wine in the garden that smelt pleasantly of box, and apples, and sweet-briar warmed in the sun.

After they had finished their wine the Duke brushed the crumbs of wafer from his knee and got up, but he waved his hand to his gentlemen, and taking Darcy's arm shoved him gently in the direction of the orchard. 'Now,' thought Darcy, 'we're coming at it,' and he was right. After a turn taken together, in which Norfolk spoke loudly of his own new grafted apple-trees at Framlingham, he dropped his voice and asked Darcy did he know that the Cardinal's Grace had returned.

'Yea, I heard.'

Norfolk looked down at the hooded hawk, restless, on his hand. 'Everywhere in France he was shown great honour.'

As he seemed to wait for a reply Darcy said that he supposed that was but natural, seeing he was the servant of so great a master.

'And so great a servant,' Norfolk suggested, to which Darcy said nothing.

'Yet I have heard say, "*Non est Propheta inhonoratus nisi in patria sua*,"' and the Duke looked sharply up at Darcy.

'How can that fit here, my Lord, unless the Cardinal thinks his honours — which, God knows, are many and great — are not enough for his services?'

'He did not think himself honoured when he came to the King at Richmond,' said Norfolk softly.

'Ah!' said Darcy. 'This I have not heard.'

Norfolk chuckled. 'I shall tell you. He came there in the evening, having landed from Calais that morning, straight to give account to his master, as a dutiful servant should, and supposing that he should be joyfully received at his home-coming, as one who has made this new treaty with France. And coming to the palace he sent one of his people to the King announcing his return, and asking where and at what hour he should visit His Grace. I was with the Cardinal, and I saw his gentleman go to the King, and I saw him return.'

He chuckled again, and Darcy, not seeing why, said, 'Well?'

'The Cardinal's gentleman, when he came back, was as red as those apples on the tree. Yet he only said to the Cardinal that the King would see him at once. "Where?" says he. "I will bring you to the King," says the gentleman, and they went out, and I saw the Cardinal turn to him, in going, and ask again, "Where is His Grace?" but I did not hear the answer — not then. I waited, and I saw the Cardinal come out of the palace and ride away. I asked one of his gentlemen how the King had received his master, "Right thankfully, I'll wager," says I. And he looked at me as awkwardly as if he'd stolen a purse, and said — "Right thankfully; very honourably," and got himself away from me as quick as he could.'

Darcy stopped walking, and they stood together under one of the trees, feeling the sun's warmth spatter through the leaves upon their heads.

'It's a long tale, but I come near to the end,' the Duke assured him. 'It was from my niece —' 'Mistress Anne?' put in Darcy; and, 'Mistress Anne,' Norfolk repeated. 'From her that I heard the rest. For she came to me after supper in the gallery, and showed me a new jewel she was wearing, a table emerald with three hanging pearls, very pretty, very costly. She'd had it, she said, of the King's Grace that evening, and many gracious words with it. "And kisses not a few," says I, whereat she laughed, and did not deny it.

'"And then," says she, "one came in from my Lord Cardinal and asked where and when he might wait on His Grace." I told her I knew what he had asked; but what had the King answered?

'"It was not the King that answered," says she. "It was I. I said to the Cardinal's gentleman, 'Where else but here should the Cardinal come? Tell him he may come here, where the King is.'"'

'"Mass!" quod I, "was not the King angry?" She laughed at that and told me, no, not angry at all, but very merry, asking her if she would be one of his Privy Council.'

'She is a very bold lady,' Darcy said, not too cordially; but then, remembering how she had discomfited the Cardinal, he laughed. 'No other would have dared.'

'Bold she is,' Norfolk said, 'and of a marvellous ready wit, and that the King loves her for. And,' he turned to Darcy, 'as I told you before, she loves not the Cardinal.' He held out his hand then, to say farewell. 'You and I think alike over one matter; we should be friends,' he said, and added, 'though not too openly.'

Darcy gave an angry laugh. 'Thomas Wolsey knows that I love him little, and with great reason.'

'Secret is best,' said Norfolk, and went on to his hawking.

July 25, 1531

The Duke of Norfolk, coming into the gallery that led to the King's Privy Chamber, recognized the voice of his niece, Mistress Anne Boleyn. It was raised and shrill, but he was certain it was hers, though he did not catch the words. And then, from a doorway at the far end of the great room she bounced out, cried, 'I will not! I will not! I will not!' on a rising note that ended as high as a peacock's scream, and slammed the door behind her.

The Duke made as if there were nothing strange in all this. As she swept by him with a whistling of silk, he saluted her gravely, though unnoticed; and rebuked, by a long hard look, the stares of the gentlemen and pages who had got to their feet from games of dice or cards.

He went the long length of the room slowly and with dignity, but in his mind he was wishing that the elderly and rheumatic gentleman who followed him had not arrived in time to see that bit of business, since he came as a messenger from Queen Katherine. As for his niece, the Duke thought, 'Mass! The girl's out of her wits. She'll lose all by this manner.'

'Wait here, Sir,' he said to the elderly gentleman, and knocking gently on the door, went into the Privy Chamber.

The King stood looking out of the window. He did not turn, and the sunshine, streaming past him, threw his broad shadow across the strewn rushes on the floor.

'Your Grace,' said Norfolk, down on one knee, 'here is a gentleman come with greetings and a letter from the Queen, who — — '

Then he saw that the King had his dagger out in his hand, and was stabbing with it at the wooden sill of the open window. The silent violence of that repeated gesture was like a blow across Norfolk's mouth. He gasped and was silent.

'By God's Death!' The King plunged in the dagger and wrenched it out again. 'She will not. Will she not?' He swung round suddenly on Norfolk. 'This girl's your niece. Yours! Did you teach her this manner duty? The Queen never spoke to me so. I've made — I can unmake her.'

Norfolk's eyes flinched from the King's face. He muttered something about 'love' and 'loyalty' and held out the Queen's letter. When the King whipped it out of his hand and flung back to the window Norfolk told himself that soldiers, aye, brave men, men that feared nothing, were afraid of their Prince, so great is the majesty of kings. Yet he felt the flush on his cheekbones, and was glad that none had been there to see and to hear.

The King said 'Tchah!' and crumpled the letter into a ball. 'A very dutiful letter. She asks how I do, laments that I left her at Windsor without the consolation of bidding farewell. Very dutiful!' He dropped the crumpled paper on the floor and set his foot on it. 'And it's she that will have me cited to Rome, and thinks I'll forgive. God's Blood! I'll not see her face again.'

He sent Norfolk away and remained alone in the small sunny room where still lay a scatter of bright silks and a piece of embroidery that Mistress Anne had thrown down when their quarrel had begun. The King tramped to and fro, rolling a little in his walk, concocting in his mind the cruellest answer to the Queen's letter that he could devise. There were two women who crossed him, and he would make one pay for both. For already an uneasiness was growing in his mind and a restless craving. Supposing that other should — mad wench — leave him after all? He could not endure the thought.

February 24, 1533

Lord Darcy sat in the house at Stepney reading a book of devotion by the light of the branch of wax candles which stood behind his chair. He kept his eyes on the page faithfully enough, but his mind wandered. Thoughts about Templehurst mingled with his meditations on mortality: the roof of the great chamber that needed mending, the young fawns that should be fed in the lower close; or there would come clear and near before the eye of his mind a glance of the Chequer Chamber window, of the steps going down to the Chapel, of the trees beyond the distant river, sleeping on a summer evening with the light dying behind them.

At last he dropped the book beside the chair and went over to the window. Outside the rain fell, steady and dark; it leaked through the casements, running in heavy drops along the iron bars of the windows and splashing down on the sill. In places it bubbled and spat upwards from the corner of the window frames. The gentlemen who were with him in the room watched him, then turned back to their occupations.

'By the Rood!' said Darcy, half aloud, 'I would I were at home in the North Country.'

He did not turn when someone knocked at the door, supposing it to be the servants with more lights; but as well as the lights they brought in his brother-in-law, Lord Sandys of the Vine, who slung off his heavy red felt coat which was dark across the shoulders where the rain had soaked in, and below that all silvery with the standing drops. He shook it before he tossed it to one of the gentlemen, and the wet flew off it and spattered the dogs that had run forward to greet him, so that they backed away.

He kissed Darcy, and said, holding him hard by the shoulder and looking him in the eye, 'I'm soaked to the bone. Will you lend me a dry gown to put on?'

'That I will. Come within.' Darcy led him towards the door of his bed-chamber, then, over his shoulder, bade one of the gentlemen, 'Bring light, James.'

In the bed-chamber, when James had lit the fire, and set candles, Darcy took Sandys by the arm and brought him to the high-backed bench in front of the hearth where two green cushions were set, worked with the Buck's Head in silver.

'Now tell me your news,' said he.

Sandys leaned towards him so that their shoulders touched, and said in a low voice, 'She is with child.'

'You mean the King's — —'

'Sh!' Sandys looked over his shoulder at the gentleman, leaning against the door, and paring his nails with a little knife.

'Keep me the door, James,' said Darcy, and when the young gentleman had gone out — 'Well then, the Marchioness of Pembroke.'

Sandys nodded, and spat in the fire. 'Nan Boleyn,' he said.

'Who told you it?'

'She did.'

'She? Told you?'

'She told us all — all that were waiting outside the King's Chamber.'

'Who?'

'God's Body! a dozen or so — Exeter, Huntingdon, Norfolk, Wyatt too.'

'Who was her lover once.'

'They say so.'

'Well I can believe it. And it's not *credo quia impossibile est.*'

Sandys shrugged and went on.

'I was talking with Wyatt as we warmed our hands at a brazier, when the door of the King's Chamber opens, and out prances my Lady Marchioness, the Queen's jewels all over her, aye, even some I can remember to have seen Her Grace wear when first she came from Spain. And this one had more too; they say the King gives her jewels every day. She'd as many as the Virgin of Conques.

'So out she comes, twisting her hands together like this,' and he wrung his hands daintily together.

'She looks round at us all, and then cries out to Wyatt, naming him by name — "Sir Thomas! Sir Thomas! By the Holy Virgin you'll not guess what the King says." Wyatt began to stroke his beard like he does when he's thinking out one of his pretty sayings, but she didn't give him time.

' "You know what I told you yesterday, how sharply I long for apples? I told His Grace, and he says it means I am with child," and back she skipped into the Privy Chamber, cackling like a hen.'

'God's Soul!' said Darcy, 'and did she clap her hands to her belly like that?'

'She did, Tom.'

They sat together in silence for quite a long time before Sandys murmured, 'Will he marry her?' and then answered his own question. 'But he cannot, unless the Pope at last should give sentence against the Queen.'

Darcy leaned his head near and spoke with his lips close to Sandys' ear. 'I was told — but did not then believe it — —'

'Tell me first who told you.'

'No, never mind. I was told that about a month ago now this new Archbishop, Cranmer, married them. It was very secret, but folks will talk.'

'But,' persisted Sandys, 'no Archbishop can, while the appeal lies at Rome.'

Darcy looked at him with his head tipped back and angry dancing lights in his eyes.

'You may say he cannot, but this Cranmer will do it. And will declare the King's first marriage void, if he is set up to judge in the cause.'

'I know,' said Sandys, 'that he was Nan Boleyn's father's chaplain. But he cannot. It is not possible.'

Darcy laughed at him, but grimly.

'You shall see what he can do, and what the King can do now that this child is begotten.'

June 8, 1533

This Sunday, the next after the Queen's coronation, almost everybody went to Court, and Lord Darcy one of them. As he paused on the landing of a stairway, Master Cromwell came out from a door which he locked carefully behind him. He seemed greatly pleased to see Darcy, and urged him to 'Come up, my Lord, come up,' as though he spoke for the King.

They went on up the stairs together, and Darcy saw that Cromwell had a little crimson velvet casket in his hand, a pretty thing with gilt hinges and a tiny gilt key.

'A jewel for Her Grace,' said Cromwell. 'The King sent for it, and it came but yesterday.' He stopped at the next window, and opened the box in the sunshine. Darcy bent his head and saw a great emerald flash back the light and hold it in depths of under-sea green that glowed as if with fire. There were three pearls hanging from it, large and elongated, the shape of plovers' eggs.

'Hm!' he said, though not much interested, 'pretty.'

'And of great price.' Cromwell prodded it with a forefinger. He had fat hands, with dimples at the knuckle joints, yet they looked strong too. 'It was the Princess Dowager's. She brought it from Spain. It was a jewel, perhaps, of those Kings of the Indies. Now His Grace will give it to Queen Anne.'

He shut the box, and they went on together. Darcy guessed that Cromwell expected him to say something, either to approve or deplore, or discretely to turn the conversation. He did none of these, being too honest to approve, too wary to deplore, and at once too practised and too bold to fear a silence.

He had thought that when they reached the Presence Chamber Cromwell would leave him, but instead the Master of the Jewels laid a hand lightly on his arm, and twinkling at him with the smile that Darcy could not dislike, said that he would he were of the number of my Lord's friends, few men of these days being so stout and honest. 'And,' said he, 'as I would earn your love I will essay a small thing thereto. I will bring you, without pain of waiting, at once to His Grace.' And he began to push his way, not roughly yet with determination, between the wide puffed shoulders of the men, and the spreading stiff gowns of the women, crowded into the long room and all looking towards the far end, where hung the cloth of estate above the King's chair. Darcy followed him, but not now liking either him or the times in which such an upstart could lead a nobleman to his Prince's presence.

When they reached it the chair of estate was empty, and Cromwell, catching the eye of a gentleman in silver and green who stood on guard at a closed door, led Darcy there, knocked, and went in.

The room was small, hot with sunshine, and fragrant with strewn flowers and perfumes of musk, ambergris, and orris. There were two small chairs, covered with purple velvet and fringed with silver, set below one of the

windows, and the King's Grace and the Queen sat on them. The King's
hand with its rings was laid on hers or touching or toying with her all the
time, whether he greeted Darcy or spoke to the French Ambassador or
argued with her father about the voice of one of the singing boys of the
Children of the King's Chapel.

Cromwell knelt, and presented the jewel to the Queen. 'It is,' said he,
'a gift from His Grace.'

'For me,' she cried, and turning her head tipped up her face to the King
who hung over her. Darcy thought, 'She knows what will prick a man
to desire.'

The King lifted the jewel out of the box. He leaned closer and set the
chain about her neck. Then he must settle the jewel so that the mid-most
pearl hung plump above the cleft between her breasts, which showed where
the jewelled edge of her gown ended. His fingers lingered on her flesh;
she let herself droop towards him.

'A born harlot!' Darcy thought, and guessed that Cromwell thought no
other, though the Master of the Jewels kissed her hand and took leave
with due humility.

But he had to acknowledge that she had wit, for she began to talk about
her coronation in the Abbey of Westminster, and had them all laughing
because she so pricked through the splendours and solemnities that she
pierced to the folk behind them, and as she talked these were no more
reverend than a rout of villagers at a May Game.

When she finished, '. . . And so we came away to dinner,' the King
wiped his eyes, though his bulk still shook with diminishing gusts of laughter. He flung his arm across her shoulders and bade her tell them more.
'What of the dinner?' he pressed her.

She let herself be pulled towards him, then put both hands on his breast
and pushed him away.

'No, but I'll tell you what I saw at the Abbey. But you'll be angry.'

'Not with you, Sweetheart.'

'Faith! but you will. You'll say, "To the Tower with her." '

'Madcap!' The King looked about at them all, and then again at the
Queen's father, a mass of slashed green velvet and cloth of gold, set upon
a pair of thin legs.

'This daughter of yours!' he cried dotingly, and then to her, 'Well, you
little rebel? I shall not be angry. Or you shall have a pardon.'

'Shall I? But you will be angry. See. I will wager you a prince to a collar
of rubies that you are angry.'

'A prince? How will you pay with a prince?'

'The prince I bear in my belly.'

'Ho!' the King laughed. 'You'll pay with him at your time, will you, nill you?'

'And isn't he enough to wager against a collar of rubies?'

The King swore by St. Edward that he would be enough, and then asked again, 'Sweet, what did you see? Tell us now.'

'I saw jewels.'

'God's body! so you should. Here have I been writing orders to Master Cromwell for this, that and t'other for you. And now to-day I have given you the emerald. My Lord,' said the King to Darcy, in high good humour, 'should these not be enough?'

'Sir,' Darcy answered, 'if women be as insatiate as the sea, it is that they know our weakness, and their own worth,' and on the last he bowed to the Queen. She inclined her head but he had seen her eye snap at his guarded courtliness.

The King however was growing impatient.

'Jewels?' he urged. 'Are there not some few on the crown and the sceptre?'

She pouted her lips, and blew all those away with scorn.

'Jewels! Not those. But the jewels on the shrine. Jewels in the Lord Abbot's mitre. Jewels in his staff. And there was a great ruby in the cross on the altar. I saw none in the crown nor in sceptre like to these.'

The King had withdrawn his arm from her neck.

'I think, Madame,' he said, 'that you forget.'

She flashed a look at Darcy that said, 'You would be glad to hear me rebuked,' and then turned her eyes, sparkling and reckless, upon the King.

'You owe me a ruby collar, for indeed you are angry.'

'The Devil I do!' The King got up quickly, but she did not move. He turned back. 'One day, Madame, you'll go too far.'

'And then,' she smiled at him, 'you will send to Ampthill and bring Dame Katherine back.'

The King had been angry, but now it was as if he had been hit with a stone between the eyes. He looked at her, but if he hoped to beat down her glance he failed. Darcy thought. 'She can stare like any cat.' And it was with the same bland sweetness of malice.

The King went back to his chair.

'I believe you would not fear the devil.'

'Not if he wore a beard. And shall I have my rubies?'

'Ask the Keeper of the Jewels.'

'Not the Abbot of Westminster?'

The Queen's father cried, in an agony, 'Peace, girl! Madame, I pray you, peace!' but the Queen did not so much as look at him.

'You'll get none of my Lord Abbot.' The King's tone was gruff.

'These monks,' the Queen murmured softly, 'have all, and give nought. And the King can't take. Yet the Cardinal took.'

'Body of God!' the King turned on her. 'The Cardinal took only a few little Priories, some of an ill name. But to speak of Westminster! By the Blood of Hales!' he cried, 'I won't have this talk.' He got up and went out of the room with his arrogant walk, swinging his wide, white satin shoulders.

When Darcy stood waiting for his litter and looking at all the coming and going in the Great Courtyard between the Palace and Master Holbein's new gallery and gate, he found Cromwell at his elbow, and thought as he greeted him, 'How the man sticks!'

'How sweet is the sunshine,' Cromwell said, as though in idlest talk. 'Truly I think this fair summer shows that God's favour is upon this marriage. That, and already so blessed a hope of issue.'

'Already,' Darcy repeated drily.

'Ah! my Lord, how I love the bluntness of you men of the North Country. But at least,' he murmured, 'at least, even you, my Lord, will confess we have a Queen now, young, witty, beautiful, and, let us hope, fruitful.'

'And bold,' said Darcy. 'She wants the King to do with the Abbey of Westminster what the Cardinal did with the Priories.'

'She said that, did she?' Cromwell remarked, in a tone almost innocent of meaning, and yet something in Darcy's brain pricked an ear, and he thought, 'It's not the first time that same has been said, nor was she the first to say it.' He was just thinking that this man was perhaps more dangerous, though not greater, than the Cardinal, when Cromwell spoke again.

'But, my Lord, there's a thing I'd ask of you. That young gentleman in Candlewick Street the other day, did you see his face?'

When Darcy did not answer he went on, 'I thought I had heard his voice before. I'm sure I have heard it.' He rapped with his knuckles on his forehead, and then bit at them angrily. 'It was a voice that one should remember, and I cannot.'

He waited, and then ran on again, begging pardon for keeping my Lord when his litter waited, 'But it would be well I should know of any young gentleman so quick, bold, forward, as that one seemed to be. It was a young gentleman, you said?'

'*You* said,' Darcy corrected him; and then with a sharp smile, 'Master

Cromwell, if I tell you, shall I have the reward they proclaimed for those who informed against any that speak evil of this marriage?' He looked at Cromwell, and laughed; the Keeper of the Jewels was not often out of countenance, but now he was quite taken aback. He began to justify himself; it was necessary, he said, that quiet should be kept.

'Therefore I keep watch. People murmur at this marriage. Her Grace was displeased that so few caps came off, and there was so little shouting when she passed through the city. And there's a nun in Kent sees visions — foretells the King's death — ' He paused and seemed to recollect himself, and laughed. 'So perhaps I make too much of the idle jest of a saucy young man.'

Darcy said, 'Perhaps,' in a tone that made Cromwell glance at him sharply, and then they parted. As Darcy looked back from below the new Gateway arch, he stood there, still sunning himself on the steps, a sober, quiet figure, in his grey silk and black fur. Darcy thought he was like one of those floating spots which trouble a distempered vision, and which the eye can neither quite catch, nor yet be rid of.

September 6, 1533

Queen Anne lay propped up with pillows in the carved, painted and gilded bed that had been brought from the King's Great Wardrobe for the occasion of the birth of the heir. The rings of the curtains, drawn wide apart now, were of silver gilt and ran along silver gilt rods. The hangings of the bed were of white and green brocaded velvet, and the counterpane which they had thrown over the bed for the King's visit was of cloth of gold. It lay very heavy upon the Queen, making her think of the leaden shrouds in which the dead are wound — the great dead, who lie in proud tombs — but as cold as any beggar. Her cheeks and eyes were still bright with fever, and fancies such as these, each of them tainted with horror, filled her mind with moving shadows. Beside her, upon a cushion of cloth of gold, lay the small tight shape of the one-day-old child, swaddled to the neck, and wearing a little tight cap exquisitely worked in silk. Between the swaddling bands and the cap, the puckered, querulous, aged face was of a dusky red.

There was a stir at the door, and one of her gentlemen announced the King. He came down the length of the chamber, tall and immensely broad in his puffed and slashed doublet of sanguine velvet, which to her fancy suddenly took on the likeness of raw, bloodied flesh, while the white satin that showed at the slashes was white bone. He came alone, having, by a motion of his hand, stayed those that were following him. The Queen's people, seeing this, also drew away. They stood in two groups, not mingling, hers by the hearth, his just inside the door.

But she was looking only at the King. He came on, his head a little bent, his shoulders swinging, till he stood beside the bed. He asked courteously and formally, after her health. She said she did well. He said that he rejoiced therefor. She thanked him for his gracious visit. He said that she should command him in anything she wished. She replied that there was nothing she desired but only his gracious favour. That, he told her, she had, and promised that not only in the Royal Chapel, but in all churches and chantries, her welfare should be petitioned for. Then he went away.

Her ladies came back. They removed the heavy coverlet and laid over her instead one of velvet brocaded in a pattern of true lovers' knots and roses. One of them asked her, 'Shall we leave with you this noble lady?' rocking in her arms the child who had wakened with a shrill, piping cry.

'No,' said the Queen, 'I shall sleep.'

She shut her eyes so that they should think she slept. He had not touched, he had not once looked at the miserable little creature that had caused her all that wasted pain. She could, for the present at least, feel nothing but loathing for the girl who should have been a boy.

August 20, 1534

The King came in to sup with the Queen in her apartments. In the antechamber one of her ladies was playing on the virginals, others were reading, or whispering together; two of the youngest were playing with a kitten. Everything seemed as usual, but when the King had looked sharply round, not one of them, as they rose to curtsey, would meet his eye. He indicated with a wave of his hand that no one should follow him into the Privy Chamber beyond, and went by quickly.

The Queen sat there, alone, between the yellow candles and a lowering red sunset. She got up from her chair and curtseyed very low; her eyes were on the ground but at the look of her the King knew that he had guessed right, and that though in the antechamber all seemed pleasant pastime and cheerfulness, a storm had raged here lately. Besides, it had by no means escaped his notice that one of the Queen's Maids who should have been in attendance was not.

'Madame,' he said, lowering his head, and going straight at the point, 'where is — —'

The Queen did not even give him time to speak the girl's name.

'She is not here. She is not here,' she burst out; and now she raised her eyes and braved him. 'I will not have her here. Oh! I know. Jesu! But I can see. And I'll have no rutting here among my maids. She shall go home.' She gave a sudden sharp cackle of laughter. 'Christ! Now you will say that it means nothing that you must sit by her, and lean over her and paw her — Ah!'

She stopped because he had moved so abruptly.

'No, Madame,' he said, not speaking loudly at all, but — she could not help herself. She started back as if he had raised his fist to her, and could only hope he did not see how fast her breath went.

'No, Madame, I shall not say that. But I shall remind you of what I have done in raising you, and what you were before I raised you. And I shall counsel you to be content with what I have done, the more because if it were to do again, I would not do it.'

He smiled at her unpleasantly, and she covered her face with her hands, and sank into the chair again. She looked beaten, but as she sobbed, partly from the trembling of her nerves, and partly for design, she had indeed snatched her courage to her again.

'It is my great love — my great love for Your Grace,' she murmured.

He began to fidget about the room, and she let her sobs cease, but she fetched a trembling sigh.

He said, 'Well, well. Come to supper.'

She caught his hand and kissed it, and then covered her mouth with her fingers, because he had pulled away from her so sharply that the claw setting of a great ruby on his finger had torn her lip.

February 2, 1535

That same afternoon Mr. Thomas Cromwell brought the French Envoy to Queen Anne. She was in one of the smaller rooms leading off the Presence Chamber, yet the room was large enough to have two fireplaces, one at each end, and for thirty or forty people to be able to divide themselves into two quite separate groups. The larger group by far was that about the King, who stood with his back to one of the fires, pulling tight his white satin trunks across his broad backside, and now and again bending slightly forward, the more exquisitely to toast his rear.

The Queen sat beside the fire at the farther end of the room with a lute on her knee, and some of her ladies and a few young gentlemen about her. The fire sent out puffs and gushes of sweetness for they had not long since scattered spices on the logs.

One of the young gentlemen near the Queen had the King's monkey by its chain, and he and a gentlewoman were feeding it with sweetmeats while most of the rest looked on and laughed. As M. Palamèdes came near he noticed that the Queen was watching the monkey too, but with loathing; and so intently that she did not see the two gentlemen approach.

As they paused the strange creature sidled over to the Queen till it stood crouching before her. She shrank back. 'Mother of God! I hate monkeys!' It laid one of its long, wrinkled, dark grey hands on the strings of the lute, and with the other grabbed a sweetmeat in the Queen's fingers. Then it was away, with its paw at its mouth. The discordant twang of the strings under the tiny clutching fingers was echoed by a cry from the Queen, who brought her own hand up to her mouth in a gesture strangely like that of the animal.

'Oh! He scratches,' she said, just as M. Palamèdes bowed and went down on one knee.

Neither he nor Cromwell missed the start that the Queen gave. Cromwell glanced round at those standing near; he did no more but it was enough. The group about the fire broke up and drew away, leaving the three of them alone.

As the Queen's hand lay upon Gontier's and he stooped to kiss it he knew it was trembling. He lifted his head, and his eyes, caught by the shifting sparkle of jewels, rested for a second on her bosom. Her blood-red velvet gown, brocaded with gold, had an edging of pearls and small sapphires along which the firelight ran with a broken flash, quickly gone, and then running again from point to point in time with the Queen's quick breathing. The woman, M. Palamèdes realized, was panting — no less — yet when he looked in her face she smiled, and as she spoke in French of how she had loved France, and how ill she now used his lovely French tongue, she laughed, shrilly, a laugh with as little meaning as the strained smile, while her eyes darted past his head to watch what was going on at the farther end of the room.

Then, with desperate urgency, but always with that same smile on her face and with laughter that tinkled emptily, she began to press him 'to use dispatch in this business of the marriage of my daughter the Princess Elizabeth's Grace.' Dispatch! Dispatch! That was the word, over and over. 'For if you do not I shall be in worse danger than before I was married. Worse danger!' She laughed with fear looking through the mask of her face. Her head jerked and she craned her neck to see beyond him. Gontier felt his flesh creep, and yet he knew that nothing had happened of more moment than that the musicians in the room beyond were tuning their instruments and that the King had moved away from the other hearth.

The Queen held out her hand; the Frenchman bent and kissed it again and felt her nails nip into his flesh.

'I dare not speak longer,' she said breathlessly. 'I cannot tell you more. The King is watching us. Someone said I should not anger him. But if I did not he would think I am afraid.' She seemed to choke, then said, 'As (dear Mother of God!) I am afraid.'

She did not seem to know that she was still clutching his hand, but he freed it gently and asked if he might wait on Her Grace another day.

'No. No. I can't see you again — or write — or stay longer. He has gone. They are dancing already.'

She sprang up, laughing again. The room was nearly empty. Only a few of her ladies were there to follow her as she moved towards the door through which came the sound of fiddles and recorders.

May 2, 1536

The Groom Porter went first down the stair in the White Tower, with the keys he carried lightly chiming one against the other. Then came Mr. Lieutenant of the Tower, Sir William Kingston, and after him Queen Anne, with her ladies, scared and white, following close. At the low round arch of the stair, that burrowed both up and down through the huge walls, the Queen seemed to stumble, and stayed, laying her hand upon the rough cold skin of the stone while her ladies bunched together behind her.

'Down?' she cried.

Sir William, already going down, said over his shoulder, 'If you please, Madame.'

But the Queen still stood, clutching at the wall, and looking down into the twilight of the stair.

'Shall I go into a dungeon?'

Sir William's voice came hollowly from below them. 'No, Madame. You shall go into the lodging you lay in at your coronation.'

At that she let out a cry.

'It is too good for me,' she said, and began to go down, but weeping now, and trembling, and crying, 'Jesu have mercy on me.'

In the great chamber where she had lain before her coronation there were ashes of a dead fire on the hearth, and candles that had guttered low before they had been blown out. For a moment she thought, as she stood in the doorway. 'They have not touched it since that night,' and that the candles were those that had then made a glancing golden haze, and the cold ashes the ashes of the fire that had hissed and spurted out sweetness to the room from the spices that were cast on it. She moved on a few paces into the room and then could hold herself up no longer, but went down on her knees, crying again and again, 'Jesu have mercy on me!'

Sir William drove her women towards her. They took her hands and after dealing with her a little, quieted her. He, at the door, was for turning his back and going away, since this was now no chamber of audience; but the Queen cried to him, begging him to move the King's Highness to let her have the sacrament in the chamber with her. 'That I may pray for mercy,' said she, still shaking so that he could see her flesh tremble. 'For I am clear from the company of man, as for sin, as I am clear from you, and am the King's true wedded wife.'

Then she put aside the women, and came close to him, catching his wrist and peering into his face. 'Mr. Kingston, do you know why I am here?'

'No,' said he, lying.

She began to ask him of the King, of her father and of her brother, and Kingston did what he could to keep to the letter of truth and yet hide from her, what he knew well, that her brother, Lord Rochford, was already in the Tower. And, lest she should ask more, he tried to loosen her hand from his arm and begone, but she would not let him go.

'For,' said she, 'I hear say I shall be accused with three men. And I can say no more but nay. Without I shall open my body,' and at that she tore at the breast of her gown, and, as she met his eyes, huddled it together again, turning her head aside and crying, 'Oh! Norris, hast thou accused me? Thou art in the Tower with me, and thou and I shall die together,' and then, all in a jumble, spoke of Mark Smeton the spinet player, and my Lady of Worcester, and of the child that had never seen the light.

'Mr. Kingston,' she cried at last, 'shall I have justice?'

'The poorest subject the King hath,' he told her, 'hath justice.'

At that she threw up her arms and began to laugh, so that he thought it best to leave her, with however little courtesy. When he had shut the door behind him he could not hear the voices of her women, trying to compose her, but her laughter only.

The Trial of Atahualpa

by Edgar Maass

> 1533 The Spanish conquistadors were courageous
> and cruel men, inspired equally by greed for gold
> and by religious fanaticism. Francisco Pizarro was
> able to conquer Peru because he twice betrayed the
> Inca Atahualpa: first by inviting him to dinner as
> an honored guest and then holding him for ransom;
> second by "trying" Atahualpa on absurd charges and
> murdering him after the ransom, a room full of gold,
> had been paid.

We arrived at the main room of the House of the Snake where
the trial was to be held. Don Francisco Pizarro and Don Diego de Almagro
sat beside each other on the high podium. Before them, a few steps lower
down, was a long table lighted from above by a shaft of light. Both the
Captains — or judges — were hidden in shadow. Around the table, turned
toward the judges, sat our Dominicans and Don Pedro de Candía, Master
Pérez, Gonzalo Pizarro and Master Riquelme, the Crown treasurer attached to the expedition, who had come along from San Miguel with
Almagro. Farther back, by themselves, sat several cavaliers. I thought I
recognized Juan and Pedro Pizarro among them. On the table was a gay
Indian blanket, and on this cover was a lone object, the only piece of
evidence, it seemed, the dog-eared Bible bound in pigskin that belonged to
Father Vicente.

The strong column of light streaming in through the ceiling illuminated
the faces of the men around the table in every detail, showed every fold
and wart as in a Flemish painting. Only the judges were really obscured.
Their faces were white blurs framed by their beards, and the rest of their
bodies were hidden from view.

Gonzalo Pizarro wore a splendid doublet made of gold brocade that
contrasted beautifully with his blue-black hair. He looked so handsome
that he would have taken any woman's breath away. He seemed to be in
charge of affairs at the table. He was just taking a document from the
hands of Master Pérez when his glance fell on Diego and me. He got up,
surprised, and said, "Welcome to the proceedings, Don Pedro. I'm glad
to see you're able to stand on two feet again. But are you sure you want to

watch this boring business when you're really not well yet? I purposely neglected telling you anything about what was going on."

"I'm healthy enough for this," I told him. "It's a question of the company's welfare, isn't it?"

"As you want," said Gonzalo drily. "Give Don Pedro a place at the table, will you? Just as you want. Only, I thought . . ."

"Thank you all the same, Gonzalo," I explained. "I brought my friend, Master Diego de Vargas, to take my place at the table. He will act as counsel for the king."

"The Inca's acts speak for themselves. There is no need for a defense counsel," Gonzalo said harshly, and looked up at the judges for support.

"Then if there is no need for a defense, there is no need for a prosecution," I answered with equal stubbornness. "In fact, in that case the whole trial is useless. But you have assigned a prosecutor, have you not?"

"Master Riquelme is the prosecutor," said Gonzalo coldly. "Master Pérez will be his assistant. But Master Diego cannot be made a defense counsel. He knows nothing about Spanish law."

"I have studied the law in Salamanca," said Diego. "I have often served as a notary, drawing up wills, contracts and other legal documents."

"But you have never served as a counsel," objected Gonzalo.

"Was Master Riquelme ever a prosecutor before?" inquired Diego. "Was Don Diego de Almagro ever a judge?"

"Master Riquelme is the Crown treasurer," said Gonzalo. "Don Diego de Almagro is the alcalde of Tumbez."

"And I am Don Pedro de Cordova's secretary," said Diego. "Beyond that I am a bachelor of the seven humanities."

"You may be," said Gonzalo, "but you won't have much chance to be clever today." He threw the paper onto the table. "Well, never mind. If you want to, take your place. You can be the defense counsel. Are you aware of what the indictment contains?"

"No, I am not," said Diego. "And the first thing I beg is that the court will postpone the trial so that I can consult with my client about its contents. It looks rather voluminous to me."

"Why, man, that's impossible," said Gonzalo, his temper rising all the while. "The lives of nearly five hundred Spaniards depend on the speedy outcome of this trial. This isn't any pleading about a will or a bill owed for forty-five years. You can't spin this business out making jokes a rod long. This is a matter of life and death."

"The weightier the issue, the more reason for measured consideration," said Diego.

"There can't be any postponement," said Almagro out of the shadows. "The court refuses to allow it."

"Is it impossible to postpone the trial because then Don Hernando de Soto will be back from Guamachucho?" inquired Diego.

There was a mutter of anger in the room. Diego Almagro got up and shouted, "The court forbids that kind of language. Keep to the subject, or keep your mouth closed."

"We are not prejudiced," said the Captain-General.

"I take the question back," said Diego. "I'll substitute a new one. How does it happen that this court dares to sit in judgment over a sovereign? A king may be judged only by those of his own rank. In this case it would have to be Don Carlos, or the Inca's own chieftans, perhaps."

"That's so much lawyers' gabble," commented Diego de Almagro. "We'll never get anywhere at this rate."

"I beseech the court to take the Inca Atahualpa to Spain," interposed Diego de Vargas, "so that he may stand trial before Don Carlos, or before a court appointed by the crown."

"We are all appointed by Don Carlos as it is. We have commissions to prove it," said Almagro.

"You have commissions to humiliate and murder kings?" asked Diego.

There was a great uproar after this. I heard cries of "Throw the bastard out," "Put him in chains," "Kill the interfering dog." And so on. Diego smiled palely. He was now caught up by his purpose, like an actor on the stage.

The Captain-General pounded for order. "Quiet, quiet," he shouted. "I warn you, Master Diego, either measure your words more carefully and pay more attention to the dignity of this court, or you will find yourself in trouble. I have already told you once. We are not prejudiced, and all that we want is justice to be done. If you persist in insulting those of us assembled here, I shall be forced to have you thrown out of the room."

"I regret the harshness of my address," said Diego. "But I beg to state for consideration that I do not consider this court in order and properly authorized by law."

"That view cannot be accepted," shouted Master Riquelme.

But the Captain-General nodded his head. "Write down his objections; take them down," he said. And so Master Pérez did this.

The indictment of Atahualpa was then read aloud, and I shall not attempt to repeat it in detail for it was four pages long. The four most serious accusations:

Ad primum: The accused was a heathen follower of gods and demons, and followed heretical customs, insofar as he kept concubines, calling them his wives.

Ad secundum: The accused had violated the royal decree of Tavanta-Suyu; with treachery and force he had persecuted the royal party, and finally caused Huáscar to lose his life by drowning.

Ad tertium: He had used his illegally acquired royal power to disperse gold and other riches of the land among his relatives, followers and other creatures unworthy of such perquisites, to the detriment of the commonalty and of the royal treasury of Castile.

Ad quartum: He had planned uprisings and war against the Spanish crusaders, and had gone so far as to collect great hosts of Caribs in the neighborhood of Guamachucho.

Now the prosecutor, Riquelme, began to tell the most revolting tales of the Inca's heathen practices. He mentioned numerous human sacrifices, and went on at length about the immoral behavior of the accused in *puncto feminae.* This was a bad example to his people and to the Spanish soldiery, the prosecutor declared. At this Father Vicente nodded vigorously in approval.

Then Diego said, "We know less than nothing about the gods and demons of this land. All that we know is that the accused according to his own lights honors the sun as a benevolent power and as one of his ancestors. This to be sure is a grievous error. But it is the common superstition of the land. We should have to wipe the whole population of the country off the face of the earth if doing this is a crime. But that would be impossible. Neither the Inca nor his subjects had ever heard before of the true religion. They never had a chance, and should not be judged on the score of belief until given full opportunity to mend their ways."

At this point Father Vicente broke in. He said sharply, "I have been talking to the Inca for more than six months about the true belief. He listens to me and understands what I say. But he absolutely refuses to change his beliefs and to be baptized. He prefers to remain up to his neck in the muck of heresy."

"Six months is no time at all in such matters," said Diego to this. "It took the saints centuries before the greater part of the Roman people under Emperor Constantine embraced the only true faith. Even after that there was Julian the Apostate, who would certainly have uprooted Christianity if it had not been foreordained to endure forever. And if the saints, men of purity and insight, had to work centuries to achieve their ends, and this among an enlightened people, then our Dominicans, for all their zeal, cannot expect to arrive at the same results in six months of working among simple barbarians. Such impatience, however intelligible it may be, however much it may spring from zeal, nevertheless to the layman's eyes borders on blasphemy. The greatest truth in the world is not to be inculcated in a few days.

"And so far as the concubinage of the Inca is concerned, I hold that to be of no relevancy. Consider the Patriarch Abraham, who had two wives, Sarah and Hagar. Think of Jacob, who entered into marriage with both Leah and Rachel and other lesser wives as well, wives in common law. I beg to draw your attention to the woman of Samaria who spoke to our Lord. She had once had five men. Since all these men and women are considered to be pleasing in the sight of God, I fail to see any mortal sin in the conjugal excess of the Inca. Furthermore, his wives are not come to him through his lusts. They are part of the royal establishment, his servants. His father, Huayna Capac, and his brother, Huáscar, both of these also had many wives."

The Captain-General bent forward. "But you admit, counsel for the defense," he said, "that the Inca Atahualpa is a heathen and that he has married many wives?"

"That I do admit," answered Diego reluctantly. He looked steadily at the Captain-General. Riquelme, the prosecutor, tittered at the exchange.

And now for a long time there ensued an argument over whether Atahualpa was a real king or only an usurper. This was very hard to decide. The principal difficulty depended on the fact that no one had ever learned anything about Huayna Capac's will except through hearsay. Diego lost no time in pointing this out, and also in bringing to the court's attention that hearsay also had it that Huáscar was the one who had really begun the war, who had assumed the initiative. He had occupied a part of Quito, the inheritance of Atahualpa.

The argument lasted so long that at last the Captain-General interposed and advised the prosecutor and the counsel for the defense that court would quash this particular part of the charges. Diego turned to me and smiled. He had won an important point. It was his first score.

Riquelme saw the two of us exchange looks and he shouted, "But we shall never drop the charge of fratricide!"

"Then prove the charge," said Diego.

"No, prove the Inca's innocence," said Riquelme. "That's your task, to prove he's innocent."

"Gladly," replied Diego, "I'll be glad to accommodate the court. At the time of Huáscar's death, the Inca was our prisoner. Huáscar died a hundred miles away from Caxamalca. No matter how sleepy our guards may be, I doubt that Atahualpa could have made a two-hundred-mile round trip and his absence not have been noted."

Some of the cavaliers laughed at this sally. I took heart, for it is always good when a man's argument can tickle the sense of humor against odds.

Riquelme cut in violently. "I didn't say that Atahualpa killed his brother with his own hand. I say that he instigated the murder. It was he who hatched and directed the scheme."

"Then why don't you express yourself more precisely, my honored colleague?" said Diego.

There was more laughter at this, and Don Francisco called for order.

"Pray, tell me what makes you think that the Inca planned the murder?" inquired Diego politely.

"The death of Huáscar was to his advantage," said Riquelme.

"So that he could have himself accused of murder and risk his life before this court, perhaps?" asked Diego.

"I mean to say it happened just at the time when the Captain-General was beginning negotiations with Huáscar," continued Riquelme, very softly.

"But that proves nothing," retorted Diego.

"It is a clear indication of intent," declared Riquelme.

"All that it is, is evidence that a wish for Huáscar's death might have arisen in Atahualpa's mind. But it is not evidence that such a wish actually did arise. And it is still less evidence that any such wish was ever carried out," said Diego.

"Then who else would have wanted to kill him?" asked Riquelme, his voice edged with sarcasm and anger.

"I am not by any means convinced that Huáscar actually was murdered," said Diego. "He might quite as well have been the victim of an unfortunate accident."

The Captain-General now rose. "So you believe the Inca when he says that Huáscar was careless? You believe it was an accident! Speak up."

"The explanation is at least as good as Master Riquelme's circumstantial evidence," said Diego, giving way.

"I want to know whether you believe it," insisted Pizarro.

"It isn't my task to express my opinions and my beliefs," retorted Diego, somewhat lamely. "I am defendng the Inca, no more. I maintain that what has been offered is not evidence, but the flimsiest of hearsay. There is nothing that inclines to establish the Inca's guilt beyond exception."

"We're bogging down again," objected Diego Almagro. "Nothing but lawyers' hairsplittings!"

Again the Captain-General turned to Diego. "You will admit," he said, "that there is a possibility the Inca had his brother Huáscar murdered?"

"There is such a possibility, of course," Diego said.

"You admit further, do you not," Pizarro insisted, "that this possibility develops into a probability when the circumstances, the time and so on are taken into consideration?"

"The probability is not very great," Diego said. "The Inca surely must have said to himself that he must suffer the Spaniards' revenge when unable to defend himself. He could better have waited until his hands were untied to even scores. And besides, men are never judged on mere probabilities."

"It's enough for me, Master Diego, that you have admitted the possibility and the probability of the deed," said the Captain-General quickly. "Put down Master Diego's statement on the record, Master Pérez. Leave the judging to us, if you please."

Diego sought my eyes, and shrugged his shoulders very lightly. He had lost this score, and lost badly. But he made one more sally. "I still hold," he said loudly, "that this court is not fitted to judge the differences of two pretenders to the crown of Tavanta-Suyu. It is quite possible that Huáscar received the customary punishment of the land for his attempt at usurpation."

The audience began to whisper busily.

Now the third point in the charge was arrived at. The two lawyers took up the matter of the Inca's supposed wasteful expenditures. Master Riquelme spent a great deal of wind on this issue attempting to prove how unworthy subjects had received enormous benefits in land and gold.

"As a sovereign," Diego retorted, "the Inca had a right to give away land and gold at his will, and to whom he wanted. He has also paid us Spaniards vast amounts of gold. If we refuse to recognize his right to dispense his wealth, then of course we must return what we have received."

"Sweet Lord Jesus asleep in the manger!" roared Almagro. "Whoever heard of such a stupid thing? Since when have we Spaniards troubled our heads about the prerogatives of infidels and Indians? What do we care

about the law of a heathen land when it comes to doing something to lift
still higher the crown of Castile?"

"If you do not admit the possibility of justice," Diego said harshly, "then
you are wasting your time trying to punish an apparent crime, as in this
instance."

"The man is talking like a fool," shouted Almagro. "He makes my head
go round. He is trying to make us all dance to his tune like a pack of idiots."

"That's right," chorused the audience. "He's merely trying to make sport
of the judges."

The Captain-General pulled Almagro by the sleeve and forced him back
to the bench. He was very angry with everybody at this point.

"I say that the court will cast out this section of the charge," the Captain-General said. "But not because I am moved by the argument of the
counsel for the defense. The whole question is closely related to the point
of whether Atahualpa was the lawful king. If he were, then he would have
certain right to dispose of his goods and benefits as he chose."

"And that is that," echoed Diego.

I was amazed at the Captain-General. Outside of Diego he appeared
to be the only man in this curious court who was able to think with any
logic at all. Yet at the same time this frightened me. I saw that it boded
ill for the Inca, far more so than the simple impatience of Almagro.

Now the supposed uprising planned by Atahualpa became the subject
of discussion. Master Riquelme named off the great armies which were re-
putedly assembled ready to fall on us. He could not prevent himself from
portraying the horrible fate that was in store for us when we fell into the
hands of the Caribs.

"But all that is so much imagining," objected Diego. "It is the fancy of
frightened men that is at work. We haven't the slightest piece of evidence
that any enemy is marching toward Caxamalca. And even if that were the
case, it would still have to be demonstrated that the Inca had a hand in it."

"In that you differ with the Captain-General," said Riquelme. "Don
Francisco Pizarro has doubled the watch; he has sent out men to reconnoiter; he has ordered that the horses be kept constantly saddled and in
readiness for battle."

"Foresight is the mother of wisdom," agreed Diego. "But Don Francisco's
general precautions against danger are no proof in themselves that this
peril actually exists. On the contrary! The mere fact that the Captain-
General has sent out a party to reconnoiter is demonstration that at the

bottom he doubts these rumors, that he is merely looking for visual proof. Otherwise would he risk some of his best men?"

Master Riquelme was checkmated. He lifted up his thin shoulders, and looked at the Captain-General, seeking help. There was a painful silence in the room. It appeared as if this most important part of the indictment had proved untenable.

Slowly the Captain-General rose and said, "You must admit, Master Diego, that the Inca is the focus, the middle point, the inmost center of all possible revolt?"

"Yes, yes," shouted Gonzalo in relief, seeing which way the wind was blowing. "You've got to admit that!"

"But I do not and cannot admit it," said Diego boldly. "I maintain that the Inca is the very center of peace and order in this land. It is my belief, quite opposite, that we tarry here in safety in Caxamalca only by virtue of his person. Were it not for his hand, that he has yet to raise against us, we should not be here at all. The Inca's death is the worst luck that could possibly befall us. That is what I believe in my heart. I do not agree with this hypothesis, Captain-General. And others besides me have felt the same way. For example, Don Hernando, your own brother."

"I can vouch for that," I said, unable any longer to hold my tongue.

The Captain-General was taken aback at this unexpected resistance.

"Don Hernando Pizarro is not among us," said Almagro, coming to Pizarro's rescue. "When he left the most serious developments were not so much as suspected."

"But nothing of importance has happened since he left," interposed Diego. "I beg the gathering to consider the advice of the man who is not here. A single word from a nobleman is of more weight than a tumult of rumor from the mob."

"That is going too far," said Almagro. "I demand that this man be taken from the room. He has insulted me."

"Calm yourself," said Don Francisco Pizarro to the infuriated Almagro. He did not look at him, but simply waved him to his seat with a hand held backward. "My brother Hernando is very dear to me. I respect his every word. Since Master Diego has brought his words to my attention, things begin to look a little different. I think we shall adjourn this court."

"What!" shouted Almagro, unable to contain himself. "And what about the thirty thousand Caribs?"

"Yes, what about them?" said Master Riquelme.

"The thirty thousand Caribs are part of a fairy tale!" shouted Diego de Vargas.

"This run-down scholiast is ridiculing me," said Almagro.

"Wait until Don Hernando de Soto comes back," said Diego, "and then you will see right enough that the Caribs are nothing but the blue mist that hangs over the mountains."

"The court can no longer continue," said Don Francisco coldly. "Everything depends on the news that Don Hernando de Soto brings back with him. When he comes back we'll take up where we left off."

"Just a minute," roared Almagro. "What about your promise that we would soon leave for Cuzco? What about me? How am I going to be repaid for my trouble? How can we go to Cuzco while Atahualpa is still alive? You're a rich man, Francisco. You've had your share. You've got fifty-seven thousand gold pesos. But I, your old friend, have got exactly nothing. I'm poor. Cuzco is my only hope in the world. And the gold in the temples . . ."

"Think of Don Carlos," pursued Master Riquelme. "Think of what he will say! The day will come when the King of Spain will demand reckoning for your having caused him to lose so much land and gold. This Inca cannot live."

"And what about God? What about Him?" shrieked Father Vicente. He got up and leaned forward at the table. "It has been clearly demonstrated that Atahualpa is a miserable heretic, and we all know that he leads a filthy life with his women. Even his own defender admits he may have taken his brother's life. How do you think it will be if you have to face God after letting these vile sins continue?"

"I shall judge when Don Hernando de Soto has returned," said Pizarro flatly.

"The punishment of heretics and sinners against the dictates of our Holy Mother the Roman Catholic Church cannot be delayed!" screamed the priest. "Spiritual works must not be pursued in such a lackadaisical fashion, no matter how one goes about worldly matters. Thousands and thousands of benighted souls can be destroyed by this heretic in a single hour if he gets loose, and so perish forever. You would not endure a leper among your friends and comrades. Much less should you endure the heretic in our midst."

"What can I do?" said the Captain-General. "No matter which course I take — postponement or judgment — it will be bad."

"Think only of your honor," cried Juan Pizarro, who had moved up to the table so that his young face was limned in the light streaming in from above.

"Is it a part of honor to forget one's friends?" said Diego Almagro.

"Nobody has honor unless he serves the King and Castile," added Riquelme.

"Outside the pale of the Church there is no honor," said Father Vicente.

"You are like a swarm of gnats," said the Captain-General. "What is the just way out?"

"There is no way out," said Father Vicente in triumph. "There is only a choice between good and evil. You must make this choice now, today."

And now Don Francisco chanced to turn toward me. "You have said nothing all this time," he declared. "Why don't you lend your voice to this tumult? Everyone else is advising me, why not you, my young friend? You had a great teacher. When you were a boy you sat among knights at the table. What do you say?"

"It appears you have made your own decision," I told him. "The charges have crumbled into so much dust."

Thereupon Gonzalo Pizarro got up to have his say. He was very impressive in his gold brocade doublet. From his girdle hung a dagger in a golden sheath. "We are all one, and must be," he said pleasantly. "Why should we turn and rend each other? Actually, none of us is worrying about honor or shame, about justice or injustice. It doesn't make a jot of difference whether Atahualpa is a heretic or a saint. It is simply this. What are we going to get out of it? What is our advantage and our power?"

"Well said," shouted Almagro.

"Then the whole trial is a monstrous lie," I said with equal vehemence.

"Justice and injustice are only devices, excuses," said Gonzalo. "We all are aware of that. When the rich judge the poor for reaching their hands towards their property in order to eat and live, is that then justice? Where does it lie, this justice? All of us are men, rich and poor, mighty and humble. By rights we should all be poor, weak and humble, as our Lord Jesus Christ would have it. Riches, power and superior position are all injustices of one sort or another. And too long have they lain a leaden weight on the Pizarro family.

"Must I remind you, brothers, how men have looked down on us? Must I call to your attention that we have starved like mangy dogs? Have you forgotten, Francisco, that your ten years of service in the Indies was rewarded by a strip of swamp fit for nothing but to breed mosquitoes? Now we have opportunity within our hands, right before us. Shall we act like cringing animals and prick up our ears at the cry of justice? We must act in good style. We must bear ourselves like rich men, like the soldiers and noblemen that we are. Let go these hollow words about honor, justice, sin and the like. They mean nothing except among slaves. Let us do what we must do."

"Bravo, bravo!" roared Almagro. "Gonzalo has spoken what was on the tip of my tongue."

"Only Atahualpa stands in our way," said Gonzalo. "Only he separates us from the riches of Cuzco. On that account he is guilty of a crime against us Pizarros and our friends. He would be still guilty no matter if a thousand charges collapsed. The fact remains he is unjust to the Pizarros. Therefore he must die."

"I will have no part in this murder!" I shouted. I turned to leave the room, overcome with emotion.

"Not so quickly, my young friend," said Gonzalo. He smiled quietly. "You made an agreement with us. You signed your name. You got your share of the gold. You must also take a share of the unpleasant duties of our expedition."

"What are you talking about?" I said, seething with anger now. "Did I not take my share of battle? Did I not ride out as a messenger and risk my neck more than any of you? Have you faced any more danger than I?"

"Nobody knows that better than I do," agreed Gonzalo. "Nobody holds you in greater esteem than I, Don Pedro. But this is one more danger, and this added danger must be shared. For it is quite possible that at the moment you are of more value to the expedition than you were at Puná or Tumbez. Many a man dares to face an enemy in mortal combat. It is much harder to face the evil whispers of the mob, to run the risk of a bad reputation."

"Do you mean to imply I am afraid, Gonzalo?" I asked. I could feel myself getting dizzy with wrath.

"I didn't say that," admitted Gonzalo. He shrugged his shoulders.

"It is against all spiritual and human justice," I said. "It is a shame, a travesty of honor — this trial. I shall have no part in it. Not if I die for it!"

"What do you mean?" shouted Gonzalo bitterly. "You talk like a fool. Where did you, personally, get the right to invade this country? What right had you to slaughter the Indians in the plaza? What right have you to hold the Indians' gold? Every step you took with us, and did not once question the justice of it! Now you fall back! What's wrong with you? You are talking like a child."

"Gonzalo!" said the Captain-General. "Watch what you are saying."

I hung my head and accepted the denunciation without a word. I felt that I was beyond injury. "The right to conquer this land is found in the words of our Lord," I said weakly. "Christ said, Go into all lands and baptize them. And likewise it was permissible to take up arms when Atahualpa threw the Bible on the ground. . . ."

"Don't be a long-eared ass," said Gonzalo. "Are you making it up as you go along? And what about the gold? Have you an excuse for that, too?"

"Forget about the gold," said the Captain-General. "It has nothing to do with what we're talking about."

"Don Pedro is right," said Father Vicente. "The justification for our deeds comes directly from God. Only one point is left unfulfilled. He will never be satisfied so long as Atahualpa lives and the demons' temple of the sun stands in Cuzco. And Gonzalo is right, too. The Lord said, You will be hated by all the world because of my name. But who endures to the end, he will be saved. We must submit to the appearance of injustice and we must put up with dishonor and whisperings. The Kingdom of God will shine forth that much brighter in the end."

My head was on my chest. Never before had I felt so confused and utterly bereft. In vain I tried to find objections to Father Vicente's cunning arguments. Then suddenly Doña Isabella's parting words came to my mind — "Pedro, the Cardinal wants you as his conscience." It came to me with such force that I started, and involuntarily turned half-around as if I had heard it over my shoulder. I looked closely at the Captain-General, trying to see him with new eyes. He was standing in the half-darkness talking busily with Diego Almagro. He had little resemblance to the Cardinal, to Antonio de Guevara. He would never understand such a train of thought. I felt there was only one thing for me to do, give back my share of gold on the spot. And it was both greed and the fear of being laughed at that finally prevented me from taking this drastic action.

That is one of the worst threats to virtue, being laughed at. Wickedness and lies seem so natural, so inevitable, have such an apparent correspondence with reality that more often than not goodness seems to be allied with stupidity. The truth as often as not looks for all the world like an extravagant exception to what counts and holds good among men. Truth really is not of this world. It comes naked from heaven. It arouses as much ribaldry and astonishment as would a naked savage parading in the market place of a Spanish city. And yet, a little thought makes it clear that there is nothing laughable in the naked human body, which was formed by God. Much less ridiculous is the naked spirit and truth among men, when stripped of prejudice and superficialities.

But when the moment of decision came for me I failed, I was mute, and I did nothing.

The Captain-General and Diego Almagro now returned to the council, diverting further attention from me. In his hand the leader had the itemized indictment against the Inca. We were all standing at attention. Pizarro began to speak.

"We judges find the accused, the Inca Atahualpa, guilty of the following crimes. He is a heretic and a follower of demons. He has entered into marriage with more than one wife. Furthermore, he is a fratricide. He has acted treasonably toward Don Carlos, whose vassal he is, insofar as he has assembled thirty thousand Caribs at Guamachucho against me, the emissary of the Crown."

The Captain-General fell silent. The indictment slipped from his hands to the table.

Diego Almagro, close by the Captain-General, said, "We judges find the Inca Atahualpa guilty of all these crimes. We sentence him to death. Since he is a heretic, he shall be led this night into the market place of Caxamalca, and there consumed by flame."

My legs began to turn to water, and I had trouble holding myself upright. Diego de Vargas took my arm. He whispered, "We did all that was possible. It simply did not suffice." Then he turned to the men assembled around the table, and said in a clear voice that was unmistakable, "For the last time I protest that this trial was illegal."

But no one paid the slightest attention to him. The papers were quickly collected. Father Vicente took his Bible and his crucifix. Nobody looked very long at anyone else. Soon the room was empty.

Two hours after sunset the horns were blown in the triangular plaza of Caxamalca. Once more we lined up in ranks, as we had when the gold was partitioned among us. Every fifth man held a flaming torch in his hand. The faggots burned fitfully, crackling noisily in the puffy breeze. A heavy pall of gray smoke hovered above us, and when it parted we could see the immense stars of the southern sky. On the same place where the gold had been parceled out now stood a heavy stake, in front of which bundles of wood and dried grasses had been piled.

The Inca was led out of the House of the Snake. He walked slowly, heavily. His feet were chained together. At his right walked Father Vicente, Bible in hand, the crucifix about his neck. At the Inca's left walked the

Captain-General. They reached the middle of the plaza. We stood stiff and silent, all under the same spell. We could all plainly hear the Inca's chains clanking on the stones, and the snapping of the torches.

Father Vicente talked rapidly to the Inca, but he seemed not to be heard. Atahualpa's face was turned away. He was grim and stubborn. He was the Indian warrior, inured to administering and enduring cruelties both. He looked at the stake, the piles of dry wood. There was cold contempt on his face. He looked around, and in his own language said plainly, "Is Chasca here?"

"I am here," I said, and went up to him.

He looked at me closely, laid his hand on my shoulder. "It is all true," he said. "The star did not lie."

My heart was sick as I peered into the Indian face. I thought how these fine features, the slender body would be all ashes in less than an hour. The eyes would never glisten and command again, the voice never speak. The horror of the murder pressed down on me like a hill. Had not Laanta told how Mamapacha had made men mortal in order that they might have cause to love each other? My mind raced, trying to think of some escape. There was none, I saw. A mysterious will had ordained it.

"Chasca," said Atahualpa, "my kingdom is gone. My people are dispersed. My warriors are not by my side. Everything has come to an end. Even the sun has turned his face away."

"But it is night," I whispered to him.

"Yes, it is night," he said; "the hour of the invisible god has come." He removed his hand from my shoulder and pointed to the stake.

"I am afraid to fall into the hands of your god," he went on to say quietly. "He is the powerful one, I see that. I am going to die, Chasca. Then the great mountains will be gone; they will vanish as the dew vanishes in the morning. The sun will go out, the moon and all the stars. There will be no more earth, and no more sea. There will be no more children playing, no more girls' laughter, no more clatter among the people and the roar of battle. All that, everything, will be gone and past. And my own body, that too will be gone. It will disappear and the wind will blow its ashes away. And then soon I shall see the unseen face of your god. Already I have an idea how terrible he will be. I see him like a cliff rising out of the mists. I have dreamed about him."

"Master," I said, "there is still time left. Accept our faith and allow yourself to be baptized."

This last word I spoke in Spanish, for I had not invented any Quicha equivalent to describe the Sacrament. Father Vicente caught on to what I was saying. He whispered loudly to me, "If he lets himself be baptized, he need not submit to the ordeal of death at the stake. I'll see it's made easier for him."

I told the Inca what the priest had said to me.

"But what does it really matter how a man dies?" the Inca inquired ironically.

"But now you believe in the unseen god, do you not?" I persisted.

"Yes, my gods have forsaken me," he agreed slowly. "The kingdom of the sun has collapsed, and with it the sun. Pachacamac has turned his face away. Even Mamapacha, the earth, is cold and indifferent. Tell them, Chasca, that I want to be baptized."

The Inca's announcement evoked great excitement among the cavaliers and soldiers. The Dominicans hastened to get out wax candles and light them. They had long since made preparations for this event. They brought baptismal water in an old silver vase. Father Vicente drew on priest's vestments over his monk's robe. Almagro talked wildly to the Captain-General who listened and now and then shook his head. "But we have no choice," I heard Almagro say, his voice rising in pitch. "It's absolutely a necessity . . . unavoidable. There's still the treason charge, even if he does become a Christian."

"I can find no fault with him now," the Captain-General whispered back hoarsely.

Thereupon Riquelme, the Crown treasurer, mixed himself into the council, and said. "Anyone who protects a man accused of high treason is suspect of the same crime. Don Carlos will demand severe reckoning of you and your family if you change your verdict."

The Captain-General looked at Riquelme, and deliberately spat at the ground before his feet. He looked blackly at Almagro and said, "Let it go, then. Let it go."

It was the night of the twenty-ninth day of August in the year of our Lord fifteen hundred and thirty-three, the night after the feast of John the Baptist. On that night the name of the Inca, Atahualpa, king of Tavana-Suyu, was changed to Juan de Atahualpa. Diego de Vargas and I stood by as his godfathers, while the men undid the chains binding his feet. We kneeled down and folded our hands as Father Vicente sprinkled his head with the blessed water.

Father Vicente opened his leather-bound Bible, and read out of the chapter of Luke about John the Baptist, how he was reared in the wilderness on the other side of the Jordan, and how he nourished himself with grass-hoppers and wild honey.

The words came to me from a great distance. I did not understand their sense. The voices of those who call in the wilderness are always understood only when it is too late, it seems. The story seemed an irrelevant tale out of times irrevocably past; it seemed bizarre, almost laughable, when I feebly tried to imagine the actual hairy, unwashed saint. But I must have had some intimation of the inner meaning of the story, and the words must have made some impression on me. For even to this day, without ever having read them since, I can repeat the story word for word without faltering.

And so the words came out of Father Vicente's mouth, and he, I am sure, was no more aware than I of what he was saying. He intoned loudly, ". . . whose fan is in his hand, and he will purge his floor, and will gather the wheat into his house; but the chaff he will burn up with unquenchable fire that cannot be put out. . . ."

The Dominican let the little Bible sink to arm's length. He then raised his right hand, and said, "The Holy Mother, the Roman Catholic Church, absolves you, Juan de Atahualpa, of all heresy, and receives her beloved child into her bosom. All sins that ye have ever committed are now absolved. . . ."

"What is he saying?" muttered Almagro hoarsely. "Did you hear what he just said?"

Father Vicente turned and measured the Captain contemptuously. "From the standpoint of the Church," he said, "Juan de Atahualpa is as innocent as a babe in the cradle. That is the Sacrament. That is what it means."

"But what about treason . . . he murdered his brother," said Diego Almagro.

"That is no concern of mine," retorted Father Vicente, "for secular justice is outside my province. It is none of my affair what you others do."

"It must be done. We cannot draw back now." It was Almagro again. "My God! Everything will be the same as ever!"

The men in the plaza were silent. The houses and the men alike were motionless, breathless, like figures painted on a board. Only the sound of the faggots was audible.

And now Diego Almagro screwed up his courage, and shouted in his high voice, "Juan de Atahualpa is condemned to die by the garrote. The executioner will do his duty."

I stood near Atahualpa as if rooted to the spot. My limbs were solid lumps of lead, and the sweat trickled down my forehead. Three dark figures moved quickly to the center of the market place. They threw aside their cloaks, and among them I recognized Miguel Estete. With practiced movements they pushed the Inca back up against the stake. Then Miguel Estete cast a length of fine rope about the Inca's throat, and twisted it tight with a little stick.

"My children," cried the Inca, "Chasca, my children . . ." Only these words and then all sound died in his throat. For a moment there was a violent gurgling and groaning. Blood spurted out of the beautiful nose. The body died slowly, in heavy cramps that came regularly, as they come to a woman in travail. At last there was no more sound.

The strangler stepped back, eased off a few turns on the stick, and let the body hang thus from the stake. It seemed as if the Inca were staring at the ground with enormously bulging eyes.

Miguel Estete turned to the Captain-General. "The task is finished, my lord," he said. He rolled down his sleeves over hairy forearms.

The Captain-General made no reply. He stood erect, very tall, gray and stony. Tears rolled down his cheeks. I looked closer. It was really so. The Captain-General was weeping. It was terrifying to see, for not a muscle in his face had changed. He did not appear to be aware even that he was weeping, as if something in him he had never suspected was weeping for him. The old man, the conquistador, the founder of cities, was weeping like the rock in the fairy tale.

He observed the corpse at last and commanded that the trumpets be blown.

The horns blew. According to the old custom they blew, half merrily.

Then the soldiers were dismissed, and they all returned to their quarters. A good meal was all prepared, and the beakers that had belonged to the Inca passed from mouth to mouth, filled with foaming chicha. Among the company there arose a spirit of gladness, of joy, almost. It was infectious. The men began to make little jokes and laugh. Now that the Inca was dead, all the fears dissolved, and we were free. The decision had been made, and it worked a miracle. In the distance, far on the other side of the mountains, golden Cuzco beckoned. The way was free to the temples of gold, to all the treasure, to new women. The way was free once more.

After a time I returned to the plaza in the company of Diego de Vargas. Two soldiers had been posted as a guard of honor for the dead king. They were talking in the manner of soldiers, philosophizing about the world.

"It's a shame, if you stop to think of it," one of them declared, "taking any man's life. Especially when you think that it's all a man has, just one life."

"You're right, friend," agreed the other. He was chewing on a crust of bread to ward off the chill of the night and keep himself occupied. "When I was a boy I used to run off to see every hanging and burning. But now I wouldn't walk around the corner to see the best of hangings. I'm tired of executions — there are too many of them; they're becoming too much of a good thing. Besides, when I think how I'm going to rattle on my deathbed just like that Indian bastard. . . ."

I looked at the dead man. He was still sagged down in the same position, his head on his chest. I felt sure that his neck was stretching, that very soon his forehead would be touching his toes. I had to look away. Then I saw that we Spaniards were not alone with the Inca in the market place. All around, before the houses, against the walls, in corners and doorways, crouched countless Indians. They hardly stirred, did not utter a word to one another, just sat and looked. They were as quiet as a thousand cats stalking a mouse. I wondered whether it was curiosity or love for the dead man that had brought them back to the city. Was it wordless grief or hatred for us that was heavy in their hearts?

Diego and I relieved the guards and kept watch the night through. We loosened the thong about the Inca's neck. We laid the body on a pile of Indian blankets. But we were too late, really, for *rigor mortis* had already set in, and the Inca lay so drawn together that his corpse was like an old man's. The silent crouching multitude did not stir.

Midnight Experiences of
Jean-Marie Baptiste des-Essars

by Maurice Hewlett

1566   Mary Queen of Scots, young, beautiful, reckless and Catholic, hated her foolish husband, Henry,
Lord Darnley, and was in turn hated by many of the
most powerful of the Scots Protestant nobles. On the
night of March 9, 1566, David Rizzio, Mary's Italian
secretary, was murdered in Mary's presence in Holyrood Palace in Edinburgh. The murderers' motives
are still debated by historians. Des-Essars was Mary's
French page.

On that appointed night of Saturday, the 9th of March — a blowy,
snowy night, harrowing for men at sea, with a mort of vessels pitching
at their cables in Leith Roads — Des-Essars was late for his service. He
should have come on to the door at ten o'clock, and it wanted but two
minutes to that when he was beating down the Castle hill in the teeth
of the wind.

Never mind his errand, and expect fibs if you ask what had kept him.
Remember that he was older at this time than when you first saw him,
a French boy 'with smut-rimmed eyes,' crop-headed, pale, shrewd, and
reticent. That was a matter of three years ago: the Queen was but nineteen and he four years younger. He was eighteen now, and may have had
evening affairs like other people, no concern of yours or mine. Whatever
they may have been, they had kept him unduly; he had two minutes and
wanted seven. He drew his bonnet close, his short cape about him, and
went scudding down the hill as fast as the snow would let him in shoes
dangerously thin for the weather, but useful for tiptoe purposes. The snow
had been heaped upon the cawsey, but in the street trodden, thawed, and
then frozen again to a surface of ice. From it came enough light to show
that few people were abroad, and none lawfully, and that otherwise it
was infernally dark. A strangely diffused, essential light it was, that of the
snow. It put to shame three dying candles left in the Luckenbooths and
the sick flame of an oil lamp above the Netherbow Port. After passing
that, there was no sign of man or man's comforts until you were in the
Abbey precincts.

Des-Essars knew — being as sharp as a needle — that something was changed the moment he reached those precincts; knew by the pricking of his skin, as they say. A double guard set; knots of men-at-arms; some horses led about; low voices talking in strange accents, — something was altered. Worse than all this, he found the word of the night unavailing: no manner of entry for him.

'My service is the Queen's honourable sir,' he pleaded to an unknown sentry, who wore (he observed) a steel cap of unusual shape.

The square hackbutter shook his head. 'No way in this night, Frenchman.'

'By whose orders, if you please?'

'By mine, Frenchman.'

Here was misfortune! No help for it, but he must brave what he had hoped to avoid — his superior officer, to wit.

'If it please you, sir,' he said, 'I will speak with Mr. Erskine in the guard-room.'

'Mr. Airrskin!' was the shocking answer — and how the man spoke it! — 'Mr. Airrskin! He's no here. He's awa'. So now off with ye, Johnny Frenchman.' The man obviously had orders: but whose orders?

Des-Essars shrugged. He shivered also, as he always did when refused anything — as if the world had proved suddenly a chill place. But really the affair was serious. Inside the house he must be, and that early. Driven to his last resource, he walked back far enough for the dark to swallow him up, returned upon his tracks a little way so soon as the hackbutter had resumed his stamping up and down; branched off to the right, slipping through a ruinous stable, blown to pieces in former days by the English; crossed a frozen cabbage garden which, having been flooded, was now a sheet of cat-ice; and so came hard upon the Abbey wall. In this wall, as he very well knew, there were certain cavities, used as steps by the household when the gateways were either not convenient or likely to be denied: indeed, he would not, perhaps, have cared to reckon how many times he had used them himself. Having chipped the ice out of them with his hanger, he was triumphantly within the pale, hopping over the Queen's privy garden with high-lifted feet, like a dog in turnips. To win the palace itself was easy. It was mighty little use having friends in the kitchen if they could not do you services of that kind.

He had to find the Queen, though, and face what she might give him, but of that he had little fear. He knew that she would be at cards, and too full of her troubles and pains to seek for a new one. It is a queer reflection that he makes in his Memoirs — that although he romantically

loved the Queen, he had no scruples about deceiving her and few fears
of being found out, so only that she did not take the scrape to heart. 'She
was a goddess to me,' he says, 'in those days, a remote point of my adoration. A young man, however, is compact of two parts, an earthly and a
spiritual. If I had exhibited to her the frailties of my earthly part it would
have been by a very natural impulse. However, I never did.' This is a
digression: he knew that she would not fret herself about him and his affairs just now, because she was ill, and miserable about the King. Throwing a kiss of his hand, then, to the yawning scullery-wench, who had had
to get out of her bed to open the window for him, he skimmed down the
corridors on a light foot, and reached the great hall. He hoped to go tiptoe
up the privy stair and gain the door of the cabinet without being heard.
When she came out she would find him there, and all would be well. This
was his plan.

It was almost dark in the hall, but not quite. A tree-bole on the hearth
was in the article of death; a few thin flames about the shell of it showed
him a company of men in the corner by the privy stair. Vexatious! They
were leaning to the wall, some sitting against it; some were on the steps
asleep, their heads nodding to their knees. He was cut off his sure access,
and must go by the main staircase — if he could. He tried it, sidling along
by the farther wall; but they spied him, two of them, and one went to cut
him off. A tall enemy this, for the little Frenchman; but luckily for him it
was a case of boots against no boots where silence was the essence of the con-
tract. Des-Essars, his shoes in his hand, darted out into the open and raced
straight for the stair. The enemy began his pursuit — in riding-boots. Heavens! the crash and clatter on the flags, the echo from the roof! It would
never do: hushed voices called the man back; he went tender-footed, finally stopped. By that time the page was up the stair, pausing at the top
to wipe his brows and neck of cold sweat, and to wonder as he wiped
what all this might mean. Double guard in the court — strange voices —
the word changed — Mr. Erskine away! No sentry in the hall, but, instead,
a cluster of waiting, whispering men — in riding boots — by the privy stair!
The vivacious young man was imaginative to a fault; he could construct
a whole tragedy of life and death out of a change in the weather. And
here was a fateful climax to the tragedy of a stormy night! First, the stress
of the driving snow — whirling, solitary, forlorn stuff! — the apprehension
of wild work by every dark entry. Passing the Tolbooth, a shriek out of
the blackness had sent his heart into his mouth. There had been fighting, too, in Sim's Close. He had seen a torch flare and dip, men and women

huddled about two on the ground; one grunting, 'Tak' it! Tak' it! and the other, with a strangled wail, 'Oh, Jesus!' Bad hearing all this — evil preparation. Atop of these apparitions, lo! their fulfilment: stroke after stroke of doom. Cloaked men by the privy stair — *Dieu de Dieu!* His heart was thumping at his ribs when he peeped through the curtain of the Queen's cabinet and saw his mistress there with Lady Argyll and the Italian. 'Blessed Mother!' he thought, 'here's an escape for me. I had no notion the hour was so late.' What he meant was, that the rest of the company had gone. He had heard that Lord Robert Stuart and the Laird of Criech were to sup that night. Well, they had supped and were gone! It must be on the stroke of midnight.

The Queen, as he could see, lay back in her elbow-chair, obviously suffering, picking at some food before her, but not eating any. Her lips were chapped and dry; she moistened them continually, then bit them. Lady Argyll, handsome, strong-featured, and swarthy, sat bolt upright and stared at the sconce on the wall; and as for the Italian, he did as he always did, lounged opposite his Queen, his head against the wainscot. Reflective after food, he used his toothpick, but no other ceremony whatsoever. He wore his cap on his head, ignored Lady Argyll — half sister to the throne — and when he looked at her Majesty, as he often did, it was as a man might look at his wife. She, although she seemed too weary or too indifferent to lift her heavy eyelids, knew perfectly well that both her companions were watching her: Des-Essars was sure of that. He watched her himself intensely, and only once saw her meet Davy's eye, when she passed her cup to him to be filled with drink, and he, as if thankful to be active, poured the wine with a flourish and smiled in her face as he served her. She observed both act and actor, and made no sign, neither drank from the cup now she had it; but sank back to her wretchedness and the contemplation of it, being in that pettish, brooding habit of mind which would rather run on in a groove of pain than brace itself to some new shift. As he watched what was a familiar scene to him, Des-Essars was wondering whether he should dare go in and report what he had observed in the hall. No! on the whole he would not do that. Signior Davy, who was a weasel in such a field as a young man's mind, would assuredly fasten upon him at some false turn or other, never let go, and show no mercy. Like all the underlings of Holyrood he went in mortal fear of the Italian, though, unlike any of them, he admired him.

The little cabinet was very dim. There were candles on the table, but none alight in the sconces. From beyond, through a half-open door, came the drowsy voices of the Queen's women, murmuring their way through two more hours' vigil. Interminable nights! Cards would follow supper, you must know, and Signior Davy would try to outsit Lady Argyll. He always tried, and generally succeeded.

The Queen shifted, sighed, and played hasty tunes with her fingers on the table: she was never still. It was evident that she was at once very wretched and very irritable. Her dark-red gown was cut low and square, Venetian mode: Des-Essars could see quite well how short her breath was, and how quick. Yet she said nothing. Once she and Lady Argyll exchanged glances; the Mistress of the Robes inquired with her eyebrows, the Queen fretfully shook the question away. It was an unhappy supper for all but the graceless Italian, who was much at his ease now that he had unfastened some of the hooks of his jacket. The French lad, who had always been in love with his mistress and yet able to criticize her — as a Protestant may adore the Virgin Mary — admits that at this moment of her life, in this bitter mood, he found her extremely piquant. 'This pale, helpless, angry, pretty woman!' he exclaims upon his page. He would seldom allow that she was more than just a pretty woman; and now she was a good deal less. Her charms for him had never been of the face — she had an allure of her own. 'Mistress Seton was lovely, I consider, my Lady Bothwell most beautiful, and Mistress Fleming not far short of that: but the Queen's Majesty — ah! the coin from Mr. Knox's mint rang true. Honeypot! Honeypot! There you had her essence: sleepy, slow, soft sweetness — with a sharp aftertaste, for all that, to prick the tongue and set it longing.'

More than nice considerations, these, which the stealthy opening of a door and a step in the passage disturbed. Des-Essars would have straightened himself on that signal, to stand as a page should stand in the view of any one entering. Then he saw, out of the corner of his eye, the King go down the little stair. It must be the King, because — to say nothing of the tall figure, small-headed as it was, — he had seen the long white gown. The King wore a white quilted-silk bedgown, lined with ermine. At the turning of the stair Des-Essars saw him just glance backwards over his shoulder towards the cabinet, but, being stiff within the shadow of the curtain, was not himself seen. After that furtive look he saw him go down the privy stair, his hand on the rope. Obviously he had an assignation with some woman below.

Before he had time to correct this conclusion by the memory of the cloaked men in the hall, he heard returning steps — somebody, this time, coming up the steps; no! there were more than one — two or three at least. He was sure of this — his ears had never deceived him — and yet it was the King alone who appeared at the stair-head with a lighted taper in his hand, which he must have got from the hall. He stood there for a moment, his face showing white and strained in the light, his mouth open, too; then, blowing out his taper, he came directly to the curtain of the Queen's cabinet, pulled it aside and went in. He had actually covered Des-Essars with the curtain without a notion that he was there; but the youth had had time to observe that he was fully dressed beneath his gown, and to get a hot whiff of the strong waters in his breath as he passed in. Urgent to see what all this might mean, he peeped through the hangings.

Lady Argyll rose up slowly when she saw the King, but made no reverence. Very few did in these days. The Italian followed her example, perfectly composed. The Queen took no notice of him. She rested as she had been, her head on the droop, eyebrows raised, eyes fixed on the disordered platter. The King, whose colour was very high, came behind her chair, stooped, and put his arm round her. His hand covered her bosom. She did not avoid, though she did not relish this.

'Madam, it is very late,' he said, and spoke breathlessly.

'It is not I who detain you,' said she.

'No, madam, no. But you do detain these good servants of yours. Here is your sister of Argyll; next door are your women. And so it is night after night. I think not of myself.'

She lifted her head a little to look up sideways — but not at him. 'You think of very little else, to my understanding. Having brought me to the state where now I am, you are inclined to leave me alone. Rather, you *were* inclined; for this is a new humour, little to my taste.'

'I should be oftener here, believe me,' says the King, still embracing her, 'if I could feel more sure of a welcome — if all might be again as it was once between you and me.'

She laughed, without mirth; then asked, 'And how was it — once?'

The King stooped down and kissed her forehead, by the same act gently pushing back her head till it rested on his shoulder.

'This it was once, my Mary,' he said; and as she looked up into his face, wondering over it, searching it, he kissed her again. 'Thus it was once,' he repeated in a louder voice; and then, louder yet, 'Thus, O Queen of Scots!'

Once more he kissed her, and once more cried out, 'O Queen of Scots!' Then Des-Essars heard the footsteps begin again on the privy stair, and saw men come into the passage — many men.

Three of them, in cloaks and steel bonnets, came quickly to the door, and passed him. They went through the curtain. These three were Lord Ruthven, Ker of Fawdonsyde, and Mr. Archibald Douglas. Rigid in his shadow, Des-Essars watched all.

Seeing events in the Italian's eyes, rather than with her own — for Signior Davy had narrowed his to two threads of blue — the Queen lifted her head from her husband's arm and looked curiously round. The three stood hesitant within the door; Ruthven had his cap on his head, Fawdonsyde his, but Archie showed his grey poll. Little things like these angered her quickly; she shook free from the King and sat upright.

'What is this, my Lord Ruthven? You forget yourself.'

'Madam —' he began; but Douglas nudged him furiously.

'Your bonnet, man, your bonnet!'

The Queen had risen, and the fixed direction of her eyes gave him understanding.

'Ah, my knapscall! I do as other do, madam,' he said, with a meaning look at the Italian. 'What is pleasant to your Majesty in yonder servant should not be an offence in a councillor.'

'No, no, ma'am, nor it should not,' muttered Fawdonsyde, who nevertheless, doffed his bonnet.

The King was holding her again, she staring still at the scowling man in steel. 'What do you want with me, Ruthven?' she said. She had very dry lips.

He made a clumsy bow. 'May it please your Majesty,' he said, 'we are come to rid you of this fellow Davy, who has been overlong familiar here, and overmuch — for your Majesty's honour.'

She turned her face to the King, whose arm still held her — a white, strong face.

'You,' she said fiercely, 'what have you to do in this? What have you to say?'

'I think with Ruthven — with all of them — my friends and well-wishers. 'Tis the common voice: they say I am betrayed, upon my soul! I cannot endure — I entreat you to trust me —' He was incoherent.

She broke away from his arm, took a step forward and put herself between him and the three. She was so angry that she could not find words. She stammered, began to speak, rejected what words came. The Italian took off his cap and watched Ruthven intently. The moment of pause that ensued was broken by Ruthven's raising his hand, for the Queen flashed out, 'Put down your hand, sir!' and seemed as if she would have struck him. Fawdonsyde here cocked his pistol and deliberately raised it against the Queen's person. 'Treason! treason!' shrieked Des-Essars from the curtain, and blundered forward to the villain.

But the Queen had been before him; at last she had found words, and deeds. She drew herself up, quivering, went directly towards Fawdonsyde, and beat down the point of the pistol with her flat hand. 'Do you dare so much? Then I dare more. What shameless thing do you here? If I had a sword in my hand — ' Here she stopped, tongue-tied at what was done to her.

For Ruthven, regardless of majesty, had got her round the middle. He pushed her back into the King's arms; and "Take your wife, my lord,' says he; 'take your good-wife in your arms and cherish her, while we do what must be done.'

The King held her fast in spite of her struggles. At that moment the Italian made a rattling sound in his throat and backed from the table. Archie Douglas stepped behind the King, to get round the little room; Ruthven approached his victim from the other side; the Italian pulled at the table, got it between himself and the enemy, and overset it: then Lady Argyll screamed, and snatched at a candlestick as all went down. It was the only light left in the room, held up in her hand like a beacon above a tossing sea. Where was Des-Essars? Cuffed aside to the wall, like a rag doll. The maids were packed in the door of the bedchamber, and one of them had pulled him into safety among them.

All that followed he marked: how the frenzied Italian, hedged in between Douglas and Ruthven, vaulted the table, knocked over Fawdonsyde, and then, whimpering like a woman, crouched by the Queen, his fingers in the pleats of her gown. He saw the King's light eyelashes blink, and heard his breath come whistling through his nose; and that pale, disfigured girl, held up closely against her husband, moaning and hiding her face in his breast. And now Ruthven, grinning horribly, swearing to himself, and Douglas, whining like a dog at a rat-hole, were at their man's hands, trying to drag him off. Fawdonsyde hovered about, hopeful to help. Lady Argyll held up the candle.

Douglas wrenched open one hand, Ruthven got his head down and bit the other till it parted.

'*Oh Dio! O Dio!*' long shuddering cries went up from the Italian as they dragged him out into the passage, where the others waited.

It was dark there, and one knew not how full of men; but Des-Essars heard them snarling and mauling like a pack of wolves; heard the scuffling, the panting, the short oaths — and then a piercing scream. At that there was silence; then some one said, as he struck, 'There! there! Hog of Turin!' and another (Lindsay), 'He's done.'

The King put the Queen among her maids in a hurry, and went running out into the passage as they were shuffling the body down the stair. Des-Essars just noticed, and remembered afterwards, his naked dagger in his hand as he went out helter-skelter after his friends. Upon some instinct or other, he followed him as far as the head of the stair. From the bottom came up a great clamour — howls of execration, one or two cries for the King, a round of welcome when he appeared. The page ran back to the cabinet, and found it dark.

It was bad to hear the Queen's laughter in the bedchamber — worse when that shuddered out into moaning, and she began to wail as if she were keening her dead. He could not bear it, so crept out again to spy about the passages and listen to the shouting from the hall. 'A Douglas! a Douglas!' was the most common cry. Peeping through a window which gave on to the front, he saw the snowy court ablaze with torches, alive with men, and against the glare the snowflakes whirling by, like smuts from a burning chimney. It was clear enough now that the palace was held, all its inmates prisoners. But what seemed more terrifying than that was the emptiness of the upper corridors, the sudden hush after so much riot — and the Queen's moan, haunting all the dark like a lost soul.

It was so bad up there that the lad, his brain on fire, felt the need of any company — even that of goalers. No one hindering, he crept down the privy stair, — horribly slippery it was, and he knew why, — hoping to spy into the hall; and this also he was free to do, since the stair-foot was now unguarded. He found the hall crowded with men; great torches smoking to the rafters; a glow of light on shields and blazonry, the banners and achievements of dead kings. In the stir of business the arras surged like the waves of the sea. A furious draught blew in from the open doors, to which all faces were turned. Men craned over each others' backs to look there. Des-Essars could not see the King; but there at the entry was the Earl of Morton in his armour, two linkmen by him. He was reading from a bill: in front of him was a clear way; across it stood the Masters of Lindsay and Ruthven, and men in their liveries, halberds in their hands.

'Pass out, Earl of Atholl,' he heard Lord Morton say; 'Pass out, Lord of Tuillibardine': and then, after a while of looking and pointing, he saw the grizzled head and square shoulders of my Lord Atholl moving down the lane of men, young Tullibardine uncovered beside him.

'Pass out, Pitcur; pass out, Mr. James Balfour; pass out, the Lord Herries.' The same elbowing in the crowd: three men file out into the scurrying snow — all the Queen's friends, observe.

Near to Des-Essars a man asked of his neighbour, 'Will they let by my Lord Huntley, think you?'

The other shook his head. 'Never! He'll keep company with the Reiver of Liddesdale, be sure.'

The Reiver was Lord Bothwell, of course, who Des-Essars knew to be in the house. 'Good fellow-prisoners for us,' he thought.

'Pass out, Mr. Secretary, on a fair errand.'

There was some murmuring at this; but the man went out unmolested, with a sweep of the bonnet to my Lord Morton as he passed. Des-Essars saw him stop at the first taste of the weather and cover his mouth with his cloak — but he waited for no more. A thought had struck him. He slipped back up the puddled stair, gained the first corridor, and, knowing his way by heart, went in and out of the passages until he came to a barred door. Here he put his ear to the crack and listened intently.

For a long time he could hear nothing on either side the door; but by and by somebody with a light — a man — came to the farther end of the passage and looked about, raising and dipping his lantern. That was an ugly moment! Crouched against the wall, he saw the lamp now high now low, and marked with a leaping heart how nearly the beams reached to where he lay. He heard a movement behind the door, too, but had to let it go. Not for full three minutes after the disappearance of the watchman did he dare put his knuckles to the door, and tap, very softly, at the panel. He tapped and tapped. A board creaked; there was breathing at the door. A voice, shamming boldness, cried, 'Qui est?'

Des-Essars smiled. 'C'est toi, Paris?'

His question was answered by another. 'Tiens, qui est ce drôle?'

Paris, for a thousand pound! Knocking again, he declared himself. 'It is I, Paris — M. Des-Essars.'

'M. Baptiste, your servant,' then said Paris through the door.

'My lord is a prisoner, Paris?'

'Not for the first time, my dear sir.'

'How many are you there?'

'Four. My lord, and M. de Huntly, myself, Jock Gordon.'

'Well, you should get out — but quickly, before they have finished in the hall. They are passing men out. Be quick, Paris — tell my lord.'

'Bravo!' says Paris. 'We should get out — and quickly! By the chimney, sir? There is no chimney. By the window? There is but one death for every man, and one neck to be broke.'

'You will break no necks at all, you fool. Below these windows is the lions' house.'

Paris thought. 'Are you sure of that?'

'Sure! Oh, Paris, make haste!'

Again Paris appeared to reflect; and then he said, 'If you are betraying a countryman of yours, M. Des-Essars, and your old patron also, you shall never see God.'

Des-Essars wrung his hands. 'You fool! You fool! Are you mad? Call my lord.'

'Wait,' said Paris. In a short time, the sound of heavy steps. Ah, here was my lord!

''Tis yourself, Baptiste?'

'Yes, yes, my lord.'

'Have they finished with Davy?'

'My God, sir!'

'What of the Queen?'

'Her women have her.'

'Now, Baptiste. You say the lion-house is below these windows. Which windows? There are four.'

'The two in the midst, my lord. My lord, across the Little Garden — in a straight line — there are holes in the wall.'

'Oho! You are a brave lad. Go to your bed.'

Jean-Marie Baptiste Des-Essars went back to the Queen's side. At the door of the cabinet he found Adam Gordon in a fit of sobs. 'Oh, my fine man,' says the French lad, stirring him with his foot, 'leave tears to the women. This is men's business.'

Adam lifted up his stricken face. 'Where have you been cowering, traitor?'

Jean-Marie laughed grimly. 'I have been saving Scotland,' he said, 'whilst you were blubbering here.'

Adam Gordon, being up by now, knocked Jean-Marie down.

'I excused him readily, however,' he writes in his Memoirs, 'considering the agitation we all suffered at the time. And where he felled me there I lay, and slept like a child.'

New Plymouth

by Ernest Gébler

> 1620   While the Mayflower lay off the coast of Cape
> Cod awaiting the return of an exploring party Doro-
> thy, wife of William Bradford, disappeared — pre-
> sumably a suicide by drowning. Bradford became the
> great governor of Plymouth Colony. Jones, the ship's
> master, had cheated the Pilgrims by deliberately ar-
> ranging to land them far to the North of the site
> agreed upon.

A sailor's shout rang out, "There's our bird winging home!" followed
by excited voices, and a moment later the pounding of feet coming up the
hatches. Gilbert crossed the deck and stood in the press of women watching the shallop round Long Point and sail in, bending on the wind. The
figures in her waved and shouted and the ship answered with an outcry
of hallooings, women's glad high voices and children's excited shrieks.

Nearer, and those on the ship could count the returning explorers.
Twenty. They were all come home: old John Carver, hat bound into a
bonnet with his scarf; the big, brash, grinning young carpenter, hero of
the broken beam; Edward Winslow; the ship's mates: Hopkins, Billington,
White. Quickly the women picked them all out. "Isaac Allerton's there,
man, be easy." "I see your man, Edward!" They were all there.

Soon boat and ship saw each other's faces. Sailors ran up the ratlines.
Mr. Jones ascended to the poop from his cabin.

"There is William Bradford — wearing the orange shirt his Dorothy dyed
sticking out at his neck." A guilty silence seemed to spread in quick, shocked
waves out around the woman who had so thoughtlessly spoken. Mr.
Brewster's tall form pushed forward to the rail, mute pain on his large,
lined face, to be the first to greet his difficult protégé, his namesake William,
and somehow, with God's help, ease the blow.

"Arrows!" Hopkins yelled, himself like some savage of dark face and
wild eye and black lank locks. "The savage men tried their hand with us —
and we frightened them to the middle of yesterday. Arrows!" He waved
the bundle of arrows aloft. The shallop came alongside, full of red, wind-
whipped faces, every man an experienced, confident traveller and conqueror.

Now we will come heart to heart, William thought, thinking of Dorothy, as he had thought all across the harbour. A woman's lot was hard. They would give each other more. He would make it up to her in little ways.

"We have found our harbour," they shouted. "The land the good Lord left over for us since the beginning of the world!"

Bradford forced himself to sit on in the stern and appear calm, strong, while the others jostled good-humoredly to get up on board, so that he was the last to ascend the boarding ladder and throw his muddy-breeched leg over the side. White, Billington, Allerton, they were all with their women and children; shouting, hugging, tears — indulgence not quite to his taste or approval. Mr. Brewster faced him; and was here taking him with an arm around his shoulder and drawing him aside beneath the projecting weather-beaten deck of the poop.

"It is true — we have found our harbour, sir, we have found our home. A harbour to take this ship in comfort. And there is cleared ground." He could not keep the note of triumph from his voice. "And good soil, where corn is grown."

The older man was strangely silent, wetting his upper lip beneath his brown and white moustache with the tip of his tongue. William remembered Dorothy and looked about quickly. "Dorothy? She is well? I have not seen her." The old man gripped his arm so tightly that it hurt. In his eyes he saw a fullness, as of tears.

"Our Dorothy has gone, Will. How, we don't know, but gone she is to eternity," the old man said, speaking faintly, close into his face, searching his eyes with helpless pity. For though he had thought of many words to say at that moment to prepare the way, he knew then that it was better that way, to say it simply and directly. "She is drowned since Monday gone, as if the earth had opened and swallowed her."

Mr. Jones, coming down off the poop deck to the waist, paused near by, and seeing close up the frozen staring face, rawboned, harsh-featured as if with all the suffering of common man moulded in the likeness of a driven animal, that was the younger man, and the open-mouthed, helpless face of the old bearded one, hurried uneasily among the gabbling throng.

"No, no — leave me to be alone," Bradford said at last, thickly, through his squeezing, choking throat. He turned to go below into the darkness, so that no one should see, not even the older man he so loved, what must by all tokens happen to him very soon — the frozen immobility inside melting, the welling up of what was underneath, his collapse into womanly weeping. He went down the stairs slowly.

The bulwarks were breast-high; through months of storm and tossing no one had fallen overboard; how then could one fall overboard in a calm harbour? She had taken her own life, the most heinous crime possible to a human creature in all the calendar of sins then known to Christian man. He passed in a cloud across the hold, descended again into complete darkness. And down again, until he was in the cargo hold. There he stumbled about with little half-formed cries, seeking a corner in which to hide; finally, falling on his knees, covering his face with his hands and bending forward half doubled up, he slowly banged his head against a barrel of meal, calling her name aloud.

On deck, the prevailing genius for organizing took a hand in the telling of what had been seen and done, Governor Carver being deputed to tell the tale as a single voice and straighten out the tangled threads being so wildly flung about the deck by everyone all at once.

Gilbert stood by his brother and Mr. Jones and listened to the surprisingly gentlemanly voice soothe the rough throng, listened and did not hear, like some savage intruder, passive, tight-mouthed, arms folded in his blankets, staring across the dark water at the lonely Cape whereon was his fancied lovers' bower in the hollow by Corn Hill.

"By their noise," Mr. Carver was saying, speaking of the savages' attack, "we guessed them to be forty or fifty; though some thought that they were many more. Edward Winslow thinks they were at first trying their kind of magic, to send us back over the seas from whence we came. But how no single one of us was hit when the arrows came so thick we know not, unles it was of God — for these savages must know how to hit the fleet-running deer, as their very lives depend on it. So how it was that no one of us came to be struck, while our capes hanging by were hit many times through and through, we know not — unless it was, as Edward swears, nothing of their design at all to wound us, but to fright us from their places of habitation. But however it is, we mean to give them a wide berth for a long time, to let them cool, before we go near them again to render accounts for their corn. But of the harbour! . . . Well, the harbour is a most hopeful place, full of byways, sideways, banks, islands, with the greatest flocks of wild fowl we saw anywhere, and cannot but be a natural ground for all the fish, in their seasons. There is there an abundance of mussels, the biggest and best we've yet seen — we'll not fall down while we can make a mussel stew! And signs of lobsters and crabs there are many. And there the ship may go straight without delay, to a better shelter than this. Mr. Jones may have no fear on that score."

"The land is excellent black mould," Edward Winslow continued the story. "We roamed it all about, seven or eight miles, without seeing a single sign of savage or of their houses — only where corn had in years past been planted. The river is not navigable, it is true. But there are plenty of small running brooks to the sea, of very sweet, fresh water. Some great oaks, pines, walnut, beech, ash, birch, hazel and the sassafras tree, for medicine oil to ship to England."

"With vines everywhere," Mr. Carver resumed. "Cherry trees, plum trees, and many others which we knew not. Oh, and herbs we found! Yes, in winter. Strawberry leaves, sorrel, watercresses and — what do you think? Beds and beds of wild leek and onions. And there is excellent clay for pots, that we washed with like it were soap. But above all there is the cleared land, and the brook to come up in our boats to it. There is a hill on which we think to set up the big guns, our own big magic, which will command all round about and from where you can look far over the ocean and see even this place of Cape Cod. So there, with God's help, we must go, without delay."

Gardens to make, houses, fishing, furs; but go across the bay and the new life in harbour and forest could begin tomorrow! And Mr. Clarke was there to testify, as had surely been the very purpose behind sending him out, that the new harbour was fit to shelter the ship. Mr. Jones withdrew from the waist deck; the women were raising their voices and calling for him to up anchor and sail then and there . . . He went into the poop without mentioning that entry into New Plymouth Harbour must wait on a following wind, in fear that the excited women would somehow set upon him and tear him in pieces if he announced any such thing. And a nice state of affairs, he thought, when Christopher Jones ran from his own decks in face of mere women; and stranger still by the same token that he found himself more concerned for them than put out. How times changed, indeed! May God send me my east wind, he prayed, and felt a greater depth of satisfaction in the prayer than he had ever had before; as if it was the very first prayer of his life; which indeed it was, in a sense.

Midmorning, Saturday, December sixteenth, the wind blowing at last from out the quarter necessary to get the *Mayflower* into the new harbour twenty-five miles across the bay, the ship's already green and slimed cables were wound in and the anchor lifted. With the shallop sailing ahead and the longboat tugging at a tow-rope behind, she moved out from the shelter of the Cape, awakened from her sleep, and became again the old live ship, creaking her timbers, singing in her shrouds and butting doggedly at the waves.

The die was cast, the spot of earth chosen; and Fate perhaps had already drawn lots for who should live and who go to the wall, for scarce one half were to reach victory in the unequal struggle of will and idea against physical circumstance, the greater number destined to defeat by death taking off their weakened, half-starved bodies. Four months and eleven days had come and gone since the ship had sailed out down Southampton Water in August sunshine, with thirty-four men settlers, sixteen bondmen and hired hands, twenty women and thirty-two children, to try to make the first English settlement in New England.

Being on a dead course for the harbour's mouth with a following wind, the mainsails prevented Mr. Jones from seeing his objective while standing on the poop, so he came down and went forwards into the bows. In the forepeak crouched a cold sailor with leaded line ready in his purple fingers. And standing in the shelter of the forecastle house were William Brewster, John Carver and Samuel Fuller.

"An hour will see us in," the Master said, in answer to a question put to him by Sam. "If the wind holds; it's but a freak wind." He stood with his back to them, small round body tightly filling out his leather jacket, his hands, blackly ingrained with charcoal, clasped behind him, legs apart, peering through red-rimmed, half-shuttered eyes at the looming coast ahead.

They had apparently come to accept his making landfall so far to the north, he felt, as a thing forced upon him — as he was believing more and more every day himself by a not unusual process of dismissing certain hard facts out of hand — and appeared to be prepared to make the best of a bad job. And in point of fact it might yet be proved that he and he alone had saved all their lives by that very act of putting in straight to land. To go south, looking for Hudson's river, would have meant a further and fatal delay and expense of supplies. But the margin of food he had thus saved them might be the very means by which they were enabled to tide over into the summer. Moreover, *he* could not be blamed for the *Speedwell's* defection, consequent loss of food and space, and addition of more mouths to feed.

He had done them wrong, he did not deny that to himself, and had tried to believe that they were many times damned and dangerous men. But that was all behind. He was growing, so mad was the world, to crave their respect and friendship; certainly of Brewster, Carver, Sam Fuller — and, perhaps, Winslow . . . Bradford alone appeared bent on keeping him an enemy, but the death of his wife seemed to be working a change in him. So that all in all the coming days looked hopeful.

"We were just now discussing our harbour, Mr. Jones," Sam said. "We all think it must be the place named by Captain Smith 'New Plymouth.' Your Mr. Clarke is of that opinion too. We have all been great readers in years past of the discoveries made in America — you can well imagine why! And Mr. Brewster in point of fact had his well-thumbed copy of Smith's *Discoveries* packed up in England at a friend's house, to ship with us, but . . . well" — Mr. Fuller nudged Mr. Brewster slyly — "he had to leave in something of a hurry."

"I remember to have had some of Smith's charts myself," the Master admitted, "and do recall that he named the place New Plymouth. But names are made by use, and I see nothing against your giving it a new name."

"New Plymouth . . ." Mr. Brewster said. "It is a good name. And I remember, as if it had been a sign, that we were handled very kindly in the old Plymouth."

"It is Captain Smith's name," the Master said distastefully.

"Nevertheless," Mr. Carver said, "we do not suppose names will be worrying us a week or a month from now. Patience works all."

On the waist deck John leaned over the side and looked forward at the shallop dipping ahead; and, as many another, the end of the sea voyage in sight, his thought turned back to some of the things that had led him to it and that had happened during it. It was a strange thing, he felt, how just some certain scenes and faces stuck in the memory, were always to hand for an odd moment, as it were, when much else that at the time had struck home as being of great import seemed to want to be forgotten. There was the dead face of the old geographer, laid out on his four-poster to be washed for burial. A sight he was sure he would not forget as long as he lived. Perhaps it was the way you came on them out of the blue. The way he had come on poor Mrs. Dorothy on the quay with tears in her eyes, as if she knew even at that early day that she was going to the fishes. How came it that he remembered as clear as if it was yesterday, William Bradford's stiff walk towards them across the cobbles — and that he wore an orange shirt? Or old Brewster's apple cheeks as he chucked the sheet from him in the sail locker? He'd far sooner remember Priscilla's face during the times she was being nice to him . . . Plainly there was no sense to what you remembered and what you didn't when it came of its own.

The cold had got into him; he clapped his arms, and went to go below for a while; but saw Priscilla standing in the poop passage, with a long black cape on and a shawl about her head. "If you come and look dead forward you'll see where the harbour is," he said to her.

She nodded out at the sailors on the deck. "They will not let us go out when the sails are to be swung, you know as well as I do; especially a woman."

"They will not let? Who are they to let? What if I let you? Come out, Miss Muffet. The sails are set." He took her by the arm and drew her across the deck. "There is a fine open hill there, that we walked up and saw all the country round abouts; and the which you may walk up before the day is out, if you're lucky and have me take you ashore."

"Are there rocks and trees?"

"Big trees, real trees, not the like of them we've left behind. Mostly the shore is sandy inside the harbour, but that's only the shore. There's a lot of mud and trash right up to the land when the tide be out."

"They say there are black clouds of birds."

"Oh, birds aplenty, birds you've never seen. And wolves to be howling behind the hill."

Robert Coppin was above on the poop, his large hands in leather mittens gripping the lateen halyards, with the helmsman below holding the ship before the wind. He glanced down at their backs with a curl of his thick lip.

Out from beneath the poop stepped William Brandford, and went to the side. He glanced forward, but for the rest of the short while he stayed above looked back fixedly at the fading outline of the head of Cape Cod. When it had dropped out of sight he returned below, and sat down beneath the shoe-shaped lamp near the galley door. The ache and heavy-headed bewilderment that had lain on him over the past two days was passing. What eased her death for him most was the belief that she had taken her own life, a deed which he held unforgivable by either God or man. Then he remembered that he should make some notes in his pocket book. Someday he would set down a history of it all, and shew the world what was done and what was suffered — what was fit to be shewn. Under "Deaths," he wrote, "December 11th. Dorothy, Wife to Mr. William Brad-ford"; and hoped in his simplicity that by dismissing her thus and speaking of her no more she was out of his life and thoughts from thenceforward. There was work enough for hand and mind amongst the people; he got up and went over to a settler, who lay sick, and forced himself to talk to him.

Now over a third of all the settlers had signs of scurvy, and it was already foreseen that the healthy would spend as much of their time nursing as in building houses. Each man had only to look in his wife's, child's, or neighbour's face, to see the result of being cramped for four months in a dark, damp, smoky hold on a daily bowl of porridge and a scrap of dried meat. They reminded each other of nothing so much as poor half-killed gypsies after a spell in prison, with their lanky greasy hair and yellow smoked faces.

Further down the hold Gilbert lay propped on his elbow, with his brother Edward sitting on the side of his pallet. While the people waited in nervous impatience for the end of the last lap of the voyage, while the ship's cook in the galley listened to the wise talk of little Ellen Moore, John succeeded again with Miss Mullins, and the Captain and Sam Fuller talked in shouts in the bows, while William Bradford forced himself to what he conceived to be his stern duty, Gilbert told his brother of Dorothy and himself, in a rambling hoarse whisper. And Edward said that while he understood how such things happened he must banish it from mind. It had been difficult enough getting him into the company at the start, Gilbert not being a person with either a shilling in his pocket or a conviction in his head; and so far his lazy conduct had done everything except prove him a man of worth. But if it leaked out that Mrs. Bradford's death had been occasioned by him in any way at all he might as well stay on the boat and go back to England. Not that he believed him to be responsible for her death; but others might not think so.

"Banish the thought? Tell me to fly like a bird and I'll do that too!" But he could say no more. Telling Edward had been a mistake; this was an absolute thing that had happened to him; words had no power to relieve or comfort; he could only go on twisting about in the dark of his mind, or give it up, as she had done. Well, he thought bitterly, men were never so badly off that they couldn't find means to hurt themselves further. But how could he have foreseen, even though he had gone on in it against his reason, that it would end in the cutting off of the sweetest being he had ever known? "Dust hath closed Helen's eye."

Opening up the harbour mouth, the mainsails were reefed to the usual accompaniment of shouts from the sailors, hauling, pulling, and squeaking of blocks. The ship, following the shallop closely, made straight in through a channel of deep water, between stretches of tide-exposed sand-bank and the harbour's two low, protecting sandy arms.

Inside, her drift carried her around in a wide arc to the left, topsails flapping loose, the sailors on the spars leaning over to gather them up. The shallop rowed on, behind the harbour's left-hand spit, and waited, marking where the *Mayflower* must come to anchor. An incoming tide let the ship's weight carry her on. Very slowly she drifted around the long arm of sand, sea grass and a few twisted bushes — another bit of Cape Cod — and her anchors were let go, dropping through twenty feet of water into mud and sand.

It was eleven o'clock forenoon, Saturday, December sixteenth, the tide one hour past low water.

Cold and quiet, the men and women came up on deck, and with drawn faces looked about their new haven, their journey's end.

Between the ship and the open sea was a long, low arm of sand; they were in a calm channel of water, perhaps a hundred feet wide, that ran along on the inside of the spit. In the opposite direction and exposed by the tide there stretched from inner water to shore proper a mile of un-even mud flats, intersected by innumerable runnels and pools. It looked immense, abandoned by God and man since the waters of the Flood re-ceded and exposed a drowned world. Patched with salt grass and drying seaweed; here and there the bones of large fishes lay on the sand and mud, festooned with decaying green and brown ribbons. Mud, eelgrass, pools, runnels, seaweed stretched flatly across the harbour to the right almost as far as the eye could see; through it a shallow stream wound from the river mouth to where the ship had come to anchor. But over beyond, the solid land rolled down to the shore, a virgin land of forest, hill and swamp that after Cape Cod looked, even in the distance, a very paradise. And God sent the snow away.

In the air, above the spit behind, gulls stood in the cold northern wind and cried; from far off came the quacking of duck. Otherwise there was no sign of life, no smoke of savage fire to be seen anywhere through the bright winter air; here, if anywhere, they should have the world to them-selves, if God would but keep the wild men away also.

No sooner were the anchors down than the Master came back to the leaders. When he spoke to John Carver his hoarse voice was uncertain and his weak light-coloured eyes searched their faces anxiously.

"The wind changes," Mr. Jones said. "Another hour and we should not have got in! I hope in God you inspected this place well, Mr. Carver, I hope in God it will do for you . . ."

The Master of the ship stood foursquarely before them and addressed them, anxious for their welfare. There could no longer be any doubt about his attitude then, whatever it had been before. Surprise and gratification stayed their answering him immediately. William Brewster glanced at John Carver, and Samuel Fuller twitched a drop from the end of his long nose and gazed upon the Master as pleased as if he saw a lost child return. Mr. Jones thought he felt the eyes of others on him from behind, their crowding about, curious of what was passing between him and the leaders; but he gripped his courage tight, determined there and then to begin establishing himself with William Brewster and his companions, if it cost him his life.

"*It is land*," John Carver said cautiously, his silver beard ruffled in the breeze. "And it is for land we come, to make our homes. Let all examine it, and answer for themselves."

Sharp and clear, above the low voices of the settlers packed on the waist deck on the other side of the forcastle house and the sailors' shouts and calls, the Captain and the leaders, standing in the bows, heard a loud, ribald voice ring out:

"Reef 'em fer easy flyin', lads, this is their graveyard we're comed to. We'll be out for home in a week an' they can set in buryin' each t'other!"

It was Coppin, standing halfway up the ratlines, shouting to the sailors tying up the main topsail. Such callous joking was common among the sailormen, and none had ever given it much heed, least of all the Captain. But there they saw him stiffen and his face suffuse with blood.

"Very true," Sam Fuller said dryly, to the Master. "Land is of two particular uses to men — to live by and to bury each other in."

The Sack of Magdeburg

by Daniel Defoe

> 1631 The butchery and devastation of the Thirty
> Years War were so great that the population of Ger-
> many has been estimated to have been reduced by
> half. In the following excerpt the author of *Robinson
> Crusoe* lets an imaginary observer describe one of
> the most horrible atrocities of the war. Defoe always
> wrote fiction as if it were fact, one of the earliest
> methods of writing historical novels.

By virtue of these passes I got into the Imperial Army, under Count
Tilly, then at the siege of Magdeburg, May the 2nd.

I confess I did not foresee the fate of this city, neither, I believe, did
Count Tilly himself expect to glut his fury with so entire a desolation, much
less did the people expect it. I did believe they must capitulate, and I
perceived by discourse in the army that Tilly would give them but very
indifferent conditions; but it fell out otherwise. The treaty of surrender
was, as it were, begun, nay, some say concluded, when some of the out-
guards of the Imperialists finding the citizens had abandoned the guards
of the works, and looked to themselves with less diligence than usual, they
broke in, carried an half-moon, sword in hand, with little resistance; and
though it was a surprise on both sides, the citizens neither fearing, nor
the army expecting the occasion, the garrison, with as much resolution
as could be expected under such a fright, flew up to the walls, twice beat
the Imperialists off, but fresh men coming up, and the administrator of
Magdeburg himself being wounded and taken, the enemy broke in, took
the city by storm, and entered with such terrible fury, that, without respect to age or condition, they put all the garrison and inhabitants, man,
woman, and child, to the sword, plundered the city, and when they had
done this set it on fire.

This calamity sure was the dreadfullest sight that ever I saw; the rage
of the Imperial soldiers was most intolerable, and not to be expressed. Of
25,000, some said 30,000 people, there was not a soul to be seen alive, till
the flames drove those that were hid in vaults and secret places to seek
death in the streets rather than perish in the fire. Of these miserable creatures some were killed too by the furious soldiers, but at last they saved

the lives of such as came out of their cellars and holes, and so about two thousand poor desperate creatures were left. The exact number of those that perished in this city could never be known, because those the soldiers had first butchered the flames afterwards devoured.

*   *   *

Being upon the works of the fort, on a sudden I heard the dreadfullest cry raised in the city that can be imagined; 'tis not possible to express the manner of it, and I could see the women and children running about the streets in a most lamentable condition.

The city wall did not run along the side where the river was with so great a height, but we could plainly see the market place and the several streets which run down to the river. In about an hour's time after this first cry all was confusion; there was little shooting, the execution was all cutting of throats and mere house murders. The resolute garrison, with the brave Baron Falkenberg, fought it out to the last, and were cut in pieces, and by this time the Imperial soldiers having broke open the gates and entered on all sides, the slaughter was very dreadful. We could see the poor people in crowds driven down the streets, flying from the fury of the soldiers, who followed butchering them as fast as they could, and refused mercy to anybody, till driving them to the river's edge, the desperate wretches would throw themselves into the river, where thousands of them perished, especially women and children. Several men that could swim got over to our side, where the soldiers not heated with fight gave them quarter, and took them up, and I cannot but do this justice to the German officers in the fort: they had five small boats, and they gave leave to the soldiers to go off in them, and get what booty they could, but charged them not to kill anybody, but take them all prisoners.

Nor was their humanity ill rewarded, for the soldiers, wisely avoiding those places where their fellows were employed in butchering the miserable people, rowed to other places, where crowds of people stood crying out for help, and expecting every minute to be either drowned or murdered; of these at sundry times they fetched over nearly six hundred, but took care to take in none but such as offered them good pay.

Never was money or jewels of greater service than now, for those that had anything of that sort to offer were soonest helped.

There was a burgher of the town who, seeing a boat coming near to him, but out of his call, by the help of a speaking trumpet, told the soldiers in it he would give them 20,000 dollars to fetch him off. They rowed close to the shore, and got him and his wife and six children into the boat, but such throngs of people got about the boat that had like to have sunk her, so that the soldiers were fain to drive a great many out again by main force, and while they were doing this some of the enemies coming down the street drove them all into the water.

The boat, however, brought the burgher and his wife and children safe, and though they had not all that wealth about them, yet in jewels and money he gave them so much as made all the fellows rich.

I cannot pretend to describe the cruelty of this day: the town by five in the afternoon was all in a flame; the wealth consumed was inestimable, and a loss to the very conqueror. I think there was little or nothing left but the great church and about a hundred houses.

This was a sad welcome into the army for me, and gave me a horror and aversion to the emperor's people, as well as to his cause. I quitted the camp the third day after this execution, while the fire was hardly out in the city; and from thence getting safe-conduct to pass into the Palatinate, I turned out of the road at a small village on the Elbe, called Emerfield, and by ways and towns I can give but small account of, having a boor for a guide, who we could hardly understand, I arrived at Leipsic on the 17th of May.

Endicott and the Red Cross

by Nathaniel Hawthorne

1634 The Puritans of Massachusetts Bay Colony were marvelously courageous and independent, and harshly bigoted also. Both aspects of the Puritan character are revealed in this story by a great American writer whose own mind was haunted by the Puritan obsession with sin and guilt.

At noon of an autumnal day, more than two centuries ago, the English colors were displayed by the standard-bearer of the Salem train band, which had mustered for martial exercise under the orders of John Endicott. It was a period when the religious exiles were accustomed often to buckle on their armor and practice the handling of their weapons of war. Since the first settlement of New England, its prospects had never been so dismal. The dissensions between Charles the First and his subjects were then, and for several years afterwards, confined to the floor of Parliament. The measures of the king and ministry were rendered more tyrannically violent by an opposition which had not yet acquired sufficient confidence in its own strength to resist royal injustice with the sword. The bigoted and haughty primate, Laud, Archbishop of Canterbury, controlled the religious affairs of the realm and was consequently invested with powers which might have wrought the utter ruin of the two Puritan colonies, Plymouth and Massachusetts. There is evidence on record that our forefathers perceived their danger, but were resolved that their infant country should not fall without a struggle, even beneath the giant strength of the king's right arm.

Such was the aspect of the times when the folds of the English banner, with the Red Cross in its field, were flung out over a company of Puritans. Their leader, the famous Endicott, was a man of stern and resolute countenance, the effect of which was heightened by a grizzled beard that swept the upper portion of his breastplate. This piece of armor was so highly polished that the whole surrounding scene had its image in the glittering steel. The central object in the mirrored picture was an edifice of humble architecture, with neither steeple nor bell to proclaim it — what nevertheless it was — the house of prayer. A token of the perils of the wilderness was seen in the grim head of a wolf, which had just been slain

374

within the precincts of the town, and, according to the regular mode of claiming the bounty, was nailed on the porch of the meetinghouse. The blood was still plashing on the doorstep. There happened to be visible, at the same noontide hour, so many other characteristics of the times and manners of the Puritans that we must endeavor to represent them in a sketch, though far less vividly than they were reflected in the polished breastplate of John Endicott.

In close vicinity to the sacred edifice appeared that important engine of Puritanic authority, the whipping post — with the soil around it well trodden by the feet of evil-doers who had there been disciplined. At one corner of the meetinghouse was the pillory, and at the other the stocks; and, by a singular good fortune for our sketch, the head of an Episcopalian and suspected Catholic was grotesquely encased in the former machine; while a fellow-criminal, who had boisterously quaffed a health to the king, was confined by the legs in the latter. Side by side on the meetinghouse steps stood a male and a female figure. The man was a tall, lean, haggard personification of fanaticism, bearing on his breast this label: A WANTON GOSPELER, which betokened that he had dared to give interpretations of Holy Writ, unsanctioned by the infallible judgment of the civil and religious rulers. His aspect showed no lack of zeal to maintain his heterodoxies, even at the stake. The woman wore a cleft stick on her tongue, in appropriate retribution for having wagged that unruly member against the elders of the church; and her countenance and gestures gave much cause to apprehend that the moment the stick should be removed a repetition of the offense would demand new ingenuity in chastising it.

The above-mentioned individuals had been sentenced to undergo their various modes of ignominy for the space of one hour at noonday. But among the crowd were several whose punishment would be lifelong; some whose ears had been cropped, like those of puppy dogs; others whose cheeks had been branded with the initials of their misdemeanors; one with his nostrils slit and seared; and another with a halter around his neck, which he was forbidden to take off, or to conceal beneath his garments. Methinks he must have been grievously tempted to affix the other end of the rope to some convenient beam or bough. There was likewise a young woman, with no mean share of beauty, whose doom it was to wear the letter A on the breast of her gown, in the eyes of all the world and her own children. And even her own children knew what that initial signified. Sporting with her infamy, the lost and desperate creature had embroidered the fatal token in scarlet cloth, with golden thread and the nicest art of needlework; so that the capital A might have been thought to mean Admirable, or anything rather than Adulteress.

Let not the reader argue, from any of these evidences of iniquity, that the times of the Puritans were more vicious than our own, when, as we pass along the very street of this sketch, we discern no badge of infamy on man or woman. It was the policy of our ancestors to search out even the most secret sins, and expose them to shame, without fear or favor, in the broadest light of the noonday sun. Were such the custom now, perchance we might find materials for a no less piquant sketch than the above.

Except the malefactors whom we have described, and the diseased or infirm persons, the whole male population of the town, between sixteen years and sixty, were seen in the ranks of the train band. A few stately savages, in all the pomp and dignity of the primeval Indian, stood gazing at the spectacle. Their flint-headed arrows were but childish weapons compared with the matchlocks of the Puritans, and would have rattled harmlessly against the steel caps and hammered iron breastplates which inclosed each soldier in an individual fortress. The valiant John Endicott glanced with an eye of pride at his sturdy followers, and prepared to renew the martial toils of the day.

"Come, my stout hearts!" quoth he, drawing his sword. "Let us show these poor heathen that we can handle our weapons like men of might. Well for them if they put us not to prove it in earnest!"

The iron-breasted company straightened their line, and each man drew the heavy butt of his matchlock close to his left foot, thus awaiting the orders of the captain. But as Endicott glanced right and left along the front, he discovered a personage at some little distance with whom it behooved him to hold a parley. It was an elderly gentleman, wearing a black cloak and band, and a high-crowned hat, beneath which was a velvet skullcap, the whole being the garb of a Puritan minister. This reverend person bore a staff, which seemed to have been recently cut in the forest, and his shoes were bemired, as if he had been traveling on foot through the swamps of the wilderness. His aspect was perfectly that of a pilgrim, heightened also by an apostolic dignity. Just as Endicott perceived him, he laid aside his staff and stopped to drink at a bubbling fountain which gushed into the sunshine about a score of yards from the corner of the meetinghouse. But ere the good man drank, he turned his face heavenward in thankfulness, and then, holding back his gray beard with one hand, he scooped up his simple draught in the hollow of the other.

"What, ho! good Mr. Williams," shouted Endicott. "You are welcome back again to our town of peace. How does our worthy Governor Winthrop? And what news from Boston?"

"The governor hath his health, worshipful sir," answered Roger Williams, now resuming his staff and drawing near. "And for the news, here is a letter, which, knowing I was to travel hitherward today, his excellency committed to my charge. Belike it contains tidings of much import; for a ship arrived yesterday from England."

Mr. Williams, the minister of Salem, and of course known to all the spectators, had now reached the spot where Endicott was standing under the banner of his company, and put the governor's epistle into his hand. The broad seal was impressed with Winthrop's coat of arms. Endicott hastily unclosed the letter, and began to read; while, as his eye passed down the page, a wrathful change came over his manly countenance. The blood glowed through it, till it seemed to be kindling with an internal heat; nor was it unnatural to suppose that his breastplate would likewise become red hot with the angry fire of the bosom which it covered. Arriving at the conclusion, he shook the letter fiercely in his hand, so that it rustled as loud as the flag above his head.

"Black tidings these, Mr. Williams," said he; "blacker never came to New England. Doubtless you know their purport?"

"Yes, truly," replied Roger Williams; "for the governor consulted, respecting this matter, with my brethren in the ministry at Boston and my opinion was likewise asked. And his excellency entreats you by me that the news be not suddenly noised abroad, lest the people be stirred up unto some outbreak, and thereby give the king and the archbishop a handle against us."

"The governor is a wise man, and a meek and moderate," said Endicott, setting his teeth grimly. "Nevertheless, I must do according to my own best judgment. There is neither man, woman, nor child in New England but has a concern as dear as life in these tidings; and if John Endicott's voice be loud enough, man, woman, and child shall hear them. Soldiers, wheel into a hollow square! Ho, good people! Here are news for one and all of you."

The soldiers closed in around their captain; and he and Roger Williams stood together under the banner of the Red Cross; while the women and the aged men pressed forward, and the mothers held up their children to look Endicott in the face. A few taps of the drum gave signal for silence and attention.

"Fellow-soldiers, fellow-exiles," began Endicott, speaking under strong excitement, yet powerfully restraining it, "wherefore did ye leave your native country? Wherefore, I say, have we left the green and fertile fields, the cottages, or, perchance, the old gray halls, where we were born and bred, the churchyards where our forefathers lie buried? Wherefore have we come hither to set up our own tombstones in a wilderness? A howling wilderness it is! The wolf and the bear meet us within halloo of our dwellings. The savage lieth in wait for us in the dismal shadow of the woods. The stubborn roots of the trees break our plowshares, when we would till the earth. Our children cry for bread, and we must dig in the sands of the seashore to satisfy them. Wherefore, I say again, have we sought this country of a rugged soil and wintry sky? Was it not for the enjoyment of our civil rights? Was it not for liberty to worship God according to our conscience?"

"Call you this liberty of conscience?" interrupted a voice on the steps of the meetinghouse.

It was the Wanton Gospeler. A sad and quiet smile flitted across the mild visage of Roger Williams. But Endicott, in the excitement of the moment, shook his sword wrathfully at the culprit, an ominous gesture from a man like him.

"What hast thou to do with conscience, thou knave?" cried he. "I said liberty to worship God, not license to profane and ridicule Him. Break not in upon my speech, or I will lay thee neck and heels till this time tomorrow! Hearken to me, friends, nor heed that accursed rhapsodist. As I was saying, we have sacrificed all things, and have come to a land whereof the Old World hath scarcely heard, that we might make a new world unto ourselves, and painfully seek a path from hence to Heaven. But what think ye now? This son of a Scotch tyrant — this grandson of a papistical and adulterous Scotch woman, whose death proved that a golden crown doth not always save an anointed head from the block — — "

"Nay, brother, nay," interposed Mr. Williams, "thy words are not meet for a secret chamber, far less for a public street."

"Hold thy peace, Roger Williams!" answered Endicott imperiously. "My spirit is wiser than thine for the business now in hand. I tell ye, fellow-exiles, that Charles of England, and Laud, our bitterest persecutor, arch-priest of Canterbury, are resolute to pursue us even hither. They are taking counsel, saith this letter, to send over a governor-general, in whose breast shall be deposited all the law and equity of the land. They are minded, also, to establish the idolatrous forms of English Episcopacy; so that, when Laud shall kiss the Pope's toe, as Cardinal of Rome, he may deliver New England, bound hand and foot, into the power of his master!"

A deep groan from the auditors — a sound of wrath, as well as fear and sorrow — responded to this intelligence.

"Look ye to it, brethren," resumed Endicott with increasing energy. "If this king and this archprelate have their will, we shall briefly behold a cross on the spire of this tabernacle which we have builded, and a high altar within its walls, with wax tapers burning round it at noonday. We shall hear the sacring bell, and the voices of the Romish priests saying the mass. But think ye, Christian men, that these abominations may be suffered without a sword drawn? without a shot fired? without blood spilt, yea, on the very stairs of the pulpit? No, be ye strong of hand and stout of heart! Here we stand on our own soil, which we have bought with our goods, which we have won with our swords, which we have cleared with our axes, which we have tilled with the sweat of our brows, which we have sanctified with our prayers to the God who brought us hither. Who shall enslave us here? What have we to do with this mitred prelate, with this crowned king? What have we to do with England?"

Endicott gazed round at the excited countenances of the people, now full of his own spirit, and then turned suddenly to the standard-bearer, who stood close behind him.

"Officer, lower your banner!" said he.

The officer obeyed; and, brandishing his sword, Endicott thrust it through the cloth, and, with his left hand, rent the Red Cross completely out of the banner. He then waved the tattered ensign above his head.

"Sacrilegious wretch!" cried the high churchman in the pillory, unable longer to restrain himself, "thou hast rejected the symbol of our holy religion!"

"Treason, treason!" roared the royalist in the stocks. "He hath defaced the king's banner!"

"Before God and man, I will avouch the deed," answered Endicott. "Beat a flourish, drummer! Shout, soldiers and people! in honor of the ensign of New England. Neither Pope nor Tyrant hath part in it now!"

With a cry of triumph the people gave their sanction to one of the boldest exploits which our history records. And forever honored be the name of Endicott! We look back through the mists of ages, and recognize, in the rending of the Red Cross from New England's banner, the first omen of that deliverance which our fathers consummated, after the bones of the stern Puritan had lain more than a century in the dust.

The Apprentice

by Hilaire Belloc

1649 More than two hundred years after Defoe described historical events from the point of view of an imaginary observer Hilaire Belloc used the same technique in a series of fictionalized sketches called *The Eye-Witness*. One of the most perfect is this in which a harness-maker's apprentice watches the execution of Charles I on a scaffold outside Whitehall Banqueting Hall in London.

Men were well into the working week; it was a Tuesday and apprentices were under the hard eyes of their masters throughout the City of London and in the rarer business places that elbowed the great palaces along the Strand. The sky was overcast and the air distastefully cold, nor did anything in the landscape seem colder than the dark band of the river under those colourless and lifeless January clouds.

Whether it were an illusion or a reality, one could have sworn that there was a sort of silence over the houses and on the families of the people; one could have sworn that men spoke in lower tones than was their custom, and that the streets were emptier. The trial and the sentence of the king had put all that great concourse of men into the very presence of Death.

The day wore on; the noise of the workmen could be heard at the scaffold by Whitehall; one hour was guessed at and then another; rumours and flat assertions were busy everywhere, especially among the young, and an apprentice to a harness-maker in the Water Lane, near Essex House, knew not what to believe. But he was determined to choose his moment and to slip away lest he should miss so great a sight. The tyranny of the army kept all the city in doubt all day long, and allowed no news; none the less, from before noon there had begun a little gathering of people in Whitehall, round the scaffold at which men were still giving the last strokes of the hammer. Somewhat after noon a horseshoe of cavalry assembled in their long cloaks and curious tall civilian hats; they stood ranked, with swords drawn, all round the platform. Their horses shifted uneasily in the cold.

The harness-maker's apprentice found his opportunity; his master was called to the door for an order from Arundel House, and the lad left his bench quickly, just as he was, without hat or coat, in the bitter weather, and darting through the side door ran down through the Water Gate and down its steps to the river. The tide was at the flood and his master's boat lay moored. He cast her off and pulled rapidly up the line of gardens, backing water when he came to the public stairs just beyond Whitehall. He quickly tied the painter and ran up breathless to Whitehall Gate, fearing he might have missed his great expectation. He was in ample time.

It was perhaps half-past three o'clock when he got through the gate and found himself in the press of people. Far off to the left, among the soldiery that lined the avenue from the park to the Mall, and so to St. James's, a continuous roll of drums burdened the still air.

The crowd was not very large, but it filled the space from the gate to the scaffold and a little beyond, save where it was pressed outward by the ring of cavalry. It did not overflow into the wide spaces of the park, though these lay open to Whitehall, nor did it run up towards Charing Cross beyond the Banqueting Hall.

The apprentice was not so tall as the men about him; he strained and elbowed a little to see, and he was sworn at. He could make out the low scaffold, a large platform all draped in black, with iron staples, and a railing round it; it covered the last three blank windows of Whitehall, running from the central casement until it met the brick house at the north end of the stonework; there the brickwork beneath one of the windows had been taken out so as to give access through it from the floor within to the scaffold on the same level without; and whispers round told the apprentice, though he did not know how much to trust them, that it was through this hasty egress that the king would appear. Upon the scaffold itself stood a group of men, two of them masked, and one of the masked ones, of great stature and strong, leant upon the axe with his arm crossed upon the haft of it. A little block, barely raised above the floor of the platform, he could only see by leaping on tip-toe, catching it by glimpses between the heads of his neighbours or the shoulders of the cavalry guard; but he noticed in those glimpses how very low it was, and saw, ominous upon it, two staples driven as though to contain the struggler. Before it, so that one kneeling would have his face toward the palace and away from the crowd, was a broad footstool covered with red velvet, and making a startling patch upon all that expanse of black baize.

It was cold waiting; the motionless twigs of the small bare trees in the park made it seem colder still. The three-quarters struck in the new clock behind him upon Whitehall Gate, but as yet no one had appeared.

In a few moments, however, there was a movement in the crowd, heads turning to the right, and a corresponding backing of the mounted men to contain the first beginnings of a rush, for the commanders of the army feared, while they despised, the popular majority of London; and the wealthy merchants, the allies of the army, had not joined this common lot. This turning of faces towards the great blank stone wall of the palace was caused by a sound of many footsteps within. The only window not masked with stone, the middle window, was that upon which their gaze universally turned. They saw, passing it very rapidly, a group of men within; they were walking very sharply along the floor (which was here raised above the level of the window itself and cut the lower panes of it); they were hurrying towards the northern end of the great Banqueting Hall. It was but a moment's vision, and again they appeared in the open air through the broken brickwork at the far end of the stone façade.

For a moment the apprentice saw clearly the tall king, his face grown old, his pointed beard left full, his long features not moved. The great cloak that covered him, with the Great Star of the Garter upon the left shoulder, he drew off quickly and let fall into the hands of Herbert. He wore no hat; he stepped forward with precision towards the group of executioners, and a little murmur ran through the crowd.

The old bishop, moving his limbs with difficulty, but suppliant and attendant upon his friend, stood by in an agony. He helped the king to pull off his inner coat until he stood conspicuous in the sky-blue vest beneath it, and round his neck a ribbon and one ornament upon it, a George carved in onyx. This also he removed and gave to the bishop, while he took from his hands a little white silken cap and fixed it firmly upon his long and beautiful hair. From beneath the sky-blue of his garment, at the neck and at the wrists, appeared frills of exquisite linen and the adornment of lace. He stood for a few moments praying, then turned and spoke as though he were addressing them all. But the apprentice, though he held his breath, and strained to hear, as did all others about him, could catch no separate word, but only the general sound of the king's voice speaking. The movement of the horses, the occasional striking of a hoof upon the setts of the street, the distance, covered that voice. Next, Charles was saying something to the masked man, and a moment later he was kneeling upon the footstool. The apprentice saw him turn a moment and spread his arms out as an example of what he next should do; he bent him toward the block — it was too low; he lay at full length, and the crowd lifted and craned to see him in this posture.

The four heavy strokes of the hour struck and boomed in the silence. The hands of the lying figure were stretched out again, this time as a final signal, and right up in the air above them all the axe swung, white against the grey sky, flashed and fell.

In a moment the group upon the scaffold had closed round, a cloth was thrown, the body raised, and among the hands stretched out to it were the eager and enfeebled hands of the bishop, trembling and still grasping the George.

A long moan or wail, very strange and dreadful, not very loud, rose from the people now that their tension was slackened by the accomplishment of the deed. And at once from the north and from the south, with such ceremony as is used to the conquered, the cavalry charged right through, hacking and dispersing these Londoners and driving them every way.

The apprentice dodged and ran, his head full of the tragedy and bewildered, his body in active fear of the horses that pursued flying packets of the crowd down the alleyways of the offices and palace buildings.

He went off by a circuitous way to find, not his master's house after such an escapade, but his mother's, where she lived beyond St. Martin's.

The dusk did not long tarry; as it gathered and turned to night small flakes of snow began to fall and lie upon the frozen ground.

Mrs. Oliver Cromwell

by Margaret Irwin

> 1658   Oliver Cromwell, soldier, statesman, revolu-
> tionist, Puritan reformer, and Lord Protector of Eng-
> land was a great man. He was also a ruthless zealot
> responsible for the murder of Charles I and for mas-
> sacres in Ireland. What did the woman who knew
> him best and who still loved him think of him?

She was not called by that name now. That was why she said it to
herself with longing and regret mingled with awe, as she thought of those
long quiet days when she had been plain Mrs. Oliver Cromwell, living
in the flat fen country round Cambridge, bearing one child after another,
four boys, four girls, and filling up the sleepy, happy months of pregnancy
(for all that she could never get over her tendency to be sick during them —
a tendency that her mother-in-law was inclined to regard as modern fad-
dishness and weakness of nerves) with the simple duties of bottling fruit
and salting mutton for the winter, going through the store cupboards,
the still-room and the linen-room in company with the ignorant country
girls that she and her mother-in-law always succeeded in turning into good
maids. Their round faces had shone at her in anxious good humour, their
round foolish mouths dropped slow words in the thick accent of the Eastern Counties, their big hands were occupied with all the same things that
occupied herself — solid, satisfying things: round heavy jars with the children like flies round them ("Now, Dick, now, Betty, take your fingers out
of that, Miss Pry!"), juicy hams swinging from the great beam in the ceiling, smooth glossy white baby linen and pillow-cases all woven by herself on her little hand-loom that stood always in the chimney-corner of
the big room, marble slabs spread with thick dough to turn into crisp warm
loaves and towering piecrusts by the time they reached the table, and
Oliver's face would light up behind them, saying, "Ah, there's nothing like
a good beefsteak pie! Who wants your foreign kickshaws?"
And then he would chaff her or his mother and pull little Betty's hair,
teasing her in the flattering way that encouraged even while he rebuked
her pertness, and quite forget that he had tramped in a rage about something or other — the Spanish army in Germany or the Prayer Book in Scotland, or some such matter that always seemed to be putting men into rages,

— leaving the marks of his muddy boots all over the newly scrubbed flag-stones, and even his mother not daring to call and tell him to go and take them off before he went on saying all he wanted about the Pope or the Emperor or the King; though what had Kings or Emperors to do with them, Mrs. Oliver had sometimes asked herself in a rare spasm of irrita-tion: — and now remembered that silent question as if it had tempted all their future fate to fall upon them.

What had Kings and Emperors to do with them now? Just this — that Oliver had cut off his own King's head; had made all other Kings, and the Emperor, yes, and the Pope, acknowledge his supremacy; that he him-self had been offered the Crown of England.

Mrs. Oliver Cromwell was now the wife of His Highness the Lord Pro-tector of England, whom all the nations of Europe delighted to honor. The royal palaces of Whitehall and Hampton Court were Oliver's town and country houses now; he drove from one to the other attended by a body of life-guards in scarlet, a host of lackeys, and fifty gentlemen-in-waiting dressed, as became the personal attendants of a Puritan ruler, in sober colours, black and grey, but splendid with silver trimmings. His court held more sumptuous state than many foreign monarchs; his stud of horses was finer than any ever owned by an English King; his envoys were given such honours abroad as even the Emperor's did not receive.

And this very year, 1658, a superb embassy of nobles had arrived from France, bearing a jewelled sword of honor to Oliver as "the most invin-cible of Sovereigns." The young French King, Louis XIV, was to have headed the embassy himself, an honour unheard of till now, but it reached only the stage of being heard of, for King Louis caught the smallpox at the last moment and had to remain at home — a bitter disappointment to Oliver's daughters, though Oliver himself declared he minded far more when the pack of wild reindeer collected so carefully for him by the young Queen Christina of Sweden to give a new zest to his hunting, was inad-vertently devoured by wolves before starting for England.

"Our dear dad is unlucky with royalty," Betty had said in her wicked way — "perhaps it is no wonder."

No one else in the family circle would dare or care to say such a thing, but Betty knew neither fear nor reverence; and perhaps that was why her father, stern, deeply, even wildly, religious man, adored his second daugh-ter above all his children: for not only was she the prettiest and the wit-tiest and the one that he loved best, but she gave him continual anxiety for her spiritual welfare. He was always telling his wife to counsel "poor

Betty" "against worldly vanities and worldly company, which I doubt she is too subject to."

She undoubtedly was. She had married a Royalist rake ("a debauched unworthy cavalier," Lucy Hutchinson, the family friend and unfailing critic, had called him), and then discovered that he was stupid as well; but it cannot be said that her disappointment preyed on her. Her dresses were the talk of London, who had plenty of opportunity to observe them when the sisters drove about the streets in state, — Biddy, the eldest, in yellow silk petticoats, and Betty, the next in age, in gorgeous green gowns. The two younger girls had both married last year into the old Royalist nobility, and there had been something of the old Royalist festivity again over the ceremonies, with mixed dancing all night in Whitehall Palace to a band of forty-eight violins.

That had been Betty's doing again, and shocked many of the faithful terribly. This splendid court was not only, like all courts, "a court of sin and vanity," but "the more abominable because they had not quite cast away the name of God but profaned it by taking it in vain among them." Very thoroughly they profaned it, for three hours on end when John Howe preached his sermons, and however gay were the supper-tables with music and fine dresses and great foreign figures, there was always a psalm at the beginning. It was hard that this should make only an added reproach from the godly.

Nor was it their only complaint. Oliver had always inveighed against class distinctions and titles, and declared openly in council that "we shall do no good until we have done away with lords," but now he was accepting one title after another, roystering it in the King's own palaces, and it was observed that though some of the old comrades whom he had raised from being draymen or cobblers to the rank of major-generals were present at his daughters' weddings, their wives were not.

"Where are the wives of the major-generals?" Betty was asked, with no kind intention.

"Washing their dishes at home, I expect, as they used to do!" she tossed back, with the malicious laughter glinting out of her eyes and jerking up her defiant little chin, and away she danced, with curls dancing on her white neck as soft as little brown clouds, and the old men who watched her said to each other, "There goes Elizabeth Cromwell. Did you ever see Elizabeth Stuart?" and fell silent, thinking of the wild gaiety and loveliness of the dead King Charles' sister, the luckless Queen of Bohemia, of whom this girl had reminded them.

But proud, pious Lucy Hutchinson, who never went out if she could help it, except to church, widow of that strict and noble Puritan Colonel Hutchinson who had died in Oliver's service, called Oliver's daughters, "insolent fools." And kind friends thought it their duty to report it to Oliver's wife, with sundry other such comments, and tell her that her daughters were good girls doubtless, but careless and giddy as girls were apt to be when they had had their heads a little turned, and could not realize the offence and scandal they caused — yes, scandal, it was really necessary to say that harsh word, for just think of all the talk there had been about poor Bridget and the wicked Duke of Buckingham, when of course there was not a word of truth in the report that he had come over to England in disguise for the last Royalist plot and employed his spare time in seducing Bridget Ireton, the daughter of the Lord Protector and wife of his right-hand man.

"There wasn't a word of truth in it. There might have been a faint shadow of it if they had substituted the name Betty for Biddy," said Elizabeth, when her horrified mother had told her the gossip as an awful warning; and then actually went on to say quite coolly and casually that it was she who had encountered the Duke of Buckingham in his very thin disguise ("He's too vain of his looks to give himself a proper one") and had flirted with him in front of her foolishly gaping husband, Mr. Claypole. That had been quite enough to make the fatuous duke boast in his cups of the conquest he had made of old Noll's daughter, and, since it was more piquant to have made a conquest of the daughter who was married to a pious Puritan leader rather than the one who was married to "a debauched unworthy cavalier," to transfer the fame of his favours from Betty Claypole to Biddy Ireton.

And Betty could not be made to see that it mattered what they said.

"Think if your father had heard of it! He would sooner see his daughters dead at his feet. Indeed" — with a sudden hushed sinking from high drama into shocked reality — "I think he might have killed you."

"I think he might," murmured Betty with rather oddly shining eyes. Her mother looked at her sharply. The girl seemed positively to delight in thinking how far she could anger her father. She knew that she alone had the power to anger him so far, and her mother, knowing it, felt a deep insurgent wave of jealousy rise up within her, and at once translated it into indignation that Elizabeth should wish to torment her father, who was already tormented past endurance by the cares and responsibilities of the State. "Poor Betty" indeed! It was "Poor Oliver" rather, bewitched and plagued and hoodwinked by his unruly daughter.

But before she could collect her reasons for righteous wrath, and the words to clothe them in, Betty was fleeting on, shaking off all this preaching, telling her mother that the world was changing and that it was of no use to try to hold it back, that nobody now took themselves seriously as Father and his kind had done: "they went to war for their principles, they said; well, that was very pleasant for them, they had their war and their principles, and out of them Father has won his principality and power — but he can't expect all of us to feel the same as he did. He's done it all, and all we can do is to enjoy it, so let us enjoy it all we can and not mind about sour old cats like Lucy Hutchinson, who will say horrible things of us however virtuous we are. Do you know what she said of you, yes, you, my sweet Mammy, you perfect-wife-and-mother — not that you were an insolent fool, nor anything against your character, but worse, oh much worse: she said that 'grandeur sat as ill on you as scarlet on an ape'!"

Silence fell between the two women like a stone. The daughter's chatter had stopped as sharply as if it were snapped off, as indeed it was, for she had never meant to punish her mother's mild scolding so far; she stopped, unable for all her bravado to meet her mother's eyes, and busied herself with her shoe-string, while over her bright head the older woman's face looked blankly at the opposite wall, the candid eyes a little duller, the full, rather heavy cheeks sagging a little more, and that the only sign of recognition she gave of the blow that had been dealt her.

Yes, Betty was right, and her mother knew it; what had been said of her mother was far worse than anything anyone could say of herself.

Even their enemies had had to admit that the Lord Protector bore himself nobly in the midst of state and splendour; but the Lord Protector's wife would never look nor be anything more than the plain Mrs. Oliver Cromwell who had mended her husband's shirts and tried to get him to change his collar more often, and not to offend people by speaking his mind so freely or so coarsely, or by neglecting to answer their letters.

Indeed, looking back on those long quiet days which had then seemed so anxious and busy, and now seemed so carefree, she wondered if she were now not only no more than the Mrs. Oliver Cromwell of those days, but had become much less. For though she had never attempted to meddle with Oliver's politics and other activities, or even to understand them, — her rare questions in the middle of his discussions with his friends being generally interrupted by his mother's gentle reminder, "Hush, my dear, the men are talking," — yet she had been of much more use to him then as his wife than she could be now. She had borne his children and shared his delight in them — though he had always liked the girls best and been more severe and impatient with the boys; and she had comforted him as best she could, when two of the boys had died, and his bereaved affection, aggravated by remorse for his intolerance, had driven him nearly out of his mind with his agony of stormy grief.

Their local doctor, Dr. Simcott, had told her that but for her, Oliver would most certainly have gone mad, not only then, but when everything was going most smoothly and happily — and he would suddenly turn and rend it all up by the roots in a frantic access of religious terrrors. In the middle of the night he would wake her up, convinced that he was dying and in danger of hell fire, and off she would send one of the sleepy herd-boys with a lantern for Dr. Simcott, whose language nearly matched the patient's own when he had got out of bed and come and examined him and told him there was nothing the matter with him.

"Most splenetic," that was Dr. Simcott's professional opinion, and he advised Oliver to go up to London and consult some fashionable physician who made a specialty of these new-fangled nerve cases. So Oliver saw the King's own doctor, Sir Theodore Mayerne, who said it was a bad case of melancholia, and could do nothing for it.

Even Oliver's mother, who had influenced him as his wife could never do, who had lived with him and his family until she died a few years ago, and to whom he had gone for a good-night talk every evening of his life when he was at home, however crowded his day had been with public cares, even she had not been able to do anything for him when those dreadful fits of dull despair had surged up over him. Only Oliver's wife could do anything, by doing nothing, by being there, acquiescent, adoring, as tender of him as of her youngest baby at her breast, knowing that his need of her was as deep and helpless, as utterly dependent.

He had hoped that in escaping from England he might escape himself; that they might all emigrate to America, that unexplored land of freedom and promise where everything was new and untouched as at the beginning of the world, and he could make what he would of it, instead of having to put up with what other men had made of England. His cousin, John Hampden, had bought a grant of land in Massachusetts as a speculation, and the two had often discussed the possibility of shaking off the unjust laws and taxes of England and moving there with their families.

"Your mother would be too old for such a change," murmured Oliver's wife hopefully; but Oliver told her in his crude fashion that his mother had guts enough for anything. She had, but they were not required for America, for England gave enough employment for Oliver's discontented energies instead; when Parliament decided to raise arms against the King, he raised his own troop of horse from Cambridgeshire and became in turn Captain, Colonel, General, General-in-Chief and Lord Protector, and there was neither need nor time nor thought left for America.

Yes, there was still some thought of it, but it was in Mrs. Oliver's mind, not his. What difference would it have made if they had carried out their plan and gone to Massachusetts? Presumably the Civil War in England would have ended quite soon in a Royalist victory, King Charles would have still been alive and on the throne, still ruling as much as possible without a Parliament, just as poor Oliver found it necessary to do, for he was continually having to turn out Parliament for not voting as he wished. They were even making trouble over his proposal to sell as building property that royal hunting-park of Hyde Park, which King Charles had been such a fool as to give gratis to his people for every Tom, Dick and Harry to disport himself in. It was sheer democracy, and "Democracy," said Oliver, "is the creed of all poor men and all bad men."

"And poor men are as bad as bad men," Betty had supplemented in a solemn voice, but her father did not rebuke her sarcasm, for he knew it to be true. His family had been exceedingly rich ever since his great-great-great-uncle Thomas Cromwell had given it some very wealthy Church lands in Henry VIII's time, and they had been all the better for it. It was solid wealth that made fine men, not old families and grand titles.

He himself had to take the title of Lord Protector because he had to take something, but he would not take that of King, nor the yet more grandiloquent offer of Emperor of the West. Somehow, thought Mrs. Oliver, if they had only gone to America, he might still have won that last title, and it would not have been so hard for her to bear in a brand new country as the title of Lord Protector in this old, subtle, smiling, sneering land of England.

Oliver soared from strength to strength, he had burst his swaddling-bands and his desperate need of her in the old quiet days; but she could not grow with him, she could not supply the further needs that now beset him, as he changed from the wealthy but simple country gentleman to the great prince. He needed a queen now for his wife, brilliant and gay, a match for him in wits and fearlessness. Grandeur sat on Betty as easily as on a queen. And thinking of Betty in her emerald gown, and the blow she had so lightly struck her, and thinking back to the old quiet days when Oliver's mother had been always with them, she thought that perhaps, after all, she had never really been all that Oliver had wanted as a wife, had never been much more than a sort of secondary mother, who could comfort and satisfy but never excite him or stir him to the depths or heights of his nature.

But had he ever allowed her to do so? There were times when his strength and the suggestion of hidden, uncontrollable forces in his nature had made her long to let go of all the self-restraint she had been taught to think the noblest duty of woman — times when she had forgotten all their anxious perpetual care of the soul, and thought it enough at that moment to live only in and for the body. He had checked her and made her feel ashamed; she was his virtuous wife and the mother of his children, training herself to be the worthy successor of his mother who slept under their roof; she must not forget this nor tempt him to forget it.

But he had starved for her to do so, she knew that, now when it was too late, now when she was no longer Mrs. Oliver Cromwell, but only the clumsy awkward out-of-place wife of the magnificent Lord Protector, on whom her borrowed finery sat as ill as scarlet on an ape.

That phrase would not let her alone, it stung her into walking up and down the splendid panelled galleries at Hampton Court where huge King Harry had walked, and Queen Elizabeth, and the slight figure of King Charles, gazing at the many lovely pictures he had collected; it echoed in her ear, whispering, "Here you are, poor ape, where your betters have trod, and do you hope to fashion yourself in their image?"

She did not, though she did try to collect pictures, hoping to replace a few of the many beauties of King Charles' collection which Oliver had sold. He was passionately fond of music, relaxing under it and losing himself in a kind of dream, and had installed two organs at Hampton Court, though Betty declared that organs gave only the mush of music. But, for the other arts, he read nothing but the Bible, and of pictures he asked only that they should represent something he knew, even if it were his own face and his own warts, for he told his portrait-painter Lely on no account to leave them out. So his wife had little encouragement in her attempt to carry on the work of King Charles, though she did her best by making conscientious enquiries of the foreign ambassadors as to the leading painters in their countries.

To what purpose? King Charles was dead, beheaded by her husband's orders. Her husband reigned in his stead, and they lived in the palaces that had been his home. She could have nothing else to do with King Charles or his work. It began to oppress her unbearably that they should walk and talk and sleep and eat in the royal palaces where King Charles had lived. There at Whitehall was the room where he had taken leave of his children and stepped out through a window to walk briskly to the scaffold. When the axe fell on him, the watching crowd had sent up a groan that had echoed to the ends of the world. Far away in India a king had forbidden any of his subjects, on pain of death by torture, even to mention the horror of that deed done on a cold January day in England. All Europe was aghast. Yet now all Europe acclaimed Oliver in terms of rapturous compliment, because he had shown that he could master her with his army as he had mastered England. Did that, then, prove that Oliver had been right to do that thing?

She dared not ask that of Oliver, who had once answered all her questions. But his answers to this one were too various. At one time he wrote publicly that Charles' death would be "honoured by Christians and feared by tyrants," but at another, to a private friend, that "perhaps there is no other way out."

How could the way out matter, if it were not the right way? Then the individual soul, their dearest concern, was no longer of first account; right and wrong had become mere quibbles; it was, Oliver had said, a matter of stern necessity.

Once upon a time, no necessity could have been sterner than the dividing line between right and wrong.

And looking back to the old quiet days when this had been so, as she heard the psalm rise in full-throated unction round her at the beginning of a rich banquet in King Charles' palace, while the soberly sumptuous pages stood with piously bowed heads over the gold dishes containing the first pineapples ever brought to England, she found her clasped hands grown strangely cold and felt as though the ground beneath her gave her no foothold, and the strong voices round her were more hollow than the mocking wind, for where was it that they stood and praised God? Here in King Charles' palace, on his grave that they had dug, and on the grave of their old simple belief in right and wrong.

Oliver *must* be right. If only he himself were sure of it. But she remembered his hysterical horseplay at the time of the King's death-sentence — how he had forced one man down into his chair with shouts of laughter and held him there until he signed it, and spattered the face of another with ink — and knew it was because he was desperately at variance with himself. Never had she put the confidence in Oliver's heartiness that other people had done, exclaiming what a great boy he was when he flung cushions at their heads or chased them round the room to pommel them. His horseplay, like his foul language (never blasphemy, but plain dirt), was the momentary relief of a spirit pent up with perilous matter. She could not resolve his doubts, nor her own. She could only hide them, and herself, and she hid them whenever she could in a pleasant country house near Amersham which she had bought two years ago as a retreat for herself and her daughters from the bustle of London and royal palaces, if only for a few days at a time. It was not more than half a day's ride on a good horse from London; Oliver himself might jog down at times and snatch more rest than he could in his Saturday-to-Monday visits to Hampton Court.

But he never seemed to have the time, and the girls were always occupied with a host of engagements, and Dick, their elder son, could never be dug out of his own country estates near Bath, and Henry, their second, was busy in Ireland ruling the country his father had conquered. Still it was peace unutterable to go by herself to the Woodrow High House and sit in its little oak rooms and walk in its walled gardens looking over the wooded hills of Buckinghamshire, and never be reminded of the grandeur that had once clothed a slaughtered king, and now sat on herself like scarlet on an ape.

And it was there behind the house in the rare afternoon sunshine of that cold July of 1658 that she walked and brushed soapsuds on to the greenfly of her rose trees, and thought of all these things.

Until, hearing a heavy step on the gravel, she looked up with a world of fear in her heart, and saw Oliver coming towards her with bowed massive shoulders as of some great wounded beast dragging his weary weight over the ground, and heard, as clearly as if he said it aloud, a sentence he had written to her years ago, "I grow an old man."

She ran to meet him, she took his hands and asked him what had happened, why he had come. He did not even hear her question and she did not repeat it, for his face made her dread the answer. She turned and led him into the house and poured him out ale, and put bread and butter and ham in front of him as in the old days, and while she did so she thought of all the things that could have happened to hurt him. His health had given her anxiety for years, he had fits of ague which this cold spring had increased, he suffered from gout and the stone, and he had had two driving accidents in the last few years, when his coach had been knocked to pieces and he himself had miraculously escaped, but badly shaken up. He looked as though he had had some such jar now, and yet, as she waited for some word from him in the silence, she knew that the shock, however far it would reach in time through his nerves and sinews, was not as yet to his body but to his soul.

And now, hurriedly marshalling them in array, she thought of their children and wondered which of them could have dealt him this blow; had Betty run away with the Duke of Buckingham, or Dick, his heir to England, disappointed him even more deeply than he had yet done by his cloddish indifference to affairs of State, his single-minded devotion to country sports? "I would not have one Englishman killed to keep me in power," Dick had once said, and his father had despaired of him after that.

But it was not Dick. Dick could not bring this heavy anguish to his father's eyes.

Oliver drank his ale and took a piece of bread but did not eat it, only crumbled it between his fingers. Not raising his eyes from it, he said in a low voice, "Is it possible to fall from grace?"

He had never asked her a question that she could remember, but he was not asking it of her, but of God. She answered as firmly as she could, "It is not possible."

"Then I am still in grace," he said, "for I know that once I was."

She sat beside him and said, "Will you not tell me?" but still he did not look at her; he sighed, and his breath caught on a groan of pain, and he broke it to cry out, "It is a fearful thing to fall into the hands of the living God."

Then Oliver thought he was dying, not, as in the old days, of his fancied terrors, but because he knew he was ill, so ill that he must die. "What is it?" she cried. "Why do you think you are dying?"

Her voice was sharp with anxiety, it had the shrill note of the scold in it that used to enforce her commands to him to be more careful of his health, and it startled him into the old compliance to her. He was aware of her now, looking at her, trying to spare her something, — if only he could see that this suspense was torturing her worse than any news!

"God has chastened our family very sorely," he said; "we do not deserve the world's envy — and perhaps we deserve no better. Betty is very ill," he added in an undertone.

She had known it all along. But why had Oliver not gone straight to Betty at Hampton Court, instead of here to herself? She asked him and he said, "I came for you." And suddenly he slipped from the seat beside her and was kneeling with his head on her lap, enclosing her body with his arms and shaking it with his sobs as he used to do in the old quiet days of her peace and his torment. In that instant, all the years rolled back; he needed her again, then, as utterly as of old, and as of old had no need even to appeal to her. He had come for her, and that was enough.

For him, but not for her. Time flew so fast now, she must keep something of this moment to treasure it inside her to the end of her life. Clasping that bowed, grizzled head to her, she whispered, "You still love me — ?"

He raised his head, and his savage and resolute eyes looked into hers. "You are dearer to me than any creature," he told her.

She had that to keep with her when Oliver died on the third of September, just four weeks after his daughter's death.

The Famous Mr. Joseph Addison

by *William Makepeace Thackeray*

1704 Colonel Henry Esmond, writing the story of
his life in his old age, here comes to his acquaintance
with one of the most eminent writers of Queen Anne's
reign. Esmond was home from the wars after fighting
in the Duke of Marlborough's celebrated victory at
Blenheim. Richard Steele was the junior partner in
the distinguished literary firm of Addison and Steele.

The gentlemen-ushers had a table at Kensington and the Guard a
very splendid dinner daily at St. James' at either of which ordinaries
Esmond was free to dine. Dick Steele liked the Guard table better than
his own at the gentlemen-ushers', where there was less wine and more
ceremony; and Esmond had many a jolly afternoon in company of his
friend, and a hundred times at least saw Dick into his chair. If there is
verity in wine, according to the old adage, what an amiable-natured character Dick's must have been! In proportion as he took in wine he overflowed with kindness. His talk was not witty so much as charming. He
never said a word that could anger anybody, and only became the more
benevolent the more tipsy he grew. Many of the wags derided the poor
fellow in his cups, and chose him as a butt for their satire: but there was
a kindness about him, and a sweet playful fancy, that seemed to Esmond
far more charming than the pointed talk of the brightest wits with their
elaborate repartees and affected severities. I think Steele shone rather than
sparkled. Those famous *beaux-esprits* of the coffee-houses (Mr. William
Congreve, for instance, when his gout and his grandeur permitted him to
come among us) would make many brilliant hits — half-a-dozen in a night
sometimes — but, like sharpshooters, when they had fired their shot, they
were obliged to retire under cover until their pieces were loaded again,
and wait till they got another chance at their enemy; whereas Dick never
thought that his bottle companion was a butt to aim at — only a friend
to shake by the hand. The poor fellow had half the town in his confidence;
everybody knew everything about his loves and his debts, his creditors
or his mistress' obduracy. When Esmond first came on to the town, honest
Dick was all flames and raptures for a young lady, a West India fortune,
whom he married. In a couple of years the lady was dead, the fortune was

396

all but spent, and the honest widower was as eager in pursuit of a new paragon of beauty as if he had never courted and married and buried the last one.

Quitting the Guard table one Sunday afternoon, when by chance Dick had a sober fit upon him, he and his friend were making their way down Germain Street, and Dick all of a sudden left his companion's arm, and ran after a gentleman who was poring over a folio volume at the book-shop near to St. James' Church. He was a fair, tall man, in a snuff-colored suit, with a plain sword, very sober, and almost shabby in appearance — at least when compared to Captain Steele, who loved to adorn his jolly round person with the finest of clothes, and shone in scarlet and gold lace. The Captain rushed up, then, to the student of the book-stall, took him in his arms, hugged him, and would have kissed him — for Dick was always hugging and bussing his friends — but the other stepped back with a flush on his pale face, seeming to decline this public manifestation of Steele's regard.

"My dearest Joe, where hast thou hidden thyself this age?" cries the Captain, still holding both his friend's hands: "I have been languishing for thee this fortnight."

"A fortnight is not an age, Dick," says the other, very good-humoredly. (He had light-blue eyes, extraordinarily bright, and a face perfectly regular and handsome, like a tinted statue.) "And I have been hiding myself — where do you think?"

"What! not across the water, my dear Joe?" says Steele, with a look of great alarm: "thou knowest I have always — "

"No," says his friend, interrupting him with a smile: "we are not come to such straits as that, Dick. I have been hiding, sir, at a place where people never think of finding you — at my own lodgings, whither I am going to smoke a pipe now and drink a glass of sack: will your honor come?"

"Harry Esmond, come hither," cries out Dick. "Thou hast heard me talk over and over again of my dearest Joe, my guardian angel?"

"Indeed," says Mr. Esmond, with a bow, "it is not from you only that I have learnt to admire Mr. Addison. We loved good poetry at Cambridge as well as Oxford; and I have some of yours by heart, though I have put on a red coat . . . 'O qui canoro blandius Orpheo vocale ducis carmen'; shall I go on, sir?" says Mr. Esmond, who indeed, had read and loved the charming Latin poems of Mr. Addison, as every scholar of that time knew and admired them.

"This is Captain Esmond, who was at Blenheim," says Steele.

"Lieutenant Esmond," says the other, with a low bow, "at Mr. Addison's service."

"I have heard of you," says Mr. Addison, with a smile; as indeed, everybody about town had heard that unlucky story of Esmond's dowager aunt and the Duchess.

"We were going to the 'George' to take a bottle before the play," says Steele: "wilt thou be one, Joe?"

Mr. Addison said his own lodgings were hard by, where he was still rich enough to give a good bottle of wine to his friends; and invited the two gentlemen to his apartment in the Haymarket, where we accordingly went.

"I shall get credit with my landlady," says he, with a smile, "when she sees two such fine gentlemen as you come up my stair." And he politely made his visitors welcome to his apartment, which was indeed but a shabby one, though no grandee of the land could receive his guests with a more perfect and courtly grace than this gentleman. A frugal dinner, consisting of a slice of meat and a penny loaf, was awaiting the owner of the lodgings. "My wine is better than my meat," says Mr. Addison; "my Lord Halifax sent me the Burgundy." And he set a bottle and glasses before his friends, and ate his simple dinner in a very few minutes, after which the three fell to and began to drink. "You see," says Mr. Addison, pointing to his writing-table, whereon was a map of the action at Hochstedt, and several other gazettes and pamphlets relating to the battle, "that I, too, am busy about your affairs, Captain. I am engaged as a poetical gazetteer, to say truth, and am writing a poem on the campaign."

So Esmond, at the request of his host, told him what he knew about the famous battle, drew the river on the table *aliquo mero*, and with the aid of some bits of tobacco-pipe, showed the advance of the left wing, where he had been engaged.

A sheet or two of the verses lay already on the table beside our bottles and glasses, and Dick having plentifully refreshed himself from the latter, took up the pages of manuscript, wrote out with scarce a blot or correction, in the author's slim, neat handwriting, and began to read therefrom with great emphasis and volubility. At pauses of the verse, the enthusiastic reader stopped and fired off a great salvo of applause.

Esmond smiled at the enthusiasm of Addison's friend. "You are like the German Burghers," says he, "and the Princes on the Mozelle: when our army came to a halt, they always sent a deputation to compliment the chief, and fired a salute with all their artillery from their walls."

"And drunk the great chief's health afterward, did not they?" says Captain Steele, gaily filling up a bumper; — he never was tardy at that sort of acknowledgement of a friend's merit.

"And the Duke, since you will have me act his Grace's part," says Mr. Addison, with a smile, and something of a blush, "pledged his friends in return. Most Serene Elector of Covent Garden, I drink to your Highness' Health," and he filled himself a glass. Joseph required scarce more pressing than Dick to that sort of amusement; but the wine never seemed at all to fluster Mr. Addison's brains; it only unloosed his tongue: whereas Captain Steele's head and speech were quite overcome by a single bottle.

No matter what the verses were, and, to say truth, Mr. Esmond found some of them more than indifferent, Dick's enthusiasm for his chief never faltered, and every line from Addison's pen Steele found a master-stroke. By the time Dick had come to that part of the poem wherein the bard describes as blandly as though he were recording a dance at the opera, or a harmless bout of bucolic cudgeling at a village fair, that bloody and ruthless part of our campaign, with the remembrance whereof every soldier who bore a part in it must sicken with shame — when we were ordered to ravage and lay waste the Elector's country; and with fire and murder, slaughter and crime, a great part of his dominions was overrun; — when Dick came to the lines:

> In vengeance roused the soldier fills his hand
> With sword and fire, and ravages the land,
> In crackling flames a thousand harvests burn,
> A thousand villages to ashes turn.
> To the thick woods the woolly flocks retreat,
> And mixed with bellowing herds confusedly bleat.
> Their trembling lords the common shade partake,
> And cries of infants sound in every brake.
> The listening soldier fixed in sorrow stands,
> Loth to obey his leader's just commands.
> The leader grieves, by generous pity swayed,
> To see his just commands so well obeyed; —

by this time wine and friendship had brought poor Dick to a perfectly maudlin state, and he hiccupped out the last line with a tenderness that set one of his auditors a-laughing.

"I admire the license of your poets," says Esmond to Mr. Addison. (Dick,

after reading the verses, was fain to go off, insisting on kissing his two
dear friends before his departure, and reeling away with his periwig over
his eyes.) "I admire your art: the murder of the campaign is done to military music, like a battle at the opera, and the virgins shriek in harmony
as our victorious grenadiers march into their villages. Do you know what
a scene it was?" — (by this time, perhaps, the wine had warmed Mr.
Esmond's head too) — "what a triumph you are celebrating? what scenes
of shame and horror were enacted, over which the commander's genius
presided, as calm as though he didn't belong to our sphere? You talk of
the 'listening soldier fixed in sorrow,' the 'leader's grief swayed by generous pity': to my belief the leader cared no more for bleating flocks than he
did for infants' cries, and many of our ruffians butchered one or the other
with equal alacrity. I was ashamed of my trade when I saw those horrors
perpetrated which came under every man's eyes. You hew out of your
polished verses a stately image of smiling victory! I tell you 'tis an uncouth,
distorted, savage idol; hideous, bloody, and barbarous. The rites performed
before it are shocking to think of. You great poets should show it as it is —
ugly and horrible, not beautiful and serene. Oh, sir, had you made the
campaign, believe me, you never would have sung it so."

During this little outbreak, Mr. Addison was listening, smoking out of
his long pipe, and smiling very placidly. "What would you have?" says
he. "In our polished days, and according to the rules of art, 'tis impossible
that the Muse should depict tortures or begrime her hands with the horrors of war. These are indicated rather than described; as in the Greek
tragedies, that, I daresay, you have read (and sure there can be no more
elegant specimens of composition), Agamemnon is slain, or Medea's children destroyed, away from the scene; — the chorus occupying the stage
and singing of the action to pathetic music. Something of this I attempt,
my dear sir, in my humble way: 'tis a panegyric I mean to write, and not
a satire. Were I to sing as you would have me, the town would tear the
poet in pieces, and burn his book by the hands of the common hangman.
Do you not use tobacco? Of all the weeds grown on earth, sure the nico-
tian is the most soothing and salutary. We must paint our great Duke,"
Mr. Addison went on, "not as a man, which no doubt he is, with weak-
nesses like the rest of us, but as a hero. 'Tis in a triumph, not a battle, that
your humble servant is riding his sleek Pegasus. We College poets trot,
you know, on very easy nags; it hath been time out of mind, part of the
poet's profession to celebrate the actions of heroes in verse, and to sing
the deeds which you men of war perform. I must follow the rules of my

art, and the composition of such a strain as this must be harmonious and majestic, not familiar, or too near the vulgar truth. *Si parva licet:* if Virgil could invoke the divine Augustus, a humbler poet from the banks of the Isis may celebrate a victory and a conqueror of our own nation, in whose triumphs every Briton has a share, and whose glory and genius contributes to every citizen's individual honor. When hath there been, since our Henrys' and Edwards' days, such a great feat of arms as that from which you yourself have brought away marks of distinction? If 'tis in my power to sing that song worthily, I will do so, and be thankful to my Muse. If I fail as a poet, as a Briton at least I will show my loyalty, and fling up my cap and huzza for the conqueror:

> ... Rheni pacator et Istri
> Omnis in hoc uno variis discordia cessit
> Ordinibus: la tatur eques, plauditque senator,
> Votaque patricio certant plebeia favori."

"There were as brave men on that field," says Mr. Esmond (who never could be made to love the Duke of Marlborough, nor to forget those stories which he used to hear in his youth regarding that great chief's selfishness and treachery) — "There were men at Blenheim as good as the leader, whom neither knights nor senators applauded, nor voices plebian or patrician favored, and who lie there forgotten, under the clods. What poet is there to sing them?"

"To sing the gallant souls of heroes sent to Hades!" says Mr. Addison, with a smile. "Would you celebrate them all? If I may venture to question anything in such an admirable work, the catalogue of ships in Homer hath always appeared to me as somewhat wearisome: what had the poem been, supposing the writer had chronicled the names of captains, lieutenants, rank and file? One of the greatest of a great man's qualities is success; 'tis the result of all the others; 'tis a latent power in him which compels the favor of the gods, and subjugates fortune. Of all his gifts I admire that one in the great Marlborough. To be brave? Every man is brave. But in being victorious, as he is, I fancy there is something divine. In presence of the occasion, the great soul of the leader shines out, and the god is confessed. Death itself respects him, and passes by him to lay others low. War and carnage flee before him to ravage other parts of the field, as Hector from before the divine Achilles. You say he hath no pity: no more have the gods, who are above it, and super-human. The fainting battle gathers strength at his aspect; and, wherever he rides, victory charges with him."

A couple of days after, when Mr. Esmond revisited his poetic friend, he found this thought, struck out in the fervor of conversation, improved and shaped into those famous lines, which are in truth the noblest in the poem of the "Campaign." As the two gentlemen sat engaged in talk, Mr. Addison solacing himself with his customary pipe, the little maid-servant that waited on his lodging came up, preceding a gentleman in fine laced clothes, that had evidently been figuring at Court or a great man's levee. The courtier coughed a little at the smoke of the pipe, and looked around the room curiously, which was shabby enough, as was the owner in his worn snuff-colored suit and plain tie-wig.

"How goes on the *magnum opus*, Mr. Addison?" says the Court gentleman, on looking down at the papers that were on the table.

"We were but now over it," says Addison (the greatest courtier in the land could not have a more splendid politeness, or greater dignity of manner). "Here is the plan," says he, "on the table: *hac ibat Simois*, here ran the little river Nebel: *hic est Sigeia tellus*, here are Tallard's quarters, at the bowl of this pipe, at the attack of which Captain Esmond was present. I have the honor to introduce him to Mr. Boyle; and Mr. Esmond was but now depicting *aliquo proelia mixta mero*, when you came in." In truth, the two gentlemen had been so engaged when the visitor arrived, and Addison in his smiling way speaking of Mr. Webb, colonel of Esmond's regiment (who commanded a brigade in the action, and greatly distinguished himself there), was lamenting that he could find never a suitable rhyme for Webb, otherwise the brigade should have had a place in the poet's verses. "And for you, you are but a lieutenant," says Addison, "and the Muse can't occupy herself with any gentleman under the rank of a field officer."

Mr. Boyle was all impatient to hear, saying that my Lord Treasurer and my Lord Halifax were equally anxious; and Addison, blushing, began reading of his verses, and, I suspect, knew their weak parts as well as the most critical hearer. When he came to the lines describing the angel that

> Inspired repulsed battalions to engage,
> And taught the doubtful battle where to rage,

he read with great animation, looking at Esmond, as much as to say, "You know where that simile came from — from our talk, and our bottle of Burgundy, the other day."

The poet's two hearers were caught with enthusiasm, and applauded the verses with all their might. The gentleman of the Court sprang up in great delight. "Not a word more, my dear sir," says he. "Trust me with the papers — I'll defend them with my life. Let me read them over to my Lord Treasurer, whom I am appointed to see in half-an-hour. I venture to promise, the verses shall lose nothing by my reading, and then, sir, we shall see whether Lord Halifax has a right to complain that his friend's pension is no longer paid." And without more ado, the courtier in lace seized the manuscript pages, placed them in his breast with his ruffled hand over his heart, executed a most gracious wave of the hat with the disengaged hand, and smiled and bowed out of the room, leaving an odor of pomander behind him.

"Does not the chamber look quite dark?" says Addison, surveying it, "after the glorious appearance and disappearance of that gracious messenger? Why, he illuminated the whole room. Your scarlet, Mr. Esmond, will bear any light; but this threadbare old coat of mine, how very worn it looked under the glare of that splendor! I wonder whether they will do anything for me," he continued. "When I came out of Oxford into the world, my patrons promised me great things; and you see where their promises have landed me, in a lodging up two pair of stairs, with a sixpenny dinner from the cook's shop. Well, I suppose this promise will go after the others, and fortune will jilt me, as the jade has been doing any time these seven years. 'I puff the prostitute away'" says he, smiling, and blowing a cloud out of his pipe. "There is no hardship in poverty, Esmond, that is not bearable; no hardship even in honest dependence that an honest man may not put up with. I came out of the lap of Alma Mater, puffed up with her praises of me, and thinking to make a figure in the world with the parts and learning which had got me no small name in our College. The world is the ocean, and Isis and Charwell are but little drops, of which the sea takes no account. My reputation ended a mile beyond Maudlin Tower; no one took note of me; and I learned this at least, to bear up against evil fortune with a cheerful heart. Friend Dick hath made a figure in the world, and has passed me in the race long ago. What matters a little name or a little fortune? There is no fortune that a philosopher cannot endure. I have been not unknown as a scholar, and yet forced to live by turning bear-leader, and teaching a boy to spell. What then? The life was not pleasant, but possible — the bear was bearable. Should this venture fail, I will go back to Oxford: and some day, when you are a general, you shall find me a curate in a cassock and bands, and I shall welcome your honor to my cottage in the country, and to a mug of penny ale. 'Tis not poverty that's the hardest to bear, or the least happy lot in life," says Mr. Addison, shaking the ash out of his pipe. "See, my pipe is smoked out. Shall we have another bottle? I have still a couple in the cupboard, and of the right sort. No more? Let us go abroad and take a turn on the Mall, or look in at the theater and see Dick's comedy. 'Tis not a masterpiece of wit: but Dick is a good fellow, though he doth not set the Thames on fire."

Within a month after this day, Mr. Addison's ticket had come up a prodigious prize in the lottery of life. All the town was in an uproar of admiration of his poem, the "Campaign," which Dick Steele was spouting at every coffee-house in Whitehall and Covent Garden. The wits on the other side of Temple Bar saluted him at once as the greatest poet the world had seen for ages; the people huzzaed for Marlborough and for Addison, and, more than this, the party in power provided for the meritorious poet, and Mr. Addison got the appointment of Commissioner of Excise, which the famous Mr. Locke vacated, and rose from this place to other dignities and honors; his prosperity from henceforth to the end of his life being scarcely ever interrupted. But I doubt whether he was not happier in his garret in the Haymarket, than ever he was in his splendid palace at Kensington; and I believe the fortune that came to him in the shape of the countess his wife, was no better than a shrew and a vixen.

Retreat from St. Francis:
The Last Four Days

by Kenneth Roberts

1759   After destroying the Indian town of St. Francis near the St. Lawrence in a surprise raid, Major Robert Rogers led his 140 Rangers south in a desperate retreat. Eighteen days later, with forty Rangers killed by Indians and the rest half dead of starvation, they reached the junction of the Ammonoosuc and Connecticut Rivers. There a relief force with ample supplies was supposed to meet them. It did not.

On the 25th the rain stopped and we began to build the raft. The task of rolling the twelve sound logs across the intervale and into the Connecticut seemed, in the beginning, beyond our powers; for at the smallest exertions our muscles quivered and relaxed, so that we could neither grip with our hands nor set our feet firmly against the ground.

Each log resisted us, as might a giant boulder. In the end we learned to kneel before a log and roll it toward us, a few inches at a time — five men to a log that one man, ordinarily, could easily have handled alone.

Those who were weaker cut alder and willow shoots, and dug roots of the red spruce. The spruce roots, knotted together, made lashings as tough as ropes; and the alder and willow shoots, laced from log to log and bound with spruce roots, held the logs firmly.

As a support for ourselves we lashed a spruce sapling across the middle of the raft, leaving a row of branches standing straight up like the teeth of a comb; and to these branches we tied our muskets, powder-horns, haversacks and blankets, to keep them from the water. For paddles we cut young swamp maples, lacing their end-crotches with spruce roots.

All the time we groaned and whimpered as we worked; for so bungling and futile seemed our labor that we feared it would never be done. Yet it *was* done on the morning of the 26th, and the raft wasn't a bad one. The dry logs made it float well. When we tried it, with Billy at one end as a look-out, Ogden and I on either side with paddles, and Rogers in the stern with a pole for pushing, she rode high, without dipping as small rafts often do.

We made a final effort, through the 26th, to find a deer, a porcupine, even a rabbit for food, but never a thing did we see — possibly because all our senses were dulled: perhaps because of our blundering movements; but more likely, it seemed to us, because of the frightening odor of anxiety and despair that must have emanated from our sorry company.

When at night Captain Jacobs and Konkapot came back last of all, empty-handed, Rogers refused to wait longer. At dawn on the 27th Grant and Avery went with us to the raft, while the others hobbled and wavered along behind, straggling like lost sheep. At the water's edge Rogers turned suddenly on Grant. "Repeat your orders."

Grant made an effort to stand straight. "I'm in charge. I'm to keep the men alive till food gets here. I'm to make the men dig bulbs every afternoon. I'm to send out hunting parties every morning." He paused and looked numbly at his feet.

"Whether they want to go or not," Rogers said sharply.

"Yes," Grant said, "whether — whether they want to go or not."

"And whatever they shoot," Rogers said, "you're to save some of it for Farrington, Curgill, Campbell, Evans and their parties. There's forty of 'em, and they'll have to eat when they get here. Something's got to be saved for those men. Bear 'em in mind all the time! Understand?"

Grant and Avery nodded.

"What else?" Rogers asked patiently.

"If I bring all of 'em in safe, you'll make me a Captain," Grant said.

"Just your orders, Lieutenant," Rogers said. "Don't try to think of anything but your orders. What are the rest of your orders?"

The other men, tattered, stooped, haggard specters in the gray dawn, had come to the edge of the bank. They stared down at Rogers, slack-lipped, dull-eyed.

Grant rubbed a claw-like hand over his face. "I'm to stay here ten days. I'm to tell Farrington, Curgill, Campbell and Evans that you'll be back in ten days."

"Ten days from today," Rogers said.

"Yes," Grant said. "You'll be back ten days from today."

"I'll be back ten days from today," Rogers repeated. "Ten days from today you'll have all you can eat."

"What'll we do if you don't get back?" Avery asked.

"You heard me," Rogers said. "I'll be back. All you've got to do is wait! Just wait!"

He motioned Ogden, the little Indian boy and me to get aboard the raft, edged it into deeper water, and crawled aboard himself. "Push us off," he told Grant.

We moved out into the current. Without a word, without any sound at all, the horde of tatterdemalions, crouching on the bank, watched us go. Their gaunt eyes followed us with a weary, dumb anxiety; and I thought perhaps they were wondering, as I was, whether our wabbly craft, when she reached midstream, would hold together.

We thrust and thrust with our porous paddles, but they took no grip on the water, and I had to go down on one knee to keep from slipping overboard.

"She's all right now," Rogers said. "Let her go!"

We stopped paddling. The raft, slowly turning and sidling, began to move downstream swiftly; and all at once there was mist and distance between us and the men we were leaving. To us it was as though we left them helpless behind bars, listless animals in cages. Some of them at the brown river's edge, fumbled in the shallows as bears do. They looked enlarged, grotesque, not human.

When we passed through riffles, the raft undulated and water spurted between the logs. If we stood, we were dizzy; if we lay down, we were drenched and nearly frozen. We relieved each other at the steering pole, and on relinquishing it hooked our arms around the uprights of the center sapling and clung there like draggled, crucified scarecrows. When the current threw the raft toward either shore, we crawled to the edges and plied our flimsy paddles furiously until it was back in midstream once more.

It turned and twisted, facing now up river and now down; coasted around sharp bends: through valleys whose sides rose steeply: past intervales miles in width.

The sky was the color of skimmed milk, and the sun no brighter or warmer than a pewter button. There was a peculiar penetrating bitterness to the air; and every breath I took seemed to lodge behind my eyeballs and make them ache. From the chill that lay above that dark stream, we might have been passing through a valley of invisible ice.

"There's cold weather coming," Rogers said. "We'll have to lay up at night; and when we do, we'll tie her in quick water, where she won't get ice-bound."

We went ashore on a sandy spit where a brook ran in, and anchored by pushing stakes around the raft; but no sort of anchorage we could devise was satisfactory. Neither Rogers nor Ogden said anything about what would happen if the raft froze in the shallows, or got away from us. None of us had much to say about anything; but in my own mind there was no doubt what would happen.

"What we better do," Rogers said, "is cut wood for a fire and fence. Then we can make some sort of rope, and I'll tie it to me."

A fire and fence is only used when there's danger of freezing. The fence is of brush, two feet high: the fire burns before it, and those who lie between the fire and the fence are warm — provided they have enough firewood.

While we built fire and fence, Billy cut flexible twigs, and later we braided them together until they were long enough to reach the raft; then made one end fast to the center sapling; the other end to Rogers' waist.

As Rogers had predicted, that night was a bad one — so bad that when we had finished cutting brush for the fence, we had trouble chopping firewood. Our wet clothes were frozen stiff, and we would have been glad for the warmth that comes with hard work, but to swing a hatchet was difficult. By slow hacking — waiting a little and then hacking a little — we felled one tree, a dead one; and when it was down, I knew how women feel when they burst into tears after a long trying day's back-breaking over a washtub.

That one tree was gone before daylight. To rise and stamp our feet for warmth seemed beyond our powers. We could only roll ourselves closer and closer to the ashes of the fire; until at last, when morning came, we were lying in them.

I had dreamt all night, over and over, that the raft was gone: that it was floating far downstream, piled high with dead Indians with staring white eyes crawling all over them; and when I woke, I'd just seen John Singleton Copley pointing at those eye-spangled corpses after promising to teach me how to paint the riffles of a river with a paddle dipped in blood.

The biting cold had held, and next morning, to save ourselves from slipping overboard, we had almost constantly to chip ice from the logs; but we made progress and came disastrously to White River Falls in the Connecticut River before noon.

Rogers had told us dully we had to look out for the falls: he wasn't sure the raft could get through them. He had droned the words "Watch out for the falls; watch out for the falls!" until they buzzed unendingly in my head. Even the waves of the Connecticut, slapping against the raft, seemed to mutter "Look out for the falls; look out for the falls!"

Just how we saved ourselves from going over the falls with the raft, I'll never know. One moment the river was clear and open ahead: the next moment Billy was piping something in a feeble voice, while Rogers shouted "Push! Push! Left! Push to the left!" Before us hung a cloud of white mist, boiling upward, and below the rolling vapor there were glimpses of broken and foamy water — downhill stretches of horribly speeding silver.

I splashed with my makeshift paddle until I thought my eyes would burst from my head. I heard straining grunts from Ogden; saw Rogers on his knees, poling like a madman.

The raft trembled, surged and heaved, spun round in a sinister hurry; and all too close we heard the dismaying great solid sound of a whole river plunging to a lower level. The shore was close, but not close enough. The raft wouldn't go to it.

"Get your guns and jump!" Rogers cried. "Take everything! Take mine! Jump!" He tried to wedge the pole against the bottom. I heard it split.

Ogden and I wrenched muskets, blankets and powder-horns from the fence of branches in the center of the raft. I saw Billy, a brown streak, leaping into the brown icy torrent, and then I was conscious myself of the shock of that same cold and speeding brownness all over me, and of uneven rocks beneath my feet; then of being swept under, and of clinging, even so, to a monstrous load of muskets and blankets that I was expected to save, whether I drowned or not.

A hand grasped my shirt and pulled me upright. Rogers had me, and he had Ogden too. Billy, in the shallows, helped us with the blankets and muskets, and then we were all in the chill mud of the river bank, with the noise of the falls in our ears, and complete anguish in our souls.

"Look!" Rogers shouted, and we saw the raft, midway of the sloping water, rise on edge and turn completely over. It appeared again, broken in the middle, V-shaped, like a cabin roof. A log burst from it and stood upright. What had been a raft became loose logs which rolled and tossed in a creamy smother; hung for a moment on the lip of the falls; then vanished.

"We're lucky," Rogers said. "It looks to me like a good sign, our not staying on that raft any longer."

Somewhere I have heard that after the first three days of fasting a man has no further desire for food, and that after thirty days he feels no discomfort whatever: that his brain is clear, his body pure, and his endurance almost unlimited. I suspect that statement in toto. I don't believe in the benefits of fasting, and ever since I tried it in the company of Major Robert Rogers on the St. Francis Expedition, I have been strongly opposed to it.

After we had seen the logs of our raft plunge over the edge of the falls, we dragged ourselves higher up the bank, dropped to the ground and lay there. Even Rogers was supine for a time — though not for long. He got to his knees. "This is no place to stay," he said. "We can't stay anywhere without a fire. We'd freeze. There'll be wood on the bank below the falls." He stood up, swaying. "That's where we go next," he said. "Come on."

We crawled after him; and it was as he said. There was wood in plenty along the shore beyond the falls, though not such wood as would build a raft. There were whole trees, hard wood for the most part, and waterlogged; windrows of twigs and branches; untold quantities of splintered pines of varying sizes, shattered by the ice-jams of the previous springs.

Rogers shook his head when he had crawled over the largest of those wood-heaps. "The only thing we can do today," he told us, "is try to get warm. Maybe tomorrow we can figure out something better."

We built ourselves another fence and a roaring fire of driftwood; then stripped ourselves and dried our shredded blankets and our sorry remnants of garments. So tattered and so rotted were those wretched rags that they were next to worthless as covering, and worse than worthless as protection against cold.

Our persons, in a way, were as bad as our clothes. I was ashamed, almost, to look at Rogers and Ogden. Their scrawny bodies seemed caricatures of what they ought to be — like bodies formed by a sculptor with no knowledge of anatomy. Their muscles were stringy as those of a skun wildcat: their knees and elbows strangely knobby: their stomachs hollowed and their ribs protuberant like those of a hake that has lain for days upon a beach.

Rogers was covered with scars — red scars, blue scars, white scars. Some were bullet wounds, while others looked as though made by the claws or teeth of animals. Ogden's two bullet-holes, so recently healed, were a flaming purple, rimmed with crimson.

When the strips we called our clothes were dry, we huddled close to the fire, listening to the everlasting roar of White River Falls. The fire warmed me, and drugged by that warmth and the thunder in my ears, I neither knew how we could move from where we were, nor did I care.

It was a good thing for us, in a way, that we were wrecked at White

River Falls. If the falls had not been there to provide us with windrows of firewood: if we had spent the night in a spot where we would have had only the fuel that we cut, we would probably have died of exhaustion and cold. Our exertions on the raft had drained us of our last reserves of strength, and it was beyond our power to drive a hatchet into a tree. As for the cold, it was so bitter that in the morning the mist from the falls had cased every branch and rock and dead leaf in a glittering envelope of ice.

We lay beside the fire until the sun had come up to take off the knife-like bite of the air.

"We'll have to eat," Rogers said. "If we don't get something in us we can't stick on the raft."

"What raft?" Ogden said.

"We'll get a raft," Rogers said.

"I don't know how," Ogden said. "If I try to swing a hatchet, I'll cut off my legs."

"Don't worry about that," Rogers said. "I'll get the raft if you'll find the food. Listen!"

Behind us, on the dark slope of the valley, a red squirrel chirred. Far away another answered. We could hear them chipping and chapping at each other: I knew just how they looked, jerking their tails and sliding spasmodically around tree-trunks with outspread legs.

"There's the food," Rogers said. "There's only one good mouthful to a roasted red squirrel, even if he's hit in the head, but all we need is a few good mouthfuls."

"I guess we can knock down a few," Ogden said. "I don't know about getting 'em back here, if I shoot more than one. One's about all I can carry." He reached for his musket. "We better draw our loads and reload," he told me. "We can't afford to miss."

"Before you go," Rogers told us, "help me with the wood. There's only one way to get trees for a raft, and that's to burn 'em down."

We stacked piles of firewood at the base of six spruces near the water's edge: then dragged ourselves up the bank, leaving Rogers and Billy crawling from pile to pile, kindling the fires that were to fell the trees we no longer had the strength to hack down ourselves.

Ogden and I shot five squirrels during the morning, and found it difficult — not only because we couldn't hurry to a squirrel when we heard one, but because we had to wait for the squirrels to sit still: then shoot from a rest because of being unable to hold the sights steady unless we did so. Hunger cramps caught us with increasing frequency, and if a hunger cramp took hold while we were drawing a bead on a squirrel, there was nothing to do but double up and wait until it went away.

We came back, late in the morning, to find Rogers and Billy still nursing the fires at the bases of the six dry trees.

We skinned and roasted the squirrels, dividing the fifth one equally; and while we picked the meat from their mouse-like bodies, one of the trees came down with a crash.

Rogers drove us out again as soon as we had eaten. "Keep on hunting," he told us. "Shoot anything you find. I'll have these trees burned into lengths by the time you get back."

It seemed to me I couldn't drag my legs up the slope of that valley again, but somehow we did it, using our muskets as walking sticks and leaning frequently against trees. So far as I could feel, my roast squirrel had done me no good: I needed a side of mutton or a cow's hind-quarter to quiet the aching void within me. I thought bitterly of Cap Huff's idle remark about a goose being a little more than one man could eat alone, but not quite enough for two. How little Cap had known of hunger! A whole goose would no more than take the edge off my appetite.

Not far from us a partridge went out of a thicket with a thunderous roar. From the blundering sound he made among the branches, I was sure he had lit at no great distance.

"He's in a tree," I whispered to Ogden. Ordinarily the breast of a partridge makes a toothsome preliminary to a simple meal; but as a meal itself it's not worth considering. Just now, however, this partridge seemed more desirable than anything on earth.

"Can you see him?" Ogden asked faintly.

I said I couldn't, but knew about where he was.

"Go ahead and get him," Ogden said. "I'll move off to the left and make a noise doing it, so he'll watch me. You sneak around and take him in the rear."

He lowered himself among the dead leaves and threw his arms and legs about, making feeble moaning sounds. I hoped the partridge would find such a noise impressive as I crept around the thicket and stood watching breathlessly. The trees were naked: leafless. In none of them could I see anything that looked like a bird, and I was about to call to Ogden when I saw a movement at one end of a swelling on the branch of an oak. It was the partridge, cocking an eye at Ogden's strange behaviour.

I found a good rest, took careful aim and let him have it. When he scaled away from the limb on a long slant, Ogden and I stumbled as fast as we could to where he came down. It was rocky ground, clear of heavy undergrowth, and dotted with an occasional juniper bush and a thin covering of leaves; but the partridge was nowhere in sight.

"You sure he came down here?" Ogden asked.

I said I was; that he was hit hard.

"Yes, I saw him. I guess he was hit all right," Ogden agreed, "but I don't believe he came down here. We'd see him if he had. He must have gone beyond those rocks."

We went there and searched; we walked in circles, sought beneath every juniper; almost looked under every fallen leaf; but we found nothing.

"You're sure he came down at all?" Ogden asked finally.

I just nodded. The thought of losing that partridge shut off my voice completely; I was afraid that if I tried to speak, I'd sob instead.

Ogden, hollow-eyed, stared at the ground. "Guess you — guess you missed him," he said in a whisper. And then his wretched staring eyes seemed to enlarge. "Well, if that don't beat all!"

He was staring at a flat juniper that had a few brown oak leaves on it. Before my eyes the oak leaves magically altered and became a partridge — an enormous cock partridge, with ruff-feathers four inches long and a tail the size of a fan. We must have walked across him and around him twenty times.

I went down on my knees and picked him up. He was still warm — the fattest, most beautiful, angelic partridge I had ever seen. The musket ball had broken his back and left his breast untouched.

I looked up at Ogden. "I'm mighty glad you found him, Captain. Mighty glad."

"I *knew* you hit him," Ogden said. "That was a might pretty shot, Langdon — the best shot I ever hope to see."

When we returned to the falls, all six trees were down, and under each burned two fires, so as to separate them into proper lengths for a raft. Rogers sat at the edge of the stream, his forehead resting on his drawn-up knees, and beside him lay Billy, asleep.

The Major looked up. He was a sight. His face and hands were black with soot: as black as Pomp Whipple's; and his eyes glared at us whitely, looking to see whether we had shot anything. I slipped the partridge's head from under my belt and held it up for him to see.

"Oh, by God!" he whispered. "Let's eat it before our luck changes!"

We ate the intestines first, washed and placed on a hot stone to roast. Then we had half a squirrel apiece, cut along the backbone. The partridge was more difficult to divide evenly. Having agreed that a newly shot partridge is better raw than cooked, we seared him no more than enough to hold the meat together. Then we took off the breasts and, after considerable discussion and measuring, split them in what we agreed were equal parts. The carcass, mattering less, was quartered without argument.

Before we slept that night the twelve fires had done their work, and twelve logs lay on the bank, with nothing more to be done to them except get them into the water and fasten them together into a raft. To me, that night, the task appeared about as easy as pushing a porcupine through a musket barrel.

Nowadays whenever I dream of the building of that second raft, I wake myself up by whimpering aloud, because I've been straining to move a vast log that will not budge, yet must, or death awaits me.

We drove stakes in shallow water where the bottom was soft. Then we inched a log to the bank, tumbled it to the shingle, and worried it into the stream. We couldn't roll it, because we had to leave protruding branches for binding the raft together.

In moving a log, we worked however we could: levering it with stakes: sliding it over driftwood: lying on our backs to ease our hunger cramps, and pushing with heels or shoulders, so that from head to foot we were black with soot.

When we had a log in the water, we drew it to the fixed stakes, which held it in place while we went for another log. To each one we fastened a hazel switch, so there might be something by which to seize and guide it if it broke loose; and Billy stood guard at the stakes to do what he could in case they gave way.

It was noon before we had finished our labors, lashed our muskets and other wretched belongings to the uprights, cut new paddles and woven a long rope of hazel shoots.

Rogers insisted on the rope. "We don't want this one to get away from us," he muttered over and over. "We really got to keep hold of *this* one." We thought he was right about that. We couldn't have made a third raft.

Whether it was because of the steadily increasing cold — a cold that threatened snow — or the long struggle with the logs, I cannot say; but whatever advantage we had gained from our mouthful of partridge and two mouthfuls of squirrel had now been lost. We were finished; if our lives depended on our marching a mile, we couldn't have done it.

By the time we started, poor young Billy had bad cramps and couldn't even sit upright, so we laid him on some spruce tips in the middle of the raft. With his sharp nose, his closed eyes, his mouth stretched tight over his teeth, and his dusky color, he looked tragically like a mummy without its wrappings.

We worked free of the stakes, poled ourselves slowly into mid-stream and sank breathless on the raft, regardless of the icy water that welled up between the logs to soak our trembling bodies. Some day, I thought, I must paint a picture of this and call it Purgatory; and then I realized such a picture would have little meaning: it couldn't show the endlessness of these journeyings — the eternal wetness and shiverings, the aching bruises to soul and body, the everlasting hunger, everlasting toil, and everlasting exhaustion.

Rogers got to his knees, and I heard him say something about falls. The word shocked me into full consciousness. "Falls?" I asked. "More falls?"

"Not bad ones," he said thickly. "Just little falls. Wattoquitchey Falls, seven miles from here. Fifty yards long. Maybe we can ride 'em."

Ogden and I struggled painfully to our feet.

"For God's sake," Ogden said, "why didn't we go there to build the raft?"

"I said 'seven miles,'" Rogers reminded him. "You couldn't march seven miles. And what about him?" He pointed at Billy. "Why, maybe I couldn't even hardly do it myself."

"Can we see these falls before we're on top of 'em?" I asked.

"See 'em?" Rogers said. "We've *got* to see 'em haven't we?"

We strained our eyes downstream. A few snowflakes drifted out of the heavy sky, and from the surface of the eddying brown water rose a vapor like a faint ghost of the mist that had billowed up from White River Falls. The thought of more falls was sheerly nauseating, and I knew that if the snow came down too thickly, we might not see them until too late. . . .

Rogers broke the silence at the end of three miles. "Maybe we can ride 'em," he said again. He repeated the words in another quarter-hour. Those falls, I realized, hadn't been out of his mind all day. That was why he had insisted on making the rope of hazel switches. I wondered what would happen if we couldn't ride them; but I didn't dare ask.

We sighted the falls through thickening snowflakes at three o'clock, and paddled the raft over toward the left bank, so we might have opportunity to see how they looked.

At first I thought we might indeed possibly ride them, for their total drop was only about ten feet; and the quick water wasn't over fifty yards long. The closer we came, however, the more apparent it was that the raft would never get down safely unless every possible ounce of weight was removed from it. Gouts of foam shot up from the middle of the rapids, proving that the ledges beneath were sharp and dangerous; we could hardly hope to live if the raft broke up or spilled us in that turmoil.

We let the draft drop down to within a few yards of the quick water, laid one end of it against the bank and held it there with our paddles. We could see the pool at the bottom — a brown, deep pool, streaked with streamers of foam.

"I don't believe we'd better try it," Rogers said.

"Somebody's got to," Ogden said wearily. "It's the only chance we've got."

"No it isn't," Rogers said. "The best chance is for me to go down to that pool and try to catch her when she comes down."

Ogden, seized with a cramp, clutched his middle. "You can't!"

Rogers seemed not to hear him. "That's what we'll do. Take Billy ashore. Take the muskets and the rest of the stuff. I'll hold her while you do it."

Ogden hesitated.

"Captain Ogden!" Rogers said sharply. "You heard me!"

Ogden moved quickly to obey. We hurriedly collected our rusty muskets, our soaked and tattered rags of blankets, and all our other accouterments that now were rubbish; then, taking Billy by his pipestem arms, we dragged him to the bank, where he lay all asprawl, no better than a shrivelled little red corpse. At Rogers' orders we made fast the rope of hazel shoots to the stoutest of the uprights; and Ogden tested the rope while I fastened our paddles to the raft's protruding branches. The rope was firm as a cable.

"Now for God's sake!" Rogers said, "don't let go that rope till I give the signal. It'll take me some time to reach the pool, and I got to undress. When I hold up my arm, turn her loose. Let the rope trail. If I miss the raft, maybe I can catch the rope." He fastened his own paddle beside ours and went ashore.

I joined Ogden, and together we clung to the rope. The raft plucked insistently at it, as if eager to be gone from us.

Picking up his musket, powder-horn and other belongings, Rogers went slowly from our sight into the dark woods, walking crouched over. The snowflakes had thickened, helping to hide him from us; and I thought it likely that I'd heard his voice for the last time.

The raft seemed more and more determined to swing out into the stream and go down the falls. For fear it might pull us off our feet and drag us into the rapids, we sat in the shallows, water up to our waists, our feet wedged against rocks.

"I'll bet my way was best," Ogden muttered. "One of us ought to *tried* to ride down on it. If the Major gets a stomach cramp when he's swimming to it — " He was silent. There wasn't much more to say.

At the edge of the pool the bushes moved apart, and Rogers, a dim figure through the steadily-falling snow, could be seen peering along the shore to left and right, seeking, evidently, for a suitable position. Then he went back into the bushes, and reappeared nearer us, crawling out on a flat rock. With agonizing slowness he put down his musket, blanket, knapsack and powder-horn and painfully undressed.

He crouched at the edge of the rock, staring up at the falls — a lonely, naked, helpless atom in that immensity of roaring white water, drifting snowflakes, screaking forest and towering dark hills. Then he held up his arm and waved.

We let go the rope and floundered to our feet. The raft swung slowly broadside to the current and moved downstream. When it reached the quick water, it bobbed on the white riffles; flung itself forward.

It rolled and rocked. Halfway down it nosed completely under: a surge of white foam swept it from end to end. It rose again, reeling and sliding in the surges, and seemed to fling itself breathlessly to the bottom of the long slope. It plunged heavily into the swirling pool, and hung there, tilted forward, half under water. We looked to see it fall apart, but with labored slowness it came to the surface, turning gently among the clots and streaks of froth.

Rogers lowered himself from the rock. He swam arduously, with awkward jerks, as if his rump strove to rise and force his head under. He stopped once, freed his face from gouts of foam, and rolled on his side to look for the raft, which, again in the grip of the current, moved more rapidly.

He altered his course and swam spasmodically on. He found himself so close to it that he clutched for a log — clutched and missed. He kicked again; got a hand on the raft: another hand. He hung there for a time, his chin on the edge, his legs and body carried beneath the logs by the current; and I, watching him, felt my muscles quake; for I knew that no mere human, with an icy torrent plucking at his starved and weakened limbs, could cling for long to those charred tree-trunks. As if in answer to my fears, he struggled sluggishly, hitched himself along with fumbling hands, gripped one of the branches we had left as uprights on the logs, and drew himself partly from the water, so that his upper body lay upon the raft — lay so long motionless, that I thought he was sped. Then we saw that he was making futile upward movements with his knee. It caught the edge eventually, and he squirmed aboard to lie flat.

"I never thought he'd make it!" Ogden whispered; and I shaking all over, found that my tongue and throat were dry as chips.

Now Rogers had got to his knees, and we saw him unlash a paddle from the uprights, and begin to work slowly toward shore.

Driftwood from Wattoquitchey Falls warmed us and kept us alive that night; and with the first faint grayness of that miserable last day of October — miserable and yet ever-memorable — we put Billy in the middle of the raft, with our blankets under and over him, and pushed out into midstream. The snow had ceased, and had been followed by a wind so bitter that it cut and slashed us like frigid knife-blades.

There were no more falls between Wattoquitchey and Number Four: no more quick water, Rogers said — no, there was nothing but the malignant cold, which seemed determined to finish what the French and the Indians and the evil spirits of the forests and streams had tried so hard to do to us.

But on both sides the intervales grew broader: the hills retreated; and though the glacial wind could thus howl at us unrestrained, we thought it had the voice of a raging demon of the wilderness, frantic to see us at last slipping from his grasp.

Out of his streaming eyes, Rogers stared at the widening intervales. "We're going to make it," he said. "By God, I believe we're going to make it!"

It was mid-afternoon when he seized Ogden by the arm. "Look!" he cried. "Look!" He doubled over with a cramp; but thus bent he pointed awkwardly, like an actor playing the part of a hunchback. On the river bank, a hundred yards ahead, two men with axes suddenly stood.

"Why," Ogden said incredulously, "it's people again!" But I don't think Rogers could speak at all, and I know I couldn't.

The two strange, strange figures, men that weren't skeletons, men that were clothed, men that swung axes easily in ruddy strength and health — those two unbelievable men saw us, and came back along the bank, hurrying toward us.

"Don't tell 'em anything," Rogers warned us huskily as we swung the raft in toward the shore. "I'll do the talking. Don't tell anyone a damned thing till we find out all about the dirty skunk that ran off with our food!"

One of the men splashed toward us, caught our rope of hazel switches and drew us to land.

"Where's Number Four?" Rogers asked.

They just stared.

"I'm Rogers," Rogers said. "Where's Number Four?"

"Rogers!" one of the men said, and a kind of horror was in his face. "You say you're Rogers?"

"I do!"

"I've often seen you," the man said swallowing. "It's hard to believe!" He shook his head. "We heard you was dead, Major; and I guess it's true! You was! But anyhow, you're at Number Four, Major. It's right here, and we'll help you to the fort!"

With that, slipping and splashing in excitement, they gave us the unfamiliar help of muscular arms and got us off the raft, lifted Billy to the bank, put our belongings in a heap, and made the raft fast to a stake. They gawked at the burned ends of the logs and at the alder and hazel withes that held them together, and kept staring at Rogers as if he'd been a hippogriff.

We sat down just beyond the water's edge and watched them as they made the raft fast.

"Happen to have anything to eat?" Rogers asked them, whereupon, after another look at him, they sprang up the bank and departed, running. They were back in five minutes, bringing with them a bottle and a third of rum and a piece of bread the size of my fist. "That's all we got, Major," one said. "We're out chopping wood and et the rest, but there's plenty supplies at the fort. There's turnips and fresh pork."

Rogers broke the bread in four pieces. "Why, it's bread!" he said. He gave us our portions, took a mouthful of rum, then went over and looked at Billy. He poured a little rum between his lips. When Billy opened his eyes and coughed, he gave him the bread and passed us the bottle.

That mouthful of bread moistened by rum had incredible sweetness and savor. I could feel it moving warmly inside me, as though hastening to assure my cramped and aching stomach, my thumping heart, my laboring lungs and my shivering body that their long agony was over.

"Now we'll go up to the fort," Rogers told the staring woodcutters. "Guess maybe you'd better help us a little. Leave our stuff here: then come back for it. One of you carry this Indian boy. Then we'll just lean on the two of you."

One of the men picked up Billy and carried him. The other gave Ogden and me each a shoulder, and Rogers staggered along, now and then bumping into the man who carried the Indian boy; and thus we set off for the fort, which we could see, low and square, in the middle of its dismal, snow-covered clearing — that same peaceful clearing I had idly sketched on a warm September evening less than two months ago.

There was no sentry at the gate of the fort; no one on the small parade ground on which the snow had been trodden to dirty, frozen slush. Our helpers took us across the parade to the log barrack in the center. A squat tower of hewn plank rose from its northern end. The man on whom Ogden and I leaned pulled the latchstring of the door and kicked it open. In a broad stone fireplace opposite the door a fire burned, and at either end of the room were rows of bunks. In front of the fire a blanket was spread on the floor, and around it were a dozen Provincials, rolling dice.

They looked up. One said angrily, "Keep that door shut!"

"This here's Major Rogers," one of the woodcutters said in a voice that choked with excitement.

The Provincials got slowly to their feet and faced us, stared at us and frowned with unbelief, then seemed to see something terrifying.

"Who's in command of this fort?" Rogers asked.

"We don't know his name, Major," a soldier said huskily. "We're strangers here."

"Go get him," Rogers ordered.

Three Provincials jumped together for the door at the end of the room, jostling and tripping in their haste.

Rogers walked drunkenly to a bench, and the staring soldiers fell away before him.

"Put Billy on the blanket and go back and get our muskets," Rogers told the woodcutters.

Ogden and I got to the bench with difficulty. The feel of a roof over my head and of a closed room, warmed by a fire, almost suffocated me.

The door at the end of the room burst open. A stolid-looking man in a wrinkled blue uniform peered at us, blinking. "Which?" he asked. "Which one?" He came to us. "They said Major Rogers! None of *you* are Major Rogers!"

"I'm Rogers," the Major said. "Now here: write down what I say. I can't repeat. What's your name?"

"Bellows," the officer said, "in charge of the King's stores." He clapped his hands to his pockets, looked confused, then hurried from the room. When he returned he had pencil and paper. "We didn't know —" he stammered. "We heard — where did you — — "

"Get canoes," Rogers said. "Load 'em with food. Send 'em up river. Mouth of the Ammonoosuc."

"These men are Provincials," Bellows said apologetically. "They're bound home. There's only — — "

"Get settlers," Rogers said. "Good canoemen. Hire 'em!"

"It's pretty bad weather," Bellows said doubtfully. "Maybe when it clears off — "

Rogers rose wavering to his feet, then straightened himself to his full height and seemed to fill the room. In a strained, hoarse voice he said: "Today! Today! Now! Can't you realize there's a hundred Rangers at the mouth of the Ammonoosuc, starving! Get men and pay 'em! Get all the settlers into the fort! Call 'em in! Drum 'em up! I'll talk to 'em! For Christ's sake, get started!"

Bellows stared at him wildly: rushed back to the door and shouted a name, adding, at the top of his lungs, "Assembly! Assembly!"

Three private soldiers tumbled into the room, one a drummer. At a gesture from Bellows he ran out on the parade ground, fumbling with his drum braces. His drum rolled and rumbled, sending chills down my spine.

To one of the other soldiers Bellows shouted, "Run to Mrs. Bellows. Get a pail of milk and a bottle of my rum."

"And some bread," Ogden said.

"All the bread she's got!" Bellows shouted.

Rogers sank down on the bench, rubbing his gaunt face with huge skeleton hands, ran his fingers through his hair. "Write an order for the food to go up river. What you got in this place?"

"Pork," Bellows said. "Fresh beef. Turnips."

"How much bread you got?"

"Not much," Bellows said. "These Provincial — — "

"Provincials be damned! Let 'em go without! Put all the food you can find in those canoes, and send out for more. Send out for everything there is! Those men of mine are going to be fed, or by God I'll raid every house in the settlement!"

The drum rattled and rolled, rumbled and banged.

Bellows scribbled hastily on a sheet of paper and sent the third soldier flying from the barrack with it. There were people crowding in at the door, goggling at us.

Rogers raised his voice to be heard over the continuous rolling of the drum. "Tell me something," he said to Bellows. "Supplies of food were to meet us at the mouth of the Ammonoosuc. They were sent, weren't they?"

"Oh yes," Bellows replied, and he looked frightened. "They were in charge of Lieutenant Stephens."

"So? What did he do with 'em?"

"He brought 'em back," Bellows said. "He waited several days; then he thought you and your command must have been wiped out — and he heard firing one morning and thought it might be French and Indians, so he decided he'd better start for home."

"Listen," Rogers said, and he spoke as much to the settlers and Provincials who had crowded in through the doorway as he did to Bellows. "We finished St. Francis for you. There isn't any more St. Francis, and you can begin to move up that way and clear the land and live in peace whenever you're a mind to. But this Lieutenant Stephens who got frightened and took our food away when we were firing muskets to show him we were coming — we'll have to have a settlement with him. He isn't here, is he?"

"No," Bellows said tremulously. "He's gone back to Crown Point. You'll be going that way, too, Major, I take it?"

"No, not till afterwards," Rogers answered in a choking voice.

The crowding people started stupidly at him as he stood before them in the firelight, unbelievably gaunt, barefooted, covered with bruises, tattered strips of strouding sagging around his legs. The shredded buckskin leggins hung loosely on his emaciated flanks; singular torn bits of garments concealed little of his ribs and bony chest: his hands were scarred, burned, sooty and pitch-stained from his labors with the raft.

"No, we'll see Lieutenant Stephens at Crown Point afterwards," Rogers said. "Now get me some beef — fat beef. I'm going back to the Ammonoosuc myself."

The Last of the Jacobites
by Sir Walter Scott

1765? According to unverifiable legends Charles Edward Stuart, the Young Pretender who led the unsuccessful insurrection of 1745, returned to England at a later date. In one of Walter Scott's finest novels, *Redgauntlet*, Charles does return and keeps a rendezvous with a group of his Jacobite supporters at a lonely inn near the Scots border. Redgauntlet, the ardent leader of the Jacobites, has kidnaped his nephew, Darsie Latimer, in the hope of enlisting him in the Stuart cause.

Redgauntlet next led the way into a very small room; adjoining which, but divided by a partition, was one of apparently larger dimensions; for they heard the trampling of the heavy boots of the period, as if several persons were walking to and fro, and conversing in low and anxious whispers.

"Here," said Redgauntlet to his nephew, as he disencumbered him from the riding-skirt and the mask, "I restore you to yourself, and trust you will lay aside all effeminate thoughts with this feminine dress. Do not blush at having worn a disguise to which kings and heroes have been reduced. It is when female craft or female cowardice find their way into a manly bosom, that he who entertains these sentiments should take eternal shame to himself for thus having resembled womankind. Follow me, while Lilias remains here. I will introduce you to those whom I hope to see associated with you in the most glorious cause that hand ever drew sword in."

Darsie paused. "Uncle," he said, "my person is in your hands; but remember, my will is my own. I will not be hurried into any resolution of importance. Remember what I have already said — what I now repeat — that I will take no step of importance but upon conviction."

"But canst thou be convinced, thou foolish boy, without hearing and understanding the grounds on which we act?"

So saying, he took Darsie by the arm, and walked with him to the next room — a large apartment, partly filled with miscellaneous articles of commerce, chiefly connected with contraband trade; where, among bales and barrels, sat, or walked to and fro, several gentlemen, whose manners and looks seemed superior to the plain riding-dresses which they wore.

There was a grave and stern anxiety upon their countenances, when, on Redgauntlet's entrance they drew from their separate coteries into one group around him, and saluted him with a formality, which had something in it of ominous melancholy. As Darsie looked around the circle, he could discern in it few traces of that adventurous hope which urges men upon desperate enterprises; and began to believe that the conspiracy would dissolve of itself, with the necessity of his placing himself in direct opposition to so violent a character as his uncle, and incurring the hazard with which such opposition must needs be attended.

Mr. Redgauntlet, however, did not, or would not, see any such marks of depression of spirit amongst his coadjutors, but met them with cheerful countenance and a warm greeting of welcome. "Happy to meet you here, my lord," he said, bowing low to a slender young man. "I trust you come with the pledges of your noble father, of B———, and all that loyal house. — Sir Richard, what news in the west? I am told you had two hundred men on foot to have joined when the fatal retreat from Derby was commenced. When the White Standard is again displayed, it shall not be turned back so easily, either by the force of its enemies, or the falsehood of its friends. — Doctor Grumball, I bow to the representative of Oxford, the mother of learning and loyalty. — Pengwinion, you Cornish chough, has this good wind blown you north? — Ah, my brave Cambro-Britons, when was Wales last in the race of honour?"

Such and such-like compliments he dealt around, which were in general answered by silent bows; but when he saluted one of his own countrymen by the name of MacKellar, and greeted Maxwell of Summertrees by that of Pate-in-Peril, the latter replied, "that if Pate were not a fool, he would be Pate-in-Safety;" and the former, a thin old gentleman, in tarnished embroidery, said bluntly, "Ay, troth, Redgauntlet, I am here just like yourself; I have little to lose — they that took my land the last time, may take my life this; and that is all I care about it."

The English gentlemen, who were still in possession of their paternal estates, looked doubtfully on each other, and there was something whispered among them of the fox which had lost his tail.

Redgauntlet hastened to address them. "I think, my lords and gentlemen," he said, "that I can account for something like sadness which has crept upon an assembly gathered together for so noble a purpose. Our numbers seem, when thus assembled, too small and inconsiderable to shake the firm-seated usurpation of a half century. But do not count us by what we are in thew and muscle, but by what our summons can do among our countrymen. In this small party are those who have power to raise battalions, and those who have wealth to pay them. And do not believe our friends who are absent are cold or indifferent to the cause. Let us once light the signal, and it will be hailed by all who retain love for the Stuart, and by all — a more numerous body — who hate the Elector. Here I have letters from — — "

Sir Richard Glendale interrupted the speaker. "We all confide, Redgauntlet, in your valour and skill — we admire your perseverance; and probably nothing short of your strenuous exertions, and the emulation awakened by your noble and disinterested conduct, could have brought so many of us, the scattered remnant of a disheartened party, to meet together once again in solemn consultation; — for I take it, gentlemen," he said, looking round, "this is only a consultation."

"Nothing more," said the young lord.

"Nothing more," said Doctor Grumball, shaking his large academical peruke.

And "Only a consultation," was echoed by the others.

Redgauntlet bit his lips. "I had hopes," he said, "that the discourses I have held with most of you, from time to time, had ripened into more maturity than your words imply, and that we were here to execute as well as to deliberate; and for this we stand prepared. I can raise five hundred men with my whistle."

"Five hundred men!" said one of the Welsh squires; "Cot bless us! and, pray you, what good could five hundred men do?"

"All that priming does for the cannon, Mr. Meredith," answered Redgauntlet; "it will enable us to seize Carlisle, and you know what our friends have engaged for in that case."

"Yes — but," said the young nobleman, "you must not hurry us on too fast, Mr. Redgauntlet; we are all, I believe, as sincere and truehearted in this business as you are, but we will not be driven forward blindfold. We owe caution to ourselves and our families, as well as to those whom we are empowered to represent on this occasion."

"Who hurries you, my lord? Who is it that would drive this meeting forward blindfold? I do not understand your lordship," said Redgauntlet.

"Nay," said Sir Richard Glendale, "at least do not let us fall under our old reproach of disagreeing among ourselves. What my lord means, Redgauntlet, is, that we have this morning heard it is uncertain whether you could even bring that body of men whom you count upon; your country-

men, Mr. MacKellar, seemed, just before you came in, to doubt whether
your people would rise in any force, unless you could produce the authority of your nephew."

"I might ask," said Redgauntlet, "what right MacKellar, or any one,
has to doubt my being able to accomplish what I stand pledged for? —
But our hopes consist in our unity. — Here stands my nephew. — Gentlemen, I present to you my kinsman, Sir Arthur Darsie Redgauntlet of
that Ilk."

"Gentlemen," said Darsie, with a throbbing bosom, for he felt the crisis
a very painful one, "Allow me to say, that I suspend expressing my sentiments on the important subject under discussion, until I have heard those
of the present meeting."

"Proceed in your deliberations, gentlemen," said Redgauntlet; "I will
show my nephew such reasons for acquiescing in the result, as will entirely remove any scruples which may hang around his mind."

Dr. Grumball now coughed, "shook his ambrosial curls," and addressed
the assembly.

"The principles of Oxford," he said, "are well understood, since she was
the last to resign herself to the Arch-Usurper — since she has condemned,
by her sovereign authority, the blasphemous, atheistical, and anarchical
tenets of Locke, and other deluders of the public mind. Oxford will give
men, money and countenance, to the cause of the rightful monarch. But
we have been often deluded by foreign powers, who have availed themselves of our zeal to stir up civil dissensions in Britain, not for the advantage of our blessed though banished monarch, but to engender disturbances
by which they might profit, while we, their tools, are sure to be ruined.
Oxford, therefore, will not rise, unless our Sovereign comes in person to
claim our allegiance, in which case, God forbid we should refuse him
our best obedience."

"It is a very good advice," said Mr. Meredith.

"In troth," said Sir Richard Glendale, "it is the very keystone of our enterprise, and the only condition upon which I myself and others could
ever have dreamt of taking up arms. No insurrection which has not Charles
Edward himself at its head, will ever last longer than till a single foot-
company of redcoats march to disperse it."

"This is my own opinion, and that of all my family," said the young
nobleman already mentioned; "and I own I am somewhat surprised at
being summoned to attend a dangerous rendezvous such as this, before

something certain could have been stated to us on this most important preliminary point."

"Pardon me, my lord," said Redgauntlet; "I have not been so unjust
either to myself or my friends — I had no means of communicating to our
distant confederates (without the greatest risk of discovery) what is known
to some of my honourable friends. As courageous, and as resolved, as when
twenty years since, he threw himself into the wilds of Moidart, Charles
Edward has instantly complied with the wishes of his faithful subjects.
Charles Edward is in this country — Charles Edward is in this house! —
Charles Edward waits but your present decision, to receive the homage
of those who have ever called themselves his loyal liegemen. He that would
now turn his coat, and change his note, must do so under the eye of his
sovereign."

There was a deep pause. Those among the conspirators whom mere
habit, or a desire of preserving consistency, had engaged in the affair, now
saw with terror their retreat cut off; and others, who at a distance had regarded the proposed enterprise as hopeful, trembled when the moment
of actually embarking in it was thus unexpectedly and almost inevitably
precipitated.

"How now, my lords and gentlemen!" said Redgauntlet; "Is it delight
and rapture that keep you thus silent? where are the eager welcomes that
should be paid your rightful King, who a second time confides his person
to the care of his subjects, undeterred by the hairbreadth escapes and severe privations of his former expedition? I hope there is no gentleman here
that is not ready to redeem, in his Prince's presence, the pledge of fidelity
which he offered in his absence?"

"I, at least," said the young nobleman, resolutely, and laying his hand
on his sword, "will not be that coward. If Charles is come to these shores,
I will be the first to give him welcome, and to devote my life and fortune
to his service."

"Before Cot," said Mr. Meredith, "I do not see that Mr. Redcantlet has
left us any thing else to do."

"Stay," said Summertrees, "there is yet one other question. Has he brought
any of those Irish rapparees with him, who broke the neck of our last
glorious affair?"

"Not a man of them," said Redgauntlet.

"I trust," said Dr. Grumball, "that there are no Catholic priests in his
company? I would not intrude on the private conscience of my Sovereign,

but, as an unworthy son of the Church of England, it is my duty to consider her security."

"Not a Popish dog or cat is there, to bark or mew about his Majesty," said Redgauntlet. "Old Shaftesbury himself could not wish a prince's person more secure from Popery — which may not be the worst religion in the world, notwithstanding. Any more doubts, gentlemen? can no more plausible reasons be discovered for postponing the payment of our duty, and discharge of our oaths and engagements? Meantime your King waits your declaration — by my faith he hath but a frozen reception!"

"Redgauntlet," said Sir Richard Glendale, calmly, "your reproaches shall not goad me into any thing of which my reason disapproves. That I respect my engagement as much as you do, is evident, since I am here, ready to support it with the best blood in my veins. But has the King really come hither entirely unattended?"

"He has no man with him but young _____, as aide-de-camp, and a single valet-de-chambre."

"No _man;_ — but, Redgauntlet, as you are a gentleman, has he no _woman_ with him?"

Redgauntlet cast his eyes on the ground and replied, "I am sorry to say — he has."

The company looked at each other, and remained silent for a moment. At length Sir Richard proceeded. "I need not repeat to you, Mr. Redgauntlet, what is the well-grounded opinion of His Majesty's friends concerning that most unhappy connexion; there is but one sense and feeling amongst us upon the subject. I must conclude that our humble remonstrances were communicated by you, sir, to the King?"

"In the same strong terms in which they were couched," replied Redgauntlet. "I love his Majesty's cause more than I fear his displeasure."

"But, apparently, our humble expostulation has produced no effect. This lady, who has crept into his bosom, has a sister in the Elector of Hanover's Court, and yet we are well assured that every point of our most private communication is placed in her keeping."

"_Varium et mutabile semper femina,_" said Dr. Grumball.

"She puts his secrets into her work-bag," said Maxwell; "and out they fly whenever she opens it. If I must hang, I would wish it to be in somewhat a better rope than the string of a lady's hussey."

"Are you, too, turning dastard, Maxwell?" said Redgauntlet, in a whisper.

"Not I," said Maxwell; "let us fight for it, and let them win and wear us; but to be betrayed by a brimstone like that — — "

"Be temperate, gentlemen," said Redgauntlet; "the foible of which you complain so heavily has always been that of kings and heroes; which I feel strongly confident the King will surmount, upon the humble entreaty of his best servants, and when he sees them ready to peril their all in his cause, upon the slight condition of his resigning the society of a female favorite, of whom I have seen reason to think he hath been himself for some time wearied. But let us not press upon him rashly with our well-meant zeal. He has a princely will, as becomes his princely birth, and we, gentlemen, who are royalists, should be the last to take advantage of circumstances to limit its exercise. I am as much surprised and hurt as you can be, to find that he has made her the companion of his journey, increasing every chance of treachery and detection. But do not let us insist upon a sacrifice so humiliating, while he has scarce placed a foot upon the beach of his kingdom. Let us act generously by our Sovereign; and when we have shown what we will do for him, we shall be able, with better face, to state what it is we expect him to concede."

"Indeed, I think it is but a pity," said MacKellar, "when so many pretty gentlemen are got together, that they should part without the flash of a sword among them."

"I should be of that gentleman's opinion," said Lord _____, had I nothing to lose but my life; but I frankly own, that the conditions on which our family agreed to join having been, in this instance, left unfulfilled, I will not peril the whole fortunes of our house on the doubtful fidelity of an artful woman."

"I am sorry to see your lordship," said Redgauntlet, "take a course which is more likely to secure your house's wealth than to augment its honours."

"How am I to understand your language, sir?" said the young nobleman, haughtily.

"Nay, gentlemen," said Dr. Grumball, interposing, "do not let friends quarrel; we are all zealous for the cause — but truly, although I know the license claimed by the great in such matters, and can, I hope, make due allowance, there is, I may say, an indecorum in a prince who comes to claim the allegiance of the Church of England, arriving on such an errand with such a companion —*si non casté, cauté, tamen.*"

"I wonder how the Church of England came to be so heartily attached to his merry old namesake," said Redgauntlet.

Sir Richard Glendale then took up the question, as one whose authority and experience gave him right to speak with much weight.

"We have no leisure for hesitation," he said; "it is full time that we decide what course we are to hold. I feel as much as you, Mr. Redgauntlet, the delicacy of capitulating with our Sovereign in his present condition. But I must also think of the total ruin of the cause, the confiscation and bloodshed which will take place among his adherents, and all through the infatuation with which he adheres to a woman who is the pensionary of the present minister, as she was for years Sir Robert Walpole's. Let his Majesty send her back to the continent and the sword on which I now lay my hand shall instantly be unsheathed, and, I trust, many hundred others at the same moment."

The other persons present testified their unanimous acquiescence in what Sir Richard Glendale had said.

"I see you have taken your resolutions, gentlemen," said Redgauntlet; "unwisely, I think, because I believe that, by softer and more generous proceedings, you would have been more likely to carry a point which I think as desirable as you do. But what is to be done if Charles should refuse, with the inflexibility of his grandfather, to comply with this request of yours? Do you mean to abandon him to his fate?"

"God forbid!" said Sir Richard, hastily; "and God forgive you, Mr. Redgauntlet, for breathing such a thought. No! I for one will, with all duty and humility, see him safe back to his vessel, and defend him with my life against whoever shall assail him. But when I have seen his sails spread, my next act will be to secure, if I can, my own safety, by retiring to my house; or, if I find our engagement, as is too probable, has taken wind, by surrendering myself to the next Justice of Peace, and giving security that hereafter I shall live quiet, and submit to the ruling powers."

Again the rest of the persons present intimated their agreement in opinion with the speaker.

"Well, gentlemen," said Redgauntlet, "it is not for me to oppose the opinion of every one; and I must do you the justice to say, that the King has, in the present instance, neglected a condition of your agreement, which was laid before him in very distinct terms. The question now is, who is to acquaint him with the result of this conference? for I presume you would not wait on him in a body to make the proposal, that he should dismiss a person from his family as the price of your allegiance."

"I think Mr. Redgauntlet should make the explanation" said Lord _____. "As he has, doubtless, done justice to our remonstrances by communicating them to the King, no one can, with such propriety and force, state the natural and inevitable consequence of their being neglected."

"Now, I think," said Redgauntlet, "that those who make the objection should state it; for I am confident the King will hardly believe, on less authority than that of the heir of the loyal House of B——, that he is the first to seek an evasion of his pledge to join him."

"An evasion, sir!" repeated Lord ————, fiercely. "I have borne too much from you already, and this I will not endure. Favour me with your company to the downs yonder."

Redgauntlet laughed scornfully, and was about to follow the fiery young man, when Sir Richard again interposed. "Are we to exhibit," he said, "the last symptoms of the dissolution of our party, by turning our swords against each other? — Be patient, Lord ————; in such conferences as this, much must pass unquestioned which might brook challenge elsewhere. There is a privilege of party as of parliament — men cannot, in emergency, stand upon picking phrases. — Gentlemen, if you will extend your confidence in me so far, I will wait upon his Majesty, and I hope my Lord ———— and Mr. Redgauntlet will accompany me. I trust the explanation of this unpleasant matter will prove entirely satisfactory, and that we shall find ourselves at liberty to render our homage to our Sovereign without reserve, when I for one will be the first to peril all in his just quarrel."

Redgauntlet at once stepped forward. "My lord," he said, "if my zeal made me say any thing in the slightest degree offensive, I wish it unsaid, and ask your pardon. A gentleman can do no more."

"I could not have asked Mr. Redgauntlet to do so much," said the young nobleman, willingly accepting the hand which Redgauntlet offered. "I know no man living from whom I could take so much reproof without a sense of degradation, as from himself."

"Let me then hope, my lord, that you will go with Sir Richard and me to the presence. Your warm blood will heat our zeal — our colder resolves will temper yours."

The young lord smiled, and shook his head. "Alas! Mr. Redgauntlet," he said, "I am ashamed to say, that in zeal you surpass us all. But I will not refuse this mission, provided you will permit Sir Arthur, your nephew, also to accompany us."

"My nephew?" said Redgauntlet, and seemed to hesitate, then added, "Most certainly. — I trust," he said looking at Darsie, "he will bring to his Prince's presence such sentiments as fit the occasion."

It seemed however to Darsie, that his uncle would rather have left him behind, had he not feared that he might in that case have been influenced by, or might perhaps himself influence, the unresolved confederates with whom he must have associated during his absence.

"I will go," said Redgauntlet, "and request admission."

In a moment after he returned, and without speaking, motioned for the young nobleman to advance. He did so, followed by Sir Richard Glendale and Darsie, Redgauntlet himself bringing up the rear. A short passage, and a few steps, brought them to the door of the presence-chamber, in which the Royal Wanderer was to receive their homage. It was the upper loft of one of those cottages which made additions to the Old Inn, poorly furnished, dusty, and in disorder; for rash as the enterprise might be considered, they had been still careful not to draw the attention of strangers by any particular attentions to the personal accommodation of the Prince. He was seated, when the deputies, as they might be termed, of his remaining adherents entered; and as he rose, and came forward and bowed, in acceptance of their salutation, it was with a dignified courtesy which at once supplied whatever was deficient in external pomp, and converted the wretched garret into a saloon worthy of the occasion.

It is needless to add, that he was the same personage already introduced in the character of Father Buonaventure, by which name he was distinguished at Fairladies. His dress was not different from what he then wore, excepting that he had a loose riding-coat of camlet, under which he carried an efficient cut-and-thrust sword, instead of his walking rapier, and also a pair of pistols.

Redgauntlet presented to him successively the young Lord _____, and his kinsman, Sir Arthur Darsie Redgauntlet, who trembled as, bowing and kissing his hand, he found himself surprised into what might be construed an act of high treason, which yet he saw no safe means to avoid.

Sir Richard Glendale seemed personally known to Charles Edward, who received him with a mixture of dignity and affection, and seemed to sympathize with the tears which rushed into that gentleman's eyes as he bid his Majesty welcome to his native kingdom.

"Yes, my good Sir Richard," said the unfortunate Prince, in a tone melancholy, yet resolved, "Charles Edward is with his faithful friends once more — not, perhaps, with his former gay hopes which undervalued danger, but with the same determined concept of the worst which can befall him, in claiming his own rights and those of his country."

"I rejoice, sire — and yet, alas! I must also grieve, to see you once more on the British shores," said Sir Richard Glendale, and stopped short — a tumult of contradictory feelings preventing his further utterance.

"It is the call of my faithful and suffering people which alone could have induced me to take once more the sword in my hand. For my own part,

Sir Richard, when I have reflected how many of my loyal and devoted friends perished by the sword and by proscription, or died indigent and neglected in a foreign land, I have often sworn that no view to my personal aggrandizement should induce me to agitate a title which has cost my followers so dear. But since so many men of worth and honour conceive the cause of England and Scotland to be linked with that of Charles Stuart, I must follow their brave example, and, laying aside all other considerations, once more stand forward as their deliverer. I am, however, come hither upon your invitation; and as you are so completely acquainted with circumstances to which my absence must necessarily have rendered me a stranger, I must be a mere tool in the hands of my friends. I know well I never can refer myself implicitly to more loyal hearts or wiser heads, than Herries Redgauntlet, and Sir Richard Glendale. Give me your advice, then, how we are to proceed, and decide upon the fate of Charles Edward."

Redgauntlet looked at Sir Richard, as if to say, "Can you press any additional or unpleasant condition at a moment like this?" And the other shook his head and looked down, as if his resolution was unaltered, and yet as feeling all the delicacy of the situation.

There was a silence, which was broken by the unfortunate representative of an unhappy dynasty, with some appearance of irritation. "This is strange, gentlemen," he said; "you have sent for me from the bosom of my family, to head an adventure of doubt and danger; and when I come, your own minds seem to be still irresolute. I had not expected this on the part of two such men."

"For me, sire," said Redgauntlet, "the steel of my sword is not truer than the temper of my mind."

"My Lord ————'s and mine are equally so," said Sir Richard; "but you had in charge, Mr. Redgauntlet, to convey our request to his Majesty, coupled with certain conditions."

"And I discharged my duty to his Majesty and to you," said Redgauntlet.

"I looked at no condition, gentlemen," said their King, with dignity, "save that which called me here to assert my rights in person. *That* I have fulfilled at no common risk. Here I stand to keep my word, and I expect of you to be true to yours."

"There was, or should have been something more than that in our proposal, please your Majesty," said Sir Richard. "There was a condition annexed to it."

"I saw it not," said Charles, interrupting him. "Out of tenderness towards the noble hearts of whom I think so highly, I would neither see nor read any thing which could lessen them in my love and my esteem. Conditions can have no part betwixt Prince and subject."

"Sire," said Redgauntlet, kneeling on one knee, "I see from Sir Richard's countenance he deems it my fault that your Majesty seems ignorant of what your subjects desired that I should communicate to your Majesty. For Heaven's sake! for the sake of all my past services and sufferings, leave not such a stain upon my honour! The note, Number D., of which this is a copy, referred to the painful subject to which Sir Richard again directs your attention."

"You press upon me, gentlemen," said the Prince, colouring highly, "recollections, which, as I hold them most alien to your character, I would willingly have banished from my memory. I did not suppose that my loyal subjects would think so poorly of me, as to use my depressed circumstances as a reason for forcing themselves into my domestic privacies, and stipulating arrangements with their King regarding matters, in which the meanest hinds claim the privilege of thinking for themselves. In affairs of state and public policy, I will ever be guided as becomes a prince, by the advice of my wisest counsellors; in those which regard my private affections, and my domestic arrangements, I claim the same freedom of will which I allow to all my subjects, and without which a crown were less worth wearing than a beggar's bonnet."

"May it please your Majesty," said Sir Richard Glendale, "I see it must be my lot to speak unwilling truths; but believe me, I do so with as much profound respect as deep regret. It is true, we have called you to head a mighty undertaking, and that your Majesty, preferring honour to safety, and the love of your country to your own ease, has condescended to become our leader. But we also pointed out as a necessary and indispensable preparatory step to the achievement of our purpose — and, I must say, as a positive condition of our engaging in it — that an individual, supposed, — I presume not to guess how truly, — to have your Majesty's more intimate confidence, and believed, I will not say on absolute proof, but upon the most pregnant suspicion, to be capable of betraying that confidence to the Elector of Hanover, should be removed from your royal household and society."

"This is too insolent, Sir Richard!" said Charles Edward. "Have you inveigled me into your power to bait me in this unseemly manner? — And you, Redgauntlet, why did you suffer matters to come to such a point as this, without making me more distinctly aware what insults were to be practised on me?"

"My gracious Prince," said Redgauntlet, "I am so far to blame in this, that I did not think so slight an impediment as that of a woman's society could have really interrupted an undertaking of this magnitude. I am a plain man, sire, and speak but bluntly; I could not have dreamt but what, within the first five minutes of this interview, either Sir Richard and his friends would have ceased to insist upon a condition so ungrateful to your Majesty, or that your Majesty would have sacrificed this unhappy attachment to the sound advice, or even to the over-anxious suspicions, of so many faithful subjects. I saw no entanglement in such a difficulty, which on either side might not have been broken through like a cobweb."

"You were mistaken, sir," said Charles Edward, "entirely mistaken — as much so as you are at this moment, when you think in your heart my refusal to comply with this insolent proposition is dictated by a childish and romantic passion for an individual. I tell you, sir, I could part with that person to-morrow, without an instant's regret — that I have had thoughts of dismissing her from my court, for reasons known to myself; but that I will never betray my rights as a sovereign and a man, by taking this step to secure the favour of any one, or to purchase that allegiance, which, if you owe it to me at all, is due to me as my birthright."

"I am sorry for this," said Redgauntlet; "I hope both your Majesty and Sir Richard will reconsider your resolutions, or forbear this discussion, in a conjuncture so pressing. I trust your Majesty will recollect that you are on hostile ground; that our preparations cannot have so far escaped notice as to permit us now with safety to retreat from our purpose; insomuch, that it is with the deepest anxiety of heart I foresee even danger to your own royal person, unless you can generously give your subjects the satisfaction, which Sir Richard seems to think they are obstinate in demanding."

"And deep indeed your anxiety ought to be," said the Prince. "Is it in these circumstances of personal danger in which you expect to overcome a resolution, which is founded on a sense of what is due to me as a man or a prince. If the axe and scaffold were ready before the windows of Whitehall, I would rather tread the same path with my great-grandfather, than concede the slightest point in which my honour is concerned."

He spoke these words with a determined accent, and looked around him on the company, all of whom (excepting Darsie, who saw, he thought, a fair period to a most perilous enterprise) seemed in deep anxiety and confusion. At length, Sir Richard spoke in a solemn and melancholy tone.

"If the safety," he said, "of poor Richard Glendale were alone concerned in this matter, I have never valued my life enough to weigh it against the

slightest point of your Majesty's service. But I am only a messenger — a
commissioner, who must execute my trust, and upon whom a thousand
voices will cry Curse and woe, if I do it not with fidelity. All of your adherents, even Redgauntlet himself, see certain ruin to this enterprise — the
greatest danger to your Majesty's person — the utter destruction of all your
party and friends, if they insist not on the point, which, unfortunately,
your Majesty is so unwilling to concede. I speak it with a heart full of anguish — with a tongue unable to utter my emotions — but it must be spoken
— the fatal truth — that if your royal goodness cannot yield to us a boon
which we hold necessary to our security and your own, your Majesty with
one word disarms ten thousand men, ready to draw their swords in your
behalf; or, to speak yet more plainly, you annihilate even the semblance
of a royal party in Great Britain."

"And why do you not add," said the Prince, scornfully, "that the men
who have been ready to assume arms in my behalf, will atone for their
treason to the Elector, by delivering me up to the fate for which so many
proclamations have destined me? Carry my head to St. James's, gentlemen; you will do a more acceptable and a more honourable action, than,
having inveigled me into a situation which places me so completely in
your power, to dishonour yourselves by propositions which dishonour me."

"My God, sire!" exclaimed Sir Richard, clasping his hands together, in
impatience, "of what great and inexpiable crime can your Majesty's ancestors have been guilty, that they have been punished by the infliction
of judicial blindness on their whole generation! — Come, my Lord _____,
we must to our friends."

"By your leave, Sir Richard," said the young nobleman, "not till we have
learned what measures can be taken for his Majesty's personal safety."

"Care not for me, young man," said Charles Edward; "when I was in
the society of Highland robbers and cattle-drovers, I was safer than I now
hold myself among the representatives of the best blood in England. —
Farewell, gentlemen — I will shift for myself."

"This must never be," said Redgauntlet. "Let me that brought you to
the point of danger, at least provide for your safe retreat."

So saying, he hastily left the apartment, followed by his nephew. The
Wanderer, averting his eyes from Lord _____ and Sir Richard Glendale,
threw himself into a seat at the upper end of the apartment, while they,
in much anxiety, stood together, at a distance from him, and conversed
in whispers.

They Fight the Serapis

by Herman Melville

> 1779 The War of the American Revolution was not
> materially affected by John Paul Jones' greatest na-
> val victory; nor did Jones' triumph receive adequate
> recognition in America. But today Jones is regarded
> by many as America's greatest naval hero. This ac-
> count of the defeat of the *Serapis* by the *Bon Homme
> Richard* is taken from Herman Melville's only full-
> length historical novel, *His Fifty Years of Exile (Israel
> Potter)*. It contains some typically Melvillian prose.

The battle between the *Bon Homme Richard* and the *Serapis* stands
in history as the first signal collision on the sea between the Englishman
and the American. For obstinacy, mutual hatred, and courage, it is without precedent or subsequent in the story of ocean. The strife long hung
undetermined, but the English flag struck in the end.

There would seem to be something singularly indicatory in this engagement. It may involve at once a type, a parallel, and a prophecy. Sharing
the same blood with England, and yet her proved foe in two wars — not
wholly inclined at bottom to forget an old grudge — intrepid, unprincipled,
reckless, predatory, with boundless ambition, civilized in externals but a
savage at heart, America is, or may yet be, the Paul Jones of nations.

Regarded in this indicatory light, the battle between the *Bon Homme
Richard* and the *Serapis* — in itself so curious — may well enlist our interest.

Never was there a fight so snarled. The intricacy of those incidents which
defy the narrator's extrication, is not illy figured in that bewildering inter-
tanglement of all the yards and anchors of the two ships, which confounded
them for the time in one chaos of devastation.

Elsewhere than here the reader must go who seeks an elaborate version
of the fight, or, indeed, much of any regular account of it whatever. The
writer is but brought to mention the battle because he must needs follow,
in all events, the fortunes of the humble adventurer whose life he records.
Yet this necessarily involves some general view of each conspicuous inci-
dent in which he shares.

Several circumstances of the place and time served to invest the fight
with a certain scenic atmosphere casting a light almost poetic over the

437

wild gloom of its tragic results. The battle was fought between the hours of seven and ten at night; the height of it was under a full harvest moon, in view of thousands of distant spectators crowning the high cliffs of Yorkshire.

From the Tees to the Humber, the eastern coast of Britain, for the most part, wears a savage, melancholy, and Calabrian aspect. It is in course of incessant decay. Every year the isle which repulses nearly all other foes, succumbs to the Attila assaults of the deep. Here and there the base of the cliffs is strewn with masses of rock, undermined by the waves, and tumbled headlong below, where, sometimes the water completely surrounds them, showing in shattered confusion detached rocks, pyramids, and obelisks, rising half-revealed from the surf — the Tadmores of the wasteful desert of the sea. Nowhere is this desolation more marked than for those fifty miles of coast between Flamborough Head and the Spurm.

Weathering out the gale which had driven them from Leith, Paul's ships for a few days were employed in giving chase to various merchantmen and colliers; capturing some, sinking others, and putting the rest to flight. Off the mouth of the Humber they ineffectually manoeuvred with a view of drawing out a king's frigate, reported to be lying at anchor within. At another time a large fleet was encountered, under convoy of some ships of force. But their panic caused the fleet to hug the edge of perilous shoals very nigh the land, where, by reason of his having no competent pilot, Paul durst not approach to molest them. The same night he saw two strangers further out at sea, and chased them until three in the morning, when, getting pretty nigh, he surmised that they must needs be vessels of his own squadron, which, previous to his entering the Firth of Forth, had separated from his command. Daylight proved this supposition correct. Five vessels of the original squadron were now once more in company. About noon a fleet of forty merchantmen appeared coming round Flamborough Head, protected by two English men-of-war, the *Serapis* and *Countess of Scarborough*. Descrying the five cruisers sailing down, the forty sail, like forty chickens, fluttered in a panic under the wing of the shore. Their armed protectors bravely steered from the land, making the disposition for battle. Promptly accepting the challenge, Paul, giving the signal to his consorts, earnestly pressed forward. But, earnest as he was, it was seven in the evening ere the encounter began. Meantime his comrades, heedless of his signals, sailed independently along. Dismissing them from present consideration, we confine ourselves, for a while, to the *Richard* and the *Serapis*, the grand duellists of the fight.

The *Richard* carried a motley crew, to keep whom in order one hundred and thirty-five soldiers — themselves a hybrid band — had been put on board, commanded by French officers of inferior rank. Her armament was similarly heterogeneous; guns of all sorts and calibres; but about equal on the whole to those of a thirty-two-gun frigate. The spirit of baneful intermixture pervaded this craft throughout.

The *Serapis* was a frigate of fifty guns, more than half of which individually exceeded in calibre any one gun of the *Richard*. She had a crew of some three hundred and twenty trained man-of-war's men.

There is something in a naval engagement which radically distinguishes it from one on the land. The ocean, at times, has what is called its *sea* and its *trough of the sea;* but it has neither rivers, woods, banks, towns, nor mountains. In mild weather it is one hammered plain. Stratagems, like those of disciplined armies — ambuscades, like those of Indians, are impossible. All is clear, open, fluent. The very element which sustains the combatants, yields at the stroke of a feather. One wind and one tide at one time operate upon all who here engage. This simplicity renders a battle between two men-of-war, with their huge white wings, more akin to the Miltonic contests of archangels than to *the comparatively squalid* tussles of earth.

As the ships neared, a hazy darkness overspread the water. The moon was not yet risen. Objects were perceived with difficulty. Borne by a soft moist breeze over gentle waves, they came within pistol-shot. Owing to the obscurity, and the known neighborhood of other vessels, the *Serapis* was uncertain who the *Richard* was. Through the dim mist each ship loomed forth to the other vast, but indistinct, as the ghost of Morven. Sounds of the trampling of resolute men echoed from either hull, whose tight decks dully resounded like drum-heads in a funeral march.

The *Serapis* hailed. She was answered by a broadside. For half an hour the combatants deliberately manoeuvred, continually changing their position, but always within shot fire. The *Serapis* — the better sailer of the two — kept critically circling the *Richard,* making lunging advances now and then, and as suddenly steering off; hate causing her to act not unlike a wheeling cock about a hen, when stirred by the contrary passion. Meantime, though within easy speaking distance, no further syllable was exchanged; but an incessant cannonade was kept up.

At this point, a third party, the *Scarborough,* drew near, seemingly desirous of giving assistance to her consort. But thick smoke was now added to the night's natural obscurity. The *Scarborough* imperfectly discerned two ships, and plainly saw the common fire they made; but which was which, she could not tell. Eager to befriend the *Serapis*, she durst not fire a gun, lest she might unwittingly act the part of a foe. As when a hawk and a crow are clawing and beaking high in the air, a second crow flying near, will seek to join the battle, but finding no fair chance to engage, at last flies away to the woods; just so did the *Scarborough* now. Prudence dictated the step; because several chance shots — from which of the combatants could not be known — had already struck the *Scarborough*. So, unwilling uselessly to expose herself, off went for the present this baffled and ineffectual friend.

Not long after, an invisible hand came and set down a great yellow lamp in the east. The hand reached up unseen from below the horizon, and set the lamp down right on the rim of the horizon, as on a threshold; as much as to say, Gentlemen warriors, permit me a little to light up this rather gloomy looking subject. The lamp was the round harvest moon; the one solitary foot-light of the scene. But scarcely did the rays from the lamp pierce that languid haze. Objects before perceived with difficulty, now glimmered ambiguously. Bedded in strange vapors, the great foot light cast a dubious, half demoniac glare across the waters, like the phantasmagoric stream sent athwart a London flagging in a night-rain from an apothecary's blue and green window. Through this sardonical mist, the face of the Man-in-the-Moon — looking right towards the combatants, as if he were standing in a trap-door of the sea, leaning forward leisurely with his arms complacently folded over upon the edge of the horizon — this queer face wore a serious, apishly self-satisfied leer, as if the Man-in-the-Moon had somehow secretly put up the ships to their contest, and in the depths of his malignant old soul was not unpleased to see how well his charms worked. There stood the grinning Man-in-the-Moon, his head just dodging into view over the rim of the sea: — Mephistopheles prompter of the stage.

Aided now a little by the planet, one of the consorts of the *Richard*, the *Pallas*, hovering far outside the fight, dimly discerned the suspicious form of a lonely vessel unknown to her. She resolved to engage it, if it proved a foe. But ere they joined, the unknown ship — which proved to be the *Scarborough* — received a broadside at long gun's distance from another consort of the *Richard*, the *Alliance*. The shot whizzed across the broad interval like shuttlecocks across a great hall. Presently the battledores of both batteries were at work, and rapid compliments of shuttlecocks were very promptly exchanged. The adverse consorts of the two main belligerents fought with all the rage of those fiery seconds who in some desperate duels make their principal's quarrel their own. Diverted from the *Richard* and the *Serapis* by this little by-play, the Man-in-the-Moon, all eager to see what it was, somewhat raised himself from his trap-door with an added grin on his face. By this time, off sneaked the *Alliance*, and down swept the *Pallas*, at close quarters engaging the *Scarborough;* an encounter destined in less than an hour to end in the latter ship's striking her flag.

Compared to the *Serapis* and the *Richard*, the *Pallas* and the *Scarborough* were as two pages to two knights. In their immature way they showed the same traits as their fully developed superiors.

The Man-in-the-Moon now raised himself still higher to obtain a better view of affairs.

But the Man-in-the-Moon was not the only spectator. From the high cliffs of the shore, and especially from the great promontory of Flamborough Head, the scene was witnessed by crowds of the islanders. Any rustic might be pardoned his curiosity in view of the spectacle presented. Far in the indistinct distance fleets of frightened merchantmen filled the lower air with their sails, as flakes of snow in a snowstorm by night. Hovering undeterminedly, in another direction, were several of the scattered consorts of Paul, taking no part in the fray. Nearer, was an isolated mist, investing the *Pallas* and *Scarborough* — a mist slowly adrift on the sea, like a floating isle, and at intervals irradiated with sparkles of fire and resonant with the boom of cannon. Further away, in the deeper water, was a lurid cloud, incessantly torn in shreds of lightning, then fusing together again, once more to be rent. As yet this lurid cloud was neither stationary nor slowly adrift, like the first-mentioned one; but, instinct with chaotic vitality, shifted hither and thither, foaming with fire, like a valiant water-spout careening off the coast of Malabar.

To get some idea of the events enacting in that cloud, it will be necessary to enter it; to go and possess it, as a ghost may rush into a body, or the devils into the swine, which running down the steep place perished in the sea; just as the *Richard* is yet to do.

Thus far the *Serapis* and the *Richard* had been manoeuvring and chasséing to each other like partners in a cotillion, all the time indulging in rapid repartee.

But finding at last that the superior manageableness of the enemy's ship enabled him to get the better of the clumsy old Indiaman, the *Richard*, in taking position, Paul, with his wonted resolution, at once sought to neutralize this, by hugging him close. But the attempt to lay the *Richard* right across the head of the *Serapis* ended quite otherwise, in sending the enemy's

jib-boom just over the *Richard*'s great tower of Pisa, where Israel was stationed; who, catching it eagerly, stood for an instant holding to the slack
of the sail, like one grasping a horse by the mane prior to vaulting into
the saddle.

"Aye, hold hard, lad," cried Paul, springing to his side with a coil of
rigging. With a few rapid turns he knitted himself to his foe. The wind
now acting on the sails of the *Serapis* forced her, heel and point, her entire length, cheek by jowl, alongside the *Richard*. The projecting cannon
scraped; the yards interlocked; but the hulls did not touch. A long lane
of darkling water lay wedged between like that narrow canal in Venice
which dozes between two shadowy piles, and high in air is secretly crossed
by the Bridge of Sighs. But where the six yard-arms reciprocally arched
overhead, three bridges of sighs were both seen and heard, as the moon
and wind kept rising.

Into that Lethean canal — pond-like in its smoothness as compared with
the sea without — fell many a poor soul that night; fell, forever forgotten.

As some heaving rent coinciding with a disputed frontier on a volcanic
plain, that boundary abyss was the jaws of death to both sides. So contracted was it, that in many cases the gun-rammers had to be thrust into
the opposite ports, in order to enter to muzzles of their own cannon. It
seemed more an intestine feud, than a fight between strangers. Or, rather,
it was as if the Siamese Twins, oblivious of their fraternal bond, should
rage in unnatural fight.

Ere long, a horrible explosion was heard, drowning for the instant the
cannonade. Two of the old eighteen-pounders — before spoken of, as having been hurriedly set up below the main deck of the *Richard* — burst all
to pieces, killing the sailors who worked them, and shattering all that part
of the hull, as if two exploded steam-boilers had shot out of its opposite
sides. The effect was like the fall of the walls of a house. Little now upheld the great tower of Pisa but a few naked crow stanchions. Thenceforth,
not a few balls from the *Serapis* must have passed straight through the
Richard without grazing her. It was like firing buck-shot through the ribs
of a skeleton.

But, further forward, so deadly was the broadside from the heavy batteries of the *Serapis* — levelled point-blank, and right down the throat and
bowels, as it were, of the *Richard* — that it cleared everything before it.
The men on the *Richard*'s covered gun-deck ran above, like miners from
the fire-damp. Collecting on the forecastle, they continued to fight with
grenades and muskets. The soldiers also were in the lofty tops, whence

they kept up incessant volleys, cascading their fire down as pouring lava from cliffs.

The position of the men in the two ships was now exactly reversed. For while the *Serapis* was tearing the *Richard* all to pieces below deck, and had swept that covered part almost of the last man, the *Richard's* crowd of musketry had complete control of the upper deck of the *Serapis*, where it was almost impossible for man to remain unless as a corpse. Though in the beginning, the tops of the *Serapis* had not been unsupplied with marksmen, yet they had long since been cleared by the over-mastering musketry of the *Richard*. Several, with leg or arm broken by a ball, had been seen going dimly downward from their giddy perch, like falling pigeons shot on the wing.

As busy swallows about barn-eaves and ridge-poles, some of the *Richard's* marksmen, quitting their tops, now went far out on their yard-arms, where they overhung the *Serapis*. From thence they dropped hand-grenades upon her decks, like apples, which growing in one field fall over the fence into another. Others of their band flung the same sour fruit into the open ports of the *Serapis*. A hail-storm of aerial combustion descended and slanted on the *Serapis*, while horizontal thunderbolts rolled crosswise through the subterranean vaults of the *Richard*. The belligerents were no longer, in the ordinary sense of things, an English ship and an American ship. It was a co-partnership and joint-stock combustion-company of both ships; yet divided, even in participation. The two vessels were as two houses, through whose party-wall doors have been cut; one family (the Guelphs) occupying the whole lower story; another family (the Ghibellines) the whole upper story.

Meanwhile, determined Paul flew hither and thither like the meteoric corposant-ball, which shiftingly dances on the tips and verges of ships' rigging in storms. Wherever he went, he seemed to cast a pale light on all faces. Blacked and burnt, his Scotch bonnet was compressed to a gunwad on his head. His Parisian coat, with its gold-laced sleeve laid aside, disclosed to the full the blue tattooing on his arm, which sometimes in fierce gestures streamed in the haze of the cannonade, cabalistically terrific as the charmed standard of Satan. Yet his frenzied manner was less a testimony of his internal commotion than intended to inspirit and madden his men, some of whom seeing him, in transports of intrepidity stripped themselves to their trousers, exposing their naked bodies to the as naked shot. The same was done on the *Serapis*, where several guns were seen surrounded by their buff crews as by fauns and satyrs.

At the beginning of the fray, before the ships interlocked, in the intervals of smoke which swept over the ships as mist over mountain-tops, affording open rents here and there — the gun-deck of the *Serapis,* at certain points, showed, congealed for the instant in all attitudes of dauntlessness, a gallery of marble statues — fighting gladiators.

Stooping low and intent, with one braced leg thrust behind, and one arm thrust forward, curling round towards the muzzle of the gun, there was seen the *loader,* performing his allotted part; on the other side of the carriage, in the same stooping posture, but with both hands holding his long black pole, pike-wise, ready for instant use — stood the eager *rammer and sponger;* while at the breech, crouched the wary *captain of the gun,* his keen eye, like the watching leopard's burning along the range; and behind all, tall and erect, the Egyptian symbol of death, stood the *matchman,* immovable for the moment, his long-handled match reversed. Up to their two long death-dealing batteries, the trained men of the *Serapis* stood and toiled in mechanical magic of discipline. They tended those rows of guns, as Lowell girls the rows of looms in a cotton factory. The Parcae were not more methodical; Atropos not more fatal; the automaton chess-player not more irresponsible.

"Look, lad; I want a grenade, now, thrown down their main hatchway. I saw long piles of cartridges there. The powder monkeys have brought them up faster than they can be used. Take a bucket of combustibles, and let's hear from you presently."

These words were spoken by Paul to Israel. Israel did as ordered. In a few minutes, bucket in hand, begrimed with powder, sixty feet in air, he hung like Apollyon from the extreme tip of the yard over the fated abyss of the hatchway. As he looked down between the eddies of smoke into that slaughterous pit, it was like looking from the verge of a cataract down into the yeasty pool at its base. Watching his chance, he dropped one grenade with such faultless precision, that, striking its mark, an explosion rent the *Serapis* like a volcano. The long row of heaped cartridges was ignited. The fire ran horizontally, like an express on a railway. More than twenty men were instantly killed: nearly forty wounded. This blow restored the chances of battle, before in favor of the *Serapis.*

But the drooping spirits of the English were suddenly revived, by an event which crowned the scene by an act on the part of one of the consorts of the *Richard,* the incredible atrocity of which has induced all humane minds to impute it rather to some incomprehensible mistake than to the malignant madness of the perpetrator.

The cautious approach and retreat of a consort of the *Serapis*, the *Scarborough*, before the moon rose, has already been mentioned. It is now to be related how that, when the moon was more than an hour high, a consort of the *Richard*, the *Alliance*, likewise approached and retreated. This ship, commanded by a Frenchman, infamous in his own navy, and obnoxious in the service to which he at present belonged; this ship, foremost in insurgency to Paul hitherto, and which, for the most part, had crept like a poltroon from the fray; the *Alliance* now was at hand. Seeing her, Paul deemed the battle at an end. But to his horror, the *Alliance* threw a broadside full into the stern of the *Richard*, without touching the *Serapis*. Paul called to her, for God's sake to forbear destroying the *Richard*. The reply was, a second, a third, a fourth broadside, striking the *Richard* ahead, astern, and amidships. One of the volleys killed several men and one officer. Meantime, like carpenters' augers, and the sea-worm called Remora, the guns of the *Serapis* were drilling away at the same doomed hull. After performing her nameless exploit, the *Alliance* sailed away, and did no more. She was like the great fire of London, breaking out on the heel of the great Plague. By this time, the *Richard* had so many shot-holes low down in her hull, that like a sieve she began to settle.

"Do you strike?" cried the English captain.

"I have not yet begun to fight," howled sinking Paul.

This summons and response were whirled on eddies of smoke and flame. Both vessels were now on fire. The men of either knew hardly which to do; strive to destroy the enemy, or save themselves. In the midst of this, one hundred human beings, hitherto invisible strangers, were suddenly added to the rest. Five score English prisoners, till now confined in the *Richard*'s hold, liberated in his consternation by the master at arms, burst up the hatchways. One of them, the captain of a letter of marque, captured by Paul, off the Scottish coast, crawled through a port, as a burglar through a window, from the one ship to the other, and reported affairs to the English captain.

While Paul and his lieutenants were confronting these prisoners, the gunner, running up from below, and not perceiving his official superiors, and deeming them dead, believing himself now left sole surviving officer, ran to the tower of Pisa to haul down the colors. But they were already shot down and trailing in the water astern, like a sailor's towing shirt. Seeing the gunner there, groping about in the smoke, Israel asked what he wanted.

At this moment the gunner, rushing to the rail, shouted "Quarter! quarter!" to the *Serapis*.

"I'll quarter ye," yelled Israel, smiting the gunner with the flat of his cutlass.

"Do you strike?" now came from the *Serapis*.

"Aye, aye, aye!" involuntarily cried Israel, fetching the gunner a shower of blows.

"Do you strike?" again was repeated from the *Serapis;* whose captain, judging from the augmented confusion on board the *Richard,* owing to the escape of the prisoners, and also influenced by the report made to him by his late guest of the port-hole, doubted not that the enemy must needs be about surrendering.

"Do you strike?"

"Aye! — I strike *back*," roared Paul, for the first time now hearing the summons.

But judging this frantic response to come, like the others, from some unauthorized source, the English captain directed his boarders to be called, some of whom presently leaped on the *Richard*'s rail, but, throwing out his tattooed arm at them, with a sabre at the end of it, Paul showed them how boarders repelled boarders. The English retreated, but not before they had been thinned out again, like spring radishes, by the unfaltering fire from the *Richard*'s tops.

An officer of the *Richard,* seeing the mass of prisoners delirious with sudden liberty and fright, pricked them with his sword to the pumps, thus keeping the ship afloat by the very blunder which had promised to have been fatal. The vessels now blazed so in the rigging that both parties desisted from hostilities to subdue the common foe.

When some faint order was again restored upon the *Richard* her chances of victory increased, while those of the English driven under cover, proportionately waned. Early in the contest, Paul, with his own hand, had brought one of his largest guns to bear against the enemy's main-mast. That shot had hit. The mast now plainly tottered. Nevertheless, it seemed as if, in this fight, neither party could be victor. Mutual obliteration from the face of the waters seemed the only natural sequel to hostilities like these. It is, therefore, honor to him as a man, and not reproach to him as an officer, that, to stay such carnage, Captain Pearson, of the *Serapis,* with his own hands hauled down his colors. But just as an officer from the *Richard* swung himself on board the *Serapis,* and accosted the English captain, the first lieutenant of the *Serapis* came up from below inquiring whether the *Richard* had struck, since her fire had ceased.

So equal was the conflict that, even after the surrender, it could be, and was, a question to one of the warriors engaged (who had not happened to see the English flag hauled down) whether the *Serapis* had struck to the *Richard* or the *Richard* to the *Serapis*. Nay, while the *Richard*'s officer was still amicably conversing with the English captain, a midshipman of the *Richard*, in act of following his superior on board the surrendered vessel, was run through the thigh by a pike in the hand of an ignorant boarder of the *Serapis*. While, equally ignorant, the cannons below deck were still thundering away at the nominal conqueror from the batteries of the nominally conquered ship.

But though the Serapis had submitted, there were two misanthropical foes on board the *Richard* which would not so easily succumb — fire and water. All night the victors were engaged in suppressing the flames. Not until daylight were the flames got under; but though the pumps were kept continually going, the water in the hold still gained. A few hours after sunrise the *Richard* was deserted for the *Serapis* and the other vessels of the squadron of Paul. About ten o'clock the *Richard*, gorged with slaughter, wallowed heavily, gave a long roll, and blasted by tornadoes of sulphur, slowly sunk, like Gomorrah, out of sight.

The loss of life in the two ships was about equal; one-half of the total number of those engaged being either killed or wounded.

In view of this battle one may ask — What separates the enlightened man from the savage? Is civilization a thing distinct, or is it an advanced stage of barbarism?

Monseigneur in Town

by Charles Dickens

> 1780 Among the causes of the French Revolution, social, economic, and political, were the arrogance, the extravagant ostentation and the frivolous uselessness of the nobility. In this chapter two noblemen, one a great figure at the Court of Versailles, and one a haughty marquis temporarily out of favor, represent their class.

Monseigneur, one of the great lords in power at the Court, held his fortnightly reception in his grand hotel in Paris. Monseigneur was in his inner room, his sanctuary of sanctuaries, the Holiest of Holiests to the crowd of worshippers in the suite of rooms without. Monseigneur was about to take his chocolate. Monseigneur could swallow a great many things with ease, and was by some few sullen minds supposed to be rather rapidly swallowing France; but, his morning's chocolate could not so much as get into the throat of Monseigneur, without the aid of four strong men besides the Cook.

Yes, it took four men, all four ablaze with gorgeous decoration, and the Chief of them unable to exist with fewer than two gold watches in his pocket, emulative of the noble and chaste fashion set by Monseigneur, to conduct the happy chocolate to Monseigneur's lips. One lackey carried the chocolate-pot into the sacred presence; a second, milled and frothed the chocolate with the little instrument he bore for that function; a third, presented the favoured napkin; a fourth (he of the two gold watches), poured the chocolate out. It was impossible for Monseigneur to dispense with one of these attendants on the chocolate and hold his high place under the admiring Heavens. Deep would have been the blot upon his escutcheon if his chocolate had been ignobly waited on by only three men; he must have died of two.

Monseigneur had been out at a little supper last night where the Comedy and the Grand Opera were charmingly represented. Monseigneur was out at a little supper most nights, with fascinating company. So polite and so impressible was Monseigneur, that the Comedy and the Grand Opera had far more influence with him in the tiresome articles of state affairs and state secrets, than the needs of all France. A happy circumstance for

France, as the like always is for all countries similarly favoured! — always was for England (by way of example), in the regretted days of the merry Stuart who sold it.

Monseigneur had one truly noble idea of general public business, which was, to let everything go on in its own way; of particular public business, Monseigneur had the other truly noble idea that it must all go his way — tend to his own power and pocket. Of his pleasures, general and particular, Monseigneur had the other truly noble idea, that the world was made for them. The text of his order (altered from the original by only a pronoun, which is not much) ran: 'The earth and the fulness thereof are mine, saith Monseigneur.'

Yet, Monseigneur had slowly found that vulgar embarrassments crept into his affairs, both private and public; and he had, as to both classes of affairs, allied himself perforce with a Farmer-General. As to finances public, because Monseigneur could not make anything at all of them, and must consequently let them out to somebody who could; as to finances private, because Farmer-Generals were rich, and Monseigneur, after generations of great luxury and expense, was growing poor. Hence Monseigneur had taken his sister from a convent, while there was yet time to ward off the impending veil, the cheapest garment she could wear, and had bestowed her as a prize upon a very rich Farmer-General, poor in family. Which Farmer-General, carrying an appropriate cane with a golden apple on the top of it, was now among the company in the outer rooms, much prostrated before by mankind — always excepting superior mankind of the blood of Monseigneur, who, his own wife included, looked down upon him with the loftiest contempt.

A sumptuous man was the Farmer-General. Thirty horses stood in his stables, twenty-four male domestics sat in his halls, six body-women waited on his wife. As one who pretended to do nothing but plunder and forage where he could, the Farmer-General — howsoever his matrimonial relations conduced to social morality — was at least the greatest reality among the personages who attended at the hotel of Monseigneur that day.

For the rooms, though a beautiful scene to look at, and adorned with every device of decoration that the taste and skill of the time could achieve, were, in truth, not a sound business; considered with any reference to the scarecrows in the rags and night-caps elsewhere (and not so far off, either, but that the watching towers of Notre Dame, almost equi-distant from the two extremes, could see them both), they would have been an exceedingly uncomfortable business — if that could have been anybody's business, at the house of Monseigneur. Military officers destitute of military knowledge; naval officers with no idea of a ship; civil officers without a notion of affairs; brazen ecclesiastics, of the worst world worldly, with sensual eyes, loose tongues, and looser lives; all totally unfit for their several callings, all lying horribly in pretending to belong to them, but all nearly or remotely of the order of Monseigneur, and therefore foisted on all public employments from which anything was to be got, these were to be told off by the score and the score. People not immediately connected with Monseigneur of the State, yet equally unconnected with anything that was real, or by lives passed in travelling by any straight road to any true earthly end, were no less abundant. Doctors who made great fortunes out of dainty remedies for imaginary disorders that never existed, smiled upon their courtly patients in the ante-chambers of Monseigneur. Projectors who had discovered every kind of remedy for the little evils with which the state was touched, except the remedy of setting to work in earnest to root out a single sin, poured their distracting babble into any ears they could lay hold of, at the reception of Monseigneur. Unbelieving Philosophers who were remodelling the world with words, and making card-towers of Babel to scale the skies with, talked with Unbelieving Chemists who had an eye on the transmutation of metals, at this wonderful gathering accumulated by Monseigneur. Exquisite gentlemen of the finest breeding — which was at that remarkable time — and has been since — to be known by its fruits of indifference to every natural subject of human interest, were in the most exemplary state of exhaustion, at the hotel of Monseigneur. Such homes had these various notabilities left behind them in the fine world of Paris, that the spies among the assembled devotees of Monseigneur — forming a goodly half of the polite company — would have found it hard to discover among the angels of that sphere one solitary wife, who, in her manners and appearance, owned to being a Mother. Indeed, except for the mere act of bringing a troublesome creature into this world — which does not go far towards the realization of the name of mother — there was no such thing known to the fashion. Peasant women kept the unfashionable babies close, and brought them up, and charming grand-mammas of sixty dressed and supped as at twenty.

The leprosy of unreality disfigured every human creature in attendance upon Monseigneur. In the outermost room were half a dozen exceptional people who had had, for a few years, some vague misgiving in them that things in general were going rather wrong. As a promising way of setting them right, half of the half-dozen had become members of a fantastic sect of Convulsionists, and were even then considering within themselves whether they should foam, rage, roar and turn cataleptic on the spot — thereby setting up a highly intelligible finger-post to the Future, for Monseigneur's guidance. Besides these Dervishes, were other three who had rushed into another sect, which mended matters with a jargon about 'the Centre of Truth': holding that Man had got out of the Centre of Truth — which did not need much demonstration — but had not got out of the Circumference, and that he was to be kept from flying out of the Circumference, and was even to be shoved back into the Centre, by fasting and seeing of spirits. Among these, accordingly, much discoursing with spirits went on — and it did a world of good which never became manifest.

But, the comfort was, that all the company at the grand hotel of Monseigneur were perfectly dressed. If the Day of Judgement had only been ascertained to be a dress day, everybody there would have been eternally correct. Such frizzling and powdering and sticking up of hair, such delicate complexions artificially preserved and mended, such gallant swords to look at, and such delicate honour to the sense of smell, would surely keep anything going, for ever and ever. The exquisite gentlemen of the finest breeding wore little pendant trinkets that chinked as they languidly moved; these golden fetters rang like precious little bells; and what with that ringing, and with the rustle of silk and brocade and fine linen, there was a flutter in the air that fanned Saint Antoine and his devouring hunger far away.

Dress was the one unfailing talisman and charm used for keeping all things in their places. Everybody was dressed for a Fancy Ball that was never to leave off. From the Palace of the Tuileries, through Monseigneur and the whole Court, through the Chambers, the Tribunals of Justice, and all society (except the scarecrows), the Fancy Ball descended to the Comon Executioner: who, in pursuance of the charm, was required to officiate 'frizzled, powdered, in a gold-laced coat, pumps, and white silk stockings.' At the gallows and the wheel — the axe was a rarity — Monsieur Paris, as it was the episcopal mode among his brother Professors of the provinces, Monsieur Orleans, and the rest, to call him, presided in this dainty dress. And who among the company at Monseigneur's reception in that seventeen hundred and eightieth year of our Lord, could possibly doubt, that a system rooted in a frizzled hangman, powdered, gold-laced, pumped, and white-silk stockinged, would see the very stars out!

Monseigneur having eased his four men of their burdens and taken his chocolate, caused the doors of the Holiest of Holiests to be thrown open, and issued forth. Then, what submission, what cringing and fawning, what servility, what abject humiliation! As to bowing down in body and spirit, nothing in that way was left for Heaven — which may have been one among other reasons why the worshippers of Monseigneur never troubled it.

Bestowing a word of promise here and a smile there, a whisper on one happy slave and wave of the hand on another, Monseigneur affably passed through his rooms to the remote region of the Circumference of Truth. There, Monseigneur turned, and came back again, and so in due course of time got himself shut up in his sanctuary by the chocolate sprites, and was seen no more.

The show being over, the flutter in the air became quite a little storm, and the precious little bells went ringing downstairs. There was soon but one person left of all the crowd, and he, with his hat under his arm and his snuff-box in his hand, slowly passed among the mirrors on his way out.

'I devote you,' said this person, stopping at the last door on his way, and turning in the direction of the sanctuary, 'to the Devil!'

With that, he shook the snuff from his fingers as if he had shaken the dust from his feet, and quietly walked downstairs.

He was a man of about sixty, handsomely dressed, haughty in manner, and with a face like a fine mask. A face of a transparent paleness; every feature in it clearly defined; one set expression on it. The nose, beautifully formed otherwise, was very slightly pinched at the top of each nostril. In those two compressions, or dints, the only little change that the face ever showed, resided. They persisted in changing colour sometimes, and they would be occasionally dilated and contracted by something like a faint pulsation: then, they gave a look of treachery, and cruelty, to the whole countenance. Examined with attention, its capacity of helping such a look was to be found in the line of the mouth, and the lines of the orbits of the eyes, being much too horizontal and thin; still, in the effect the face made, it was a handsome face, and a remarkable one.

Its owner went downstairs into the courtyard, got into his carriage, and drove away. Not many people had talked with him at the reception; he had stood in a little space apart, and Monseigneur might have been warmer in his manner. It appeared under the circumstances, rather agreeable to him to see the common people dispersed before his horses, and often barely escaping from being run down. His man drove as if he were charging an enemy, and the furious recklessness of the man brought no check into the face, or to the lips, of the master. The complaint had sometimes made itself audible, even in that deaf city and dumb age, that, in the narrow streets without footways, the fierce patrician custom of hard driving endangered and maimed the mere vulgar in a barbarous manner. But few cared enough for that to think of it a second time, and, in this matter, as in all others, the common wretches were left to get out of their difficulties as they could.

With a wild rattle and clatter, and an inhuman abandonment of consideration not easy to be understood in these days, the carriage dashed through the streets and swept around corners, with women screaming before it, and men clutching each other and clutching children out of its way. At last, swooping at a street corner by a fountain, one of its wheels came to a sickening little jolt, and there was a loud cry from a number of voices, and the horses reared and plunged.

But for the latter inconvenience, the carriage probably would not have stopped; carriages were often known to drive on, and leave their wounded behind, and why not? But the frightened valet had got down in a hurry, and there were twenty hands at the horses' bridles.

'What has gone wrong?' said Monsieur, calmly looking out.

A tall man in a night-cap had caught up a bundle from among the feet of the horses, and had laid it on the basement of the fountain, and was down in the mud and wet, howling over it like a wild animal.

'Pardon, Monsieur the Marquis!' said a ragged and submissive man, 'it is a child.'

'Why does he make that abominable noise? Is it his child?'

'Excuse me, Monsieur the Marquis — it is a pity — yes.'

The fountain was a little removed; for the street opened, where it was, into a space some ten or twelve yards square. As the tall man suddenly got up from the ground, and came running at the carriage, Monsieur the Marquis clapped his hand for an instant on his sword-hilt.

'Killed!' shrieked the man, in wild desperation extending both arms at their length above his head and staring at him. 'Dead!'

The people closed round, and looked at Monsieur the Marquis. There was nothing revealed by the many eyes that looked at him but watchfulness and eagerness; there was no visible menacing or anger. Neither did the people say anything; after the first cry, they had been silent, and they remained so. The voice of the submissive man who had spoken, was flat and tame in its extreme submission. Monsieur the Marquis ran his eyes over them all, as if they had been mere rats come out of their holes.

He took out his purse.

'It is extraordinary to me,' said he, 'that you people cannot take care of yourselves and your children. One or the other of you is for ever in the way. How do I know what injury you have done my horses. See! Give him that.'

He threw out a gold coin for the valet to pick up, and all the heads craned forward that all the eyes might look down at it as it fell. The tall man called out again with a most unearthly cry, 'Dead!'

He was arrested by the quick arrival of another man, for whom the rest made way. On seeing him, the miserable creature fell upon his shoulder, sobbing and crying, and pointing to the fountain, where some women were stooping over the motionless bundle, and moving gently about it. They were as silent, however, as the men.

'I know all, I know all,' said the last comer. 'Be a brave man, my Gaspard! It is better for the poor little play-thing to die so, than to live. It has died in a moment without pain. Could it have lived an hour as happily?'

'You are a philosopher, you there,' said the Marquis, smiling. 'How do they call you?'

'They call me Defarge.'

'Of what trade?'

'Monsieur the Marquis, vendor of wine.'

'Pick up that, philosopher and vendor of wine,' said the Marquis, throwing him another gold coin, 'and spend it as you will. The horses there; are they right?'

Without deigning to look at the assemblage a second time, Monsieur the Marquis leaned back in his seat, and was just being driven away with the air of a gentleman who had accidentally broken some common thing, and had paid for it, and could afford to pay for it; when his ease was suddenly disturbed by a coin flying into his carriage, and ringing on its floor.

'Hold!' said Monsieur the Marquis. 'Hold the horses! Who threw that?'

He looked to the spot where Defarge the vendor of wine had stood, a moment before; but the wretched father was grovelling on his face on the pavement in that spot, and the figure that stood beside him was the figure of a dark stout woman, knitting.

'You dogs,' said the Marquis, but smoothly, and with an unchanged front, except as to the spots on his nose: 'I would ride over any of you very willingly, and exterminate you from the earth. If I knew which rascal threw at the carriage, and if that brigand were sufficiently near it, he should be crushed under the wheels.'

So cowed was their condition, and so long and hard their experience of what such a man could do them, within the law and beyond it, that not a voice, or a hand, or even an eye was raised. Among the men, not one. But the woman who stood knitting looked up steadily, and looked the Marquis in the face. It was not for his dignity to notice it; his contemptuous eyes passed over her, and over all the other rats; and he leaned back in his seat again, and gave the word, 'Go on!'

He was driven on, and other carriages came whirling by in quick succession; the Minister, the State-Projector, the Farmer-General, the Doctor, the Lawyer, the Ecclesiastic, the Grand Opera, the Comedy, the whole Fancy Ball in a bright continuous flow, came whirling by. The rats had crept out of their holes to look on, and they remained looking on for hours; soldiers and police often passing between them and the spectacle, and making a barrier behind which they slunk, and through which they peeped. The father had long ago taken up his bundle and hidden himself away with it, when the women who had tended the bundle while it lay on the base of the fountain, sat there watching the running of the water and the rolling of the Fancy Ball — when the one woman who had stood conspicuous, knitting, still knitted on with the steadfastness of Fate. The water of the fountain ran, the swift river ran, the day ran into evening, so much life in the city ran into death according to rule, time and tide waited for no man, the rats were sleeping close together in their dark holes again, the Fancy Ball was lighted up at supper, all things ran their course.

The Fall of the Bastille
by Charles Dickens

1789 From the miserable inhabitants of the Saint
Antoine slum quarter of Paris the mobs were organized which captured the royal prison called the Bastille and which later applauded the executions in the
Place de la Concorde. M. and Mme. Defarge were
leaders of the mob, which Dickens sometimes calls
Saint Antoine as if it were a single individual thirst-
ing for vengeance.

Saint Antoine had been, that morning, a vast dusky mass of scarecrows heaving to and fro, with frequent gleams of light above the billowy
heads, where steel blades and bayonets shone in the sun. A tremendous
roar arose from the throat of Saint Antoine, and a forest of naked arms
struggled in the air like shrivelled branches of trees in a winter wind: all
the fingers convulsively clutching at every weapon that was thrown up
from the depths below, no matter how far off.

Who gave them out, whence they last came, where they began, through
what agency they crookedly quivered and jerked, scores at a time, over
the heads of the crowd, like a kind of lightning, no eye in the throng could
have told; but, muskets were being distributed — so were cartridges, powder and ball, bars of iron and wood, knives, axes, pikes, every weapon
that distracted ingenuity could discover or devise. People who could lay
hold of nothing else, set themselves with bleeding hands to force stones
and bricks out of their places in walls. Every pulse and heart in Saint Antoine was on high-fever strain and at high-fever heat. Every living creature
there held life as of no account, and was demented with a passionate readiness to sacrifice it.

As a whirlpool of boiling waters has a centre point, so, all this raging
circled round Defarge's wine shop, and every human drop in the cauldron
had a tendency to be sucked towards the vortex where Defarge himself,
already begrimed with gunpowder and sweat, issued orders, issued arms,
thrust this man back, dragged this man forward, disarmed one to arm another, laboured and strove in the thickest of the uproar.

'Keep near to me, Jacques Three,' cried Defarge; 'and do you, Jacques

One and Two, separate and put yourselves at the head of as many of these patriots as you can. Where is my wife?'

'Eh, well! Here you see me!' said madame, composed as ever, but not knitting to-day. Madame's resolute right hand was occupied with an axe, in place of the usual softer implements, and in her girdle were a pistol and a cruel knife.

'Where do you go, my wife?'

'I go,' said madame, 'with you at present. You shall see me at the head of women, by and by.'

'Come then!' cried Defarge, in a resounding voice. 'Patriots and friends, we are ready! The Bastille!'

With a roar that sounded as if all the breath in France had been shaped into the detested word, the living sea rose, wave on wave, depth on depth, and overflowed the city to that point. Alarm-bells ringing, drums beating, the sea raging and thundering on its new beach, the attack begun.

Deep ditches, double drawbridge, massive stone walls, eight great towers, cannon, muskets, fire and smoke. Through the fire and through the smoke — in the fire and in the smoke, for the sea cast him up against a cannon, and on the instant he became a cannonier — Defarge of the wine shop worked like a manful soldier, two fierce hours.

Deep ditch, single drawbridge, massive stone walls, eight great towers, cannon, muskets, fire and smoke. One drawbridge down! 'Work, comrades all, work! Work, Jacques One, Jacques Two, Jacques One Thousand, Jacques Two Thousand, Jacques Five-and-Twenty Thousand; in the name of all the Angels or the Devils — which you prefer — work!' Thus Defarge of the wine shop, still at his gun, which had long grown hot.

'To me, women!' cried madame his wife. 'What! We can kill as well as the men when the place is taken!' And to her, with a shrill thirsty cry, trooping women variously armed, but all armed alike in hunger and revenge.

Cannon, muskets, fire and smoke; but, still the deep ditch, the single drawbridge, the massive stone walls, and the eight great towers. Slight displacements of the raging sea, made by the falling wounded. Flashing weapons, blazing torches, smoking wagon-loads of wet straw, hard work at neighbouring barricades in all directions, shrieks, volleys, execrations, bravery without stint, boom smash and rattle, and the furious sounding of the living sea; but, still the deep ditch, and the single drawbridge, and the massive stone walls, and the eight great towers, and still Defarge of the wine shop at his gun, grown doubly hot by the service of Four fierce hours.

A white flag from within the fortress, and a parley — this dimly perceptible through the raging storm, nothing audible in it — suddenly the sea rose immeasurably wider and higher and swept Defarge of the wine shop over the lowered drawbridge, past the massive stone outer walls, in among the eight great towers surrendered!

So resistless was the force of the ocean bearing him on, that even to draw his breath or turn his head was as impracticable as if he had been struggling in the surf at the South Sea, until he was landed in the outer courtyard of the Bastille. There, against an angle of a wall, he made a struggle to look about him. Jacques Three was nearly at his side; Madame Defarge, still heading some of her women, was visible in the inner distance, and her knife was in her hand. Everywhere was tumult, exultation, deafening and maniacal bewilderment, astounding noise, yet furious dumb-show.

'The prisoners!'

'The records!'

'The secret cells!'

'The instruments of torture!'

'The prisoners!'

Of all these cries, and ten thousand incoherencies, 'The prisoners!' was the cry most taken up by the sea that rushed in, as if there were an eternity of people, as well as of time and space. When the foremost billows rolled past, bearing the prison officers with them, and threatening them all with instant death if any secret nook remained undisclosed, Defarge laid his strong hand on the breast of one of these men — a man with a grey head, who had a lighted torch in his hand — separated him from the rest and got him between himself and the wall.

'Show me the North Tower!' said Defarge. 'Quick!'

'I will faithfully,' replied the man, 'if you will come with me. But there is no one there.'

'What is the meaning of One Hundred and Five, North Tower?' asked Defarge. 'Quick!'

'The meaning, monsieur?'

'Does it mean a captive, or place of captivity? Or do you mean that I shall strike you dead?'

'Kill him!' croaked Jacques Three, who had come close up.

'Monsieur, it is a cell.'

'Show it me!'

'Pass this way, then.'

Jacques Three, with his usual craving on him, and evidently disappointed by the dialogue taking a turn that did not seem to promise blood-shed, held by Defarge's arm as he held by the turnkey's. Their three heads had been close together during this brief discourse, and it had been as much as they could do to hear one another, even then: so tremendous was the noise of the living ocean, in its irruption into the fortress, and its in-undation of the courts and passages and staircases. All around outside, too, it beat the walls with a deep, hoarse roar, from which, occasionally, some partial shouts of tumult broke and leaped into the air like spray.

Through gloomy vaults where the light of day had never shone, past hid-eous doors of dark dens and cages, down cavernous flights of steps, and again up steep rugged ascents of stone and brick, more like dry water-falls than staircases, Defarge, the turnkey, and Jacques Three, linked hand and arm, went with all the speed they could make. Here and there, espe-cially at first, the inundation started on them and swept by; but when they had done descending, and were winding and climbing up a tower, they were alone. Hemmed in here by the massive thickness of walls and arches, the storm within the fortress and without was only audible to them in a dull, subdued way, as if the noise out of which they had come had almost de-stroyed their sense of hearing.

The turnkey stopped at a low door, put a key in a clashing lock, swung the door slowly open, and said, as they all bent their heads and passed in — —

'One hundred and five, North Tower!'

There was a small, heavily grated, unglazed window high in the wall, with a stone screen before it, so that the sky could only be seen by stoop-ing low and looking up. There was a small chimney, heavily barred across, a few feet within. There was a heap of old feathery wood-ashes on the hearth. There was a stool, and table, and a straw bed. There were the four blackened walls, and a rusted iron ring in one of them.

'Pass that torch slowly along these walls, that I may see them,' said Defarge to the turnkey.

The man obeyed, and Defarge followed the light closely with his eyes.

'Stop! — Look here, Jacques!'

'A.M.!' croaked Jacques Three, as he read greedily.

'Alexandre Manette,' said Defarge in his ear, following the letters with his swart forefinger, deeply engrained with gunpowder. 'And here he wrote "a poor physician." And it was he, without a doubt, who scratched a cal-endar on this stone. What is that in your hand? A crowbar? Give it me!'

He had still the linstock of his gun in his own hand. He made a sudden exchange of the two instruments, and turning on the worm-eaten stool and table, beat them to pieces in a few blows.

'Hold the light higher!' he said, wrathfully, to the turnkey. 'Look among those fragments with care, Jacques. And see! Here is my knife' — throwing it to him — 'rip open that bed, and search the straw. Hold the light higher, you!'

With a menacing look at the turnkey he crawled upon the hearth, and, peering up the chimney, struck and prised at its sides with the crowbar, and worked at the iron grating across it. In a few minutes, some mortar and dust came dropping down, which he averted his face to avoid; and in it, and in the old wood-ashes, and in a crevice in the chimney into which his weapon had slipped or wrought itself, he groped with a cautious touch.

'Nothing in the wood, and nothing in the straw, Jacques?'

'Nothing.'

'Let us collect them together, in the middle of the cell. So! Light them, you!'

The turnkey fired the little pile, which blazed high and hot. Stooping again to come out at the low-arched door, they left it burning, and retraced their way to the courtyard; seeming to recover their sense of hearing as they came down, until they were in the raging flood once more.

They found it surging and tossing, in quest of Defarge himself. Saint Antoine was clamorous to have its wine-shop keeper foremost in the guard upon the governor who had defended the Bastille and shot the people. Otherwise, the governor would not be marched to the *Hotel de Ville* for judgment. Otherwise, the governor would escape, and the people's blood (suddenly of some value, after many years of worthlessness) be unavenged.

In the howling universe of passion and contention that seemed to encompass this grim old officer conspicuous in his grey coat and red decoration, there was but one quite steady figure, and that was a woman's. 'See, there is my husband!' she cried, pointing him out. 'See Defarge!' She stood immovable close to the grim old officer, and remained immovable close to him; remained immovable close to him through the streets, as Defarge and the rest bore him along; remained immovable close to him when he was got near his destination, and began to be struck at from behind; remained immovable close to him when the long-gathering rain of stabs and blows fell heavy; was so close to him when he dropped dead under it, that, suddenly animated, she put her foot upon his neck, and with her cruel knife — long ready — hewed off his head.

The hour was come, when Saint Antoine was to execute his horrible idea of hoisting up men for lamps to show what he could be and do. Saint Antoine's blood was up, and the blood of tyranny and domination by the iron hand was down — down on the steps of the *Hotel de Ville* where the governor's body lay — down on the sole of the shoe of Madame Defarge where she had trodden on the body to steady it for mutilation. 'Lower the lamp yonder!' cried Saint Antoine, after glaring round for a new means of death; 'here is one of his soldiers to be left on guard!' The swinging sentinel was posted, and the sea rushed on.

The sea of black and threatening waters, and of destructive upheaving of wave against wave, whose depths were yet unfathomed and whose forces were yet unknown. The remorseless sea of turbulently swaying shapes, voices of vengeance, and faces hardened in the furnaces of suffering until the touch of pity could make no mark on them.

But, in the ocean of faces where every fierce and furious expression was in vivid life, there were two groups of faces — each seven in number — so fixedly contrasting with the rest, that never did sea roll which bore more memorable wrecks with it. Seven faces of prisoners, suddenly released by the storm that had burst their tomb were carried high overhead; all scared, all lost, all wandering and amazed, as if the Last Day were come, and those who rejoiced around them were lost spirits. Other seven faces there were, carried higher, seven dead faces, whose drooping eye-lids and half-seen eyes awaited the Last Day. Impassive faces, yet with a suspended — not yet abolished — expression on them; faces rather, in a fearful pause, as having yet to raise the dropped lids of the eyes, and bear witness with the bloodless lips, 'THOU DIDST IT!'

Seven prisoners released, seven gory heads on pikes, the keys of the accursed fortress of the eight strong towers, some discovered letters and other memorials of prisoners of old time, long dead of broken hearts — such, and such-like, the loudly echoing footsteps of Saint Antoine escort through the Paris streets in mid July, one thousand seven hundred and eighty-nine. Now, Heaven defeat the fancy of Lucie Darnay, and keep these feet far out of her life! For, they are headlong, mad and dangerous; and in the years so long after the breaking of the cask at Defarge's wine-shop door, they are not easily purified when once stained red.

Haggard Saint Antoine had had only one exultant week in which to soften his modicum of hard and bitter bread to such extent as he could, with the relish of fraternal embraces and congratulations, when Madame Defarge sat at her counter, as usual, presiding over the customers. Madame

Defarge wore no rose in her head, for the great brotherhood of Spies had become, even in one short week, extremely chary of trusting themselves to the saint's mercies. The lamps across his streets had a portentously elastic swing with them.

Madame Defarge, with her arms folded, sat in the morning light and heat, contemplating the wine shop and the street. In both, there were several knots of loungers, squalid and miserable, but now with a manifest sense of power enthroned on their distress. The raggedest night-cap, awry on the wretchedest head, had this crooked significance in it: 'I know how hard it has grown for me, the wearer of this, to support life in myself; but do you know how easy it has grown for me, the wearer of this, to destroy life in you?' Every lean bare arm, that had been without work before, had this work always ready for it now, that it could strike. The fingers of the knitting women were vicious, with the experience that they could tear. There was a change in the appearance of Saint Antoine; the image had been hammering into this for hundreds of years, and the last finishing blows had told mightily on the expression.

Madame Defarge sat observing it, with such suppressed approval as was to be desired in the leader of the Saint Antoine women. One of her sisterhood knitted beside her. The short, rather plump wife of a starved grocer, and the mother of two children withal, this lieutenant had already earned the complimentary name of The Vengeance.

'Hark!' said The Vengeance. 'Listen, then! Who comes?'

As if a train of powder lain from the outermost bound of the Saint Antoine Quarter to the wine-shop door, had been suddenly fired, a fast-spreading murmur came rushing along.

'It is Defarge,' said madame. 'Silence, patriots!'

Defarge came in breathless, pulled off a red cap he wore and looked around him! 'Listen, everywhere!' said madame again. 'Listen to him!' Defarge stood, panting, against a background of eager eyes and open mouths, formed outside the door; all those within the wine shop had sprung to their feet.

'Say then, my husband. What is it?'

'News from the other world!'

'How, then?' cried madame, contemptuously. 'The other world?'

'Does everybody here recall old Foulon, who told the famished people that they might eat grass, and who died, and went to Hell?'

'Everybody!' from all throats.

'The news is of him. He is among us!'

'Among us!' from the universal throat again. 'And dead?'

'Not dead! He feared us so much — and with reason — that he caused himself to be represented as dead, and had a grand mock-funeral. But they have found him alive, hiding in the country, and have brought him in. I have seen him but now, on his way to the *Hotel de Ville*, a prisoner. I have said that he had reason to fear us. Say all! *Had* he reason?'

Wretched old sinner of more than threescore years and ten, if he had never known it yet, he would have known it in his heart of hearts if he could have heard the answering cry.

A moment of profound silence followed. Defarge and his wife looked steadfastly at one another. The Vengeance stooped, and the jar of a drum was heard as she moved it at her feet behind the counter.

'Patriots!' said Defarge, in a determined voice, 'are we ready?'

Instantly Madame Defarge's knife was in her girdle; the drum was beating in the streets, as if it and a drummer had flown together by magic; and The Vengeance, uttering terrific shrieks, and flinging her arms about her head like all the forty Furies at once, was tearing from house to house, rousing the women.

The men were terrible, in the bloody-minded anger with which they looked from windows, caught up what arms they had, and came pouring down into the streets; but, the women were a sight to chill the boldest. From such household occupations as their bare poverty yielded, from their children, from their aged and their sick crouching on the bare ground famished and naked, they ran out with streaming hair, urging one another, and themselves, to madness with the wildest cries and actions. Villain Foulon taken, my sister! Old Foulon taken, my mother! Miscreant Foulon taken, my daughter! Then, a score of others ran into the midst of these, beating their breasts, tearing their hair, and screaming, Foulon alive! Foulon who told the starving people they might eat grass! Foulon who told my old father that he might eat grass, when I had no bread to give him! Foulon who told my baby it might suck grass, when these breasts were dry with want! O mother of God, this Foulon! O Heaven, our suffering! Hear me, my dead baby and my withered father: I swear on my knees, on these stones, to avenge you on Foulon! Husbands, and brothers, and young men, Give us the blood of Foulon, Give us the head of Foulon, Give us the heart of Foulon, Give us the body and soul of Foulon, Rend Foulon to pieces, and dig him into the ground, that grass may grow from him! With these cries, numbers of the women, lashed into blind frenzy, whirled about, striking and tearing at their own friends until they dropped into a passionate swoon, and were only saved by the men belonging to them from being trampled under foot.

Nevertheless, not a moment was lost; not a moment! This Foulon was at the *Hotel de Ville,* and might be loosed. Never, if Saint Antoine knew his own sufferings, insults, and wrongs! Armed men and women flocked out of the Quarter so fast, and drew even these last dregs after them with such a force of suction, that within a quarter of an hour there was not a human creature in Saint Antoine's bosom but a few old crones and the wailing children.

No. They were all by that time choking the Hall of Examination, where this old man, ugly and wicked, was, and overflowing into the adjacent open space and streets. The Defarges, husband and wife, The Vengeance, and Jacques Three, were in the first press, and at no great distance from him in the Hall.

'See!' cried madame, pointing with her knife. 'See the old villain bound with ropes. That was well done to tie a bunch of grass upon his back. Ha, ha! That was well done. Let him eat it now!' Madame put her knife under her arm, and clapped her hands as at a play.

The people immediately behind Madame Defarge, explaining the cause of her satisfaction to those behind them, and those again explaining to others, and those to others, the neighboring streets resounded with the clapping of hands. Similarly, during two or three hours of drawl, and the winnowing of many bushels of words, Madame Defarge's frequent expressions of impatience were taken up, with marvellous quickness, at a distance: the more readily, because certain men who had by some wonderful exercise of agility climbed up the external architecture to look in from the windows, knew Madame Defarge well, and acted as a telegraph between her and the crowd outside the building.

At length the sun rose so high that it struck a kindly ray as of hope or protection, directly down upon the old prisoner's head. The favour was too much to bear; in an instant the barrier of dust and chaff that had stood surprisingly long, went to the winds, and Saint Antoine had got him!

It was known directly, to the furthest confines of the crowd. Defarge had but sprung over a railing and a table, and folded the miserable wretch in a deadly embrace — Madame Defarge had but followed and turned her hand in one of the ropes with which he was tied — The Vengeance and Jacques Three were not yet up with them, and the men at the windows had not yet swooped into the hall, like birds of prey from their high perches — when the cry seemed to go up, all over the city, 'Bring him out! Bring him to the lamp!'

Down, and up, and head foremost on the steps of the building; now, on his knees; now, on his feet; now, on his back; dragged, and struck at, and stifled by the bunches of grass and straw that were thrust into his face by hundreds of hands; torn, bruised, panting, bleeding, yet always entreating and beseeching for mercy; now full of vehement agony of action, with a small clear space about him as the people drew one another back that they might see; now, a log of dead wood drawn through a forest of legs; he was hauled to the nearest street corner where one of the fatal lamps swung, and there Madame Defarge let him go — as a cat might have done to a mouse — and silently and composedly looked at him while they made ready, and while he besought her: the women passionately screeching at him all the time, and the men sternly calling out to have him killed with grass in his mouth. Once, he went aloft, and the rope broke, and they caught him shrieking; twice, he went aloft, and the rope broke, and they caught him shrieking; then, the rope was merciful, and held him, and his head was soon upon a pike, with grass enough in the mouth for all Saint Antoine to dance at the sight of.

Nor was this the end of the day's bad work, for Saint Antoine so shouted and danced his angry blood up, that it boiled again, on hearing when the day closed in that the son-in-law of the dispatched, another of the people's enemies and insulters, was coming into Paris under a guard five hundred strong, in cavalry alone. Saint Antoine wrote his crimes on flaring sheets of paper, seized him — would have torn him out of the breast of an army to bear Foulon company — set his head and heart on pikes, and carried the three spoils of the day in Wolf-procession through the streets.

Not before dark night did the men and women come back to the children, wailing and breadless. Then, the miserable baker's shops were beset by long files of them, patiently waiting to buy bad bread; and while they waited with stomachs faint and empty, they beguiled the time by embracing one another on the triumphs of the day, and achieving them again in gossip. Gradually, these strings of ragged people shortened and frayed away; and then poor lights began to shine in high windows, and slender fires were made in the streets, at which neighbours cooked in common, afterwards supping at their doors.

Scanty and insufficient suppers those, and innocent of meat, as of most other sauce to wretched bread. Yet, human fellowship infused some nourishment into the flinty viands, and struck some sparks of cheerfulness out of them. Fathers and mothers who had had their full share in the worst of the day, played gently with their meagre children; and lovers, with such a world around them and before them, loved and hoped.

It was almost morning, when Defarge's wine shop parted with its last knot of customers, and Monsieur Defarge said to madame his wife, in husky tones, while fastening the door:

'At last it is come, my dear!'

'Eh well!' returned madame. 'Almost.'

Saint Antoine slept, the Defarges slept: even The Vengeance slept with her starved grocer, and the drum was at rest. The drum's was the only voice in Saint Antoine that blood and hurry had not changed. The Vengeance, as custodian of the drum, could have awakened him up and had the same speech out of him as before the Bastille fell, or old Foulon was seized; not so with the hoarse tones of the men and women in Saint Antoine's bosom.

Ten Thousand and Five Francs

by Marjorie Coryn

> 1795 Letizia, indomitable widow of the Corsican patriot, Carlo Bonaparte, was living in Marseilles with her younger children. She had heard nothing from her second son, Napoleon, since he had dashed off to Paris hoping to mend his damaged military prospects. Fréron, one of the terrorists of the Revolution, had been responsible for frightful massacres in Marseilles and Toulon.

> A mother of eight children can never be avaricious.
>
> Letizia

The commissary Fréron kissed her hand. He was Madame Bonaparte's humble servitor, he was hers to command. . . . No, she was not to disturb herself, he knew the way out. And he was gone as he had come, courteous, gentle-spoken, deferentially familiar. From his manner, you might think he'd been the most regular of visitors, instead of never having been near them for six months, not since Napoleon went to Paris — speaking vaguely of over-work and ill-health, but making no excuses, giving no explanations. He'd known that she was there with only Louis by way of a man — Napoleon in Paris, Lucien at St. Chaumans in the starvation job he'd managed to get for himself, Joseph off in Genoa on his mother-in-law's business — yet for six months he might not have been aware that she and her family existed.

He couldn't be expected to compromise himself, Lucien said — but surely they were as compromising now as they had ever been — more, for Napoleon wasn't even a General on half-pay now, but an officer struck off the Army lists, finished, done for, because he wouldn't do what they wanted him to do in the Vendée. An opportunist, Joseph had called him — but what opportunity could he hope to find in that dungeon-like apartment, among her young children, and she with barely a week's money left in her purse? Unless Lucien — but no, she'd heard from him only the day before, there was nothing new or hopeful in his dreary, pen-scratching life of a little clerk. And he hadn't asked after her other children, save vaguely, hoping they were well, and giving her no time to answer — no, not even Paulette.

Paulette — Paulette was sixteen, Fréron over forty — yet as Lucien said, she was a girl who would need an older man for husband. She was almost unmanageable now, and when you couldn't spare the money to give a girl pleasure at home, nor the time to make sure she didn't find it elsewhere, an early marriage had its advantages. Most people would say that a girl without a *dot*, or any hope of ever catching one, was more than lucky in attracting so rich a catch as Fréron, a fine handsome man into the bargain, and after all only in his prime.

A hyena, Napoleon had called him, stinking of death — but certainly the only odour he'd left behind him today was of lavender-water and scented powder. He'd talked about that, too, about the bloodshed, with that respectfully intimate little smile he had, as though you were the only person he could really explain himself to. He'd always abhorred the Terror, he said, but — what would you? — he'd been obliged to kill, for such was the law. And it would have been cowardly, would it not, to have refused to serve such a law, when by so doing he would have left it in the hands of monsters who would have turned it against the innocent as well as the guilty? For himself, he felt well repaid for the horrors he'd forced himself to endure if, by plunging his hands into a river of blood, he'd been able to drag a few hundred innocent victims safely ashore.

That might be true — there might be something in it — but it didn't explain what he'd come for. . . . She picked up the bottle of wine from the table and put it carefully away in the buffet. She'd sent Catherine out for it — good wine, so that Fréron shouldn't think that she couldn't afford to offer decent refreshment to a guest. Catherine was always willing to run errands, never off gadding somewhere when you wanted her, like Paulette, or thinking it beneath her dignity, like Elisa. There was no denying it, it made a difference having Catherine about the house. She was willing, competent, cheerful — and after all, even if she couldn't read or write, a woman who knew how to manage a house, and did it, was more successful in life than a statesman who thought he knew how to manage a country and made a mess of it. She sometimes thought Lucien didn't quite appreciate the girl — it was a pity they couldn't be together, her cheerful common-sense would be good for him.

There were Jerome's school-books left out on the table. He'd taken advantage of Fréron's visit to abandon them. A book of mathematics, propped up against the cruet — he took no care of his things, he'd get it spotted with oil. She picked it up. Behind it was another book, open at the middle, *The Marvelous Exploits of the Great Cartouche.* It didn't look like a school-book, but you could never tell these days, since the Revolution there had been so many great men, all of them marvels until the next one came along, that you couldn't be expected to remember all their names.

She was worried about Jerome. He and Caroline were as ignorant as fisher-children. It didn't matter so much for a girl, but for a man a knowl-edge of names and dates and figures was like a dress-sword — useless in itself, but stamping him a gentleman. She'd tried to get Lucien to teach him, as Napoleon had done for Louis — but Lucien knew so much him-self that he had no patience with ignorance, even in a child. He'd called Jerome a thick-headed little dunce, and Jerome had called him a conceited prig, and there the matter had ended. She herself could do nothing but try to see that he sat before his books for a certain number of hours a day — and she somehow doubted that this Cartouche book. . . .

Jerome had come too late — there was no king to pay for his schooling, no father to educate him at home, no money to pay for teaching. You couldn't ask Joseph to help in that, you couldn't let him, it would be like bargaining for him with his wife, like saying, "I've given you my son, now pay for him." Not that the Clarys were mean — there were all those invi-tations to meals that had to be refused because they couldn't be returned — but Julie had married Joseph, not the whole Bonaparte family. Daughters-in-law weren't like sons-in-law, you couldn't accept help from them. Fréron . . .

She'd called Fréron a weather-cock, but he wasn't that really, he was more like the needle of a compass; you turned a compass about in your hands, and the needle seemed to point north, and Fréron's north was suc-cess. He'd pointed at Robespierre, at Barras — and now he seemed to be pointing at a Bonaparte — but which Bonaparte? Not Napoleon — Napoleon tramping the streets of Paris without overcoat or gloves, his boots grey because he couldn't afford blacking to hide the cracks, lodging in a squalid attic, eating only one meal a day and pawning his watch — his father's watch — to pay even for that.

She knew these things from Panoria — Panoria whom she remembered as an excited girl of her own age, going off to France to marry a French-man, a Monsieur Permon, and who was now a middle-aged widow with two grown children of her own. She'd been glad to know Panoria was in

Paris, somebody to keep an eye on Napoleon, to give her news of him. She wasn't always so glad to have the news now — not that she'd want to be without it.

No, it wasn't news of that kind that would interest Fréron — Napoleon kicking his heels in the ante-chamber of the Ministry for War, only in the end to be struck off the lists. . . . What could those men in Paris be thinking of? — snatching at wretched twenty-year-old boys, and ignoring an experienced officer who asked nothing better than to serve. It was fortunate they ran only the government of the country and not its kitchens, with their wasting of green fruit while the ripe was left to rot. Not that she hadn't been right to make him go to Paris — she was still sure of that — yet, if she had it to do again, perhaps. . . .

But, be that as it might, it couldn't be Napoleon that the needle of Fréron's compass was pointing to. Joseph? Joseph was well-off for a Bonaparte, but he could be no more than a sprat in Fréron's financial waters. There was only Lucien, then. . . . He'd said nothing, but then he'd said nothing before the Paoli affair either. She'd thought of him poked away in those mean little villages, unable to get his foot on the ladder — and perhaps all this time he'd been. . . . Barras would soon fall, he'd always said, like all the leaders who'd gone before him. And it couldn't go on forever — some day there must be a man capable of governing the country . . . . Lucien understood why all those other men had failed, he'd always been able to see their mistakes, to explain what he would have done in their place. Perhaps now he was going to be able to show what he could do, instead of only talking about it. Perhaps in the future. . . .

She had always tried not to think of the future. Like a trapped animal she had lain very still, with the snare of fear about her throat, as though by ignoring it, it might somehow not be there. The faint jerk of hope upon it brought with it the panic-knowledge of its reality. It was there, the blank terror of a future that was already tomorrow — when it became today, when the choking pressure of poverty became the stranglehold of utter destitution. . . .

The morrow came, not panic-white, but with a brave flash of blue and gold through the grey October weather. A lean and swaggering man on a lean and swaggering horse, both of them stiff with mud and the self-importance of the military. . . . Less than three days from Paris to Marseilles — the Citizeness would know what that meant if she'd ever tried it herself, the roads being what they were at this time of year. As the Citizeness must also know, that was the habit of Colonel Murat's Hussars, to ride as though they had a red-hot devil up pillion behind them — but then, of course, you weren't a Murat Hussar if anything living could pass you on the road, except naturally the Citizen Colonel himself, whose devil was in his own belly, saving your respect. Ha! If you'd seen us snatch the guns from the Sablons Park and bring them to the Tuileries at dead of night — light Hussars bringing heavy artillery through the streets of Paris at the charge. . . . Oh, one understood she could scarcely believe the thing possible, not having seen it. It just showed that, where cavalry was concerned, there was nothing the Citizen Murat couldn't do, from tight-rope walking to moving mountains. So here was the packet for the Citizeness straight from Paris, with the seals still upon it — and if she would sign the receipt, it should be back in Paris before the ink was dry.

A flat packet, fastened with green ribbon and red seals — a printed paper with crossed flags at the top of it, and underneath, "French Republic, One and Indivisible"; a dangerous-looking document to sign, when you weren't always sure of the more difficult French words — and you couldn't very well ask a common soldier, however much gold braid he had on his chest. You couldn't ask him either whether he expected a tip, and how much. Probably not, so gorgeously dressed a person — and better to be thought mean than ignorant, especially when you possessed exactly five francs in the whole world, and didn't know whether what he'd brought from Paris was worth it.

She went to the sideboard for pen and ink. Fréron's wine — it was still there. That would do. It was good wine — too good, probably. But the man had come quite a long way — and it'd keep him busy, so that he wouldn't watch while she got through the nervous business of putting her signature to his paper.

She sanded the wet ink, gave him his receipt. He took it, setting down his glass and saluting. He was stiffer, less talkative in his going than he had been in his coming. Perhaps after all she ought to have given him — Still, he'd only done what he was already well paid for doing.

Looking up through the basement window, she saw the two long booted legs striding toward the four mud-splashed legs of the waiting horse — saw, too, the flicker of a blue skirt. Paulette knew when there was a uniform in the neighborhood as surely as a cat knows when there's fish in the kitchen. The booted legs paused for a moment, then with a sudden leap they forked the saddle, without so much as touching the stirrups. The horse's forelegs reared out of sight, while its back legs beat frantically on the cobblestones, twisting around and about in a sort of heathen dance. It was curious the effect Paulette had on men, at the mere sight of her they seemed instantly to be seized with an imperative desire to *do* something. If that had been Elisa's skirt out there, the blue and gold young man wouldn't have found it necessary to leap like a frog, nor to make his horse behave like a jumping-jack.

There was the packet from Paris to be faced. Ill news, they said, like a crow, travels fast and straight. Less than three days — nothing but bad news had come out of Paris yet, and certainly none had come faster. . . . She'd put away the wine first. She held up the bottle to the light of the window. It didn't seem possible — just in the moment she had taken to write her name, and Fréron had only had one small glass, she not more than two fingers for courtesy's sake. . . . Well, you got a sou back on the empty bottle anyway.

The packet — criss-crossed with green ribbon, knotted at every crossing, sealed at every knot, in the extravagant way that men had, so that even if you did manage to get the knots undone the ribbon was so waxsoaked that it was impossible to make any use of it. Real silk it was, too, it went to your heart to take the scissors to it.

She'd never seen so much money all together in her life — a packet of bills as thick as a small book — the whole tied together with still more green ribbon. On the top of it was a letter, addressed to the Citizen Joseph Bonaparte. So that was it — business affairs of Joseph's — of the Clarys. That was all. She sat down quickly. Her knees had suddenly begun to shake so that they wouldn't support her, which was absurd, now that her fear was gone. A business letter for Joseph, nothing more terrible than that.

She must read it. Joseph being in Italy, she must see what she was to do with all that money. The writing looked like the tracings a wasp makes on a white plate after it's crawled out of the blackberry jam. Nobody else wrote so badly as that. The signature — a tall, aggressive N, followed by a wavering line — a signature that looked like nothing so much as a snake rearing a threatening head. Had Napoleon gone into the soap business, then? If he'd found a client for Joseph with as much money to spend as all that. . . .

"14th Vandémiaire, Year IV, at two o'clock in the morning," she read. In proper Christian reckoning, that meant the 6th of October, 1795. He still had his pernicious habit then of getting up in the middle of the night to write his letters, instead of doing it by daylight as any sane person would do. No wonder he could never get any meat on his bones:

> My dear brother: It is all over, and my first thought is to give you the news. The Royalists of the Sections were becoming more obstreperous every day. The Government ordered the Lapelletier Section to disarm. Instead, they attacked the troops sent to carry out the order. It is said that Menou, the Commander of the troops, is a traitor; in any case, he was dismissed on the spot. The Government named Barras Commander-in-Chief, and me his second in command. We took our dispositions; the mob attacked us in the Tuileries . . .

She glanced rapidly ahead. There was nothing about soap or business in the letter, as she had hoped there might be — only another street-fight, like those of Ajaccio:

> . . . the artillery from the Sablons, at midnight . . . a whiff of grape-shot. Now we've disarmed them, and peace is restored. . . .

Not soap, no, but artillery. Men never really grew up, they went on playing the same games they'd played as children. A little boy, he'd dragged a wooden cannon about the streets of Ajaccio; now, a man, he dragged bronze cannon about the streets of Paris. All that happened was that their toys became bigger, more expensive, more destructive. In Ajaccio he'd ruined his clothes, at Toulon he'd nearly lost his leg . . . "Thirty of our men killed." . . . She searched anxiously through the untidy jumble of pen-strokes. "As for me, I haven't a scratch — my luck is in." . . .

That, then, was all right. Whatever the trouble was in Paris that he'd managed to get himself mixed up in, he'd at least come out of it with a whole skin. "My luck is in." His luck again, not Lucien's — never Lucien's. . . . Less than three days, the soldier had said, boasting that nobody could pass him on the road. Yet somebody or something had. Fréron knew yesterday, and he'd followed his compass-needle that always pointed towards his polar-star, success. "My luck is in."

"Remember me to Julie." . . . The end of the letter — no word for her, nothing. . . . Then her eye caught a scrawled postscript at the foot of the page. "Don't worry about the family. I'm sending Mother 10,000 francs with this packet."

Ten thousand francs. . . . She picked up the packet, feeling the solid weight and thickness of it. It was like holding a strong, comforting hand —a hand that had loosed the snare about her throat, so that at last she could breathe again.

Ten thousand francs! If she'd known, she could have given that soldier her five francs. Yet after all, it was better to have ten thousand and five francs, than just a round ten thousand.

The Dark Country

by Conrad Richter

1795? The Luckett family were woodsies, among
the very first who ventured on foot into the ancient
forests of Ohio to live among the wild creaters and
the Indians. This is what it was like tramping through
the gloom, looking for a place to cut down a few
trees and call the clearing home.

It seemed strange the next few days when Sayward recollected the
vision and realized that now they were down under that ocean of leaves.
A red-tailed hawk screeching high over the tree-tops would hardly reckon
there was a road down here. You had to be a porcupine rooting under
the branches to find it or the black cat of the forest that could see in the
dark and that some called the fisher fox.

This place, Jary quavered to Sayward, must be the grandaddy of all the
forests. Here the trees had been old men with beards when the woods in
Pennsylvania were still whips. Sayward watched her mother puttering
along between the great shaggy butts that dripped with moss and moisture.
All day she could see Jary's sunken eyes keep watching dully ahead for
some sign that they might be coming out under a bit of sky.

Down in Pennsylvania you could tell by the light. When a faint white
drifted through the dark forest wall ahead, you knew you were getting to
the top of a hill or an open place. You might come out in a meadow or
clearing, perhaps even in an open field with the corn making tassels and
smelling sweet in the sun. But away back here across the Ohio, it had no
fields. You tramped day long and when you looked ahead, the woods were
dark as an hour or a day ago.

Sayward could feel the woods most when the time came to step a few
feet into the brush. Sometimes Sulie or Genny ran in after her. Sometimes
she went alone. The family bobbed on in single file and in a lick or two
the forest had swallowed them up. While she waited here with the green
leaves brushing her skin, with the monster brown trunks close enough to
touch and all around her those wild unkempt graves of ancient wind-falls,
she minded what her father had once told her.

He had been tramping with his gun in the black forest when he felt it.
He was a grown man and had followed the woods since he was a boy, and

yet something came over him in those dark pines and hemlocks where the sun never came so that he wanted to run. He had hardly seen even a piney squirrel all day, and he saw nothing afterwards.

"I was so afeard I broke out in a sweat," he said.

Two hunters from the West Branch told him they knew what he meant. What made it they didn't know. It came over them no place but the deep woods. When pressed, Worth reckoned it might be a panther following his scent, for panthers were curious about humans. A while back he had circled in a tracking snow and found where one of the long yellow beasts had been snuffing behind him on his trail.

But Sayward had the feeling her father hadn't said what lay deepest in his mind. Alone here in these woods sometimes she could feel it. The trace was gone as if it had never been. The only roads were the deer paths. They looked like humans had made them. They coaxed you to come on. They'd lead you to a clearing, they said. They'd take you clear out of the woods. But well she knew that once she followed, they would twist and turn and circle on themselves and peter out in the middle of some swamp. Nothing moved in here. Even the green daylight stood still. The moss was thick and soft as a pallet. It invited you to lay down, and yet Sayward's feet wanted to run.

"It's nothin' but the woods fever," she would tell herself and make that self stand there and count clock time before she let her legs go. She stood up so stout, the skirt of her shortgown flared out a little in front. Between strong cheek bones her eyes looked at you blue and straight as whortleberries, and her hair hung in yellow braids heavy as hawsers on a Monongahela keel boat.

It was good to get back to the Indian trace after that. Human feet had packed it and like human feet it was never still, turning and dodging to miss the butts of the big trees. It pleased her to catch up to the family and hear the young ones crowing and quarreling over the droppings of some fox, wolf, coon or fisher fox in the trace, or to see her father point where a beast had stood on its hind legs and sharpened its claws in long scratches on the bark of a tree.

Some of the young ones would guess "painter" and some "link," meaning the black-browed catamount with hair on the balls of its feet.

"I reckon it was no more'n a bobcat," Jary would say soothingly, for she liked to think there was no savage beast in these woods as big as Sulie.

"It was a big black bear!" little Sulie herself would call out and look quickly behind her. Nothing could ever come big enough for Sulie, though it might come too close.

Generally Worth would wait to tell them what it was until the pack had come down off his shoulders. Camp and household chores blew out of his mind like down out of a thistle, but he never forgot a lick that had to do with the woods. When his tongue was supple, he could sit on a log by the campfire and go back over the day's tramp, naming every sign and the beast that had made it together with the trees that stood by. Most times he even said whether it was made by a he or she one.

Once they came to a fork in the trace where a child's skull hung on a pole and the beech trees were carved with sign.

"Kin you read it?" little Wyitt asked, standing there with his fur cap askew high on the shock of his sandy hair.

"Oh, I kin read it all right," his father said evasively. He went from tree to tree, standing in front of each and rubbing his beard. He told them the lefthand fork kept to the woods and the righthand one, if he minded right, led to Sandusky and the English seas.

Sayward saw a faint light break on her mother's face here in this shadowy, shut-in place.

"I heerd," she said, "it's fine livin' in the open prairie by the English seas."

"It's too fur for you, Jary," Worth told her.

"I'm stout," she said, straightening. "I kin walk a long ways."

"The game's cleaned out up there."

"You mought git wild bulls in the open prairies," she told him.

But Worth didn't hold much to that. How could he swap talk with any of the foreign Indians up there? Now Delaware was second nature to him for wasn't he part Delaware himself? And Shawnee he could get along with.

In the end they took the lefthand fork, and the light faded from Jary's face. All that day and the next the forest continued to thicken. None but Worth had ever laid eyes on such trees. A black walnut stood along the trace and three of them couldn't reach around it. No, they had to get a fourth to span it. Still bigger buttonwoods stood rooted on a creek's bank. Worth reckoned the heaviest close to fifteen feet through. He bragged he could drive two yoke of oxen past each other and never get off that stump.

Jary's face had gone cruelly bleak at the talk of oxen in this wild place. She peered dully at the nameless stream. The giant trees reached over and covered it from either side. Even in the middle the water looked dark as old Virginia tobacco.

"Ain't it got sun in these woods, Worth?" she complained, her eyes hard on him like her enemy. And when he had shed his pack and gone nosing downstream with his gun and Sarge, "If anything happens me, Saird, don't let him always have his way. You'll never get the chance to see Pennsylvany again."

"I mought never want to go back," Sayward encouraged her.

"Don't talk about the old state thataway." Jary sat the log, her face slanted down, her head giving at every beat of the blood in her gaunt neck. "I knowed it that day on the ferry I made all your beds wrong for you. Now you'll have to sleep in 'em as best you kin."

A long time afterward they heard Worth faintly hallooing down the stream.

"What kin he see in here?" Jary muttered.

"He mought have found some riffles we kin cross without gittin' wet to our middles," Sayward said. Together she and Achsa managed their father's heavy pack between them. When they reached him, far off the trace, the stream was still deep and slow with flecks of brown foam.

"Hain't you got eyes in your heads?" Worth put at them, puffing on his clay, his own eyes sharp and knowing in his beard.

Sayward expected at first the black soil where he stood was scattered with small gray stone. Then she saw they were the shed horns of deer. Most of them were broken up. Porcupines, squirrels and other woods creatures had eaten them through. And yet so many pieces lay around that at one place they made a thin drift like the gray leavings of last year's snow. It was plain even to little Sulie's wide eyes that herds of deer had been coming here for many winters to shed. Most every tree you looked at was rubbed smooth in places as their old axe handle.

Worth said little but the smoke came fast from his bearded lips. He showed them what he called a shovel horn and a blue horn and one on which he counted thirteen points. In the crotch of a tree where some Indian must have hung them he fetched out two unbroken gray moose horns. When he set them on the ground and put their tips together, all the young ones save Sayward could walk under.

"By the tarnal!" he kept saying.

He took them where the dark stream emptied in a log-choked river. Down the river path he fetched them to a small run and up that run to a strong spring cradled in the knees of an old beech. The ground hereabouts was black as charcoal and the timber the densest stand Sayward had yet seen. God Almighty, she expected, would have to take an axe here if He wanted to look up and see the firmament He made. The big butts stood shoulder to shoulder, and something came in Jary's sunken eyes as if she had found herself in a herd of those great foreign elephant beasts she had told her young ones a hundred times she had once seen splashing through the mud of a Lancaster street fair.

She looked around her in a sort of terror.

"You don't aim to stay here, Worth! Where'd you git sticks for a cabin? It'd take you all winter a-maulin' those big butts."

"Oh, it's got light timber here and yonder," Worth said. He looked up tolerantly at the wild grape and other creepers roping tree to tree with sloping leafy thatches that shut out every wandering speck of God's free air.

Jary opened her mouth no more except to swoop in what breath she could in this choked-up place. She had had her say and what good did it do her? The time to have set herself against this place was away back in the old state when Worth claimed the squirrels were leaving the country. Now she and her young ones were here and here likely they would stay.

The sun must have been straight overhead, for at one place a shaft of light filtered through. It was pale and thin but it looked golden as a guinea. For a hundred feet it fell straight to the ground. Woods flies were rising and falling in it. Jary watched them. When they dropped, they seemed to be falling down some deep, dark well. And she and her young ones, she told herself, were on the bottom.

The Little Tyke

by Conrad Richter

1797? Now there were other families in the forest, but not so many that the woods were much changed. A body could count on trouble. If it weren't folks acting cussed it would be the cruelty of the woods striking at people, even at children like little Sulie.

Sayward wished that Buckman Tull had kept what day it was to himself. She would rather not have known that she and her father had made this out against Louie Scurrah on a Friday. The Tulls were bighead and always had to show they knew the most. They never let you forget they had an almanac and that it came all the way from the Bay State. Now Portius Wheeler came from down there himself and you'd never know it from him. But the Tulls couldn't pass the time without fetching in the day of the week.

"How are you, this fine Friday mornin'?" Buckman Tull had called out big as you please as he went by to the post.

Sayward didn't mind them telling her when it was the Lord's day. The better the day, the better the deed. Any washing she did on the Sabbath would be cleaner and sweeter-smelling and bleached whiter even though it had no sun handy to hang it in. But Fridays were not like other days of the week. No, Friday was the deil's day, for the Lord was massacred on it. Oh, it could be fair enough one place on a Friday, but other places in the world it would be black and bitter as death.

Never mind, Sayward told herself. If she couldn't change the day, she would have to let it go. It appeared fair enough here in this Northwest country today. Achsa's axe rang out like a man's while she chopped supper wood. Genny hummed while she rolled the leaves soft in their beds and lugged the bedding in. And Wyitt and Sulie ran off early on their chore of fetching the cows. When it got late and they didn't come in, Sayward didn't think much about it. She and the other girls pulled stools to their supper. But once it was dark, she reckoned she'd go over to the Coven-hovens and see what was keeping them.

Then she looked up and saw Wyitt silent and pale as tallow at the door. His bare legs were black muddy to the knees.

"Whar's Sulie at?" Genny cried at him first.

"Ain't she here?" he said, but you could see the way his look went around the cabin that he didn't expect her.

"Whar'd you leave her?" Sayward asked sharply.

Wyitt stood just inside the doorway. He acted like he was scared to come in his own pappy's house. The cows, he said, had never been out so far. He and Sulie couldn't hear a bell till they climbed atop a sharp hill. Away down on the other side they found them in some gat brush off from the flies. But when they drove them out, the cows wouldn't make for the settlement. No, they had it in their heads to go the other way. He beat them over their stubborn horns with a club and still they would go away from home.

He promised Sulie they would get fagged after a while and then he could turn them. But she was scared to go further in the Shawnee country. He could go on with them if he wanted, she said; she would take the path back and tell Mrs. Covenhoven.

The cows kept right on with Wyitt scrambling behind. They forded a river and wound through places he had never seen before. It was dark when he saw a light ahead. This was one of the Shawnee towns, he expected. He saw a strange log barn, and a strange white man came out with a light. Wyitt asked him could he tell him where he and his cows were at. The man looked at him. He said didn't he know where he was at? This was the Covenhoven improvement and these were their cows he had fetched home.

"It was Mister Covenhoven hisself!" Achsa jeered in her man's voice. "The cows fetched you home and you never knowed it."

"Then whar's Sulie?" Genny cried.

"I expect Sulie kin take keer of her own self," Sayward said, holding her voice and face calm. "You and Achsa stay here. Wyitt kin eat his supper. Then me and him'll go out and git her. If he kin show me the way."

"I kin show you the way we went out," the boy said. "But I kain't the way the cows brung me home."

Before Wyitt got up from the table, big John Covenhoven came stooping in the door. His wife sent him over to see if Sulie had shown up. He said he better go along. Sayward dropped some dry candlewood and pine knots in her greasy leather apron. Wyitt lit a stick at the fireplace and went ahead. Sometimes he whirled around a pine knot or a sliver of candlewood and sometimes a bunch of shell-bark torn off on the way.

More than once he stopped to make sure he wasn't turned around again. Sayward told herself that never had she seen any of this strange black woods before tonight. They went over runs and wet places, up hill and down and up again till Wyitt said this was the knoll he and Sulie had heard the bells from. He was sure as could be and if they couldn't find his and Sulie's barefoot tracks in the soft ground, it must be the deil had his foot over them.

They built a fire there atop the hill and kept it going to guide Sulie's little feet through the night. One time or another they would go to the end of the firelight.

"Whoooo-hooooo!" Sayward would send her strong call into the black woods.

"Suuuu-lieeee!" Wyitt would yell as if splitting his throat would fetch her in.

All that answered were echoes, and that, they knew was the woods mocking them. Out in the darkness they could hear the night birds and beasts going about their business like nothing had happened. The big-eared owl some called the Hill Hooter bit off his hoots calm and steady as always and his barred relation dragged out the last of his arrogantly. Now and then wolves howled far off and once came a distant wail through the woods like a panther or catamount. Or it might have been only the red fox that Worth said could give you the worst scare of any beast in the woods when it wanted. Oh, the wild creatures gave no notice at all that they saw the red light of the fire up on this hill. They went prowling their rounds as if no little tyke had been lost in the woods and didn't know the way home in the dark to her pappy's.

It started to rain and in her mind Sayward could see little Sulie, a bedraggled mite somewhere out in this wide bush. Where was she at, she would be asking herself, and would ever she see sisters and brother again? She couldn't take her sopping wet clothes off her little body tonight and snuggle down safe and dry in her loft bed under the roof her pappy had made with his axe, frow and augur. No, she must crawl in a dead, hollow tree like a bear or up a live one like a marten. Up a tree she might be safe enough, should she but recollect she is no young gabby bird that can hold on to a limb with its toes while it sleeps. If she as much as halfdozed, down she might come. And sit on a rock and wait till they came and fetched her.

John Covenhoven said hadn't they better go home on account of the rain?

"I ain't sugar and salt. I won't melt," Sayward told him.

She was all for pushing further on, but the rain put out their torches. They had to wait for daylight to look for the place Sulie and Wyitt had

parted, and then Wyitt couldn't find the gat brush where the cows had
stood off from the flies. When they got home to the cabin, no tuckered-out
and brier-scratched little tyke was waiting for them, but Genny and Achsa
hadn't lacked someone to talk to. When her man didn't come, Mrs. Covenhoven had bridled a horse and ridden over. And when he wasn't back by
early dawn, she had ridden on to the Tulls and Harbisons to sound
the alarm.

The settlers answered the summons like the blowing of a great hunting horn. No church bell could have drawn them as hard as such a heart-
break thing. Jake Tench and the bound boy, almost the last to hear, were
the first to come. Billy Harbison fetched his hounds and tied them to a
young dogwood from where they made it ring around the cabin. Tod
Wylder rode his dun ox over with his wife on behind. A gaunt Kentucky
woman came on foot with her man and her fourth baby. She was nursing it as she stepped dark as an Indian woman across the doorway, her
breast white as milk beside the brown face, her eyes deep in their hollow
sockets. Little Mathias and his boy came. The MacWhirters and the
McFalls tramped together through the woods with all their five or six boys.
And there were some the Lucketts had only heard about and never
seen before.

It made you feel better with so many around, Sayward thought. The
littlest ones didn't know what it was all about and ripped and tore like
they were at a frolic. But the older ones stood here and yonder, quiet as
could be, the boys with their pappies, the girls with their mams in the
cabin. The women had lots to ask about this thing. Each time a fresh one
came, they listened to the story over again, and their eyes kept stirred up
and glowing.

Outside the men stood in a hard knot, making men's talk, chewing off
tobacco, telling of bodies they knew had been lost. Their eyes were alive
in their sober faces, and now and then when one of them rubbed over
his mouth with his hand, rumpling his beard if he had any and spitting
copiously, he would cast around to see if his own youngest was all right,
making like a grimace to cover it up, but there was no humor in it.

Jake Tench put a brighter face on them after the MacWhirters and
the McFalls came.

"Never you mind, Saird," he called in at the door. "Jude MacWhirter
kin find a young 'un for you. Now John Covenhoven couldn't find one
behind his own choppin' block."

The men's mouths opened round to laugh at this joke on the childless

Covenhovens. Judah MacWhirter had six or seven living and only God knew how many dead back in Kentucky. The women in the house laughed, too, pulling down their faces at each other, for behind the chopping log was where they told their youngest that babies came from. For a while now it was more like usual in the Luckett cabin and out. The men told lighter stories and slapped their legs. But the woods closed around this place too thick and dark to last. It hadn't a field here nor tame bush, not a clearing or patch of sky a human could call his own. No, this cabin was owned soul and body by the great woods that ran on and on to the prairies by the English Lakes and to the Spanish Settlements on the Illinois.

Buckman Tull was the first to hear and the last to come. Billy Harbison loosed his hounds and they were ready to start. It didn't seem they cared if Wyitt went along or not to show them the way. They would go out in the woods and find out for themselves what happened to this young one that she didn't come home. The women crowded out of the door to watch them go. They looked like Sinclair's army, men and boys, with rifles and clubs, in boots and bare feet, shoepacks and moccasins. Buckman Tull had on his soldier coat with his horn slung over one shoulder and it was he who took charge.

"They'll fetch your young-un back," Ellen MacWhirter comforted Sayward. "If she ain't been killed by some wild creater."

But all they fetched back next day was news of a barefoot young one's track by a run. It might have been Sulie's toes in the black mud, and it might have been the youngest MacWhirter's boy's. At the blast of the horn they had all run up and tramped it out before they could measure. The day after they found nothing.

Oh where, Sayward cried in her mind, was her father? Why did he have to be off now when they needed him most? They were out of fresh meat with all these mouths to feed. And Sulie's bed in the loft was slept in by strangers. Didn't he know his favorite young one was lost out in the woods while he wandered around digging in the dirt for roots for the pigtail people!

When he did come home, she pitied him hard. The second evening little Hughie McFall ran in saying that a strange man was outside. Sayward thought one of the other women could talk to him. Then she looked up and Worth stood in the doorway, his bag of sang roots weighting his back, his rifle in his hand.

"What fetches all these folks?" he asked sternly of Genny who was nearest him in the crowded cabin.

When she shrank back and wouldn't answer, his eyes moved on past Wyitt and Achsa till he found Sayward at the fire.

"Whar's Sulie?" he asked louder.

"She never came home with the cows," Sayward told him.

He gave a start like a beast in a trap when it gets the first lick with the club.

"When was this?" And when Sayward told him, "She ain't out in the woods yit?"

The neighbor folks all watched him, pitying him as Sayward told the story. She had told it so often, the words were worn to her tongue like Worth's pipestem to his teeth. Several times he groaned, and Sayward guessed he was thinking how it might have been different if he had stayed to home. She and John Covenhoven and Wyitt had done what they could that first night, but Worth could find his way through the woods like a lynx in the dark. The first night little Sulie couldn't have been far off. Now only God knew where she had wandered and to what end she had come.

When she finished, he looked like he had been dram drinking.

"Whar's Louie?" he wanted to know.

She didn't answer.

"You'd better git him." He wouldn't meet her eyes. "Louie mought know. He mought a seed her."

Louie Scurrah came early next morning. He wore a buck tail like it was some kind of frolic.

"So you wouldn't git me before!" the hard look he gave Sayward said.

Oh, you could see he knew he had been slighted and now they'd had to send for him. It made him cocky as all get out. He set himself in charge and told the men why they hadn't got anywhere. It was plain Buckman Tull didn't like this. Today, Louie said, they would stretch a line with every man and boy six poles apart. They would whoop at each other to keep the line straight and when somebody found a sign, Buckman Tull would blow his horn. Buckman Tull sat up and nodded. That, you could tell, satisfied him. And if they fired off their rifles, Louie went on, that would mean they had found the young one.

"Dead or alive," he said, looking hard at Sayward.

Wouldn't they need every human they could get, Achsa put to him. You could see she hankered to go along. Every last man and boy, Louie told her. But not women and girls. They were no good in the woods. They only made it harder. If women found a sign, they would run ahead and screech for the young one till it would hide, if it were around. No, the place for a girl was women's work at home.

Achsa's black eyes burned back at him. You could tell she reckoned it easy enough to be a man and go out in the woods whooping to keep in line and beating the bushes for a little tyke in a red dress that by this time the brush must have whipped halfways off her back. You did no whooping at women's work. No, you stooped by the fire till your face singed and your leg muscles ached so folks got enough to eat. And you heard no horn. All you listened to was women's talk from daylight to dark.

The women hardly stirred foot outside the cabin, yet it hadn't one who didn't have her notion why they hadn't found little Sulie. Tod Wylder's woman told about a boy called Chris that had been lost in the woods back in York state. This was in the olden times. When they found him, a panther had scratched leaves over what was left of him till it would get back that way again, and that's why it took so long to find him. Then Sally Harbison was acquainted with a lost girl it took four years to find down in Virginia. An Indian had shot her for a deer and buried her so the whites wouldn't find out. But her grave fell in and when they dug it up, they found the bullet in her breast bone.

God help you, getting lost in the woods was a fearsome thing, old Granny MacWhirter said. She had toothless gums and on the back of her head a white knit cap that was all yellow with age and hair grease. She was lost once herself for forty-eight hours.

"They's only one word for it," she bobbed her head, "and that's lostness. Even a growed woman keeps a runnin' and stumblin' till she's wore out. The smartest man gits fogged. He kain't see straight any more. He goes crazy with bein' lost, and that's what he does. If he comes on a trace he tromped every day, he don't know it any more. Let him take it, and his craziness takes the wrong end. He thinks his own tracks an hour past are the tracks of some man he never seed or knowed. Let him hear man, woman or young'un a comin', and he runs and hides. He ain't human no more. He's nothin' but a wild creater. Git him home and the whole world's turned around end for end. The sun's in the wrong place. It rises in the west and sets in the east. The North Star's away down yonder."

She knew a case once in Kentucky pitiful to tell. A young boy was lost seventeen days. They found him digging up acorns like a squirrel with its paws and wilder than anything in the woods. He tried to bite the thumb off his own pappy and run off. Once he was home, they reckoned he would come back to his old life, but he never owned his own sister or mother.

He wouldn't sleep in a bed, and he dirtied the house like a hound. What end he came to she didn't hear, but the doctors knew nothing to do for a case like that.

"Sometimes," Granny MacWhirter bobbed her cap and worked her lips and drew down her face at you, "it's a good thing if you don't find a lost young'un!"

"Once they're out too long," Mrs. McFall said, wiping her eyes, "I'd as soon see them dead and buried. That's easier to stand than this waitin' around and never knowin'."

But Sayward reckoned different. She wouldn't mind if their little Sulie snapped at them like a pet fox for a while, just so they found her alive. She always snapped some anyhow. A little more would be of no account. And sooner never find her than see her dead and buried. So long as you never knew, you could keep on hoping, if it was a score of years. Once you saw a body put underground, that was an end to it and to a little part inside of you that died too.

How many times the horn blew that day they didn't know, for it was too far to hear. The men must have camped out somewhere in the woods that night. You could see this wasn't going to be over and done with easy like Louie Scurrah thought. In the morning Achsa, Cora MacWhirter and some of the other big girls made the rounds of the improvements that had stock to tend. They fetched back food and bedding. The men did not come back that night either. But a few nights following, when they were all down on pallets on the floor like so many logs jammed side by each at a rolling, they heard a whooping. Genny's hands trembled so she could hardly pull on her shortgown. She thought they had Sulie.

It was old Hugh McFall and Hen Giddings whooping before they got to the cabin so the women and young ones wouldn't get scared. They had come back to see if the women folks were all right and the stock tended. They would take back some meal to the woods tomorrow. Sayward threw wood on the fire for light and got them rations. After their bellies were filled, they told what they knew.

No, they hadn't come on the young one yet. But that Louie Scurrah had a lynx eye in the woods. You needn't be out long to know he'd been raised by the Delawares. Between him and Worth they had no need of Billy Harbison's hounds. The first day Louie found spicewood chewed by some other creature than a deer, for it had teeth marks on the upper side of the twig. And Worth picked up a red thread torn off a black haw.

Oh, those two could follow where you could see nothing. And every sign they came on, the young one was further and further from home. They found where she ate wild cherries and whortleberries and here she crossed the runs. You could see her foot plain as could be in the sand. The third day they came on a nest of old leaves where she spent the night. She must have camped here more than one day, for her little feet had beaten a path in a heavy stand of timber. Now what do you reckon she had in there?

Old Hugh, who was telling it, settled himself. He blinked solemn as an owl.

You'd never guess it, he said. Louie Scurrah found it himself and had Buckman Tull blow his horn. When they all came up, he took them in and asked did they see anything. So help him, if there wasn't a little bitty play house made of sticks in that big timber! It had bark on the roof and a doorway in the middle. Inside it had a bed of leaves and a block of wood for a trencher with a scrap off a young one's dress for a fancy trencher cloth. It even had a nosegay of flowers. Anybody could see right off a mite of a girl had done this. Away back here in the wilderness, far from any human cabin, she had made herself a little house just like her pappy's. You might reckon a big bearded fellow like Jake Tench wouldn't mind looking at such. But when Worth raised up and called out to the woods, "Sulie! Sulie! Be you still alive?" Jake had to walk himself off in the bush.

Genny couldn't listen any more. She buried her head in the bed clothing. Achsa's brown face twisted up in cruel lumps. Sayward turned hard to the fire because like Jake she couldn't stop her eyes. "Sulie! Sulie! Be you still alive?" she called out in her mind with her father. Out there in the great woods, further than any of them had ever been except maybe one or two, their little Sulie had built a play house to recollect how she and Wyitt and Genny and Achsa had run and played together by this cabin. Wasn't it just like her? Who but little Sulie would put a nosegay in a play house or make up a trencher with a fine red cloth? She was ever saying grand things that no one dared think of but she and her Granmam Powelly who lived in a story-and-a-half chipped-log house across the road from Granpappy's gunsmith's shop along the Conestoga.

Sayward wished she could see for herself that little play house Sulie had made. She'd give all she had if Hugh McFall and Hen Giddings would take her back with them when they went. Those men would need a woman if ever they found Sulie. God knows that after all these days she would be a poor little bag of bones. She would need special waiting on. Men would not know how.

But old Hugh McFall and Hen Giddings went back to the woods without saying a word, no not a word. They went alone at daylight, and that was the last the women saw of them for a week.

Once upon a time Sayward wished she had a clock. Mrs. Covenhoven had one, and Portuis Wheeler, the bound boy said, carried a pocket clock that struck the hours though it was no bigger than his fist. A clock, Sayward reckoned, was almost human, for it had face, hands and sense to tell the time. No doubt it was a friendly face to have around and to hear it ticking sociably through the day and night. But a human could tell time the best, for some hours were fast and some were slow. Now you could tell nothing from Sayward's face, but the hours of this last week were the longest in all her born days. This was time in her life, she thought, she would never want to go back to and live again.

You would expect, Genny said, that since they found Sulie's play house, it wouldn't take long till they found the little tyke herself. But it didn't work out that way. No, it seemed the deil had done it like this just to work up their hopes and then let them fall through. The men said there was a plain track of Sulie going into that place but none going out. Like a pack of hounds trying to find the lost scent, they made bigger and bigger circles around, but one cold track was all they could find. It was almost like an eagle had swooped down by her play house and carried her off, leaving never a sign on the ground.

In worn-out bunches the men and boys straggled back. They said they had done all mortal men could do. They had tramped the woods from Dan to Beersheba. They had tramped it further than any young one could travel on its own shanks. They had raked it with a fine tooth comb. All they had found were horse tracks and a place where some strange Indians had made fire for the night.

"The young-un's a gone Josie," Jude MacWhirter shook his shaggy head. "They ain't no use a huntin' what ain't thar."

Now little Sulie's bed up in the loft lay empty and lonesome again. Only Worth and Louie Scurrah had not come back. No, they had stuck to the woods like stubborn hounds that can't be clubbed into giving up the scent. There wasn't a fresh bone or dust of meal left in the cabin, but Sayward reckoned they could make out by their selves. The young ones could pick berries and fish the river with whang leather outlines. Wyitt could snare rabbits, and she could cut out the summer worms. Maybe, too, a body could take a rock and keep still long enough in the woods to call a turkey or kill a cock pheasant when he came strutting to his log.

But the hungry young ones were glad enough to lay eyes on Louie

Scurrah at the cabin door one morning. Flowers sprang out on Genny's white cheeks though it would be an hour before she should taste the venison slung in a red summer hide on his back. No meat ever came in handier but Sayward begrudged him sorely that it wasn't their Sulie he had fetched back. Never would she forgive him that.

He said he and Worth had followed the tracks of the horseback Indians till they separated and petered out. Back on the Miami River he had to give up, but Worth wouldn't come home. No, he said he couldn't look at his cabin now with his littlest gone. Now that he was out this far, he would keep on beating the woods for her till he reached the grandaddy of rivers. Always had Worth wanted to lay eyes on that long river frozen in winter in one end while the other end has flowers and palm trees on either bank.

"He said one man could keep his cabin in meat till he got back," Louie told her.

Sayward's face was tight-lipped and cruel. She had not a word to say as she got a roast ready, for what could you say to a man who had beat the woods for your littlest sister that was likely dead, then fetched meat home for your living sisters and brother to eat. Oh, she would feed their empty bellies with smoking, hot flesh till their cheeks stuck out again, but it would be bitter enough meat to her. Dinner done she scrubbed what little she had to scrub and took herself off by her lonesome to the woods where she could work this thing off with her legs.

Everywhere she went the trees stood around her like a great herd of dark beasts. Up and up shot the heavy butts of the live ones. Down and down every which way on the forest floor lay the thick rotting butts of the dead ones. Alive or dead, they were mostly grown over with moss. The light that came down here was dim and green. All day even in the cabin you lived in a green light. At night that changed. By day you looked paler than you really were. By night the fire gave you a ruddy glow. She always waited for night time when little Sulie had looked to be ailing. Likely it was only the woods light. By firelight she would be well again.

Oh, it was a cruel thing for the trees to do this to a little girl who had never harmed them more than to shinny up their branches or swing on a creeper. Some claimed the trees were softhearted as humans. They said the pole of the cross had been cut from pine and that's why the pine was always bleeding. The crosspiece, they claimed, was from quaking ash. The quaking ash has shook ever since, and never can it live now more than the thirty-three years of the Lord.

Likely as not, Sayward told herself, a tree might tremble and bleed for the son of the Almighty who could heave it out by its roots with His breath or smack it down with His thunder. But neither pine nor quaking ash would give a hait for a poor little girl wandering around lost in the woods crying for her sisters and pappy who never came to answer. And the birds and beasts would be as bad. Oh, she heard Genny sing a catch once where the birds and beasts covered up the lost Babes in the Woods with leaves. But that was just a pretty song. Any woodsy knew that the corbies would sit around in a ring waiting to pick out the poor little Babes in the Woods's eyes. And if any beast covered them up with leaves it would be the panther so he could come back and munch at their starved little hams another day.

Back along the Conestoga the trees seemed tame enough. Out here they were wild trees. Even in the daytime you could feel something was watching you. When you went through the woods it followed sly as a fox and stealthy as a Shawnee. Leave your cabin for a season and it would choke it around with brush. Likely you would find trees growing out of your bed when you got back.

H.M.S. Sutherland

by C. S. Forester

1810   Captain Horatio Hornblower habitually concealed his nervous tension and general pessimism
beneath a mask of cold composure. A near genius in
battle action, he was much more considerate of his
crews than were most of his fellow captains in the
British navy of Nelson's time. Here he is about to
sail for the Mediterranean to take part in the blockade of Napoleonic France.

Captain Horatio Hornblower was reading a smudgy proof which
the printers had just sent round to his lodgings.

"To all Young Men of *Spirit*," he read. "Seamen, Landsmen, and Boys,
who wish to strike a Blow for Freedom and to cause the Corsican Tyrant
to wish that he had never dared the Wrath of these British Isles. His Majesty's ship *Sutherland* of two decks and seventy four guns is at present
commissioning at Plymouth, and a few *Vacancies* still exist to complete
her Crew. Captain *Horatio Hornblower* in command has lately returned
from a Cruise in the *South Sea* during which in command of the Frigate
Lydia of thirty six guns, he engaged and *sank* the Spanish vessel *Natividad*
of two decks and more than *twice the force*. The Officers, Petty Officers,
and Men of the *Lydia* have all joined him in the *Sutherland*. What Heart
of Oak can resist this Appeal to Join this Band of Heroes and Share with
them the new Glories which await them? Who will teach Monsieur *Jean
Crapaud* that the Seas are *Britannia's* where no Frog-eating *Frenchman*
can show his Face? Who wishes for a Hatful of Golden Louis d'or for *Prize
money?* There will be *Fiddlers* and *Dancing* every evening, and Provision
at *sixteen* ounces to the Pound, the Best of Beef, the Best of Bread, and
Grog at midday every Day of the Week and *Sundays,* all in addition to
the *Pay* under the *Warrant* of His Most Gracious Majesty King *George!*
In the *Place* where this notice is read can be found an Officer of His Majesty's Ship *Sutherland* who will enlist any *Willing Hearts* Who Thirst for
Glory."

Captain Hornblower struggled against hopelessness as he read the proof.
Appeals of this sort were to be read in dozens in every market town. It
hardly seemed likely that he could attract recruits to a humdrum ship of

the line when dashing frigate captains of twice his reputation were scouring the country and able to produce figures of prize money actually won in previous voyages. To send four lieutenants, each with half a dozen men, round the southern counties to gather recruits in accordance with this poster was going to cost him practically all the pay he had accumulated last commission, and he feared lest it should be money thrown away.

Yet something had to be done. The *Lydia* had supplied him with two hundred able-bodied seamen (his placard said nothing of the fact that they had been compulsorily transferred without a chance of setting foot on English soil after a commission of two years' duration) but to complete his crew he needed another fifty seamen and two hundred landsmen and boys. The guardship had found him none at all. Failure to complete his crew might mean the loss of his command, and from that would result unemployment and half-pay — eight shillings a day — for the rest of his life. He could form no estimate at all of with how much favour he was regarded at the Admiralty, and in the absence of data it was natural to him to believe that his employment hung precariously in the balance.

Anxiety and strain brought oaths to his lips as he tapped on the proof with his pencil — silly blasphemies of whose senselessness he was quite well aware even as he mouthed them. But he was careful to speak softly; Maria was resting in the bedroom through the double doors behind him, and he did not want to rouse her. Maria (although it was too early to be certain) believed herself to be pregnant, and Hornblower was sated with her cloying tenderness. His irritation increased at the thought of it; he hated the land, the necessity of recruiting, the stuffy sitting-room, the loss of the independence he had enjoyed during the months of his last commission. Irritably he took his hat and stole quietly out. The printer's messenger was waiting, hat in hand, in the hall. To him Hornblower abruptly handed back the proof with a curt order for one gross of placards to be struck off, and then he made his way into the noisy streets.

The toll keeper at the Halfpenny Gate Bridge at sight of his uniform let him through without payment; a dozen watermen at the ferry knew him as the Captain of the *Sutherland* and competed to catch his eye — they could expect an ample fee for rowing a Captain to his ship up the long length of the Hamoaze. Hornblower took his seat in a pair-oared wherry; it gave him some satisfaction to say no word at all as they shoved off and began the long pull through the tangle of shipping. Stroke oar shifted his quid and was about to utter some commonplace or other to his passenger, but at sight of his black brow and ill-tempered frown he thought

better of it and changed his opening word to a self-conscious cough —
Hornblower, acutely aware of the byplay although he had spared the man
no open glance, lost some of his ill temper as a result. He noticed the play
of muscles in the brown forearms as the man strained at his oar; there was
tattooing on the wrist, and a thin gold ring gleamed in the man's left ear.
He must have been a seaman before he became a waterman — Hornblower
longed inexpressibly to have him haled on board when they should reach
the *Sutherland;* if he could only lay his hands on a few dozen prime seamen his anxiety would be at an end. But the fellow of course would have
a certificate of exemption, else he would never be able to ply his trade
here in a port where a quarter of the British Navy came seeking for men.

The victualling yard and dockyard as they rowed past were swarming
with men, too, all of them able-bodied, and half of them seamen — ship-
wrights and riggers — at whom Hornblower stared as longingly and as helplessly as a cat at goldfish in a bowl. The rope walk and the mast house, the
sheer hulk and the smoking chimneys of the biscuit bakery went slowly by.
There was the *Sutherland,* riding to her moorings off Bull Point; Hornblower, as he gazed at her across the choppy water, was conscious of a
queer admixture of conservative dislike in the natural pride which he felt
in his new command. Her round bow looked odd at a time when every
British-built ship of the line had the beak head to which his eye had long
grown accustomed; her lines were ungainly and told their tale (as Hornblower noticed every time he looked at her) of more desirable qualities
sacrificed for shallow draught. Everything about her — save for the lower
masts which were of English origin — proved that she was Dutch-built,
planned to negotiate the mud banks and shallow estuaries of the Dutch
coast. The *Sutherland,* in fact, had once been the Dutch 74 *Eendracht,*
captured off the Texel, and, now rearmed, the ugliest and least desirable
two-decker in the Navy List.

God help him, thought Hornblower, eyeing her with a distaste accentu-
ated by his lack of men to man her, if ever he should find himself trying
to claw off a lee shore in her. She would drift off to leeward like a cocked-
hat paper boat. And at the subsequent courtmartial nobody would believe
a word of the evidence regarding her unweatherly qualities.

"Easy!" he snapped at the wherrymen, and the oars ceased to grind in
the rowlocks as the men rested; the sound of the waves slapping the sides
of the boat became suddenly more apparent.

As they drifted over the dancing water Hornblower continued his discontented examination. She was newly painted, but in as niggardly a fashion

as the dockyard authorities could manage — the dull yellow and black was unrelieved by any white or red. A wealthy captain and first lieutenant would have supplied the deficiency out of their own pockets, and would have shown a lick of gold leaf here and there, but Hornblower had no money to spare for gold leaf, and he knew that Bush, who kept four sisters and a mother on his pay, had none either — not even though his professional future depended in some part on the appearance of the *Sutherland*. Some captains would by hook or by crook have cozened more paint — gold leaf too, for that matter — out of the dockyard, as Hornblower ruefully told himself. But he was not good at cozening; not the prospect of all the gold leaf in the world could lead him to slap a dockyard clerk on the back and win his favour with flattery and false bonhomie; not that his conscience would stop him, but his self-consciousness would.

Someone on deck had spied him now. He could hear the pipes twittering as preparations were made to receive him. Let 'em wait a bit longer; he was not going to be hurried today. The *Sutherland*, riding high without her stores in her, was showing a wide streak of her copper. That copper was new, thank God. Before the wind the ugly old ship might show a pretty turn of speed. As the wind swung her across the tide she revealed her run to him. Looking over her lines, Hornblower occupied his mind with estimates of how to get the best performance out of her. Twenty-two years of seagoing experience helped him. Before his mind's eye he called up a composite diagram of all the forces that would be at work on her at sea — the pressure of the wind on her sails, the rudder balancing the headsails, the lateral resistance of the keel, the friction of the skin, the impact of waves against her bows. Hornblower sketched out a preliminary trial arrangement, deciding just how (until practical tests gave him more data) he would have the masts raked and the ship trimmed. But next moment he remembered bitterly that at present he had no crew to man her, and that unless he could find one all these plans would be useless.

"Give way," he growled to the wherrymen, and they threw their weight on the oars again.

"Easy, Jake," said bow oar to stroke, looking over his shoulder.

The wherry swung round under the *Sutherland's* stern — trust those men to know how a boat should be laid alongside a ship of war — giving Hornblower a sight of the stern gallery which constituted to Hornblower one of the most attractive points about the ship. He was glad that the dockyard had not done away with it, as they had done in so many ships of the line. Up in that gallery he would be able to enjoy wind and sea and sun, in a privacy unattainable on deck. He would have a hammock chair made for use there. He could even take his exercise there, with no man's eye upon him — the gallery was eighteen feet long, and he would only have to stoop a little under the overhanging cove. Hornblower yearned inexpressibly for the time when he would be out at sea, away from all the harassing troubles of the land, walking his stern gallery in the solitude in which alone he could relax nowadays. Yet without a crew all this blissful prospect was withheld from him indefinitely. He must find men somewhere.

He felt in his pockets for silver to pay the boatmen, and although silver was woefully short his self-consciousness drove him into overpaying the men in the fashion he attributed to his fellow captains of ships of the line.

"Thank 'ee, sir. Thank 'ee," said stroke oar, knuckling his forehead.

Hornblower went up the ladder and came in through the entry port with its drab paint where in the Dutchmen's time gilding had blazed bravely. The pipes of the boatswain's mates twittered wildly, the marine guard presented arms, the side boys stood rigidly at attention. Gray, master's mate, — lieutenants kept no watch in harbour, — was officer of the watch and saluted as Hornblower touched his hat to the quarterdeck. Hornblower did not condescend to speak to him, although Gray was a favourite of his; the rigid guard he kept on himself for fear of unnecessary loquacity forbade. Instead he looked round him silently.

The decks were tangled with gear as the work of rigging the ship proceeded, but the tangle, as Hornblower was careful to note, carried under its surface the framework of orderliness. The coils of rope, the groups at work on the deck, the sailmaker's party sewing at a topsail on the forecastle, gave an impression of confusion, but it was disciplined confusion. The severe orders which he had issued to his officers had borne fruit. The crew of the *Lydia*, when they had heard that they were to be transferred bodily to the *Sutherland* without even a day on shore, had nearly mutinied. They were in hand again now.

"Master-at-arms wishes to report, sir," said Gray.

"Send for him, then," answered Hornblower.

The master-at-arms was the warrant officer responsible for enforcing discipline, and was a man new to Hornblower, named Price. Hornblower concluded that he had allegations of indiscipline to lodge, and he sighed even while he set his face in an expression of merciless rigidity. Probably it would a matter of flogging, and he hated the thought of the blood and the agony. But, at the beginning of a commission like this, with a restive crew under his orders, he must not hestitate to flog if necessary — to have the skin and flesh stripped from the offender's backbone.

Price was coming along the gangway now at the head of the strangest procession. Two by two behind him came a column of thirty men, each one handcuffed to his neighbour, save for the last two who clanked drearily along with leg irons at their ankles. Nearly all of them were in rags, and the rags had no sort of nautical flavour about them at all. The rags of a great many of them were sacking, some had corduroy, and Hornblower, peering closer, saw that one wore the wrecks of a pair of moleskin breeches. Yet another wore the remains of what had once been a respectable black broadcloth suit — white skin showed through a rent in the shoulder. All of them had stubbly beards, black, brown, golden, and grey, and those who were not bald had great mops of tangled hair. The two ship's corporals brought up the rear.

"'Alt," ordered Price. "Orf 'ats."

The procession shuffled to a halt, and the men stood sullenly on the quarterdeck. Some of them kept their eyes on the deck, while the others gaped sheepishly round them.

"What the devil's all this?" demanded Hornblower, sharply.

"New 'ands, sir," said Price. "I signed a receipt to the sodgers what brought 'em, sir."

"Where did they bring them from?" rasped Hornblower.

"Exeter assizes, sir," said Price, producing a list. "Poachers, four of 'em. Waites, that's 'im in the moleskin breeches, sir, 'e was found guilty of sheepstealing. That 'un in black, 'is crime's bigamy, sir — 'e was a brewer's manager before this 'appened to 'im. The others is larceny mostly, sir, 'cept for them two in front what's in for rick burning and t'other two in irons. Robbery with violence is what they done."

"Ha — h'm," said Hornblower, wordless for the moment. The new hands blinked at him, some with hope in their eyes, some with hatred, some with indifference. They had chosen service at sea rather than the gallows, or transportation, or the gaol. Months in prison awaiting trial accounted for their dilapidated appearance. Here was a fine addition to the ship's company, thought Hornblower, bitterly — budding mutineers, sullen skulkers, half-witted yokels. But hands they were and he must make the most of them. They were frightened, sullen, resentful. It would be worth trying to win their affection. His naturally humanitarian instincts dictated the course he decided to pursue after a moment's quick thinking.

"Why are they still handcuffed?" he demanded, loud enough for them all to hear. "Release them at once."

"Begging your pardon, sir," apologised Price. "I didn't want to without orders, sir, seeing what they are and 'ow they come 'ere."

"That's nothing to do with it," snapped Hornblower. "They're enlisted in the King's service now. And I'll have no man in irons in *my* ship unless he's given *me* cause to order it."

Hornblower kept his gaze from wavering towards the new hands, and steadily addressed his declamation to Price — it was more effective delivered that way, he knew, even while he despised himself for using such rhetorical tricks.

"I never want to see new hands in the charge of the master-at-arms again," he continued, hotly. "They are recruits in an honourable service, with an honourable future before them. I'll thank you to see to it another time. Now find one of the purser's mates and see that each of these men is properly dressed in accordance with my orders."

Normally it might be harmful to discipline to rate a subordinate officer in front of the men, but in the case of the master-at-arms Hornblower knew that little damage was being done. The men would come to hate the master-at-arms anyway sooner or later — his privileges of rank and pay were given him so that he might be a whipping boy for the crew's discontent. Hornblower could drop the rasp from his voice and address the hands directly, now.

"A man who does his duty as best he can," he said, kindly, "has nothing to fear in this ship, and everything to hope for. Now I want to see how smart you can look in your new clothes, and with the dirt of the place you have come from washed off you. Dismiss."

He had won over some of the poor fools, at least, he told himself. Some of the faces which had been sullen with despair were shining with hope now, after this experience of being treated as men and not as brutes — for the first time for months, if not the first time in their lives. He watched them off the gangway. Poor devils; in Hornblower's opinion they had made a bad bargain in exchanging the gaol for the navy. But at least they represented thirty out of the two hundred and fifty additional human bodies which he needed to drag at ropes and to heave at capstan bars so as to take this old *Sutherland* out to sea.

Lieutenant Bush came hastening onto the quarterdeck, and touched his hat to his captain. The stern swarthy face with its incongruous blue eyes broke into a smile just as incongruous. It gave Hornblower a queer twinge, almost of conscience, to see the evident pleasure which Bush experienced at sight of him. It was odd to know that he was admired — it might even be said that he was loved — by this very capable sailor, this splendid disciplinarian and fearless fighter who boasted so many of the good qualities in which Hornblower felt himself to be lacking.

"Good morning, Bush," he said. "Have you seen the new draft?"

"No, sir. I was rowing guard for the middle watch and I've only just turned out. Where do they hail from, sir?"

Hornblower told him, and Bush rubbed his hands with pleasure.

"Thirty!" he said. "That's rare. I never hoped for more than a dozen from Exeter assizes. And Bodmin assizes open today. Please God we get another thirty there."

"We won't get topmen from Bodmin assizes," said Hornblower, comforted beyond measure at the equanimity with which Bush regarded the introduction of gaolbirds into the *Sutherland's* crew.

"No, sir. But the West India convoy's due this week. The guards ought to nab two hundred there. We'll get twenty if we get our rights."

"M'm," said Hornblower, and turned away uneasily. He was not the sort of captain — neither the distinguished kind nor the wheedling kind — who could be sure of favours from the Port Admiral. "I must look round below."

Captain Hornblower was walking up and down his quarterdeck amid all the last-minute bustle of getting ready for sea. He was raging to himself at the length of time necessary for these final preparations, although he knew quite well that every factor causing delay was susceptible to a reasonable explanation. Two thirds of the men scurrying about the decks, urged on by the cane of Harrison the boatswain and the rope's ends of the petty officers, were landsmen most of whom until lately had never seen the sea, let alone been in a ship. The simplest order left them merely bewildered, and they had to be led to their tasks and the ropes actually put into their hands; even then they were far more inefficient than trained seamen, because they had not learned the knack of throwing all their weight simultaneously on the rope and walking away with it. And having once set them heaving, it was hard for a petty officer to remember that a shout of "Avast" or "Belay" meant nothing to them. More than once the few trained seamen among them, obeying promptly, were thrown off their feet and trampled upon by the rush of landsmen still heaving away. On one occasion of this sort a water butt while being hove up by a whip to the main yard-arm had simply gone away with a run again, and only the mercy of Providence had saved it from going clean through the bottom of the longboat overside.

It was owing to Hornblower's own orders that the water was so late in being brought aboard. Water left months in cask became so foul and so crawling with living things that he had put off bringing it aboard until the last possible moment. Even a gain of a day or two was desirable. That twelve tons of biscuit had also been delayed was the result of the usual incompetence of the victualling yard, whose officials seemed incapable of reading or writing or figuring. The complication due to the fact that a shore boat with captain's stores was having to be unloaded at the same time, and its precious cargo passed carefully down the after hatchway, was due to the Patriotic Fund's delay in sending down to him the sword value one hundred guineas which he had been awarded for his fight with the *Natividad*. No shopkeeper or ship chandler would give credit to a captain about to sail on a new commission. The sword had only arrived yesterday, barely in time for him to pledge it with Duddingstone the chandler, and Duddingstone had only grudgingly given him credit on it, forcing him to promise faithfully to redeem it at the earliest opportunity.

"A sight too much writing on this for me," said Duddingstone, pointing with a stubby forefinger at the wordy legend which the Patriotic Fund had had engraved, at vast expense, upon the blue steel of the blade.

Only the gold on hilt and scabbard and the seed pearls on the pommel had any intrinsic value. Duddingstone, to give him his due, had been quite right in saying that it was hardly worth forty guineas' credit at his shop, even allowing for his profit and the chance of its being redeemed. But he had kept his word and had sent off the stores at dawn next morning — one more complication in the business of preparing for sea.

Along the gangway Wood the purser was dancing with rage and anxiety.

"God damn and blast all you ham-fisted yokels!" he was saying. "And you, sir, down there. Take that grin off your face and be more careful, or I'll have you clapped under hatches to sail with us today. Easy, there, easy! Christ, rum at seven guineas an anker isn't meant to be dropped like pig iron!"

Wood was supervising the loading of the rum. The old hands were doing their best to make sure that the clumsiness of the new ones would result in the staving of a keg or two, so as to swill from the leaks, and the grinning lightermen overside were abetting them. Hornblower could see by the red faces and uncontrollable hilarity that some of the men had succeeded in getting at the spirits, despite Wood's eagle eye and the marine sentries on guard; but he had no intention of interfering. It would merely compromise his dignity to try to keep sailors from stealing rum if they had the barest opportunity — no one had ever yet succeeded in that task.

From his position of vantage beside the quarterdeck rail he looked down upon a curious bit of byplay on the main deck. A bewildered young giant — a tin miner, Hornblower guessed, from his biceps — had rounded upon Harrison, apparently driven frantic by the volley of orders and blasphemy hurled at him. But Harrison at forty-five had fought his way up to boatswain's rank through hundreds of such encounters, and in his prime might have contested for the highest honours of the prize ring. He slipped the Cornishman's clumsy punch and felled him with a crashing blow on the jaw. Then without ceremony he seized him by the scruff of the neck and kicked him across the deck to the tackle which was waiting. Dazed, the Cornishman took hold with the others and heaved with them, while Hornblower nodded approvingly.

The Cornishman had made himself liable to "death, or such less penalty," as the Articles of War said, by raising his hand to his superior officer. But it was not the moment to invoke the Articles of War, even though they had been read over to the Cornishman last night on his compulsory enlistment. Gerard had sailed round with the longboat and had raided Redruth and Camborne and St. Ives, taking each place by surprise and returning with fifty stout Cornishmen who could hardly be expected yet to appreciate the administrative machinery of the service which they had joined. In a month's time, perhaps, when everyone on board would have learnt the heinousness of such an offence, a courtmartial might be needed and a flogging — death, perhaps — but at the present time it was best to do what Harrison had just done, and crack the man on the jaw and set him to work again. Hornblower found time to thank God he was a captain and out of the hurly-burly, for any attempt on his part at cracking men on the jaw would be a lamentable failure, he knew.

He shifted his weight from one leg to the other, and was reminded of the fact that he was horribly tired. Night after night now he had not slept, and his days had been spent in all the numerous activities necessitated by commissioning a ship of the line. The nervous tension induced by his worrying about Lady Barbara and Maria, by money troubles and manning troubles, had prevented him from leaving the details to Bush and Gerard even though he knew they were perfectly capable of dealing with everything. Worry and anxiety would not allow him to rest, and had goaded him into activity. He felt sick and stupid and weary. Day after day he had longed for the moment when he should get to sea, and could settle down into the comfortable solitude which surrounds a ship's captain, leaving all his shore worries behind him, even leaving Lady Barbara behind him.

He had the sense to realise that this new meeting with her had thoroughly upset him. He had given up as insoluble the problem of whether or not she had secured his nomination to the *Sutherland;* he had tried his hardest to combat his consuming jealousy of her husband. He had persuaded himself in the end that what he wanted more than anything else was to escape from her, just as he wanted to escape from Maria's cloying sweetness and lovable stupidity, from all the complex misery of life on land. He had yearned for the sea as a castaway yearns for a drink of water. Two days ago the prospect of thus standing on the deck in the final bustle of departure seemed marvellously desirable to him. Now, he realised with a gulp, he was not quite so sure. It was like having a limb torn out by the roots to be leaving Lady Barbara like this. And, oddly enough, he was distressed at leaving Maria, too. There would be a child born before he could be home again, a child well over a year old, running about, perhaps even saying its first few words. Maria would have to go through her pregnancy and confinement without his moral support; and he knew, despite the brave way in which she had dismissed the subject, and despite her stout-hearted good-bye, how much she would miss him. It was that which made it so painful to leave her.

With all her courage her lips had trembled and her eyes had been wet when she lifted her face to him, in the sitting-room of their lodgings; they had agreed long ago that it was foolish to prolong the pangs of parting by her accompanying him on board. Even then the urge to be off had still been strong enough to take him from her arms without a pang, but it was different now. Hornblower mentally spurned himself as a sentimental fool, and glanced impatiently up at the masthead vane. Without a doubt, the wind was backing northerly. If it should come round to north or nor'east the admiral would be anxious to start. The convoy, and the *Pluto* and *Caligula,* were assembled now, or pretty nearly, in Cawsand Bay; if the admiral decided not to wait for the stragglers he would be irritated at the *Sutherland's* delay, be it never so unavoidable.

"Keep the men to it, Mr. Bush," shouted Hornblower.

"Aye aye, sir," answered Bush, patiently.

That patience in his voice irritated Hornblower further. It implied a slight rebuke, a rebuke only apparent to Bush and Hornblower. Hornblower knew that Bush was working as hard as he could, and that he was working the men as hard as he could, too. Hornblower's order had been a mere manifestation of impatience, and Bush knew it. Hornblower was annoyed with himself for having so unguardedly broken his rule of never saying an unnecessary word to his officers, and by way of advancing a reason for having spoken he went down below to his cabin, as he had not intended to do.

The sentry stood aside for him as he entered the door of his sleeping cabin on the half deck. There was plenty of room here; even the presence of a twelve-pounder left ample space for his cot and his desk and his chest. Polwheal had set everything to rights here already; Hornblower passed through into the main cabin. Here there was ample room, too; the Dutchmen who designed the *Sutherland* had lofty ideas regarding the comfort of the captain. The cabin extended across the whole width of the stern, and the great stern windows gave plenty of light. The stone-coloured paint made the cabin sunny and cheerful, and the black bulks of a twelve-pounder on each side made an effective colour scheme. A couple of hands were standing by Polwheal in here while he lay on his stomach packing away cases of wine into the lockers. Hornblower glared at them, realising that he could not yet retire to the solitude of the stern gallery while he should be under their observation through the stern windows.

He went back to the sleeping gallery and threw himself with a sigh on his cot, but his restlessness brought him to his feet again and across to his desk. He took out a crackling document and sat down to look through it again.

Orders to the Inshore Squadron, Western Mediterranean, by Sir Percy Gilbert Leighton, K.B., Rear Admiral of the Red, Commanding.

There was nothing unusual about them at all — night signals, private signals, British, Spanish and Portuguese; rendezvous in case of separation; a line or two regarding the tactics to be adopted in the event of encountering while with the convoy a hostile squadron of any force. The flagship would accompany the Lisbon convoy of transports into the Tagus — calling for orders, presumably; the *Caligula* was to take the storeships *Harriet* and *Nancy* to Port Mahon; the *Sutherland* was to escort the East Indiamen as far as Latitude 35° before heading for the Straits, to the final rendezvous off Palamos Point. Captains of His Britannic Majesty's ships were informed that the coast of Andalusia, with the exception of Cadiz and Tarifa, was in the hands of the French, and so also was the coast of Catalonia from the frontier to Tarragona. At the same time captains entering any Spanish port whatever must take the most careful precautions lest the French should be in occupation there. The attached schedule of instructions to masters of ships in the convoy was mostly repetition of all this.

But to Hornblower, musing over these orders, they told a very full and complicated story. They told how, although Trafalgar had been fought five years back, and although England was maintaining at sea the greatest fleet the world had ever seen, she was still having to strain every nerve in the struggle. The Corsican was still building fleets in nearly every port in Europe, Hamburg, Antwerp, Brest, Toulon, Venice, Trieste, and a score of places in between, so that outside every port storm-beaten squadrons of English battleships had to maintain an unceasing watch — a hundred and twenty ships of the line could be found employment, if they could have been spared, on the blockade alone, without regard to the other duties. And at the same time every creek and fishing harbour along half the coasts of Europe maintained privateers, even if hardly better than big rowboats full of men, always ready to dash out and capture the helpless British merchant ships to be found in every sea. To guard against these depredations British frigates had to maintain unceasing patrol, and no King's ship could be despatched on any mission whatever without taking advantage of the opportunity given to convoy merchant shipping on part of their journey at least. In this war against the world only the most careful and scientific distribution of force could prevail, and now, mustering all her strength, England was taking the offensive. Her armies were on the march in Spain, and three ships of the line, scraped together from other duties from which they might just be spared, were being sent to attack the vulnerable flank which Bonaparte had incautiously exposed by his advance into the Peninsula. The *Sutherland* was destined to be the point of the spearhead which was making the thrust against the tyranny which dominated all Europe.

All very well, said Hornblower to himself. Automatically he was pacing up and down again, his head bent under the deck beams, and his walk limited to four strides between the twelve-pounder and the door. It was an honourable and responsible position, and yet he had not the men to man his ship. To make or set sail in the way it should be done in a King's ship — or rather, with the rapidity and facility which might make the difference between defeat and victory — called for two hundred and fifty trained seamen. And if all the trained men were aloft at once there would be none at the guns. To serve the guns, if both broadsides were in action at once, called for four hundred and fifty men — two hundred of them he admitted, might be untrained — and nearly a hundred more carrying powder and engaged upon necessary duties about the ship.

He had a hundred and ninety trained men from the *Lydia* and a hundred and ninety raw landsmen. During the commissioning of the *Sutherland* only twenty old *Lydias* had deserted, abandoning two years' pay and risking the penalty of a thousand lashes, and he knew he was lucky at that. Some captains would have lost two thirds of their crews during as long a stay as this in a home port. But those twenty missing men would have been desperately useful now. He was a hundred and seventy men — a hundred and seventy *trained* men — short of complement. In six weeks he might drill his landsmen, all except that proportion of hopeless ones, diseased, crippled, or idiotic whom he could expect to find among them, into passable seamen and gunners. But in less than six weeks, possibly in less than three, he would be in action on the coast of Spain. By tomorrow night, even, he might be at grips with the enemy — the wind was backing towards the east and might bring out a French squadron of ships of the line from Brest, evading the blockading squadron, and crammed with men, to fall upon such a tempting prize as the East India convoy. What chance would the *Sutherland* stand, yard-arm to yard-arm with a French first rate, with only two thirds of her proper crew, and half of them seasick?

Hornblower clenched his fists again, boiling with exasperation at the thought. It was he who would be held responsible for any disaster, who would have to sustain the contempt or the pity — either alternative horrible to contemplate — of his brother captains. He yearned and hungered for men, more passionately than ever miser desired gold, or a lover his mistress. And now he had no more chance of finding any. Gerard's raid upon St. Ives and Redruth had been his last effort; he knew that he had been fortunate to get as many as fifty men from there. There would be no chance of obtaining any from the convoy. Government transports to Lisbon, Government storeships to Port Mahon, East India Company's ships — he could not take a man from any of those. He felt like a man in a cage.

He went across to his desk again and took out his private duplicate of the ship's watch bill, which he and Bush had sat up through most of the night to draw up. It was largely upon that watch bill that the efficiency of the ship would depend in her short-handed condition; the trained men had to be distributed evenly over every strategic point, with just the right proportion of landsmen to facilitate training and yet not to impede the working of the ship. Foretop, maintop, and mizzen top; forecastle and afterguard; every man had to be assigned a duty, so that whatever evolution out of the thousand possible was being carried out, in fair weather or foul, in daylight or darkness, he would go to his position without confusion or waste of time, knowing exactly what he had to do. He had to have his place at the guns allotted him under the command of the officer of his division.

Hornblower looked through the watch bill again. It was satisfactory as far as it went. It had a kind of card-castle stability — adequate enough at first sight, but incapable of standing any strain or alteration. Casualties or disease would bring the whole thing down in ruins. He flung the watch bill down as he remembered that, if the cruise were a healthy one, he might expect one death every ten days from accident or natural causes without regard to hostile action. Fortunately it was the unseasoned men who were the more likely to die.

Hornblower cocked his ear at the din on the main deck. The hoarse orders, the pipes of the boatswain's mates, and the stamp-and-go of many feet told him that they were heaving up the longboat from overside. A strange squeaking, unlike that of the sheaves in the blocks, which had reached him for some time and which he had been unable to identify so far, he suddenly realised was the noise of the various families of pigs — captain's stores and wardroom stores — at last come on board. He heard a sheep bleating and then a cock crowing to the accompaniment of a roar of laughter. He had brought no cock along with his hens; it must belong to someone in the wardroom or the midshipmen's berth.

Someone thumped on the cabin door, and Hornblower snatched up his papers and dropped into his chair. Not for worlds would he be seen standing up and obviously awaiting the hour of departure with discomposure.

"Come in!" he roared.

A scared young midshipman put his head round the door — it was Longley, Gerard's nephew, newly come to sea.

"Mr. Bush says the last of the stores are just coming on board, sir," he piped.

Hornblower eyed him with a stony indifference which was the only alternative to grinning at the frightened little imp.

"Very good," he growled, and busied himself with his papers.

"Yes, sir," said the boy, after a moment's hesitation, withdrawing.

"Mr. Longley!" roared Hornblower.

The child's face, more terrified than ever, reappeared round the door.

"Come inside, boy," said Hornblower testily. "Come in and stand still. What was it you said last?"

"Er — sir — I said — Mr. Bush — — "

"No, nothing of the sort. What was it you said *last?*"

The child's face wrinkled into the extreme of puzzlement, and then cleared as he realised the point of the question.

"I said, 'Yes sir,' " he piped.

"And what ought you to have said?"

"Aye aye, sir."

"Right. Very good."

"Aye aye, sir."

That boy had a certain amount of quickness of wit, and did not allow fright to bereave him entirely of his senses. If he learned quickly how to handle the men he would make a useful warrant officer. Hornblower put away his papers and locked his desk; he took a few more turns up and down his cabin, and then, a sufficient interval having elasped to conserve his dignity, he went up to the quarterdeck.

"Make sail when you're ready, Mr. Bush," he said.

"Aye aye, sir. Easy with those falls there, you — you — — "

Even Bush had reached the condition when there was no more savour in oaths. The ship was in a horrible state of muddle, the decks were filthy, the crew exhausted. Hornblower stood with his hands behind him in a careful attitude of Olympian detachment as the order was given for all hands to make sail, and the petty officers drove the crew, stupid with weariness, to their stations. Savage, the senior midshipman, whom Hornblower had seen grow from boyhood to manhood under his eye, came shouting for the afterguard to man the main topsail halliards. Savage was wan and his eyes were bloodshot; a night of debauchery in some foul haunt in Plymouth had not left him in the best of condition. As he shouted he put his hand to his temple, where clearly the din he was making was causing him agony. Hornblower smiled to himself at the sight — the next few days would sweat him clean again.

"Captain of the afterguard!" yelled Savage, his voice cracking. "I don't see the afterguard coming aft! Quicker than that, you men! Clap on the main topsail halliards, there! I say, you master-at-arms. Send the idlers aft. D'ye hear, there!"

A boatswain's mate headed a rush to the mizzen rigging at Hornblower's elbow. Hornblower saw young Longley standing hesitating for a second, looking up at the men preceding him, and then, with a grimace of determination, the boy leaped for the ratlines and scrambled up after them. Hornblower appreciated the influences at work upon him — his fear of the towering height above him, and then his stoical decision that he could follow wherever the other men could venture. Something might be made of that boy.

Bush was looking at his watch and fuming to the master.

"Nine minutes already! God, look at them! The marines are more like sailors!"

The marines were farther aft, at the mizzen topsail halliards. Their booted feet went clump-clump-clump on the deck. They did their work like soldiers, with soldierly rigidity, as if at drill. Sailors always laughed at that, but there was no denying that at the present moment it was the marines who were the more efficient.

The hands scurried from halliards to braces. A roar from Harrison forwards told that the mooring was slipped, and Hornblower, casting a final glance up at the wind vane, saw that the wind had backed so far easterly that rounding Devil's Point was not going to be simple. With the yards braced round the *Sutherland* turned on her keel and slowly gathered way. Women's screeches and a fluttering of handkerchiefs from the shore boats told how some of the wives whom Hornblower had turned out twenty-four hours ago had put off to say good-bye. Close overside he saw a woman in the stern sheets of a boat blubbering unashamed, her mouth wide open and the tears running like rivers. It was no more than an even chance that she would ever see her man again.

"Keep your eyes inboard, there!" yelled Harrison, who had detected some member of the crew waving farewell. Every man's attention must be kept strictly to the business in hand now.

Hornblower felt the ship heel as Bush directed her course as near to the wind as she would lie; with Devil's Point ahead, and an unfamiliar ship to handle, it was clearly as well to get as far to windward as possible. That heeling of the ship awakened a storm of memories. It was not until one was in a ship under sail, with the deck unstable under one's feet, and the familiar rattle of the blocks and piping of the rigging in one's ears, that the thousand and one details of life at sea became vivid and recognisable again. Hornblower found himself swallowing hard with excitement.

They were shaving the Dockyard Point as closely as possible. Most of the dockyard hands left their work to stare at them, stolidly, but not a soul among them raised a cheer. In seventeen years of warfare they had seen too many King's ships putting out to sea to be excited about this one. Hornblower knew that he ought to have a band on board, to strike up "Britons, Strike Home" or "Come cheer up, my lads, 'tis to glory we steer," but he had no band; he had not the money for one, and he was not going to call on the marine fifer or the ship's fiddler to make a tinny little noise at this moment. Stonehouse Pool was opening up before them now, and beyond it lay the roofs of Plymouth. Maria was there somewhere; perhaps she could see the white topsails, close-hauled to the wind. Perhaps Lady Barbara was there, looking out at the *Sutherland*. Hornblower gulped again.

A little flaw of wind, blowing down Stonehouse Pool, took the ship nearly aback. She staggered until the helmsman allowed her to pay off. Hornblower looked round to starboard. They were coming dangerously close in to Cremyll — he had been correct in his surmise that the *Sutherland* would make plenty of leeway. He watched the wind, and the set of the tide off the point. He looked ahead at Devil's Point on the starboard bow. It might be necessary at any moment to put the ship about and beat up to north-ward again before breasting the tide once more. At the very moment when he saw that they would weather the point he saw Bush raise his head to bark the orders to go about.

"Keep her steady as she goes, Mr. Bush," he said; the quiet order was an announcement that he had taken charge, and Bush closed the mouth which had opened to give the order.

They cleared the buoy a bare fifty yards from any danger, with the water creaming under the lee now as she lay over to the fresh breeze. Hornblower had not interfered to demonstrate the superiority of his seamanship and judgment, but merely because he could not stand by and watch something being done a little less artistically than was possible. In the cold-blooded calculation of chances he was superior to his lieutenant, as his ability at whist proved. Hornblower stood sublimely unconscious of his motives; in fact he hardly realised what he had done — he never gave a thought to his good seamanship.

They were heading straight for the Devil's Point now; Hornblower kept his eye on it as they opened up the Sound.

"You can put the helm aport now," he said. "And set the t'gallant sails, Mr. Bush."

With the wind abeam they headed into the Sound, the rugged Staddon Heights to port and Mount Edgecumbe to starboard. At every yard they advanced towards the open sea the wind blew fresher, calling a keener note from the rigging. The *Sutherland* was feeling the sea a little now, heaving perceptibly to the waves under her bows. With the motion, the creaking of the wooden hull became audible — noticeable on deck, loud below until the ear grew indifferent to the noise.

"God blast these bloody farmers!" groaned Bush, watching the way in which the topgallant sails were being set.

Drake's Island passed away to windward; the *Sutherland* turned her stern to it as with the wind on her port quarter she headed down the Sound. Before the topgallant sails were set they were abreast of Picklecomb Point and opening up Cawsand Bay. There was the convoy — six East India-men with their painted ports like men of war, all flying the gridiron flag of the Honourable Company and one sporting a broad pendant for all the world like a king's commodore; the two naval storeships and the four transports destined for Lisbon. The three-decker *Pluto* and the *Caligula* were rolling to their anchors to seaward of them.

"Flagship's signalling, sir," said Bush, his glass to his eye. "You ought to have reported it a minute ago, Mr. Vincent."

The *Pluto* had not been in sight more than thirty seconds, but there was need for promptness in acknowledging this, the first signal made by the Admiral.

"*Sutherland's* pendant, sir," said the unfortunate signal midshipman, staring through his glass. "Negative. No. 7. Number Seven is 'Anchor,' sir."

"Acknowledge," snapped Hornblow. "Get those t'gallants in again and back the main topsail, Mr. Bush."

With his telescope Hornblower could see men racing up the rigging of the ships. In five minutes both the *Pluto* and the *Caligula* had a cloud of canvas set.

"They commissioned at the Nore, blast 'em," growled Bush.

At the Nore, the gateway of the busiest port in the world, ships of the Royal Navy had the best opportunity of completing their crews with prime seamen taken from incoming merchant vessels, in which it was not necessary to leave more than half a dozen hands to navigate their ships up to London river. In addition, the *Pluto* and *Caligula* had enjoyed the advantage of having been able to drill their crews during the voyage down channel. Already they were standing out of the bay. Signals were soaring up the flagship's halliards.

"To the convoy, sir," said Vincent. "Make haste. Up anchor. Make all sail con-conformable with the weather, sir. Jesus, there's a gun."

An angry report and a puff of smoke indicated that the admiral was calling pointed attention to his signals. The Indiamen, with their heavy crews and man-o'-war routine, were already under weigh. The storeships and transports were slower, as was only to be expected. The other ships were backing and filling outside for what seemed an interminable time before the last of them came creeping out.

" 'Nother signal from the flagship, sir," said Vincent, reading the flags and then hurriedly referring to the signal book. "Take up stations as previously ordered."

That would be to windward of the convoy, and, with the wind abaft as it was, in the rear. Then the ships of war could always dash down to the rescue if a Frenchman tried to cut off one of the convoy under their noses. Hornblower felt the freshening breeze on his cheek. The flagship's topgallants were set, and, as he looked, he saw her royals being spread as well. He would have to conform, but with the wind increasing as it was he fancied that it would not be long before they would have to come in again. Before nightfall they would be reefing topsails. He gave the order to Bush, and watched while the crew gathered at Harrison's bellow of "All hands make sail." He could see the landsmen flinch, not unnaturally — the Sutherland's main royal yard was a hundred and ninety feet above the deck and swaying in a dizzy circle now that the ship was beginning to pitch to the Channel rollers.

Hornblower turned his attention to the flagship and the convoy; he could not bear the sight of frightened men being hounded up the rigging by petty officers with rope's ends. It was necessary, he knew. The Navy did not — of necessity could not — admit the existence of the sentences "I cannot" and "I am afraid." No exceptions could be made, and this was the right moment to grain it into men who had never known compulsion before that every order must be obeyed. If his officers were to start with leniency, leniency would always be expected, and leniency, in a service which might at any moment demand of a man the willing sacrifice of his life, could only be employed in a disciplined crew which had had time to acquire understanding. But Hornblower knew, and sympathised with, the sick terror of a man driven up to the masthead of a ship of the line when previously he had never been higher than the top of a haystack. It was a pitiless, cruel service.

"Peace'll be signed," grumbled Bush to Crystal, the master, "before we make sailors out of these clodhoppers."

A good many of the clodhoppers in question had three days before been living peacefully in their cottages with never a thought of going to sea. And here they were under a grey sky, pitching over a grey sea, with a keener breeze than ever they had known blowing round them, overhead the terrifying heights of the rigging, and underfoot the groaning timbers of a reeling ship.

They were well out to sea now, with the Eddystone in sight from the deck, and under the pressure of the increased sail the *Sutherland* was growing lively. She met her first big roller, and heaved as it reached her bow, rolled, corkscrew fashion, as it passed under her, and then pitched dizzily as it went away astern. There was a wail of despair from the waist.

"Off the decks, there, blast you!" raved Harrison. "Keep it off the decks!"

Men were being seasick already, with the freedom of men taken completely by surprise. Hornblower saw a dozen pale forms staggering and lurching towards the lee rails. One or two men had sat down abruptly on the deck, their hands to their temples. The ship heaved and corkscrewed again, soaring up and then sinking down again as if she would never stop, and the shuddering wail from the waist was repeated. With fixed and fascinated eyes Hornblower watched a wretched yokel vomiting into the scuppers. His stomach heaved in sympathy, and he found himself swallowing hard. There was sweat on his face although he suddenly felt bitterly cold.

He was going to be sick, too, and that very soon. He wanted to be alone, to vomit in discreet privacy, away from the amused glances of the crowd on the quarterdeck. He braced himself to speak with his usual stern indifference, but his ear told him that he was only achieving an unsuccessful perkiness.

"Carry on, Mr. Bush," he said. "Call me if necessary."

He had lost his sea legs, too, during this stay in harbour — he reeled as he crossed the deck, and he had to cling with both hands to the rail of the companion. He reached the half deck safely and lurched to the after-cabin door, stumbling over the coaming. Polwheal was laying dinner at the table.

"Get out!" snarled Hornblower, breathlessly. "Get out!"

Polwheal vanished, and Hornblower reeled out into the stern gallery, fetching up against the rail, leaning his head over towards the foaming wake. He hated the indignity of seasickness as much as he hated the misery of it. It was of no avail to tell himself, as he did, despairingly, while he clutched the rail, that Nelson was always seasick, too, at the beginning of a voyage. Nor was it any help to point out to himself the unfortunate coincidence that voyages always began when he was so tired with excitement and mental and physical exertion that he was ready to be sick anyway.

It was true, but he found no comfort in it as he leaned groaning against the rail with the wind whipping round him.

He was shivering with cold now as the nor'easter blew; his heavy jacket was in his sleeping cabin, but he felt he could neither face the effort of going to fetch it, nor call Polwheal to bring it. And this, he told himself with bitter irony, was the calm solitude for which he had been yearning while entangled in the complications of the shore. Beneath him the pintles of the rudder were groaning in the gudgeons, and the sea was seething yeastily in white foam under the counter. The glass had been falling since yesterday, he remembered, and the weather was obviously working up into a nor'easterly gale. Hounded before it, across the Bay of Biscay, he could see no respite before him for days, at this moment when he felt he could give everything he had in the world for the calm of the Hamoaze again.

His officers were never sick, he thought resentfully, or if they were they were just sick and did not experience this agonising misery. And forward two hundred seasick landsmen were being driven pitilessly to their tasks by overbearing petty officers. It did a man good to be driven to work despite his seasickness, always provided that discipline was not imperilled thereby as it would be in his case. And he was quite, quite sure that not a soul on board felt as miserable as he did, or even half as miserable. He leaned against the rail again, moaning and blaspheming. Experience told him that in three days he would be over all this and feeling as well as ever in his life, but at the moment the prospect of three days of this was just the same as the prospect of an eternity of it. And the timbers creaked and the rudder groaned and the wind whistled and the sea hissed, everything blending into an inferno of noise as he clung shuddering to the rail.

Hornblower took a last pull at his cigar when he heard the drum beating to divisions. He exhaled a lungful of smoke, his head thrown back, looking out from under the cove of the stern gallery up at the blissful blue sky, and then down at the blue water beneath, with the dazzling white foam surging from under the *Sutherland's* counter into her wake. Overhead he heard the measured tramp of the marines as they formed up across the poop deck, and then a brief shuffle of heavy boots as they dressed their line in obedience to the captain's order. The patter of hundreds of pairs of feet acted as a subdued accompaniment as the crew formed up round the decks. When everything had fallen still again Hornblower pitched his cigar overboard, hitched his full-dress coat into position, settled his cocked hat on his head, and walked with dignity, his left hand on his sword-hilt, forward to the half deck and up the companion ladder to the quarterdeck. Bush was there, and Crystal and the midshipmen of the watch. They saluted him, and from farther aft came the snick-snack-snick of the marines presenting arms.

Hornblower stood and looked round him in leisurely fashion; on this Sunday morning it was his duty to inspect the ship, and he could take advantage of the fact to drink in all the beauty and the artistry of the scene. Overhead the pyramids of white canvas described slow cones against the blue sky with the gentle roll of the ship. The decks were snowy white — Bush had succeeded in that in ten days' labour — and the intense orderliness of a ship of war was still more intense on this morning of Sunday inspection. Hornblower shot a searching glance from under lowered eyelids at the crew ranged in long single lines along the gangways and on the main deck. They were standing still, smart enough in their duck frocks and trousers. It was their bearing that he wished to study and that could be done more effectively in a sweeping glance from the quarterdeck than at the close range of the inspection. There could be a certain hint of insolence in the way a restive crew stood to attention, and one could perceive lassitude in a dispirited crew. He could see neither now, for which he was thankful.

Ten days of hard work, of constant drill, of unsleeping supervision, of justice tempered by good humour, had done much to settle the hands to their duty. He had had to order five floggings three days ago, forcing himself to stand apparently unmoved while the whistle and crack of the cat-o'-nine-tails sickened his stomach. One of those floggings might do a little good to the recipient — an old hand who had apparently forgotten what he had learned and needed a sharp reminder of it. The other four would do none to the men whose backs had been lacerated; they would never make good sailors and were mere brutes whom brutal treatment could at least make no worse. He had sacrificed them to show the wilder spirits what might happen as a result of inattention to orders — it was only by an actual demonstration that one could work on the minds of uneducated men. The dose had to be prescribed with the utmost accuracy, neither too great nor too small. He seemed, so his sweeping glance told him, to have hit it off exactly.

Once more he looked round to enjoy the beauty of it all — the orderly ship, the white sails, the blue sky; the scarlet and pipeclay of the marines, the blue and gold of the officers; and there was consummate artistry in the subtle indications that despite the inspection the real pulsating life of the ship was going on beneath it. Where four hundred and more men stood at attention awaiting his lightest word, the quartermaster at the wheel with his mind on the binnacle and the leach of the main course, the lookouts at the masthead, and the officer of the watch with his telescope were living demonstrations of the fact the ship must still be sailed and the King's service carried on.

Hornblower turned aside to begin his inspection. He walked up and down the quadruple ranks of the marines, but although he ran his eye mechanically over the men he took notice of nothing. Captain Morris and his sergeants could be relied upon to attend to details like the pipeclaying of belts and the polishing of buttons. Marines could be drilled and disciplined into machines in a way sailors could not be; he could take the marines for granted and he was not interested in them. Even now, after ten days, he hardly knew the faces and names of six out of the ninety marines on board.

He passed on to the lines of seamen, the officers of each division standing rigidly in front. This was more interesting. The men were trim and smart in their whites — Hornblower wondered how many of them ever realised that the cost of their clothing was deducted from the meagre pay they received when they were paid off. Some of the new hands were horribly sunburned, as a result of unwise exposure to the sudden blazing sun of yesterday. A blond burly figure here had lost the skin from his forearms as well as from his neck and forehead. Hornblower recognised him as Waites, condemned for sheepstealing at Exeter assizes — that explained the sunburn, for Waites had been blanched by months of imprisonment awaiting trial. The raw areas looked abominably painful.

"See that this man Waites," said Hornblower to the petty officer of the division, "attends the surgeon this afternoon. He is to have goose grease for those burns, and whatever lotions the surgeon prescribes.

"Aye aye, sir," said the petty officer.

Hornblower passed on down the line, scanning each man closely. Faces well remembered, faces it was still an effort to put a name to. Faces that he had studied two years back in the far Pacific on board the *Lydia*, faces he had first seen when Gerard brought back his boatload of bewildered captives from St. Ives. Swarthy faces and pale, boys and elderly men, blue eyes, brown eyes, grey eyes. A host of tiny impressions were collecting in

Hornblower's mind; they would be digested together later during his solitary walks in the stern gallery, to form the raw material for the plans he would make to further the efficiency of his crew.

"That man Simms ought to be rated captain of the mizzentop. He's old enough now. What's this man's name? Dawson? No, Dawkins. He's looking sulky. One of Goddard's gang — it looks as if he's still resenting Goddard's flogging. I must remember that."

The sun blazed down upon them, while the ship lifted and swooped over the gentle sea. From the crew he turned his attention to the ship — the breechings of the guns, the way the falls were flemished down, the cleanliness of the decks, the galley and the forecastle. At all this he need only pretend to look — the skies would fall before Bush neglected his duty. But he had to go through with it, with a show of solemnity. Men were oddly influenced — the poor fools would work better for Bush if they thought Hornblower was keeping an eye on him, and they would work better for Hornblower if they thought he inspected the ship thoroughly. This wretched business of capturing men's devotion set Hornblower smiling cynically when he was unobserved.

"A good inspection, Mr. Bush," said Hornblower, returning to the quarterdeck. "The ship is in better order than I hoped for. I shall expect the improvement to continue. You may rig the church now."

It was a God-fearing Admiralty who ordered church service every Sunday morning, otherwise Hornblower would have dispensed with it, as befitted a profound student of Gibbon. As it was, he had managed to evade having a chaplain on board — Hornblower hated parsons. He watched the men dragging up mess stools for themselves, and chairs for the officers. They were working diligently and cheerfully, although not with quite that disciplined purposefulness which characterised a fully trained crew. His coxswain Brown covered the compass box on the quarterdeck with a cloth, and laid on it, with due solemnity, Hornblower's Bible and prayer book. Hornblower disliked these services; there was always the chance that some devout member of his compulsory congregation might raise objections to having to attend — Catholic or Nonconformist. Religion was the only power which could ever pit itself against the bonds of discipline; Hornblower remembered a theologically minded master's mate who had protested against his reading the benediction, as though he, the King's representative at sea — God's representative, when all was said and done — could not read a benediction if he chose!

He glowered at the men as they settled down, and began to read. As the thing had to be done, it might as well be done well, and, as ever, while he read he was struck once more by the beauty of Cranmer's prose and the deftness of his adaptation. Cranmer had been burned alive two hundred and fifty years before — did it benefit him at all to have his prayer book read now?

Bush read the lessons in a tuneless bellow as if he were hailing the foretop. Then Hornblower read the opening lines of the hymn, and Sullivan the fiddler played the first bars of the tune. Bush gave the signal for the singing to start — Hornblower could never bring himself to do that; he told himself he was neither a mountebank nor an Italian opera conductor — and the crew opened their throats and roared it out.

But even hymn singing had its advantages. A captain could often discover a good deal about the spirits of his crew by the way they sang their hymns. This morning either the hymn chosen was specially popular or the crew were happy in the new sunshine, for they were singing lustily, with Sullivan sawing away at an ecstatic obligato on his fiddle. The Cornishmen among the crew apparently knew the hymn well, and fell upon it with a will, singing in parts to add a leavening of harmony to the tuneless bellowing of the others. It all meant nothing to Hornblower — one tune was the same as another to his tone-deaf ear, and the most beautiful music was to him no more than comparable to the noise of a cart along a gravel road. As he listened to the unmeaning din, and gazed at the hundreds of gaping mouths, he found himself wondering as usual whether or not there was any basis of fact in this legend of music — whether other people actually heard something more than mere noise, or whether he was the only person on board not guilty of willful self-deception.

Then he saw a ship's boy in the front row. The hymn meant something to him, at least. He was weeping broken-heartedly, even while he tried to keep his back straight and to conceal his emotions, with the big tears running down his cheeks and his nose all beslobbered. The poor little devil had been touched in one way or another — some chord of memory had been struck. Perhaps the last time he had heard that hymn was in the little church at home, beside his mother and brothers. He was homesick and heartbroken now. Hornblower was glad for his sake as well as for his own when the hymn came to an end; the next ceremony would steady the boy again.

He took up the Articles of War and began to read them, as the Lords Commissioners of the Admiralty had ordained should be done each Sunday in every one of His Britannic Majesty's ships. He knew the solemn sentences by heart at this, his five hundredth reading, every cadency, every turn of phrase, and he read them well. This was better than any vague religious service or Thirty Nine Articles. Here was a code in black and white, a stern, unemotional call to duty pure and simple. Some Admiralty clerk or pettifogging lawyer had had a gift of phrasing just as felicitous as Cranmer's. There was no trumpet call about it, no claptrap appeal to sentiment; there was merely the cold logic of the code which kept the British Navy at sea, and which had guarded England during seventeen years of a struggle for life. He could tell by the deathlike stillness of his audience as he read that their attention had been caught and held, and when he folded the paper away and looked up he could see solemn, set faces. The ship's boy in the front row had forgotten his tears. There was a faraway look in his eyes; obviously he was making good resolutions to attend more strictly to his duty in future. Or perhaps he was dreaming wild dreams of the time to come when he would be a captain in a gold-laced coat commanding a seventy four, or of brave deeds which he would do.

In a sudden revulsion of feeling Hornblower wondered if lofty sentiment would armour the boy against cannon shot — he remembered another ship's boy who had been smashed into a red jam before his eyes by a shot from the *Natividad*.

Borodino

by Leo Tolstoy

1812 Borodino, fought shortly before his entry into Moscow, was just barely a victory for Napoleon and a costly one. Tolstoy describes it according to his personal theories about war, history and the ineffectuality of great men, including Napoleon. Count Pierre Bezuhov, an amiable, bungling Russian civilian, watched some of the fiercest fighting as an interested observer.

Many historians say that the French did not win the battle of Borodino because Napoleon had a cold, and that if he had not had a cold the orders he gave before and during the battle would have been still more full of genius and Russia would have been lost and the face of the world would have been changed. To historians who believe that Russia was shaped by the will of one man — Peter the Great — and that France from a republic became an empire and French armies went to Russia at the will of one man — Napoleon — to say that Russia remained a power because Napoleon had a bad cold on the 24th of August may seem logical and convincing.

If it had depended on Napoleon's will to fight or not to fight the battle of Borodino, and if this or that other arrangement depended on his will, then evidently a cold affecting the manifestation of his will might have saved Russia, and consequently the valet who omitted to bring Napoleon his waterproof-boots on the 24th would have been the saviour of Russia. Along that line of thought such a deduction is indubitable, as indubitable as the deduction Voltaire made in jest (without knowing what he was jesting at) when he said that the Massacre of St. Bartholomew was due to Charles IX's stomach being deranged. But to men who do not admit that Russia was formed by the will of one man, Peter I, or that the French Empire was formed and the war with Russia begun by the will of one man, Napoleon, that argument seems not merely untrue and irrational, but contrary to all human reality. To the question of what causes historic events another answer presents itself, namely, that the course of human events is predetermined from on high — depends on the coincidence of the wills of all who take part in the events, and that a Napoleon's influence on the course of these events is purely external and fictitious.

Strange as at first glance it may seem to suppose that the Massacre of St. Bartholomew was not due to Charles IX's will, though he gave the order for it and thought it was done as a result of that order; and strange as it may seem to suppose that the slaughter of eighty thousand men at Borodino was not due to Napoleon's will, though he ordered the commencement and conduct of the battle and thought it was done because he ordered it; strange as these suppositions appear, yet human dignity — which tells me that each of us is, if not more at least not less a man than the great Napoleon — demands the acceptance of that solution of the question, and historic investigation abundantly confirms it.

At the battle of Borodino Napoleon shot at no one and killed no one. That was all done by the soldiers. Therefore it was not he who killed people.

The French soldiers went to kill and be killed at the battle of Borodino not because of Napoleon's orders but by their own volition. The whole army — French, Italian, German, Polish and Dutch — hungry, ragged and weary of the campaign felt at the sight of an army blocking their road to Moscow that the wine was drawn and must be drunk. Had Napoleon then forbidden them to fight the Russians, they would have killed him and have proceeded to fight the Russians because it was inevitable.

When they heard Napoleon's proclamation offering them, as compensation for mutilation and death, the words of posterity about their having been in the battle before Moscow, they cried 'Vive l'Empereur!' just as they cried 'Vive l'Empereur!' at the sight of the portrait of the boy piercing the terrestrial globe with a toy stick, and just as they would have cried 'Vive l'Empereur!' at any nonsense that might be told them. There was nothing left for them to do but cry 'Vive l'Empereur!' and go to fight, in order to get food and rest as conquerors in Moscow. So it was not because of Napoleon's commands that they killed their fellow men.

And it was not Napoleon who directed the course of the battle, for none of his orders were executed and during the battle he did not know what was going on before him. So the way in which these people killed one another was not decided by Napoleon's will but occurred independently of him, in accord with the will of hundreds of thousands of people who took part in the common action. It *only seemed* to Napoleon that it all took place by his will. And so the question whether he had or had not a cold has no more historic interest than the cold of the least of the transport soldiers.

Moreover the assertion made by various writers that his cold was the cause of his dispositions not being as well planned as on former occasions, and of his orders during the battle not being as good as previously, is quite baseless, which again shows that Napoleon's cold on the 26th of August was unimportant.

The dispositions cited above are not at all worse, but are even better than previous dispositions by which he had won victories. His pseudo-orders during the battle were also no worse than formerly, but much the same as usual. These dispositions and orders only seem worse than previous ones because the battle of Borodino was the first Napoleon did not win. The profoundest and most excellent dispositions and orders seem very bad, and every learned militarist criticizes them with looks of importance, when they relate to a battle that has been lost, and the very worst dispositions and orders seem very good, and serious people fill whole volumes to demonstrate their merits, when they relate to a battle that has been won.

The dispositions drawn up by Weyrother for the battle of Austerlitz were a model of perfection for that kind of composition, but still they were criticized — criticized for their very perfection, for their excessive minuteness.

Napoleon at the battle of Borodino fulfilled his office as representative of authority as well as, and even better than, at other battles. He did nothing harmful to the progress of the battle; he inclined to the most reasonable opinions, he made no confusion, did not contradict himself, did not get frightened or run away from the field of battle, but with his great tact and military experience carried out his role of appearing to command, calmly and with dignity.

On returning from a second careful inspection of the lines, Napoleon remarked:

'The chessmen are set up, the game will begin to-morrow!'

Having ordered punch and summoned de Beausset, he began to talk to him about Paris and about some changes he meant to make in the Empress's household, surprising the prefect by his memory of minute details relating to the Court.

He showed an interest in trifles, joked about de Beausset's love of travel, and chatted carelessly, as a famous, self-confident surgeon who knows his job does when turning up his sleeves and putting on his apron while a patient is being strapped to the operating-table. 'The matter is in my hands and is clear and definite in my head. When the time comes to set to work I shall do it as no one else could, but now I can jest, and the more I jest and the calmer I am the more tranquil and confident you ought to be, and the more amazed at my genius.'

Having finished his second glass of punch, Napoleon went to rest before the serious business which, he considered, awaited him the next day. He was so much interested in that task that he was unable to sleep, and in spite of the cold which had grown worse from the dampness of the evening, he went into the large division of the tent at three o'clock in the morning, loudly blowing his nose. He asked whether the Russians had not withdrawn, and was told that the enemy's fires were still in the same places. He nodded approval.

The adjutant in attendance came into the tent.

'Well, Rapp, do you think we shall do good business today?' Napoleon asked him.

'Without doubt, sire,' replied Rapp.

Napoleon looked at him.

'Do you remember, sire, what you did me the honour to say at Smolensk?' continued Rapp. 'The wine is drawn and must be drunk.'

Napoleon frowned, and sat silent for a long time leaning his head on his hand.

'This poor army!' he suddenly remarked. 'It has diminished greatly since Smolensk. Fortune is frankly a courtesan, Rapp. I have always said so and I am beginning to experience it. But the Guards, Rapp, the Guards are intact?' he remarked interrogatively.

'Yes, sire,' replied Rapp.

Napoleon took a lozenge, put it in his mouth and glanced at his watch. He was not sleepy and it was still not nearly morning. It was impossible to give further orders for the sake of killing time, for the orders had all been given and were now being executed.

'Have the biscuits and rice been served out to the regiments of the Guards?' asked Napoleon sternly.

'Yes, sire.'

'The rice too?'

Rapp replied that he had given the Emperor's order about the rice, but Napoleon shook his head in dissatisfaction as if not believing that his order had been executed. An attendant came in with punch. Napoleon ordered another glass to be brought for Rapp, and silently sipped his own.

'I have neither taste nor smell,' he remarked, sniffing at his glass. 'This cold is tiresome. They talk about medicine — what is the good of medicine when it can't cure a cold! Corvisart gave me these lozenges but they don't help at all. What can doctors cure? One can't cure anything. Our body is a machine for living. It is organized for that, it is its nature. Let life go on in it unhindered and let it defend itself, it will do more than if you paralyse it by encumbering it with remedies. Our body is like a perfect watch that should go for a certain time; the watchmaker cannot open it, he can only adjust it by fumbling, and that blindfold . . . Yes, our body is a machine for living, that is all.'

And having entered on the path of definition, of which he was fond, Napoleon suddenly and unexpectedly gave a new one.

'Do you know, Rapp, what military art is?' asked he. 'It is the art of being stronger than the enemy at a given moment. That's all.'

Rapp made no reply.

'Tomorrow we shall have to deal with Kutuzov!' said Napoleon. 'We shall see! Do you remember at Brannau he commanded an army for three weeks and did not once mount a horse to inspect his entrenchments. . . . We shall see!'

He looked at his watch. It was still only four o'clock. He did not feel sleepy. The punch was finished and there was still nothing to do. He rose, walked to and fro, put on a warm overcoat and a hat, and went out of the tent. The night was dark and damp, a scarcely perceptible moisture was descending from above. Near by, the camp-fires were dimly burning among the French Guards, and in the distance those of the Russian line shone through the smoke. The weather was calm, and the rustle and tramp of the French troops already beginning to move to take up their position was clearly audible.

Napoleon walked about in front of his tent, looked at the fires and listened to these sounds, and as he was passing a tall guardsman in a shaggy cap, who was standing sentinel before his tent and had drawn himself up like a black pillar at the sight of the Emperor, Napoleon stopped in front of him.

'What year did you enter the service?' he asked with that affectation of military bluntness and geniality with which he always addressed the soldiers.

The man answered the question.

'Ah! One of the old ones! Has your regiment had its rice?'

'It has, your Majesty.'

Napoleon nodded and walked away.

At half-past five Napoleon rode to the village of Shevardino. It was growing light, the sky was clearing, only a single cloud lay in the east. The abandoned camp-fires were burning themselves out in the faint morning light.

On the right a single deep report of a cannon resounded and died away in the prevailing silence. Some minutes passed. A second and third report shook the air, then a fourth and fifth boomed solemnly near by on the right.

The first shots had not yet ceased to reverberate before others rang out and yet more were heard mingling with and overtaking one another.

Napoleon with his suite rode up to the Shevardino Redoubt where he dismounted. The game had begun.

Having reached the knoll, Pierre sat down at one end of a trench surrounding the battery, and gazed at what was going on around him with an unconsciously happy smile. Occasionally he rose and walked about the battery still with that same smile, trying not to obstruct the soldiers who were loading, hauling the guns and continually running past him with bags and charges. The guns of that battery were being fired continually one after another with a deafening roar, enveloping the whole neighborhood in powder-smoke.

In contrast with the dread felt by the infantrymen placed in support, here in the battery where a small number of men busy at their work were separated from the rest by a trench, every one experienced a common and as it were family feeling of animation.

The intrusion of Pierre's non-military figure in a white hat made an unpleasant impression at first. The soldiers looked askance at him with surprise and even alarm as they went past him. The senior artillery officer, a tall, long-legged, pock-marked man, moved over to Pierre as if to see the action of the farthest gun and looked at him with curiosity.

A young round-faced officer, quite a boy still and evidently only just out of the Cadet College, who was zealously commanding the two guns entrusted to him, addressed Pierre sternly.

'Sir,' he said, 'permit me to ask you to stand aside. You must not be here.'

The soldiers shook their head disapprovingly as they looked at Pierre. But when they had convinced themselves that this man in the white hat was doing no harm, but either sat quietly on the slope of the trench with a shy smile, or, politely making way for the soldiers, paced up and down the battery under fire as calmly as if he were on a boulevard, their feeling of hostile distrust gradually began to change into a kindly and bantering sympathy, such as soldiers feel for their dogs, cocks, goats and in general for the animals that live with the regiment. The men soon accepted Pierre into their family, adopted him, gave him a nickname ('our gentleman'), and made kindly fun of him among themselves.

A shell tore up the earth two paces from Pierre and he looked around with a smile as he brushed from his clothes some earth it had thrown up.

'And how's it you're not afraid, sir, really now?' a red-faced, broad-shouldered soldier asked Pierre, with a grin that disclosed a set of round, white teeth.

'Are you afraid, then?' said Pierre.

'What else do you expect?' answered the soldier. 'She has no mercy, you know! When she comes spluttering down, out go your innards. One can't help being afraid,' he said laughing.

Several of the men, with bright kindly faces, stopped beside Pierre. They seemed not to have expected him to talk like anybody else, and the discovery that he did so delighted them.

'It's the business of us soldiers. But in a gentleman it's wonderful! There's a gentleman for you!'

'To your places!' cried the young officer to the men gathered round Pierre.

The young officer was evidently exercising his duties for the first or second time, and therefore treated both his superiors and the men with great precision and formality.

The booming cannonade and the fusillade of musketry was growing more intense over the whole field, especially to the left where Bagration's *flèches* were, but where Pierre was the smoke of the firing made it almost impossible to distinguish anything. Moreover his whole attention was engrossed by watching the family circle — separate from all else — formed by the men in the battery. His first unconscious feeling of joyful animation produced by the sights and sounds of the battlefield was now replaced by another, especially since he had seen that soldier lying alone in the hayfield. Now, seated on the slope of the trench, he observed the faces of those around him.

By ten o'clock some twenty men had already been carried away from the battery; two guns were smashed and cannon-balls fell more and more frequently on the battery, and spent bullets buzzed and whistled around. But the men in the battery seemed not to notice this, and merry voices and jokes were heard on all sides.

'A live one!' shouted a man as a whistling shell approached.

'Not this way! To the infantry!' added another with loud laughter, seeing the shell fly past and fall into the ranks of their supports.

'Are you bowing to a friend, eh?' remarked another, chaffing a peasant who ducked low as a cannon-ball flew over.

Several soldiers gathered by the wall of the trench, looking out to see what was happening in front.

'They've withdrawn the front line, it has retired,' said they, pointing over the earthwork.

'Mind your own business,' an old sergeant shouted at them. 'If they've retired it's because there's work for them to do farther back.'

And the sergeant, taking one of the men by the shoulders, gave him a shove with his knee. This was followed by a burst of laughter.

'To the fifth gun, wheel it up!' came shouts from one side.

'Now then, all together like bargees!' rose the merry voices of those who were moving the gun.

'Oh, she nearly knocked our gentleman's hat off!' cried the red-faced humorist, showing his teeth and chaffing Pierre. 'Awkward baggage!' he added reproachfully to a cannon-ball that struck a cannon-wheel and a man's leg.

'Now then, you foxes!' said another, laughing at some militiamen who, stooping low, entered the battery to carry away the wounded man.

'So this gruel isn't to your taste? Oh, you crows! You're scared!' they shouted at the militiamen who stood hesitating before the man whose leg had been torn off.

'There lads . . . oh, oh!' they mimicked the peasants, 'they don't like it at all!'

Pierre noticed that after every ball hit the redoubt, and after every loss, the liveliness increased more and more.

As the flames of the fire hidden within come more and more vividly and rapidly from an approaching thunder-cloud, so, as if in opposition to what was taking place, the lightning of hidden fire growing more and more intense glowed in the faces of these men.

Pierre did not look out at the battlefield and was not concerned to know what was happening there; he was entirely absorbed in watching this fire which burnt ever more brightly and which he felt was flaming up in the same way in his own soul.

At ten o'clock the infantry that had been among the bushes in front of the battery and along the Kamenka streamlet retreated. From the battery they could be seen running back past it carrying their wounded on their muskets. A general with his suite came to the battery, and after speaking to the colonel gave Pierre an angry look and went away again having ordered the infantry supports behind the battery to lie down, so as to be less exposed to fire. After this from amid the ranks of infantry to the right of the battery came the sound of a drum and shouts of command, and from the battery one saw how those ranks of infantry moved forward.

Pierre looked over the wall of the trench, and was particularly struck by a pale young officer who, letting his sword hang down, was walking backwards and kept glancing uneasily around.

The ranks of the infantry disappeared amid the smoke but their long-drawn shout and rapid musketry firing could still be heard. A few minutes later crowds of wounded men and stretcher-bearers came back from that direction. Projectiles began to fall still more frequently in the battery. Several men were lying about who had not been removed. Around the cannon the men moved still more briskly and busily. No one any longer took notice of Pierre. Once or twice he was shouted at for being in the way. The senior officer moved with big, rapid strides from one gun to another with a frowning face. The young officer, with his face still more flushed, commanded the men more scrupulously than ever. The soldiers handed up the charges, turned, loaded, and did their business with strained smartness. They gave little jumps as they walked, as though they were on springs.

The storm-cloud had come upon them, and in every face the fire which Pierre had watched kindle, burnt up brightly. Pierre was standing beside the commanding officer. The young officer, his hand to his shako, ran up to his superior.

'I have the honour to report, sir, that only eight rounds are left. Are we to continue firing?' he asked.

'Grape-shot!' the senior shouted, without answering the question, looking over the wall of the trench.

Suddenly something happened: the young officer gave a gasp, and bending double sat down on the ground like a bird shot on the wing. Everything became strange, confused and misty in Pierre's eyes.

One cannon-ball after another whistled by and struck the earthwork, a soldier or a gun. Pierre, who had not noticed these sounds before, now heard nothing else. On the right of the battery soldiers shouting 'Hurrah!' were running not forwards but backwards, it seemed to Pierre.

A cannon-ball struck the very end of the earthwork by which he was standing, crumbling down the earth; a black ball flashed before his eyes and at the same instant plumped into something. Some militiamen who were entering the battery ran back.

'All with grape-shot!' shouted the officer.

The sergeant ran up to the officer and in a frightened whisper informed him (as a butler at dinner informs his master that there is no more of some wine asked for) that there were no more charges.

'The scoundrels! What are they doing?' shouted the officer turning to Pierre.

The officer's face was red and perspiring and his eyes glittered under his frowning brow.

'Run to the reserves and bring up the ammunition-boxes!' he yelled, angrily avoiding Pierre with his eyes and speaking to his men.

'I'll go,' said Pierre.

The officer, without answering him, strode across to the opposite side.

'Don't fire. . . . Wait!' he shouted.

The man who had been ordered to go for ammunition stumbled against Pierre.

'Eh, sir, this is no place for you,' said he, and ran down the slope.

Pierre ran after him, avoiding the spot where the young officer was sitting.

One cannon-ball, another, and a third flew over him, falling in front, beside and behind him. Pierre ran down the slope. 'Where am I going?' he suddenly asked himself when he was already near the green ammunition-wagons. He halted irresolutely, not knowing whether to return or go on. Suddenly a terrible concussion threw him backwards to the ground. At the same instant he was dazzled by a great flash of flame, and immediately a deafening roar, crackling and whistling, made his ears tingle.

When he came to himself he was sitting on the ground leaning on his hands; the ammunition-wagons he had been approaching no longer existed, only charred green boards and rags littered the scorched grass, and a horse, dangling fragments of its shafts behind it, galloped past, while another horse lay, like Pierre, on the ground, uttering prolonged and piercing cries.

Beside himself with terror Pierre jumped up and ran back to the battery, as to the only refuge from the horrors that surrounded him.

On entering the earthwork he noticed that there were men doing something there but that no shots were being fired from the battery. He had no time to realize who these men were. He saw the senior officer lying on the earth wall with his back turned as if he were examining something down below, and that one of the soldiers he had noticed before was struggling forward shouting 'Brothers!' and trying to free himself from some men who were holding him by the arm. He also saw something else that was strange.

But he had not time to realize that the colonel had been killed, that the soldier shouting 'Brothers!' was a prisoner, and that another man had been bayoneted in the back before his eyes, for hardly had he run into the redoubt before a thin, sallow-faced, perspiring man in a blue uniform rushed on him sword in hand, shouting something. Instinctively guarding against the shock — for they had been running together at full speed before they saw one another — Pierre put out his hand and seized the man (a French officer) by the shoulder with one hand and by the throat with the other. The officer, dropping his sword, seized Pierre by his collar.

For some seconds they gazed with frightened eyes at one another's unfamiliar faces, and both were perplexed at what they had done and what they were to do next. 'Am I taken prisoner or have I taken him prisoner?' each was thinking. But the French officer was evidently more inclined to think he had been taken prisoner because Pierre's strong hand, impelled by instinctive fear, squeezed his throat ever tighter and tighter. The Frenchman was about to say something, when just above their heads, terrible and low, a cannon-ball whistled, and it seemed to Pierre that the French officer's head had been torn off, so swiftly had he ducked it.

Pierre too bent his head and let his hands fall. Without further thought as to who had taken whom prisoner, the Frenchman ran back to the battery and Pierre ran down the slope stumbling over the dead and wounded who, it seemed to him, caught at his feet. But before he reached the foot of the knoll he was met by a dense crowd of Russian soldiers who, stumbling, tripping up, and shouting, ran merrily and wildly towards the battery. (This was the attack for which Ermolov claimed the credit, declaring that only his courage and good luck made such a feat possible: it was the attack in which he was said to have thrown some St. George's Crosses he had in his pocket into the battery for the first soldiers to take who got there.)

The French who had occupied the battery fled, and our troops shouting 'Hurrah!' pursued them so far beyond the battery that it was difficult to call them back.

The prisoners were brought down from the battery and among them was a wounded French general, whom the officers surrounded. Crowds of wounded — some known to Pierre and some unknown — Russians and French, with faces distorted by suffering, walked, crawled, and were carried on stretchers, from the battery. Pierre again went up onto the knoll where he had spent over an hour, and of that family circle which had received him as a member he did not find a single one. There were many dead whom he did not know, but some he recognized. The young officer still sat in the same way, bent double, in a pool of blood at the edge of the earth wall. The red-faced man was still twitching, but they did not carry him away.

Pierre ran down the slope once more.

'Now they will stop it, now they will be horrified at what they have done!' he thought, aimlessly going towards a crowd of stretcher-bearers moving from the battlefield.

But behind the veil of smoke the sun was still high, and in front and especially to the left, near Semenovsk, something seemed to be seething in the smoke, and the roar of cannon and musketry did not diminish, but even increased to desperation like a man who, straining himself, shrieks with all his remaining strength.

The chief action of the Battle of Borodino was fought within the seven thousand feet between Borodino and Bagration's *flèches*. Beyond that space there was, on the one side a demonstration made by the Russians with Uvarov's cavalry at midday, and on the other side, beyond Utitsa, Poniatowski's collision with Tuchkov; but these two were detached and feeble actions in comparison with what took place in the centre of the battlefield. On the field between Borodino and the *flèches*, beside the wood, the chief action of the day took place on an open space visible from both sides, and was fought in the simplest and most artless way.

The battle began on both sides with a cannonade from several hundred guns.

Then when the whole field was covered with smoke, two divisions, Campan's and Dessaix's, advanced from the French right, while Murat's troops advanced on Borodino from their left.

From the Shevardino Redoubt where Napoleon was standing the *flèches* were a verst away, and it was more than two versts as the crow flies to Borodino, so that Napoleon could not see what was happening there, especially as the smoke mingling with the mist hid the whole locality. The soldiers of Dessaix's division advancing against the *flèches* could only be seen till they had entered the hollow that lay between them and the *flèches*. As soon as they had descended into the hollow, the smoke of the guns and musketry on the *flèches* grew so dense that it covered the whole approach on that side of it. Through the smoke glimpses could be caught of something black — probably men — and at times the glint of bayonets. But whether they were moving or stationary, whether they were French or Russian, could not be discovered from the Shevardino Redoubt.

The sun had risen brightly and its slanting rays struck straight into Napoleon's face as, shading his eyes with his hand, he looked at the *flèches*. The smoke spread out before them, and at times it looked as if the smoke were moving, at times as if the troops moved. Sometimes shouts were heard through the firing, but it was impossible to tell what was being done there.

Napoleon, standing on the knoll, looked through a field-glass, and in its small circlet saw smoke and men, sometimes his own and sometimes Russians, but when he looked again with the naked eye, he could not tell where what he had seen was.

He descended the knoll and began walking up and down before it.

Occasionally he stopped, listened to the firing, and gazed intently at the battlefield.

But not only was it impossible to make out what was happening from where he was standing down below, or from the knoll above on which some of his generals had taken their stand, but even from the *flèches* themselves — in which by this time there were now Russian and now French soldiers, alternately or together, dead, wounded, alive, frightened or maddened — even at those *flèches* themselves it was impossible to make out what was taking place. There for several hours amid incessant cannon and musketry fire, now Russians were seen alone, now Frenchmen alone, now infantry and now cavalry: they appeared, fired, fell, collided, not knowing what to do with one another, screamed and ran back again.

From the battlefield adjutants he had sent out, and orderlies from his marshals, kept galloping up to Napoleon with reports of the progress of the action, but all these reports were false, both because it was impossible in the heat of battle to say what was happening at any given moment, and because many of the adjutants did not go to the actual place of conflict but reported what they had heard from others; and also because while an adjutant was riding the couple of versts to Napoleon circumstances changed and the news he brought was already becoming false. Thus an adjutant galloped up from Murat with tidings that Borodino had been occupied and the bridge over the Kolocha was in the hands of the French. The adjutant asked whether Napoleon wished the troops to cross it? Napoleon gave orders that the troops should form up on the farther side and wait. But before that order was given — almost as soon in fact as the adjutant had left Borodino — the bridge had been retaken by the Russians and burnt, in the very skirmish at which Pierre had been present at the beginning of the battle.

An adjutant galloped up from the *flèches* with a pale and frightened face and reported to Napoleon that their attack had been repulsed, Campan wounded, and Davout killed; yet at the very time the adjutant had been told that the French had been repulsed, the *flèches* had in fact been re-captured by other French troops, and Davout was alive and only slightly bruised. On the basis of these necessarily untrustworthy reports Napoleon gave his orders, which had either been executed before he gave them, or could not be and were not executed.

The marshals and generals, who were nearer to the field of battle but, like Napoleon, did not take part in the actual fighting and only occasion-ally went within musketry range, made their own arrangements without asking Napoleon and issued orders where and in what direction to fire and where cavalry should gallop and infantry should run. But even their orders, like Napoleon's, were seldom carried out, and then but partially. For the most part things happened contrary to their orders. Soldiers or-dered to advance ran back on meeting grape-shot; soldiers ordered to re-main where they were, suddenly seeing Russians unexpectedly before them, sometimes rushed back and sometimes forward, and the cavalry dashed without orders in pursuit of the flying Russians. In this way two cavalry regiments galloped through the Semenovsk hollow and as soon as they reached the top of the incline, turned round and galloped full speed back again. The infantry moved in the same way, sometimes running to quite other places than those they were ordered to go to. All orders as to where and when to move the guns, when to send infantry to shoot or horsemen to ride down the Russian infantry — all such orders were given by the officers on the spot nearest to the units concerned, without asking either Ney, Davout, or Murat, much less Napoleon. They did not fear getting into trouble for not fulfilling orders or for acting on their own initi-ative, for in battle what is at stake is what is dearest to man — his own life, and it sometimes seems that safety lies in running back, sometimes in running forward; and these men who were right in the heat of the battle acted according to the mood of the moment. In reality, however, all these movements forward and backward did not improve or alter the position of the troops. All their rushing and galloping at one another did little harm, the harm of disablement and death was caused by the balls and bullets that flew over the fields on which these men were floundering about. As soon as they left the place where the balls and bullets were flying about, their superiors, located in the background, re-formed them and brought them under discipline, and under the influence of that discipline led them back to the zone of fire, where under the influence of fear of death they lost their discipline and rushed about according to the chance promptings of the throng.

Napoleon's generals — Davout, Ney and Murat, who were near that region of fire and sometimes even entered it — repeatedly led into it huge masses of well-ordered troops. But contrary to what had always happened in their former battles, instead of the news they expected of the enemy's flight, these orderly masses returned thence as disorganized and terrified mobs. The generals re-formed them, but their numbers constantly decreased. In the middle of the day Murat sent his adjutant to Napoleon to demand reinforcements.

Napoleon sat at the foot of the knoll, drinking punch, when Murat's adjutant galloped up with an assurance that the Russians would be routed if his Majesty would let him have another division.

'Reinforcements?' said Napoleon in a tone of stern surprise, looking at the adjutant — a handsome lad with long black curls arranged like Murat's own — as though he did not understand his words.

'Reinforcements!' thought Napoleon to himself. 'How can they need reinforcements when they already have half the army directed against a weak, unentrenched Russian wing?'

'Tell the King of Naples,' said he sternly, 'that it is not noon yet, and I don't yet see my chess-board clearly. Go! . . .'

The handsome boy-adjutant with the long hair sighed deeply without removing his hand from his hat, and galloped back to where men were being slaughtered.

Napoleon rose and having summoned Caulaincourt and Berthier began talking to them about matters unconnected with the battle.

In the midst of this conversation, which was beginning to interest Napoleon, Berthier's eyes turned to look at a general with a suite, who was galloping towards the knoll on a lathering horse. It was Belliard. Having dismounted he went up to the Emperor with rapid strides, and in a loud voice began boldly demonstrating the necessity of sending reinforcements. He swore on his honour that the Russians were lost if the Emperor would give another division.

Napoleon shrugged his shoulders and continued to pace up and down without replying. Belliard began talking loudly and eagerly to the generals of the suite around him.

'You are very fiery, Belliard,' said Napoleon, when he again came up to the general. 'In the heat of a battle it is easy to make a mistake. Go and have another look and then come back to me.'

Before Belliard was out of sight, a messenger from another part of the battlefield galloped up.

'Now then, what do you want?' asked Napoleon in the tone of a man irritated at being continually disturbed.

'Sire, the prince . . .' began the adjutant.

'Asks for reinforcements?' said Napoleon with an angry gesture.

The adjutant bent his head affirmatively and began to report, but the Emperor turned from him, took a couple of steps, stopped, came back, and called Berthier.

'We must give reserves,' he said, moving his arms slightly apart. 'Who do you think should be sent there?' he asked of Berthier (whom he subsequently termed 'that gosling I have made an eagle').

'Send Claparède's division, sire,' replied Berthier, who knew all the divisions and battalions by heart.

Napoleon nodded assent.

The adjutant galloped to Claparède's division and a few minutes later the Young Guards stationed behind the knoll moved forward. Napoleon gazed silently in that direction.

'No!' he suddenly said to Berthier. 'I can't send Claparède. Send Friant's division.'

Though there was no advantage in sending Friant's division instead of Claparède's, and even an obvious inconvenience and delay in stopping Claparède and sending Friant now, the order was carried out exactly. Napoleon did not notice that in regard to his army he was playing the part of a doctor who hinders by his medicines — a role he so justly understood and condemned.

Friant's division disappeared as the others had done, into the smoke of the battlefield. From all sides adjutants continued to arrive at a gallop and as if by agreement all said the same thing. They all asked for reinforcements and all said that the Russians were holding their positions and maintaining a hellish fire under which the French army was melting away.

Napoleon sat on a camp-stool, wrapped in thought.

M. de Beausset, the man so fond of travel, having fasted since morning, came up to the Emperor and ventured respectfully to suggest lunch to his Majesty.

'I hope I may now congratulate your Majesty on a victory?' said he.

Napoleon silently shook his head in negation. Assuming the negation to refer only to the victory and not to the lunch, M. de Beausset ventured with respectful jocularity to remark that there is no reason for not having lunch when one can get it.

'Go away . . .' exclaimed Napoleon suddenly and morosely, and turned aside.

A beatific smile of regret, repentance and ecstasy, beamed on M. de Beausset's face and he glided away to the other generals.

Napoleon was experiencing a feeling of depression like that of an ever-lucky gambler who, after recklessly flinging money about and always winning, suddenly just when he has calculated all the chances of the game, finds that the more he considers his play the more surely he loses.

His troops were the same, his generals the same, the same preparations had been made, the same dispositions, and the same proclamation *courte et énergique,* he himself was still the same: he knew that and knew that he was now even more experienced and skillful than before. Even the enemy was the same as at Austerlitz and Friedland — yet the terrible stroke of his arm had supernaturally become impotent.

All the old methods that had been unfailingly crowned with success: the concentration of batteries on one point, an attack by reserves to break the enemy's lines and cavalry attack by 'the men of iron,' all these methods had already been employed, yet not only was there no victory, but from all sides came the same news of generals killed and wounded, of reinforcements needed, or the impossibility of driving back the Russians, and of disorganization among his own troops.

Formerly, after he had given two or three orders and uttered a few phrases, marshals and adjutants had come galloping with congratulations and happy faces, announcing the trophies taken, the corps of prisoners, bundles of enemy eagles and standards, cannon and stores, and Murat had only begged leave to loose the cavalry to gather in the baggage-wagons. So it had been at Lodi, Marengo, Arcola, Jena, Austerlitz, Wagram and so on. But now something strange was happening to his troops.

Despite news of the capture of the *flèches,* Napoleon saw that this was not the same, not at all the same, as what had happened in his former battles. He saw that what he was feeling was felt by all the men about him experienced in the art of war. All their faces looked dejected, and they all shunned one another's eyes — only a de Beausset could fail to grasp the meaning of what was happening.

But Napoleon with his long experience of war well knew the meaning of a battle not gained by the attacking side in eight hours, after all efforts had been expended. He knew that it was a lost battle and that the least accident might now — with the fight balanced on such a strained centre — destroy him and his army.

When he ran his mind over the whole of this strange Russian campaign in which not one battle had been won, and in which not a flag, or cannon, or army corps, had been captured in two months, when he looked at the concealed depression on the faces around him and heard reports of the Russians still holding their ground — a terrible feeling like a nightmare took possession of him, and all the unlucky accidents that might destroy him occurred to his mind. The Russians might fall on his left wing, might break through his centre, he himself might be killed by a stray cannon-ball. All this was possible. In former battles he had only considered the possibilities of success, but now innumerable unlucky chances presented themselves, and he expected them all. Yes, it was like a dream in which a man fancies that a ruffian is coming to attack him, and raises his arm to strike that ruffian a terrible blow which he knows should annihilate him, but then feels that his arm droops powerless and limp like a rag, and the horror of unavoidable destruction seizes him in his helplessness.

The news that the Russians were attacking the left flank of the French army aroused that horror in Napoleon. He sat silently on a camp-stool below the knoll, with head bowed and elbows on his knees. Berthier approached and suggested that they should ride along the line to ascertain the position of affairs.

'What? What do you say?' asked Napoleon. 'Yes, tell them to bring me my horse.'

He mounted and rode towards Semenovsk.

Amid the powder-smoke, slowly dispersing over the whole space through which Napoleon rode, horses and men were lying in pools of blood, singly or in heaps. Neither Napoleon nor any of his generals had ever before seen such horrors or so many slain in such a small area. The roar of guns, that had not ceased for ten hours, wearied the ear and gave a peculiar significance to the spectacle, as music does to *tableaux vivants*. Napoleon rode up the high ground at Semenovsk, and through the smoke saw ranks of men in uniform of a colour unfamiliar to him. They were Russians.

The Russians stood in serried ranks behind Semenovsk village and its knoll, and their guns boomed incessantly along their line and sent forth clouds of smoke. It was no longer a battle: it was a continuous slaughter which could be of no avail either to the French or the Russians. Napoleon stopped his horse and again fell into the reverie from which Berthier had aroused him. He could not stop what was going on before him and around him and was supposed to be directed by him and to depend on him, and from its lack of success this affair, for the first time, seemed to him unnecessary and horrible.

One of the generals rode up to Napoleon and ventured to offer to lead the Old Guard into action. Ney and Berthier, standing near Napoleon, exchanged looks and smiled contemptuously at this general's senseless offer.

Napoleon bowed his head and remained silent a long time.

'At eight hundred leagues* from France, I will not have my Guard destroyed!' he said, and turning his horse rode back to Shevárdino.

The terrible spectacle of the battlefield covered with dead and wounded, together with the heaviness of his head and the news that some twenty generals he knew personally had been killed or wounded, and the consciousness of the impotence of his once mighty arm, produced an unexpected impression on Napoleon who usually liked to look at the killed and wounded, thereby, he considered, testing his strength of mind. This day the horrible appearance of the battlefield overcame that strength of mind which he thought constituted his merit and his greatness. He rode hurriedly from the battlefield and returned to the Shevardino knoll, where he sat on his campstool, his sallow face swollen and heavy, his eyes dim, his nose red, and his voice hoarse, involuntarily listening, with downcast eyes, to the sounds of firing. With painful dejection he awaited the end of this action, in which he regarded himself as a participant and which he was unable to arrest. A personal, human feeling for a brief moment got the better of the artificial phantasm of life he had served so long. He felt in his own person the sufferings and death he had witnessed on the battlefield. The heaviness of his head and chest reminded him of the possibility of suffering and death for himself. At that moment he did not desire Moscow, or victory, or glory (what need had he for any more glory?). The one thing he wished for was rest, tranquility and freedom. But when he had been on the Semenovsk heights the artillery commander had proposed

(* The French *lieue*, or league, is about two and a half miles, so Napoleon's calculation was that he was two thousand miles' march from home.)

to him to bring several batteries of artillery up to those heights to strengthen the fire on the Russian troops crowded in front of Knyazkovo. Napoleon had assented and had given orders that news should be brought him of the effect those batteries produced.

An adjutant came now to inform him that the fire of two hundred guns had been concentrated on the Russians, as he had ordered, but that they still held their ground.

'Our fire is mowing them down by rows, but still they hold on,' said the adjutant.

'They want more!' said Napoleon in a hoarse voice.

'Sire?' asked the adjutant, who had not heard his remark.

'They want more!' croaked Napoleon frowning. 'Let them have it!'

Even before he gave that order the thing he did not desire, and for which he gave the order only because he thought it was expected of him, was being done. And he fell back into that artificial realm of imaginary greatness, and again — as a horse walking a treadmill thinks it is doing something for itself — he submissively fulfilled the cruel, sad, gloomy and inhuman role predestined for him.

And not for that day and hour alone were the mind and conscience darkened of this man on whom the responsibility for what was happening lay more than on all the others who took part in it. Never to the end of his life could he understand goodness, beauty, or truth, or the significance of his actions which were too contrary to goodness and truth, too remote from everything human, for him ever to be able to grasp their meaning. He could not disavow his actions, belauded as they were by half the world, and so he had to repudiate truth, goodness and all humanity.

Not only on that day, as he rode over the battlefield strewn with men killed and maimed (by his will as he believed), did he reckon as he looked at them how many Russians there were for each Frenchman and, deceiving himself, find reason for rejoicing in the calculation that there were five Russians for every Frenchman. Not on that day alone did he write in a letter to Paris that 'the battlefield was superb,' because fifty thousand corpses lay there, but even on the island of St. Helena in the peaceful solitude where he said he intended to devote his leisure to an account of the great deeds he had done, he wrote:

'The Russian war should have been the most popular war of modern times: it was a war of good sense, for real interests, for the tranquility and security of all; it was purely pacific and conservative.

'It was a war for a great cause, the end of uncertainties and the beginning of security. A new horizon and new labours were opening out, full of well-being and prosperity for all. The European system was already founded; all that remained was to organize it.'

Several tens of thousands of the slain lay in diverse postures and various uniforms on the fields and meadows belonging to the Davydov family and to the Crown serfs — those fields and meadows where for hundreds of years the peasants of Borodino, Gorki, Shevardino and Semenovsk had reaped their harvests and pastured their cattle. At the dressing-stations the grass and earth were soaked with blood for a space of some three acres around. Crowds of men of various arms, wounded and unwounded, with frightened faces, dragged themselves back to Moshaysk from the one army, and back to Valuevo from the other. Other crowds, exhausted and hungry, went forward led by their officers. Others held their ground and continued to fire.

Over the whole field, previously so gaily beautiful with the glitter of bayonets and cloudlets of smoke in the morning sun, there now spread a mist of damp and smoke and a strange acid smell of saltpetre and blood. Clouds gathered and drops of rain began to fall on the dead and wounded, on the frightened, exhausted and hesitating men, as if to say: 'Enough, men! Enough! Cease . . . bethink yourselves! What are you doing?'

To the men of both sides alike, worn out by want of food and rest, it began equally to appear doubtful whether they should continue to slaughter one another; all the faces expressed hesitation, and the question arose in every soul: 'For what, for whom, must I kill and be killed? . . . You may go and kill whom you please, but I don't want to do so any more!' By evening this thought had ripened in every soul. At any moment these men might have been seized with horror at what they were doing, and might have thrown up everything and run away anywhere.

But though towards the end of the battle the men felt all the horror of what they were doing, though they would have been glad to leave off, some incomprehensible, mysterious power continued to control them, and they still brought up the charges, loaded, aimed, and applied the match, though only one artilleryman survived out of every three, and though they stumbled and panted with fatigue, perspiring and stained with blood and powder. The cannon-balls flew just as swiftly and cruelly from both sides, crushing human bodies, and that terrible work which was not done by the will of a man but at the will of Him who governs men and worlds, continued.

Any one looking at the disorganized rear of the Russian army would have said that if only the French made one more slight effort, it would disappear; and any one looking at the rear of the French army would have said that the Russians need only make one more slight effort and the French would be destroyed. But neither the French nor the Russians made that effort, and the flame of battle burnt slowly out.

The Russians did not make that effort because they were not attacking the French. At the beginning of the battle they stood blocking the way to Moscow and they still did so at the end of the battle as at the beginning. But even had the aim of the Russians been to drive the French from their positions, they could not have made this last effort, for all the Russian troops had been broken up, there was no part of the Russian army that had not suffered in the battle, and though still holding their positions they had lost one half of their army.

The French, with the memory of al their former victories during fifteen years, with the assurance of Napoleon's invincibility, with the consciousness that they had captured part of the battlefield and had lost only a quarter of their men and still had their Guards intact, twenty thousand strong, might easily have made the effort. The French who had attacked the Russian army in order to drive it from its position ought to have made that effort, for as long as the Russians continued to block the road to Moscow as before, the aim of the French had not been attained and all their efforts and losses were in vain. But the French did not make that effort. Some historians say that Napoleon need only have used his Old Guards, who were intact, and the battle would have been won. To speak of what would have happened had Napoleon sent his Guards is like talking of what would happen if autumn became spring. It could not be. Napoleon did not give his Guards, not because he did not want to, but because it could not be done. All the generals, officers and soldiers of the French army knew it could not be done, because the flagging spirit of the troops would not permit it.

It was not Napoleon alone who had experienced that nightmare feeling of the mighty arm being stricken powerless, but all the generals and soldiers of his army whether they had taken part in the battle or not, after all their experience of previous battles — when after one-tenth of such efforts the enemy had fled — experienced a similar feeling of terror before an enemy who after losing HALF his men, stood as threateningly at the end as at the beginning of the battle. The moral force of the attacking French army was exhausted. Not that sort of victory which is defined by the capture of pieces of material fastened to sticks, called standards, and of the ground on which the troops had stood and were standing, but a moral victory that convinces the enemy of the moral superiority of his opponent and of his own impotence, was gained by the Russians at Borodino. The French invaders, like an infuriated animal that has in its onslaught received a mortal wound, felt that they were perishing, but could not stop, any more than the Russian army, weaker by one-half, could help swerving. By the impetus gained, the French army was still able to roll forward to Moscow, but there, without further effort on the part of the Russians, it had to perish, bleeding from the mortal wound it had received at Borodino. The direct consequence of the battle of Borodino was Napoleon's senseless flight from Moscow, his retreat along the old Smolensk road, the destruction of the invading army of five hundred thousand men, and the downfall of Napoleonic France, on which at Borodino for the first time the hand of an opponent of stronger spirit had been laid.

The Warrior's Soul

by Joseph Conrad

> 1812   The retreat of Napoleon's Grand Army from
> Moscow was a horror compounded of attacks by Rus-
> sian troops and by Russian guerrillas, starvation, and
> the snow and cold of winter. This is the background
> of one of the finest of Conrad's short stories.

The old officer with long white moustaches gave rein to his indignation.

"Is it possible that you youngsters should have no more sense than that! Some of you had better wipe the milk off your upper lip before you start to pass judgment on the few poor stragglers of a generation which has done and suffered not a little in its time."

His hearers having expressed much compunction the ancient warrior became appeased. But he was not silenced.

"I am one of them — one of the stragglers, I mean," he went on patiently. "And what did we do? What have we achieved? He — the great Napoleon — started upon us to emulate the Macedonian Alexander, with a ruck of nations at his back. We opposed empty spaces to French impetuosity, then we offered them an interminable battle so that their army went at last to sleep in its positions lying down on the heaps of its own dead. Then came the wall of fire in Moscow. It toppled down on them.

"Then began the long rout of the Grand Army. I have seen it stream on, like the doomed flight of haggard, spectral sinners across the inner-most frozen circle of Dante's Inferno, ever widening before their despairing eyes.

"They who escaped must have had their souls doubly riveted inside their bodies to carry them out of Russia through that frost fit to split rocks. But to say that it was our fault that a single one of them got away is mere ignorance. Why! Our own men suffered nearly to the limit of their strength. Their Russian strength!

"Of course our spirit was not broken; and then our cause was good — it was holy. But that did not temper the wind much to men and horses.

"The flesh is weak. Good or evil purpose, Humanity has to pay the price. Why! In that very fight for that little village of which I have been telling you we were fighting for the shelter of those old houses as much as victory. And with the French it was the same.

"It wasn't for the sake of glory, or for the sake of strategy. The French knew that they would have to retreat before morning and we knew perfectly well that they would go. As far as the war was concerned there was nothing to fight about. Yet our infantry and theirs fought like wild cats, or like heroes if you like that better, amongst the houses — hot work enough — while the supports out in the open stood freezing in a tempestuous north wind which drove the snow on earth and the great masses of clouds in the sky at a terrific pace. The very air was inexpressibly sombre by contrast with the white earth. I have never seen God's creation look more sinister than on that day.

"We, the cavalry (we were only a handful), had not much to do except turn our backs to the wind and receive some stray French round shot. This, I may tell you, was the last of the French guns and it was the last time they had their artillery in position. Those guns never went away from there either. We found them abandoned next morning. But that afternoon they were keeping up an infernal fire on our attacking column; the furious wind carried away the smoke and even the noise but we could see the constant flicker of the tongues of fire along the French front. Then a driving flurry of snow would hide everything except the dark red flashes in the white swirl.

"At intervals when the line cleared we could see away across the plain to the right a sombre column moving endlessly; the great rout of the Grand Army creeping on and on all the time while the fight on our left went on with a great din and fury. The cruel whirlwind of snow swept over that scene of death and desolation. And then the wind fell as suddenly as it had arisen in the morning.

"Presently we got orders to charge the retreating column; I don't know why unless they wanted to prevent us from getting frozen in our saddles by giving us something to do. We changed front half right and got into motion at a walk to take that distant dark line in flank. It might have been half-past two in the afternoon.

"You must know that so far in this campaign my regiment had never been on the main line of Napoleon's advance. All these months since the invasion the army we belonged to had been wrestling with Oudinot in the north. We had only come down lately, driving him before us to the Beresina.

"This was the first occasion, then, that I and my comrades had a close view of Napoleon's Grand Army. It was an amazing and terrible sight. I had heard of it from others; I had seen the stragglers from it; small bands of marauders, parties of prisoners in the distance. But this was the very column itself! A crawling, stumbling, starved, half-demented mob. It issued from the forest a mile away and its head was lost in the murk of the fields. We rode into it at a trot, which was the most we could get out of our horses, and we stuck in that human mass as if in a moving bog. There was no resistance. I heard a few shots, half a dozen perhaps. Their very senses seemed frozen within them. I had time for a good look while riding at the head of my squadron. Well, I assure you, there were men walking on the outer edge so lost to everything but their misery that they never turned their heads to look at our charge. Soldiers!

"My horse pushed over one of them with his chest. The poor wretch had a dragoon's blue cloak, all torn and scorched, hanging from his shoulders and he didn't even put his hand out to snatch at my bridle and save himself. He just went down. Our troopers were pointing and slashing; well, and of course at first I myself . . . What would you have! An enemy is an enemy. Yet a sort of sickening awe crept into my heart. There was no tumult — only a low deep murmur dwelt over them interspersed with louder cries and groans while that mob kept on pushing and surging past us, sightless and without feeling. A smell of scorched rags and festering wounds hung in the air. My horse staggered in the eddies of swaying men. But it was like cutting down galvanized corpses that didn't care. Invaders! Yes . . . God was already dealing with them.

"I touched my horse with the spurs to get clear. There was a sudden rush and a sort of angry moan when our second squadron got into them on our right. My horse plunged and somebody got hold of my leg. As I had no mind to get pulled out of the saddle I gave a back-handed slash without looking. I heard a cry and my leg was let go suddenly.

"Just then I caught sight of the subaltern of my troop at some little distance from me. His name was Tomassov. That multitude of resurrected bodies with glassy eyes was seething round his horse as if blind, growling crazily. He was sitting erect in his saddle, not looking down at them and sheathing his sword deliberately.

"This Tomassov, well, he had a beard. Of course we all had beards then. Circumstances, lack of leisure, want of razors, too. No, seriously, we were a wild-looking lot in those unforgotten days which so many, so very many of us did not survive. You know our losses were awful, too. Yes, we looked wild. *Des Russes sauvages* — what!

"So he had a beard — this Tomassov I mean; but he did not look *sauvage*. He was the youngest of us all. And that meant real youth. At a distance he passed muster fairly well, what with the grime and the particular stamp of that campaign on our faces. But directly you were near enough to have a good look into his eyes, that was where his lack of age showed, though he was not exactly a boy.

"Those same eyes were blue, something like the blue of autumn skies, dreamy and gay, too — innocent, believing eyes. A topknot of fair hair decorated his brow like a gold diadem in what one would call normal times.

"You may think I am talking of him as if he were the hero of a novel. Why, that's nothing to what the adjutant discovered about him. He discovered that he had a 'lover's lips' — whatever that may be. If the adjutant meant a nice mouth, why, it was nice enough, but of course it was intended for a sneer. That adjutant of ours was not a very delicate fellow. 'Look at those lover's lips,' he would exclaim in a loud tone while Tomassov was talking.

"Tomassov didn't quite like that sort of thing. But to a certain extent he had laid himself open to banter by the lasting character of his impressions which were connected with the passion of love and, perhaps, were not of such a rare kind as he seemed to think them. What made his comrades tolerant of his rhapsodies was the fact that they were connected with France, with Paris!

"You of the present generation, you cannot conceive how much prestige there was then in those names for the whole world. Paris was the center of wonder for all human beings gifted with imagination. There we were, the majority of us young and well connected, but not long out of our hereditary nests in the provinces; simple servants of God; mere rustics, if I may say so. So we were only too ready to listen to the tales of France from our comrade Tomassov. He had been attached to our mission in Paris the year before the war. High protections very likely — or maybe sheer luck.

"I don't think he could have been a very useful member of the mission because of his youth and complete inexperience. And apparently all his time in Paris was his own. The use he made of it was to fall in love, to remain in that state, to cultivate it, to exist only for it in a manner of speaking.

"Thus it was something more than a mere memory that he had brought with him from France. Memory is a fugitive thing. It can be falsified, it can be effaced, it can be even doubted. Why! I myself come to doubt sometimes that I, too, have been in Paris in my turn. And the long road there with battles for its stages would appear still more incredible if it were not for a certain musket ball which I have been carrying about my person

ever since a little cavalry affair which happened in Silesia at the very beginning of the Leipsic campaign.

"Passages of love, however, are more impressive perhaps than passages
of danger. You don't go affronting love in troops as it were. They are rarer,
more personal and more intimate. And remember that with Tomassov all
that was very fresh yet. He had not been home from France three months
when the war began.

"His heart, his mind were full of that experience. He was really awed
by it, and he was simple enough to let it appear in his speeches. He considered himself a sort of privileged person, not because a woman had
looked at him with favour, but simply because, how shall I say it, he had
had the wonderful illumination of his worship for her, as if it were heaven
itself that had done this for him.

"Oh yes, he was very simple. A nice youngster, yet no fool; and with
that, utterly inexperienced, unsuspicious, and unthinking. You will find
one like that here and there in the provinces. He had some poetry in him
too. It could only be natural, something quite his own, not acquired. I suppose Father Adam had some poetry in him of that natural sort. For the
rest un Russe sauvage as the French sometimes call us, but not of that
kind which, they maintain, eats tallow candle for a delicacy. As to the
woman, the French woman, well, though I have also been in France with
a hundred thousand Russians, I have never seen her. Very likely she was
not in Paris then. And in any case hers were not the doors that would
fly open before simple fellows of my sort, you understand. Gilded salons
were never in my way. I could not tell you how she looked, which is strange
considering that I was, if I may say so, Tomassov's special confidant.

"He very soon got shy of talking before the others. I suppose the usual
campfire comments jarred his fine feelings. But I was left to him and truly
I had to submit. You can't very well expect a youngster in Tomassov's
state to hold his tongue altogether; and I — I suppose you will hardly
believe me — I am by nature a rather silent sort of person.

"Very likely my silence appeared to him sympathetic. All the month of
September our regiment, quartered in villages, had come in for an easy
time. It was then that I heard most of that — you can't call it a story. The
story I have in my mind is not in that. Outpourings, let us call them.

"I would sit quite content to hold my peace, a whole hour perhaps, while
Tomassov talked with exaltation. And when he was done I would still
hold my peace. And then there would be produced a solemn effect of silence which, I imagine, pleased Tomassov in a way.

"She was of course not a woman in her first youth. A widow, maybe. At any rate I never heard Tomassov mention her husband. She had a salon, something very distinguished; a social centre in which she queened it with great splendour.

"Somehow I fancy her court was composed mostly of men. But Tomassov, I must say, kept such details out of his discourses wonderfully well. Upon my word I don't know whether her hair was dark or fair, her eyes brown or blue; what was her stature, her features, or her complexion. His love soared above mere physical impressions. He never described her to me in set terms; but he was ready to swear that in her presence everybody's thoughts and feelings were bound to circle round her. She was that sort of woman. Most wonderful conversations on all sorts of subjects went on in her salon: but through them all there flowed unheard like a mysterious strain of music the assertion, the power, the tyranny of sheer beauty. So apparently the woman was beautiful. She detached all these talking people from their life interests, and even from their vanities. She was a secret delight and a secret trouble. All the men when they looked at her fell to brooding as if struck by the thought that their lives had been wasted. She was the very joy and shudder of felicity and she brought only sadness and torment to the hearts of men.

"In short, she must have been an extraordinary woman, or else Tomassov was an extraordinary young fellow to feel in that way and to talk like this about her. I told you the fellow had a lot of poetry in him and observed that all this sounded true enough. It would be just about the sorcery a woman very much out of the common would exercise, you know. Poets do get close to truth somehow — there is no denying that.

"There is no poetry in my composition, I know, but I have my share of common shrewdness, and I have no doubt that the lady was kind to the youngster, once he did find his way inside her salon. His getting in is the real marvel. However, he did get in, the innocent, and he found himself in distinguished company there, amongst men of considerable position. And you know what that means: thick waists, bald heads, teeth that are not — as some satirist puts it. Imagine amongst them a nice boy, fresh and simple, like an apple just off the tree; a modest, good-looking, impressionable, adoring young barbarian. My word! What a change! What a relief for jaded feelings! And with that, having in his nature that dose of poetry which saves even a simpleton from being a fool.

"He became an artlessly, unconditionally devoted slave. He was rewarded by being smiled on and in time admitted to the intimacy of the

house. It may be that the unsophisticated young barbarian amused the
exquisite lady. Perhaps — since he didn't feed on tallow candles — he satisfied some need of tenderness in the woman. You know, there are many
kinds of tenderness highly civilized women are capable of. Women with
heads and imagination, I mean, and no temperament to speak of, you understand. But who is going to fathom their needs or their fancies? Most
of the time they themselves don't know much about their innermost
moods, and blunder out of one into another, sometimes with catastrophic
results. And then who is more surprised than they? However, Tomassov's
case was in its nature quite idyllic. The fashionable world was amused.
His devotion made for him a kind of social success. But he didn't care.
There was his one divinity, and there was the shrine where he was permitted to go in and out without regard for official reception hours.

"He took advantage of that privilege freely. Well, he had no official
duties, you know. The Military Mission was supposed to be more complimentary than any thing else, the head of it being a personal friend of
our Emperor Alexander; and he, too, was laying himself out for successes
in fashionable life exclusively — as it seemed. As it seemed.

"One afternoon Tomassov called on the mistress of his thoughts earlier
than usual. She was not alone. There was a man with her, not one of the
thick-waisted, bald-headed personages, but a somebody all the same, a
man over thirty, a French officer who to some extent was also a privileged intimate. Tomassov was not jealous of him. Such a sentiment would
have appeared presumptuous to the simple fellow.

"On the contrary he admired that officer. You have no idea of the French
military men's prestige in those days, even with us Russian soldiers who
had managed to face them perhaps better than the rest. Victory had marked
them on the forehead — it seemed for ever. They would have been more
than human if they had not been conscious of it; but they were good comrades and had a sort of brotherly feeling for all who bore arms, even if
it was against them.

"And this was quite a superior example, an officer of the major-general's
staff, and a man of the best society besides. He was powerfully built, and
thoroughly masculine, though he was as carefully groomed as a woman.
He had the courteous self-possession of a man of the world. His forehead,
white as alabaster, contrasted impressively with the healthy colour of his face.

"I don't know whether he was jealous of Tomassov, but I suspect that
he might have been a little annoyed at him as at a sort of walking ab-

surdity of the sentimental order. But these men of the world are impenetrable, and outwardly he condescended to recognize Tomassov's existence even more distinctly than was strictly necessary. Once or twice he had offered him some useful worldly advice with perfect tact and delicacy. Tomassov was completely conquered by that evidence of kindness under the cold polish of the best society.

"Tomassov, introduced into the *petit salon,* found these two exquisite people sitting on a sofa together and had the feeling of having interrupted some special conversation. They looked at him strangely, he thought; but he was not given to understand that he had intruded. After a time the lady said to the officer — his name was De Castel — 'I wish you would take the trouble to ascertain the exact truth as to that rumour.'

" 'It's much more than a mere rumour,' remarked the officer. But he got up submissively and went out. The lady turned to Tomassov and said: 'You may stay with me.'

"This express command made him supremely happy, though as a matter of fact he had had no idea of going.

"She regarded him with her kindly glances, which made something glow and expand within his chest. It was a delicious feeling, even though it did cut one's breath short now and then. Ecstatically he drank in the sound of her tranquil, seductive talk full of innocent gaiety and of spiritual quietude. His passion appeared to him to flame up and envelop her in blue fiery tongues from head to foot and over her head, while her soul reposed in the centre like a big white rose. . . .

"H'm, good this. He told me many other things like that. But this is the one I remember. He himself remembered everything because these were the last memories of that woman. He was seeing her for the last time though he did not know it then.

"M. De Castel returned, breaking into that atmosphere of enchantment Tomassov had been drinking in even to complete unconsciousness of the external world. Tomassov could not help being struck by the distinction of his movements, the ease of his manner, his superiority to all the other men he knew, and he suffered from it. It occurred to him that these two brilliant beings on the sofa were made for each other.

"De Castel sitting down by the side of the lady murmured to her discreetly, 'There is not the slightest doubt that it's true,' and they both turned their eyes to Tomassov. Roused thoroughly from his enchantment he became self-conscious; a feeling of shyness came over him. He sat smiling faintly at them.

"The lady without taking her eyes off the blushing Tomassov said with a dreamy gravity quite unusual to her:

" 'I should like to know that your generosity can be supreme — without a flaw. Love at its highest should be the origin of every perfection.'

"Tomassov opened his eyes wide with admiration at this, as though her lips had been dropping real pearls. The sentiment, however, was not uttered for the primitive Russian youth but for the exquisitely accomplished man of the world, De Castel.

"Tomassov could not see the effect it produced because the French officer lowered his head and sat there contemplating his admirably polished boots. The lady whispered in a sympathetic tone:

" 'You have scruples?'

"De Castel, without looking up, murmured: 'It could be turned into a nice point of honour.'

"She said vivaciously: 'That surely is artificial. I am all for natural feelings. I believe in nothing else. But perhaps your conscience . . .'

"He interrupted her: 'Not at all. My conscience is not childish. The fate of those people is of no military importance to us. What can it matter? The fortune of France is invincible.'

" 'Well then . . .' she uttered, meaningly, and rose from the couch. The French officer stood up, too. Tomassov hastened to follow their example. He was pained by his state of utter mental darkness. While he was raising the lady's white hand to his lips he heard the French officer say with marked emphasis:

" 'If he has the soul of a warrior (at that time, you know, people really talked in that way), if he has the soul of a warrior he ought to fall at your feet in gratitude.'

"Tomassov felt himself plunged into even denser darkness than before. He followed the French officer out of the room and out of the house; for he had a notion that this was expected of him.

"It was getting dusk, the weather was very bad, and the street was quite deserted. The Frenchman lingered in it strangely. And Tomassov lingered, too, without impatience. He was never in a hurry to get away from the house in which she lived. And besides, something wonderful had happened to him. The hand he had reverently raised by the tips of its fingers, had been pressed against his lips. He had received a secret favour! He was almost frightened. The world had reeled — and it had hardly steadied itself yet. De Castel stopped short at the corner of the quiet street.

" 'I don't care to be seen too much with you in the lighted thoroughfares, M. Tomassov,' he said in a strangely grim tone.

" 'Why?' asked the young man, too startled to be offended.

" 'From prudence,' answered the other curtly. 'So we will have to part here; but before we part I'll disclose to you something of which you will see at once the importance.'

"This, please note, was an evening in late March of the year 1812. For a long time already there had been talk of a growing coolness between Russia and France. The word war was being whispered in drawing rooms louder and louder, and at last was heard in official circles. Thereupon the Parisian police discovered that our military envoy had corrupted some clerks at the Ministry of War and had obtained from them some very important confidential documents. The wretched men (there were two of them) had confessed their crime and were to be shot that night. To-morrow all the town would be talking of the affair. But the worst was that the Emperor Napoleon was furiously angry at the discovery, and had made up his mind to have the Russian envoy arrested.

"Such was De Castel's disclosure; and though he had spoken in low tones Tomassov was stunned as by a great crash.

" 'Arrested,' he murmured, desolately.

" 'Yes, and kept as a state prisoner — with everybody belonging to him. . . .'

"The French officer seized Tomassov's arm above the elbow and pressed it hard.

" 'And kept in France,' he repeated into Tomassov's very ear, and then letting him go stepped back a space and remained silent.

" 'And it's you, you, who are telling me this!' cried Tomassov in an extremity of gratitude that was hardly greater than his admiration for the generosity of his future foe. Could a brother have done for him more! He sought to seize the hand of the French officer, but the latter remained wrapped up closely in his cloak. Possibly in the dark he had not noticed the attempt. He moved back a bit and in his self-possessed voice of a man of the world, as though he were speaking across a card table or something of the sort, he called Tomassov's attention to the fact that if he meant to make use of the warning the moments were precious.

" 'Indeed they are,' agreed the awed Tomassov. 'Good-bye then. I have no word of thanks to equal your generosity; but if ever I have an opportunity, I swear it, you may command my life. . . .'

"But the Frenchman retreated, had already vanished in the dark lonely street. Tomassov was alone, and then he did not waste any of the precious minutes of that night.

"See how people's mere gossip and idle talk pass into history. In all the memoirs of the time if you read them you will find it stated that our envoy had a warning from some highly placed woman who was in love with him. Of course it's known that he had successes with women, and in the highest spheres, too, but the truth is that the person who warned him was no other than our simple Tomassov — an altogether different sort of lover from himself.

"This then is the secret of our Emperor's representative's escape from arrest. He and all his official household got out of France all right — as history records.

"And amongst that household there was our Tomassov of course. He had, in the words of the French officer, the soul of a warrior. And what more desolate prospect for a man with such a soul than to be imprisoned on the eve of war; to be cut off from his country in danger, from his military family, from his duty, from honour, and — well — from glory, too.

"Tomassov used to shudder at the mere thought of the moral torture he had escaped; and he nursed in his heart a boundless gratitude to the two people who had saved him from that cruel ordeal. They were wonderful! For him love and friendship were but two aspects of exalted perfection. He had found these fine examples of it and he vowed them indeed a sort of cult. It affected his attitude towards Frenchmen in general, great patriot as he was. He was naturally indignant at the invasion of his country, but this indignation had no personal animosity in it. His was fundamentally a fine nature. He grieved at the appalling amount of human suffering he saw around him. Yes, he was full of compassion for all forms of mankind's misery in a manly way.

"Less fine natures than his own did not understand this very well. In the regiment they had nicknamed him the Humane Tomassov.

"He didn't take offence at it. There is nothing incompatible between humanity and a warrior's soul. People without compassion are the civilians, government officials, merchants and such like. As to the ferocious talk one hears from a lot of decent people in war time — well, the tongue is an unruly member at best, and when there is some excitement going on there is no curbing its furious activity.

"So I had not been very surprised to see our Tomassov sheathe deliberately his sword right in the middle of that charge, you may say. As we rode away after it he was very silent. He was not a chatterer as a rule, but it was evident that this close view of the Grand Army had affected him deeply, like some sight not of this earth. I had always been a pretty tough individual myself — well, even I . . . and there was that fellow with a lot of poetry in his nature! We rode side by side without opening our lips. It was simply beyond words.

"We established our bivouac along the edge of the forest so as to get some shelter for our horses. However, the boisterous north wind had dropped as quickly as it had sprung up, and the great winter stillness lay on the land from the Baltic to the Black Sea. One could almost feel its cold, lifeless immensity reaching up to the stars.

"Our men had lighted several fires for their officers and had cleared the snow around them. We had big logs of wood for seats; it was a very tolerable bivouac upon the whole, even without the exultation of victory. We were to feel that later, but at present we were oppressed by our stern and arduous task.

"There were three of us round my fire. The third one was that adjutant. He was perhaps a well-meaning chap but not so nice as he might have been had he been less rough in manner and less crude in his perceptions. He would reason about people's conduct as though a man were as simple a figure as, say, two sticks laid across each other; whereas a man is much more like the sea whose movements are too complicated to explain, and whose depths may bring up God only knows what at any moment.

"We talked a little about that charge. Not much. That sort of thing does not lend itself to conversation. Tomassov muttered a few words about a mere butchery. I had nothing to say. As I told you I had very soon let my sword hang idle at my wrist. That starving mob had not even *tried* to defend itself. Just a few shots. We had two men wounded. Two! . . . and we had charged the main column of Napoleon's Grand Army.

"Tomassov muttered wearily: 'What was the good of it?' I did not wish to argue, so I only just mumbled: 'Ah, well!' But the adjutant struck in unpleasantly:

" 'Why, it warmed the men a bit. It has made me warm. That's a good enough reason. But our Tomassov is so humane! And besides he has been in love with a French woman, and thick as thieves with a lot of Frenchmen, so he is sorry for them. Never mind, my boy, we are on the Paris road now and you shall soon see her!' This was one of his usual, as we believed them, foolish speeches. None of us but believed that the getting to Paris would be a matter of years — of years. And lo! less than eighteen months afterwards I was rooked of a lot of money in a gambling hell in the Palais Royal.

"Truth, being often the most senseless thing in the world, is sometimes revealed to fools. I don't think that adjutant of ours believed in his own words. He just wanted to tease Tomassov from habit. Purely from habit. We of course said nothing, and so he took his head in his hands and fell into a doze as he sat on a log in front of the fire.

"Our cavalry was on the extreme right wing of the army, and I must confess that we guarded it very badly. We had lost all sense of insecurity by this time; but still we did keep up a pretence of doing it in a way. Presently a trooper rode up leading a horse and Tomassov mounted stiffly and went off on a round of the outposts. Of the perfectly useless outposts.

"The night was still, except for the crackling of the fires. The raging wind had lifted far above the earth and not the faintest breath of it could be heard. Only the full moon swam out with a rush into the sky and suddenly hung high and motionless overhead. I remember raising my hairy face to it for a moment. Then, I verily believe, I dozed off, too, bent double on my log with my head towards the fierce blaze.

"You know what an impermanent thing such slumber is. One moment you drop into an abyss and the next you are back in the world that you would think too deep for any noise but the trumpet of the Last Judgment. And then off you go again. Your very soul seems to slip down into a bottomless black pit. Then up once more into a startled consciousness. A mere plaything of cruel sleep one is, then. Tormented both ways.

"However, when my orderly appeared before me, repeating: 'Won't your Honour be pleased to eat? . . . Won't your Honour be pleased to eat? . . .' I managed to keep my hold of it — I mean that gaping consciousness. He was offering me a sooty pot containing some grain boiled in water with a pinch of salt. A wooden spoon was stuck in it.

"At that time these were the only rations we were getting regularly. Mere chicken food, confound it! But the Russian soldier is wonderful. Well, my fellow waited till I had feasted and then went away carrying off the empty pot.

"I was no longer sleepy. Indeed, I had become awake with an exaggerated mental consciousness of existence extending beyond my immediate surroundings. Those are but exceptional moments with mankind, I am glad to say. I had the intimate sensation of the earth in all its enormous expanse wrapped in snow, with nothing showing on it but trees with their straight stalk-like trunks and their funeral verdure; and in this aspect of general mourning I seemed to hear the sighs of mankind falling to die in the midst of a nature without life. They were Frenchmen. We didn't hate them; they did not hate us; we had existed far apart — and suddenly they had come rolling in with arms in their hands, without fear of God, carrying with them other nations, and all to perish together in a long, long trail of frozen corpses. I had an actual vision of that trail: a pathetic multitude of small dark mounds stretching away under the moonlight in a clear, still, and pitiless atmosphere — a sort of horrible peace.

"But what other peace could there be for them? What else did they deserve? I don't know by what connection of emotions there came into my head the thought that the earth was a pagan planet and not a fit abode for Christian virtues.

"You may be surprised that I should remember all this so well. What is a passing emotion or half-formed thought to last in so many years of a man's changing, inconsequential life? But what has fixed the emotion of that evening in my recollection so that the slightest shadows remain indelible was an event of strange finality, an event not likely to be forgotten in a life-time — as you shall see.

"I don't suppose I had been entertaining those thoughts more than five minutes when something induced me to look over my shoulder. I can't think it was a noise; the snow deadened all the sounds. Something it must have been, some sort of signal reaching my consciousness. Anyway, I turned my head, and there was the event approaching me, not that I knew it or had the slightest premonition. All I saw in the distance were two figures approaching in the moonlight. One of them was our Tomassov. The dark mass behind him which moved across my sight were the horses which his orderly was leading away. Tomassov was a very familiar appearance, in long boots, a tall figure ending in a pointed hood. But by his side advanced another figure. I mistrusted my eyes at first. It was amazing! It had a shining crested helmet on its head and was muffled up in a white cloak. The cloak was not as white as snow. Nothing in the world is. It was white more like mist, with an aspect that was ghostly and martial to an extraordinary degree. It was as if Tomassov had got hold of the God of War himself. I could see at once that he was leading this resplendent vision by the arm. Then I saw that he was holding it up. While I stared and stared, they crept on — for indeed they were creeping — and at last they crept into the light of our bivouac fire and passed beyond the log I was sitting on. The blaze played on the helmet. It was extremely battered and the frost-bitten face, full of sores, under it was framed in bits of mangy fur. No God of War this, but a French officer. The great white cuirassier's cloak was torn, burnt full of holes. His feet were wrapped up in old sheep-skins over remnants of boots. They looked monstrous and he tottered on them, sustained by Tomassov who lowered him most carefully on to the log on which I sat.

"My amazement knew no bounds.

" 'You have brought in a prisoner,' I said to Tomassov, as if I could not believe my eyes.

"You must understand that unless they surrendered in large bodies we made no prisoners. What would have been the good? Our Cossacks either killed the stragglers or else let them alone, just as it happened. It came really to the same thing in the end.

"Tomassov turned to me with a very troubled look.

" 'He sprang up from the ground somewhere as I was leaving the out-post,' he said. 'I believe he was making for it, for he walked blindly into my horse. He got hold of my leg and of course none of our chaps dared touch him then.'

" 'He had a narrow escape,' I said.

" 'He didn't appreciate it,' said Tomassov, looking even more troubled than before. 'He came along holding to my stirrup leather. That's what made me so late. He told me he was a staff officer; and then talking in a voice such, I suppose, as the damned alone use, a croaking of rage and pain, he said he had a favour to beg of me. A supreme favour. Did I un-derstand him, he asked in a sort of fiendish whisper.

" 'Of course I told him that I did. I said: *Oui, je vous comprends.*'

" 'Then,' said he, 'do it. Now! At once — in the pity of your heart.'

"Tomassov ceased and stared queerly at me above the head of the prisoner.

"I said, 'What did he mean?'

" 'That's what I asked him,' answered Tomassov in a dazed tone, 'and he said that he wanted me to do him the favour to blow his brains out. As a fellow soldier,' he said. 'As a man of feeling — as — as a humane man.'

"The prisoner sat between us like an awful gashed mummy as to the face, a martial scarecrow, a grotesque horror of rags and dirt, with awful living eyes, full of vitality, full of unquenchable fire, in a body of horrible affliction, a skeleton at the feast of glory. And suddenly those shining un-extinguishable eyes of his became fixed upon Tomassov. He, poor fellow, fascinated, returned the ghastly stare of a suffering soul in that mere husk of a man. The prisoner croaked at him in French.

" 'I recognize, you know. You are her Russian youngster. You were very grateful. I call on you to pay the debt. Pay it, I say, with one liberating shot. You are a man of honour. I have not even a broken sabre. All my being recoils from my own degradation. You know me.'

"Tomassov said nothing.

" 'Haven't you got the soul of a warrior?' the Frenchman asked in an angry whisper, but with something of a mocking intention in it.

" 'I don't know,' said poor Tomassov.

"What a look of contempt that scarecrow gave him out of his unquenchable eyes. He seemed to live only by the force of infuriated and impotent despair. Suddenly he gave a gasp and fell forward writhing in the agony of cramp in all his limbs; a not unusual effect of the heat of a campfire. It resembled the application of some horrible torture. But he tried to fight against the pain at first. He only moaned low while we bent over him so as to prevent him rolling into the fire, and muttered feverishly at intervals: *Tuez moi, tuez moi . . .'* till, vanquished by the pain, he screamed in agony, time after time, each cry bursting out through his compressed lips.

"The adjutant woke up on the other side of the fire and started swearing awfully at the beastly row that Frenchman was making.

" 'What's this? More of your infernal humanity, Tomassov,' he yelled at us. 'Why don't you have him thrown out of this to the devil on the snow?'

"As we paid no attention to his shouts, he got up, cursing shockingly, and went away to another fire. Presently the French officer became easier. We propped him up against the log and sat silent on each side of him till the bugles started their call at the first break of day. The big flame, kept up all through the night, paled on the livid sheet of snow, while the frozen air all round rang with the brazen notes of cavalry trumpets. The Frenchman's eyes, fixed in a glassy stare, which for a moment made us hope that he had died quietly sitting there between us two, stirred slowly to right and left, looking at each of our faces in turn. Tomassov and I exchanged glances of dismay. Then De Castel's voice, unexpected in its renewed strength and ghastly self-possession, made us shudder inwardly.

" '*Bonjour, messieurs.'*

"His chin dropped on his breast. Tomassov addressed me in Russian.

" 'It is he, the man himself . . .' I nodded and Tomassov went on in a tone of anguish: 'Yes, he! Brilliant, accomplished, envied by men, loved by that woman — this horror — this miserable thing that cannot die. Look at his eyes. It's terrible.'

"I did not look, but I understood what Tomassov meant. We could do nothing for him. This avenging winter of fate held both the fugitives and the pursuers in its iron grip. Compassion was but a vain word before that unrelenting destiny. I tried to say something about a convoy being no doubt collected in the village —but I faltered at the mute glance Tomassov gave me. We knew what those convoys were like: appalling mobs of hopeless wretches driven on by the butts of Cossacks' lances, back to the frozen inferno, with their faces set away from their homes.

"Our two squadrons had been formed along the edge of the forest. The minutes of anguish were passing. The Frenchman suddenly struggled to his feet. We helped him almost without knowing what we were doing.

"'Come,' he said, in measured tones. 'This is the moment.' He paused for a long time, then with the same distinctness went on: 'On my word of honour, all faith is dead in me.'

"His voice lost suddenly its self-possession. After waiting a little while he added in a murmur: 'And even my courage. . . . Upon my honour.'

"Another long pause ensued before, with a great effort, he whispered hoarsely: 'Isn't this enough to move a heart of stone? Am I to go on my knees to you?'

"Again a deep silence fell upon the three of us. Then the French officer flung his last word of anger at Tomassov.

"'Milksop!'

"Not a feature of the poor fellow moved. I made up my mind to go and fetch a couple of our troopers to lead that miserable prisoner away to the village. There was nothing else for it. I had not moved six paces towards the group of horses and orderlies in front of our squadron when . . . but you have guessed it. Of course. And I, too, I guessed it, for I give you my word that the report of Tomassov's pistol was the most insignificant thing imaginable. The snow certainly does absorb sound. It was a mere feeble pop. Of the orderlies holding our horses I don't think one turned his head round.

"Yes. Tomassov had done it. Destiny had led that De Castel to the man who could understand him perfectly. But it was poor Tomassov's lot to be the predestined victim. You know what the world's justice and mankind's judgment are like. They fell heavily on him with a sort of inverted hypocrisy. Why! That brute of an adjutant himself, was the first to set going horrified allusions to the shooting of a prisoner in cold blood! Tomassov was not dismissed from the service of course. But after the siege of Dantzig he asked for permission to resign from the army, and went away to bury himself in the depths of his province, where a vague story of some dark deed clung to him for years.

"Yes. He had done it. And what was it? One warrior's soul paying its debt a hundredfold to another warrior's soul by releasing it from a fate worse than death — the loss of all faith and courage. You may look on it in that way. I don't know. And perhaps poor Tomassov did not know himself. But I was the first to approach that appalling dark group on the snow: the Frenchman extended rigidly on his back, Tomassov kneeling on one knee rather nearer to the feet than to the Frenchman's head. He had taken his cap off and his hair shone like gold in the light drift of flakes that had begun to fall. He was stooping over the dead in a tenderly contemplative attitude. And his young, ingenuous face, with lowered eyelids, expressed no grief, no sternness, no horror — but was set in the repose of a profound, as if endless and endlessly silent, meditation."

A Border Family

by Robert Louis Stevenson

> 1813   The Scots who lived near the English border
> were cattle thieves and feudists by what they be-
> lieved to be natural right. Their tradition of violence
> persisted into the opening years of the nineteenth
> century, as is shown in this account of the Elliotts of
> Cauldstaneslap, old Gilbert and his sons, "The Four
> Black Brothers."

Such an unequal intimacy [between master and servant] has never
been uncommon in Scotland, where the clan spirit survives; where the
servant tends to spend her life in the same service, a helpmeet at first, then
a tyrant, and at last a pensioner; where, besides, she is not necessarily destitute of the pride of birth, but is, perhaps, like Kirstie, a connection of
her master's, and at least knows the legend of her own family, and may
count kinship with some illustrious dead. For that is the mark of the Scot
of all classes: that he stands in an attitude towards the past unthinkable
to the Englishmen, and remembers and cherishes the memory of his for-
bears, good or bad; and there burns alive in him a sense of identity with
the dead even to the twentieth generation. No more characteristic instance
could be found than in the family of Kirstie Elliott. They were all, and
Kirstie the first of all, ready and eager to pour forth the particulars of their
genealogy, embellished with every detail that memory had handed down
or fancy fabricated; and, behold! from every ramification of that tree there
dangled a halter. The Elliotts themselves have had a chequered history;
but these Elliotts deduced, besides, from three of the most unfortunate of
the border clans — the Nicksons, the Ellwalds and the Crozers. One an-
cestor after another might be seen appearing a moment out of the rain
and the hill mist upon his furtive business, speeding home, perhaps, with a
paltry booty of lame horses and lean kine, or squealing and dealing death
in some moorland feud of the ferrets and the wildcats. One after another
closed his obscure adventures in mid-air, triced up to the arm of the royal
gibbet or the Baron's dule-tree. For the rusty blunderbuss of Scots criminal justice, which usually hurts nobody but jurymen, became a weapon
of precision for the Nicksons, the Ellwalds, and the Crozers. The exhil-
aration of their exploits seemed to haunt the memories of their descend-

560

ants alone, and the shame to be forgotten. Pride glowed in their bosoms
to publish their relationship to "Andrew Ellwald of the Laverockstanes,
called 'Unchancy Dand,' who was justifeed wi' seeven mair of the same
name as Jeddart in the days of King James the Sax." In all this tissue of
crime and misfortune, the Elliotts of Cauldestaneslap had one boast which
must appear legitimate: the males were gallows-birds, born outlaws, petty
thieves, and deadly brawlers; but according to the same tradition, the females were all chaste and faithful. The power of ancestry on the character is not limited to the inheritance of cells. If I buy ancestors by the gross
from the benevolence of Lion King at Arms, my grandson (if he is Scottish) will feel a quickening emulation of their deeds. The men of the
Elliotts were proud, lawless, violent as of right, cherishing and prolong-
ing a tradition. In like manner with the women. And the woman, essentially passionate and reckless, who crouched on the rug, in the shine of
the peat fire, telling these tales, had cherished through life a wild integrity of virtue.

Her father Gilbert had been deeply pious, a savage disciplinarian in
the antique style, and withal a notorious smuggler. "I mind when I was
a bairn getting mony a skelp and being shoo'd to bed like pou'try," she
would say. "That would be when the lads and their bit kegs were on the
road. We've had the riffraff of two-three counties in our kitchen, mony's the
time, betwix' the twelve and the three; and their lanterns would be standing in the forecourt, ay, a score o' them at once. But there was nae ungodly
talk permitted at Cauldstaneslap; my father was a consistent man in walk
and conversation; just let slip an aith, and there was the door to ye! He
had that zeal for the Lord, it was a fair wonder to hear him pray, but the
faimily has aye had a gift that way." This father was twice married, once
to a dark woman of the old Ellwald stock, by whom he had Gilbert, presently of Cauldstaneslap; and, secondly, to the mother of Kirstie. "He was
an auld man when he married her, a fell auld man wi' a muckle voice —
you could hear him rowting from the top o' the kye-stairs," she said; "but
for her, it appears, she was a perfit wonder. It was gentle blood she had,
Mr. Archie, for it was your ain. The country-side gaed gyte about her and
her gowden hair. Mines is no to be mentioned wi' it, and there's few
weemen has mair hair than what I have, or yet a bonnier colour. Often
would I tell my dear Miss Jeannie — that was your mother, dear, she was
cruel ta'en up about her hair, it was unco tender, ye see — 'Houts, Miss
Jeannie,' I would say, 'just fling your washes and your French dentifrishes
in the back o' the fire, for that's the place for them; and awa' down to a

burnside, and wash yersel in cauld hill water, and dry your bonny hair in the caller wind o' the muirs, the way that my mother aye washed hers, and that I have aye made it a practice to have washen mines — just you do what I tell ye, my dear, and ye'll give me news of it! Ye'll have hair, and routh of hair, a pigtail as thick's my arm,' I said, 'and the bonniest colour like the clear gowden guineas, so as the lads in kirk'll no can keep their eyes off it!' Weel, it lasted out her time, puir thing! I cuttit a lock of it upon her corp that was lying there sae cauld. I'll show it ye some of thir days if ye're good. But, as I was sayin,' my mither — — "

On the death of the father there remained golden-haired Kirstie, who took service with her distant kinsfolk, the Rutherfords, and black-a-vised Gilbert, twenty years older, who farmed the Cauldstaneslap, married, and begot four sons between 1773 and 1784, and a daughter, like a postscript, in '97, the year of Camperdown and Cape St. Vincent. It seemed it was a tradition of the family to wind up with a belated girl. In 1804, at the age of sixty, Gilbert met an end that might be called heroic. He was due home from market any time from eight at night till five in the morning, and in any condition from the quarrelsome to the speechless, for he maintained to that age the goodly customs of the Scots farmer. It was known on this occasion that he had a good bit of money to bring home; the word had gone round loosely. The laird had shown his guineas, and if anybody had but noticed it, there was an ill-looking, vagabond crew, the scum of Edinburgh, that drew out of the market long ere it was dusk and took the hill-road by Hermiston, where it was not to be believed that they had lawful business. One of the country-side, one Dickieson, they took with them to be their guide, and dear he paid for it! Of a sudden, in the ford of the Broken Dykes, this vermin clan fell on the laird, six to one, and him three parts asleep, having drunk hard. But it is ill to catch an Elliott. For awhile, in the night and the black water that was deep as to his saddle-girths, he wrought with his staff like a smith at his stithy, and great was the sound of oaths and blows. With that the ambuscade was burst, and he rode for home with a pistol-ball in him, three knife-wounds, the loss of his front teeth, a broken rib and bridle, and a dying horse. That was a race with death that the laird rode! In the mirk night, with his broken bridle and his head swimming, he dug his spurs to the rowels in the horse's side, and the horse, that was even worse off than himself, the poor creature! screamed out loud like a person as he went, so that the hills echoed with it, and the folks at Cauldstaneslap got to their feet about the table and looked at each other with white faces. The horse fell dead at the yard gate, the laird won the length of the house and fell there on the threshold. To the son that raised him he gave the bag of money. "Hae," said he. All the way up the thieves had seemed to him to be at his heels, but now the hallucination left him — he saw them again in the place of the ambuscade — and the thirst of vengeance seized on his dying mind. Raising himself and pointing with an imperious finger into the black night from which he had come, he uttered the single command, "Broken Dykes," and fainted. He had never been loved, but he had been feared in honour. At that sight, at that word, gasped out at them from a toothless and bleeding mouth, the old Elliott spirit awoke with a shout in the four sons. "Wanting the hat, continues my author, Kirstie, whom I but haltingly follow, for she told this tale like one inspired, "wanting guns, for there wasnae twa grains o' pouder in the house, wi' nae mair weapons than their sticks into their hands, the fower o' them took the road. Only Hob, and that was the eldest, hunkered at the door-sill where the blood had rin, fyled his hand wi' it, and haddit it up to Heeven in the way o' the auld Border aith. 'Hell shall have her ain again this nicht!' he raired, and rode forth upon his errand." It was three miles to Broken Dykes, down-hill, and a sore road. Kirstie has seen men from Edinburgh dismounting there in plain day to lead their horses. But the four brothers rode it as if Auld Hornie were behind and Heaven in front. Come to the ford, and there was Dickieson. By all tales, he was not dead, but breathed and reared upon his elbow, and cried out to them for help. It was at a graceless face that he asked mercy. As soon as Hob saw, by the glint of the lantern, the eyes shining and the whiteness of the teeth in the man's face, "Damn you!" says he; "ye hae your teeth, hae ye?" and rode his horse to and fro upon that human remnant. Beyond that, Dandie must dismount with the lantern to be their guide; he was the youngest son, scarce twenty at the time. "A' nicht long they gaed in the wet heath and jennipers, and whaur they gaed they neither knew nor cared, but just followed the bluidstains and the footprints o' their faither's murderers. And a' nicht Dandie had his nose to the grund like a tyke, and the ithers followed and spak' naething, neither black nor white. There was nae noise to be heard, but just the sough of the swalled burns, and Hob, the dour yin, risping his teeth as he gaed." With the first glint of the morning they saw they were on the drove road, and at that the four stopped and had a dram to their breakfasts, for they knew that Dand must have guided them right, and the rogues could be but little ahead, hot foot for Edinburgh by the way of the Pentland Hills. By eight o'clock they had word of them — a shepherd had seen four men "uncoly mishandled" go by in the last hour. "That's yin a piece," says Clem, and swung his cudgel. "Five o' them!" says Hob. "God's death, but the faither was a man! And him drunk!" And then there befell them what my author termed "a sair misbegowk," for they were overtaken by a posse of mounted neighbours come to aid in the pursuit. Four sour faces looked on the reinforcement. "The deil's broughten you!" said Clem, and they rode thenceforward in the rear of the party with hanging heads. Before ten they had found and secured the rogues, and by three of the afternoon, as they rode up the Vennel with their prisoners, they were aware of a concourse of people bearing in their midst something that dripped. "For the boady of the saxt," pursued Kirstie, "wi' his head smashed like a hazel-nit, had been a' that nicht in the chairge o' Hermiston Water, and it dunt-ing it on the stanes, and grunding it on the shallows, and flinging the deid thing heels-ower-hurdie at the Fa's o' Spango; and in the first o' the day Tweed had got a hold o' him and carried him off like a wind, for it was uncoly swalled and raced wi' him, bobbing under braesides, and was long playing with the creature in the drumlie lynns under the castle, and at the hinder end of all cuist him up on the starling of Crossmichael brig. Sae there they were a' thegither at last (for Dickieson had been brought in on a cart long syne), and folk could see what mainner o' man my brither had been that had held his head again sax and saved the siller, and him drunk!" Thus died of honourable injuries and in the savour of fame Gilbert Elliott of the Cauldstaneslap; but his sons had scarce less glory out of the business. Their savage haste, the skill with which Dand had found and followed the trail, the barbarity to the wounded Dickieson (which was like an open secret in the county) and the doom which it was currently supposed they had intended for the others, struck and stirred popular imagination. Some century earlier the last of the minstrels might have fash-ioned the last of the ballads out of that Homeric fight and chase; but the spirit was dead, or had been reincarnated already in Mr. Sheriff Scott, and the degenerate moorsmen must be content to tell the tale in prose and to make of the "Four Black Brothers" a unit after the fashion of the "Twelve Apostles" or the "Three Musketeers."

Robert, Gilbert, Clement, and Andrew — in the proper Border diminu-tive, Hob, Gib, Clem, and Dand Elliott — these ballad heroes had much in common; in particular, their high sense of the family and the family honour; but they went diverse ways, and prospered and failed in different businesses. According to Kirstie, "they had a' bees in their bonnets but Hob." Hob the laird was, indeed, essentially a decent man. An elder of the Kirk, nobody had heard an oath upon his lips, save, perhaps, thrice or so at the sheepwashing, since the chase of his father's murderers. The figure he had shown on that eventful night disappeared as if swallowed by a trap. He who had ecstatically dipped his hand in the red blood, he who had ridden down Dickieson, became, from that moment on, a stiff and rather graceless model of the rustic proprieties; cannily profiting by the high war prices, and yearly stowing away a little nest-egg in the bank against calamity; approved of and sometimes consulted by the greater lairds for the massive and placid sense of what he said, when he could be induced to say anything; and particularly valued by the minister, Mr. Torrance, as a right-hand man in the parish, and a model to parents. The transfiguration had been for the moment only; some Barbarossa, some old Adam of our ancestors, sleeps in all of us till the fit of circumstance shall call it into action; and for as sober as he now seemed, Hob had given once for all the measure of the devil that haunted him. He was married, and, by reason of the effulgence of that legendary night, was adored by his wife. He had a mob of little lusty, barefoot children who marched in a caravan the long miles to school, the stages of whose pilgrimage were marked by acts of spoliation and mischief, and who were qualified in the country-side as "fair pests." But in the house, if "faither was in," they were quiet as mice. In short, Hob moved through life in a great peace — the reward of any one who shall have killed his man, with any formidable and figurative circumstance, in the midst of a country gagged and swaddled with civilisation.

It was a current remark that the Elliotts were "guid and bad, like sanguishes"; and certainly there was a curious distinction, the men of business coming alternately with the dreamers. The second brother, Gib, was a weaver by trade, had gone out early into the world to Edinburgh, and come home again with his wings singed. There was an exaltation in his nature which had led him to embrace with enthusiasm the principles of the French Revolution, and had ended by bringing him under the hawse of my Lord Hermiston in the furious onslaught of his upon the Liberals, which sent Muir and Palmer into exile and dashed the party into chaff. It was whispered that my lord, in his great scorn for the movement, and prevailed upon a little by a sense of neighbourliness, had given Gib a hint.

Meeting him one day in the Potterrow, my lord had stopped in front of him. "Gib, ye eediot," he had said, "what's this I hear of you? Poalitics, poalitics, poalitics weaver's poalitics, is the way of it, I hear. If ye are nae a' thegether dozened with eediocy, ye'll gang your ways back to Cauld-staneslap, and ca' your loom, and ca' your loom, man!" And Gilbert had taken him at the word and returned, with an expedition almost to be called flight, to the house of his father. The clearest of his inheritance was that family gift of prayer of which Kirstie had boasted; and the baffled poli-tician now turned his attention to religious matters — or, as others said, to heresy and schism. Every Sunday morning he was in Crossmichael, where he had gathered together, one by one, a sect of about a dozen persons, who called themselves "God's Remnant of the True Faithful," or, for short, "God's Remnant." To the profane, they were known as "Gib's Deils." Baillie Sweedie, a noted humourist in the town, vowed that the proceed-ings always opened to the tune of "The Deil Fly Away with the Excise-man," and that sacrament was dispensed in the form of hot whisky toddy; both wicked hits at the evangelist, who had been suspected of smuggling in his youth, and had been overtaken (as the phrase went) on the streets of Crossmichael one Faire day. It was known that every Sunday they prayed for a blessing on the arms of Bonaparte. For this, "God's Remnant," as they were "skailing" from the cottage that did duty for a temple, had been repeatedly stoned by the bairns, and Gib himself hooted by a squad-ron of Border volunteers in which his own brother, Dand, rode in a uniform and with a drawn sword. The "Remnant" were believed, besides, to be "antinomian in principle," which might otherwise have been a serious charge, but the way public opinion then blew it was quite swallowed up and forgotten in the scandal about Bonaparte. For the rest, Gilbert had set up his loom in an outhouse at Cauldstaneslap, where he laboured as-siduously six days of the week. His brothers, appalled by his political opin-ions and willing to avoid dissension in the household, spoke but little to him; he less to them, remaining absorbed in the study of the Bible and almost constant prayer. The gaunt weaver was dry-nurse at Cauldstaneslap, and the bairns loved him dearly. Except when he was carrying an infant in his arms, he was rarely seen to smile — as, indeed, there were few smilers in that family. When his sister-in-law rallied him, and proposed that he should get a wife and bairns of his own, since he was so fond of them, "I have no clearness of mind upon that point," he would reply. If nobody called him to dinner, he stayed out. Mrs. Hob, a hard, unsympathetic woman, once tried the experiment. He went without food all day, but at dusk, as the light began to fail him, he came into the house of his own accord, looking puzzled. "I've had a great gale of prayer upon my speerit," said he. "I canna mind sae muckle's what I had for denner." The creed of God's Remnant was justified in the life of its founder. "And yet I dinna ken," said Kirstie. "He's maybe no more stockfish than his neeghbours! He rode wi' the rest o' them, and had a good stamach to the work, by a' that I hear! God's Remnant! The deil's clavers! There wasna muckle Christianity in the way Hob guided Johnny Dickieson, at the least of it; but Guid kens! Is he a Christian even? He might be a Mahommedan or a Deevil or a Fireworshiper, for what I ken."

The third brother had his name on a door-plate, no less, in the city of Glasgow. "Mr. Clement Elliott," as long as your arm. In his case, that spirit of innovation which had shown itself timidly in the case of Hob by the admission of new manures, and which had run to waste with Gilbert in subversive politics and heretical religions, bore useful fruit in many ingenious mechanical improvements. In boyhood, from his addiction to strange devices of sticks and string, he had been counted the most eccentric of the family. But that was all by now, and he was a partner of his firm, and looked to die a baillie. He too had married, and was rearing a plentiful family in the smoke and din of Glasgow; he was wealthy, and could have bought out his brother, the cock-laird, six times over, it was whispered; and when he slipped away to Cauldstaneslap for a well-earned holiday, which he did as often as he was able, he astonished the neighbours with his broadcloth, his beaver hat, and the ample plies of his neckcloth. Though an eminently solid man at bottom, after the pattern of Hob, he had contracted a certain Glasgow briskness and *aplomb* which set him off. All the other Elliotts were as lean as a rake, but Clement was laying on fat, and he panted sorely when he must get into his boots. Dand said, chuckling: "Ay, Clem has the elements of a corporation." "A provost and corporation," returned Clem. And his readiness was much admired.

The fourth brother, Dand, was a shepherd to his trade, and by starts, when he could bring his mind to it, excelled in the business. Nobody could train a dog like Dandie; nobody, through a peril of great storms in the winter time, could do more gallantly. But if his dexterity were exquisite, his diligence was but fitful; and he served his brother for bed and board, and a trifle of pocketmoney when he asked for it. He loved money well enough, knew very well how to spend it, and could make a shrewd bargain when he liked. But he preferred a vague knowledge that he was well to windward to any counted coins in the pocket; he felt himself richer so. Hob would expostulate: "I'm an amateur herd," Dand would reply: "I'll keep your sheep to you when I'm so minded, but I'll keep my liberty too. Thir's no man can coandescend on what I'm worth." Clem would expound to him the miraculous results of compound interest, and recommend investments. "Ay, man?" Dand would say, "and do you think, if I took Hob's siller, that I wouldna drink it or wear it on the lassies? And, anyway, my kingdom is no of the world. Either I'm a poet or else I'm nothing." Clem would remind him of old age. "I'll die young, like Robbie Burns," he would say stoutly. No question but he had a certain accomplishment in minor verse. His "Hermiston Burn," with its pretty refrain —

> I love to gang thinking whaur ye gang linking,
> Hermiston burn, in the howe;

his "Auld, auld Elliotts, clay-cauld Elliotts, dour, bauld Elliotts of auld," and his really fascinating piece about the Praying Weaver's Stone, had gained him in the neighbourhood the reputation, still possible in Scotland, of a local bard; and, though not printed himself, he was recognised by others who were and who had become famous. Walter Scott owed to Dandie the text of the "Raid of Wearie" in the *Minstrelsy* and made him welcome at his house, and appreciated his talents, such as they were, with all his usual generosity. The Ettrick Shepherd was his sworn crony; they would meet, drink to excess, roar out their lyrics in each other's faces, and quarrel and make it up again till bedtime. And besides these recognitions, almost to be called official, Dandie was made welcome for the sake of his gift through the farmhouses of several contiguous dales, and was thus exposed to manifold temptations which he rather sought than fled. He had figured on the stool of repentance, for once fulfilling to the letter the tradition of his hero and model. His humorous verses to Mr. Torrance on that ocasion — "Kenspeckle here my lane I stand" — unfortunately too indelicate for further citation, ran through the country like a fiery cross; they were recited, quoted, paraphrased, and laughed over as far away as Dumfries on the one hand and Dunbar on the other.

These four brothers were united by a close bond, the bond of that mutual admiration — or rather mutual hero-worship — which is so strong among the members of secluded families who have much ability and little culture. Even the extremes admired each other. Hob, who had as much poetry as the tongs, professed to find pleasure in Dand's verses; Clem, who had no more religion than Claverhouse, nourished a heartfelt, at least an open-mouthed, admiration of Gib's prayers; and Dandie followed with relish the rise of Clem's fortunes. Indulgence followed hard on the heels of admiration. The laird, Clem, and Dand, who were Tories and patriots of the hottest quality, excused to themselves, with a certain bashfulness, the radical and revolutionary heresies of Gib. By another division of the family, the laird, Clem, and Gib, were were men exactly virtuous, swallowed the dose of Dand's irregularities as a kind of clog or drawback in the mysterious providence of God affixed to bards, and distinctly probative of poetical genius. To appreciate the simplicity of their mutual admiration, it was necessary to hear Clem, arrived upon one of his visits, and dealing in a spirit of continuous irony with the affairs and personalities of that great city of Glasgow where he lived and transacted business. The various personages, ministers of the church, municipal officers, mercantile big-wigs, whom he had occasion to introduce, were all alike denigrated, all served but as reflectors to cast back a flattering side-light on the house of Cauldstaneslap. The Provost, for whom Clem by exception entertained a measure of respect, he would liken to Hob. "He minds me o' the laird there," he would say. "He has some of Hob's grand, whum-stane sense, and the same way with him of steiking his mouth when he's no very pleased." And Hob, all unconscious, would draw down his upper lip and produce, as if for comparison, the formidable grimace referred to. The unsatisfactory incumbent of St. Enoch's Kirk was thus briefly dismissed: "If he had but twa fingers o' Gib's he would waken them up." And Gib, honest man! would look down and secretly smile. Clem was a spy whom they had sent out into the world of men. He had come back with the good news that there was nobody to compare with the Four Black Brothers, no position that they would not adorn, no official that it would not be well they should replace, no interest of mankind, secular or spiritual, which would not immediately bloom under their supervision. The excuse of their folly is in two words: scarce the breadth of a hair divided them from the peasantry. The measure of their sense is this: that these symposia of rustic vanity were kept entirely within the family, like some secret ancestral practice. To the world their serious faces were never deformed by the suspicion of any simper of self-contentment. Yet it was known. "They hae a guid pride o' themsel's!" was the word in the country-side.

Lastly, in a Border story, there should be added their "two-names." Hob was The Laird. "Roy ne puis, prince ne daigne"; he was the laird of Cauldstaneslap — say fifty acres — *ipsissimus*. Clement was Mr. Elliott, as upon his door-plate, the earlier Dafty having been discarded as no longer applicable, and indeed only a reminder of misjudgment and the imbecility of the public; and the youngest, in honour of his perpetual wanderings, was known by the sobriquet of Randy Dand.

It will be understood that not all this information was communicated by the aunt, who had too much of the family failing herself to appreciate it thoroughly in others. But as time went on, Archie began to observe an omission in the family chronicle.

"Is there not a girl too?" he asked.

"Ay. Kirstie. She was named from me, or my grandmother at least — it's the same thing," returned the aunt, and went on again about Dand, whom she secretly preferred by reason of his gallantries.

"But what is your niece like?" said Archie at the next opportunity.

"Her? As black's your hat! But I dinna suppose she would maybe be what you would ca' *ill-looked* a' thegither. Na, she's a kind of handsome jaud — a kind o' gipsy," said the aunt, who had two sets of scales for men and women — or perhaps it would be more fair to say that she had three, and the third and the most loaded was for girls.

"How comes it that I never see her in church?" said Archie.

" 'Deed, and I believe she's in Glesgie with Clem and his wife. A heap good she's like to get of it! I dinna say for men folk, but where weemen folk are born, there let them bide. Glory to God. I was never far'er from here than Crossmichael."

In the meantime it began to strike Archie as strange, that while she thus sang the praises of her kinsfolk, and manifestly relished their virtues and (I may say) their vices like a thing creditable to herself, there should appear not the least sign of cordiality between the house of Hermiston and that of Cauldstaneslap. Going to church of a Sunday, as the lady housekeeper stepped with her skirts kilted, three tucks of her white petticoat showing below, and her best India shawl upon her back (if the day were fine) in a pattern of radiant dyes, she would sometimes overtake her relatives preceding her more leisurely in the same direction. Gib of course was absent; by skriegh of day he had been gone to Crossmichael and his fellow heretics; but the rest of the family would be seen marching in open order: Hob and Dand, stiff-necked, straight-backed six-footers, with severe dark faces, and their plaids about their shoulders; the convoy of children scattering (in a state of high polish) on the wayside, and every now and again collected by the shrill summons of the mother; and the mother herself, by a suggestive circumstance which might have afforded matter of thought to a more experienced observer than Archie, wrapped in a shawl nearly identical with Kirstie's but a thought more gaudy and conspicuously newer. At the sight, Kirstie grew more tall — Kirstie showed her classical profile, nose in air and nostril spread, the pure blood came in her cheek evenly in a delicate living pink.

"A braw day to ye, Mistress Elliott," said she, and hostility and gentility were nicely mingled in her tones. "A fine day, mem," the laird's wife would reply with a miraculous curtsey, spreading the while her plumage — setting off, in other words, and with arts unknown to the mere man, the pattern of her India shawl. Behind her, the whole Cauldstaneslap contingent marched in closer order, and with an indescribable air of being in the presence of the foe; and while Dandie saluted his aunt with a certain familiarity as of one who was well in court, Hob marched on in awful immobility. There appeared upon the face of this attitude in the family the consequences of some dreadful feud. Presumably the two women had been principals in the original encounter, and the laird had probably been drawn into the quarrel by the ears, too late to be included in the present skin-deep reconciliation.

"Kirstie," said Archie one day, "what is this you have against your family?"

"I dinna complean," said Kirstie, with a flush. "I say naething."

"I see you do not — not even good-day to your own nephew," said he.

"I hae naething to be ashaimed of," said she. "I can say the Lord's prayer with a good grace. If Hob was ill, or in preeson or poverty, I would see to him blithely. But for curtchying and complimenting and colloguing, thank ye kindly!"

Archie had a bit of a smile: he leaned back in his chair. "I think you and Mrs. Robert are not very good friends," says he slyly, "when you have your India shawls on?"

She looked upon him in silence, with a sparkling eye but an indecipherable expression; and that was all that Archie was ever destined to learn of the battle of the India shawls.

"Do none of them ever come here to see you?" he inquired.

"Mr. Archie," said she, "I hope that I ken my place better. It would be a queer thing, I think, if I was to clamjamfry up your faither's house . . .

that I should say it! — wi' a dirty, black-a-vised clan, no ane o' them it was worth while to mar soap upon but just mysel'! Na, they're all damni-feed wi' the black Ellwalds. I have nae patience wi' black folks." Then, with a sudden consciousness of the case of Archie, "No that it maitters for men sae muckle," she made haste to add, "but there's naebody can deny that it's unwomanly. Long hair is the ornament o' woman ony way; we've good warrandise for that — it's in the Bible — and wha can doubt that the Apostle had some gowden-haired lassie in his mind — Apostle and all, for what was he but just a man like yersel'?"

Sioux

by A. B. Guthrie, Jr.

1830 Many weeks out of St. Louis up the Missouri into buffalo and Indian country, the keelboat Mandan was tied to the banks for the night. Jourdonnais hoped to trade his cargo of whiskey to the Blackfeet for beaver plews and a big profit. Dick Summers, an experienced Mountain Man, was his hunter. Boone Caudill and Jim Deakins, youngsters from Kentucky, would be hunters and Mountain Men, too, someday, if they could stay alive long enough to learn what Summers could teach them.

Boone picked his way among the sleeping men. Jourdonnais' face, faintly horned with the spikes of his mustache, was a dark circle against his darker robe. He was snoring the long deep snore of a man worn out.

"I got you a Hawken," Summers said from the keelboat, keeping his voice low. He handed a gun and horn and pouch over the side to Boone. "It's the real beaver, for buffler or anything."

Boone hefted the rifle and tried it at his shoulder. It was heavier than Old Sure Shot, and it was a flintlock, not a cap and ball, but it felt good to him — well-balanced and stout, like a piece a man could depend on.

A kind of flush was coming into the sky, not light yet but not dark, either. The men lying in their blankets looked big, like horses or buffalo lying down. The mast of the keelboat, dripping with dew, glistened a little. Boone could hear the water lapping against the sides of the Mandan. Farther out, the river made a quiet, busy murmur, as if it were talking to itself of things seen upcountry. Once in a while one of the men groaned and moved, easing his muscles on the earth.

"It's winter ground mostly," said Summers, coming down from the boat, "but might be we can get our sights on one."

They started up the river, moving out from the fringe of trees to the open country at the base of the hills, hearing a sudden snort and the sound of flight from a thicket. "Elk," said Summers. "Poor doin's, to my way of thinking, if there's aught else about. We'll git one, if need be. They're plenty now."

"Poor? I was thinkin' they're tasty, the ones we shot so far."

"Nigh anything's better. Dog, for a case. Ever set your teeth in fat pup?"

Summers made a noise with his lips. "Or horse? A man gets a taste for it.
And beaver tail! I'm half-froze for beaver tail. And buffler, of course, fat
fleece and hump rib and marrow bones too good to think of."

"That's best, I reckon."

"You reckon wrong. Painter meat, now, that's some. Painter meat, that's
top, now." Summers' moccasined feet seemed to make no noise at all. "But
meat's meat, snake meat or man meat or what."

Boone turned to study the hunter's lined and weathered face, wondering if he had eaten man meat, seeing an arm or leg browning and dripping
over the fire.

"Injuns like dead meat. You'll see 'em, towin' drawned buffler to shore,
buffler that would stink a man out of a skunk's nest. This nigger's et skunk,
too. It ain't so bad, if he ain't squirted. The Canadians, now, they set a
heap of store by it. It's painter meat to them."

The stars had gone out, and the sky was turning a dull white, like scraped
horn. A low cloud was on fire to the east, where the sun would come up.
Boone could make out the trees, separate from each other now and standing against the dark hills — short, squatty trees, big at the base, which
could hold against the wind. They walked slow, just dragging along, while
Summers' eyes kept poking ahead and the light came on and Boone could
follow the Missouri with his eye, on and on until it got lost in a far tumble
of hills. The ground was spotted in front of them with disks of old buffalo
manure under which the grass and weeds grew white, as in a root house.
When he turned one over with his toe, little black beetles scurried out
into the grass.

"Ain't any fresh," he said. His eyes searched the hills and the gullies
that wormed up through them from the river bottom. "Reckon we won't
find any?"

Summers didn't answer right away. He would look east, up on the slope
of the hills and west to the woods and river and beyond them to where
other hills rose up, making a cradle for the Missouri, and sometimes his
eyes would stop and fix on something, as if it might be game or Indians,
and go on after a while and stop again. Boone tried to see what he was
seeing, but there was only the river winding ahead and the slopes of the
hills and the gullies cutting into them and here and there a low tree, flattened at the top, where birds were chirping.

Half the sun was showing, shining in the grass where the dew was
beaded. There wasn't a cloud in all the sky, not even a piece of one now

that the one to the east had burned out, and the air was still and waiting-like, as if it were worn out and resting up for a blow.

"Sight easier to kill game along the river, where a man don't have to tote it," Summers said, following the valley with his eyes. "Let's point our stick up, anyway." He turned and started uphill.

From the top Boone could see forever and ever, nearly any way he looked. It was open country, bald and open, without an end. It spread away, flat now and then rolling, going on clear to the sky. A man wouldn't think the whole world was so much. It made the heart come up. It made a man little and still big, like a king looking out. It occurred to Boone that this was the way a bird must feel, free and loose, with the world to choose from. Nothing moved from sky line to sky line. Only down on the river he could see the keelboat showing between the trees, nosing up river like a slow fish. He marked how she poked ahead. He looked on to the tumble of hills that closed in on the river and wondered if she could ever get that far.

Summers had halted, his nose stuck out, like a hound feeling for a scent. "Air's movin' west, if it's movin' at all, I'm thinkin'. All right." He stepped out again, walking with a loose, swift ease.

The sun got up, hot and bright as steel. Off a distance the air began to shimmer in it. Summers kept along the crest of the hills, going slow when they came in sight of a gully or a swale.

It was in one of them that they saw the buffalo, standing quiet with its head down, as if its thoughts were away off. Summers' hand touched Boone's arm. "Old bull," he said, "but meat's meat." The bull lifted his great head and turned it toward them, looking, his beard hanging low.

"He seen us," Boone whispered. "He'll make off."

"Shoo!" said Summers, putting his hand on the lifted barrel of Boone's rifle. "They can't see for nothin', and hearin' don't mean a thing to 'em. It's all right, long as he don't get wind of us." He started forward, walking slow. "You kin shoot him."

"Now?"

"Wait a spell."

The bull didn't move. He stood with his head turned and down, as if for all his blindness, he knew they were there. Boone's mind went back to his blind Aunt Minnie who could always tell when someone was around. Her head would pivot and her face would wait, while she looked out of eyes that didn't see.

"Take your wipin' stick. Make a rest. Like this." Summers put the stick out at arm's length and had Boone hold it with his left hand and let the rifle lie across his wrist. "Let 'im have it."

The rifle bucked against Boone's shoulder, cracking the silence. The ball made a gut-shot sound, and a little puff of dust came from the buffalo, as if he had been hit with a pebble. For an instant he stood there looking dull and sad, as if nothing had happened, and then he broke into a clumsy gallop, heading out of the gully. Boone watched him, and heard another crack by his side and saw the bull break down at the knees and fall ahead on his nose. He lay on his side, his legs waving, his breath making a snore in his nose.

Summers was reloading, grinning as he did so. "Too high." Boone felt naked in the bright blue gaze of his eyes, as if what he felt in his mind was standing out for the hunter to see. Summers' face changed. "Don't think nothin' of it. Nigh everybody shoots high, first time. Just a hand and a half above the brisket, that's the spot. It's a lesson for you. Best to load up again, afore anything."

Quicker than Boone could believe, Summers charged his gun. He hitched his pouch and powder horn around, drew the stopper from the horn with his teeth, put the mouth of it in his left hand, and with his right turned the horn up. He was ramming down his load before Boone got his powder measured out.

The buffalo's eyes were fading. They looked soft now, deep and soft with the light going out of them. His legs still waved a little. Summers put his knife in his throat. "We'll roll him over, and this child'll show you how to get at good feedin'." He planted the four legs out at the sides, so that the buffalo seemed to have been squashed down from above. The hunter's knife flashed in the sun. It made a cut crosswise on the neck, and Summers grabbed the hair of the boss with his other hand and separated the skin from the shoulder. He laid the skin open to the tail and peeled it down the sides, spreading it out. "Can't take much," he said, chopping with his hatchet. "Tongue and liver and fleece fat and such. Or maybe one of us best go and git some help from the boat. Wisht we had a pack mule."

"There's a wolf."

Summers looked around at the grinning face that watched them from behind a little rise. "Buffler wolf. White wolf." He spoke in jerks while his knife worked. "I seen fifteen-twenty of 'em circled round sometimes."

"Don't you never shoot 'em?"

"Have to be nigh gone for meat. Ain't enough powder and ball on the Missouri to shoot 'em all."

Boone found a rock and pitched it at the wolf. The head disappeared behind the rise and came into sight again a jump or two away.

Summers kept looking up from his butchering, turning to study every direction, and then going back to the bull again. "See them cayutes?" Boone watched them slink up, their feet moving as if they ran a twisting line, their eyes yellow and hungry. They came closer than the wolf and sat down. Their tongues came out and dripped on the grass. "Watch!" Summers threw a handful of gut toward them. The bigger one darted in, seized the gut, and made off, but he hadn't got far before the wolf jumped on him and took it away. The coyote came back and sat down again. "Happens every time," said Summers. He had the liver out, and the gall bladder. He cut a slice of liver and dipped it in the bladder and poked it in his mouth, chewing and gulping while he worked. "For poor bull, it ain't so bad. Want some?"

Boone took a slice. While he was making himself chew on it, he saw the cloud of dust. It came from behind a little pitch of land maybe two miles to the north, and it wasn't a cloud so much as a vapor, a wisp that he expected to disappear like a fleck in the eye. He wondered whether to point it out to Summers. The wisp came on to the top of the pitch. There was a movement under it. He said then, "Reckon you catched sight of that?"

Summers looked long, the knife idle in his hand. "I be dogged! Hold still now! It's brown skin, sure as I be, but maybe just Puncas." After what seemed to Boone a long time, he added, "Let's back up toward cover. We can cache, maybe. Here's a hoss as don't like it."

He peeled off his shirt and spread it on the ground and put on it the parts of the carcass he had cut out to save, folding the shirt over afterward. Boone narrowed his eyes against the glare. Those were horses under the dust cloud, with riders on them.

"Might be we can git back with this here," said Summers. "They seen us all right." He lifted his parcel. "Poor doin's, anyhow, to let Injuns think you're runnin'. Even the squaws get braved up then, and full of hell. Ease away, now." His voice was sure and quiet.

Boone scanned the river, looking for the *Mandan*. "Ain't hardly had time to pull this fur," said Summers, "with no breeze to help."

They dropped down behind the crest of the hills, out of sight of the Indians. "Hump it! Hump it some!" They broke for the thin timber two hundred yards and more away, with Summers holding his bundle out from him so as not to hinder his leg.

"I'll take 'er," Boone panted, but Summers only shook his head.

"All right." Summers slowed to an unhurried walk. The Indians came to the top of the hill and halted, outlined against the sky.

"We'll make peace sign." Summers put his parcel down and fired his rifle at the sky. Afterwards, he took his pipe out and held it high for the Indians to see.

The Indians looked and talked among themselves, until one of them yelled and all joined in, a kind of high, quavering yell. They sent their horses down the bluff, the hoofs making a clatter in a patch of stones.

"Gimme your Hawken and load this 'un." They were still a throw away from the fringe of woods along the river. Summers took the wiping stick from its slot while he watched. "Sioux, by beaver, or this nigger don't know Injun. They can't circle us here, anyways. Git ready, old hoss, but hold fire till I give the sign." He planted his wiping stick out before him and laid the rifle on its rest. "That's it, hoss, and line your sights on the belly, not the head."

A hundred and fifty yards away the Indians pulled up. Boone counted them. Twelve men. They were naked from the waist up, unless a man counted the feathers stuck in their hair. Their skin looked smooth and soft, like good used leather. It would make a better strop than the one he'd left in Louisville. Three or four had guns in their hands, and the others bows. Their horses minced around as they waited.

"It ain't a war party, anyhow," Summers said, as if he was making talk at night around the fire.

"How can a body tell?"

"No paint. No shields. They're huntin', I'm thinkin'."

Summers stood up. His voice went out, rough and steady and strong, in language Boone didn't understand, and his hands made movements in front of him.

The Indians listened, sitting their horses as if they were grown on them. Sometimes as the horses moved Boone could see the Indians' hair, hanging far down in plaits. The foremost of them, though, the one who seemed to be the leader, had chopped it off short.

Summers' voice came to a halt. To Boone he said, "A man never knows about Sioux."

The Indians sat their milling horses. Their heads moved, and their hands, as they talked to one another. The Indian with the short hair rode out.

The tail of some animal hung from his moccasin. His voice was stronger than Summers' and came more from his chest.

"Asks if we're squaws, to run," Summers translated. "And what have we got for presents? His tongue is short but his arm is long, and he feels blood in his eye."

The Indian halted, waiting for Summers' reply. "I'm thinkin' they just met up with an enemy and got the worst of the tussle. That makes 'em mean as all hell. I'll tell 'em our tongues ain't so long either, but our guns is a heap longer'n them crazy fusees." His voice went out again.

Suddenly, while the rest watched, the Indian with the short hair let out a yell and put his horse to a gallop, coming straight at them. He was low on his horse, just the top of him showing and the legs at the sides.

Summers dropped to one knee again and leveled his gun, and nothing seemed to move about him except the end of the barrel bearing on the rider. Boone was down, too, with his rifle up, seeing the outflung hoofs of the horse and the flaring nostrils. He would be on them in a shake. The horse bore out a little, and the cropped head moved, and the black of a barrel came over the horse's neck. Summers' rifle spoke, and in a wink the horse was running free, shying out in a circle and going back. The Indian lay on his belly. He didn't move. "That's one for the wolves," Summers said. His hand came over and gave Boone the empty rifle and took the loaded one and drew away with it. "Load up!"

The Indians had sat, watching the one and yelling for him. They hushed when he fell and then all began to yell again, the voices rising shrill and falling. They set their horses to a run streaking to one side and then the other, not coming directly at Boone and Summers, but working closer as the line went back and forth. Sometimes one, bolder than the rest, would charge out of the line and come nearer, waving his gun or bow while he shouted, and then go back to the line again. "Hold your sights on one," said Summers, "the one on the speckled pony. Hold fire till I tell you. Then plumb center with it." He had taken his pistols from his belt and had them out before him, ready to his hand.

The Indians made themselves small on the horses, swinging to the off side as they turned. "Shoo!" Summers said. "They can't ride for nothin'. Can't shine with Comanches, or even Crows."

"Why'n't they charge, all of 'em?"

Summers' eye ran along the barrel of his gun. "They got no stummick for that kind of doin's, save once in a while one likes to shine alone, like that nigger out there."

A rifle cracked, and in front of them the ground exploded in a little blast of dust. "Steady. Time to go ag'in." Out of the corner of his eye Boone saw smoke puff from the gun. A running horse stumbled and fell. The Indians shouted, higher and wilder. The fallen horse lay on its rider. Boone saw the rider, just the head and jerking hands of him beyond the horse, trying to pull his leg free. Summers handed over the empty rifle. Two Indians flew to the one who was down, slipped from the off sides of their horses, and, stooping behind the downed horse, rolled the withers up. The fallen rider tried to arise and went off crawling, dragging one leg.

The others, driven back a little by the shot, began to come in again, working to and fro. One of them bobbed up and swung his rifle over. The ball sang past Boone. He had the rifle primed again, and the Indian on the speckled pony on his sights. "Kin I shoot one?" He didn't wait. The sights seemed to steady of themselves and fixed just above the pony's neck. His finger bore on the trigger, like it had a mind of its own. The rifle jumped.

"I be dogged."

The speckled pony shied off. Behind him a man squirmed on the ground, squirmed and got up and went back, bent at the middle.

"Slicker'n ice, Caudill."

The Indians bunched up, talking and gesturing. "They had nigh enough, I'm thinkin'," said Summers, raising his cheek from his rifle. He added, "For now."

"That's the boat."

The trumpet had sounded, cutting through the still air, rolling up river and out to the hills and coming back on itself. Boone saw the *Mandan*. The oars made little even flashes as the men laid them back. Someone was busy in the bow. It looked like Jourdonnais. It was him, working at the swivel gun, which was a bar of light in the bow. The Indians looked, holding their horses tight, easing them backward away from the river. The swivel belched smoke, and the sound of it came to them, a rolling boom like thunder. Jourdonnais got busy with it again.

"First shot was just to skeer 'em. Second'll be business."

But the Sioux drew off, turning back and shouting and shaking their arms as they went. Boone watched them long enough to see that they picked up the two crippled warriors.

Summers put his pistols back in his belt and fitted his wiping stick to his rifle. He and Boone walked ahead, to the Indian who lay still in the grass. Summers stooped over. His knife cut into the scalp and made a rough circle, from which the blood beaded. He got hold of the Indian's short hair and tore the circle loose, leaving the piece of skull naked and raw. "Take his gun. This injun's had a grief lately. Some of his kin's gone under — a brother, maybe. That's why he chopped his tails off. Looks recent, don't it? Like as not it just happened. That's why they was so froze for our scalps, so's they wouldn't have to go home beaten and with nary thing to shine with." He went back and picked up his bundle of meat, carrying scalp and bundle in one hand.

The *Mandan* pulled in, so close they could hop aboard. Jourdonnais' bold, dark face questioned Summers. The Creoles looked at him, too, their eyes big and watchful like the eyes of a frog ready to jump if a man took another step.

Summers said, "We put one under and winged two." The barrel of his rifle swung toward Boone. "There's a hoss as'll shoot plumb center." In tones that Boone barely overheard he went on, "We ain't seen the last of 'em, I'm thinkin'."

Summers was right; but for a day and part of another, while they went by the Rivière à Jacques and headed on toward the L'Eau Qui Court, Jourdonnais told himself that he wasn't. There wasn't one sign of Indian, not even to Summers, who watched the shores, hour after hour, searching with his trained gray eye. Summers' face was sober, but not worried. Jourdonnais wondered if he ever worried, this big, loose-built man who was like a wise old dog. Watching him, gazing down from his place at the steering oar, Jourdonnais wondered that Summers had gone in with him. Summers didn't care for money or a nice house or pretties for a wife, if he had one. He lived like a wild thing, to eat and frolic and keep his scalp, not thinking from one day to another, not putting by against the future. If Jourdonnais hadn't found him fresh back from a good hunt in the country of the Arapahoes, Summers wouldn't have had money to put into cargo, the way he was spending it. As it was, Jourdonnais in his desperate need for funds had had to beg, holding out the possibilities of rich profits in the Trois Fourches. Looking at Summers, seeing the alert face that was untroubled by regrets or ambition, Jourdonnais thought that Summers had joined him for the fun rather than the profit. He was glad that Summers was an easy man, without the dark strain of violence that ran so often in mountain men.

He was thankful, too, for the favor of the wind, grudging and unreliable as it was. It would take a gun, almost, to drive the Creoles to the bank now. He wouldn't order them to tow unless he had to. A hundred Indians could hide in one small thicket and kill the crew to the last man as they pulled up to it. It was good that the river was down. The time was coming on to June, and the Missouri would flood again when the snow in the mountains ran off.

As much as he could, Jourdonnais kept the *Mandan* to the left bank, away from the side on which Summers and Caudill had come up against the Indians. Sometimes he put the crew out with the cordelle on the long sand bars that divided the current, lying in the water like the backs of hogs cooling off in the muck. The men rowed, each with a rifle by his side, and for all of Summers' looking, they looked, too, putting only half their attention on the oars and the other half on the bank, as if every bush hid an Indian. Sometimes Jourdonnais felt ashamed for his people, who had neither bravery nor pride like Americans.

"The Sioux go away, eh, Summers?"

Summers came over and leaned against the cargo box and gave a half-shake of his head. "They're like to pop up on a bank any time and rain arrers down on us. Now's when we need two boats, one on each side, the other lookin' out for us and us lookin' out for them. We can see the far shore a heap better'n this one. I'm thinkin' they're comin' along, maybe lookin' for a way acrost."

The hunter looked down from his six feet and said something in Indian to little Teal Eye, who was standing by her lodge with one hand on the box letting the breeze blow her. She answered and let her gaze slide back to the shore.

"You sure about Sioux?" Jourdonnais asked. "They make no trouble for long time."

Summers' tone had a faint edge. "This child ought to know a Sioux."

Jourdonnais agreed, smiling to soften the other's irritation. "You have sleep with them enough? Maybe *beaucoup* Sioux babies by Summers?"

The hunter didn't answer at once, and when he did speak it was to explain. "Sioux or what, two white men alone make Injuns itchy."

"So?"

"They had blood in their eye to boot, I'm thinkin'." He pointed to the scalp that had been tucked under a lashing, raw side up, to dry. A big blue-green fly, shining with bloat, was working on it. "Hair's cut short. Means that hoss was grievin'."

"Yes."

"Injuns ain't never so mean as when they've took a beatin'. They're half-froze to make up for it, don't matter on who."

They pulled up to a sand bar for the night. The river ran on both sides of it, making an island — a flat little island on which the willows had commenced to poke up. It might wash away with the next high water. The wind played among the willows and picked up the sand and threw it at them, so that there was sand in the eye and in the meat and in the beds. Pambrun had set up his stove on top of the cargo, in a box filled with sand. Here in the middle of the river the Creoles felt safe. Some of them took off their clothes and sported in the water. That was one thing about his people, Jourdonnais thought; they had the light heart. He let himself have one of the Spanish segars that he reserved for special occasions, though he hardly felt right in smoking it. A man could keep himself poor, letting small money get away from him. "By damn," he said to Romaine while he wiped an eye, "the wind blow the gnat off and the sand on. One damn thing or another." As the night began to close down Pambrun set out his fishlines, baited with bird gut.

They stood watches that night and went on before the sun was up, their bellies working on catfish and roast liver and tenderloin that was half-raw and tough but full of strength. Great yellow-breasted larks sang as the sun came up, and with his fowling piece Summers shot half a dozen prairie hens that had watched them from an island, their heads up and turning until the bird shot knocked them over.

There was no wind at all in the early morning, and the river seemed to have a new strength, as if it had just awakened to find how far they had invaded her. The absence of a breeze, the renewed force of the current, the Indians maybe somewhere along the bank, all seemed to Jourdonnais, squirming at the helm, the proof of conspiracy against him. *Enfant de garce*, wasn't the river easier above the Jacques, always! He thought of distance as the enemy, as a slow and crawling thing that stood between him and a new house and money in pocket and the big men of St. Louis saying "Monsieur Jourdonnais." The left bank lay open, inviting him to tow. He motioned Summers to him.

"The cordelle?" He was asking for advice. He motioned toward the bare bank.

Summers' chin closed, so that his mouth was the thin mouth of thought. "Put in," he said at last. "This child'll scout. See me wave, send the crew out." He lifted his gun that seemed always in his hand now and refreshed the priming. "Better send a hunter with 'em, to boot." Before he started for the shore he studied it. "All right." Jourdonnais saw that they had scared up a heron, which flopped away with its legs out, using them for a rudder.

It seemed a long time before he saw Summers again, standing half a mile up on a little tongue of land, motioning them on. Jourdonnais said, "The cordelle. We tow," loud enough for the oarsmen in the bow to hear him. The men's eyes went to the bank and then to him. They got themselves up, as if they had weights in their pants. "*Non!* Not the guns. *Mon Dieu,* you think to pull with rifles in the hands?" They stood shifting from foot to foot, muttering to themselves. "Summers, he's looking ahead. I send Caudill with you, to lead. Here, all have a drink. It is all right."

The woods were still, but not too still. Things moved in them and made noises, a brown thrush flitting in a thicket of buffalo berry, a coyote trotting at the edge of the meadow that flowed out from the trees and led on up to the hills, a bunch of magpies cawing in a tangled cottonwood. Summers' eye caught the movement of the thrasher. It was no more than a shadow passing in shadows, but he saw it and identified the bird, and his eye climbed the bushes until it found the nest. The magpies were a brood. The young ones made an unsure clamor, like boys with their voices changing.

Summers went on, letting a part of his mind roam and keeping a part of it open for the messages of the woods. A man had to learn to divide his mind that way, to think and remember in some far-off part of it and yet to note and feel what was going on about him, and to be ready to act without thinking. The far-off part of his mind saw Caudill aiming at the Indian, his face set and maybe a little pale but not scared. Caudill, for all he was an odd and silent boy, would make a mountain man. Maybe so would Deakins, though he didn't seem cut out so clear for it. Trading would suit him; he got along with people. It was something, what traders would do to make money — like Jourdonnais stewing over his nickels. Christ, even when you had a heap of beaver what did you have?

He went to the water line and motioned an "All right," waiting for Jourdonnais' answering wave, and then let the woods swallow him again and that far piece of his mind go on with its thinking. He knew he wasn't a mountain man as some men were. He liked to get to St. Louis once in a while and sleep in a sure-enough bed, with a white woman that smelled of perfume instead of grease and diamond-willow smoke. He didn't mind farming, too much. It was still getting outside. And he hadn't lost his taste for bread and salt and pies and such. They were a heap better than squaw meat, which men had been known to butcher and eat, probably after bedding with the squaws first.

Above him, out at the edge of the brush, a curlew was calling. Its sharp two-toned cry seemed to hang in the air. He caught a glimpse of it, with its wings outspread and just the tips of them fluttering as it glided. He waited for it to land, waited for the muted little trill that would tell him it was aground again and satisfied. The bird's shadow sped along the leaves over his head. It hadn't lighted. It wasn't going to light. The two-toned cry kept sounding, as if something had stumbled on the nest.

Summers waited and watched and after a while moved ahead again, going as softly as a man could. Except for the curlew and the magpies that were half a mile behind him now, the woods had no voice at all, and no movement. He came to a small open space and stood at the edge of it, unmoving except for his eyes. Through a screen of brush he could see a patch of the river shaded by the trees above him. The water seemed still as pond water, gathered in a small elbow in the bank. While he watched, a mallard hen came into the patch, swimming steadily downstream, watching for the string of ducklings that trailed behind her. They didn't make a sound.

Summers thought, "Injuns about, sure as God," but still he didn't move. A man couldn't run off yelling Injun without knowing where they were and who and how many. After a while he slipped ahead again, and stopped, and went on. A willow branch made a little whisking noise along his buckskin. He halted and put it back of him and waited again. The curlew was still circling, still crying about her nest.

The boats were stowed carefully in the brush, so as not to be seen from the river. There were seven of them in sight, the round bullboats of the upper Missouri, each made from the hide of a single bull stretched over a willow frame. They appeared old and were wet yet, but not dripping, as if they had been used the night before and hadn't had time to dry out there in the shade. Summers looked at them through a clump of low willow. He made out a moccasined track pointed upstream.

After what seemed a long time, he crouched down and sidled over toward the bank of the river. He thrust his head from the brush slowly, like a squirrel peeking from behind a limb, knowing it was movement and not shape that caught the eye. Up the current, less than an arrow shot away, the river made a slow turn. The willows grew lush there, probably where a tree had gone over and caught the sand and made a bank. The boat towers would have clear going until they got there.

Summers couldn't see anything among the willows, not so much as a branch bent out of shape or the grass trampled where a man might have gone through, but he knew the Sioux were there.

He brought his head back, still slowly, and turned about, to see an Indian screened in the brush only an arm's length away. Two black stripes ran down the Indian's cheeks. They pulled downward as the Indian caught his movement. There was one still instant — a flash of seeing, in which nothing moved or sounded — and then the Indian jerked up his battleax. Summers leaped to one side, hearing the empty whistle of the club before it thrashed the brush. There wasn't room or time for the rifle. Summers dropped it and leaped ahead, straight through the thin willows at the Indian, trying to beat the second swing of the club. The Sioux grunted and went down over a root, chopping with the bladed club as he fell. Summers felt the point of it stabbing his left shoulder. He got hold of the hand. His right hand went down for his knife. The Indian gave a sudden heave, snapping himself at the crotch. They rolled over, Summers underneath now, hugging the Indian to cramp his swing. He knew he ought to call out, to warn the crew oncoming with the cordelle. He felt the Indian's legs on either side of his knee and jerked the knee up. The force of it pounded the Indian ahead. The Indian let out a grunt that settled into a thin whine. Summers got his knife then, got it out and around and brought it down, feeling it hit and skid and go on. The Indian flopped from him and lay straining and got himself on his butt and sat, unable to do more. Summers was on his feet. He had his right hand back, with the knife in it.

The Sioux's fingers lay loose around the handle of his tomahawk. Summers thought his eyes were like a dog's, like a pitiful goddam dog's. He had to let him have it. The eyes followed Summers arm up to the knife, waiting for it to come down. The far-off part of Summers' mind told him again he wasn't a real mountain man. Eyes like a goddam hound's. The knife went in easy this time.

Summers wrenched himself around and lurched through the brush to the shore. He could feel his shirt sticking to his back. The boatmen strung along the cordelle pulled up, their mouths dropping open, as he burst out almost on top of them. He made himself be deliberate. "Back!" he said. "Quick, but be careful!" He heard the Indians begin to shout behind him, from the clustered willow. Their arrows made a small fluttering noise, and their fusils boomed. He thought, "Injuns always use a heap too much powder," while he shouted at the Creoles, trying to put order in their flight. They had turned like sheep and started to run and fallen down and run again and fallen, as the fleeter overran the others. He was shouting, more to himself than to them, "Easy! You French sons of bitches." An arrow was sticking from Labadie's arm, but it didn't stop his running. It just made him yell. Christ, a man would think it had him in the heart!

The Indians shouted louder, but not from the willow any more and not like men standing still. Summers could hear them breaking through the brush, their cries broken by the jolt of their feet. The Creoles were a frantic tangle down the bank. Closer, Caudill stood, his dark eye fixed along the rifle barrel, and behind him was Deakins, unarmed but waiting. "Hump it!" cried Summers, humping it himself. The *Mandan* lay like a dead duck at the edge of the stream, her sail down and useless as a broken wing. Free from the tow-line, she was settling back with the current and pulling out, drawing away from them. While Summers watched, he saw Romaine splash into the water and run up on the bank and take a snub on a tree, and then splash back to the *Mandan* as if the devil was on his tail.

"Go on!" shouted Summers. "Hump it, you goddam fools!"

Caudill's rifle went off almost in his face, and then they were running at his sides, Caudill and Deakins were, running and looking back. An arrow whizzed over their heads and buried its head in a tree before them. A rifle spoke again, sounding as if it had been fired right behind their heads. "Goddam it, run, you boys!" Summers felt his legs playing out on him. His head was dauncy, as if it wasn't fixed rightly to his neck. All of a sudden he realized he was old. It was as if all his life he had run among the sleeping dogs of the years and now at last they had wakened all at once and seized on him. He knew he couldn't make it. "Git on, you two," he panted. Back of him he could see the Indians, running in the open now and yelling their heads off, sure that they would get him.

And then the swivel spoke. The black smoke belched out of it, cored at first with fire, and hung in a black cloud, tattering at the edges as the air played with it. The shot silenced the yells of the Indians and the footsteps. When Summers looked back he couldn't see a Sioux, except for two that lay there for the wolves. After a while, above the slowed sound of his own moccasins, he heard them again, but thin this time and lost in the brush. He called to Jourdonnais. "Let's move on up and get them scalps. They'll help a heap with the Rees and Blackfeet."

Spring Song

by Walter D. Edmonds

> 1845? Customs change as society itself changes. When most Americans lived on the land isolated from all save a few neighbors the authority of adults over children was absolute. To escape adult cruelty, children used to run away to sea, to the city, or to the West. Rose's escape was possible because she lived close to the banks of the old Erie Canal.

I

Her day began at five when she came down to get her uncle's morning coffee. It was bitter cold then and the gray shadows that crossed the valley before dawn reached just to the window sills. The kitchen was full of the languid old smells that are born in a house between the end of night and the beginning of day.

She wore a white nightgown under one of her uncle's worn-out coats. The nightgown was thin and outgrown, and, with the largeness of the coat, it made her look timidly aware of herself. She slippered over to the stove in the half light, laid kindling and paper, bent over, struck a match.

After a moment a thin sputtering began in the firebox, and she removed the lid again and carefully placed the wood. Leaving the draft open, she filled the coffeepot from the bucket of water by the sink and measured the ground coffee in her hand. Then she set the pot on the stove, and, taking up the bucket, went out through the snow to the pump.

She placed the bucket under the spout and stood awhile, motionless and straight. Sixteen years old, in the house she seemed a frightened child; now all at once, as she gazed over the valley, she was older. For an instant her body had promise of stature and fine proportions. With her long braid of wheat-colored hair coming forward over the front of the coat and the rise of her breast as her lungs tasted the damp air, she was alien to the hand of man as it showed in the bleak brown house and the old red barn near her.

Of all her toil-burdened day, this hour was her own. She could see ahead of her the hills beyond the valley. Her eyes followed the downward curve, picking out here and there dim buildings of other farms. There was no life visible about them, and her gaze went to the bottom of the valley. Here under the snow she could trace the course of the empty canal and its attendant towpath. It was silent now with the bitter hush of winter, but in a little while, she knew, the water would come, bringing the boats and the faint sound of horns.

The bed of the canal led her eyes southward down the valley to a group of old beeches. When the canal emerged beyond them, it came to the first locks leading it down into the gorge to the Mohawk Valley, and the great cities, Rome and Syracuse and Utica. She had heard of them and they had been called places of sin. She was told that she had come from one of them, but she could not remember which one, for it had been too long ago. Only now in the hovering breathlessness of dawn she felt them stirring in her. A pale flush crept into her white cheeks, and the dim light, kind to her blue eyes, showed no fear. Slender, fair-colored, she suggested in that instant the moonlight in the beeches and the old things of earth, perpetually new.

The excitement went. Her thin shoulders slumped suddenly; she felt the cold. Heavy footfalls were thumping across the kitchen floor. The pump rattled and creaked as she worked it; the water came at last in lazy glittering gushes.

Her left arm stretched out shoulder-high, she carried the bucket indoors. The fire in the stove roared hollowly as she set down the bucket; she cast a covert glance at the man before the stove. He seemed aware of her glance, for he said without turning, "You're late again to-day."

She made no answer, and he said, "It's got to stop."

He was a man of slight build, but his gray eyes had the hardness of cut glass. When the coffee boiled, he poured himself a cup, drank it quickly, and went out to the barn.

The girl went over to the stove and took down her clothes from a peg. She dressed quickly without enjoying the warmth. Then she set about getting breakfast. As she turned the potatoes, she kept an eye on the bedroom door. Suddenly a woman called, "Is it warm yet?"

The girl replied, "Yes."

The woman yawned audibly and could be heard turning over.

"Bring me some coffee," she said.

The girl obediently filled a cup and took it in. In the big double walnut bed, with its garnish of carved pears, lay a woman with reddish hair and a full red mouth. Her brown eyes had a chill on them which even the languor of the warm bed could not hide. She stretched out a plump white arm and her little finger curled tightly as she took the cup. "Hold the saucer," she commanded, and the girl, with skill of long practice, followed the cup back and forth from a comfortable position on the patched quilt to the red mouth.

When she had finished the woman let herself fall back against a pillow and sighed elaborately. She was one on whom false refinement sat too heavily. She resented her life on the farm, but, because she feared her husband, she let resentment fall upon the girl.

Lying under the covers, she gave the child her orders for the morning. "Scald the churn," she said. "And after breakfast you can kill and pick them hens in the coop. We'll want 'em for dinner. I'll have the cream ready then for churning."

She turned to the wall.

"How long's Jed been out?"

"Five minutes," said the girl.

"All right. Call me when he lets the horses out to the trough."

She would be ready when her husband came to breakfast.

The sun was rising now and the shadow of the brown house was walking into the valley beside the shadow of the barn. While the girl laid the breakfast for two (they did not allow her to eat with them) she watched the sunlight finding its way across the snow. The slight mist of morning was wavering over the bed of the canal and stealing away upstream with a faint jerky motion that could be seen only by eyes looking for this very thing. She had seen it waver so for two mornings. This was the third. In the winter the mist settled and went southward; but when spring came it would begin its run into the hills. Then the canal would open.

It was the sight of boats moving on the water that gave relief to the monotony of her drab days. She had been born outside the law to the woman's only sister; and when her mother died her aunt and uncle had adopted her. They did not actually abuse her; but they were wearing out her spirit.

II

They had only beaten her twice, when she tried to run away. The second time they had trailed her through the woods with the Kentucky coon dog kept chained throughout the year. She was ten then, and in the dark woods she could hear his baying and the weird echoing of it ahead of her in the dark branches. When he found her he had danced round her, barking happily, until her uncle came with his lantern to drive her home to weeks of bitter penance.

For five years she had gone to school up the valley; but the other children knew her story, and it was almost a relief each day to return to the bitter house.

On Sundays they took her to church. She rode by herself in the back seat of the surrey, holding the big Bible on her knees, keeping her eyes on the floor when they stopped for conversation.

But one day she had looked up as they crossed the canal bridge that led to their own road. It was in the autumn. A boat was going under, drawn by a chestnut team. Behind the horses walked a big man, black-bearded, with the shoulders of a bull. He swore when the wagon suddenly rattled the planks over his head, a hot oath of surprise, and from the far side returned her uncle's cold stare. Then he caught her eye and smiled — a wide smile that flashed in his black beard; and the kindness of it left her tremulous.

Her aunt turned around to see her watching him.

"Rose!" she said sharply.

The girl dropped her eyes again. And her aunt said to her uncle, "We've got to be careful." It had come to her that the girl could look pretty. Thereafter she took pleasure in exacting menial service from the child about her person. She seldom let her leave the house alone; and when they went out in the evening to a meeting she locked the girl in.

But the girl rode home with tremulousness still on her. When she stepped from the surrey she found a weakness in her knees, and she slipped and muddied her dress. She spent a long hour cleaning it under her aunt's eye; but for once she found the painful supervision pleasant.

She had always liked the boats, but since that Sunday morning she had had the big chestnut team to look for. And at times she saw them with the man walking at their heels. She could see his black beard way across the valley and she learned to know the note of the horn an old man blew from the deck. It was not the ordinary horn that boaters carried; it was a long curving silver thing and it blew in a lower scale, not loud, but with a slow suggestive note that carried to the heart of things.

Rose recognized it one night. Something insistent in it had penetrated her sleep, and when she slipped out of her attic bed she found moonlight on the valley, and a silver sheen on the twigs of the beech grove. While she watched, she saw the night lantern stealing from behind the trees, and the sound of the horn came to her then, low and insistent, and she felt afraid. She thought of him walking with long strides of his heavy legs, his great shoulders bent, and she saw in her mind's eye the black beard, and the black hair on his arms, and all the great bulk of him.

Suddenly the light had stopped, and she had heard the horn again as if it called. The fear went from her. She crossed to her door, but it was locked. She returned noiselessly to the window to see the distant light once more moving.

Thereafter, all through the autumn, her door was locked at night. Only when the winter came did they leave it unlocked. For with the canal frozen in and the boats still, there was no escape for her.

Escape. She had run away as a little child, twice. She had been caught. Now for four months the snow shut her in. Falling steadily, a little at a time by day. . . .

Her mother had called her Rose, a name of which her uncle disapproved. She had a vague memory of a small room, with noise beyond the garish curtains, and a tall woman gracefully lying in a bed and a man who came to see her. He must have been handsomely dressed, for the woman was very proud of him. . . .

Her uncle was late to supper; but when he came he told his wife that in the morning boats would clear from Rome. The locktenders had come back to their shanties. Down the gorge you could see supper smokes against the sky.

That night they had rain. She lay awake listening to the drumming on the roof and the steady chatter of drops from the eaves. She heard her uncle climb the stairs to lock her in and she lay still until he had gone down.

It rained all next day, a gray wall that seemed to shut the farm in upon itself, and the woman nagged the girl without rest.

"She's sullen," she said to her husband at supper. "I thought she was going to answer back."

Her uncle stared at the girl's bent shoulders.

"She's going to need a hiding," he said. But he set her to picking over the seed potatoes in the cellar.

She worked by the light of a candle beside the bins. The hound who had tracked her down years before, an old dog now, with silver on his muzzle, came down and sat beside her. He patted the floor with his tail once or twice; then stretched out with his chin resting on the toe of her slipper. It was dead still, and the hard earth floor had a nasty smell. Outside the rain had stopped, and the air was getting cold.

Only twice was she disturbed. Once when her uncle came to the head of the stairs and stood looking down on her small bent back. He went away without speaking.

The second time, it was a sound, the low insistent note of a horn. She recognized it, and her shoulders straightened as if the sound had physical touch. The hound heard it also, for he lifted his head and she saw his old nostrils working. It came again into the walls of the cellar, and the sound of it hung in the damp air all around her, until she seemed to hear it singing in her head.

III

There were hired help to cook for. The crops were going in. The long furrows were black in the meadows and the teams went slowly back and forth all day. Men sowed the grain, walking in long strides and giving the seed in wide swoops of their right hands. They did not notice her as she moved timidly about the kitchen at meal times. In her old print dress, with her childlike braid on her back, she gave nothing to interest them. Her eyes kept to the floor. Only when she was alone did she lift them to the window. . . . She saw him twice again, moving heavily behind his team, and her heart swelled.

The men talked after they had eaten. They sat around with their pipes, the smell of the fields still on them. While she washed the dishes she could listen to their speaking. Generally it was of crops or horse trades or stories out of the woods; but once they told about a fight between one of their friends and a boater.

"A great mammoth," they called him. He had beaten their man badly.

"The bearded son . . ." they said; and described him, hating him aloud. . . . But she knew who he was and treasured their ill-nature.

It was the first warm night of spring, with a few small stars a prelude to the moon. She watched them from the bed. Below her the house slept noisily. She could hear heavy snores from the rooms of the hired help. Her uncle had gone off to town after supper; he had not yet returned. And her aunt had forgotten to lock her in.

The girl got out of bed and dressed. Then she went down the stairs a step at a time, feeling patiently for the creaks in the treads, pressing close to the wall. There was no one to hear her in the hall, and she crept to the kitchen. The floor creaked at her first step; she stopped as if frozen.

The low light of the lamp showed her in her white Sunday dress, in stocking feet, her blue eyes filmed and her lower lip drawn in against her teeth. Her thin figure was straight and tense; for a time she gave no sign of breathing.

The latch clicked as she turned the knob, and she stood still again with the lamplight on her back and the kitchen all but behind her. But the house slept steadily, and she stepped outside. The old hound, chained to the stoop, whined faintly. She went over to him and stroked his ears. She remembered how he had found her once before, and she decided this time she would take him with her. She unfastened the snap and walked to the stoop edge. He went ahead of her, dancing stiffly on old legs.

The valley was quite still; but there was a movement in the shadows and the moon came over the trees. Slowly the light was born; the woods took shape, and far down the valley a wash of silver touched the beeches. She was shaking. It did not seem that she could take her feet from the last step. There was a loneliness in the dark worse than the sleeping clamor of the house. It was still.

Then far up the valley she heard the horn. The low clear sound of it brought her courage.

She stooped swiftly for her shoes, and remembered that they were lying by her bed. Then the horn sounded again, far away, plaintive, insistent, and she looked up to see a lantern coming swiftly along the road, touching a horse's flank and the shining wet ruts; and when it turned a corner she had a glimpse of its red eye in the dark.

Panic swept her. She ran downhill like a white shadow under the moon, and when she reached the fence the house looked far back and high above her. A cow, heavy with her calf, lifted her head and blew out a misty breath, thick with the new grass smell, and waited for her word. But she was watching the barn.

The wagon wheeled up to the door and the horse stopped. She had a moment's view of her uncle's back and the dark quarters of the horse, and they were gone. And she ran again.

The rain upon the ground was cold, and the stones bruised her feet, but she felt neither. She splashed through a small brook with the water coming to her knees, icy cold, and she halted again.

The house was merely a dark square against the hillside, with the moon touching the chimney top. Then as she watched a high shrill whistling broke out for the hound. He pressed against her leg, glancing up in the shadows, and she felt him sway to his wagging tail.

She fled to the beech grove at her back. As soon as she was among the trees, the sound of the whistling was cut off.

In her sudden plunge into the grove she had lost her direction; and now she ran, blind with fear, and at her heels the old hound who years before had been so glad to catch her. She ran until her heart ached and a dry pain entered her throat.

She came to the edge of a small circular clearing, where the moon was bright and a gnarled tree stood, the mother of the grove. It was not slender and straight as the other trees, but heavy upon its roots, and its branches stretched over the ground. She fell down under it, lying flat on her breast, with her arms out before her, quivering. After a while she looked up to see the old hound gazing back into the woods.

His tail wagged excitedly and he lifted his chin and barked. Following his eyes, she saw a yellow lantern light swooping into the limbs overhead. Great shadows came to life; she heard the stamp of men. The hound barked again and one of the men shouted: "The dog's found her."

She would have cried out but for her hopelessness. She only lay silent before the tree, breathing as if she prayed. . . .

And then into the clearing an old buck rabbit hopped, bright-eyed, his ears high; and the hound greeted him like a friend.

"She's run again."

The man swore as he turned to cut across the angle made by the rabbit. "Bear right!" he shouted.

In a moment they were gone. The lights flickered in the branches and went out. The shadows sank into the ground.

IV

The stillness returned to the clearing with the white light of the moon, and with it came also the beginning of sound. Far away in the swamp a frog tried its pipe, very low and shy, a single note. And presently it tried again and then it was still.

The girl pulled her arms under her eyes where she lay and began to cry, and the strength she had had went out of her like water running. She could not have stirred then if the men had burst upon her with their lights and shouting. Even her sobs were slow dead things.

She was tired, so tired that her senses could tell her nothing. She could not tell at which point she had entered the clearing. There was only the moon, and the old tree casting its shadow on its roots, and far away the single note of a frog.

She must have lain beneath the tree for a long time, for when at last she heard it she was cold. It came low to the earth, with the smell of leaves and old things of the trees, slow and gentle, as if the man had breathed into the horn.

She got to her knees and faced the sound, for it was easy to find. It came again, and she rose to her feet and went toward it out of the clearing, through the woods. There were old things in her, but she did not care. Among the beeches it did not matter what had been right in the cold brown house where men lived righteously.

She walked as if she walked blindly, for twigs bent across her cheeks. She did not seem to feel the strokes. Her wet hair shone pale as the dress upon her shoulders. It too was wet with the dew and spotted brown where she had lain beneath the tree. It hung close to her, showing her thin child's body. Her feet fell into a path that deer might have made and it brought them straight to the canal.

The water flowed quietly with a black sheen round the curve. As she stood on the towpath she could hear the mutter of it in the bank-side grass, and she saw the water weeds weaving from side to side. Here and there the moonlight caught the arrow-headed ripples. It flowed out of the stillness of the grove with the trees thick along the towpath, giving darkness, and it went past her feet southward under the moon, a thread of silver. Far down she could see the sky upon the water where it entered the gorge.

Then above the curve her ears caught the tread of horses coming toward her. With them came once more the sound of the horn, and she knew it was he.

Till that moment it seemed simple to her. There would be no need of talking, she had thought. All through the winter it seemed to her that she belonged to him. She would be there, and he would take her and put her aboard with no word spoken.

But when the team appeared in the arm of the curve, their necks bent before the collars and the towline a thread of silver behind them, drawing on something still out of sight, she was afraid. He came upon her in the shadow without seeing her. But the horses stopped and snorted at her gently, letting out steam from their nostrils. Then he stood before her looking down, his heavy legs wide apart, his broad hat back on his head, his long whip looped on his shoulder, and his black beard sweeping his shirt; and the bigness of him came over her like a blanket.

"Hullo," he said. "Who're you?"

She said, "I'm Rose."

His voice rumbled to himself deep in him. He said over his shoulder, "Put her in a minute, Pete, and look at this."

The old blunt bow of the boat came into sight with its own momentum, cuddling a ripple before it, and the lantern burning on the stern threw a light against the trees.

An old man jumped ashore with a rope in his hand and hitched it to a tree. Then he joined them. A horn hung in a silver circle over his arm and as he walked he blew gently in the mouthpiece, and a low note went ahead of him, like the sleepy murmur of bees. He was a little man with silver hair and a face smooth and alert as a squirrel's. He wore a red waistcoat to his thighs and he stood beside the driver's arm.

"Hullo," he said. "Who're you?"

She said once more, "I'm Rose."

She could not say any more; it was all she had to say; but she looked at them with a silent hopefulness.

"Jeepers!" he said after a while.

The old man echoed, "Cripus!"

They exchanged glances.

"What're you doing here?" he asked her.

"I've run away again," she said.

"They caught you before?"

"Two times."

"What did they do to you?" asked the old man.

She did not answer.

The boater rumbled in his black beard. It was like thunder on the earth at night.

"They would do that," said the old man, Pete.

"Why did you find me?" he asked, bending his black beard toward her. A shiver passed up her, and she barely whispered, "I heard the horn."

He looked at the old man. Pete touched the horn with his mouth, and it seemed to her that the sound hung around them both.

A thought came to him; he asked, "Was it you they're after, them with lanterns and the hound?" He tilted his head back toward the grove.

"Yes," she said; "but it's a rabbit now."

Suddenly they heard the happy cry of the hound coming toward them.

He swore deep in his chest. "I've seen him. I'd run away, too. Get aboard with Pete, Rose."

She felt the blood flooding to her hair. Then his arm was about her and
he had hoisted her to his shoulder. The old man went back and jumped
nimbly to the deck.

He said, "We'll push on past the combines. Then we'll eat, and we'll
haul all night. I'm working down below this summer."

He handed her up and the old man took her.

"Will you cook for us, Rose?"

"Yes."

"Keep inside the cabin, then. We'll look out for you."

"Sure," said Pete. "If he comes we'll give him a twister."

He touched his horn again and the team started of their own accord.

"Better get down," said the old man. "They'd see you here in the light."

As she went down the narrow stairs, she felt the old boat move under her.

"There's some supper on the stove you might keep your eye on," Pete
called after her.

V

A glass-bowled lamp lighted the cabin from its bracket on the wall. The
little cookstove to the right of the stairs had the air hot and filled the room
with a comfortable smell of potatoes heating in a pan. There were old
green curtains drawn across the windows.

She went forward softly as she had in the kitchen in the gaunt house
above the valley. Her eyes explored the sleeping cuddy with its three bunks,
two made up with soiled blankets; she observed the old dust and the old
food smells of the wood; and her eye fell on the table, let down on
its hinges from the wall, with the grimy salt and pepper shakers set back
in the shelf behind it. It was dirty and full of the odor of men living alone;
but it brought her a great comfort, and by degrees her back straightened
and her eyes grew bright. It was comfortable and friendly for all the dirt,
and its warmth went through her. . . . It was a place for her to live.

Her heart hurt with its gratitude. He had taken her in with nothing.
She thought of the words of the hired man, "You're pretty, Rose." She
looked at herself in the small mirror and her small face grew pink.

"We'll look out for you," he had said.

The old boat moved along, and as they went she heard beyond the window the same frog in the far swamp finding his song. While she listened,
he found it; confidence crept into the clear notes, and suddenly other voices

took it up, and the sound of their singing came closer until it went with them along the water, voice upon voice uplifted.

Overhead she heard Pete, the old man, sound his horn loud for the lock, and she knew that the grove was left behind, and the hunting men, and the bay of the running hound, and the old buck rabbit leaping.

The boat sank down between the walls and went on, and again the horn blew from the lock, and again they sank and went on, and the bitter farm lay far back in the high valley.

It came to her then in the cabin that she looked upon her house; and there was work for her to do. When she looked between the curtains, she could see him walking behind the heavy rumps of his horses, his great shoulders bent and his whip wound round his arm. Overhead she heard the shifting of the old man's feet, and from time to time the old insistence of the horn. In a while they would come down; they would look to her for food.

She stood there before the stove, minding the potatoes, and as her senses found root in the cabin she smelled cheese. A smile curved her child's mouth and she went to the cupboard and found there what she wanted.

So while they went on she worked, until her back ached from beating in the bowl and bending over the oven. But the ache pleased her, for she knew that she was working well. Beside herself, it was the only gift she had to bring him.

Outside, the team stopped and the boat went to the bank. She heard the horses come aboard and settle down in their stalls and Pete go forward to help feed them. She did not hear them talking, only the deep mutter of his voice.

"I wisht he'd come after us," he said to Pete, "so I could've told him a few things, and hit him once."

"I'd've told him a few things," the old man echoed him. "He's as low as they come."

And he brought a sweet note from the horn.

"What'll you do with her?" the old man asked.

"We'll let her stay."

"She's pretty," said the old man.

"She ain't only a child," he growled.

She did not hear him, for she was bending before the oven. But when they sat down at the table, and she laid the eggs and potatoes before them, the old man hung up the horn with a fond glance at it, and said conversationally, tucking his handkerchief into his shirt collar, "I used to know your ma, Rose. She was a famous lady down there, and well liked." She looked up at the boater and he nodded his black beard.

"I knowed her, too," he said. "She was a beautiful woman."

She felt the blood rush into her face.

They waited with their eyes on hers. All at once a dark look came over his face.

"Set down and eat," he said. And the old man growled to himself and cast his eye to the horn.

Then shyly she went to the stove and brought forth the pie to set it before him, and her heart sang because she saw that it was good.

The old man cleared his throat and cocked his eye, and he said, "I've allus held there'd be cows in Heaven, just for a cheese pie."

But he said nothing. Only when she ventured to lift her eyes to him, he gave her a wide white smile through his beard. . . .

So they went on after a while, refreshed, with a warm rain washing the deck; and she went to sleep in the bunk, with the sound of frogs singing, the soft voice of the water on the planks, and the low note of the horn.

Chickamauga

by Thomas Wolfe

> 1863 The Civil War, the most deeply felt experience in American history, has inspired a vast literature. Many of the Civil War books are good and a few are fine. But nothing I know of surpasses this brilliant story, a triumph of the creative imagination in its suggestion of the quality of the typical Confederate soldier and the nature of the war he fought.

On the seventh day of August, 1861, I was nineteen years of age. If I live to the seventh day of August this year I'll be ninety-five years old. And the way I feel this mornin' I intend to live. Now I guess you'll have to admit that that's goin' a good ways back.

I was born up at the Forks of the Toe River in 1842. Your grandpaw, boy, was born at the same place in 1828. His father, and mine too, Bill Pentland — *your* great-grandfather, boy — moved into that region way back right after the Revolutionary War and settled at the Forks of Toe. The real Indian name fer hit was Estatoe, but the white men shortened hit to Toe, and hit's been known as Toe River ever since.

Of course hit was all Indian country in those days. I've heared that the Cherokees helped Bill Pentland's father build the first house he lived in, where some of us was born. I've heared, too, that Bill Pentland's grandfather came from Scotland back before the Revolution, and that thar was three brothers. That's all the Pentlands that I ever heared of in this country. If you ever meet a Pentland anywheres you can rest assured he's descended from one of those three.

Well, now, as I was tellin' you, upon the seventh day of August, 1861, I was nineteen years of age. At seven-thirty in the mornin' of that day I started out from home and walked the whole way in to Clingman. Jim Weaver had come over from Big Hickory where he lived the night before and stayed with me. And now he went along with me. He was the best friend I had. We had growed up alongside of each other: now we was to march alongside of each other fer many a long and weary mile — how many neither of us knowed that mornin' when we started out.

Hit was a good twenty mile away from where we lived to Clingman, and I reckon young folks nowadays would consider twenty mile a right smart walk. But fer people in those days hit wan't anything at all. All of us was good walkers. Why, Jim Weaver could keep goin' without stoppin' all day long.

Jim was big and I was little, about the way you see me now, except that I've shrunk up a bit, but I could keep up with him anywheres he went. We made hit into Clingman before twelve o'clock — hit was a hot day, too — and by three o'clock that afternoon we had both joined up with the Twenty-ninth. That was my regiment from then on, right on to the end of the war. Anyways, I was an enlisted man that night, the day that I was nineteen years of age, and I didn't see my home again fer four long years.

Your Uncle Bacchus, boy, was already in Virginny: we knowed he was thar because we'd had a letter from him. He joined up right at the start with the Fourteenth. He'd already been at First Manassas and I reckon from then on he didn't miss a big fight in Virginny for the next four years, except after Antietam where he got wounded and was laid up fer four months.

Even way back in those days your Uncle Bacchus had those queer religious notions that you've heard about. The Pentlands are good people, but everyone who ever knowed 'em knows they can go queer on religion now and then. That's the reputation that they've always had. And that's the way Back was. He was a Russellite even in those days: accordin' to his notions the world was comin' to an end and he was goin' to be right in on hit when hit happened. That was the way he had hit figgered out. He was always prophesyin' and predictin' even back before the war, and when the war came, why, Back just knowed that this was hit.

Why, law! He wouldn't have missed that war fer anything. Back didn't go to war because he wanted to kill Yankees. He didn't want to kill nobody. He was as tender-hearted as a baby and as brave as a lion. Some fellers told hit on him later how they'd come on him at Gettysburg, shootin' over a stone wall, and his rifle bar'l had got so hot he had to put hit down and rub his hands on the seat of his pants because they got so blistered. He was singin' hymns, they said, with tears a-streamin' down his face — that's the way they told hit, anyway — and every time he fired he'd sing another verse. And I reckon he killed plenty because when Back had a rifle in his hands he didn't miss.

But he was a good man. He didn't want to hurt a fly. And I reckon the reason that he went to war was because he thought he'd be at Armageddon.

That's the way he had hit figgered out, you know. When the war came, Back said: "Well, this is hit, and I'm a-goin' to be thar. The hour has come," he said, "when the Lord is goin' to set up His kingdom here on earth and separate the sheep upon the right hand and the goats upon the left — jest like hit was predicted long ago — and I'm a-goin' to be thar when hit happens."

Well, we didn't ask him which side *he* was goin' to be on, but we all knowed which side without havin' to ask. Back was goin' to be on the *sheep* side — that's the way *he* had hit figgered out. And that's the way he had hit figgered out right up to the day of his death ten years ago. He kept prophysyin' and predictin' right up to the end. No matter what happened, no matter what mistakes he made, he kept right on predictin'. First he said the war was goin' to be the Armageddon day. And when that didn't happen he said hit was goin' to come along in the eighties. And when hit didn't happen then he moved hit up to the nineties. And when the war broke out in 1914 and the whole world had to go, why Bacchus knowed that *that* was hit.

An no matter how hit all turned out, Back never would give in or own up he was wrong. He'd say he'd made a mistake in his figgers somers, but that he'd found out what hit was and that next time he'd be right. And that's the way he was up to the time he died.

I had to laugh when I heard the news of his death, because of course, accordin' to Back's belief, after you die nothin' happens to you for a thousand years. You jest lay in your grave and sleep until Christ comes and wakes you up. So that's why I had to laugh. I'd a-give anything to've been there the next mornin' when Back woke up and found himself in heaven. I'd've give anything just to've seen the expression on his face. I may have to wait a bit but I'm goin' to have some fun with him when I see him. But I'll bet you even then he won't give in. He'll have some reason fer hit, he'll try to argue he was right but that he made a little mistake about hit somers in his figgers.

But Back was a good man — a better man than Bacchus Pentland never lived. His only failin' was the failin' that so many Pentlands have — he went and got queer religious notions and he wouldn't give them up.

Well, like I say then, Back was in the Fourteenth. Your Uncle Sam and Uncle George was with the Seventeenth, and all three of them was in Lee's Army in Virginny. I never seed nor heared from either Back or Sam fer the next four years. I never knowed what had happened to them

or whether they was dead or livin' until I got back home in '65. And of
course I never heared from George again until they wrote me after Chancellorsville. And then I knowed that he was dead. They told hit later when
I came back home that hit took seven men to take him. They asked him
to surrender. And then they had to kill him because he wouldn't be taken.
That's the way he was. He never would give up. When they got to his
dead body they told how they had to crawl over a whole heap of dead
Yankees before they found him. And then they knowed hit was George.
That's the way he was, all right. He never would give in.

He is buried in the Confederate cemetery at Richmond, Virginny.
Bacchus went through thar more than twenty years ago on his way to the
big reunion up at Gettysburg. He hunted up his grave and found out
where he was.

That's where Jim and me thought that we'd be too. I mean with Lee's
men, in Virginny. That's where we thought that we was goin' when we
joined. But, like I'm goin' to tell you now, hit turned out different from
the way we thought.

Bob Saunders was our captain; L. C. McIntyre our major; and Leander
Briggs the colonel of our regiment. They kept us thar at Clingman fer
two weeks. Then they marched us into Altamont and drilled us fer the
next two months. Our drillin' ground was right up and down where Parker
Street now is. In those days thar was nothing thar but open fields. Hit's
all built up now. To look at hit today you'd never know thar'd ever been
an open field thar. But that's where hit was, all right.

Late in October we was ready and they moved us on. The day they
marched us out, Martha Patton came in all the way from Zebulon to see
Jim Weaver before he went away. He'd known her fer jest two months;
he'd met her the very week we joined up and I was with him when he
met her. She came from out along Cane River. Thar was a camp revival
meetin' goin' on outside of Clingman at the time, and she was visitin' this
other gal in Clingman while the revival lasted; and that was how Jim
Weaver met her. We was walkin' along one evenin' towards sunset and
we passed this house where she was stayin' with this other gal. And both
of them was settin' on the porch as we went past. The other gal was fair,
and she was dark: she had black hair and eyes, and she was plump and
sort of little, and she had the pertiest complexion, and the pertiest white
skin and teeth you ever seed; and when she smiled there was a dimple
in her cheeks.

Well, neither of us knowed these gals, and so we couldn't stop and talk to them, but when Jim saw the little 'un he stopped short in his track like he was shot, and then he looked at her so hard she had to turn her face. Well, then, we walked on down the road a piece and then Jim stopped and turned and looked again, and when he did, why, sure enough, he caught *her* lookin' at him too. And then her face got red — she looked away again.

Well, that was where she landed him. He didn't say a word, but Lord! I felt him jerk there like a trout upon the line — and I knowed right then and thar she had him hooked. We turned and walked on down the road a ways, and then he stopped and looked at me and said:

"Did you see that gal back thar?"

"Do you mean the light one or the dark one?"

"You know damn good and well which one I mean," said Jim.

"Yes, I seed her — what about her?" I said.

"Well, nothin' — only I'm a-goin' to marry her," he said.

I knowed then that she had him hooked. And yet I never believed at first that hit would last. Fer Jim had had so many gals — I'd never had a gal in my whole life up to that time, but Lord! Jim would have him a new gal every other week. We had some fine-lookin' fellers in our company, but Jim Weaver was the handsomest feller that you ever seed. He was tall and lean and built just right, and he carried himself straight as a rod: he had black hair and coal-black eyes, and when he looked at you he could burn a hole through you. And I reckon he'd burned a hole right through the heart of many a gal before he first saw Martha Patton. He could have had his pick of the whole lot — a born lady-killer if you ever seed one — and that was why I never thought that hit'd last.

And maybe hit was a pity that hit did. Fer Jim Weaver until the day that he met Martha Patton had been the most happy-go-lucky feller that you ever seed. He didn't have a care in the whole world — full of fun — ready fer anything and into every kind of devilment and foolishness. But from that moment on he was a different man. And I've always thought that maybe hit was a pity that hit hit him when hit did — that hit had to come jest at that time. If hit had only come a few years later — if hit could only have waited till the war was over! He'd wanted to go so much — he'd looked at the whole thing as a big lark — but now! Well, she had him, and he had her: the day they marched us out of town he had her promise, and in his watch he had her picture and a little lock of her black hair, and as they marched us out, and him beside me, we passed her, and she looked at him, and I felt him jerk again and knowed the look she gave him had gone through him like a knife.

From that time on he was a different man; from that time on he was like a man in hell. Hit's funny how hit all turns out — how none of hit is like what we expect. Hit's funny how war and a little black-haired gal will change a man — but that's the story that I'm goin' to tell you now.

The nearest rail head in those days was eighty mile away at Locust Gap. They marched us out of town right up the Fairfield Road along the river up past Crestville, and right across the Blue Ridge there, and down the mountain. We made Old Stockade the first day's march and camped thar fer the night. Hit was twenty-four miles of marchin' right across the mountain, with the roads the way they was in those days, too. And let me tell you, fer new men with only two months' trainin' that was doin' good.

We made Locust Gap in three days and a half, and I wish you'd seed the welcome that they gave us! People were hollerin' and shoutin' the whole way. All the women folk and childern were lined up along the road, bands a-playin', boys runnin' along beside us, good shoes, new uniforms, the finest-lookin' set of fellers that you *ever* seed — Lord! you'd a-thought we was goin' to a picnic from the way hit looked. And I reckon that was the way most of us felt about hit, too. We thought we was goin' off to have a lot of fun. If anyone had knowed what he was in fer or could a-seed the passel o' scarecrows that came limpin' back barefoot and half naked four years later, I reckon he'd a-thought twice before he 'listed up.

Lord, when I think of hit! When I try to tell about hit thar jest ain't words enough to tell what hit was like. And when I think of the way I was when I joined up — and the way I was when I came back four years later! When I went away I was an ignorant country boy, so tender-hearted that I wouldn't harm a rabbit. And when I came back after the war was over I could a-stood by and seed a man murdered right before my eyes with no more feelin' than I'd have had fer a stuck hog. I had no more feelin' about human life than I had fer the life of a sparrer. I'd seed a ten-acre field so thick with dead men that you could have walked all over hit without steppin' on the ground a single time.

And that was where I made my big mistake. If I'd only knowed a little more, if I'd only waited jest a little longer after I got home, things would have been all right. That's been the big regret of my whole life. I never had no education. I never had a chance to git one before I went away.

And when I came back I could a-had my schoolin' but I didn't take hit. The reason was I never knowed no better: I'd seed so much fightin' and killin' that I didn't care fer nothin'. I jest felt dead and numb like all the brains had been shot out of me. I jest wanted to git me a little patch of land somewheres and settle down and fergit about the world.

That's where I made my big mistake. I didn't wait long enough. I got married too soon, and after that the childern came and hit was root, hawg, or die: I had to grub fer hit. But if I'd only waited jest a little while hit would have been all right. In less'n a year hit all cleared up. I got my health back, pulled myself together and got my feet back on the ground, and had more mercy and understandin' in me, jest on account of all the sufferin' I'd seen, than I ever had. And as fer my head, why hit was better than hit ever was: with all I'd seen and knowed I could a-got a schoolin' in no time. But you see I wouldn't wait. I didn't think that hit'd ever come back. I was jest sick of livin'.

But as I say — they marched us down to Locust Gap in less'n four days' time, and then they put us on the cars fer Richmond. We got to Richmond on the mornin' of one day, and up to that very moment we had thought that they was sendin' us to join Lee's Army in the north. But the next mornin' we got our orders — and they was sendin' us out west. They had been fightin' in Kentucky: we was in trouble thar; they sent us out to stop the Army of the Cumberland. And that was the last I ever saw of old Virginny. From that time on we fought it out thar in the west and south. That's where we was, the Twenty-ninth, from then on to the end.

We had no real big fights until the spring of '62. And hit takes a fight to make a soldier of a man. Before that, thar was skirmishin' and raids in Tennessee and in Kentucky. That winter we seed hard marchin' in the cold and wind and rain. We learned to know what hunger was, and what hit was to have to draw your belly in to fit your rations. I reckon by that time we knowed hit wasn't goin' to be a picnic like we thought that hit would be. We was a-learnin' all the time, but we wasn't soldiers yet. It takes a good big fight to make a soldier, and we hadn't had one yet. Early in '62 we almost had one. They marched us to the relief of Donelson — but, law! They had taken her before we got thar — and I'm goin' to tell you a good story about that.

U. S. Grant was thar to take her, and we was marchin' to relieve her before old Butcher could git in. We was seven mile away, and hit was comin' on to sundown — we'd been marchin' hard. We got the order to fall out and rest. And that was when I heared the gun and knowed that Donelson had fallen. Thar was no sound of fightin'. Everything was still as Sunday. We was settin' thar aside the road and then I heared a cannon boom. Hit boomed five times, real slow like — Boom! — Boom! — Boom! — Boom! — Boom! And the moment that I heared hit, I had a premonition. I turned to Jim and I said: "Well, thar you are! That's Donelson — and she's surrendered!"

Cap'n Bob Saunders heared me, but he wouldn't believe me and he said: "You're wrong!"

"Well," said Jim, "I hope to God he's right. I wouldn't care if the whole damn war had fallen through. I'm ready to go home."

"Well, he's wrong," said Captain Bob, "and I'll bet money on hit that he is."

Well, I tell you, that jest suited me. That was the way I was in those days — right from the beginnin' of the war to the very end. If thar was any fun or devilment goin' on, any card playin' or gamblin', or any other kind of foolishness, I was right in on hit. I'd a-bet a man that red was green or that day was night, and if a gal had looked at me from a persimmon tree, why, law! I reckon I'd a-clumb the tree to git her. That's jest the way hit was with me all through the war. I never made a bet or played a game of cards in my life before the war or after hit was over, but while the war was goin' on I was ready fer anything.

"How much will you bet?" I said.

"I'll bet you a hundred dollars even money," said Bob Saunders, and no sooner got the words out of his mouth than the bet was on.

We planked the money down right thar and gave hit to Jim to hold the stakes. Well, sir, we didn't have to wait half an hour before a feller on a horse came ridin' up and told us hit was no use goin' any farther — Fort Donelson had fallen.

"What did I tell you?" I said to Cap'n Saunders, and I put the money in my pocket.

"Well, the laugh was on him then. I wish you could a-seen the expression on his face — he looked mighty sheepish, I tell you. But he admitted hit, you know, he had to own up.

"You were right," he said. "You won the bet. But — I'll tell you what I'll do!" He put his hand into his pocket and pulled out a roll of bills. "I've got a hundred dollars left — and with me hit's all or nothin'! We'll draw cards fer this last hundred, mine against yorn — high card wins!"

Well, I was ready fer him. I pulled my hundred, and I said, "Git out the deck!"

So they brought the deck out then and Jim Weaver shuffled hit and held hit while we drawed. Bob Saunders drawed first and he drawed the eight of spades. When I turned my card up I had one of the queens.

Well, sir, you should have seen the look upon Bob Saunders' face. I tell you what, the fellers whooped and hollered till he looked like he was ready to crawl through a hole in the floor. We all had some fun with him, and then, of course, I gave the money back. I never kept a penny in my life I made from gamblin'.

But that's the way hit was with me in those days — I was ready fer hit — fer anything. If any kind of devilment or foolishness came up I was right in on hit with the ringleaders.

Well, then, Fort Donelson was the funniest fight that I was ever in because hit was all fun fer me without no fightin'. And that jest suited me. And Stone Mountain was the most peculiar fight that I was in because — well, I'll tell you a strange story and you can figger fer yourself if you ever heared about a fight like *that* before.

Did you ever hear of a battle in which one side never fired a shot and yet won the fight and did more damage and more destruction to the other side than all the guns and cannon in the world could do? Well, that was the battle of Stone Mountain. Now, I was in a lot of battles. But the battle of Stone Mountain was the queerest one of the whole war.

I'll tell you how hit was.

We was up on top of the mountain and the Yankees was below us tryin' to drive us out and take the mountain. We couldn't git our guns up thar. The only gun I ever seed up thar was a little brass howitzer that we pulled up with ropes, but we never fired a shot with hit. We didn't git a chance to use hit. We no more'n got hit in position before a shell exploded right on top of hit and split that little howitzer plumb in two. Hit jest fell into two parts: you couldn't have made a neater job of hit if you'd cut hit down the middle with a saw. I'll never fergit that little howitzer and the way they split hit plumb in two.

As for the rest of the fightin' on our side, hit was done with rocks and stones. We gathered together a great pile of rocks and stones and boulders all along the top of the mountain, and when they attacked we waited and let 'em have hit.

The Yankees attacked in three lines, one after the other. We waited until the first line was no more'n thirty feet below us — until we could see the whites of their eyes, as the sayin' goes — and then we let 'em have hit. We jest rolled those boulders down on 'em, and I tell you what, hit was an awful thing to watch. I never saw no worse destruction than *that* with guns and cannon during the whole war.

You could hear 'em screamin' and hollerin' until hit made your blood run cold. They kept comin' on and we mowed 'em down by the hundreds. We mowed 'em down without firin' a single shot. We crushed them, wiped them out — jest by rollin' those big rocks and boulders down on them.

There was bigger battles in the war, but Stone Mountain was the queerest one I ever seed.

Fort Donelson came early in the war, and Stone Mountain came later towards the end. And one was funny and the other was peculiar, but thar was fightin' in between that wasn't neither one. I'm going to tell you about that.

Fort Donelson was the first big fight that we was in — and as I say, we wasn't really in hit because we couldn't git to her in time. And after Donelson that spring, in April, thar was Shiloh. Well — all that I can tell you is, we was thar on time at Shiloh. O Lord, I reckon that we was! Perhaps we had been country boys before, perhaps some of us still made a joke of hit before — but after Shiloh we wasn't country boys no longer. We didn't make a joke about hit after Shiloh. They wiped the smile off of our faces at Shiloh. And after Shiloh we was boys no longer: we was vet'ran men.

From then on hit was fightin' to the end. That's where we learned what hit was like — at Shiloh. From then on we knowed what hit would be until the end.

Jim got wounded thar at Shiloh. Hit wasn't bad — not bad enough to suit him, anyways — fer he wanted to go home fer good. Hit was a flesh wound in the leg, but hit was some time before they could git to him, and he was layin' out thar on the field and I reckon that he lost some blood. Anyways, he was unconscious when they picked him up. They carried him back and dressed his wound right thar upon the field. They cleaned hit out, I reckon, and they bandaged hit — thar was so many of 'em they couldn't do much more than that. Oh, I tell you what, in those days thar wasn't much that they could do. I've seed the surgeons workin' underneath an open shed with meat-saws, choppin' off the arms and legs and throwin' 'em out thar in a pile like they was sticks of wood, sometimes without no chloroform or nothin', and the screamin' and the hollerin' of the men was enough to make your head turn grey. And that was as much as anyone could do. Hit was live or die and take your chance — and thar was so many of 'em wounded so much worse than Jim that I reckon he was lucky they did anything fer him at all.

I heared 'em tell about hit later, how he come to, a-layin' stretched out thar on an old dirty blanket on the bare floor, and an army surgeon seed him lookin' at his leg all bandaged up and I reckon thought he'd cheer him up and said: "Oh, that ain't nothin' — you'll be up and fightin' Yanks again in two weeks' time."

Well, with that, they said, Jim got to cursin' and a-takin' on something terrible. They said the language he used was enough to make you hair stand up on end. They said he screamed and raved and reached down thar and jerked that bandage off and said — "Like hell I will!" They said the blood spouted up thar like a fountain, and they said that army doctor was so mad he throwed Jim down upon his back and sat on him and he took that bandage, all bloody as hit was, and he tied hit back around his leg again and he said: "Goddam you, if you pull that bandage off again, I'll let you bleed to death."

And Jim, they said, came ragin' back at him until you could have heared him fer a mile, and said: "Well, by God, I don't care if I do; I'd rather die than stay here any longer."

They say they had hit back and forth thar until Jim got so weak he couldn't talk no more. I know that when I come to see him a day or two later he was settin' up and I asked him: "Jim, how is your leg? Are you hurt bad?"

And he answered: "Not bad enough. They can take the whole damn leg off," he said, "as far as I'm concerned, and bury hit here at Shiloh if they'll only let me go back home and not come back again. Me and Martha will git along somehow," he said. "I'd rather be a cripple the rest of my life than have to come back and fight in this damn war."

Well, I knowed he meant hit too. I looked at him and seed how much he meant hit, and I knowed thar wasn't anything I could do. When a man begins to talk that way, thar hain't much you can say to him. Well, sure enough, in a week or two, they let him go upon a two months' furlough and he went limpin' away upon a crutch. He was the happiest man I ever seed. "They gave me two months' leave," he said, "but if they jest let me git back home old Bragg'll have to send his whole damn army before he gits me out of thar again."

Well, he was gone two months or more, and I never knowed what happened — whether he got ashamed of himself when his wound healed up all right, or whether Martha talked him out of hit. But he was back with us again by late July — the grimmest, bitterest-lookin' man you ever seed. He wouldn't talk to me about hit, he wouldn't tell me what had happened, but I knowed from that time on he'd never draw his breath in peace until he left the Army and got back home fer good.

Well, that was Shiloh, that was the time we didn't miss, that was where we lost our grin, where we knowed at last what hit would be until the end.

I've told you of three battles now, and one was funny, one was strange, and one was — well, one showed us what war and fightin' could be like. But I'll tell you of a fourth one now. And the fourth one was the greatest of the lot.

We seed some big fights in the war. And we was in some bloody battles. But the biggest fight we fought was Chickamauga. The bloodiest fight I ever seed was Chickamauga. Thar was big battles in the war, but thar never was a fight before, thar'll never be a fight again, like Chickamauga. I'm goin' to tell you how hit was at Chickamauga.

All through the spring and summer of that year Old Rosey follered us through Tennessee.

We had him stopped the year before, the time we whupped him at Stone's River at the end of '62. We tard him out so bad he had to wait. He waited thar six months at Murfreesboro. But we knowed he was a-comin' all the time. Old Rosey started at the end of June and drove us out of Shelbyville. We fell back on Tullahoma in rains the like of which you never seed. The rains that fell the last week in June that year was terrible. But Rosey kept a-comin' on.

He drove us out of Tullahoma too. We fell back across the Cumberland, we pulled back behind the mountain, but he follered us.

I reckon thar was fellers that was quicker when a fight was on, and when they'd seed just what hit was they had to do. But when it came to plannin' and a-figgerin', Old Rosey Rosecrans took the cake. Old Rosey was a fox. Fer sheer natural cunnin' I never knowed the beat of him.

While Brag was watchin' him at Chattanooga to keep him from gittin' across the Tennessee, he sent some fellers forty mile upstream. And then he'd march 'em back and forth and round the hill and back in front of us again where we could look at 'em, until you'd a-thought that every Yankee in the world was there. But, law! All that was just a dodge! He had fellers a-sawin' and a-hammerin', a-buildin' boats, a-blowin' bugles and a-beatin' drums, makin' all the noise they could — you could hear 'em over yonder gittin' ready — and all the time Old Rosey was fifty mile or more down-stream, ten mile *past* Chattanooga, a-fixin' to git over way down thar. That was the kind of feller Rosey was.

We reached Chattanooga early in July and waited fer two months. Old Rosey hadn't caught up with us yet. He still had to cross the Cumberland, push his men and pull his trains across the ridges and through the gaps before he got to us. July went by, we had no news of him. "O Lord!" said Jim, "perhaps he ain't a-comin'!" I knowed he was a-comin', but I let Jim have his way.

Some of the fellers would git used to hit. A feller'd git into a frame of mind where he wouldn't let hit worry him. He'd let termorrer look out fer hitself. That was the way hit was with me.

With Jim hit was the other way around. Now that he knowed Martha Patton he was a different man. I think he hated the war and army life from the moment that he met her. From that time he was livin' only fer one thing — to go back home and marry that gal. When mail would come and some of us was gittin' letters he'd be the first in line; and if she wrote him why he'd walk away like someone in a dream. And if she failed to write he'd jest go off somers and set down by himself: he'd be in such a state of misery he didn't want to talk to no one. He got the reputation with the fellers fer bein' queer — unsociable — always a-broodin' and a-frettin' about somethin' and a-wantin' to be left alone. And so, after a time, they let him be. He wasn't popular with most of them — but they never knowed what was wrong, they never knowed that he wasn't really the way they thought he was at all. Hit was jest that he was hit so desperate hard, the worst-in-love man that I ever seed. But, law! I knowed! I knowed what was the trouble from the start.

Hit's funny how war took a feller. Before the war I was the serious one, and Jim had been the one to play.

I reckon that I'd had to work too hard. We was so poor. Before the war hit almost seemed I never knowed the time I didn't have to work. And when the war came, why, I only thought of all the fun and frolic I was goin' to have; and then at last, when I knowed what hit was like, why, I was used to hit and didn't care.

I always could git used to things. And I reckon maybe that's the reason

that I'm here. I wasn't one to worry much, and no matter how rough the
goin' got I always figgered *I* could hold out if the others could. I let termorrer look out fer hitself. I reckon that you'd have to say I was an opti-
mist. If things got bad, well, I always figgered that they could be worse;
and if they got so bad they couldn't be no worse, why, then I'd figger that
they couldn't last this way forever, they'd have to git some better sometime later on.

I reckon towards the end thar, when they got so bad we didn't think
they'd ever git no better, I'd reached the place where I jest didn't care.
I could still lay down and go to sleep and not worry over what was goin'
to come termorrer, because I never *knowed* what was to come and so I
didn't let hit worry me. I reckon you'd have to say that was the Pentland
in me — our belief in what we call predestination.

Now, Jim was jest the other way. Before the war he was happy as a
lark and thought of nothin' except havin' fun. But then the war came and
hit changed him so you wouldn't a-knowed he was the same man.

And, as I say, hit didn't happen all at once. Jim was the happiest man
I ever seed that mornin' that we started out from home. I reckon he thought
of the war as we all did, as a big frolic. We gave hit jest about six months.
We figgered we'd be back by then, and of course all that jest suited Jim.
I reckon that suited all of us. It would give us all a chance to wear a uniform and to see the world, to shoot some Yankees and to run 'em north,
and then to come back home and lord it over those who hadn't been and
be a hero and court the gals.

That was the way hit looked to us when we set out from Zebulon. We
never thought about the winter. We never thought about the mud and
cold and rain. We never knowed what hit would be to have to march
barefoot with frozen feet and with no coat upon your back, to have to lay
down on bare ground and try to sleep with no coverin' above you, and
thankful half the time if you could find dry ground to sleep upon, and
too tard the rest of hit to care. We never knowed or thought about such
things as these. We never knowed how hit would be there in the cedar
thickets beside Chickamauga Creek. And if we had a-knowed, if someone
had a-told us, why, I reckon that none of us would a-cared. We was too
young and ignorant to care. And as fer *knowin'* — law! The only trouble
about *knowin'* is that you've got to know what knowin's *like* before you
know what knowin' *is*. Thar's no one that can tell you. You've got to know
hit fer yourself.

Well, like I say, we'd been fightin' all this time and still thar was no sign of the war endin.' Old Rosey jest kept a-follerin' us and — "Lord!" Jim would say, "will it never end?"

I never knowed myself. We'd been fightin' fer two years, and I'd given over knowin' long ago. With Jim hit was different. He'd been a-prayin' and a-hopin' from the first that soon hit would be over and that he could go back and get that gal. And at first, fer a year or more, I tried to cheer him up. I told him that hit couldn't last ferever. But after a while hit wasn't no use to tell him that. He wouldn't believe me any longer.

Because Old Rosey kept a-comin' on. We'd whup him and we'd stop him fer a while, but then he'd git his wind, he'd be on our trail again, he'd drive us back. — "O Lord!" said Jim, "will hit never stop?"

That summer I been tellin' you about, he drove us down through Tennessee. He drove us out of Shelbyville, and we fell back on Tullahoma, to the passes of the hills. When we pulled back across the Cumberland I said to Jim: "Now we've got him. He'll have to cross the mountains now to git at us. And when he does, we'll have him. That's all that Bragg's been waitin' fer. We'll whup the daylights out of him this time," I said, "and after that thar'll be nothin' left of him. We'll be home by Christmas, Jim — you wait and see."

And Jim just looked at me and shook his head and said: "Lord, Lord, I don't believe this war'll ever end!"

Hit wasn't that he was afraid — or, if he was, hit made a wildcat of him in the fightin'. Jim could get fightin' mad like no one else I ever seed. He could do things, take chances no one else I ever knowed would take. But I reckon hit was jest because he was so desperate. He hated hit so much. He couldn't git used to hit the way the others could. He couldn't take hit as hit came. Hit wasn't so much that he was afraid to die. I guess hit was that he was still so full of livin'. He didn't want to die because he wanted to live so much. And he wanted to live so much because he was in love.

. . . So, like I say, Old Rosey finally pushed us back across the Cumberland. We was in Chattanooga in July, and fer a few weeks hit was quiet thar. But all the time I knowed that Rosey would keep comin' on. We got wind of him again long in August. He had started after us again. He pushed his trains across the Cumberland, with the roads so bad, what with the rains, his wagons sunk down to the axle hubs. But he got 'em over, came down in the valley, then across the ridge, and early in September he was on our heels again.

We cleared out of Chattanooga on the eighth. And our tail end was pullin' out at one end of the town as Rosey came in through the other. We dropped down around the mountain south of town and Rosey thought he had us on the run again.

But this time he was fooled. We was ready fer him now, a-pickin' out our spot and layin' low. Old Rosey follered us. He sent McCook around down towards the south to head us off. He thought he had us in retreat but when McCook got thar we wasn't thar at all. We'd come down south of town and taken our positions along Chickamauga Creek. McCook had gone too far. Thomas was follerin' us from the north and when McCook tried to git back to join Thomas, he couldn't pass us, fer we blocked the way. They had to fight us or be cut in two.

We was in position on the Chickamauga on the seventeenth. The Yankees streamed in on the eighteenth, and took their position in the woods a-facin' us. We had our backs to Lookout Mountain and the Chickamauga Creek. The Yankees had their line thar in the woods before us on a rise, with Missionary Ridge behind them to the east.

The Battle of Chickamauga was fought in a cedar thicket. That cedar thicket, from what I knowed of hit, was about three miles long and one mile wide. We fought fer two days all up and down that thicket and to and fro across hit. When the fight started that cedar thicket was so thick and dense you could a-took a butcher knife and drove hit in thar anywheres and hit would a-stuck. And when that fight was over that cedar thicket had been so destroyed by shot and shell you could a-looked in thar any-wheres with your naked eye and seed a black snake run a hundred yards away. If you'd a-looked at that cedar thicket the day after that fight was over you'd a-wondered how a hummin' bird the size of your thumb-nail could a-flown through thar without bein' torn into pieces by the fire. And yet more than half of us who went into that thicket came out of hit alive and told the tale. You wouldn't have thought that hit was possible. But I was thar and seed hit, and hit was.

A little after midnight — hit may have been about two o'clock that mornin', while we lay there waitin' for the fight we knowed was bound to come next day — Jim woke me up. I woke up like a flash — you got used to hit in those days — and though hit was so dark you could hardly see your hand a foot away, I knowed his face at once. He was white as a ghost and he had got thin as a rail in that last year's campaign. In the dark his face looked white as paper. He dug his hand into my arm so hard hit hurt. I roused up sharp like; then I seed him and knowed who hit was.

"John!" he said—"John!"—and he dug his fingers in my arm so hard
he made hit ache—"John! I've seed him! He was here again!"

I tell you what, the way he said hit made my blood run cold. They say
we Pentlands are a superstitious people, and perhaps we are. They told
hit how they saw my brother George a-comin' up the hill one day at sunset, how they all went out upon the porch and waited fer him, how everyone, the childern and the grownups alike, all seed him as he clumb the
hill, and how he passed behind a tree and disappeared as if the ground
had swallered him—and how they got the news ten days later that he'd
been killed at Chancellorsville on that very day and hour. I've heared these
stories and I know the others all believe them, but I never put no stock
in them myself. And yet, I tell you what! The sight of that white face
and those black eyes a-burnin' at me in the dark—the way he said hit
and the way hit was—fer I could feel the men around me and hear somethin' movin' in the wood—I heared a trace chain rattle and hit was enough
to make your blood run cold! I grabbed hold of him—I shook him by the
arm—I didn't want the rest of 'em to hear—I told him to hush up——

"John, he was here!" he said.

I never asked him what he meant—I knowed too well to ask. It was
the third time he'd seed hit in a month—a man upon a horse. I didn't
want to hear no more—I told him that hit was a dream and I told him
to go back to sleep.

"I tell you, John, hit was no dream!" he said. "Oh, John, I heared hit—
and I heared his horse—and I seed him sittin' thar as plain as day—and
he never said a word to me—he jest sat thar lookin' down, and then he
turned and rode away into the woods . . . John, John, I heared him and
I don't know what hit means!"

Well, whether he seed hit or imagined hit or dreamed hit, I don't know.
But the sight of his black eyes a burnin' holes through me in the dark made
me feel almost as if I'd seed hit too. I told him to lay down by me—and
still I seed his eyes a-blazin' thar. I know he didn't sleep a wink the rest
of that whole night. I closed my eyes and tried to make him think that
I was sleepin' but hit was no use—we lay thar wide awake. And both of
us was glad when mornin' came.

The fight began upon our right at ten o'clock. We couldn't find out what
was happenin': the woods thar was so close and thick we never knowed fer
two days what had happened, and we didn't know for certain then. We
never knowed how many we was fightin' or how many we had lost. I've
heared them say that even Old Rosey himself didn't know jest what had

happened when he rode back into town next day, and didn't know that Thomas was still standin' like a rock. And if Old Rosey didn't know no more than this about hit, what could a common soldier know? We fought back and forth across that cedar thicket fer two days, and thar was times when you would be right up on top of them before you even knowed that they was thar. And that's the way the fightin' went — the bloodiest fightin' that was ever knowed, until that cedar thicket was soaked red with blood, and thar was hardly a place left in thar where a sparrer could have perched.

And as I say, we heared 'em fightin' out upon our right at ten o'clock, and then the fightin' came our way. I heared later that this fightin' started when the Yanks come down to the Creek and run into a bunch of Forrest's men and drove 'em back. And then they had hit back and forth until they got drove back themselves, and that's the way we had hit all day long. We'd attack and then they'd throw us back, then they'd attack and we'd beat them off. And that was the way hit went from mornin' till night. We piled up there upon their left: they mowed us down with canister and grape until the very grass was soakin' with our blood, but we kept comin' on. We must have charged a dozen times that day — I was in four of 'em myself. We fought back and forth across that wood until there wasn't a piece of hit as big as the palm of your hand we hadn't fought on. We busted through their right at two-thirty in the afternoon and got way over past the Widder Glenn's where Rosey had his quarters, and beat 'em back until we got the whole way cross the Lafayette Road and took possession of the road. And then they drove us out again. And we kept comin' on, and both sides were still at hit after darkness fell.

We fought back and forth across that road all day with first one side and then the tother holdin' hit until that road hitself was soaked in blood. They called that road the Bloody Lane, and that was jest the name for hit.

We kept fightin' fer an hour or more after hit had gotten dark, and you could see the rifles flashin' in the woods, but then hit all died down. I tell you what, that night was somethin' to remember and to marvel at as long as you live. The fight had set the wood afire in places, and you could see the smoke and flames and hear the screamin' and the hollerin' of the wounded until hit made your blood run cold. We got as many as we could — but some we didn't even try to git — we jest let 'em lay. It was an awful thing to hear. I reckon many a wounded man was jest left to die or burn to death because we couldn't git 'em out.

You could see the nurses and the stretcher-bearers movin' through the woods, and each side huntin' fer hits dead. You could see them movin' in the smoke an' flames, an' you could see the dead men layin' there as thick as wheat, with their corpselike faces an' black powder on their lips, an' a little bit of moonlight comin' through the trees, and all of hit more like a nightmare out of hell than anything I ever knowed before.

But we had other work to do. All through the night we could hear the Yanks a-choppin' and a-thrashin' round, and we knowed that they was fellin' trees to block us when we went fer them next mornin'. Fer we knowed the fight was only jest begun. We figgered that we'd had the best of hit, but we knowed no one had won the battle yet. We knowed the second day would beat the first.

Jim knowed hit too. Poor Jim, he didn't sleep that night — he never seed the man upon the horse that night — he jest sat there, a-grippin' his knees and starin', and a-sayin': "Lord God, Lord God, when will hit ever end?"

Then mornin' came at last. This time we knowed jest where we was and what hit was we had to do. Our line was fixed by that time. Bragg knowed at last where Rosey had his line, and Rosey knowed where we was. So we waited there, both sides, till mornin' came. Hit was a foggy mornin' with mist upon the ground. Around ten o'clock when the mist began to rise, we got the order and we went chargin' through the wood again.

We knowed the fight was goin' to be upon the right — upon our right, that is — on Rosey's left. And we knowed that Thomas was in charge of Rosey's left. And we all knowed that hit was easier to crack a flint rock with your teeth than to make old Thomas budge. But we went after him, and I tell you what, that was a fight! The first day's fight had been like playin' marbles when compared to this.

We hit old Thomas on his left at half-past ten, and Breckenridge came sweepin' round and turned old Thomas's flank and came in at his back, and then we had hit hot and heavy. Old Thomas whupped his men around like he would crack a rawhide whup and drove Breckenridge back around the flank again, but we was back on top of him before you knowed the first attack was over.

The fight went ragin' down the flank, down to the center of Old Rosey's army and back and forth across the left, and all up and down old Thomas's line. We'd hit him right and left and in the middle, and he'd come back at us and throw us back again. And we went ragin' back and forth thar like two bloody lions with that cedar thicket so tore up, so bloody and so thick with dead by that time, that hit looked as if all hell had broken loose in thar.

Rosey kept a-whuppin' men around off of his right, to help old Thomas on the left to stave us off. And then we'd hit old Thomas left of center and we'd bang him in the middle and we'd hit him on his left again, and he'd whup those Yankees back and forth off of the right into his flanks and middle as we went fer him, until we run those Yankees ragged. We had them gallopin' back and forth like kangaroos, and in the end that was the thing that cooked their goose.

The worst fightin' had been on the left, on Thomas's line, but to hold us thar they'd thinned their right out and had failed to close in on the center of their line. And at two o'clock that afternoon when Longstreet seed the gap in Wood's position on the right, he took five brigades of us and poured us through. That whupped them. That broke their line and smashed their whole right all to smithereens. We went after them like a pack of ragin' devils. We killed 'em and we took 'em by the thousands, and those we didn't kill and take right thar went streamin' back across the Ridge as if all hell was at their heels.

That was a rout if ever I heared tell of one! They went streamin' back across the Ridge — hit was each man fer himself and the devil take the hindmost. They caught Rosey comin' up — he rode into them — he tried to check 'em, face 'em round, and get 'em to come on again — hit was like tryin' to swim the Mississippi upstream on a boneyard mule! They swept him back with them as if he'd been a wooden chip. They went streamin' into Rossville like the rag-tag of creation — the worst-whupped army that you ever seed, and Old Rosey was along with all the rest!

He knowed hit was all up with him, or thought he knowed hit, for everybody told him the Army of the Cumberland had been blowed to smithereens and that hit was a general rout. And Old Rosey turned and rode to Chattanooga, and he was a beaten man. I've heard tell that when he rode up to his headquarters thar in Chattanooga they had to help him from his horse, and that he walked into the house all dazed and fuddled like, like he never knowed what had happened to him — and that he jest sat thar struck dumb and never spoke.

This was at four o'clock of that same afternoon. And then the news was brought to him that Thomas was still thar upon the field and wouldn't budge. Old Thomas stayed thar like a rock. We'd smashed the right, we'd sent it flyin' back across the Ridge, the whole Yankee right was broken into bits and streamin' back to Rossville for dear life. Then we bent old Thomas back upon his left. We thought we had him, he'd have to leave the field or else surrender. But old Thomas turned and fell back along the Ridge and put his back against the wall thar, and he wouldn't budge.

Longstreet pulled us back at three o'clock when we had broken up the right and sent them streamin' back across the Ridge. We thought that hit was over then. We moved back stumblin' like men walkin' in a dream. And I turned to Jim — I put my arm around him, and I said: "Jim, what did I say? I knowed hit, we've licked 'em and this is the end!" I never even knowed if he heared me. He went stumblin' on beside me with his face as white as paper and his lips black with the powder of the cartridge bite, mumblin' and mutterin' to himself like someone talkin' in a dream. And we fell back to position, and they told us all to rest. And we leaned thar on our rifles like men who hardly knowed if they had come out of that hell alive or dead.

"Oh, Jim, we've got 'em and this is the end!" I said.

He leaned thar swayin' on his rifle, starin' through the wood. He jest leaned and swayed thar, and he never said a word, and those great eyes of his a-burnin' through the wood.

"Jim, don't you hear me?" — and I shook him by the arm. "Hit's over, man! We've licked 'em and the fight is over! — Can't you understand?"

And then I heared them shoutin' on the right, the word came down the line again, and — Jim — poor Jim! — he raised his head and listened, and "O God!" he said, "we've got to go again!"

Well, hit was true. The word had come that Thomas had lined up upon the Ridge, and we had to go fer him again. After that I never exactly knowed what happened. Hit was like fightin' in a bloody dream — like doin' somethin' in a nightmare — only the nightmare was like death and hell. Longstreet threw us up that hill five times, I think, before darkness came. We'd charge up to the very muzzles of their guns, and they'd mow us down like grass, and we'd come stumblin' back — or what was left of us — and form again at the foot of the hill, and then come on again. We'd charge right up the Ridge and drive 'em through the gap and fight 'em with cold steel, and they'd come back again and we'd brain each other with the butt end of our guns. Then they'd throw us back and we'd reform and come on after 'em again.

The last charge happened jest at dark. We came along and stripped the ammunition off the dead — we took hit from the wounded — we had nothin' left ourselves. Then we hit the first line — and we drove them back. We hit the second and swept over them. We were goin' up to take the third and last — they waited till they saw the color of our eyes before they let us have hit. Hit was like a river of red-hot lead had poured down on us: the line melted thar like snow. Jim stumbled and spun around as if somethin' had whupped him like a top. He fell right towards me, with his eyes wide open and the blood a-pourin' from his mouth. I took one look at him and then stepped over him like he was a log. Thar was no more to see or think of now — no more to reach — except that line. We reached hit and they let us have hit — and we stumbled back.

And yet we knowed that we had won a victory. That's what they told us later — and we knowed hit must be so because when daybreak came next mornin' the Yankees was all gone. They had all retreated into town, and we was left there by the Creek at Chickamauga in possession of the field.

I don't know how many men got killed. I don't know which side lost the most. I only know you could have walked across the dead men without settin' foot upon the ground. I only know that cedar thicket which had been so dense and thick two days before you could've drove a knife into hit and hit would of stuck, had been so shot to pieces that you could've looked in thar on Monday mornin' with your naked eye and seed a black snake run a hundred yards away.

I don't know how many men we lost or how many of the Yankees we may have killed. The generals on both sides can figger all that out to suit themselves. But I know that when that fight was over you could have looked in thar and wondered how a hummin' bird could've flown through that cedar thicket and come out alive. And yet that happened, yes, and something more than hummin' birds — fer men came out, alive.

And on that Monday mornin', when I went back up the Ridge to where Jim lay, thar just beside him on a little torn piece of bough, I heard a redbird sing. I turned Jim over and got his watch, his pocket-knife, and what few papers and belongin's that he had, and some letters that he'd had from Martha Patton. And I put them in my pocket.

And then I got up and looked around. It all seemed funny after hit had happened, like something that had happened in a dream. Fer Jim had wanted so desperate hard to live, and hit had never mattered half so much to me, and now I was a-standin' thar with Jim's watch and Martha Patton's letters in my pocket and a-listenin' to that little redbird sing.

And I would go all through the war and go back home and marry Martha later on, and fellers like poor Jim was layin' thar at Chickamauga Creek.

Hit's all so strange now when you think of hit. Hit all turned out so different from the way we thought. And that was long ago, and I'll be ninety-five years old if I am livin' on the seventh day of August, of this present year. Now that's goin' back a long ways, hain't hit? And yet hit all comes back to me as clear as if hit happened yesterday. And then hit all will go away and be as strange as if hit happened in a dream.

But I have been in some big battles, I can tell you. I've seen strange things and been in bloody fights. But the biggest fight that I was ever in — the bloodiest battle anyone has ever fought — was at Chickamauga in that cedar thicket — at Chickamauga Creek in that great war.